Belle Cora

Belle Cora

PHILLIP MARGULIES

DOUBLEDAY

NEW YORK LONDON TORONTO

SYDNEY AUCKLAND

Copyright © 2014 by Phillip Margulies

All rights reserved. Published in the United States by Doubleday,
a division of Random House LLC, New York, and in Canada by
Random House of Canada Limited, Toronto,
Penguin Random House Companies.

www.doubleday.com

DOUBLEDAY and the portrayal of an anchor with a dolphin are
registered trademarks of Random House LLC.

Jacket design by Emily Mahon
Jacket photograph © Killerton, Devon, UK / National Trust Photographic
Library / Andreas von Einsiedel / The Bridgeman Art Library

LIBRARY OF CONGRESS CATALOGING-IN-PUBLICATION DATA
Margulies, Phillip, 1952–
Belle Cora / Phillip Margulies. — First edition.
pages cm
ISBN 978-0-385-53276-1 (alk. paper)
I. Title.
PS3613.A7446B45 2013
813'.6—dc23
2012048554

MANUFACTURED IN THE UNITED STATES OF AMERICA

2 4 6 8 10 9 7 5 3 1

First Edition

To Maxine

Tell me where, or in what land
is Flora, the lovely Roman,
or Archipiades, or Thaïs,
who was her first cousin;
or Echo, replying whenever called
across river or pool,
and whose beauty was more than human . . . ?

Where is that brilliant lady Heloise,
for whose sake Peter Abelard was castrated
and became a monk at Saint-Denis?
He suffered that misfortune because of his love for her.
And where is that queen who
ordered that Buridan
be thrown into the Seine in a sack? . . .

where are they, where, O sovereign Virgin? . . .

FRANÇOIS VILLON, CA. 1460

Belle Cora

Mrs. Frances Andersen had already been a New York City merchant's daughter, a farm girl, a millworker, a prostitute, a madam, a killer, a missionary, a spirit medium, a respectable society matron, and a survivor of the Great San Francisco Earthquake when she began writing the book known to us as *Belle Cora*. She completed her final draft two days before her death in 1919, and the manuscript was discovered shortly thereafter in her Sacramento hotel suite, beneath a note that said, "Hear the will before you entertain any thoughts of destroying this." As she had foreseen, the news of its existence came as an unpleasant shock to her heirs, who had had until then every reason to hope that their wealthy relative's secrets would die with her.

It would be difficult to overstate the delight the tabloid press of the 1920s took in the ensuing court battle, as famous in its day as the Fatty Arbuckle rape trial or the "Peaches" Browning divorce. Before it was over, Mrs. Andersen's sanity had been posthumously challenged, her servants had spoken on her behalf, the character of her loyal amanuensis Margaret Peabody had been attacked, members of San Francisco's most notable families had been subpoenaed, and the manuscript itself had testified to its author's mental competence much as *Oedipus at Colonus* is said to have done for the poet Sophocles. Since the purpose of this campaign was to keep *Belle Cora* a family affair, it was self-defeating from the start; Mrs. Andersen's book—its plot already boiled down to its essentials in girls' jump-rope rhymes and West Indian calypso songs, its title known to streetcar conductors and immigrant fruit peddlers—went into five printings when published in 1926 in highly abridged form by the Dial Press. The full text was harder to obtain. Scholars wishing to consult it were obliged either to visit the Bancroft Library at the University of California, Berkeley, or else to make wary use of the pirated version published by the Obelisk Press in Paris in the 1930s and smuggled into the United States in the luggage of sophisticated travelers. At last, in 1966, the U.S. Supreme Court's decision regarding *Fanny Hill* (*Memoirs v. Massachusetts,*

383 U.S. 413) prepared the way for this accurate, complete, and unexpurgated edition.

In my role as a curator for the Bancroft collection and the author of separate monographs on the careers of David Broderick and Edward McGowan, both of whom walk briefly through the pages of Mrs. Andersen's memoir, I have been fascinated by this remarkable document for years. When Sandpiper Senior Editor Morris Abramson asked me to edit the book and write the foreword, I jumped at the chance.

According to the current legal definition, *Belle Cora* is not obscene. There is no question about the redeeming social value of this work, a primary source for anyone researching antebellum New York, the "Miller heresy," the California Gold Rush, or its author, a significant historical figure in her own right; and with Victorianism's eclipse, it no longer offends contemporary community standards relating to the description or representation of sexual matters.

We are not all historians, however. It is fair to ask, now that the scandal surrounding its first publication is forgotten, and on drugstore bookracks the works of Genet and de Sade brazenly return our stare— now that we are permitted to read *Belle Cora*—why should we read it? For most of us the answer will be found in the spell its remarkable author, with her special brew of guile and honesty, is still able to cast upon us.

Like an old French postcard, *Belle Cora* has survived long enough to substitute other charms for its fading erotic appeal. Although Andersen, aka Arabella Godwin, Arabella Moody, Harriet Knowles, Arabella Talbot, Arabella Dickinson, Frances Dickinson, Arabella Ryan, and Belle Cora, was certainly a flawed human being, many readers have found her book as companionable as she herself was in her bloom ("Flaunting her beauty and wealth on the gayest thoroughfares, and on every gay occasion, with senator, judge, and citizen at her beck and call . . ."*). She was not entirely a novice when she began *Belle Cora,* having previously ghost-written two books credited to her third husband, and having published, under her own name, the considerably less candid autobiography *My Life with James Victor Andersen.* It is safe to say that nothing in those works prepared

---

* Bancroft, Hubert Howe, *Popular Tribunals,* vol. 2. (San Francisco: History Company, 1887), p. 240.

their readers for this one, with its pitiless scrutiny of matters concerning which her contemporaries maintained a systematic silence. Nostalgic without sentimentality, Mrs. Andersen has performed the feat of seeming modern to more than one generation. She speaks as clearly as ever across expanding gulfs of time, telling us what it was like to be in places long since obliterated, making the nearly impossible choices that most of us have been spared.

Prior to the publication of her memoir, the general outline of Belle Cora's moment in history was known through several multi-volume works on the subject of Gold Rush–era California, reminiscences by members and opponents of the 1856 San Francisco Vigilance Committee, and a series of articles in the *San Francisco Bulletin* by the popular feature writer Pauline Jacobson. The more personal and private events of her childhood and adolescence in New York, as astonishing in their own way as those for which historians had remembered her, were unknown until these confessions appeared.

In fact, it is one of Mrs. Andersen's unintended accomplishments to have helped correct, just as it was coming into existence, a false impression given by many books and films about the Far West—the myth of a Western type, with its own accent and code of honor, a romanticization of the old-timers and third-generation Westerners encountered by the writers and filmmakers of the 1920s. It is too easy to forget that when the West was really a frontier most of its inhabitants were new to it. They met as immigrants from many distant points of origin, as ill-assorted as the crates of shovels, cigars, pineapples, mosquito nets, and upright pianos that landed on San Francisco's chaotic shores in 1849. And they were also immigrants from another time, from decades of naïve piety, climaxing five years earlier in the bitter fiasco of Millerism, when people had stood on hills and rooftops waiting for Jesus to appear in the sky. Mrs. Andersen, in her eagerness to justify her actions, to explain how she became an immoral woman, gives us this Eastern background of the West.

It is with pride that I present, complete in one volume, the confessions of the notorious widow of the gambler Charles Cora.

Arthur Adams Baylis, Ph.D., *New York, 1967*

FRANCES ANDERSEN

BELLE
CORA

THE OBELISK PRESS

338, RUE SAINT-HONORÉ, PARIS

1933

THIS EDITION CANNOT BE BOUGHT IN ENGLAND OR U.S.A.

[facsimile of 1933 Obelisk Press cover page]

My experiences in the April 1906 earthquake in San Francisco have led me to write this book, so I suppose I'll begin there. When the first temblor came, I was in bed: it was 5:12 a.m. I was dreaming the dream I have had at least once a year for the greater part of my life, that I was an innocent farm girl in upstate New York.

In this edition of the dream, my aunt's hands were gripping my shoulders. Her husky voice implored me to wake up; there was work to be done. I kept my eyes shut, knowing very well that when I awoke I wouldn't be on the farm. She didn't understand that, naturally; she was dead. She kept shaking me. At last she pulled her arm back and struck me so hard she knocked my head against the wall, and the floor beneath us started to sway. I knew then where we really were. We were at sea, rounding the Horn.

When I awoke, chandeliers were swinging. Precious objects in breakfronts tinkled, shuddering across the shelves; thick pillars and crossbeams split and snapped. I heard shouts, screams, and dogs barking.

Feeling that any movement on my part might make the house collapse, I at first shifted only my eyes, and then turned my head carefully. The curtains had fallen from the bedroom window. I saw a patch of sky and the ornate scrollwork of the corner of the roof of the building across the street. I understood: Aunt Agatha had died long ago, my last husband more recently, and perhaps my turn had come. I'd resided in California too long to think that one big shock would be the end of it, or that there was anything to do but wait, saying goodbye: to my jewels, the house, the sky; to the sad remains of the body that used to concentrate the gaze of the crowd when I ambled down the street twirling a parasol.

After twenty-five seconds, the second shock came. "Forgive me!" I shouted. My bed hit the floor. My back and neck hurt. The canopy top was lopsided. I guessed that a lamp, and maybe part of the ceiling, had fallen on it. I was sure that if I moved I would bring it all down on me.

The window showed no roof now, only sky. I thought the building opposite had collapsed, but it was just that I was on the floor now, looking up.

The vanity table teetered like a drunk looking for a safe place to fall, causing a slow avalanche of ivory- and silver-handled combs and brushes, mirrors, china pots, carved boxes, a playbill from the San Francisco Opera. They slid to the carpet; after a brief delay the table followed them, and a big oil painting came down and its frame split. There were more shouts.

Soon I noticed that Janet, my lady's maid; Mrs. Flynn, my housekeeper; and Gerald, my butler, were in the doorway. I saw their heads over the fallen dresser. "Well, help me up," I commanded, surprised at the firmness of my voice. I was very frightened. With tense faces, they stepped carefully over and around the debris. Gerald, whose brow was bleeding, propped up the canopy, while Janet and Mrs. Flynn helped me to my feet.

"It's a miracle," I decided, meaning that I could move at all. "Let's go to the window. Thank you, I can walk by myself now."

My house stood on the highest point of California Street, in the best part of the town, and we could see for miles. To the eye not much was different: a few empty spots where there had been buildings only minutes ago; here and there a mighty pillar of smoke that brought to mind the Lord as He revealed Himself to the Israelites.

Janet, who was not yet twenty, but was shaking as if she were in her nineties, tended to Gerald's cut, while Mrs. Flynn and I went through the house to assess the damage. At exactly the same time, we turned to each other and said, "Flo." Flo was my cook. We found her in her room, snoring, mouth agape, the beached immensities of her pale, mole-flecked body halfway out of her bed. A novel lay on its face beside a toppled dresser. Flo, I remembered, was fond of Dr. Armiger's Wonderful Solution, a laudanum-spiked sleeping potion, and, to show Mrs. Flynn and, I suppose, myself that I was no longer afraid, I made a joke: "Florence Glynn, cook to the prominent Nob Hill dowager Frances Andersen, slept straight through an earthquake, thanks to DR. ARMIGER'S WONDERFUL SOLUTION," I declaimed, while Mrs. Flynn shook Flo out of her stupor. "Surely YOU deserve sleep like this." Her eyes opened.

I thought it was over except for sweeping and dusting, and some funerals of strangers. I should have known better.

The telephone was inoperative. I returned to my bedroom, Janet helped me dress, and we went out into the street, which was eerily quiet and filling up with the mighty of San Francisco: rail barons and traction magnates, real-estate moguls and silver kings, and their dependents. A goodly proportion of them were unshaven and half dressed or in their nightclothes, with their hair in disarray. They looked like children caught being bad.

My club ladies lived in this neighborhood, rich women who occupied themselves, under my despotic supervision, with charity balls, the reformation of drunkards, the alleviation of slum conditions by means of forcible exposure to fine art. Each had her specialty. I found Constance in her front yard, looking like a Pre-Raphaelite Ophelia, uncorseted, red hair loose, gripping an iron railing as if planning to cling to it should the earth move again. I found Harriet stroking the back of her twenty-two-year-old daughter, Jennifer, and speaking to her in tones appropriate to a young child.

"Mrs. Andersen, thank heaven you're all right," said Harriet—as I now know, insincerely. Harriet's husband owned the Saint Francis Hotel, and at his insistence, several years earlier she had sent Jennifer away to the Reed School in Detroit, a school, according to its statement in the advertising pages of *McClure's,* "for Nervous Children and Children Who Are Backward or Slow in Mental Development." Jennifer wasn't nervous: she was those other things, as anyone realized after two minutes in her company. She had to be watched constantly; she would cross the street in heavy traffic to inspect a steam shovel.

"It's a mercy," I rejoined, and I asked after her family and servants. In the meantime, Eleanor and Grace, also clubwomen, came up to greet us. We embraced, too. I became very conscious that this morning there had been no baths, and no talcum or perfume, and in their place were pungent aromas of sweat and fear; my nostrils also conveyed the curious information that the feebleminded Jennifer had not soiled herself, but Eleanor had. I held her long enough to whisper, "You must change your clothes, Eleanor." She flushed and whispered back that she was afraid her house would fall down. "Then use mine," I hissed. "My house is sturdy," I added, as if to say: I'm Mrs. Frances Andersen, the earthquake wouldn't dare to topple *my* house. After a moment she obeyed me.

Shortly after this, I recognized in the crowd Brigadier General Frederick Funston, acting commander of the army's Pacific Division. I liked General Funston.

"General—oh, General! What can you tell us? Have many died?"

"Mrs. Andersen."

He was panting. I now know why, having just read his highly self-serving account of that day.* He had run all the way from his home on Russian Hill to Nob Hill, and then to the army stable on Pine near Hyde. After sending a message to the commanding officer of the Presidio to report with all available troops to the chief of police at the Hall of Justice, he had walked back to the top of Nob Hill, which was to the military mind merely high ground from which to view the action. He was a tubby little fellow with narrow shoulders, a button nose—cute on a baby, embarrassing on a man—and a well-trimmed mustache and tidy beard. I guessed that he would be important today, though I didn't know how important.

"Has there been much damage, General?"

He studied me. As I said, I liked him. He didn't like me. But I knew things about him, so he had to be respectful.

"The water mains are broken. Do you know what that means, Mrs. Andersen?"

At first I didn't; but as soon as he turned his eyes toward Market Street and the great towers of smoke, I understood. The earthquake, when it ignited fires all over the city, had simultaneously wrecked the water mains, thereby crippling the fire department. Soon these expanding conflagrations would unite. They would become a monster, sucking wind from all points of the compass, marching up and down the hills, devouring all in its path. We stood in the shadow of edifices that would be heaps of ash a few days hence.

Funston foresaw that, which was smart of him. But he didn't know how to stop it, and it might have been better if he hadn't tried. This is not my judgment alone. I have spoken with experts. Since it was impossible to drown the fire, his tactic was to starve it by destroying the buildings in its path. Although this is quite the usual thing to do under those cir-

---

* Frederick Funston, "How the Army Worked to Save San Francisco," *Cosmopolitan*, July 1906, vol. 41, no. 3. —Ed.

cumstances, if it is not done just right you help the fire spread. Which is just what happened in San Francisco over the next three days. They used dynamite, black powder, and guncotton, and when they ran out of these, they rolled out the cannons and began smashing the buildings with artillery shells, and it was all worse than useless.

On Thursday morning, with the anxious assistance of the U.S. Army and the fire department, the fire reached Nob Hill and destroyed my house and the houses of most of my neighbors, leaving us with nothing but what we had been able to remove in haste.

I owe a debt to Funston, all the same; thanks to him, I began the evacuation of my own residence early. I made several trips between my house and the wharf, where Mrs. Flynn and a Pinkerton detective stood watch. I rescued my mother's diaries and letters; my brother Lewis's lucky rock, my brother Edward's false leg, and a pair of gold-handled derringers formerly the property of Charles Cora, who broke every faro bank in New Orleans, Vicksburg, and Natchez all in the same year; letters written during the Civil War by my first husband, Jeptha Talbot; my collection of portrait miniatures; my jewels and clothes; a cedarwood hope chest that had once belonged to the wife of James King of William; some other choice furniture and pictures; some old daguerreotypes and photographs; and other souvenirs.

By then the city was full of armed men. There were soldiers and militia, with orders from Mayor Schmitz authorizing them—and also the "Special Police Officers"—to shoot looters. Men of citizens' committees roamed the city, with rifles and pistols and dangerous fresh self-regard, and often I pretended to be grateful they were willing to do this odious but necessary job. I detest such men; I do not underestimate them.

People in fine clothes covered with soot were pushing hand trucks and wagons, dragging trunks, cooking on the sidewalks and the streets, and eating outdoors on card tables. They packed the squares and camped in the parks.

Everyone whose home still stood kept hoping, amid temporary victories and optimistic rumors, that the explosives would work and any minute the fire would die.

I was in the street, sitting on a broken divan from my parlor, and I was watching two thin-necked little soldiers unroll fuses leading to the foundations of my house, which I was no longer permitted to enter, when Harriet Atherton called my name. "I've lost Jenny. She's wandered off."

"Oh dear," I answered. Jenny unsupervised was cause for alarm even on a normal day in a city that was not in flames. I asked how long she'd been gone—fifteen minutes—and what she was wearing, and we rounded up Constance and Gerald. We agreed to look for her separately, covering different areas, and then to rendezvous at a spot several blocks north of where we were. In designating our meeting place, we took into account the fire's rapid march.

Even so, when we met there we were too near the blaze. Smoke stung our eyes; we could hear the fire's roar and see litter skidding down the street toward the fire. The only other people in sight were those fleeing places of still worse danger. Constance had spoken to someone who thought she had seen Jenny.

A motorcar laden with mattresses for the relief of the displaced mounted the hill. I recognized the vehicle, and its driver, a nurse who had offered me a ride earlier in the day. She was a tall, big-boned woman with a cultivated accent. I waved my arms to get her to stop.

"You shouldn't be this close," admonished the nurse, raising her motoring goggles.

"We know. This is Harriet Atherton; she's lost her daughter." I explained the situation. "I was wondering if you could help us look for her in your carriage."

"How old?" inquired the nurse.

I told her, adding, "Mentally no better than a child. Red hair in a Gibson, a yellow dress covered with soot, and a monkey face," and Harriet didn't contradict me.

The nurse commanded us, "Empty the car and get in. I'll help you find her, and then I'll get you out of here." I assumed the order to unload the car did not apply to me, since I was seventy-eight years old. When it was empty, I climbed into the tonneau, between Gerald and Constance.

A few minutes later, we were motoring down Van Ness in search of a young woman in a sooty yellow dress. We turned a corner, and it was the wrong corner: the whole block was in flames. Smoke rose, twisting like a cyclone. There was a rushing wind, its shape illustrated in turbulent debris. Telephone poles were burning and falling. I was thrust against Constance as the nurse spun the wheel. On the street we'd just left, pieces of an exploding church shot into the sky. A billboard for Pears soap caved in the hood of the motorcar. The giant upside-down eye of the baby in the Pears advertisement regarded us serenely for a moment and slid out of sight.

Steam and flames rose from the hood.

"We must leave the car. Get out. Get out," the nurse commanded. "Make haste."

We obeyed. Gerald helped me: I was trembling. So was he. We walked. The nurse told us, "Quickly, don't look back," but we had to look. The car blossomed into flame. A steel fender landed where I had been a few seconds earlier.

"Look, there! Look!" cried the nurse.

Jenny was running down the street away from the intersection where the church had exploded. Harriet screamed out her name, and her daughter turned and ran toward us, weeping with relief. She thought that finding us meant she was safe.

Harriet gripped Jenny's hand. We looked around us and at each other. We didn't know where to go. Then we *did* know—the right place to run was away from the tall, rolling breaker of black soot and smoke rapidly advancing on us. Gerald, after a hesitation for which I could hardly blame him, slung me over his shoulder and ran with me, and now he's in my will, and so shall that nurse be, if I can discover her name.

He carried me for an astonishing amount of time, two or three roaring city blocks, and at last we were far enough out for it to seem safe to put me down. We were all together—Constance, Harriet, Jennifer, the nurse, Gerald, and I—and they were all panting from the exertion, and I was panting with only the excuse of fear. I thanked Gerald, and then there was another explosion, of which I heard just the beginning, because it temporarily deafened me. Having been hurled to the ground, I rose in a gray mist of dust, through which, when it cleared, I could see just enough of Jenny's dress to identify her. Her head was under a slab of masonry. Grimacing and straining—and grunting, probably— Gerald and Constance lifted the block, forced themselves to look under it; then they put it down beside her, careful not to look again. We were in a heap of charred bricks and splintered sticks. A limestone fragment said INSTITUT, with the final "e" gone, and another said HE FINE ARTS.

The nurse stood over Harriet, who lay partly buried under bricks, coated with white dust, her upper body in an odd, broken-looking posture. Then Harriet spoke, which was startling, like a marble statue coming to life. But I was still deaf, so I couldn't hear what she said. I felt myself cough—from the dust and smoke. I wondered if my deafness would be permanent, and exactly then all the sounds came back: the crackle of the fire, the roar of wind, distant shouting, motors, bells, Constance and Gerald coughing, and Harriet's frail voice gasping, "—with Jenny. I had her. Jenny. Oh, my Jenny, my Jenny, Jenny. Tell me, Frances."

I didn't say anything. I had never permitted myself to feel anything at all for Jenny, and I had never really liked Harriet, though I felt sorry for her now.

"My foolish baby," wailed Harriet.

I decided that since she would be dead soon anyway I could lie. "She's hurt her leg. She'll have to be carried, but I don't think it's serious."

"You're a liar. Tell me."

"But, Harriet, it's the truth. Ask Constance. Constance?"

"She's just lamed," agreed Constance, with enough conviction to inspire belief in someone who wanted to live a little longer in hope.

Harriet wasn't like that. "I'm dying," she moaned. "My poor foolish baby is dead, and I'm next. Why? Why me? Why my baby?"

I tried to please her. "We're in the hands of God, Harriet." I knew how religious she was. "Whatever happens, it's God's will."

"How can it be God's will that my baby should be dead and I'm to be dead in a few minutes, good people like us, while you go on gulling the world?"

What did she mean? Did she know who I used to be? No, I decided. She just knew what I was now. She knew I was bad.

I heard Constance intervene, "Don't talk; don't tire yourself," and to me: "She doesn't know what she's saying."

"It's not so important that I deceive people, Harriet, so long as they act as if they are deceived," I said thoughtfully as the others picked up the pieces of rubble burying her. "But as to why and who, isn't that in God's hands? We are told He has His reasons for sometimes taking the good before the wicked, and that all accounts will be settled in heaven. Then you and your daughter will be among the saints, and where will I be?"

"In a lake of fire," said Harriet, and I felt as if I knew her for the first time. She was my old enemy, the Good Christian Woman.

"She's in a delirium," Constance explained anxiously. "What if you live, Harriet?" she asked, and it was quite revealing. I had not known they were so frightened of me. It was more than I had intended.

I thought: how informative earthquakes are. The locks break, the safes open, people run out of the house in their linen.

Harriet insisted, "I want the Lord to take me."

Soon enough, she took a last grimacing breath. She exhaled. The breath kept coming out of her like steam heat until it was gone, her pupils grew, she looked smaller, and none of us doubted that she was dead but we were glad to have an expert, a nurse, on hand to make it official; and to tell us that now we could leave her and save our own lives.

What do you want to know now? Did I survive? I'm writing this, aren't I? We walked to safety. The nurse returned to her job on foot. The rest of us were taken by ferry to a tent camp in Oakland. That evening, when I needed to wash my face, someone brought me a bucket of water and a cake of Pears soap.

BY FRIDAY, MRS. FLYNN HAD MANAGED to hire a wagon to take all of us—Gerald, Flo, Mrs. Flynn, and me—to a hotel in Sacramento, but first we spent a night in a camp on Lake Merritt, where people who had been destitute before the earthquake mingled indiscriminately with people of means. There were rows of squat canvas tents, long lines of people waiting to be fed, carrying the tin plates they'd been given at the end of another line, men in black coats and fedoras and bowler hats, women in long skirts and shawls, girls in jackets and short skirts, boys in short pants. Some of the children were crying or sulking; others played, as young children will amid awful disasters. We had a large satchel full of bread, jam, ham, goose-liver pâté, mustard, olives, and cheese wedges, all rescued from my larder the day before, and so we were spared the indignity of the tin plate and food line. It was another clear day, but dust was falling on us: residue of the burning city.

In the morning, Mrs. Flynn reported that she had found a driver. I was thanking her when I interrupted myself to ask, "Why is that woman staring at us?"

She was coming away from the breakfast line, tin plate laden with slop, an old woman. Her clothes were no dirtier than ours, but beneath the grime was the drabness of innumerable washdays. She had aged in a very particular way. The crow's-feet around her eyes had lengthened until they overtook the rest of her face; every wrinkle was a road to the corner of her left or right eye. Her least appetizing feature was a loose upper plate that she kept moving about in her mouth with noisy clicking and slurping.

"Belle?" she said as she came close enough to be heard without shouting. No one had called me that for many years.

"You've made a mistake," Mrs. Flynn told her.

"Belle Cora?"

She was only a few feet away now.

"Get rid of her," I commanded Mrs. Flynn, who understood the urgency of this matter immediately. Mrs. Flynn knew me from the old days.

"There's no one with that name here," said Mrs. Flynn.

"I know her! Belle, look at me."

"Get tough with her," I instructed my housekeeper.

"If you don't leave us, there'll be trouble," said Mrs. Flynn.

"I'm just a poor old woman! What are you afraid of?"

"Mrs. Andersen does not know you. She does not wish to know you. She's had a very difficult couple of days, and she simply cannot concern herself with your troubles right now. Clearly, you've had a hard time, too; we don't wish you any harm, so, please, don't persist, don't make us ask that you be removed from the camp. You don't want that. We don't want it, either. Just go. We won't say another word." Mrs. Flynn had been reaching into her bag; now she took out a five-dollar bill. "Mrs. Andersen wants you to have this."

The woman didn't have a purse or bag; she just stood there, holding the tin plate with one hand and clutching the bill with the other. She looked at it and wept. "I need it, God knows. Yesterday I'd have been too proud."

Mrs. Flynn put her arm around the woman's shoulder. "I know. I know . . ."

The woman said, "Yes, thank you, I'm sorry," and began to walk off, to my relief, but abruptly she turned and cried out: "I'm Antoinette! Don't you know me, Belle? It's Antoinette!" For a second the name meant nothing. Then it all came back. I remembered that face when men wanted to

kiss it, and how the first tentative marks that would become those loop-
ing lines would appear around her eyes when she was happy. I remembered that ruined mouth with fine teeth in it and a toothache she'd had
and a dentist I had paid to pull the tooth, and I remembered comment-
ing that women of our sort must take care of their teeth, that she should
use tooth powder and dentists and eat more white foods. I remembered
that she liked sweets, and I remembered that she liked hop.

I looked at her, and I thought, why not? What did it matter really,
after all these years, and at my advanced age, and what we'd all just been
through? What had I to lose? A great deal, in fact. But I felt for a moment
as if it were nothing, for we were in the camp, outside society, in a kind of
parenthesis cut off from the regular flow of life.

Those were my thoughts and my reasons for disregarding my policy
of over forty years, and revealing myself to someone who remembered me
by my old name.

"Antoinette," I said. "Mrs. Flynn, it's all right. Leave us alone for a
little while."

I embraced this decrepit old woman with much more emotion than
I had known when embracing my neighbors two days earlier. We felt all
the losses of the intervening years at once. We wept. I think she wept
sincerely, even though less than half an hour later she was trying to
blackmail me, as she had probably intended to do from the moment she
realized who I was.

We sat on my luggage and shared my picnic food. Chewing gave her
such trouble that I supposed she would have been happier with the mush
in the tin plate. She told me, first, of her recent adventures—she ran a
boarding house on Valencia Street, south of Market, where the earthquake itself pulled down buildings and made the street buckle.

We talked about old times, about other American women with French
names, and where they ended up, and how they died. Georgette, who had
been thrifty, became a madam in Denver, got rich, made bad investments,
took arsenic. Suzette, who would give you her shirt, ended up in a two-
bit knocking shop in New York and took some other poison—Antoinette
wasn't sure what exactly, she believed carbolic acid, very painful and
bloody—this had happened under highly theatrical circumstances in a
miserable dive on Doyers Street, with the owner, a big Irish brute, shout-

ing, "Not here, you don't!" and reaching her too late to knock the vial from her grasp. Michelle, after changing her name to "Dr. Winifred Dorcas, Discreet Female Physician," died at thirty-five, insane from syphilis (so I told Antoinette). Monique perished of a botched abortion, not at the hands of Michelle (again, my information). Francesca, after losing her arm as a consequence of wounds sustained in a knife fight with another girl, continued in the profession until she succumbed to alcoholism at the age of twenty-six. The lovely Angelique, always funny and unpredictable, became wilder and wilder, and went from house to house, and was beaten to death by a customer (or, as we'd have called him in those days, "a gentleman").

We wept over these women, for we were more sentimental now than when we were hard-hearted enough to live that life, and we said, of the many others whose ultimate fate we didn't know, that probably they had enjoyed lives of relatively normal length. We said hopefully that perhaps the reason we hadn't heard about them was that they *had* survived. They had changed their ways, and changed their names, and lived in a manner that permitted them to escape notice.

Then we talked about the men. We clucked over their deaths, too. Jim had been hanged. Bill had been shot. When we knew them, they had been incredibly young. Still, one couldn't help noticing that on the average even the most violent of the violent, reckless men we knew of had lived longer than most of the light girls. Perhaps there was hidden evidence, but certainly on the evidence known to us it was more hazardous to be a prostitute than a gunslinger. We cried over that.

Enjoying ourselves thoroughly, we reminisced about the parlor houses, saloons, and dance halls—which ones were still open, which had changed their names, which had become Chinese wet-washing factories or been demolished to make way for the houses just reduced to ashes by the fire that had turned us into refugees, and we cried over those places, too, and wondered what had become of the characters who used to frequent them.

Finally, we talked about our lives since then. I told her of my travels and my marriage. There was no way to hide the fact that I was very well-off. When it was her turn, she said she had married a miner and had been a good wife to him, and he'd been pretty reliable, although he had an irritating habit of saying, when drunk, that he didn't regret marrying her—no, sir—though all his friends told him he was a fool to do it. He had been dead for twenty years now. They'd had five children, scattered to the winds. She had invested everything in the boarding house. She'd owned the building, not the land; now she had nothing.

"We'll stay in touch now," I said, "and I'll help you."

"Well, of course you will, *Mrs. Andersen,*" she said, with a hideous grin wide enough to show, more than our previous conversation, how completely she'd ignored my advice about her teeth.

"What do you mean?"

"You know what I mean."

"Say it outright."

"I know who you are, and you will have to make it worth my while not to tell everybody."

"Oh, my dear," I said. "Oh, Antoinette. Aren't you ashamed? Wasn't I good to you? Didn't I take you out of a Stockton Street dance hall, where you were entertaining a dozen men a day in your sad ignorance of your own worth, and give you a home in the best parlor house in the city? Didn't I loan you money at no interest for your wardrobe?"

"Yes, but never mind."

"And teach you which fork to use for shrimp? And give you a French name and French lessons to multiply your earning power? Didn't I get you out of a fix now and then? Never mind all that? Remember a name I used forty-odd years ago, but forget all that?"

"That's beside the point. I can't afford to gamble on your charity in my position. Look at you, with three servants, a house on Nob Hill—"

"Not anymore."

"And fire insurance and bank accounts, and God knows what—stocks and bonds, and houses. You're headed to a hotel in Sacramento. You're rich! Richer than ever. You've always treated yourself grand, and you've always been sharp with a dollar, except for that one time with Cora. And you're respectable. They wouldn't let you near that hill, even with all your money, if they knew who you used to be, and I'll tell them if you don't treat me right."

We sat staring at each other. Finally, I asked, "You know what I was just about to do, Betsy?" That was her real name. I never heard anyone grant her the dignity of "Elizabeth"; it was always "Betsy" before it was "Antoinette." "I was about to give you the address of my son, Frank, who lives in a splendid mansion behind an iron gate, you know, just outside San Jose. He would set your silence at a higher price than I would, because he has business interests you could damage. I was going to give you his address, and telephone him about you and let you bring him your story."

She waited for me to go on. When I didn't, she inquired irritably, with an undertone of disquiet, "What do you mean? You were going to, but you changed your mind?"

"That's right, because I'm sentimental about you, Betsy, and he's such a ruthless man. No, it's all right, you needn't be frightened."

She put a hard look on her face. "You can't frighten me."

"Are you sure you're not frightened?" My tone was kindly, as though I had her best interests at heart. "You look a bit frightened." I put my hand over hers. She flinched and tried to jerk the hand away. I held it. Neither of us was strong.

Mrs. Flynn, who had been watching from a distance of four or five yards, began to approach us. I waved her back.

"Let go of me."

"Betsy, calm yourself." I shifted my grip to her wrist. "I don't want to see you hurt just because the fire unsettled you and made you say things you don't mean. You're no blackmailer. You don't have the nerve. Your pulse is fast. I bet it's faster now than it was during the earthquake. This is scarier. That was running away from danger. This is heading *into* danger. Can you do something so new, at your age? I don't think so. It's too late. Right?" Seconds passed. "To delay your answer so long is as much as to agree, Betsy."

I released her hand, and she stood up.

"Where are you going, Betsy?" I asked. "Don't run away. It's too late to run."

"Stop it," she said. "You can't bluff me."

"Betsy, Betsy, Betsy. Who's bluffing?"

She sat down again and began to weep, a poor weak old woman. I was glad. I didn't want to hurt her.

Since then, I have kept track of Betsy, not that I am afraid she may reveal my secret—she won't—but simply so that I may have the benefit of her memory when I want it. I have decided to write a true, full account of my life, which I've spent nearly half a century concealing.

Why do it? Why now? As I said at the beginning, the earthquake and fire contributed to my decision, with Harriet and "Antoinette" each doing her part to remind me that I have a lot of explaining to do. There are many crimes on my head, some known to history, others that will be revealed only with the publication of this book. I mean it to be a complete confession, which means, naturally, one with excuses, without which no confession is complete. I invite your judgment, reader.

I write these words sitting in a rattan chair on the balcony of the Belle Vista Hotel in Sacramento. I used to have a parlor house only a few blocks from here, with a winding staircase and a grand piano. How refreshing it feels to write that. The Belle Vista is a mediocre hotel. Its location, once semi-rural, is now a busy commercial district. Over the pedestrians' heads, only a few yards from where I sit, the electric wires of the streetcars crackle with alarming white and blue sparks. But I have always found crowds soothing, I am immune to noise, and my money gets me special treatment here. Janet, becoming less a lady's maid and more of a private nurse as time passes, has a room adjoining mine. Flo is in the kitchen to direct the preparation of my favorite dishes. I have moved in my furniture—choice pieces I was able to salvage—and my keepsakes, and a firm new bed from a downtown department store. Mrs. Flynn has her own room on my floor and runs errands and keeps me company. I enjoy the conversation of the drummers of sundry goods that patronize this class of hotel. Drummers will talk to anyone, and, whatever they may say to each other later, they never look skeptical when you tell them that once you were a great beauty and really (you lean forward, your reedy voice drops), really rather fast—no, it's true!

The San Francisco where I've lived so long, the golden city in which I delighted and suffered, that made me rich, adored and pampered me, and finally took it in its head to demand that in the name of decency I leave it forever so that it could become respectable, is gone utterly, never to return. A new one will be built, but who knows what my condition will be by then? I'm not likely to resume the life I had before the fire, nor do I wish to. My thoughts keep turning, half against my will, to that other, long-buried life, to the New York City of my childhood, to the pious black-clad merchants who patrolled the First Ward docks distributing tracts with titles like *Happy Poverty* and *Deleterious Consequences of Idleness and Dissipation* to men who could barely read; to the mother we all knew would die, the father whose name I could not for many years speak; the farm and village where I found an implacable enemy and a lover whom I lost and regained; and the parlor house where my illusions were stripped away—but not quite all of them, even then.

I think about these things, wishing I could send my thoughts back through the long line of my life like electricity through telegraph wire, all the way to my childhood self, to advise the little girl and the young woman. I lean forward in my chair. Do this, not that, trust this one, not that one, I want to tell her. My experiences have made me into a schemer; even in reminiscence I plot and contrive.

If it is a harbinger of mental decay that on some days it all seems realer to me than the Belle Vista Hotel, that is all the more reason to begin now, before the shadows gather. Every full-length history of the city contains some misshapen account of my story here, but they don't know it from the inside, and they certainly don't know the whole story. They don't know what brought me here. I want that told, at least after I'm dead: and this won't be published until then.

Those are my own selfish purposes for writing this book. Why anyone should read it is another matter—and here I have changed my mind. Over the years my hypocrisy has become so habitual that I was about to say something false: that, though my autobiography must touch on indecent matters, its effect would be moral. It would strip away the cheap glamour that flatters vice, and also the well-intended concealment that leaves frail young creatures unwarned and unprotected, etc. I don't really think that way. That's not the way I am made. To tell people how to behave in regard to any matter that does not immediately touch my interest is simply not in my nature. Whether some books corrupt people and others fortify them, I don't know. Perhaps they do. It is a matter of indifference to me. I just want to tell what happened.

Book One

{ 1828–1837 }

THERE IS A STORY ABOUT A GIRL who took the wrong path, and rues it all her life. She is too trusting. She is too passionate. The result: an error than can't be corrected, a stain that can't be washed out. Back on the old homestead where she grew up, no one is permitted to speak her name, and her picture is turned to the wall.

Gentlemen love this story, so when any girl in a house of mine lacked some version of it I would help her to make one up. I'd take her to a good restaurant at a quiet time of day, order something very expensive, and tell her, "You were an Ohio farm girl, and to help your folks out with the bank loan you went to work in a mill. The mill agent's son noticed you. He was very handsome. That was your downfall."

Or I'd begin, "You're from a fine old Baltimore family. Your father was a good man, except he was a bit reckless: he gambled; he was killed in a duel."

And so on. There was a time when I had three girls declaring in the face of overwhelming contrary evidence that they were the daughters of clergymen.

Why it was useful to say these things, I can only guess. God knows it wasn't to evoke pity. We weren't beggars, and the customers weren't soft-hearted. The important thing was that it worked. We knew from experience that these men paid more for the attention of a girl wrapped in the fiction that she had not chosen this life—she was unlucky, meant for something better, but here to enjoy thanks to her misfortune.

Sometimes we lied even though the truth was perfect. The pretty creature would run a fingertip along the rim of her glass and tell me, "I *was* a farm girl, but in Indiana," or "There *was* a boss's son, and a child, it *did* die, I *did* try to kill myself." I'd inquire, "Do you ever tell them that?" She'd answer, "No." I'd say, "Of course not: it's too personal. But since it resembles what they want to hear, tell them something else along those lines. That way everyone's happy."

The truth was withheld only because so much else had to be forfeited. My case was like that. I was the country girl. And before that, I was the rich girl.

TO BEGIN WITH THE FIRST STORY, I was born in 1828, into a family of pious Yankee merchants. My grandfather, a silk importer, had come to New York from Massachusetts fifteen years earlier and had prospered. He owned what was for several years the tallest building in New York City. My father was his chief clerk. My mother was an invalid, and we prayed every day that she would live and knew that she would die.

Our home was in Bowling Green, a fashionable New York City neighborhood a little past its prime. Its fine three-story buildings, with their pitched roofs and neat rows of dormer windows and wrought-iron fences, were being refashioned to live second lives as boarding houses, or being torn down entirely and replaced with hotels. I think it is because I was born there that the world has always felt old to me. The United States was young. Newspapers constantly reminded us of that. But in Bowling Green things showed signs of long use. I remember when a flood on the second floor of our house damaged a wall of the sitting room on the floor below, revealing many old layers of wallpaper, in quaint patterns, and my father told me that they had been pasted to the walls by the people who had been here before us, and deeper layers had been put there by the people who were here still earlier. How remarkable: there had been other families, surrounded by fleurs-de-lis on yellow, before that by pussy-willow twigs on green, and so on, layer on layer, back and back. Digging in the courtyard, I would find children's lost whip tops and penny dolls. Who were these children? Where were they now?

One still saw pigs in the streets, and when I look back now, their freedom to roam the nation's leading commercial city seems like proof that the United States was only half civilized; but I didn't think so, since I was a child, with no basis for comparison. So far as I knew, there had always been pigs on Broadway, along with carriages and omnibuses. It had all been there before me, in the era of fleurs-de-lis, in the era of pussy willows, forever. And if new houses were rising on new streets to the north, that, too, had been going on for ages, and no one knew how much longer it would be permitted to continue. The world would end soon, according to several upstate New York ministers.

One of my earliest memories is of the time my mother lost me on the docks; she used to make a story of this episode, stuffed with morally fortifying lessons, like all her stories, so that I remember some of it from her point of view. She left my brother Lewis in the care of the hired girl and took me to Pearl Street. It was an ambitious journey: for months, the most she had been able to manage was a trembling descent of the stairs and a brief constitutional in the park across the street, with frequent rests. Now she was feeling better, glad to be out again, strong again—maybe *all* better, cured by some miracle?—and she walked, testing herself, one step and then another, with a fierce secret joy, gripping my hand, all the way to the docks.

Since it was so long ago, I must explain that she was misbehaving—women of her class were not supposed to go to the waterfront, certainly not on foot—but my mother wished to investigate a dry-goods store known for its quality and reasonable prices. She did it with the pretext of visiting my father at his place of business. (As she explained later, she *overreached herself,* stepping out of her *sphere,* and she was punished for it.) We bought hot roasted peanuts from a pushcart. While she was talking to a clerk, I wandered out of the store and crossed the street to watch some children of the poor who lay facedown on the edge of the dock. They were holding a yard of cheap cloth beneath the water. I remember that the reflections of pilings, ropes, and masts wriggled like worms, with the children's faces seemingly contained in the cloth. Abruptly the picture disintegrated; the boys' arms were webbed with the river's slime, the cloth dripped, tiny fish writhed. I turned to speak to my mother; she wasn't there. I didn't know which of those many doors I'd come out of and had no idea how to find it.

To my left were the wooden ships, a bewildering thicket of masts, with vines of ropes and leaves of reefed sail, pigeons sitting on the yard-arms, bowsprits drawing undulating lines of shadow on the cobble-stones. To my right were three- and four-story buildings, many signs, doors and awnings—horses, wagons, dogs fighting over shreds of offal, men pushing wheelbarrows, heaving casks, spitting in doorways. I ran through all that in elemental terror, shouting "Mama! Mama!" until, with a sudden pressure beneath my arms, a man with brown teeth and rum breath, in a coarse-woven dirty shirt and pants with suspenders picked me up. He held me high, walking, while I kicked at his head. "Who lost a babe? Lost! One babe!" A little later: "What am I bid for this fine babe?"

"That's my child! Thank heavens—oh, thank you, thank you," cried my mother, who moments before had been picturing my body fished lifeless out of the water, and I was handed down to her so quickly it was almost falling. Her grip, much weaker than the rough man's, was tighter than usual for her. I could hear her quick heartbeat and wheezes—she had been running—and I did not feel entirely out of danger yet. I sensed her fear of this man, the kind of man our family considered a good object for home missionary work. When other prosperous merchants were rewarding themselves with a convivial midday libation or the comforts of home, my grandfather, accompanied by my father or one of his clerks, was busy spreading the word of God, as they believed all serious Christians should do, whatever their regular professions. In combed black hats and immaculate somber suits, they patrolled the waterfront, distributing Bibles—gripping calloused hands, saying, "Take this, sir, and may God bless you," while peering into the eyes of sailors and dockers unaccountably not reached by the Gospel after eighteen hundred years.

The next part I remember is walking up a flight of wooden stairs to the second floor of my father's workplace, which was lit partly by gaslight and partly by slanting shafts of sun from the big windows. Junior clerks sat on high stools before inclined desks, scratching out lists and letters, while my father watched from a high platform that afforded him a godlike view of their labors. When he greeted my mother, the more astute clerks removed their short-brimmed high black hats, and the others followed the example. He took me from my mother, kissed me, handed me back. He said that he was happy that she was feeling stronger, what a surprise, and she must never do it again, and then he turned to one of the clerks and told him to stop what he was doing to take us home in a company wagon.

When we were halfway down the steps, my mother apologized to the clerk and said that she must stop to rest. She sat down on the steps. I sat beside her. The clerk stood behind us, thinking God knows what. She coughed: a familiar sound. Whenever I played at being a mama, at a certain point I would interrupt my pretended chore to rest, saying, "Mercy." I would cough, with a reflective, listening, diagnostic expression, as if the cough contained a message, and put a hand on my chest or side. Then, grinding my teeth and wincing, I'd get up and return to my imaginary work.

Often I would tell my dolls to hurry up and learn to be good, since I would not always be there to teach them.

LATER IN LIFE, WHENEVER I TALKED ABOUT my mother I would begin to sob. There wouldn't be any buildup—nothing at all—then the tears. Those who knew me as a hard woman would find it distasteful. Who could blame them? How could they understand?

She had fine flaxen hair, which she kept in a severe bun under a plain bonnet. She was small and, in my early memories, pretty, with a graceful figure. (Not later; the progress of the illness made her delicate beauty shrivel.) Her nose was straight and thin; her eyes were long-lashed and bright, her lips bow-shaped; her chin was small. Her complexion was pale, except when she was feverish, at which times the black-and-white hues of her clothing contrasted with a hectic, ruddy, deceptively healthy-looking glow.

Slicing apples, sewing, polishing the candlesticks, or trimming the lamps (four duties she said were permissible for ladies), she would remark, "The Lord may take me early. Then I will be sorry not to be here with you and your brothers, but, on the other hand, I will be very glad to again see my own mother and my grandfather and my aunt"—all dead of consumption—"and of course I expect to meet you in your time. That is why you must do your duty and love God."

We believed that completely and literally. We would be reunited in heaven. That was our plan, as practical to us as "Let's meet at sundown in front of the clock tower."

Growing tired, she would rest, while I went on sewing or polishing. She'd tell me how helpful I was—what would she do without me? She would cough, intending it to be a small, cautious throat-clearing cough. The cough would have bigger ideas and go on and on, while she ran to a pail, and she would spit and study her sputum. Was it white or yellow or green? Or red—the most feared color.

In retrospect—now that "consumption" is "tuberculosis" and the diligent Dr. Koch has traced it to a microscopic bacillus—it is clear that insufficient efforts were made to save my mother's life. Even based on the knowledge then available to physicians, everything possible was not done. It never was when the sufferer was a woman. Male consumptives made survival their life's work. They went on long sea voyages. They traveled to better climes. They changed careers, shunned brain work, and sought to restore their health with vigorous labor out of doors. These measures were considered impractical for women. How could they change careers, when motherhood was their true occupation, without which their lives were empty? How could a sick woman contend with the thousand inconveniences of travel, or bear to be separated from dear friends and relations? Women were too good to do the selfish things that might have preserved them, so they weren't told to. Only seldom did doctors even advise a consumptive woman to refrain from childbearing, although they knew that each pregnancy would shorten her life.

My mother believed ardently in what was then considered to be the modern view of woman's nature—it was a relatively new idea, that women were finer than men—and if any doctor had suggested that she ought to leave her family or avoid childbirth she would have found another doctor. She had five of us: Robert, Edward, Frank, me, and, last of all, Lewis. She was found to be in the second stage of consumption soon after Edward, and each subsequent birth resulted in a permanent worsening of her condition.

Within these limits, it was her duty to improve. On Dr. Boyle's advice, she ate bland foods: wheat breads, apples, boiled rice, boiled beef. She took opium to relieve the pain and to reduce the severity of her coughs. She took calomel to relieve the constipation caused by the opium. When she was well enough, she walked or went riding. She relieved her swellings with blisters and poultices, which she became expert at preparing for anyone who wanted them, and she bled herself with leeches, the descendants of a little family of them imported from Europe, which she bred and raised at home. The leeches mated and bore their young in pond water that she kept in a porcelain tub in her bedroom. Her blood was their only food.

She belonged to a sewing circle consisting of pious Congregationalist women with consumption, whom she had come to know at church or through the recommendation of her doctors. She went to their houses;

they came to ours. Before I was seven, I attended the funerals of three of these ladies. They had sat facing each other, plying their needles, trading medical details they had learned as dutiful invalids. One by one they were put in boxes, stored in the ground, and replaced by others in earlier phases of the process.

All of these doomed women had children whom they were anxious to infuse with a full course of moral instruction in the little time that might remain. Every incident was an occasion for a lesson about piety, work, or self-effacement. Never take the best chair when someone older is present, or speak of hating things or people, or say you do not love what is given to you. Never leave chairs out of place.

For my mother's children, there was special advice on the art of being a guest. She had been only four years old herself when her own mother died. Her father had been unequal to the task of caring for her and her sister Agatha, and from an early age she had become—as she put it—a "wanderer" and a "pilgrim" in the houses of relations. She had learned to be neat, quiet, obedient, and useful. We must learn how to be like that, too.

Perhaps she and my father had decided that he wouldn't keep us after she died. In any event, we weren't merely told that acting in certain ways was wrong—we were told that it would not be tolerated by people less indulgent than our parents. She was forever teaching us how to act during long visits, so far wholly imaginary, at the houses of friends and relatives. "Try every day to cause them as little trouble as possible."

Would we wear well on long acquaintance? Naturally, she worried. We were lovable, yes, but each of us had endearing imperfections that, in her considered judgment, would not travel well.

Robert, six years my senior, found it hard to occupy a chair in a manner befitting a descendant of the Puritans. His knees would climb to his chest, or one leg would behave itself while the other leg was flung out; at the table it was always "Robert, sit up," and his posture was at its worst when he was reading, as he did every spare moment, articles about the Crusades, the habits of the pelican, the use of flying buttresses in cathedrals, the methods of snake charmers, Swedish forest fires, etc., in *The Penny Magazine of the Society for the Diffusion of Useful Knowledge,* and accounts of murders and steamship disasters in the *Sun* and the *Courier.*

My grandfather had given him a complete thirty-six-volume translation of Buffon's *Natural History,* used but in good condition, which he read with his head on the floor and his feet on the wall.

In a letter to Robert—to be opened after her death—my mother wrote: "As you grow I know you will learn how disrespectful your strange postures seem to your elders."

There was a letter like that for each of us, our mother speaking as if from the grave so that we would remember her, get a lump in our throats, and resolve to be better people. In Edward's she hopes he will learn not to tear out of the house without a goodbye, and to study harder and not tease me. In her letter to Frank she recommends that he seek vigorous outdoor work in a better clime. Frank was born with a large black birthmark directly over his heart, like a target placed there for the convenience of the Angel of Death. He was small for his age, and we used to say he could not watch the rain through a shut window without getting a fever, and wherever he is I hope he will forgive me for saying that he wet the bed occasionally until he was eight. He, too, liked to read. He liked the sea tales of Captain Marryat.

Writing to Lewis, who could not yet read, posed special problems which are reflected in her confusing advice to him. Sometimes she is writing to a little boy who loves to climb things and to look at pictures; sometimes she is addressing a young man who must be told to shun gambling hells and theaters. Lewis came too late for her really to know him. She knew only that he was beyond her control. From the moment he was able to crawl, he was busy damaging property and risking his life. It was more than she could do to keep him out of cabinets and flour bins, to keep his hand out of jars, to keep him from tossing fruit, stones, and plates from second-story windows to learn whether they would bounce, splash, or shatter. Curious and lawless, he was bitten by dogs, scratched by cats, nearly trampled by horses, had the same hand run over by another boy's hand truck and cut by an apple corer, had a bookshelf topple onto him, was burned by a hot pan, and was trapped in a trunk for three hours. By the age of four, he was covered from head to toe with tiny scars.

Since my mother could not contain Lewis, by the time he was three I took on this chore for her—watching him, teaching him, scolding him, kissing his boo-boos, making him wash his face and brush his hair every day and say his prayers each evening; punishing him—at my own discretion, which went unquestioned—by applying a stick to his bottom with all my puny might; and in the middle of the night I pulled him out of my mother and father's bed and back into mine. When I assumed these responsibilities, I was just a little girl imitating her mother; I went on because she couldn't and I was applauded for it and it made me feel important.

Once, Edward and I were walking down Broadway, and Lewis was running ahead of us. A big sow coming out from a side street knocked him down. He was sitting in the road, not yet sure if he ought to cry about this, when the sow turned and charged him again; it would, for all I know, have eaten him had I not been there. I picked up a brickbat and with a lucky shot hit the sow in the snout, whereupon it turned on me. A small barrel, thrown from a nearby wagon by a quick-thinking teamster, hit the sow on its back. The cask bounced off the animal and went rolling down the street. Carts changed course to avoid it, and the sow darted between the tall wheels of a coach and ran off "to mend its ways," said Edward, who had been laughing, like most of the onlookers.

When we got home, the story was that Lewis had almost been eaten by a pig, and that I had risked my life to save his. "Lewis has two mothers," said my father, adding that I was certainly the most courageous girl he had ever met; my mother said I was a blessing and a boon. "What would I do without you?" It was a prominent part of our family conversation for weeks. For a long time afterward, Lewis was afraid of pigs—not only of pigs in the street, but of any and all pigs, and he would not eat pork, for fear of angering the pigs. He ate ham, thinking it came from some other animal, and we would all be amused, and my father would offer him second helpings, saying, "More ham for our young Mussulman?"

Were we happy? I want to tell the truth in these pages, and so I am wary of making any period of my life appear better than it was. Everyone has troubles. When disaster strikes, it finds us in the midst of everyday cares and sorrows. But I do not want to go too far in the other direction and imply that it was all grimness, growing up in the shadow of consumption. We all thought that we belonged together, in our house in Bowling Green, with our family stories and our foolish jokes, and each of us was indispensable. My mother's illness gave me responsibilities. By the time I was five, I had given up playing with dolls. Lewis was my doll, and when I was not minding him, I was running and fetching and carrying messages and being praised for my usefulness. I considered myself wise beyond my years and braver than the common run of girls, and I honestly believed that the household would fall apart without me. "What a boon you are to me," said my mother, "I could never get along without you," and I took her at her word. Under her eye, or watched by the hired girl—the "help," as we called servants in those days—by the time I was seven I could put wood in the kitchen fireplace, bake biscuits in a Dutch oven, and make buckwheat cakes and scrambled eggs in a cast-iron skillet that I had to lift with two hands. I mended holes in stockings. I conveyed my mother's wishes to the help, and when my mother was too ill to say what she wanted done, I told them what my mother's wishes would have been.

I notice that I have not mentioned her special advice to me, in the letters I was to read after her death. What does the voice from the beyond say? She praises me for my diligence. She warns me against vanity. She tells me to be gentle, to keep my criticisms of others to myself and show the better way, if necessary, by example rather than by harsh words, and to be virtuous. I reread these letters recently, and how that felt I do not have the art to tell you. Mother, I'm sorry.

AFTER I BECAME RICH, I MADE A POINT of acquiring the surviving evidence of my life long ago in Bowling Green, as a pathetic substitute for my lost childhood there, which ended abruptly when I was nine. I have the letters my mother wrote to us, and also her diaries, which came to me under circumstances I may as well describe here, though it requires me to break away from strict chronology.

In 1884, my brother Edward died alone without heirs, with a wooden leg that he had not used in a long time, his stump being ulcerous, in a room full of empty whiskey bottles, heaps of clothes cured with pus and urine, and some old family furniture that he had given long black scars by letting cigarettes burn out on them. The police broke down the door of his apartment on Great Jones Street in New York City after a neighbor complained of the smell coming from his rooms. Handkerchiefs before their faces, they marched in to find my brother's corpse on its back, clutching a wooden leg. A window was opened, a breeze came in, a slip of paper on his dresser drew attention to itself by fluttering, and it turned out to be a bank draft from Mrs. Frances Andersen of San Francisco. Eventually, someone thought of writing to the rich woman who seemed to be supporting him and might be persuaded to pay his debts, and that is how, a few months later, I happened to receive a parcel containing the diaries: the cracked red leather covers permanently indented where for so long they had been tightly wrapped in twine, the good rag paper, the straps, which Edward had slit, neatly, because the keys were lost (probably they still exist somewhere; they are all around us, in boxes, drawers, drains, and riverbeds, these brass widowers, these useless keys to destroyed locks).

I laid my hands upon them for a while. When at last I permitted myself to open the first volume, I was a straight-backed, corseted old lady outwardly but, inside, a child desperate to be with her mother. And look how much she wrote! Alas, the length turned out to be deceptive; the details of her illness occupied half of each diary. Over and over: her lungs, her sputum, her cough, her food, how often she has bled herself. On first perusal, these passages were not without a power to awaken memory, but gradually I began to be dismayed, as I am when she copies out a hymn or lines from some dreadful book of spiritual guidance that comforted her in its time.

In the diary, which she expected to be destroyed, she discusses her children in a less guarded way than in the letters, and it is bracing to read years later if you are one of us. Ink that once sat in a bottle on her bedroom desk records her worries about Edward—blurred ink on warped pages swollen from being drenched some years ago with whiskey. (Whiskey and tears on the very pages devoted to him, while cigarettes expired on the heirloom furniture—what a maudlin debauch that must have been.)

Some entries made when I was four record the family's flight from New York City's 1832 cholera epidemic. We stayed with my aunt and uncle in their Massachusetts farmhouse, a year before they moved to western New York State. I had known about this visit but had no memory of it. When I read this part, I rose to my feet and paced the floor. Suddenly they were all present, younger than my earliest memories of them—aunt, uncle, cousins—and I couldn't do a thing about it. There my mother was, forever, playing finger games with my cousin Matthew.

When they were growing up, after the early death of their own mother, my aunt Agatha and my mother had been together sometimes, and other times apart. Both had spent their childhoods in the homes of better-off relations, bouncing from one to another. Both had tiny dowries. The great difference was that Aunt Agatha was plain, and she had not married well. I believe my mother was shocked by the fate that had befallen her sister, but she wouldn't let herself think of it. In the diary, she does not remark on the poverty, narrow-mindedness, and ignorance of Elihu, my aunt's husband. Instead, she praises them both for their hard work. They lived the old, virtuous country way, buying nothing, making everything, which kept them very busy all the time.

WE ALWAYS HAD A SERVANT—just one at any time, usually a German girl. Before I was born, my mother had formed a special prejudice against Irish help when she overheard one of them telling Robert that a medal she wore on a chain represented Saint Benedict, proof against consumption. Friends reminded her that not all the Irish were Catholics, and that, in any case, by insisting on Protestant help she was denying these girls the opportunity to benefit by our example. My mother replied that she had to take special care since, owing to her illness, her children were often in the company of the help. Native-born white American girls were considered too demanding and "ungrateful." This left Germans and colored girls. There was one colored girl, Louise, who worked for us when I was two and then went to work for my grandfather. The rest were mostly Germans, and thanks to them my brothers and I learned the names of several German towns and principalities and went around the house repeating little German phrases of shock and exasperation like "*Scheiße!*" and "*Verdammt*" and "*Verflucht nochmal!*," which the girl had uttered during kitchen mishaps.

They would be with us six months or a year or two. Then, because they found better work or a husband, or for some other reason, they'd leave,

and their time became the basis of our household's private calendar—
my mother would date a past event by saying "when we had Frieda," or
"when we had Bertha," and my father, adopting her practice and gently
mocking it, would say, "That was back in the reign of Gretchen."

The departures were usually tearful, with the help weeping as much
as the children did. If a girl left without a big tragic goodbye, it was a
betrayal; my love would sour temporarily into hatred. My mother became
attached to them, too, but she worried about their influence on us. She
was shocked when, instead of saving for their dowries or to keep their
little brothers and sisters off the streets, they spent their money on pretty
bows and hats and dresses, and used their little scraps of leisure to walk
up Broadway or Bowery or to go to dance halls or theaters. She wondered if they were subtly imparting to us (maybe just by the way they
put their weight more on one leg than the other, or arched their backs
and flung out their arms to stretch their young bones) some invisible
taint of immorality carried from the squalid districts where their families
lived.

One of them left when her belly grew, amid rebukes from my mother
("You were like a daughter to us!"), tears and defiance from the girl, and
conversations that stopped when I came into the room. My mother said
that Anna had found work in a house with more help uptown (which was
plausible: the help were always saying that we ought to ease their labor
by hiring another girl, and forever recommending friends who would
work cheaply), but my father said that Anna had taken a boat back to
Hesse. My brother Robert said, "Anna had a weak character. She fell." I
asked how and where. He said, "She fell *morally*." He refused to add to his
explanation.

After Anna, my parents made an exception and hired Sally, an American. Sally did not fuss over me like the German girls, nor was she as
pretty, but she had a careless, absentminded, amoral manner I found
relaxing. When we played, she played to win. She never used anything
as the occasion for a lesson. She took Lewis and me with her when she
did the marketing, and one day I noticed a departure from my mother's
instructions. Sally wasn't asking for the best cut of beef, but for something cheaper. When I corrected her, I saw a look pass between her and
the butcher.

My mother had told me to watch the help to make sure they weren't stealing, and had warned me of the methods they might use. Though I liked Sally, my loyalty was to my mother. I told her what I had seen, and she rose from her sickbed to interview the storekeepers and the peddlers, thereby uncovering Sally's corrupt practices, identical with those implemented on a larger scale, later in the century, by the great names in army provisioning, streetcar manufacturing, and municipal office construction. My father was tenderhearted and wanted merely to give Sally a scolding, but my mother, who took everything these girls did very personally, said that Sally had taken a low advantage of the illness in the house. So Sally was fired without notice, and my father acted the part that our ideas of the world demanded by telling her he hoped it would be a lesson to her.

I went into her room while she was packing. She had thrown her week's allotment of wood into the stove as a final gesture of defiance, and the heat was stifling. She crouched on the floor, jamming clothes into an old leather trunk that had broken straps. "You're just a dumb little girl, you didn't know any better," she said, bidding me to stand on the trunk while she secured it with rope and tugged as if she meant to strangle it. "There's things I could say. Like why I'm grudged a few coppers saved by good management, that's all it was, while doing three girls' work. Why a New York Yankee merchant's son, with a house in Bowling Green, has got to live poor as Job's turkey with one help and no carriage. Does he gamble? Has he got a gal on the side? I could say all that, but I won't. I'll put my capital into a nasty dress and go on the town."

My detection of Sally's embezzlements brought me extra attention a few days later, at Thanksgiving, a feast our family celebrated the second week of December. It was our one big holiday of the season, for in those days people of New England stock still nourished a Puritan disdain for Christmas. Since Christmas was already an elaborate affair in New York, the signs of it all around us helped to make us feel we were a colony of sober New Englanders, here on a mission in a city whose leading families cared only for money, pleasure, and appearances.

Soon after we arrived at the big house on Bond Street, with the usual round of cheerful but stiff greetings, my grandfather announced to the company that he would have a word alone with Arabella in his study. He took my hand and led me to a small, cluttered room where a window with many light-warping panes looked out on trees whose branches drooped with snow, and a yard dotted with the footprints of dogs. He took a stack of papers off a chair so that I could climb onto it, flipped back the tail of his coat, and sat down. He praised me for discovering Sally's trickery. "I could wish that my chief clerk had as sharp an eye as yours."

He asked me if I was as attentive to my Sunday-school lessons as I was to the misdeeds of the help, and I said I hoped so, and he tested me with a series of questions of advancing difficulty. I told him who made the world; I identified Adam, Eve, Cain, Noah, Lot, Joseph in Egypt, Moses, Mary, Mary's Joseph, Paul, and Peter. He nodded his approval as I affirmed—without the least idea of the implications of what I was saying—that because of Adam's disobedience we were all wicked sinners, and that every evil thought we had was our own, and every good thought we had was put there expressly by the Lord. We all deserved to go to hell, but some of us would be redeemed anyway. He asked me what I had to do to be saved, and I said, "To love God."

He started to speak, and stopped himself.

I added, "And to have the gift of the Holy Spirit."

This pleased him. "And who can have the gift of the Holy Spirit?"

"Anyone, if they sincerely repent." A lady in the sewing circle, now deceased, had laid great stress on this, and evidently it was the right thing to say. My grandfather reached forward awkwardly and patted me on the shoulder. He did not have an easy way with children. All the same, I knew he liked me. I liked him back, without ever once wondering how people could like each other if, thanks to Adam's sin, they were totally depraved and there was no good in them.

"Tell Louise I said to give you an extra helping of pudding," he said at last.

I would have gotten the extra helping anyway, but I thanked him. "Grandfather?"

"Yes, child."

"Grandfather, what does 'go on the town' mean?"

He blinked. "Who used these words?"

"Sally."

"I see."

"She said she was going to buy a nasty dress and go on the town."

"I see. Well, I suppose she meant that she would find other work," he said brightly.

My grandfather was a busy reformer. Beyond such projects as the printing of religious tracts, the building of workhouses, and campaigns to suppress drunkenness and Sabbath breaking and to abolish slavery, he was a sponsor of the Magdalene Society and other efforts to promote the reclamation of fallen women. He knew very well that "going on the town" was what girls of the laboring class said they were doing when they went out to prostitute themselves in the street.

He rose and opened the door, and I followed him back to the second-floor dining room for Thanksgiving dinner, where I ate until my stomach hurt.

The feast was marred by two incidents.

First, Lewis had used the time I spent talking to my grandfather to wander into forbidden parts of the house and was found playing with my grandmother's collection of fine lace. My grandmother had no patience for small boys. She let my mother feel her frosty displeasure for the rest of the afternoon.

Second, as is traditional at Thanksgiving, someone's feelings were hurt. That person was my father. I know because at our house that night I heard my mother consoling him in their bedroom, a wall away from the room I shared with Lewis and Frank. There was weeping, which I realized with a shock was his, and a groan of anguish, and this mysterious shout: ". . . thirty-seven!" Years later, I realized it was his age. I held my breath, and they went on talking, but I couldn't understand any more of it.

The next day, when he was having his coffee alone at the table, and reading letters that he had taken in a messy bundle out of a leather bag, I asked if I might sit with him. Yes, if I was quiet, he said. I watched him read and turn the pages and sip his coffee, and scratch his cheek, and write notes. He looked at me. I asked him if his work was very hard. I said that he must be very smart to do such work, and he smiled, saying, "Arabella, you promised not to make noise," and sent me away. My father usually showed us a cheerful face, but I know from my mother's diary that he was given to attacks of what in those days we called "the melancholy."

❧ III ❧

A FEW DAYS LATER, IT BECAME SO COLD THAT, to save wood, we moved our bedding downstairs and slept near the big sitting-room fireplace—my mother, my father, my brothers, Christina (the girl who replaced Sally), and me. We wrapped ourselves in blankets and sat on stools and chairs, faces ruddy in the firelight, and Lewis begged my father: "Tell us about the Turk."

This was a frequent request, arising out of Lewis's refusal to eat pork and my father calling him a "little Mussulman" and asking him how many wives he meant to have when he grew up. Lewis had responded with questions of his own, and in time my father's answers developed into an absurd lecture which operated powerfully on my little brother's mind. In the house and on the street, Lewis went about holding a stick for sword fighting, now pretending to be the Turk and now a doughty American sailor, the Turk's enemy, whom my father had added to the lecture in the second or third telling.

"The Turk hates houses," said my father solemnly. "He lives in a tent. He always wears a hat, even in church. He doesn't eat pork, but turkey and Turkish Delight. He has so many wives he can't remember all of their names."

"He boils you in oil!" interjected Lewis, jumping to his feet. Boiling in oil was his favorite part; often he brought it up prematurely, afraid my father would forget to include it.

"Don't interrupt, Lewis," my mother admonished him.

He sat, but as he did he confided to Frank, "He tried to make the sailor a Mussulman!"

"Let Papa tell it," said Frank, who liked this nonsense almost as much as Lewis did. My father had originally thrown in the sailor for Frank's benefit. The others in the room were Edward, mainly intent on staying warm; Robert, who lay with his back to the fire, the better to get its light onto the tiny print in *The Penny Magazine;* and Christina, whose English was limited; and my mother. They all looked up, amused by Lewis's reactions.

"That is in fact what happened to a sailor of my acquaintance who was captured by the Turk," continued my father. "The Turk said, 'Be a Mussulman or be boiled.' But this sailor had personally been handed a Bible by your grandfather—I was there; we were walking on the docks, handing out improving tracts and Bibles to drunken sailors and watching the change start to come over them by the very touch of it in their fingers—a wonderful sight to behold—and he had read his Bible and become a strong, stouthearted Christian. 'Boil me in oil?' he said. 'I double-dare you to.' 'I'll do it,' said the Turk. 'I don't believe you,' said the sailor. 'You asked for it,' said the Turk, and threw him into the bubbling pot! Oh, the poor sailor! He found it very uncomfortable. Luckily, his skin had been toughened by years of salt spray washing over him as he hauled the ropes on the deck of a two-hundred-ton three-masted brig, and he stood up to boiling in oil remarkably well, though he told me he would hate to go through it again, and I have no reason to doubt him. He was a very honest sailor, at least after he had gotten his Bible."

"I won't let the Turk boil me at all!" declared Lewis. "I'll take his sword away and cut his head off! I'll shoot him between the eyes!" My mother, who hated the Turk story both for itself—for its violence—as well as for its effects on Lewis, said he should not talk of cutting off heads and shooting, and I told him that if he kept interrupting, Papa would not be able to finish, and he managed to keep silent after that.

Later that night, as I was drifting off to sleep, I heard the wind rattling the windows and doors like a prowler trying to find one left unlocked. I heard my mother cough and sit up to spit in a pot placed nearby for this purpose. In the morning, she would look at the sputum. Now she lay in the dark, wondering what color it was, and so did I.

That night, I dreamed that Dr. Boyle had come to see her. He opened up her chest as if he were opening the doors of an armoire, and he showed us the rot inside: old bottles, bits of newsprint, creeping centipedes molded to the humps and valleys of limp brown cabbage leaves. He took out her lungs and held them up to light suddenly streaming through the window. "As I thought: phthisis in every tissue. Only the fruit of a tree in Cyprus can save her; but, inconveniently, the Turk has it. Somehow your family must obtain it from the Turk, who hates us; to get it you may have to kill him."

Lewis leapt to his feet. "I will shoot the Turk, Mama. Belle will help me to do it." She looked at him as though very sad that he should still be talking of shooting when she had told him not to, and I tried to explain that he meant merely that he would do whatever was necessary and I would help him. I tried to speak. No sound came out.

When I opened my eyes, only a few hours after I had shut them, I saw my father, Robert, Edward, and Frank all standing in the firelight, dressed for the cold in coats, scarves, and hats. It was still dark. I heard bells clanging. One of my grandfather's clerks, a young man whose hands and face shook from the cold, crouched close to the fire while giving a grim report to my father, who asked him questions. At first I did not understand, but gradually I learned that there was a fire, a big one, spreading quickly ("eating up blocks," the clerk said), near my grandfather's store. I was still muzzy-headed from sleep, and for a few moments I thought I could cheer everyone with the good news that my mother could be cured, until the urgency of my father's voice woke me fully.

"Robert, Edward, you will come with us," said my father, in a strong voice, but in a strangely pensive tone, as if it were more of a prediction than a command.

Frank said, "May I go, too, please?"

My father, after a hesitation, said yes, a decision he came to regret.

"What's happening?" asked Lewis, just woken, blinking. "What is it?"

"There's a fire on the docks," I told him, happy to have something to do—help control Lewis—and wanting to show that, though I was only seven myself, I understood what was happening and what was important. "Papa will empty the warehouse in case it catches fire. He's taking Robert and Edward and Frank."

"I'll go, too." Lewis wriggled out of Christina's grasp. "Papa, please, may I go to the fire?"

"You can go to the *next* fire," my father promised.

"I want to see *this* fire! Let me see *this* fire!"

As they got ready to leave, he kept on begging and complaining, saying he never got to go anywhere and he wouldn't be a burden. I had to hold onto him tightly until they had gone. Then I took him to the top floor of the house to look out the east-facing dormer windows; we saw no flames, only a great swath of darkness where smoke blocked out the stars. But we heard the fire's distant roar, and the bells of the fire engines, and later, as the drift to sleep disheveled my thoughts, I imagined that the bells were a magical attempt to break up the fire by tearing through its voice.

The *Herald* reported later that the fire had broken out at nine o'clock at night in the store of Comstock & Andrews, in Merchant Street, a narrow crooked lane of dry-goods merchants and auctioneers in the rear of the Merchants' Exchange. Someone had forgotten to close a gas cock when the store was shut; gas had filled the room, and when the gas reached some lit coals in the grate, it exploded. Within twenty minutes, conflagration was spreading to other blocks. Fire brigades from all over the city—later, from other cities—fought the blaze in weather so cold that the water in the hydrants had frozen. Horses dragged the engines to the East River; firemen chopped holes in the ice, linked hoses and pumps to carry the water from the river to the fire, and poured brandy into the hoses to keep the water liquid; when they pointed the hoses at the flames, the wind blew the water back in their faces as pieces of ice.

My grandfather, father, and brothers emptied the warehouse, assisted by their clerks and by anyone else willing to lend a hand. The merchants gave things away to whoever would help them save their stock. "Thank you: here's a coat, here's a hat," they would say, as heaps of goods rose in the street, acquiring a film of fine soot, and the carters charged several times their usual rate to take the heaps to safety.

My mother and I knew none of these details at the time—we were at home, worrying, until at last I fell asleep.

When I woke the next morning, my mother was coughing uncontrollably into a bowl. Her pale hands were speckled with blood. "Don't look," she gasped, "don't cry." For I was crying; I had never been so frightened for her. In a wheezy voice she gave me some instruction which I did not understand, and she had to repeat it: "Tell Sally to start the fire in my room."

When the fire had warmed my parents' room, Christina helped my mother into her bed. I stood by the door and heard again my mother call Christina "Sally."

My father sometimes went on business trips, or went early to the store, so it was not unusual to wake and find him gone in the morning, but that Frank and Edward should also be gone felt strange. My grandfather's clerk had described the fire as "eating blocks," and I had pictured it immediately as a beast; I had pictured its mouth. But I had confidence in my father, and I was not as worried as I would have been if I were older. That my mother should go to heaven while we still had need of her, that was the particular calamity threatening us from as far back as I could remember, and this morning she had vomited blood.

Wanting to fend off bad luck by being very good, and useful, I added wood to the kitchen fire and started a batch of biscuits. I had just learned how to make them.

Lewis came in and asked me, "Is the fire still burning?"

"I don't know."

"When can I see the fire?"

"I don't know. Mama is sick, Lewis."

Christina appeared in the doorway. "I'm making breakfast," I explained.

"Good," she said. "Good. Make breakfast. I go. I bring doctor."

"Oh no," I said. A doctor meant it was serious. "Oh no."

When I had finished making breakfast, I called out to Lewis to come into the kitchen, but he didn't answer, and I went to look for him. With increasing panic I searched downstairs, upstairs, in the attic, the backyard, and the street. I searched the house again, this time walking into my parents' room to see if he was with my mother.

She was in bed. Her chest heaved in shuddering breaths that seemed to require all her concentration. When I came in she opened her eyes. "What is it, Arabella?"

"I was calling Lewis for breakfast, Mama," I said.

She nodded slowly.

"May I bring you some biscuits and toast?" I asked her.

"No, thank you, Arabella."

LEWIS HAD GONE TO SEE THE FIRE; I was sure of it. On a piece of wrapping paper, I wrote a note saying that I was going to look for him; I pinned it under a candlestick on the kitchen table. I clothed myself in two of everything except my coat, into the pockets of which, wrapped in newspaper, I put the biscuits, and I went out to follow my poor foolish brother to the docks in weather so cold it had frozen every cistern and well in the city.

I wrapped my scarf around my face and walked, sometimes into the wind, over patches of dirty snow, frozen puddles, and frozen dung. Cloudy icicles as thick as a man's arm clung to the railings and shutters. Above the roofs, smoke from small, regularly spaced chimneys rose in groups of three, and a much larger column of smoke loomed beyond the houses, like the giant mother of those smaller plumes. The smoke told me where to walk.

Much sooner than I had expected, I stood among the charred ruins and knots of people guarding their belongings. The fire had stopped only a few long blocks from our house. Whenever the smoke cleared, it exhibited the shocking fact that the river was in plain sight because there were no longer any buildings to interrupt the view. It was as if the whole world had been put to the torch. Here and there a jagged, blackened section of a wall or a marble façade stood before piles containing all the nonflammable contents of the building, which had fallen through its wooden floors. Stacks of rescued goods rose higher than my head. Some were piled neatly in bales and boxes, some strewn helter-skelter. More than once I mistook some bundle on the sidewalk for the frozen body of my brother.

"Lewis!" I called out. "Lewis! Lewis, where are you?"

Iron wheels rattled on paving bricks. Bosses shouted out orders to the clerks and the laboring men. I asked men in black silk hats and capes, men in uniforms, and men who sat exhausted on the curb if they had seen a five-year-old boy with brown hair. They said yes. They had seen dozens of them.

In the street beside the smoldering ruins of a warehouse, its exterior reduced to a staring door insanely offering passage through a triangular shard of wall, I came upon some grizzled old-timers, with ripped, soiled clothing, warming themselves by a sweet-smelling fire, a tame fire, a pet fire, which they lovingly fed with morsels of wood from broken crates. "Have you seen a five-year-old boy?"

"Aye," said one of them. "Some." Since he said "aye" for "yes," I decided he must be a sailor.

I asked, "Did you see one about this tall?"

"Maybe," he said. "Are you cold? Come and warm yourself."

I was shivering, so I accepted the invitation. There were two other men, dressed in tattered coats, with dirty rags stuffed into the collars and sleeves, and rags wrapped around their wrists and the knuckles of their raw hands. A broken crate had been sacrificed to the fire. Its corners glowed orange, and the stenciled words CODDINGTON & BARROW HYSON TEA transiently swelled and shrank and shimmied in the flames.

"He has red mittens," I remembered. "Did you see a boy with red mittens?"

"Follow me," said the man. He took my hand and started walking. He was taller and younger than he had seemed a moment earlier, but very unprepossessing, with a scraggly beard, and purple bruises on his face—he fought; low people got in fights—and his tight grip hurt my hand. He scared me, but though I might with a sudden effort have pulled away, and I could certainly have screamed for help, I didn't. I was too worried about Lewis to pay much attention to my own safety. Nothing very bad had ever happened to me, and whatever else he may have been, this stranger was a grown man with a grown man's resources.

"Where are you going, Bill?" called out one of the man's companions.

"To look for the lost boy," answered the man holding my hand—Bill—and then, very oddly, he asked me: "Is he your son?"

"How can he be my son? I'm a child."

"Is that so? How old?"

"Seven and a half."

"A smart little girl?"

"I have been called so."

"Do you read?"

"Yes."

"That must be why they call you smart. What's the boy's name?"

"Lewis," I answered, and I called out, "Lewis! Lewis! Do you hear me, Lewis? Where are you, Lewis?"

"Let me call him," said Bill. "Lewis. Lewis. Come, Lewis. Come here, Lewis."

He was joking, I supposed, because he called very quietly, almost in a whisper.

"He can't hear you. You must shout," I said. "Lewis! Lewis!"

Some barrels of raw sugar had spilled out, and a few small children were scooping it into their hands and eating it. We passed a place that had been a bank. Soldiers with rifles stood before it. It did not occur to me until they were far behind us that I might have asked them for help. Anyway, perhaps Bill was helping me. He was either helping me or abducting me.

"Can you read the small sign on that lamppost?" Bill inquired.

"It says Wall Street," I answered.

"Does it? So that's what it was saying all this time."

There was no way to distinguish street from curb. I stumbled, and he picked me up and carried me in his arms, squeezing my thigh through my trousers.

He had carried me to the wharves, where stacks of stovepipe hats, barrels of rum and coffee beans, crates of pepper, heaps of silks and tweeds and calicos and chests of teas had temporarily melted the East River ice, which now tightly gripped it all and slowly bore it all away. A little farther, there was smoke, and I coughed. I knew there was something wrong with him, though I could not have told you exactly what it was, and I was becoming alarmed. In my innocence, the range of bad fates that I imagined befalling me were limited: I was afraid he would throw me into the river or the fire or enslave me, making me into one of the poor little girls I had been told of who sold hot corn or swept street corners for pennies that they brought home to their unimaginable fathers.

"B-B-Bill," I said, stuttering from cold rather than from fear, though I was scared enough. "M-my grandfather and my father hand out B-B-Bibles. On South Street and in the F-Five P-Points." I am not sure why I said this: I suppose to make him know that my family was a friend to those living in darkness—to people like him—and he should consider this before he threw me into the river. "M-maybe you have met them, Bill. My grandfather is Solomon G-Godwin, the silk importer. He has a store and warehouse on P-Pearl Street."

"Not no more he don't."

He walked to Pearl Street and stood before the remnants of a sign on half a charred wall: SO__MO_ GO_W__. Boys were poking the embers with sticks.

"Lewis!" I shouted. "That's him! Put me down!"

"Help me, Arabella," said Lewis, as if we were home and I had just come in from the next room. He was trying to work a brass-tipped cane from the embers.

"P-put me down," I commanded Bill.

"Did I find your brother for you?"

"Yes, thank you."

"And you're grateful?"

"Yes."

"And do you know how to show gratitude?"

"I'll tell my papa. My papa will give you something."

"Your papa? No. Something from you."

We were bargaining. I understood that. But what could he want from me? I had in my room some pennies, and dimes, one English shilling, books, toys, a collection of seashells; I knew he would not trust me to go home and come back with them. I had my scarf; I was unwilling to surrender it in this cold. I had biscuits in my pockets. I decided I would offer them to him, but I thought it prudent to ask first, "What do you want?"

"Give me a kiss."

Well, that cost nothing, and it was not even the first time I had made this exchange; perfectly respectable strangers, after telling me how pretty I was, had often solicited my kisses, and once I had kissed a store clerk who had afterward given me a penny, and Christina had reminded me to thank him. So now I cooperated readily; my lips grazed the sandpapery whiskers of his filthy cheek. "Not like that," he said. Gripping the back of my head with his free hand, he kissed me on the mouth, while the hand that held me from below clutched a place on my body that seemed unnecessary to the task of holding me aloft. It was as foul a surprise as you would expect it to be; and I leave you to decide, knowing what ultimately became of me, whether this strange man saw or in some mysterious way influenced my future, or whether, as I believe, it only seemed so later because of the events which I shall relate in their proper order.

At any rate, he put me down, and then I was wiping my mouth with one hand and grabbing Lewis with the other. "Lewis, we sh-shouldn't be out. We have to get home."

"In a minute," he said. "Help me."

"Nanaowowow!" I demanded. The word was elongated by my shivers, as in a game we used to play when I would shake him while he said his name and it would come out "Lllllllllooooooooo-iiiiiii-sssssss"; but the cold was our rough playmate now. There was no feeling in my fingertips, and I considered it very strange to stand surrounded by embers and worry that we might freeze before we reached our home.

"Help me," said Lewis. He meant help him get at his loot.

"Will you come with me when you have the cane?" I asked.

After a hesitation, he said, "Y-y-yes." He was shivering, too.

The cane, half buried under assorted office furniture, had a curved brass handle in the shape of a snake's head. It was the handle he wanted. I stepped tentatively on the cane. Then I stepped on it harder. Within a puff of fine ash, which expanded slowly in the air for a long time afterward, the cane snapped near the handle. I stepped again, and it broke off completely. Lewis stuffed it into a pocket already bulging and sagging with other loot.

He was trembling with the cold, and I pulled him close to me as we walked home. He told me his head hurt and asked me to pick him up. I told him that I didn't feel well either. I, too, had a headache, and I was tired. I remembered that we had missed breakfast. So we stopped to warm ourselves by the heat of a burning house, and ate cold biscuits, though neither of us was hungry.

When we reached our street I saw the doctor's carriage waiting by the black iron fence. I banged the knocker until the door opened, and Christina pulled us into the house, touching our heads and our cheeks, exclaiming over the dirt and soot that covered us.

"How is Mama?" I asked.

Christina had a careful, emphatic way of imparting information, staring into your eyes, as if she meant you to memorize her words. "The doctor is with your mama."

I started to go upstairs to see her, but Christina insisted on cleaning us up at a basin in the kitchen first. "How you both shiver!"

Christina helped us up the stairs. As we reached the landing, the boards creaked to announce the approach of Dr. Boyle, whose name had been spoken so often in our house that it had been among my first words. He was tall and stout, well dressed, ruddy, a model of health and good appetite for his patients to imitate. "So these are the young fugitives!" He beamed down at us benevolently.

Lewis began to vomit. Dr. Boyle stepped away to save his boots. He did it deftly, and with no change of expression, as if he had been expecting Lewis to vomit and it was, medically, a good sign. Then he became interested in the vomit. He sat us both on the steps. He looked at his watch while holding Lewis's wrist and feeling his forehead. Then he did the same for me and told Christina to put us to bed.

I lay beneath many blankets, shivering, half awake, and distantly aware of Christina undressing Lewis.

I dreamed of the blackened streets, the treasure drifting downriver, the smoldering ruins behind the marble pillars of the Exchange, and an angel, who with one arm wielded a sword he pointed north, east, south, and west, and with the other arm carried me safely through the air across the burning world. Worried faces surrounded me. I spat up into a bowl. Christina fed me beef broth, which I promptly spewed onto my night-shirt. My coughs carved deeper and wider spaces within my chest as if bent on hollowing me out completely. It occurred to me that I might die before my mother.

Later, using all my strength, I turned my head slowly to watch Dr. Boyle hold a candle with which he was setting bits of paper alight on Lewis's chest. He covered the paper with a wineglass. Then Dr. Boyle was holding a lancet. Lewis's blood dripped into a white china basin. With another slice of the lancet, the blood flowed.

Frank was brought in. He was sick, too. We were fed, cupped, bled, and purged.

When I was conscious once more, the other beds in the room were empty, and my mother was stroking my hair. That she was alive was wonderful, and her touch was a comfort to me; yet I knew that something terrible had happened. "What is it?" I asked weakly. "What?"

"Don't talk," she said, her eyes brimming.

Next I was sitting up in bed, eating Irish potatoes. Christina was there with my mother.

"Who?" I asked. My mother turned away.

"Your brother Frank is in heaven," said Christina.

❧ IV ❧

IT WAS NEVER DETERMINED WHAT HAD CAUSED our general attack of "fever," as Dr. Boyle called it. The suspects were bad food—maybe an inferior ham that Sally had purchased, which we had finished off the night of the fire—and bad air from an open drain. No one said the word "infection." I suppose there were doctors who thought that illnesses were contagious, but they were backward or foreign; Dr. Boyle was not one of them. He believed in ventilation.

I had a lingering bronchitis afterward, and for months I was obliged to spend several hours each day in bed or sitting in a chair. I passed the time reading books. I read *The Fairchild Family* twice. I read Genesis in the family's big picture Bible. Robert began reading *Robinson Crusoe* aloud to me, and when he wasn't there, I went on by myself. It was much harder than the Bible or *The Fairchild Family*. I remember how the last page looked, down to a little pea-soup stain, on the day I finished it, and that at first no one believed that a seven-and-a-half-year-old child had really read such a grown-up book. Eventually, I was given Frank's books.

MY GRANDFATHER WAS WELL KNOWN by this time as the abolition-ist merchant who helped to found an antislavery newspaper, and who had the minister of the Abyssinian Presbyterian Church as a guest at his table. Today it is believed that all Northerners were foes of slavery, but in fact the cause dearest to my grandfather's heart was unpopular in New York City, where many people depended for their livelihood on trade with the South. New York insurance companies had refused to take his money, and he had used a Boston firm instead; this worked to his advantage after the fire, because the New York insurers went bankrupt, and my grandfather had more capital than his competitors did during the period of rebuilding. By the following year, fifteen months after the fire, a new store and warehouse had arisen, seven stories high, the tallest edifice in the city of New York.

I have alluded to this building earlier. I heard that phrase, "the tall-est building in the city," on the lips of every member of my family very often from the time we knew that that's what it would be. We bragged to the other schoolchildren about it. I walked down the street with Lewis's hand in mine and told him that he was a lucky boy since his grandfather owned the tallest building in New York.

One day soon after it had risen to its full height, the family, all excepting my mother, made a visit to stand on the roof of the warehouse and enjoy its immensity. All around us, the grays and browns of the waterfront were replaced by the tawny hues of raw wood, and the air smelled of paint, bricks, and sawdust.

We were all panting by the time we reached the top, and as we stepped out onto the flat roof, I gripped Lewis's sweaty, slippery hand tightly. He had recently voiced the alarming opinion that a person who wished hard enough, with perfect faith, might learn to fly.

We had lived all our lives on flat land in the city, with occasional excursions to the farms of Brooklyn and New Jersey, so we were very impressed by the view from seven flights up. We could see the ships on the river, and more buildings, streets, wagons, carriages, horsecars, omnibuses, and people than our eyes had ever beheld at once. We noticed the fire's legacy in the broad swath of the city—like the track of God's paintbrush—where everything was new. Humpbacked clouds cast shadows on neighborhoods in sun and neighborhoods in rain. We found our house.

"Let go of me," Lewis demanded. "My hand hurts. I can't see."

I let go as Robert grabbed him under the armpits and jerked him up roughly onto his shoulders. "Now you're the highest one of all," said Robert.

"Jump," said Lewis.

"What?" Robert asked in bewilderment.

"Jump up."

"What?"

"To be higher. Then we'll both be higher."

"Oh," said Robert, and he jumped up and down.

I wanted my father to stop them. "Father," I said, trying to catch his eye, and I was struck by the darkness of his expression. We had all experienced sudden ambushes of dejection since Frank's death, when we were stopped in the middle of whatever we were doing by the reminder that he was not here to enjoy this moment, but waiting for us in a land beyond the sky. I assumed that my father was thinking this now, but if you had asked me even at that age I could have supplied other explanations for his gloom. His wife was dying. Earlier that year, he had been on a business trip to Cincinnati; there had not been much talk about it afterward, and there would have been if it had gone well. Though I would not have been able to put it into words back then, I knew that my father did not fit into the good, pious, humorless family into which he had been born. He was a likable man with a witty mind, but in his circle charm counted far less than business sense and high moral purpose, qualities he tried to acquire, earnestly and in vain. Many people having woes greater than his are cheerful anyway, from sheer animal spirits. That is their nature. His nature was to be melancholy.

After a while, the clouds were above us, bringing a premonition of rain. My father said it was time to go home. As soon as Lewis was on his feet he ran to the edge and dropped a large, heavy rock over the side of the warehouse. He'd hidden the rock in a pocket of his coat and brought it all this way with the express intention of dropping it from the roof.

When we got to the bottom, we found the rock broken into five pieces on the cobblestones, a yard or so away from a dead pig. Two dogs were already sniffing the corpse.

My father went into the store and gave orders for the pig to be removed.

"You killed that pig," I scolded Lewis. "It could have been a man."

"It's a pig," said Lewis in a distant, philosophical tone.

"Yes, luckily, but what if you had dropped the rock over the edge when a man was walking below? You'd have killed him!"

"Think of it, Lewis," said Edward, to tease me. "You're very young for a killer."

"It's not funny," I said.

"I could have killed a man," Lewis echoed, impressed with himself. He picked up the largest fragment of the rock.

"Put it down," I demanded.

"Oh, let him have his souvenir," said Edward. "It's done its damage."

Robert seconded him. "He knows he mustn't do that again—don't you, Lewis?"

"Yes, I know."

"He's learned his lesson. Let him have it."

"Let him," said my father absentmindedly.

The next time we had pork chops for dinner, Lewis ate his share complacently, and no one said a word, afraid to break the spell. From then on, pork was like any other meat to him, and throwing brickbats at pigs became his favorite amusement.

The piece of the rock with which he had killed the pig was forever afterward his lucky stone. It would be among his possessions for many years, with him whenever he needed luck, whenever he gambled, and whenever he killed someone.

V

ON THE DAY MY MOTHER FELL INTO her final illness—at the very moment when she was lifted for the last time onto her deathbed—I was walking home with Rebecca, a new girl at the subscription grammar school that I had been attending for three years, along with around thirty other children of the neighborhood, in the second story of the Union Presbyterian Church. The teacher, a young, choleric man, never looked at peace with himself except when he caned the boys; then he had a poetic countenance, like a concert pianist playing an exquisite passage. He didn't cane girls. For girls it was the ruler smacking the palms, which seemed to tremble with their own fear, separate from mine, as I held them out to receive correction.

My friendship with Rebecca had all the thrills and terrors of a love affair. It was she who befriended me, very actively like a practiced seducer. And virtually from the instant I surrendered, I was worried that she would realize how dull I was and regret the intense effort she had made to fascinate me, which had been so flattering because she had so many tools of fascination at her disposal. She was the daughter of a hotel proprietor, and lived at the hotel and had enjoyed a more numerous variety of amusements and met a greater variety of people than any other girl I knew. She had met Englishmen, Frenchmen, and Italians; she had been up the Hudson by steamboat; she had seen a trotting race in Brooklyn and a diorama of the Battle of New Orleans, and when I told her about the view from the tallest building in New York City, she told me of the view from a mountain. She had been to ice-cream saloons, as they were called then, and she had met a 150-year-old colored woman who was said to have been George Washington's nurse.

My own life seemed uninteresting by comparison, and when I was with Rebecca I had little to say, except to echo her opinions.

At school she would pretend to be dainty and squeamish; spotting a centipede on her trousers, she would give a shriek and beg someone to remove it. She said "limb" instead of "leg." Yet, when she was walking home with me once—her father's hotel was on the way—her vocabulary was suddenly easy and vulgar, and she took her hand out of her trouser pocket and showed me a centipede crawling over her palm.

"I'm a hypocrite," she confided proudly, as one would say, "I'm double-jointed." ("Me, too!" I almost said.)

It was from Rebecca that I first learned what men and women do with each other. She told me on our last day together.

"They do what dogs do," she said, and when I said I didn't know what she meant, she said, well, surely I had seen what the dogs in the street were doing sometimes, when people threw rocks to separate them, and parents covered the eyes of their children?

I had not. So, as we walked home, Rebecca explained. I was amazed, without really grasping the significance of the secret she had imparted to me. I was always stupid with Rebecca. I studied her speech and gestures in order to reproduce them for her approval, and I missed a great deal of what she actually said.

My life was about to be kicked in a new direction, like a child's ball, so in later years I often thought back to this moment. It was a warm spring day. Sunbeams, squeezed through tiny random openings in the canopy of sycamores, made golden disks that winked and shimmered when the wind rose, and leaf shadows stroked the back of Rebecca's yellow blouse when I was behind her and her skin when she faced me. We came to the point where we always said goodbye. We paused there. I was glad to realize that she wanted to linger, that she took pleasure in my company. We said, "See you tomorrow," and we believed it.

Walking on alone, I noticed a dog sniffing the curb. I looked at its hindquarters. While I was thus distracted, an impossible idea crept into my mind: that some of Rebecca's remarks applied to my parents.

Then I saw Dr. Boyle's carriage on the street outside the house.

I banged the brass door-knocker. Christina let me in, and there was a look on her face that I do not remember, but it caused me to cry out. "What? What is it? What?" I demanded. "What's happened?"

My brother Robert lay prostrate, sobbing, on the sofa where he usually read his newspapers and his books.

I shouted "Mama!" and turned toward the stairs, but Christina flung out an arm to stop me.

"She lives a little longer. Go to the pump," she said. "Get wash water."

I went out to the back of the house. Lewis was digging in the garden, where everything was in bloom, for it was May. He was digging a deep hole with a tin spoon. I took a bucket to the pump and pumped water until the bucket was full, and carried it to the washtub. Stupid Christina, who thought the idea that my mother was to live "a little longer" would reconcile me to spending another minute away from her, came out carrying a great heap of sheets, and, seeing the bright-red blood they were drenched in, I said, "Oh no," in a small voice. My mother had hemorrhaged from her lungs while the other children and I were filing in two rows out of our schoolroom at the back of the Union Presbyterian Church. Edward had run to fetch the doctor when Rebecca was telling me about dogs and men. Christina dumped the bedding into the washtub and said, oddly, "Good." What in the world she was thinking I have no idea, because I never thought to ask.

I felt the flimsy boards of the back porch shake under the feet of Dr. Boyle. "Let me talk to the little girl," he told Christina. He was wiping his hands with a rag. Slowly, giving a distinct impression that, for him, sitting down called for as much effort as moving a grand piano, he lowered his great bottom onto the edge of the porch and patted the place next to him. "Your mama is resting," he said when I had sat beside him. "We let her rest so that she may stay with us a little longer. There will certainly be time to say goodbye, days or more, and she may even be able to give you a few words of encouragement; I know she would use her last breath to help you in any way she can. But we must prepare."

He patted my head. I drew away, and he pulled his hand back. I didn't want him to work on my emotions, even if it would make me feel better. I wanted my mother.

"You know, I think . . ." He paused. "You know that your mother inherited a predisposition from her own mother, and she has probably suffered in some degree from consumption for over twenty years. What began it is not certain. She puts the blame on a fall from a horse; I suspect a croup when she was fourteen." He brushed a fly away from his big red face absentmindedly. "Not everyone who has a consumptive parent inherits the predisposition. We can tell, though, from the signs which God in His wisdom has placed upon the patient's face and form. Oval face, bright eyes, large pupils, clear complexion, fine hair."

I felt his gaze make the inventory of my features. I understood; this was what he had wanted to tell me. I had inherited a tendency to consumption. I had heard all that. I had dismissed it. I was strong. I was healthy.

"She has remained among us longer than expected," he went on. "I attribute her survival mainly to her dutiful attention to her own improvement. Now the time is upon us. In a sign of God's mercy, consumption has helped to make her ready. As her mortal part decays, her spiritual part beams forth with increased luster. She's three-quarters angel already, is she not?"

Oh, she was! His words took me against my will, as my own mother's words sometimes had, when she wanted me to feel contrite, and I wept on the coarse weave of Dr. Boyle's waistcoat, smelling sweat, stale tobacco, and blood.

My father had come home while Dr. Boyle was talking. Reverend Fowler, our minister, whom my mother had known for ten years, had come to sit by her bed, and Mrs. Fitch, a member of my mother's consumptive sewing circle, arrived to help Christina with the housework. At the dinner table, Dr. Boyle, Reverend Fowler, and Mrs. Fitch carried the burden of the conversation. Believing that small talk would do us good, they asked us about school, and my father about the events of the day.

Only two months after our optimistic climb to the top of my grandfather's new warehouse, the country had descended into an economic crisis, with businesses failing, banks refusing to issue specie, clerks and mechanics thrown out of work. This was discussed for a while, with Reverend Fowler asking questions and my father pulling himself out of a blue funk to answer him. The subject changed to a recent steamship explosion in which eleven men and three women had lost their lives. Then Mrs. Fitch talked about a trip she and Mr. Fitch had taken up the Hudson to attend a revival, and how many had been saved on that occasion, and she and Reverend Fowler compared the abilities of various revival speakers. I thought of the violence that sickness had wreaked upon my mother's body, that she would never see the return of good times, and of the great crossing that lay before her.

Christina came down to announce that my mother had woken and was asking for us. We all went upstairs.

Her skin was pale, the fine blue veins were numerous and prominent, and her eyes glittered in their deep cavities. Her body by this time was a bundle of sticks, a grotesque puppet cruelly burdened with a soul. Christina had wrapped her as tightly as a mummy, and only the arms lay above the blankets now; in her wrists, which projected out of the sleeves of her nightshirt, the veins and tendons were like tangled string, the knuckles too big, the fingernails flattened.

Propped up on her pillows, my mother addressed us by our names, not omitting Dr. Boyle, Mrs. Fitch, and Reverend Fowler. Her eyes moved in her immobile head as she looked at each of us in turn, and finally she said, as if surprising herself, "Frank." She tried to blink away her tears. Christina dabbed at my mother's eyes with a handkerchief. My mother said, smiling and weeping, "I'll be with him soon. If you have any messages for him, my darlings, give them to me now."

"Give him," said my father, beginning smoothly, but choking on the words, "our love," his throat constricted, and Robert said, "Yes," and Edward said, "Yes, give him our love," and we all wept.

"Mama, don't go," cried Lewis, and he began to climb into bed with her.

My father stopped him. "No, Lewis." He may have feared Lewis would tax her strength and end the life she was clinging to so feebly. Or it may have been his sense of decorum; my mother herself had very definite ideas of what was fitting at a deathbed.

Lewis kissed her cheek and begged her, "Stay with me, Mama."

She told him that she hated to leave him when he was so small, but if the Lord was calling her, there must be a good reason for it. She asked Reverend Fowler to back her up on this point, and he agreed. She told Lewis to respect his elders and obey his father and his sister and try to lighten their burdens. Then, in a weak voice, but with a confident mastery of this moment for which she had so long prepared, she moved on to Robert and Edward and to me, giving each of us a particular word of warning and encouragement.

"You will continue to take good care of your brother Lewis, Belle?"

"Yes, Mama, oh yes."

"You must always be watchful and loyal. Promise me."

I promised.

She said that we had all been a great blessing to her, that we had given her great happiness, and that thanks to us she counted herself among the most fortunate of women.

"I shall be watching you," she said, and a shudder racked her body, and her eyes shut, and I cried out, "Mama!" but Dr. Boyle went close and leaned his head next to hers, then announced, "She's sleeping."

After that we all took turns keeping vigil by her bedside, calling the others into her room when she seemed to be at a crisis, so that we should all be there when she expired. At her request, friends from her sewing circle came to say farewell. One, Mrs. Wilder, was obviously very sick herself. "You and I will not be separated long, Mrs. Wilder," my mother predicted, and Mrs. Wilder, with a rueful smile, agreed.

Giving directions from her bed, my mother dispensed presents, some she had made or purchased especially as gifts, some from among her possessions. I received her sewing kit and pins and brooches; a blank diary purchased especially for me; *Advice to a Young Married Woman,* by a minister, which she asked me not to read until I was older, though I need not necessarily wait until I was married; *Exemplary Letters for Sundry Occasions; The Whole Duty of Woman;* and some of her own volumes of Walter Scott's novels, which I might enjoy when my reading had improved. With a glance at Reverend Fowler, whose advice she had sought in this matter, she said that, for a sensible girl such as she knew me to be, novels by respectable authors could provide harmless amusement, but I must remember not to neglect my duties for them, not to demand that my life be a romance, or overstrain myself with too much reading.

She gave Robert and Edward some of her books as well, and she had bought each of them a writing kit and a copy of *Advice to a Young Man,* and she gave them decorative pincushions and other needlework she had made herself, stitching in pain so that they should have the work of their mother's hands to remember her by.

Under her direction, we read to her from the Bible and sang her favorite hymns. She conducted her leave-taking with such assurance, it began to create an illusion that she wasn't dying, that our lives had entered a permanent new phase of visiting and giving presents and praying at her bedside, with a difficult but tolerable undercurrent of dread. Then, early in the morning, with a dry gasp, she died. I was woken from my sleep to be told—"Your mother is in heaven"—by my father, who looked, most of all, weary.

MRS. FITCH STAYED ON IN THE HOUSE to help us. With my mother gone, the burden on Christina was considerably eased, my own chores were lighter, the house became noticeably cleaner and tidier, and our meals were better cooked. Mrs. Fitch sympathized tactfully, without calling attention to herself.

A few days after the funeral, we heard the cry of a rag picker, "Any old clothes, any rags, money for your old rags," and Christina went out to the street with a bundle for him; I followed her. He was a Negro man, not old, pushing a cart laden with burlap sacks stuffed with old clothes and other broken and worn-out articles. When Christina handed him the bundle, he unwrapped it, and I saw that she was giving him the sheets stained with my mother's blood, which she had not been able to wash out after all.

THAT SAME AFTERNOON, A MAN WHO I LATER LEARNED was the First Ward constable came to the house, accompanied by a clerk from Grandfather's firm, and they spoke to Mrs. Fitch alone. At dinner, we noticed the strain in her effort to be cheerful. "Are you well, Mrs. Fitch?" I asked her. She said that she had had a slight attack of her own illness, nothing serious, adding, "The young man whose visit you have noticed has told me that your father will not be home tonight. He has been called away unexpectedly."

"Where did he go?" asked Robert.

She hesitated, and then said, "Cincinnati."

"Do you know when he will return?"

"We don't know that yet," replied Mrs. Fitch.

The brevity and vagueness of her replies struck me as odd. But I was nine, and there were still many perfectly ordinary aspects of adult life that I didn't understand, so I shrugged off this little piece of strangeness that came in the midst of the great strangeness of life without my mother. My father had been to Cincinnati before.

VI

THE NEXT DAY, THE RAIN MADE a slate-colored stream along the curb and beat the flowers in the garden until their stems lay flat. Mrs. Fitch said she hoped we wouldn't mind missing a few more days of school, and she asked us to occupy ourselves in the house and to keep close to it while she went out. She left us in the charge of Christina and took a hack uptown and did not return until that evening after supper.

When she came back, she asked us to meet her in the parlor. She smiled at us. She took Lewis in her lap and stroked his hair. She looked around at us and beyond us, and it seemed several times as though she were about to speak but couldn't find the words.

"I've always liked this room," she said finally. "Of all the rooms in all the houses where our sewing circle has gathered, this is the most pleasant. And you children were always good to all of us silly, sick old ladies, and if someone gave you a little present you thanked us, and if we gave you advice, whether it was wise or not, you listened, and if you were scolded unjustly you took our infirmity into account and did not resent it. You were a credit to your mother. You were a joy to her. She often told me so. You know I loved her. I always liked your father, too, with his gentle humor and kindness." She paused, squinting. With a sigh, she pushed on: "Your grandfather I regard as a great man, and I am not alone in this. In short—forgive me—in short, you . . . you are well-brought-up children from a fine family, and wherever you go you may carry your name with pride. And—oh, mercy—mercy." She winced. "Forgive me, children. You have been through so much, and you have been so strong, and it grieves me to tell you that you must bear an even greater burden. Your father has passed on. Oh, mercy. Your father, too—it happened quickly, he took ill in Cincinnati, he took ill with a fever—he was weakened by his grief and he died quickly, without time to make arrangements for you, but he sent you his love, he spoke your names, his last thoughts were of his children."

It was different from the way it had been around my mother's death-bed. None of us wept. Even Lewis, sitting in Mrs. Fitch's lap, looked bewildered rather than grief-stricken, and as for me, I felt as if all the blood had drained from my body, and I thought to myself: She is mistaken. She is a silly old woman, just as she says. She's gotten it wrong.

"But I cannot—I ask that you do not question me further about your father's passing," Mrs. Fitch continued—as if to fend off a volley of inquiries, though none of us had said a word—"for there is very little I know of a certainty right now, and I don't want to sow confusion. Tonight you must pack, for tomorrow you are moving uptown to your grandfather's house."

Mrs. Fitch led us on a search for trunks and carpetbags and saw to it that we included our winter clothes. Eventually, our grandfather would send for the contents of the house, she said. But much of it might be stored away and hard to reach, and so, if there was anything we needed, we should take it now.

I helped Lewis pack his clothes and his toys, his presents from his mother, and his souvenirs, including his lucky rock, which at first he had me put in a box but which he decided at last to keep in his trouser pocket.

That night, in the room I shared with Lewis, after we had said our prayers, I read to him by candlelight from *Mr. Midshipman Easy* by Frank's favorite author, Captain Marryat. Frank had not lived to read this particular volume, which was published shortly after he died. In the first chapter there was a bluff joke about death and graves; neither of us commented on it. When Lewis's eyelids began to sink, I snuffed out the candle and went to my own bed.

The gas lamp outside threw a lozenge of light onto the ceiling. I heard street sounds of farewells, rolling carriage wheels, night-soil collectors scraping the pavement. In my dream, Mrs. Fitch came into the room and apologized to us; she had, in fact, been entirely mistaken about my father's death. Then I woke up, and I could not fall back to sleep.

Lewis was awake, too, and he asked if he could come into bed with me. I said yes, and we held each other. I spoke to Lewis about our grand-father's house, reminding him of it, inviting him to speculate where we would sleep when we got there.

After a silence, he asked me, "Where is Cincinnati?" and I told him that it was out west, in Ohio. Then he asked, "Is Papa in heaven?"

"So we have been told," I replied.

"No, we haven't," Lewis corrected me.

"Yes, Lewis. Mrs. Fitch said so."

"When did she say it?"

"You were there when she said it."

"I don't remember. I remember she said Papa was dead. When did she say he was in heaven, like Frank and Mama?"

I thought for a while, and finally answered, "I forget. Of course Papa is in heaven."

Another few seconds went by, and then my brother asked me, "Will we die?"

"Yes. That's why we must be good, so that when we die we will go to heaven and be with Mama and Papa and Frank."

"Will we die soon?"

"No. Not for many years."

"How do you know?"

"I know. Believe me. Why, are you afraid?"

He didn't answer.

"It's not like you to be afraid," I said. "It's you who frightens me, with your climbing, and picking fights with bigger boys, and playing with fire and knives, and running away so I can't find you, and throwing rocks at pigs. Oh, it's torture for me. How many times have I wished you were a coward."

"I'm sorry," said Lewis. "I'm sorry I frightened you. I'm sorry I was bad."

I felt his face, wet with tears, against mine. I said he was a wonderful boy and a great joy to me. He sobbed louder and held me tighter. "I'll be good. I promise. And you promise me."

"That I'll be good? What do you mean? I'm always good," I said, to make him smile, though it was only the truth.

I felt his head shaking. "Promise me you won't die."

I stroked his hair. "I promise." I kissed the top of his head, and his brow, and his cheeks, and his lips. "I promise. I promise."

A bright bar of light gradually appeared under the doorway, and there came a knock. I said, "We're awake, come in," and Robert entered, holding an astral lamp and followed by Edward. "Sleep in our room tonight," said Edward. I held the lamp while they dragged our mattresses down the hall and into their room.

We all lay there, quietly awake, until Robert suddenly spoke, saying, "We have to be faithful. We've got to stick together now," and we all murmured our assent and pledged our loyalty to one another, making childish promises never again to quarrel.

I had begun to doze when I was startled awake by the following idea: It could not be an accident that my father had taken ill so quickly after my mother died. My father and mother could not bear to be apart, and God had taken pity on them both by sending him a quick, easy death. If in His kindness to our parents God had treated us harshly, it was because he knew we could bear it. He was trying us, toughening us. He had some great purpose for us.

In the sky, they were watching us, Mama and Papa, together and glad to see that their children were being kind to each other. I pictured them. They had beautiful white wings. The stars behind their heads seemed larger because they were so near.

❧ VII ❧

IN THE EARLY AFTERNOON, WE WENT UPTOWN in a wagon from my grandfather's store. The driver was a clerk in his employ—Horace—

a young man so naturally cheerful that he could not help being wrong for the occasion: with tight, garish clothes, and a short-brimmed hat at a rakish angle.

Horace helped us load our trunks and bags. With self-conscious gallantry, he gave his hand to help Christina into the wagon.

Mrs. Fitch embraced each of us in turn, making us promise to visit and to write. She said that she was confident—knowing how well our mother had raised us—that we would try to be light burdens to our grandfather and grandmother. We would remember that they, too, had just suffered a grievous blow in the death of our parents, and we should not wear them down with anxious questions. She said, finally, eyes brimming, "We are all pilgrims and wayfarers on this earth."

And we were off. From the back of the wagon, I saw Mrs. Fitch with her fist in her mouth, and then, for the last time, the house and this familiar tree and that familiar lamp, and Bowling Green Park, getting smaller until, with a turn of the wagon, it all disappeared. We came to the corner where Rebecca and I always used to separate on our walk home, and then we passed the hotel her father owned, where she lived and conversed with travelers from all over the world; I wondered if she had heard of what had happened since we last met, and the thought of her learning of it made my throat hurt. With a collective twist, like a great ribbon, a flock of pigeons simultaneously left the roof of a building nearby and reassembled on a ledge on the other side. We went by a long, dripping ice wagon, and men with pushcarts, Jews and Negroes and Irishmen chanting little rhymes about the freshness of their fish or their skill at sharpening knives. We were being swallowed up by the vast world. Our parents in heaven watched us and approved.

Horace, perhaps nervous to be around people who had suffered a double bereavement, talked a great deal, not always appropriately; he flirted with Christina and praised our grandfather's house and congratulated us on moving there (and Robert said quietly, "Only slaves and horses should be given classical names"). We went no great distance, but it took almost an hour, because the streets were crowded with carriages and horsecars and there were many delays. At last we came to the house I had visited usually on holidays, and I savored the sweet, fleeting impression that this was another, and that later that night I would return home to my parents; and instantly, in what was not my first experience of this age-old rhythm of bereavement, I paid for that pleasant instant of forgetfulness with the reminder of the truth: *No, you won't, never, never.* My grandfather and grandmother came out to greet us, and with Horace's help we stepped down from the wagon.

My grandmother was a short, pink-faced, double-chinned woman, who always held her back very straight, as if to make up for her shortness. She smiled stiffly and sadly and lowered her head, first to me and then to Lewis, to receive our kisses. She gave us nothing more in the way of encouragement or welcome. She had just received a terrible blow, worse even than I knew, but there was more to it than that. She had never been demonstrative toward me or toward my brothers. Taking into account the formality of her class and generation, she was relatively natural with my father, but as a grandmother she was chilly, and she had always struck me as rather selfish.

My grandfather's manners were even stiffer, but his affections had a broader scope, and I knew that he did not view me merely as a difficulty thrust on him by my parents' death. When we spoke, although we were formal, we were not impersonal.

He embraced me in his usual bewildered way, as if he had never quite understood the purpose of embraces but did not want to hurt anyone's feelings by withholding them. Then he put his hands gently on my shoulders—a sincerer gesture—to hold me at the right distance to focus on my face and my eyes, and he welcomed me. He shook hands gravely in turn with Robert, Edward, and Lewis. He told us that the servants would show us our rooms, and that we should let them know that we were not loafers but serious, hardworking people, by helping them bring up our bags and trunks.

So we helped bring our belongings into our rooms, which were on the second floor, not far from the big dining room where we met on holidays. Robert and Edward were in the guest bedroom, and Lewis and Christina and I in another. From its window I could see a chestnut tree, a weeping willow, a fountain, a pool, and a garden. The linen on my bed was fresh and crisp. The rooms were more numerous and larger than we were used to; the chairs were covered with silk instead of chintz; we could go down to the kitchen at any time and get a drink with ice in it. Once we had helped to bring our luggage in, we had no work to do, for the help carried all the wood and water and did all the other work that we usually did at home. We were sad, but we were comfortable.

IT SEEMED THAT MY GRANDMOTHER HAD DECIDED to befriend me the best way she knew how, by having me accompany her as she went about her little routines and self-assigned chores. She did not have to cook or clean in any serious way, but she took upon herself the tasks she said could not be entrusted to the help, which were really the ones she simply liked to do.

So, while Christina minded Lewis, we baked and polished the silver and sewed. We made full suits of clothing from fabrics we selected—materials my grandmother possessed in abundance, drawers and drawers full of rich, heavy brocades and broadcloths, damask, jaconet, and fustians. There was a great deal of lace, which she showed me with guilty pride, explaining the astonishing and basically unjustifiable amount of work that had gone into the making of each piece, years of skilled labor concentrated in that one drawer. Collecting these fabrics was her main vice.

Because women in evangelical circles were supposed to shun vain frippery, an indulgence of this sort needed an excuse. My grandmother's was that she belonged to her church's Dorcas Society, which made clothes for the poor. (I did not ask whether she put lace and damask into these clothes, and I still don't know.) Dorcas, said my grandmother, was a Christian woman in olden times who was so good that Peter raised her from the dead.

This got me to thinking, and after a few more minutes of sewing, I asked my grandmother the name of the illness of which my father had died.

She grew still for a moment and answered tersely, "It was fever. Nothing more specific is known." A little later, she looked up again from her needle and added, "Several others in the hotel had gotten it, and the vapors from—from his person—were thought to be dangerous, and so they hurried to get him in the ground. That is why you did not go to his funeral."

"Where is he buried?"

"He was buried there."

We went on sewing in silence. We were in a drawing room on the second floor, at the back of the house. From the window I could see the lawn and garden, and Lewis with Christina and a small white dog. After another minute, I asked, "Will he be brought home?"

"Yes," she said quickly.

"When?"

"Eventually."

"Will he be buried beside my mother?"

"Yes."

I heard Lewis cough, I heard the dog bark. I looked out the window again. A bird left the windowsill with a flutter and a swoop. Farther away, the dog dropped something at Lewis's feet, and Lewis, with a stick, was poking whatever had been dropped. I asked, "Who was with him when he died?"

"I don't know."

"Did any others in the hotel die of the fever?"

"No."

We kept dipping our needles into the fabric. The bird came back. I heard it cooing. I made more stitches, and asked, "Did the fever spread? Beyond the hotel?"

"I believe it was successfully contained."

I thought more and sewed more, and finally asked, "Was it in the newspapers?"

"Stop it, I won't have it," cried my grandmother. It was so unexpected that for a moment I thought she might be speaking to a bird at the window or a servant in the next room. "Did your mother never speak to you about asking questions?"

I didn't like to hear anything that could be interpreted as a criticism of my mother. "My mother worked hard to teach me good manners."

A little more softly, she agreed, "Of course she did. Your mother was a good woman, and you are a well-behaved child. But you are being thoughtless. Remember that your father was my son, and these questions pain me."

When we went to church, my grandparents wouldn't let us speak to anyone.

Doctors visited the house to examine us—all of us. We did not know why, and I did not question it, assuming that my grandfather wished to know the condition of the new members of the household and was wealthy enough to pay doctors just to determine exactly how healthy we were. Dr. Boyle came first. Then there was a Frenchman, who used a stethoscope, a novelty in those days. It came in a felt-lined wooden carrying case and was assembled from pieces, like a clarinet. We were next seen, in turn, by a Thomsonian, a physiobotanist, and a homeopath. The homeopath gave us tiny white pills. Lewis and I both still suffered from a dry cough, which all of the physicians, whatever their system, considered to be highly significant.

We were not told the results of these observations, but a few times I heard them agreeing sagely that Lewis and I each possessed "a tubercular diathesis." I knew what this meant. It was supposed back then, before Dr. Koch, that there was a consumptive type—refined, sensitive, and attractive. Beauty of a certain kind was a seal of doom.

A few weeks after the last of the doctors, a servant told me to go to my grandfather's study. When I got there, he smiled at me, but he looked troubled, and I thought that Lewis must have broken something expensive or uttered a sentiment intolerable even in a boy of seven, and my grandmother had asked that I be spoken to about him. Dust motes rose and drifted as my grandfather moved letters and ledgers off a chair for me to sit. He asked how I was feeling. I said very well. "Good," he said. I asked the same of him, and he replied that he was in good health for a man his age.

Christina wanted me to use my influence to get her a room of her own. She had had her own room in Bowling Green and didn't see why she should have to sleep with the children in a much larger house, and she had insisted that I bring the subject up with my grandfather the next time I spoke to him. I had felt timid about passing on this request, but now I was glad to have something to say to delay whatever unpleasant subject he was about to broach.

My grandfather told me, "Christina can have Robert and Edward's room. They are going to a boarding school. I know you'll miss them, but you must realize that even if your mother and father had lived they would have gone away soon."

It was a shock. We had all just sworn to stick together. "But," I said, to show that I was reasonable, "we'll see them in the summer and on holidays."

He was still for a moment. "Perhaps," he said, and I knew it meant no. "If—if you would please, for the moment, refrain from interrupting. Your grandmother and I enjoy your company. We wish you could stay with us. But it would be selfish of us to permit it. I've made arrangements to send both you and Lewis to live with your uncle Elihu and your aunt Agatha on their farm near Livy, in western New York State, south of the canal. As you'll see when you make the trip, the distances are considerable, and the roads near the end are so rugged that travel between there and here is infrequent. It may be a long time before you see Robert and Edward again. But you'll have Lewis, and a new family closely related to you by blood."

What had I done wrong? I wanted to plead with him, but he had told me not to interrupt, and I did not want to make him angrier.

He paused. "You'll want to know why."

"Yes, Grandfather."

I was on the brink of tears; I'm sure he noticed.

"For your health. I know Dr. Boyle has explained this to you. You and Lewis are both of the consumptive type. One day, if we are not careful, you may fall ill and perish like your poor brother Frank. To you this seems a distant prospect, because now you are well—though we have all noted the dry cough, which we must take seriously because of the wasting disposition you have inherited. The future comes whatever we do, and you and your brother will have the best chance of a long life—indeed, the best chance of living to be grown—if you are taken from the city's noxious vapors and nervous stimulations."

The young child in me wanted to weep and beg, to promise that Lewis and I would be good and never do it again, whatever we had done, and make him happy that he had kept us. But a wiser part of my suddenly divided self was sure that childish emotions would be discounted. I must think.

Struggling not to seem argumentative, and yet to show myself the smart girl he had always liked, I insisted that Lewis and I were both unusually healthy children—our energy and strength often drew comment. That was why Lewis was such a handful! The coughs meant nothing. Everybody has a cough now and then. Besides: "My mother stayed here."

"And she died," said my grandfather.

"Why did she stay?"

"Because she was a good woman, and her duty was here."

"But wasn't there another reason?" I queried, drawing on conversations overheard. "Because travel is harder for women! It's not natural, it's very hard for them to leave their loved ones, their dear ones, dear to their hearts. And we're children, so it's even harder. We don't know these people."

"They're your close blood relations," he rebuked me. "You mustn't speak of them that way."

"But I don't know them. They're just names. I don't guess Lewis even knows their names. I don't mean any disrespect; it's just true. They're strangers to us. It's bad for someone with a wasting disposition to have a shock, isn't it, and wouldn't it be a shock to be sent away? It would be worse for us. It would *make* us sick. Or at least it might, and in that case why do it?"

I thought I had spoken well, and my grandfather seemed to think so, too, but it was useless. I was being told, not consulted. "Don't think the considerations you have just advanced have not occurred to us. Of course they have. We've discussed them. We've worried and fretted and prayed for guidance, and at last we have decided on this course, which is the recommendation of all the physicians who have examined you."

He reminded me that I must not argue this way with my aunt and uncle. They were country people with old-fashioned ideas.

Robert and Edward were informed at dinner, after Lewis had bolted his food and left the table, his departure accompanied, as always, by a look of relief from my grandmother.

I was dismayed to see how little the news bothered my older brothers. We must stick together, they'd said, sincerely enough, the night before we left our childhood home, but now they were looking forward to beginning their own separate lives. To make me feel better, they extolled the virtues of farm life. The golden grain! The fresh eggs and butter! The clean, healthy air!

It fell to me to tell Lewis. I emphasized the thrills of the journey, the vast distances and differing methods of conveyance: a steamboat up the Hudson, then a packet on the Erie Canal, bad roads, swamps, and mountains, in a virgin land from which the red man had been swept only a generation earlier. We traced the journey on a map. The country was smaller then, and with only a little exaggeration we could imagine that we were going out west.

AS PREPARATIONS FOR OUR DEPARTURE WERE MADE, my grandmother and I worked together to make me what she called, to excuse its extravagance, a "Sunday frock." She based it on pictures in *Godey's Lady's Book,* using the most expensive fabrics in her collection and every fancy stitch she knew.

Lewis and I were sent to a dentist, who pulled one of Lewis's teeth and filled one of mine. My grandfather had made these appointments for us on the recommendation of the famous revival preacher Charles Finney, who had once searched in vain for a dentist when he suffered a toothache in a town thirty miles north of Rochester. Finney had said that the absence of dentists was an obstacle to temperance in the West, for many good people took spirits to dull the pain caused by rotten stumps in their heads.

ONE DAY, WHEN WE WERE SEWING my "Sunday frock," my grandmother said that there was a keepsake of my mother that she had been meaning to give me. She left the room, and returned bearing an oval object the size of a pocket watch.

"Do you know what this is?" she asked me.

"Yes, ma'am," I replied.

It was a miniature, one of the tiny painted images courting couples used to exchange in those days. Once or twice during my earlier childhood, my father had shown it to me. Executed on ivory with almost inhuman patience and precision by techniques now forgotten, it was mounted in a hinged metal casing with a loop on top so that it could be worn as a locket. The cover opened like a door to a vanished day: There, behind glass, was my mother, aglow with health, in a lace cap I had seen her wear in life and a shawl I had never seen her in, holding a soft-looking leather-bound Bible. The details of the room had not been neglected. I recognized pieces of furniture now stored in a shed behind my grandfather's Bond Street house. On the reverse side, trapped in some hard transparent resin, a lock of my mother's hair had been worked into a design resembling a shock of wheat.

From the moment it passed into my hands, I thought of it as a magical connection to my mother and I felt that if I lost it I would be cursed.

❊ VIII ❊

MY UNCLE WROTE TO MY GRANDFATHER, saying he preferred for us to come after the grain harvests. Thus we lingered at the house on Bond Street for months longer, interpreting the delay as a reprieve, and hoping that my grandparents would change their minds. In September, Robert and Edward left for boarding school. On the morning of their departure, Robert made three trips to my room in order to bring me, twelve books at a time, his thirty-six volumes of Buffon's *Natural History*. They were mine now. "If you can manage to read them, you will be a savant where you are going," he said, for Robert was a snob, and, despite a serious desire to reconcile me to my fate, he simply could not refrain from making disparaging remarks about the fools he expected me to meet at my destination.

I knew the books were dear to him, and I embraced him for a long time, pressing my face against his coat. I noticed that he had grown faster than I had in the last year, and I wondered what our relative heights would be the next time we met.

When Edward heard that Robert had given me his books, he was annoyed. "Are we supposed to give presents?" he demanded. "You should have told me." He rummaged in his bags and came out with a pincushion that my mother had made with her own hands and given to him on her deathbed.

"Mother gave you that," I told him, really shocked. "You can't give that to me. You can't give that to anyone. You have to keep that forever."

"Suit yourself," he said, and gave the pincushion to Lewis instead. My parting with Edward was a good deal less sentimental than my parting with Robert. We all embraced again outside the carriage, driven by one of my grandfather's servants, and we watched them go.

Finally, the day came, early October, chilly but clear. Servants loaded our trunks, carpetbags, and portmanteaus in the back of a hack; and—hoisting Lewis up in the air by way of greeting—there was my grandfather's clerk Horace, charged with bringing us all the way to our destination in the Finger Lakes. Fool, I thought without any judgment when I saw him, because my brother Robert had twice referred to our trip here in the wagon and what a chattering fool the driver, Horace, had been. But I was glad to see him. He was familiar: indeed, Horace had a way of seeming like an old acquaintance a quarter of an hour after you met him.

As we rolled downtown, he told us that it would be easy getting help carrying our baggage onto the steamboat, because times were hard—and, in fact, when we reached the docks we were approached by men eager for day labor, some of them in fine clothes recently soiled.

On the steamboat, we pushed our way to the rail with the other passengers, men in straw hats, stovepipe hats, and caps; women whose true shapes were a mystery housed somewhere within bulky dresses with wide shoulders and leg-of-mutton sleeves and many petticoats. All of us felt the sudden jar—some staggered and grabbed the rail—and the paddle wheel churned foam, and with what tumult in my heart I cannot express, we left the island on which I had spent my whole life. As we moved upriver, the piers seemed to turn like spokes of a wagon wheel. The shores behind us began to fold upon themselves. The shores ahead began to open. The buildings nearest the shore shrank. The top story of a tall edifice rose behind them, and though I knew the North River was on the west side of the island and Pearl Street was on the east, I asked Horace if it might be my grandfather's warehouse.

"Maybe," he said.

"Do you see it, Lewis?"

"Which one?" Lewis inquired, squinting.

"Why, of course, the tallest. Is it still the tallest, Horace?"

I was looking at the building when Horace answered, "Yes," and though his voice was almost inaudible in the hubbub, it sounded strange to me. When I turned back to look at him, he was already looking at me, with a sober expression that was quite unlike him.

Later that day, I overheard passengers talking about a young woman named Victoria who a few months earlier had become the queen of

England. In all the years since that day, every time Queen Victoria has been mentioned, my mind has flickered back, however briefly, to that moment. People were friendly. Whenever they learned we were orphans, they clucked and knit their brows, and when Horace told them where we were going, they promised us that we would love it there. Men put Lewis on their shoulders and pointed out the sights on the river and the shore.

There was a merchant who, when he was told about our journey, said that he was taking almost the same route, except he was going farther, to Ohio. There would be another canal, and then Cincinnati. He was in a hurry. It would take six days.

This made me think, and a little later, as the boat was preparing to stop at West Point, I asked Horace if my father had died in Cincinnati or in some town on the way.

"In Cincinnati," answered Horace firmly.

"Are you sure, Horace? I don't see how that can be, if it takes six days to get from New York to Cincinnati. He wasn't gone that long. He was gone only two days when we heard that he had died."

"I see." He gripped my hand. "Yes, I see what you mean. But, you see, your father's business was more urgent than the business of that man, and he went by fast coach."

But when the boat had docked and we were on the pier, he said that he was not absolutely sure that my father had reached Cincinnati. It might have been on the way.

He had to tell me that, because once I started doing arithmetic I would discover that it takes three days for a fast coach to reach Cincinnati from New York. And even if in 1837 there had been rails linking the two cities, enabling the merchant to travel at today's superhuman speeds, and my father had died promptly on reaching his destination, there was no telegraph or telephone to send a report. A human being or a letter would have had to bring the news back to New York. It was simply impossible for my father to have died in Cincinnati, but I had been told a dozen times that he had, by Mrs. Fitch, by my grandfather, my grandmother, and Horace.

From this point on, I knew that I had been lied to. I didn't know what to do with this knowledge. They were all good people, these liars. I knew that they were trying to protect me, and that was frightening, because they had failed. I was unprotected from the dangerous truth, whatever it was. I wished they had lied more skillfully.

IN ALBANY, BY PREARRANGEMENT, we spent Saturday and Sunday in the house of a portly clergyman and his homely family. On Monday we started out again and had our first encounter with canal travel. I remember coming to feel that I had never known anything else but this: the laborer in muddy trousers leading a pair of horses on the shore, the long ropes sagging and tightening, the strip of brown water that ambled through the country with a strange intimacy, only the towpath separating us from a farmer's field or the center of a big town. I had become a pair of eyes, upon which God had imposed the duty to inventory Creation: this cow, this fence, these blackened stumps, this forest, this miserable log hut, this sallow woman in rags who abruptly locked eyes with me.

Horace, who had grown up on a farm, often told us how much he had liked it, and how much we would like it. He made bad jokes, some of which Lewis did not understand, and Lewis laughed anyway. Lewis pestered Horace with questions: about mountains and waterfalls, the family who apparently lived—dirty children, dog, dangling laundry, and all—on a barge coming the other way, the names of towns, the purposes of various tools, the special uses of the wood from the various trees we passed. Whenever I saw Lewis looking thoughtful, I knew he was trying to come up with a question for Horace.

In Rochester, we slept in a cheap inn, and when we woke, our legs were covered with red spots. Horace bought a horse and painted wagon and we set off south. With each mile the scenery became ruder, with more unpainted houses, crooked fences, and underfed livestock. Roads of logs shook the wagon. Roads of mud were full of sky-reflecting puddles. Horace made us walk ahead of the wagon, testing the ground with a stick. We ate at farmers' houses. We slept in the wagon. In the morning, we couldn't find Lewis. We yelled his name into the forest. Only the wind and the birds answered. Then a voice above us said, "Here I am!" His arms and legs encircled a silvery-barked branch of an old beech tree that had been shedding yellow leaves onto the road and the wagon all night. He was near the top of it. "Look at me, Horace."

"Well, well, look at Lewis." Horace clapped his hands.

"Lewis, you promised not to scare me," I reminded him.

"Watch this, Horace," cried Lewis.

"No, it's too high!" I shouted.

"You'd better come down slowly, Lewis," said Horace.

He climbed lower, then jumped, and the only reason he didn't make a hole in the wagon's flimsy roof was that he slid off it headfirst. He might have broken his neck if Horace hadn't caught him.

I didn't let myself care about Horace. Horace was temporary. I should think ahead, to my aunt and uncle. I tried to picture them. All I could see was our parents, not dead after all but hiding, living a new life as a farmer and his wife in upstate New York.

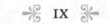

IX

THE TOWN OF LIVY BORE THE NAME of a Roman historian: so my brother Robert had said when we were discussing this trip, snobbishly adding "a fact of which I'll wager most of the villagers are innocent." It had grown up around a stream, which provided power to a sawmill, a gristmill, and a cider mill but was broken by falls that made it useless for transportation. There were several two-story clapboard houses for the local grandees, and a number of one-story and one-and-a-half-story houses. There was a wooden bridge; a livery stable; a general store; a tavern; churches for Presbyterians, Methodists, and Free Will Baptists; and a one-room schoolhouse.

On the day the painted wagon bounced over the deeply rutted road into town, I noticed only how bare it was. Little in the way of fences or grass distinguished the yards from the nameless dirt streets. Balding cows and scrawny, big-headed razorback hogs roamed them both in perfect freedom.

Horace tipped his hat to some odorous checkers-players—one missing two fingers on his right hand, another toothless, face collapsed like a decaying jack-o'-lantern—who were sitting on crates on the front porch of the general store where we stopped to ask directions. As we entered the store, the stink of whiskey breath and flatulence gave way to spices, leather, tallow, and turpentine. Ahead of us, a man and a boy brought two bushels of oak barrel staves to the jowly storekeeper, who counted them, inspected them, and discarded several of them as unusable. The man addressed the storekeeper as "Colonel." The storekeeper called the man Jake and the boy Jeptha. We witnessed a disagreement between Jake and the colonel, who smiled a lot, patted Jake on the back, and pointed out some figures in a ledger. Jake, who did not seem to like having six of the barrel staves refused—or to like being patted on the back, either—accepted the storekeeper's judgment with an almost imperceptible nod of his head. The colonel wrote in the ledger and fetched a sack of flour and a tin of patent medicine from the shelves.

The boy, Jeptha, was handsome, with black hair that looked as if it had been cut with the help of a bowl, and quick, alert blue eyes. I supposed him to be about a year older than I was. His shirt was a butternut color. His homespun woolen trousers had rolled cuffs and were held up with suspenders, all worn and soiled. In his right hand he carried a broad-brimmed straw hat. When his father's bargain with the storekeeper had been concluded, he put the hat on his head so as to leave his hands free and took a handful of broken crackers from a barrel, while Jake went to another barrel, from which a drinking cup hung on a string. Jeptha, after a nervous glance at the colonel, reached out and touched Jake's elbow. "Pa." Jake tried to box Jeptha's ears. Jeptha skipped out of reach with a calm skill that spoke of long practice, and when he had reached a place of safety, he turned around and watched his father. Putting down the sack, Jake spat a slimy wad of chewing tobacco into his hand, twisted the spigot cock, filled the cup, drank, refilled the cup, and took another. His face ruddier than it had been a moment before, he shoved the tobacco back in his mouth and wiped his hand on his pants.

The whole scene made a strong impression on me, but what I thought back on later—even more often than I remembered the missing fingers and the caved-in mouth, respectively, of the two idlers on the porch—was the look of pure disgust, strangely mature, very wrong for his age, that took possession of the boy's face while he watched his father drink, together with a weariness as if he had lived a hundred years and spent all of it in the company of this man.

Horace introduced himself to the colonel and asked for directions in the New England manner, as a hypothesis: supposing a body wanted to go from here to the Moody farm—given that set of circumstances—how might he get there?

Jeptha asked us where we were from.

"New York."

"We're in New York."

"New York *City*."

"You're going to Elihu's farm. We heard about you."

"What did you hear?" I asked.

He looked at a loss for a moment, then said irrelevantly, "I been to Rochester." When he spoke, I noticed a triangular bit of blackness caused by a slender chip in one of his top front teeth.

"We were just *in* Rochester," said Lewis.

For the moment, we were all overtaken by shyness and just listened to Horace talking to Jake and the colonel. Jeptha stared at me; it seemed like a friendly stare, but it made me a little uncomfortable. His eyes, bluer and purer every time I noticed them, had a searching gaze that made me feel a little more important when they looked my way, and challenged me to be as interesting as they seemed to find me. They were too much for me. I looked away, as if suddenly very curious about the highly miscellaneous collection of goods on the shelves and the big black cast-iron pipe of the iron heating stove. When I looked back, the boy was facing the other way, at the shelves, making Sherman's Worm Lozenges feel important and challenging them to be better worm lozenges, and I found, a little to my surprise, that I was disappointed. "How'd you chip your tooth?" I heard myself ask, just to receive again the scrutiny I had rejected before. He turned. For a while the eyes wore an empty, abstracted look, as though he had forgotten where he was and who he was. "Fell on a rock," he said finally, reaching out his hand to offer us each a couple of broken crackers. We took them and began to chew with murmurs of appreciation they did not deserve.

Horace came up to us, saying, "It's easy," meaning the way to my uncle's farm, and he tipped his hat again as we left. It seemed to me that his speech and his manners, the way he moved and stood, had changed in many small ways. He was acting like a man from the country.

As we were moving off in the wagon, Horace said, "Look at Romeo," just as I noticed Jeptha walking back and forth atop the fence, with his arms spread for balance. Twice the boy shot glances our way, though this obviously made the trick harder to do.

"He wants us to see," I said.

"No. He wants *you* to see," said Horace. In other circumstances this might have pleased me; just then I was detached from my emotions. While my mind stored away innumerable observations, mostly what I felt was the strangeness of everything.

THE ROAD THAT RAN BESIDE THE STREAM was lined with birches whose slender trunks resembled naked white arms with too many elbows. Our progress dragged the sun winking rapidly through the trees; every so often a bright ray would break through unimpeded and blind me. The whine of hidden insects grew slowly louder and slowly faded away. We came to plowed land and pastures with haystacks. "Maybe your uncle's fields," Horace speculated.

We recognized the house from a picture my uncle had drawn in a letter Horace had shown us several times on our long journey. It was really two adjoining houses, each one story plus a loft, made of unpainted clapboard, a pale gray tinted pink by the sunset. On the broad acres behind it stood a small barn, sheds, a woodpile, some huts on tall legs that I came to recognize as corncribs, a privy, and a big, well-fenced vegetable garden. I noticed a large maple whose lower limbs had been lopped off, leaving scars like a chorus of thick-lipped caroling mouths. All other trees originally found on the spot had been exterminated. There were, however, five apple trees in the part of the backyard nearest the house. As I learned later, each stood on a former location of the privy, which was moved whenever the pit beneath it filled up.

It all looked miserably haphazard, even in the picture, which did not show the stains under the windows from the pouring out of slops, the stumps grown over with fungi, the scummy puddles, the powdery wooden ash-hopper, the handmade wheelbarrow tipped over in the tall weeds, the pigs that lumbered toward the back of the house when we came near, or the large dog snarling and curling its dark-purple lips.

Horace, having prepared himself on the colonel's advice, threw the dog a piece of sausage, which the animal caught and sucked into itself noisily. He let the dog lick his hands. He scratched behind its black ears and tugged its loose neck, saying, "Good boy. Yes. Yes. Meet Lewis. Meet Arabella," until the animal permitted us to approach the house. Horace knocked, waited, lifted a wooden latch, pulled, and peered within. "Hello?" He tried the other side of the house and came back. "We'll wait inside." We went in, followed by the dog. The front room, so low that Horace could have touched the rafters, contained a long table, stools and chairs, rag carpets, a hearth with a banked fire, and a shelf with lamps, almanacs, and the family Bible, in which Horace showed me the names of my aunt and uncle and cousins. I felt uneasy, being in the house and examining the Bible of people I had never met.

Horace started dragging our trunks from the wagon and into the house, and under his supervision Lewis and I brought in the lighter baggage.

Presently, we heard the sound of wheels and hooves. We went to the door. A woman and two girls were coming up the road in a wagon.

Horace turned to us. "Stay here a moment. I'll prepare them to meet you."

What did he mean, prepare? They had been prepared with letters, hadn't they? Perhaps it had to do with some country custom unknown to me.

The wagon stopped a bit short of the house when they saw him. I could not hear what was said. It looked like an argument. The woman put her palm to her forehead, then flung it out and spoke to Horace; there was a fierce expression on her face. Turning her head, she spoke as fiercely to the children. Then she lifted the reins and drove the rest of the way to the house. The children jumped out of the wagon and stood back, while my aunt got out, walked nearer to the house, and put her hand over her heart. "Arabella? Lewis? Come here, children," she said.

She knelt to put her face level with ours and reached out slowly to touch my cheek, and then Lewis's cheek, as if in amazement. "Look at you! Each the living image of my poor sister." Her voice was raspy. "Agnes, Evangeline, say hello to your cousins."

I decided with relief that the hard look had been just for her own children, who must have done something wrong. With us her expression was gentle. That was good. In every other respect, her face disappointed me. I had known better than to tell Horace about my childish daydream that my aunt and uncle would turn out to be my parents in a new guise;

still, it had seemed not impossible that my mother and her sister might be as alike as twins. My aunt would be my mother restored to me in a rustic form; I would know then that everything was for the best and as God had planned it.

This hope was now dashed in every possible way. Where my mother had been fair, my aunt was dark, with black hair; where my mother had been small, my aunt was tall, and would have been taller still but for a noticeable twist in her spine. Her face was narrow and masculine, with a high brow like that of a balding man, a long, large nose, and deep lines flanking the mouth, which was wide with thin, tight lips. Her appearance labored under the additional burdens of a protuberant mole the size of a pea and several more the size of mustard seeds on her cheeks, and short chin-whiskers. Her clothes were of manufactured cloth, rudely sewn. She was homely even for an overworked country wife.

My girl cousins, who now approached, were much better looking. Agnes, who was my age, had dark hair like her mother but all the beauty her mother lacked, with delicate symmetrical features, perfect skin, and large liquid brown eyes, her mother's eyes, which looked lovely when set in Agnes's face—in fact, I realized when I saw them in Agnes, they were my mother's eyes. Evangeline, eight, was ruddy, with an upturned nose; her plump body seemed boneless, her movements languid.

My aunt said that she and the girls had been out to visit the ailing Mrs. Lyall, whose husband had died last year. The men and the boys were out cutting timber, she said, and they would be home soon, and we should pardon her because she had to get dinner ready. I asked if there was anything I could do, and she said, "No, bless you."

"Surely not," added Agnes, eyes melting with sympathy, "after your hard trip, and with your illness."

They had been told we had come here for our health. Horace said, "They're not sick now. But they have come a long way."

We sat down at the long table. Horace, to make the conversation go, asked Agnes and Evangeline about the farm, the neighbors, and the schoolteacher. Evangeline answered in detail, Agnes briefly. From Evangeline I learned that there were two hired hands on the farm. They had helped with the harvest, and they were staying on in the winter to cut trees and make charcoal, being paid just in room and board.

To help with the talk, I asked, "Why?"

"To help us," explained Evangeline.

"But why just for room and board?" I asked. "Why don't they want money?"

"I don't exactly know," said Evangeline, and she looked at her sister. "Why don't they want money, Agnes?"

"I guess because times are so hard," said Agnes.

Evangeline explained, "It's because times are hard."

"So they are willing to work for any crust they can get, poor souls," added Agnes, and Evangeline's mouth formed a little "o" of belated understanding.

"We stopped at the store in town before we came here," Horace informed them. "Lewis and Arabella met a boy who was there with his father, and they had just traded a load of staves, and when we left the boy was showing off for Arabella."

There was an immediate change in Agnes's expression, and I knew—how, I cannot say—that she had an idea who this boy was, and didn't want him to show off for me. "No, he wasn't," I said firmly.

"He was walking on a fence. He picked the place where we were sure to see him, didn't he, Lewis—Lewis, what was his name?"

"Jeptha," said Lewis.

"Oh, Jeptha," said Evangeline. "We know him."

"Evangeline, we should be helping Mama," interrupted Agnes.

"Mama said to talk to them," said Evangeline.

"We'll all talk more later," said Agnes. They got up—Agnes grim, Evangeline sullen—and the two sisters began setting the table with ill-assorted plates and cups and utensils.

From the porch came male voices and a great deal of stamping and gurgling. My aunt hastened out. We heard her say, "The children," among other words I could not make out, after which the men and the boys tromped heavily in.

My aunt said, "Father, my sister's children have come." That she should repeat what she had just said in the other room struck me as odd at the time, and in my memory the scene has a queer formality, like a diplomatic ritual. The meeting had been made official.

My uncle Elihu nodded, looking at us with strange, tiny eyes for several uncomfortable seconds, and then he said: "We're glad you've come

to live with us, children. I guess it will take some time for you to get used
to our ways when you've been raised another way, and maybe you'll miss
some things, but by and by you'll learn, and you'll get the idea that we're
not so bad here after all."

What kind of man was he? It was too early to tell. All I knew so far was
that his head looked small because his features were too large for it. His
mouth, nose, and ears were terribly crowded in each other's company.
The eyebrows and eye sockets were big, too, but at the eyes themselves
the generosity stopped; they were like two blind buttonholes, robbing
him of the warmth that sometimes saves homely faces. He had an odd,
hip-jutting gait, and at some later date—I do not remember when it was
or who told me—I learned that he had broken his leg once, and it had not
been set properly.

After introducing the hired hands (Sam, a Bohemian; Pat, an Irishman), my uncle introduced our boy cousins. Neither took after his parents, for both were handsome. Matthew, the elder, and the bigger of
the two, was eleven, with dark hair and brown eyes. Titus, ten, had sandy
hair.

A little later, as, with heads bowed and fingers interlaced, we asserted
our sinfulness and gratitude, I was acutely conscious of the strong body
odors which surrounded me. Everyone bathed less often back then, but
farmers, despite their strenuous duties, less often than merchants.

Supper was corn bread, dry and gummy by turns, and tasting faintly
of soap, and a greasy stew with salt pork, potatoes, and turnips, a vegetable that up till now I had been permitted to forgo. I ate it, and I told my
aunt that the supper was delicious. To make me agreeable and pleasant
in the homes of my relations had been my mother's life work.

They all used the knife to spear and convey food to their mouths. My
uncle, who had bad teeth, often found it necessary to claw a trapped mor-
sel free with his index finger, and whenever he drank water, he sloshed
it around before swallowing. The boys, to my astonishment, were each
permitted one gulp from the whiskey jug.

I looked at Horace, and he winked. I smiled to show he needn't worry
about me.

"What's your secret?" asked Elihu, smiling, with the knife before his
mouth.

"Secret, sir?" asked Horace.

"You and my niece traded a wink. What's the secret?"

"Well, sir, you've found us out. We have a secret sign between us; I was to wink if I thought that this was a fine farm and a fine family and she and her brother were going to like it fine here."

"Well, I'm glad we passed your little test," said Elihu, still smiling.

After an excruciating silence, Horace decided to laugh; the others joined him; and I laughed last, having no idea what I was laughing about, or what, really, had just occurred.

Pat asked what it had been like on the canal, and for a few minutes Horace and the hands carried the conversation. Sam had worked as a porter on the canal. Pat had been a docker in New York, where he lived on Baxter Street, and he had heard of Godwin & Co.

"The Godwin warehouse is the tallest building in the city," said Lewis.

Everyone stopped chewing.

"Jesus," said Matthew.

"Matthew," said my aunt.

"Did you hear what he said?"

"Matthew, it would be a shame if this got you a licking," said Elihu.

"The old one was burned up in the Great Fire," Lewis went on, and he proceeded to say more words in a row than he had spoken since his arrival. "I saw it burn. I helped to empty it." In fact, he had arrived when the old warehouse was in ashes. "The new one is seven stories high. We went up to the top right after it was built. It was like a mountain. We could see the ships. We could see north past the edge of the city. We were looking down on the churches. Robert put me on his shoulders. I used to go up there all the time."

He'd been to the roof only once.

"Lewis, don't talk about the warehouse anymore," said Horace.

"Why not?"

"It's bragging, Lewis."

"But it's true," said Lewis, taking the silence for fascination. And he told them that oftentimes he used to kill pigs by dropping rocks from the top of it.

Then there was more silence, which my cousin Titus was the first to break. "Arabella, how did your pa come to pass on?"

"He took ill while traveling. He was on his way to Cincinnati."

Horace abruptly began questioning Elihu about the farm, its soil, trees, crops, weather, and pests. He said that he had grown up on farms in Connecticut and Vermont where the harvest had declined each year. It was only later, when he used an idle afternoon in the city to attend a New-York State Agricultural Society lecture, that he learned in what contempt Englishmen held American farming. We bought too much land to work well. Our way with manure was too unsystematic. We should pen our animals and plant Swedish turnips. The British loved to slander our country. Yet Horace guessed that if he were ever to farm again he would try some of their methods.

Elihu inclined his head and squinted. "A lecture in the New York— what?"

"State Agricultural Society."

"Well, sir, you got me beat there. I ain't never been to one of *their* lectures."

Horace chuckled, since a joke had been intended. Elihu, whose smile ceased to put one at ease, inquired, "What's funny?" and Horace, in the depths of his good nature, found the will to say that he, Horace, was funny, for trying to teach farming to a farmer.

After the meal, my uncle told Titus to meet him on the porch. As we were helping with the dishes, we heard my uncle speaking, each word accompanied by a muffled blow and a cry of pain. "Children." Thwack. "Will." Thwack. "Learn." Thwack. "To." Thwack. "Listen." Thwack. "To." Thwack. "Their." Thwack. "Elders." Thwack. As though she were imparting a great secret, Evangeline told us that Titus was being whipped. When I asked why, she said she didn't know.

Horace and the hands slept on the other side of the house. My aunt and uncle slept in a small bedroom downstairs. The children slept in the loft, a room with a big floor but low, slanting ceilings. The whole house was really very small. Sounds carried easily in it, and we could always hear the rhythmic creak of the bed when my aunt was fulfilling her marital obligations, but we were spared this on our first night.

When we were up in the loft, I saw the trunks that Sam and Pat had brought up there after supper. They contained things that country children might never have seen. "See what we've brought from New York," I said, and, gratifyingly, my cousins crowded around a trunk. I spoke more freely with my aunt and uncle gone. I showed them the illustrations in Buffon's *Natural History,* my dress shoes, my seashell collection. I told them that, each day on the piers in New York City, barges many times larger than this house unloaded great mountains of oysters. I showed them a lace collar my grandmother had given me. I remarked on a difference between New York City and Livy. In Livy, from what I'd heard, you went to Colonel Ashton's store for everything. But in New York City, a five-block district was devoted just to the sale of carpets, and another neighborhood to ropes and other nautical things, and another to butchering, and another to carriages. I told them about Moving Day. In New York City, most people rented their homes, and the leases ended on the same day, and every first of May the streets were clogged with wagons heaped with people's belongings. But my grandfather owned our house. We had never moved, until recently.

As I spoke I thought of Rebecca, my schoolmate, who had overawed me with her experiences of mountains, racetracks, and panoramas. As Rebecca was to me, I was to my cousins. I had seen more of the world. I had an advantage, and I could subdue them, as Rebecca had subdued me. This could help reconcile me to the small house, the bad food, the loutish manners, and whatever other disappointments awaited me here.

Evangeline, curiously turning an oyster shell and making parts of it glisten in the candlelight, asked, "Did you bring any oysters with meat in them?"

Agnes said, "Don't be silly, Evangeline. Oysters would not keep on such a long journey." She looked at me with a tiny smile, that we might sigh together over Evangeline's incorrigible ignorance.

I was going to do just that—I should have—but then I had a bright idea. "Actually, oysters can be dried. Some people like them that way," and I added airily: "I wish I had thought to bring some." Evangeline's expression rebuked Agnes—see, her question had *not* been stupid!—and Agnes's face fell, and I had a tiny suspicion that I had just made an error.

"What a fancy name you have, Arabella," said Agnes. "That's not a Bible name, is it?"

"It's a name in my grandfather's family," I said.

"It sounds Spanish. It makes me think of a fine Spanish lady who wears black lace and has servants."

"It's English, I guess. The ship that first brought the Puritans to Massachusetts was the *Arbella*."

"Aren't you mistaken, Arabella?" Agnes asked as if she had caught me being naughty and was putting my little crime to me delicately.

"I don't think I am."

"If you think a little more, won't it come to mind that the ship that brought the Puritans to America was the *Mayflower*?"

My other cousins were watching us with a sudden alertness which told me that it was dangerous to disagree with Agnes, but I could not, like Horace, efface myself to the point of saying the opposite of what I believed. "You're right, Agnes. The *Mayflower* came before the *Arbella*. But my grandfather always used to remind us that the Pilgrims and the Puritans were not the same. The Pilgrims came on the *Mayflower* with Miles Standish. The Puritans came on the *Arbella* with James Winthrop. My grandfather used to tell us that every Thanksgiving. He always mentioned the ship, because of my name."

I threw in my grandfather and Thanksgiving as a sop to Agnes's pride. I didn't know all this just because I had received a better education. I knew it for these special, personal, accidental reasons.

Agnes asked, "Are you sure, Arabella?"

"So I was told."

"Is it likely, Arabella, that the Puritans, who set such store on simplicity, came on a boat with so fancy a name? How are we to explain that?"

"I can't explain it."

"Could the explanation be that you did not hear correctly?"

Did she think she could bully me into saying there was no difference between Pilgrims and Puritans? Into the silence came Matthew's derisive comment: "She's talking about her own darn name, Agnes. How dumb would she have to be to be wrong about her own name?" Agnes didn't answer, and he drove the point home: "Well, I guess you don't know everything after all, do you, Agnes."

WE KNELT BESIDE OUR BEDS. They seemed to be waiting for me to start. I said the Prayer of Agur, which my mother had taught me long ago. I prayed to be given what I needed but not more than was good for my character.

Agnes's prayer, which began after mine, was very long and specific.

She asked that Jesus lead Mr. Cooper and Mr. Talbot away from drink and ease Mrs. Slocum's rheumatism; console Mr. and Mrs. Rawley for the death of their son by drowning last year; and that Mrs. Lyall, the sick widow, recover or be granted an easy passage to the arms of the Lord; that Josh Rowen leave off swearing; that the stony hearts of Henry Rowen, Mark Taylor, Becky Forrest, and twenty others she named, including her dear cousins Lewis and Arabella, be softened into such a consistency as would enable us to receive the Holy Spirit and the believer's baptism; that the winter would not be too hard and the vegetables not run out early and the livestock not perish until the best time to slaughter them and that the meat would not spoil; that the cows keep giving good fat milk for a few more weeks, and come spring the maple sap be plentiful and sweet; that Sam and Pat be converted from popish idolatry; that the people of New York City have money again; that my grandfather's business survive and he be furthered in his great work; that the Lord guide the counsels of President Van Buren and smite the enemies of the United States.

Was that how one prayed here? Must I learn to pray like that? To my relief, Evangeline's prayers were short and the boys' were piggish grunts. I thanked Agnes for mentioning Lewis and me. I tried to make a peace offering of my thanks. I knew I had offended her.

X

LEWIS AND I SLEPT THROUGH the rooster's crow. My aunt pulled us to our feet, and we piled on clothes, and the crimes that are rumored to occur on farms were actually perpetrated: hens were distracted with corn and robbed of their eggs, cows were milked, hay was forked, pigs were swilled, all before our breakfast of watery oatmeal. Only the milk was thick and good. We were each allowed one spoonful of molasses.

At breakfast, Lewis announced that Horace would be staying on as a hired hand.

"Am I?" said Horace.

"Horace, you like farming," said Lewis. "You *told* me you did."

"Lewis, you're a fine, brave boy and you're going to be all right. You've got a new family now. You've got your sister, and four cousins, and an uncle and an aunt who will be like a ma and a pa to you. You can write me letters, and I'll write you back."

"I don't want any letter from you. I hate you." He was crying now.

"Hush, Lewis," said my aunt.

Horace picked him up. Lewis wrapped his arms around Horace's neck. "Horace, don't go. Don't go, Horace. Don't go."

My uncle said, "That's enough, Lewis. Let go," but he wouldn't, until my aunt peeled him off Horace and held him as he tried to twist away. The hands laughed. Horace looked sad. My aunt asked Titus to fetch a switch. Lewis sat, waiting sullenly, until Titus came back with a hard stick about the diameter of my index finger.

"Let me do it," I said. "I always did it at home."

My aunt looked at my uncle and then shook her head, and she gave him eight strokes on the bottom: "This. Is. To. Teach. You. How. To. Obey."

She told me later she couldn't find it in her heart to blame my mother for letting me punish my little brother. She had heard of such things in large families where the eldest children were almost grown, but she didn't approve of it, and she was happy to take this burden off my shoulders.

LEWIS WENT UP IN THE LOFT so as not to see Horace go, but he seemed to recover later, and he tagged along when the men and the boys went out to the woods with the felling saw.

The house was quiet. I showed my aunt and Agnes and Evangeline some presents my grandmother had given me to give them, the factory-made buttons, ribbons, and pins that country women craved as much as did any naked islander who might swim out to meet Captain Cook. I showed them the miniature of my mother. My aunt sighed: it was just as she remembered her sister. Agnes said, "Oh, it is so lovely. Some would charge her with vanity for putting a man to the trouble of painting it, but what a providence to have it now. I'm sure Providence made her do it, even if it struck people as vain at the time."

I supposed these insinuations about my mother were retribution for correcting Agnes about oysters and the *Mayflower* and the *Arbella*. "My mama was pretty before illness took away her beauty, but she wasn't vain. Nobody said that. My papa had one of these made of himself, too, for her to carry. I don't know what happened to it."

"Oh my," said Evangeline, as if I'd said something shocking.

"Dear Evangeline, please do remember your promise," said Agnes enigmatically.

My aunt cleaned and baked and had us fetch this and mix that, but mainly asked that we stay near so that she could hear the talk. Agnes and Evangeline told me about life in Livy. I told them about New York City.

Evangeline was amazed at everything, yet somehow not very interested. Agnes made many comments, of four general types. First, she supposed that *some* people would disapprove of the waste, frivolousness, or impiety shown by my report of city life. Second, she hoped that the country was not going to bore me. Third, whenever I mentioned my mother, she'd give me a big helping of false pity. Fourth, the next time I spoke of my father her hand flew to her mouth, and my aunt gave her a stern look.

At last there came a time that afternoon when I mentioned my grandfather's warehouse. I remember that, before I spoke the words, I knew they would make something bad happen. I spoke against my better judgment. Lewis had been exaggerating when he said he went up there all the time, I said. He'd only been up there once. But it really was the tallest building in New York City, and he really had dropped a rock from it and accidentally killed a pig that was walking below.

My aunt wiped her hands with a cloth. "Belle, come up with me." I followed her to the loft. She sat on the edge of my low bed, her knees raised awkwardly high, as she invited me to sit beside her. The bulk of her, the moles and blemishes scattered across her face, the stench of lard and sweat emanating from her clothes repulsed me and I struggled not to show it. But more than anything I was frightened. I knew that she was about to tell me something terrible.

"Someone should have told you; they *promised me* they would tell you. Until that man Horace stopped us in the wagon yesterday, we thought you were told. You can't talk about your grandpa's warehouse: you must never mention it again. You can't keep saying your pa got a fever on a business trip to Cincinnati. You can't because it ain't true, and everybody knows what really happened. It was put in the newspapers, and folks know about it because your grandpa is talked of for his crusades against drink and slavery and Sabbath breaking, and I—foolishly, vainly, I bragged about my sister's connection to him. And now you're to be punished for my vanity, because folks *know*. Your pa took his own life. The way he did it was by jumping from the top of that warehouse. It was a terrible thing for him to do, and a terrible thing for you to have to hear, and for me to have to be the one to tell you—oh my Lord, how bitter this is for me."

She tried to embrace me, but I flinched and turned away.

There was more. "He left a note," my aunt said. "He asked forgiveness. He took the blame on himself—I don't know who else he thought we'd blame—but since he left a note we know that he meant to do it. It was no accident: he jumped. We know it. Everybody knows it, so you have to."

She reached for me again. Again I jerked away from her. She said, "Belle, where are you going?" I did not know myself, nor can I report to you how it felt. I was not aware of being in myself, feeling myself, making decisions. It was a discovery to me that I was throwing on my coat and rushing down the ladder, past Agnes and Evangeline, out to the porch, down the steps, past the privy, the chicken shack, and the orchard, and across a gully by means of a ramshackle bridge made of two weathered gray planks with holes where knots had fallen out, and out into the brown fields that were full of stubble and decaying stumps.

The sky was white. I ran until I looked back and the house was small. A little farther on, the ground rose, and I was in rolling country dotted with mounds of hay. The grade of the land fell again, and when I looked back there wasn't any house. I was panting among rotten pumpkins. Collapsing, turning brown, they were oozing black juice, and I wondered why whoever had planted these pumpkins hadn't come back to harvest them. I supposed he had killed himself. I heard a scratchy voice calling my name, but again I ran.

She must have run, too, because she caught up with me. "What do you think you're doing out here? Where do you think you're going?"

"Go away. You're not my mother."

"Who said I was? Your mother's in heaven. I'm your aunt." She knelt and put her hands on my shoulders. She had hurt me and I wanted to hurt her. "You won't do. You have a man's face and a crooked back. I can't stand to look at you."

I saw the pain wash across her gaunt features, followed by anger, and was simultaneously gratified and frightened. "I'm sorry for you," she said steadily. "I don't want to punish you when you've just had a bad shock, but you can't talk that way to me."

I had taken a scary step away from the good girl I considered myself to be. A part of me wanted to fall sobbing onto her narrow bosom and be comforted. How many times I've wished I had—as I would have, if only she had waited a moment longer. But she tried to hurry it; like an impatient lover, she tried to pull me toward her; and I rebelled. "Leave me alone," I said. She persisted. I spat in her face.

She stared at me, dumbfounded. Then she released me, and one of her hands returned with a wallop on the jaw that made my head ring. She had swung wide, using her strength and weight, and with an empty look on her face she pulled her arm back and let loose a second blow, which knocked me to the ground.

"No dinner *and* no supper," she said, gasping. "You'll spend the rest of the day upstairs, thinking about what you've done. Now get up and walk ahead," she pointed. "That way. That's home now."

I got up and walked where she pointed; my head throbbed, and I was shaking. There had been no punishments like this in Bowling Green. This was life from now on. I was astonished that things could have gone so wrong between us so quickly, and wished that the last few minutes could be undone. Buried beneath it all, coloring everything, was a vision of my father hurling himself down from the roof of my grandfather's warehouse.

"I blame my sister," I heard her say from behind me. "She knew she was dying. Why didn't she prepare you better? How could she have spoiled you so?"

I turned to tell my aunt that she was wrong—that my mother had devoted her life to making me a welcome presence in the houses of my relatives.

"No sass," said my aunt. "No sass from you."

IN THE LOFT, I THOUGHT OF MY MOTHER looking down upon me: Had she seen the slaps? Then she had seen me spit in my aunt's face. What did she think of my aunt? What was her opinion of me?

I looked out the window. I thought of crawling out on the roof and escaping—it wasn't high. But where would I go? I decided to wait until everyone was asleep. I would take Lewis with me. We would bring food. We would walk to Rochester. We would beg at the farmhouses on the way, and I could get a position as a servant somewhere—I knew how to cook, clean, mend, and sew, and I had good manners, and I didn't eat very much. When we had enough money, we'd take the canal back to Albany and the steamboat down to New York City, to my grandparents' house, where they would be grateful to see that we were still alive, for by then they would have heard of our disappearance.

I knew when they told Lewis about my father. I heard him shouting, "You're lying! You're a liar!" and I heard my aunt say, "Titus, get me a switch," and a scuffle, probably Lewis running and being caught.

It was his second switching in one day. He, too, was sent to bed without supper, and we weren't allowed to speak to each other.

After sundown, the others came up to the loft. They had been forbidden to speak to us. Matthew and Titus played with marbles, by candlelight, and said only things like "Lucky shot," and "You cheated."

Then my aunt came in and told my cousins to leave. She sat down with us on the bed, saying, "We've made a bad start. There's no excuse for the way you two have acted today, and I—and you made me lose my temper. But you've been punished, and I forgive you. And you have to forgive me, because we can't go on this way."

I mumbled insincerely that I forgave her. She had us both kneel beside the bed with her and ask God to help us to be better children.

THE NEXT MORNING, SHE SAID THAT we should all be kind to each other today, in respect for the Lord's Day. We dressed for church. When my aunt saw me in the frock I'd made with my grandmother, she got a pained look on her face and said it was very pretty, it was too pretty, and the two of us went through my trunk until we found a frock that would draw less attention to me. I knew she was right—even at nine and with no experience of country people, I knew as soon as she spoke that I could not walk into their unpainted church dressed for a ball.

Matthew got the wagon ready, and my uncle drove us to the Free Will Baptist church. At the end of the journey, it stood just past a hilltop, and to spare the horses we got out and walked. I saw the spireless roof first, then the rest of the small building appeared, step by step and log by log; last came the short log sections it was perched on. Free Will Baptists, famous for adding foot washing to the customary Baptist ordinances, endured a lot of mockery from members of other churches, and the greater number who had no church. But worldly ridicule is a glory to the devout.

Outside the church, the several small families that made up the congregation were gathering, farmers and farmers' wives, and their children, all in the best and cleanest of their drab homemade clothes. The grown-ups made a dignified effort not to stare at the new arrivals, and children were cuffed and scolded for their curiosity. As the animals chewed on the tops of the fence posts or nibbled the grass, my uncle introduced us to the neighbors piecemeal, several times repeating, with slight variations, "These are my wife's sister's children you probably heard of. This here's Lewis. This here's Arabella." A sort of line began to form of people waiting to meet us, and with an expectant feeling I noticed Jacob and Jeptha, the two already known faces, waiting behind the family my uncle was talking to. A woman—skinny, with hollow cheeks and raw eyes—rested a hand briefly on Jeptha's shoulder. His mother, I guessed. Near him stood a girl I assumed to be his sister, cheerful and fresh-looking but with the gait of an old man—she dipped an extra inch on every other step—and in her hand was a cane. Jeptha was looking at me. With an admirable economy of motion, so that he did not seem to be working, he kept me in view as people passed between us. My uncle noticed that I was looking past the family he was introducing at the moment. His buttonhole eyes quizzed me, and my aunt said, "Oh, she's noticing Jacob and Jeptha; she's met them before. She met them at the store. She don't mean to be rude to you, Thomas, do you, Arabella?" and I said no, and was forgiven. I knew that Agnes's eyes were on me.

"This is Mr. Talbot, children, who you met at the store. And this is Mrs. Talbot." I greeted them, and Lewis greeted them. As when I had seen them in the store, the father and the son shared a quality of unusual alertness. The boy's alertness was curious and playful. The father's had soured into a threat. But just now he was a Sunday version of himself and greeted me with absentminded gravity. The wife must have been pretty once. I smiled at her and received a blank stare in return. Then came Jeptha, who said, quickly, "Hi, Agnes, Matthew, Evangeline," giving them about equal weight, it seemed to me, and he nodded to Lewis, and said to me, "Here we are again," and quickly introduced us to the lame girl, Becky, his sister, to his three-year-old sister Ruth, and to his brothers Ike and Ezra, and then we all went into the church, which was dark and drafty. The floor was made of rudely sawed half-logs, with wide cracks between some of them, and on some days one caught glimpses of animals skittering in the crawl spaces below.

As we walked to our family's benches, Agnes said she guessed that Horace had been right, and that Jeptha liked me.

"I don't care about boys," I declared.

The minister, William Jefferds, was a frail-looking little man in his thirties with thin sandy hair, narrow shoulders, small hands, and sad eyes behind wire-rimmed D-shaped spectacles. Titus whispered that Jefferds was also the schoolteacher. He looked too weak to do either of his jobs, but it turned out that he made good use of his frailty. People heeded his soft voice as one would attend a dying man's last words, while he delivered the gentlest and most terrifying hellfire sermon I had ever heard.

It would have gone against his temperament to rage or threaten even if he had had the strength for it. He merely explained the situation. He began with the pain. "Think how it hurts when you burn your finger or your arm. This burning is over the whole body. And it never stops. Hell is full of screaming. It would be terrible just to hear it, but maybe the damned don't notice, since they're screaming themselves."

He talked as if he were warning us against skating on a pond where the ice had broken and drowned children several years in a row. There was no censure, only dismay that in this day and age, when everything was so well understood and it was obvious what needed to be done, so many people still chose damnation. Before long, his frail voice was being joined by quiet weeping and moaning from quite a few of the men and women on the hard rough benches around me, and he began to address us by name. "Jenny Williams, do I see a tear in your eye? Are you beginning to think it over?" "John Lenox, I believe you hear me." And me: "Arabella, new to our village, so much has changed for you of late. Lean on Jesus, Arabella. He was there in New York. He is here in Livy. He'll be with you today and tomorrow. He will never leave you. He will never die." I gasped, feeling as if he had reached into my chest and grabbed my heart.

If this had been all he said, I could have accepted the invitation to be comforted, and I suppose that, at least for a time, I might have become a very religious girl. But as I was just becoming aware, there was an obstacle, and I could never get around it.

THAT AFTERNOON, MY AUNT, wanting to show me some special favor, asked me to help her with dinner. We peeled potatoes, and after a while I asked her, "Do you think my papa is in heaven?"

There was a long pause, and she said, very quietly, "I hope so."

"But what do you think? Do you think he's in hell?"

"You mustn't say such things. We don't know. He could be in heaven. We can hope it."

"But, you think, probably not."

"I would never say such a thing."

"You say my mama's in heaven, you're sure about her. I need to know what to picture when I think of my papa. Is he above me or below me?"

She seemed to be looking for an answer in the potato peels. "I asked the minister, and he said he's never read or heard in so many words that a man who takes his own life can't be saved. So there's room for us to hope, and that is what we ought to do."

"My papa was a good man."

"Nobody said he wasn't."

"He was kind to us, he only drank to be sociable, he worked hard, he walked with my grandpa along the waterfront handing out Bibles to the sailors and the dockers."

"Remember him that way. Oh, what a terrible thing. I am sorry for him."

"He wasn't a Baptist."

"That's no matter, so long as he accepted God's grace."

Keeping my voice steady, and squinting at a dark spot in the potato in my hand, I said, "I don't think he did."

My aunt didn't reply. It was perfectly clear that she didn't think he had, either.

The plan had gone awry. We would not all be together in the afterlife. I would never be able to think of my dear mother in heaven looking down at us adoringly, without thinking also of my father burning and screaming below us.

Book Two

{ 1837–1844 }

XI

MY NEW FAMILY WOULD HAVE DENIED that they intended from the first to think badly of me. And there would have been some truth in their answer. No doubt had I arrived knowing where the root cellar was and how to do half a dozen farm chores, they'd have been pleasantly surprised. As it was, I confirmed their direst suspicions. It was their politely unspoken belief that no one in New York City did honest work. My uncle knew—he had been there three times. If further proof was needed, just look at me—a girl of nine who had spent her whole life learning to put on the airs of a lady.

I had always thought of myself as a diligent little helper in a sober evangelical family, and one does not quickly abandon such a notion; still, I soon stopped defending my previous existence. To mention New York seemed always to mean saying things like "We went by omnibus," and having to explain to unsympathetic listeners what that was, and being asked how much it cost to ride in one. It meant admitting that my mother wore kid gloves whenever she went out, and that most of our washing was done by a woman who lived across town and whose name I didn't know. It meant saying that every time I had left the house I used to see strangers, because there were too many people in the city for me ever to know them all. It meant learning that there was something very wrong about my inability to appreciate the wickedness in such a state of affairs.

The girls were given charge of my farm education, a plan that put too much power in Agnes's hands: it was her way to leave crucial elements out of her instructions, and watch while I made mistakes for which she knew I would be punished.

"Show Arabella how we harvest carrots," said my aunt one day. Under Agnes's direction, I removed the straw and rags covering a patch of late carrots. The ground was hard this time of year. I softened it with water. I tugged. The wilted tops broke off in my hands. Agnes took note of this in her melodious voice (the sound of which, just saying, "Looks like rain," could make my spine straighten with alarm). "Dear Arabella," she added, "it was all right to use *all* the water, if you felt that you must, but be more careful with the tops of the carrots." To prove that it was not true when they said, "Your help makes it take longer," I clawed the ground, tugging the pale cones. A few broke in the soil. In my haste, I ended up leaving a few of the tips in. "Arabella," said Agnes, "it is true that there are plenty of carrots to eat now, but, come spring, how sorely we should miss the broken piece left in the earth to rot."

She left me. The dogs sniffed the vegetables. I threw sticks to distract them. Into the fraying straw basket went straight and crooked carrots, forked carrots with two tapering legs like armless little men, twisted, fibrous, wrinkled, bewhiskered carrots. My spirits rose. I had always been a competent little girl. I could make biscuits. I could sew a straight seam. Why shouldn't I learn to do this well?

"I know you're impatient, Arabella," said Agnes, who had returned, "but wouldn't it have been better to give the young ones a chance to grow tall like their cousin carrots? When you were in New York City, day-dreaming of your trip on a steamboat, my mother and I toiled over these plants, and it seems a shame that this will be all we get when with a little patience there could have been so much more." In my confusion, I began to put them back. "No, Arabella. The carrots won't grow now."

She never dropped her ladylike pretense that she had my best interests at heart, and even more than it infuriated me, this accomplishment amazed me: it was so much more than I could have done in her place. I was a simpler person than she was. I knew it, because I could think of nothing to say to hurt her. I simply wished her dead.

"Come," she said. I followed her to the creek, which was low this season, with its sources in the mountains frozen. Mossy roots poked from the banks. Clear water ran in rivulets and tiny whirlpools. I wished I were one of the blobs of shadow that hurried downstream, stretching and folding athletically over thousands of round and oval stones.

We washed the carrots. When we took them to the porch for drying, Agnes reported, "I fear the carrots won't last till May. Arabella got impatient and pulled the little ones." Evangeline, who was scrubbing—or, rather, gently stroking—the inside of a milk bucket, gave a cry of dismay. My aunt remarked that patience was a virtue, and when I objected that Agnes hadn't told me not to pull out the little ones, everyone looked flabbergasted by the idea that there existed in the world a person who had to be told such a thing. Agnes merely nodded and said, "Of course, Arabella is right. I should have *told* her. Punish *me*, Mama!" but my aunt said that I was the one who needed to learn.

She added that because Agnes had defended me, supper would not be withheld; there would be only the stick. "Arabella, your hands." And only three strokes: "Don't. Waste. Food." Which was preferable, you'll agree, to a wordier message, such as "This. Will. Teach. You. Not. To. Pull. The. Carrots. Out. Of. The. Ground. Before. They're. Ready. You. Naughty. Girl." There had been sentences of such savage prolixity that I still felt them when I lifted my palms to receive the next day's lesson.

Evangeline's tutelage was easier to bear. She would throw her head back to howl out my mistakes—"Mama! Arabella almost let Shadrach"—a pig—"into the cider barrel! She would have done it, but I stopped her!"—but she explained every step clearly. She was literal-minded, and I don't believe she ever had any particular feeling about me one way or another.

THE FIRST TIME AUNT AGATHA GAVE ME a shirt to mend, I went to work with a gathering confidence that improved my spirits, for in New York City I had learned to sew quite well for a girl my age, and I had by this time quite forgotten that I was good at anything. When I announced as calmly as if it were nothing special that I was done, Agnes said, "Let me see. Yes. I see. But let us not trouble my mother with it now, Arabella. I'll show it to her later."

Night fell. We all sat by the fire, and my aunt, who was in the rocker, praised my sewing and showed it to the family. Each one gripped the shirt in turn, expressing tepid approval or sullen indifference, and at last I had an opportunity to admire my own work; I took it nearer the fire. But what was this?

"What is it, Arabella?" my aunt asked.

"A mistake has been made," I said. "This isn't my sewing."

"What do you mean? Did you do the work I gave you?"

"Yes, with brown thread. This is white thread. Someone has ripped out my work and done it over."

I said it without quite believing it, ready to be shown my error.

"You must be mistaken," said my aunt soothingly. "Who would do that? Why would they do it? Evangeline? Agnes?"

Agnes bowed her head and murmured inaudibly.

"Agnes?" my aunt repeated.

Agnes showed us her glistening eyes. "It was I, Mama," she confessed. "I know I shouldn't have. But I didn't want Arabella to get in *trouble*." She turned to me and explained, "It was done so carelessly. You must learn to slow down a little and take more care."

My aunt said, "Agnes, you did wrong. Get me a switch."

We waited while Agnes hunted outside the house for a stick. She returned with one nearly as stout as the one I would have selected for her.

My aunt told me, "I would never punish you for sewing badly, so long as you did the best you could. But you have to try and do your best. I'm surprised you didn't learn to sew better in New York. You must ask Agnes to teach you."

ONE MORNING, MY EYES OPENED while the others were sleeping, and I thought of a way to show them all how wrong they were about me. I wrapped myself in the top blanket, while Lewis stirred and spoke in his sleep. (Once, I had heard him say, quite distinctly, "Broadway.") My clothes were already on. I put on my shoes, collected the irons that had warmed our beds the night before, and climbed down the ladder to put kindling on the embers in the kitchen. When the flames were going, I added a log, put some potatoes in to roast, and heated up the fire in the sitting room. By then the others would be up.

It was noticed, just once, that I had been the first awake—my aunt used my example as a means of rebuking the other children. I was gratified, but there were no more compliments. I kept doing it anyway. It felt good, it made me feel strong, to have the house to myself, the last of the night to myself.

School began in November. I remember the first day best, though perhaps it is adulterated, as such memories often are with knowledge acquired later. At any rate, this is how I recall it. There was a short period, about three weeks, when it was cold but the cows still needed our attention in the mornings. A chalky shard of the moon sat in the sky over the barn roof; a veil of frost turned weeds, sheds, and barrels a shade paler; and the frozen vegetation was springy under our feet. Steam rose from fresh dung the boys shoveled into a wheelbarrow, while the girls milked the cows, often dozing for a few seconds on the creatures' warm bellies. Twice, after I had milked a full bucket, the cow stepped forward and flicked its manure-coated tail into the milk, ruining it, and I was whipped. It was both times the same hateful cow, with whose habits my cousins were familiar. We fed the chickens, took eggs from nests scattered all over the barn and the yard, and cleaned their shack. We cleaned our shoes with sticks and grass, washed our hands and faces on the porch, just with water (soap was for clothes; the one time I used it for my face, I was punished). Then we had a breakfast—which included milk until, in December, the cows dried up—and we walked to school with hot potatoes in our pockets.

The older children went to school from mid-November to mid-March, half as long as school had lasted for me in New York City. There was also a summer session, taught by the sawmill owner's daughter, for children under eight years old; it was attended mostly by the town children who lived near enough to walk to the school by themselves.

On the way, my cousins told me about the teacher, Mr. Jefferds, whom I had already met in his capacity as pastor of our church. Everything they said would turn out to be very important, but of course I didn't know it, so I didn't give it much of my attention. I had been punished with no supper the night before, and was still hungry after breakfast. I was wondering if it would be a good idea to eat one of the potatoes now. Would I regret not having it at recess? Would Agnes or Evangeline report that I had eaten the potato prematurely, and if so, would that be grounds for a punishment? I thought mainly about this as Evangeline said that Jefferds was an exceptionally kindly teacher who only beat the children if they were bad, and he gave out tickets for special feats of learning; when you had fifty tickets, you were rewarded with a pocket-sized New Testament or, if you already had that, an Old Testament.

Titus said that Mr. Jefferds had no house of his own, and boarded for a few months at a time with the families of the students; he was always given the best food and the chair nearest the fire, because he was a mine of information and a fount of wisdom. He had studied in a college somewhere. Agnes, too, produced careful evidence that Jefferds was a fine man.

We walked on then in silence for a few minutes. Fearing ridicule almost more than a whipping, I wondered if I would be mocked should I ask whether eating the potato early was a punishable offense. Farm gave way to forest. When Matthew spoke, I realized they had all been waiting for him to speak. "Bill Jefferds is a beggar. That's all he is. Teaching school is a government job. Preachers ain't supposed to have government jobs. People round here overlook it. Why do you think they do that?" he asked, pitching a stone at a bird's nest in a birch tree, swearing when he missed it, and trying again while we waited for him. He answered himself: it was because Jefferds, who had to rest for a moment after he climbed the two steps to his pulpit, was unfit for man's work. "It's teach school or starve." The nest came down. Matthew walked on, picking it apart. "Folks round here are too honest to understand somebody like him."

These were already more words than Matthew had ever before spoken to me, and the tirade continued until we had reached our destination. I had never heard a child voice so much contempt for a grown man, let alone his family's pastor.

The schoolhouse was the one-room edifice, as plain as the house a child draws, that we see nowadays on the cover of piano sheet music for songs that mention hickory sticks and girls in calico. It had a long, pitched roof and a smoking chimney. It had once been painted red. At places that got extra wear, like the doorway, and places that for some reason got the brunt of the weather, the gray wood showed through; and the unpainted planks of the walls inside were dark with soot from the fireplace and dirt from the hands of children. There were brass hooks on the back wall for our coats, in case it should ever get warm enough for us to remove them, and an odd assortment of benches, tables, and desks, and planks and old barrels that could be assembled into makeshift desks. There were shelves, also assorted, which, when new, had lived in the houses of the miller, the storekeeper, and the sawmill owner, and there were pupils of ages ranging from eight to sixteen.

Jefferds called the roll, naming me among the "G"s as Arabella Godwin, and pausing to tell the class that they had probably heard I was the cousin of the Moody children, come here to live here with them. I looked around and I noticed Agnes staring at Jeptha. I also noticed—and the significance of this observation sank in slowly—that at least four other girls, two of them pretty (one a fourteen-year-old with hips and a bosom), were variously smiling at Jeptha, or casting sudden glances and then looking away in pretended indifference. When Jefferds got to the "T"s and Jeptha answered, Agnes watched me. I was going to look at my desk, but I decided that would be strange in itself, and I looked at him. As he said, "Here," he turned to smile at me. I tried to harden my heart against this smile, but I felt a renewed shock at his simple good looks. Then Jefferds called out, "Rebecca Talbot." My eyes sought the girl and a few seconds later, the cane. She was a little older than Lewis, a skinny girl with a plump, round, freckly face, a faded cotton dress, and a woolen shawl. According to Titus who was proving to be the only safe source of information in my uncle's house, this was her first year in the winter school. She was very talkative, always immediately in conference with other girls as soon as the teacher was absent. Everyone treated her kindly, although sometimes Matthew said unpleasant things about her to get a rise out of Jeptha. With Becky as the pretext, Jeptha and Matthew had fought three times. Each time, Matthew had been the victor.

On no day of school do we learn more than on the first day of silent panic among strange faces and unknown tacit rules, and it was on my first day in that unpainted one-room schoolhouse that I learned why Matthew hated Mr. Jefferds. The puzzle was solved all at once when, an hour after the roll was taken, I watched my cousin struggle, at the teacher's insistence, with two short paragraphs in the second-year reader. Matthew, who was big and strong and not stupid, the cock of the walk in every situation but this one, began to stammer. His face went red. For five minutes he writhed within the mild teacher's invisible talons. Released, he seemed to fall from a height and flop lifeless onto his desk. This black magic was in evidence in any encounter with books, writing, or numbers, all winter long. From a sense of duty, maybe—an honest desire to teach the smart boy who might succeed if he tried harder—Jefferds called on Matthew more often than he called on other children. I saw my cousin dread the moment and seethe with fury afterward. He was sure that the weakling in the D-shaped spectacles was deliberately humiliating him out of envy for his health and vitality. No one had ever hurt him like that. He never forgave it.

ONE DAY, TWO WEEKS LATER, Jefferds cleared his throat and announced that it was recital time. Lifting up his spectacles, he brought a ledger an inch from his nose and squinted at it in a way that was always included in the comical imitations done by the boys who rushed to sit at his desk whenever he left the room. "Ephraim Towne. Step up, Ephraim."

A skinny red-haired boy in homespun woolen trousers of a faded brown with ragged cuffs, and a homespun shirt in a faded blue, quietly rose from his desk, walked to the front of the room, and stood with his back to the fire. "Wait a moment, Ephraim," said Jefferds, squinting at the list again. "Children, as some of you may realize, this is no ordinary recital. Ephraim has forty-nine tickets carried over from last year, entitling him to"—more squinting—"a copy of the New Testament when he earns his fiftieth."

He was telling them nothing; even I knew. Titus had reminded me of it this morning—in a whisper, out of Matthew's hearing—as we were washing up: poor Ephraim Towne's excellent memory, of which he was justly proud, had gotten him into a pickle. For, if Ephraim earned his fiftieth ticket, his second reward, after the New Testament, was to be a beating from Matthew on the way home. If the future resembled the past, Matthew would take the book away from him. He would not keep it—he was no thief—and according to his odd but rigid sense of what was fitting, he couldn't destroy it, because it was Scripture. However, he could put it at the end of a high limb on a tree Ephraim wasn't brave enough to climb, or just under the roof of a notably bad-tempered farmer's barn, or some other amusing place. Matthew bullied wittily, denying his victims the consolation of considering themselves his intellectual superiors. His bullying was no impulsive product of his hurt feelings. It was a policy.

"I can't help feeling sorry for Ephraim," said Titus. He said it not as someone protesting an injustice but as someone noting the sadness of life. Matthew and Titus were very different, with different views, and at home they often quarreled; but outside things were different. Titus was small for his age, and he was considered fortunate to have Matthew for a brother.

Usually, I sat near the front of the drafty little schoolhouse, to be nearer the fire, and the better to be seen by the myopic Jefferds, who complimented my reading and spelling and penmanship and let me help the slower children with their work. But on this particular day, I had come in last and was in the back, with a good view of the whole room. I saw Ephraim's tension as he prepared to recite, and I saw enough of the faces of the assorted other pupils to get a general idea of which ones pitied him, which took a cruel pleasure in his predicament, and which ones just marveled at his temerity, as I did.

"We wait, Ephraim," said Jefferds. "We're waiting."

Staring over our heads at the knotty horizontal planks on the back wall, Ephraim recited the poem about the amazingly dutiful boy "on the burning deck," who remains in that unenviable predicament awaiting instructions from his father, who, in fact, is dead.

As he came to the end, Ephraim hesitated. He will forget, I thought. Who could blame him? Then he looked at Matthew and—immobile save for his fiercely straining lips—flung each word like a missile: "'But the noblest thing that perished there / Was that young, faithful heart!'" Children cheered, hooted, stomped, and drummed. "Well done, Ephraim," said Jefferds, handing him the book. "You've earned this. We can all learn from the courage of the boy on that ship." Matthew's friends made throat-cutting gestures. Matthew just shook his head sadly, as if disappointed in Ephraim and regretting the stern disciplinary measures that awaited them both. Jeptha's back was to me, and I could not see his look. Titus wore a faraway, daydreaming expression.

Ephraim hovered over the book until Jefferds, perhaps to answer nature's call, left the room for a few minutes. Gazing out of one of the schoolhouse's small windows, Titus said he saw a dog with a rabbit, and the rabbit's guts were hanging out, and most of the children rushed to that side of the room. I didn't want to see rabbit guts, so I was in my seat when Ephraim rose a little later than the others, leaving the book behind. I saw Jeptha pass Ephraim's desk and stuff the book into his trousers. On his way to the window, he turned to me and put his finger to his lips.

I was confused. Jeptha's theft of the book contradicted everything I had learned so far about the politics of the little schoolhouse. The boys were divided into three stable factions: one gathered around Matthew, another around Jeptha, and a third consisted of the Miller brothers, who were fearless because they were so numerous: four in the school that year, and in addition the seventeen-year-old, who had graduated the previous year, and the seven-year-old, who would enter it next year. Ephraim belonged to Jeptha's faction: why should Jeptha steal his book? It wasn't until Ephraim got back to his seat and raised no alarm about the missing book that I understood: Jeptha had taken it, with Titus's help and by prearrangement with Ephraim, to keep it out of Matthew's hands. It was to be expected that Jeptha would help Ephraim: they were friends. That Titus should take the risk of thwarting his brother was more surprising.

Later, while we trotted home through the cold, Matthew went off in the direction of Ephraim's house. "Did you tell?" Titus asked me when Agnes was out of earshot. I shook my head, and he patted my arm, and I was grateful to him for giving me the opportunity to prove that I was someone who could be trusted to keep a secret.

Well after bedtime, Matthew came up to the loft, carrying a candle and a hunk of bread, and after pulling Titus from his bed he proceeded to recite a new chapter in his, Matthew's, continuing saga: how Ephraim, in a cowardly attempt to evade his fair punishment, had taken a detour through Norris Woods and the Muskrat Pond, and Matthew had tracked him like an Indian, noticing broken twigs, pausing to listen for the sounds of crackling beneath Ephraim's worn-out shoes, which left a slightly different pattern depending upon whether Ephraim had been running, walking, leaping, or standing still in terror so great that it stopped his mind and he was just a passive vessel of fear. Matthew knew how to walk on springy matted leaves and hard roots so that he left no track. Thanks to such astounding feats of woodcraft, he had caught up with poor Ephraim, who was by then half frozen, so really it was a rescue. "You're lucky I found you," Matthew had said, giving him a sound drubbing, after which they both felt better, because of course, Matthew reminded us, there is no licking worse than the fear of a licking in those foolish enough to fear them. But Matthew had not recovered the testament.

Titus and Matthew huddled around the candle. The rest of us watched.

"Why not?" asked Titus innocently.

"He didn't have it. He had another boy hold it for him."

"That was smart. Did he say who he gave it to?"

"Well, he didn't want to say. He didn't say at first. But after a while, I guess he changed his mind, and then he did say. He gave it to Jeptha."

"I guess it was too late by then to catch up with Jeptha," said Titus.

"Yup," said Matthew. Then his arms moved. Titus, expecting it, ducked and ran for the ladder. Matthew cornered him near a dresser.

Soon Matthew had one of Titus's arms behind his back and was tugging it upward while Titus winced and cried out: "Stop it, Matt! I didn't do nothing! Stop it!"

"'Look everybody—dog with a rabbit,'" Matthew murmured. "Teach you to take sides against your own brother."

"Uncle Elihu, Matthew's hurting Titus!" I called, out of friendliness to Titus, but also lest under torture he name me among the other conspirators. My uncle shouted out for them to stop. He climbed to the loft and, talking as if they were equally responsible, said that if they didn't settle their differences peaceably they would both get a licking worse than they could give each other. And while they were on the subject, Matthew was owed a licking for coming home too late to do his chores. He would get it tomorrow. (But he didn't. My uncle made little effort to hide his preference for Matthew.)

The next day, Matthew told Agnes: "You see your sweetheart, tell him his sneaky trick has come to light, and he's going to have to take his licks. I'll attend to it when he comes over for hog killing."

Agnes, blushing, said, "He's not my sweetheart," and I thought: *It's true.*

"Oh, I know that," said Matthew, who knew many ways to be cruel.

XII

THEY SAY THAT ANIMALS DO NOT COMPREHEND the inevitability of death. One felt that keenly around the creatures who fed in happy ignorance of their fate, as the season of their killing and butchering approached. There were to be several slaughters, accompanied by feasting and drinking, on one farm and then another in our part of the country, and there was a holiday atmosphere, there was something pagan in the air, as the first of these occasions approached, and blades were sharpened, ropes mended, barrels and buckets scrubbed, and trips made into town for salt and whiskey. On the day appointed for the slaughter on my uncle's farm, two families arrived soon after dawn. Jeptha's family came after we had already started. I knew I would be mocked for turning away, so I stood where I could see everything, as the first struggling victim was manhandled to a spot beneath the old maple, and as the pig was struck between the ears with the blunt end of an ax, and struck again when the first blow proved ineffectual, and provoked into a last sad kick as a long knife penetrated its heart, at which point I sighed, sorry for the pig. Hearing a derisive snort, I glanced quickly around; Jeptha's mother was regarding me coldly. When I looked back, a stick was being thrust through the hind legs. A rope was thrown over a stout limb, men pulled the rope, the carcass ascended, its brethren squealed with human horror, Agatha moved a bucket to catch the blood, Elihu slit the throat. After a posthumous shave in the iron kettle, the hog rose again, and everyone crowded in for the disembowelment. Lewis asked me if the steam that issued from the carcass then was the soul, and I said yes; it seemed obvious.

My aunt handed Lewis a stick and told him to chase the dogs away until they could be distracted with the lungs, which were their portion. Later, when the feast began, she said that he had done well, and as a reward gave him his choice of certain fatty tidbits children crave. I coaxed him to try these delicacies, and he did, but as usual he barely ate. I told him that this was a rare occasion and he should take advantage of it. I said that at night, when I hugged him, I could feel his ribs. I said that if he did not start eating more he would stop growing and the other boys would beat him up; that he would get consumption and die. I told him things like that all the time.

He had not regained his appetite since the moment he heard of our father's suicide. The news had no other observable effect on him. He did not sulk or brood; he seemed to like the farm; he made pets of wild creatures; he tagged along behind Matthew and Titus whenever they'd let him. He was usually cheerful a half-hour after a punishment. He did not talk about New York or Mama or Papa. He ate barely enough to keep himself alive.

I watched Jeptha as we all brought our plates to the makeshift tables, which had been created by laying planks of wood over barrels. The

strangeness of this place had put me into a stupor; all my emotions were
dulled, every feeling muted and muffled, but something about this boy
broke through and seized my attention. At school I had noticed that he
was very quick, and in my only private conversation with him so far I had
learned that, like me, he had read an essay about the discoveries of Gali-
leo and an essay about the Battle of Waterloo in an older student's copy
of the fourth-year reader, though in the school he was only up to the
third-year reader. I was sure that he had read the whole series, but he kept
that to himself: he was shrewd enough to realize that having a reputation
as a scholar did a boy more harm than good around here. He was friendly
and agreeable to everyone, yet I had the feeling that he was searching, in
every spare moment, for another example of his kind.

One day he had come into school with a brooding look and sat at his
desk making fists, and at recess his sister Becky said that Jeptha and Papa
had had an awful fight the night before.

Now, though everyone knew he was going to fight Matthew today,
and everyone expected him to be beaten, he stuffed himself with pork
and Indian pudding, apparently cheerful and fearless. I hoped that he
would not spoil the effect by puking, as I had once seen a boy do under
the exact same circumstances back in the Union Presbyterian School in
New York City. Occasionally, I saw him give his father a cool glance. The
father had had more than his share of my uncle's whiskey, and I remembered that everyone said he was quarrelsome when he was drunk.

The older boys drank, too, under the protection of the fathers, who
observed sagely that the men who had never been brought up to whiskey
were the very ones who became drunkards when they grew up. It was a
constant cause of friction between Elihu and Agatha. My aunt usually
had the stronger will. He had given in to her on such large matters as
joining the Free Will Baptist church, and (I came to realize) taking in her
dead sister's children. But he held out on some things, to show he wasn't
completely tame, and this included the matter of letting Titus and Matthew drink.

Jeptha confined himself to water, saying, "I got religion," which I took
for a joke: I knew from our one conversation at school that Jeptha was an
infidel, like his father. "But don't let me stop you, Matt. Agnes, give Matt
some more of the creature."

"You want me to, Matt?" asked Agnes.

Matthew ignored her, asking Jeptha: "You think if I'm corned and you ain't it'll help you out later on?"

Jeptha said firmly, "I'm counting on it."

Matthew looked at him with pity. "I could whip you with ten drinks in me."

"Why don't you show me?"

Before Matthew could reply, Agnes filled his cup; Matthew stared down at it and looked up at his sister.

Jeptha said, "You could lick me corned? No fooling? Is that true? Show me."

"Getting me corned will make it worse for you," Matthew explained in a patient tone. "If I was corned and I tried to bloody your nose, I would hit you too hard and break it. If I was corned, I might bust you up so bad nobody could fix you."

"You're scared to hurt me? That doesn't sound like you, Matthew. I don't believe it. Does anybody believe it?" Jeptha asked the other children at the table; and they all said no, and the hands, Pat and Sam, shook their heads, too. "Look around you, Matt. They know you, too," said Jeptha. "They know what you're like. They're begging you. Drink up. Unless you're scared that if you drink you won't be able to beat me."

Matthew did look around. Everyone was nodding and saying, "Go on," and "Have another, Matt."

My aunt was staring at us from the next table. Children and men fell into guilty silence, expecting her to scold them for urging her son to drink. But she said, "Maybe they're right, Matthew. Have some more. Show them you're not scared." She announced generally, "Let nobody call my son a sissy."

Matthew certainly must have realized that his mother was hoping that whiskey *would* make him lose, thereby turning him against whiskey. Nevertheless, he raised the cup, absorbed its contents, and slapped it down to the table defiantly.

Whereupon Agnes did something that made me admire her despite myself. Locking eyes with Jeptha, she refilled Matthew's cup. We all stared at him, and he drank.

His footsteps were extremely deliberate as he and Jeptha made their way to a grassy patch between the back porch and the garden and took off their jackets, while the fathers and mothers and children gathered, including Mrs. Talbot, Becky, assorted other members of the large Talbot brood, my uncle Elihu's brother, Melanchthon, whose farm lay half a mile from ours, and his wife, Anne, and Agnes, her lips compressed, her hands alternately making fists and claws.

Matthew and Jeptha used to be great friends, according to Titus. They had hunted together, played Indian and mumblety-peg, dug for gold, and competed with each other in feats of skill, endurance, and daring. This had ended abruptly a year and a half ago, with Matthew giving as the reason that Jeptha had too weak a character to face up to his, Matthew's, superiority, and Jeptha giving as the reason that he had gotten tired of hearing Matthew talk about himself.

Jake was shouting at Jeptha, "What's the matter with you? He's whupped you twice already, you little girl, ain't you learned your lesson?" As the fight progressed, and Matthew kept swinging and missing, Jake's cry changed to "Sock him, you goddamned dancer!" And when Jeptha had Matthew's head in his arm and Matthew's face was as red as a tomato, it was "Rip him up, damn you! He whups you now, I'll whup you worse!"

Jeptha, straining and grimacing, asked, "Are you licked? Say you're licked."

Matthew sagged within Jeptha's clutches. He seemed almost to fall asleep. Suddenly he struggled again—a ruse—it didn't work.

"Are you licked?" Jeptha repeated.

"No, he ain't licked!" screamed Jake. "Do him so he knows it, you fine lady in white gloves and petticoats. You got him. Put him to some use!"

My uncle looked at Jake without speaking. My uncle's brother, Melanchthon, said, "It's all in fun, Jake."

At last, Matthew admitted defeat. Jeptha let him up. They shook hands. Matthew, in speech that was not slurred but showed effort, every word an accomplishment, said, "Well, you're . . . you're . . . famous. Famous now. Licked . . . Matt Moody. When he was so corned he couldn't . . . stand, hardly, but . . . it's a . . . Not nobody can never take that away from you. But next time we scrap . . ." He seemed to lose his train of thought.

"What?" said Jeptha impatiently, as if he could not bear to waste another minute of his life on Matthew. "You were saying. Next time we scrap. What?"

He was angry, I realized.

"I won't drink," said Matthew, and he looked around, doggedly explaining, "He got the bulge on me 'cause Agnes—she was in it with him, got me corned."

"Temperance," said Melanchthon genially. "Lesson to us all."

Jeptha had his back to Jake, who stepped forward to put an arm on his son's shoulder, possibly in congratulation. As though a spring had been released, Jeptha turned and knocked his father's hand away. Jake laughed. "Ooh, ooh, the taste of blood." Jake stood in a boxer's pose. "Go to it, killer."

"One day," said Jeptha.

"Jeptha," said his mother. "You won. Don't spoil it."

"Oh, let him be a man, Marm. Come on, boy. I'm corned, ain't I? That helps you, don't it?"

Jeptha shook his head. "Not one day when I'm old enough to beat you."

"Jeptha, you stop," said his mother sharply.

Jeptha shook his head. "One day when I'm old enough to run the farm." He slapped his palms back and forth as if he were getting rid of some dirt. "You can go live in town and drink away your days; I'll pay for the drinks." His father looked astounded. "I can hardly wait," Jeptha said, and walked off. Becky followed him with her irregular step through the frosty weeds. "Jeptha!" she called after him. "Jeptha, don't be mad. Jeptha, be happy you won." Agnes followed Becky and caught up with her, and they walked together.

"Come back, you ungrateful pup," Jake gasped, looking as if the wind had been knocked out of him. The disrespect of Jeptha's outburst, directed at a grown man, a father, who was known to have a violent temper, shocked everyone who had heard it, including me. It was a much bigger thing than the fight which had preceded it. Jake started off after his son, but his wretched wife grabbed him around the waist, virtually leaping upon him, saying "Please, Jake." He shook free of her. He pulled his arm back as if to strike her, and stopped, and we all knew it was our presence that stopped him. "I *kill* myself," he growled, "break my back, work my hands raw, die every day for all of you. And who is *he,* goddamnit? What's he ever done?"

Before this, sometimes when I was in my straw bed but not yet asleep, and the memories of my day offered nothing else to comfort me, I thought of a friendly glance this boy had tossed in my direction. Now I was glad he had not been hurt or shamed. I hoped his father would not hurt him later. But most of all I wished that, like Agnes, I had thought of a way to help. I had seen nothing to do but fret, and a girl who despised me had shown me wrong. I felt as insignificant as they all kept insisting I was.

LATER IN THE DAY, THERE WAS MORE butchering and salting, and in the evening, more feasting and drinking, and games, including wrestling and cards. Jacob and Melanchthon told funny stories which I have heard many times since then, in which Yankee farmers, by pretending to be simple, get the better of crafty storekeepers, city folk, and educated fools.

Melanchthon stayed overnight with Anne and two of their several children. Melanchthon, eight years older than Elihu, was an instructive contrast to his brother. He had been in Livy twice as long. His farm was bigger. He was a bigger man in the community. Outwardly he was a larger, older version of my uncle, with the same crowded face and buttonhole eyes, but the better you knew him, the more different he seemed, and he made a point of establishing an acquaintance quickly. Soon after we met, he told me in a whisper to keep an eye on a broom whenever a woman entered a chamber. If it moved even slightly, she was a witch. Thereafter, he winked at me and glanced at the broom whenever any female entered, including my aunt, Agnes, Evangeline, and his own wife, Anne, and daughter, Susannah, and I laughed in spite of myself.

I had heard it said that he knew the secrets of Indian medicine and had once cured a bewitched butter churn by dropping a silver dollar into it. When he arrived that morning, my aunt had extracted a promise from him to help her find a missing shawl. It was his unofficial duty to recover lost articles, using a forked stick with which in past summers he had led moonlight quests for gold, on the south sides of the local eminences that best qualified as mountains.

To crown his accomplishments, Anne, Melanchthon's second wife, was young, pretty, and friendly to me. It did not take me long to wish that

Horace had driven half a mile farther and left us at Melanchthon's farm instead of his brother's. As it was, just to know that these people existed gave me a bit of extra strength. Even here in this wilderness—where, clearly, I did not belong, where I had been sent by an error which could yet be rectified—even here, so far from civilization, there was another way to live, another way to think, another opinion to have about the merits of Arabella Godwin.

Their six-year-old daughter, Susannah, let me brush her hair. When I told her that New York City was on an island, she asked me whether it was tethered to the ocean's bottom by a stem, like a water lily, or stuck fast, like a boulder. I showed her the miniature of my mother, my Sunday frock, my seashells, and the pictures in Buffon's *Natural History*.

In the morning, I helped the grown women cut the cold fat and melt it in the big black kettle to make lard. Later, when Susannah and I were walking near the creek, we heard my aunt cry out from the other side of the house and ran, thinking someone was hurt, but it had been a cry of joy: with the help of his dowsing stick, Melanchthon had found her shawl in a pile of leaves behind a corncrib, where it must have been dragged by a dog, or perhaps by one of the very pigs whose hindquarters were hanging in the smokehouse.

❧ XIII ❧

BY FEBRUARY, THE BIG ROUND OF VISITS to other farms that had accompanied slaughtering and shelling and threshing was over and forgotten, and we lived on cornmeal and salt meat. On one of those cold, monotonous days when drifts from the previous week's snow lay against the barn as high as the windows, we came home from school to learn that a peddler had been to the house. He had been a peddler of the middling class, the kind that had no wagon, but a poor overburdened nag to carry his whole stock of goods, and the products of my aunt's trading with him included Souchong tea, spices, belt buckles, and presents for the children. For Lewis, a whittling knife; for me, pencils and paper.

I was, I will not say touched, but taken aback, that she had thought of me, that she had made this kind gesture.

A few days later, when we were by the fireside—I was sewing, my aunt was spinning—Lewis asked me to read to him from *Peter Simple,* one of Frank's books, which neither of us had looked at in a long time. We haggled for a while and at last agreed that I would read to him if he ate two slices of bread cut to the thickness of the widest part of my thumb. He crammed the food into himself and went to the loft to the trunk of books.

"It ain't here," Lewis shouted from the loft.

An odd look crossed my aunt's face. I climbed the ladder. The trunk was not quite empty: *Advice to a Young Married Woman* was there, *The Whole Duty of Woman,* and *Exemplary Letters for Sundry Occasions,* my Bible, and my diary. But the five books by Captain Marryat, the dozen by Scott, and the thirty-six volumes of Buffon's *Natural History* were all gone.

The peddler. The trading, the tea, the little presents. We had been in Livy four months by then, and I had learned to know my aunt—no great feat, she wasn't complicated, only my resentment of her prevented me from knowing her completely. I knew what had happened to those books, or at least I suspected: what she had done was so enormous, in my eyes, that it was hard to believe. Though I had hardly glanced at them since I had come here, they were precious. I was proud to own them; they represented New York City and civilization. They had all been gifts, and on their flyleaves my brother Frank, my brother Robert, and my mother had written their names in their own hand, turning the books into relics and heirlooms. My mother had given me some of those books *on her deathbed,* and my aunt knew it, because I had told her. It was a crime.

"Wait up here," I told Lewis, and I went down the ladder. "Aunt Agatha, do you know where my books are?" A few seconds went by, filled with the motion of her foot on the treadle and the airy whirring of her wheel. "Do you know, Aunt Agatha?" Still no answer.

"Come to the kitchen with me," she said, halting the wheel, and I followed her. "We'll have some tea and apple cheese, just us," she said. She put up a kettle in the kitchen fireplace for hot water, prepared some

Souchong tea, cut some of her dense, soggy bread, and opened a crock of thick brown apple cheese; she didn't begin speaking again until we were both seated on stools and facing each other at a small table.

She said that she was going to explain about the books. I must be patient and hear her out. (Although it seemed to me that I suffered in silence, I was notorious in the family for my interruptions, arguments, and excuses.)

"Some of the books you kept in your trunk were not good books for a young girl to read. I know you don't mean to do wrong by it, but many a girl has been led to ruin by novels. I guess your mother thought that there are differences between one novel and another and that these ones were all right. But she's not here now. I'm looking after you now, and I can't raise my own girls one way and you another. So that's why the peddler got those. Now, just wait awhile before you interrupt. The other books, by the Frenchman, were not for girls of any age, and especially not one apt to get consumption if she does brain work. It wasn't your mother's idea for you to have those; it was your brother Robert's, as you told me, and I guess he didn't know any better. I've looked at them." She spoke as if she had taken a great risk herself in doing that much. "They're books for a professor or a doctor, not a girl in delicate health."

I had plenty to say, but I held it back. I wish you to appreciate the effort it took for me not to object or reason or protest but instead to wait—to behave as coolly as my clever enemy, Agnes, some of whose traits I coveted.

It was a long time ago. I suppose I was angry, but what I remember best is my delight. She had done something wrong, and I could make her feel it.

Finally, she said, "Do you want to ask me something?"

A few more seconds passed. "You never told me you thought that way about the books."

"I didn't want us to argue," she said, as if that was a perfectly ethical explanation.

"You never told me not to read them."

"If you read in them somewhat before I had a chance to get rid of them, it wouldn't matter so much. It's reading them daily that makes the danger."

"Why do you send me to school if brain work is bad for me? Why do you have me learn Bible verses on Sunday? Learning Bible verses is much harder than just reading Buffon, I think. I think that, to preserve my health, I had better stop going to school, and be excused from learning verses by heart."

"Are you sassing me?"

"Oh no, Aunt Agatha. I would never sass you."

She didn't know. Sarcasm was not a weapon in her arsenal. She knew of its existence, but she really didn't understand it.

"You need to go to school to learn to write and figure, and you need to study the Bible for your salvation. Reading the Frenchman's book stirs you up to no purpose."

I nodded, and, to convince her that there were no hard feelings, I asked, "Could you tell me about the trading you did, so that when I'm grown I'll know how to trade with peddlers?"

"Of course," she said, and, warily at first but with gathering enthusiasm, proud of the bargain she'd made, she told me that the peddler had offered her twenty-five cents per book, but she had said she couldn't part with them for less than a dollar. They had eventually agreed to a half-dollar each; he had wanted to pay less for each volume of Buffon, since it was really only one long book, but she had not fallen for that, and she had held out for the full eighteen dollars for the Buffon. (I saw the sum impressed her.) He had offered her banknotes. She had insisted on real clinking coins. Five dollars and fifty cents of the total for Buffon and the other books were expended for the whittling knife, the pencil and paper, and other items, including the tea we were sipping. She had come away with all of that, plus twenty-one dollars in cash.

We sipped the tea and ate the bread, and she smiled sweetly at me, happy it had worked out so well and I had not made too big a fuss.

"This is good," I said. "Thank you, Aunt Agatha."

"You're welcome."

I let her love me a little more, and then I said, quietly but distinctly, "He cheated you," and I watched the smile fade.

"You're not old enough to know if that is true."

"My brother Robert told me what I should get for the books if I ever sold them. Not less than fifty dollars. They were a gift to him from my grandfather. He's going to be awful disappointed when I write to him that you sold the books without asking my permission, and how you let that man make a fool of you. I'm afraid he'll get angry, and if I know Robert, he'll be mean about it."

"That's enough, Arabella."

"Yes, ma'am, but let me tell you about Robert. He's an awful snob. These ignorant back-country Jonathans, he'll say, of course if they had a book the first thing they'd do is sell it, and they'd get cheated because they don't know the value that civilized people set on books. If they did, why, they wouldn't be ignorant."

Robert, I must tell you, had never mentioned what I might get for the books.

My aunt got up. "That's enough. Go upstairs."

I picked up the rest of my bread on the assumption that there would be no supper for me. "Anyhow, where's my twenty-one dollars?"

"Go upstairs, Arabella."

"Yes, ma'am. Just give me my money."

It was her turn to exercise self-control. "Arabella, I'm your aunt. If you don't agree with something I do, you can ask me why I did it. But you've got to be respectful. You're a smart girl. You know better."

"Yes, Aunt Agatha. I know the difference between what's mine and what's somebody else's."

That lay there between us for a while.

She sighed. "Get me a switch."

"To be sure, the switch. The magic stick that explains everything."

I started to run, but she caught me by the wrist; the bread fell to the floor, I shrieked, the back of her hand caught the side of my jaw. I broke free of her, trying to avoid a second blow; she always struck in twos. In fleeing, I slipped and fell backward against the stones of the fireplace, making a cut in the back of my head.

Lewis came in then, saw blood, and Agatha running toward me. He picked up a long black iron poker and swung it at her. She caught his arm and overpowered him. Pinning his arms to his sides, she called Evangeline and Agnes, who subdued him. She made a poultice for my head, using stale bread in the dressing. This worked—the wound did not fester—but still I had a permanent scar, which my hair covered up until I reached the age when my hair grew thin; and there it is today, the crooked little line inscribed on my desiccated scalp, the ancient record of an argument over the sale of Buffon's *Natural History* to a peddler in 1838. Had it been on my face, my life might have taken a different direction.

My aunt said that she did not know what to do about Lewis. She had never in her life heard of a case of a boy trying to murder his aunt—not in the sinful families that worked on the Lord's Day, not among the heathen Indians—and we mustn't speak of it. People would point to Lewis as a man and say that when he was a boy he had tried to kill his aunt with a poker. What on earth was she going to do with him? He was so small and skinny, she said, that she feared to punish him as he deserved.

She said all this out loud, to impress upon him the gravity of his crime, but her confusion was genuine. She decreed, foolishly, that he would go to bed without supper every night for a week. After three days she gave in, because he wasn't eating his dinner.

We were eating downstairs, and he was in the loft, where he spent suppertime. My aunt said, "Belle, come with me," and gave me a plate burdened with bits of salt pork, red beans, stony biscuits, and a spoon. Lewis was crouching by our trunk, guiltily hiding his marbles, which he was on his honor not to play with while he was being punished. "Sit, Lewis," she said, and he sat on his bed, and she handed him the plate, which he held indifferently. "Lewis, I want you to eat. You have to eat. If people don't eat they die." She sat on a stool facing him, looking down and up, looking at me and at him, her hands gripping and turning and squeezing each other.

"I wasn't trying to kill you," he said, just wanting to set the record straight.

"Let's say you weren't. But something very bad could have happened. And it was a shock to me that you would raise a weapon against your aunt, who is only trying to do what your poor mother would want me to do. That was very wrong. Can you see that?"

The mention of his mother had its effect. "Yes," he said, suddenly on the verge of tears. Seizing the opportunity with better instinct than was usual with her, she reached out, and he let her enfold him in her angular embrace. "That's better, that's better," she said, stroking his hair and looking alternately at him and at me. "We'll make a new beginning, each one of us. We'll each be good according to our different duties. Now, I've been praying on this matter of your books, Arabella, and I've talked it over with Elihu. We've decided to give you five dollars out of what we got from the sale of them. You may have this much, but not the whole amount, because we all have to help each other. We all have to make a contribution. Do you think that is fair, Arabella?"

"Yes, Aunt Agatha," I said, still hating her, but she was obviously relieved. She had a great innocent faith in contracts. You said a thing, under duress or not, and she considered the matter settled, and if you went back on it later, she was appalled.

Reader, do you feel sorry for her? *I* do. She wanted us all to be as happy as we could be, given that there is no real happiness this side of heaven (and her primary task, more crucial than the hard work that occupied her every waking hour, was to get us all into heaven). She did not understand exactly why it was proving difficult to be a mother to me, but she knew she had to take some of the blame. She knew she had a bad temper. It may even be that she knew, without quite admitting it to herself, that greed had helped to convince her that I was better off without Buffon's *Natural History* and the novels of Scott and Marryat. But if she regretted that decision, she did not see that it was possible for a grown-up to acknowledge fault in a dispute with a child.

That's how I see it today. At the time, I only knew that we were struggling and that any friendly gesture she made was a thrilling sign of weakness in my enemy.

❧ XIV ❧

I READ WHAT WAS LEFT OF MY LIBRARY. I read the Bible from Genesis to Kings. I read *Exemplary Letters for Sundry Occasions,* which, watered by my imagination like some highly concentrated soup stock, proved as heady a form of romantic literature for me as Captain Maryatt had once been for poor Frank. I would have copied out the letters if paper had been less dear. Instead, I memorized them, imagining as I did it the guests I invited to the banquet, the invitations I accepted, and the unsuitable ones which I graciously declined; the suitors to whose respectful approaches I was not averse, the clergyman I thanked for his kind words after my husband's death. How enviable were the lives of the fine ladies who wrote such letters! They did not boil the wash or disembowel hogs. They sat at a writing desk. They slipped off their white gloves; soft white hands trimmed the pen, dipped it, lifted it. "As I lift my pen . . ."

Following models in the book ("To Family Members Far Distant"), I wrote my first letters to Robert and Edward, and to Mrs. Fitch, and to my grandparents.

March 5, 1838
Dear Grandfather and Grandmother,

I hope this letter finds you well. As I lift my pen in this season
of snow when hoar lies on the branches my heart is warmed by
thoughts of distant Dear Ones. Time has flown since we came here.
Dear Aunt Agatha and Uncle Elihu and our cousins Agnes, Evangeline, Matthew and Titus have done much to take the place of
our old family. We have all become great friends. It has been hard
getting used to the Duties of a farm girl, but I am learning with
Cousin Agnes' kind help. She explains things so clearly one knows
just what to do. Aunt Agatha is very gentle. Evangeline guides me
by her example of hard work. I hope to be as good and clever as
she is one day. Matthew is the admiration of all the local boys on
account of his great skill at games. Titus has a remarkable head for
figures. They are both strong, healthy boys. They are attentive to
their younger cousins, making us feel safe and welcome.

Lewis enjoys the farm creatures and makes pets of wild animals.
He is still a little sad about Mother and Father and does not eat
as he should, though Aunt Agatha plies him with the most delicious dishes for she is a wonderful cook.

Soon the countryside will be in bloom; it will be time for getting
syrup from the maple trees. I look forward to seeing this miracle!

Grandmother, how are the ladies of the Dorcas Society? What
will you plant in your garden this spring? Grandfather, how is the

silk business, and the great cause of abolition? Please write, for I am eager for news of home. With fondest regards, I close,

Your loving granddaughter,
Arabella

I wrote similar letters to Robert, Edward, and Mrs. Fitch. I finished them while we were all together around the fire. My aunt, as I had expected, asked if she might know their contents. I read them aloud, and was rewarded with general expressions of approval at the letters' maturity and accuracy. Agnes and my aunt asked to read them over for themselves. I agreed. They made suggestions. Agnes hoped that I would not take it amiss, for she knew I was excessively sensitive to criticism, if she noted that I had misspelled several words—"abolition" should be "abalishin," "syrup" should be "sirrup," "garden" should be "gardin," etc.—and I should throw in some more commas for good measure, as well-bred people did. My aunt examined the letter and agreed that my spelling needed work. I thanked them both for catching these errors. My aunt said that it would be better not to worry my grandparents by telling them that Lewis wasn't eating as well as he should; we were all doing our best to encourage him to eat more; there was nothing Grandpa and Grandma could do; so perhaps I should rewrite all the letters without that in them, if I didn't mind. I said of course I didn't mind.

And indeed I did not, for they were all dummies and feints, these letters. The letter I actually wrote to my grandfather survives, and here it is, word for word.

March 5, 1838
Dear Grandfather and Grandmother,

I hope this letter finds you well. As I lift my pen in this season of snow when hoar lies on the branches my thoughts fly to better times in grandpa's dear house on Bond Street. I do not wish to trouble you when I know that your own woes lie heavy but I must tell you that our health is not improving here. The air on the farm is unwholesome. I am sure it carries disease for truth to tell we are surrounded by wretched filth. Aunt Agatha throws scraps out the

window for the pigs, so that the yard is full of disgusting pig drop-
pings, or was until most of the pigs were stuck. They died horribly
which was an awful shock to me and Lewis and can hardly have
been good for such as us who have a Wasting Disposition. The
wind carries the bad air from the "necessary" into the house. We
sleep in the loft where there is no fireplace. We shiver all night. I get
up while it is still dark and cold to make the fire. Aunt Agatha is a
bad cook and we all suffer from gripes and fluxes in consequence.
What is healthy in that? Lewis is becoming Skin and Bones. Matthew and Titus drink Rye Whiskey like grown men, a Habit I hope
your grandson Lewis shall not take up. Also Aunt Agatha told us
the truth about Father. She told us very suddenly, which was a
shock to Lewis and may be why he does not eat. They use the swich
all the time on us, even though we are good. We never had the
swich used on us much back in New York. Aunt Agatha has a bad
temper and <u>Uses Her Hands</u>. She sold my books to a peddler to get
money for her own use.

There is no room to tell you all. Some things I cannot bear to
write. If you will bring us back we shall be exemplary and careful of
our health.

Grandma, how are the ladies of the Dorcas Society? What will
you plant in your garden this spring? Grandfather, how is the silk
business, and the great Cause of abolition? Please write for I am
eager for news of home. With fondest regards I close,

Your loving granddaughter,
Arabella

Reading it over, I want to improve the letter as if the nine-year-old
child who wrote it still existed and still had the power of choice. Apart
from wanting to remove the silly echoes of *Exemplary Letters,* I want to
tell my young self that it would be better not to give every possible argument; that weak arguments discredit strong ones by casting doubt on the
writer's judgment. And that, when begging for help, it is better not at the
same time to preen, showing off your recent ladylike accomplishments,
making it seem as if you do not need help.

As soon as the weather allowed trips into town, I brought the letters to the store, where Colonel Ashton weighed them and charged me for them under my aunt's eye. Since there was no coach to Livy, they would be carried in a mailbag to the larger village of Patavium by whoever happened to be going there next, in a day or two days or a week.

Sitting by the fireside with my enemies, sewing, spinning, or hugging my skinny brother in our straw bed after saying aloud for public consumption my lying prayers, I pictured my letter being read in Bond Street. When two weeks had passed—my estimate of the time it would take the letter to reach its destination—I decided that I was free to think of my grandfather or one of his employees traveling toward us by steamboat, stagecoach, and canal packet, advancing implacably on this farm like Caesar on Gaul, come to demand the surrender of the two captives. A four-in-hand hurries in, the driver snapping the whip; customers at the general store rush to the porch; gossip spreads through the miserable town; the simple people are amazed—All this for two children! Who *are* these children?—and they realize then and forever how trivial their own lives are.

At the end of April, my uncle came back from a trip to town and handed a letter that had come and been addressed to me—it was from my grandfather. I took it up to the loft and read it in a shaft of light from the window.

April 7, 1838
Dear Arabella,

Your grandmother and I were glad to receive a letter from you, but we wish that it had been a different letter. We wish that you had waited until you were in a better mood, when you could write with more charity about your aunt and your uncle.

The parts of country life that you find so disagreeable are well known to those of us who have lived on farms. Physicians do not consider them unhealthy—quite the contrary. I myself grew up on a farm where the swine disposed of the remains of our meals and we slaughtered our own livestock. The slaughter can be unpleasant, but someone must do it if we are to have meat. My father chastised me when I failed to apply myself sufficiently to my duties, and today I am glad that he did. You say that you are punished now more often than you were in your first home. This is because your chores are different now, and it is taking you time to learn them. You will learn, and be punished less often.

If Lewis is not eating as much as he should, the reason might, as you say, be that he is sad. Or he may be unwell; I will write separately to your uncle about this. I doubt that your aunt's cooking is at fault, and that you would say so in a letter saddens me. It is very wrong to say such a thing. It does not sound like the good, grateful, sensible Arabella I know. For what is set before you, you must give thanks. You must thank God, who gave us dominion over this bountiful Earth; your uncle, whose honest labor wrested its fruits from the soil; and your aunt, who toiled over the fire to make those fruits fit to eat.

I have no doubt that it is best for you and your brother to stay with your uncle Elihu on his farm. Please do not cast about for new reasons why you should come back to New York City. Instead, apply yourself with your whole heart to making the best of things where you are. Many people bear far heavier burdens than yours without complaint. You must learn to do so, too. It is ungrateful to complain, and it is bad for your own sake to be a complainer. Try, instead, to be cheerful and a good companion. Take your sorrows to God.

I hope that you will write to me again soon, and that when you write you will tell me that you have taken my advice to heart.

Affectionately,
Solomon Godwin

I crumpled the letter and dropped it. I took it up and smoothed it out and read it again. I sat on the floor and put my arms around my shins and wept and rocked. My aunt came up the ladder and asked me what was wrong. "Have you had bad news?"

"Yes." I nodded. "A friend of mine has died. In New York. A dear friend."

"How very sad. May I see the letter?"

"No—if you don't mind—please—you would not be interested."

"A letter from York? From your grandfather? Let me be the judge. I would love to read it. We have such a hunger for news here. Oh, please let me read it, dear."

I shook my head.

"That's all right," she said. "I've read it. Your uncle and I read it."

She was smiling. She had been playing with me. I had never before known her to deploy studied cruelty. By nature, she was all too direct. But I had wounded her pride, as she had wounded mine, and we were teaching each other subtlety. "It's plain enough what you did. You wrote a letter to show us, and another to show him. What was in it we can guess from what he wrote back." The thought of it made her flush. I was afraid she would strike me, but she unleashed her anger in words, as harsh as she knew how to make them. "If only he had come! I would have told him that you were the most ungrateful child in all creation. I'd have *begged* him to take you. Please, take her! Please, don't leave this wicked girl here to poison this good family with her dishonesty and her spite! When we gave you a home, an orphan child with nothing! Oh, you're a snake in the grass! I'm glad you're not one of mine!"

She was shouting. Everyone in the house heard her. They knew everything.

SO I REMAINED. THE SPRING BLOSSOMS CAME, and I was there to be intoxicated by their perfumes, like a girl in a melodrama drugged by the villain. Later, during the prolonged emergency of haying time, I took bread and water to the store clerks and tavern workers who had left their accustomed tasks to swing the scythe. I ran barefoot down the dry path to the pond and watched the widening rings my toes made in the water, repeatedly tearing and mending a reflection of surrounding pines, while a dragonfly, like a liberated compass needle, with lacy wings and queer jeweled eyes, darted over the rippling green scum to hide among the cattails and shadows and reflections.

There were moments of peace working beside my aunt Agatha. We forgot to dislike each other. She taught me the old songs she had learned during a temporary patch of security in her nomadic New England girlhood, songs about wars and shipwrecks, men who died for love, and women ruined by men who had said they were dying for love.

I remember standing on the back porch throughout the three-act drama of a summer storm, beginning with the sporadic knock of the shutters and the springy dancing of the trees. Clouds dimmed the universe, rain hissed, lightning cracked the sky, illuminating wheat field, cornfield, fence, pasture. I jumped back at the voice of God. One by one, expanding pillars of light poked through the clouds, like phases in the building of a temple, touching a corncrib, a row of sodden haycocks, a stand of oaks.

My strongest, sweetest memories of the farm are of that first year, when I was in despair. Living without hope from moment to moment, I absorbed new sensations defenselessly, like a much younger child. It all spoke to me in some ancient, inhuman language, trying to convey an urgent message I was too ignorant to decipher. Or so it seemed: really that was just how it beguiled my attention while it sank barbed hooks into me that could never be extracted. 1838! How I despised it! How often have I longed to be back there again!

❄ XV ❄

I KNOW A MAN WHO HAD a colossal stone mansion dismantled to be taken by sea from New York to California, with every block labeled and numbered so that the house could be reassembled at its destination. Whenever in my life I have moved a great distance to a new place and new circumstances, I have felt like that house. I seem to have spent some time in pieces, waiting for certain parts to arrive by separate ships or trains, and some pieces never come and are lost to me forever. But gradually I am put together; I remember who I am, what I need, and what I must do to take care of myself.

Slowly, and in a fumbling, semiconscious way, I sought out whatever in Livy would help make the place bearable. Thus, whenever anything had to be carried to or fetched from Melanchthon's farm, I asked to be sent on the errand, happy to go where I would be given something good

to eat and I could see little Susannah, who worshipped me, and where
the story of my letter to my grandfather (told to them by my aunt in
the expectation that they would share her outrage) was an occasion for
laughter. Though she could not say it outright, I knew that Anne was
delighted that I had derided my aunt's cooking, the well-known wretch-
edness of which it was forbidden to mention.

Everything was more comfortable on Melanchthon's farm. The barn
was bigger. The crops grew in straighter rows. The fences had posts. Anne
had been raised in the country and knew which wild herbs could lend
variety to dishes, and that strawberry leaves were good for the bladder
and nettles good for ague and one should drink sassafras tea in the spring
in order to thin the blood, which grows dangerously thick each winter.

She always delayed me, taking an apparently selfish pleasure in my
company. She had me fetch the herbs and measure out the flour, and
claimed to be very impressed, and by how quickly I learned the name and
purpose of a plant or the ingredients of a dish. "Now you can teach your
aunt to make this one," she would say.

On the way back one day a voice from the sky called out to me. I
looked up and saw Jeptha sitting in the top branches of a great old maple
tree. He was directly over my head; for a moment when I regarded him
from that unusual angle his face seemed to be gripped, as in a vise, by the
soles of his bare feet. "Do you dare?" he called down to me. "No. You're
just a girl. I'll come to you."

"Wait," I said. I jumped twice and on the third jump managed to claw
my way up to the lowest branch. All the boughs nearest the ground were
too thick to grip with one hand. A fatal fall seemed possible. Yet the
higher I climbed the safer I felt because the branches were closer together,
easy to grip, and made a sort of cage whose bars would catch me if I fell.
I found a crook of branches to sit in just a few feet below the crook where
Jeptha sat.

The young branches up this high were springy and when there was a
wind, the trunk itself swayed a little.

"That was fast," said Jeptha, grabbing my hand to help me up at the
end. He was smiling for a moment, and I glimpsed the narrow gap where
a tooth was chipped. Letting go of my hand, he swept back his limp black
hair which had fallen over his eyes. For a while we discussed my brav-

ery. Then I asked how his family was. I asked hesitantly—it seemed like a weighty question—and he hesitated, too, before saying, "Good," and a moment later, as an afterthought, "As good as they know how to be."

The conversation came to halt, and I felt as I had felt in the general store half a year earlier, not knowing what to say next. The training in manners I had received in my mother's house had emphasized being seen and not heard, keeping valuable objects safe, and being generally convenient for my elders and my relations, nothing at all in the ladylike art of using questions to draw boys out. I did not think it would do to be flirtatious, to ask him, for example, if he had really been showing off for me that first day I arrived, nor did I feel sure enough of my ground to be very serious and ask him if he really meant to drive his father from the house one day. Yet there had to be talk. "We saw you in church the first day," I said. "Then we didn't see you there again, other Sundays."

He became pensive, and was quiet so long that I was going to tell him it wasn't important. But then he said, "We just came that one day to get a look at you and Lewis. We don't do a lot of church. Pa's not much on church." He stopped awhile and then went on as if he were telling a funny story: "Pa says he's waiting for the sects to settle their differences, so he can know just exactly what we all need to do to get into heaven. He tells Ma, don't worry, he's sure they'll get that chore done any day now." I couldn't tell from the way he said it what he thought of this idea, which I understood as a way to mock religion, and was clever, but also mean to his mother, for whom I harbored a mixture of pity and contempt. I hesitated to ask, but Jeptha answered my unspoken questions: "Ma prays for him, I wish he would go for her sake." After another silence he added, "Other than that, and maybe seeing you there, I'm not much on church either."

"Neither am I," I blurted out, realizing only then that it was true, and why, and I became a little sad, thinking of my own father, just at the start of his eternity of burning.

Maybe noticing the change in my mood, Jeptha suddenly asked, "What's an omnibus?" I told him, and he asked me to describe it in greater detail until he had a clearer picture of it in his mind. "And how many stories were there in your house?" and I told him three, and he asked how many people there were in New York City, and I told him what

I had learned at the school behind the Union Presbyterian Church, that it was a quarter of a million, and Jeptha said, "Liar, you're lying."

I could feel my features rearranging themselves into impassivity, as they had learned to do when it was important that other people's opinions cease to matter. Then I saw his surprise and remorse and understood that it would never have occurred to him to think anything bad of me, and cutting to the heart of it he said, "They call you a liar much in that house? Elihu? Agatha? Agnes?"

So he knew.

"Not in so many words. Mostly with silences. Changing the subject."

"Well, they—that's a shame. You know, I feel sorry for them. They don't know what they've got. They're just ignorant, I guess. If they don't hurry they'll never get to understand you at all."

I noticed the funny way he put that, if they don't hurry. "They don't want to understand me. They're in no hurry."

"Well, I am. I'm ignorant too, but at least I'm curious." He pulled a leaf off a nearby branch and dropped it, and I watched it whirl out of sight below us. "I see you, I'm thinking, there's the girl from York, she's seen things I can't even picture. What yokels we must look like to her."

Feeling that I had been released from a vow of silence, I accepted what I took as his invitation to tell him some of the things I've told you, but in reverse order, beginning with complaints about my aunt, and the incidents of the letters and the books which Aunt Agatha had sold to the peddler. I told him about the exhaustive and detailed nature of Agnes's prayers; we both laughed at that. I told him how I had learned of the manner of my father's death, and he said—about the suicide—that he had heard and it was a very sad thing to happen, and a hard thing for me to have to go through. He had used almost exactly the same words my aunt had used, but the effect on me was completely different: from him it was a comfort. Then narrating mostly backward but with some loops through time, I told him about my grandfather and grandmother, Mrs. Fitch's lie about Cincinnati—we discussed the human weakness which had led her to tell that lie, and others to endorse it, when they knew I was bound to find out the truth as soon as I reached Livy—and what my father was like, his humor, his sadness, and about my mother's death (the subject of the books came up again, which made me mention Agatha again), and then the Great Fire of New York and Frank's death. It was amazing to me to realize how much there was. It all seemed to come back in the telling, and with it a great part of my forbidden self was restored to me, making me feel stronger and braver. At a certain point, when talking of my mother, I fell silent to keep from crying, Jeptha asked me, "How much did those books your aunt sold weigh?" and when I answered that they'd been too heavy for me to lift all at once, he said pensively, "They could be in town somewhere. He wouldn't want to make his horse carry them all across the state. He paid more for them than he would have got from Colonel Ashton"—that is, at the general store—"so he probably had a customer in mind. Somebody in town." He thought more, and said, "There aren't more than five people who could afford them."

By some unspoken agreement we began talking quite pleasantly about miscellaneous trivial matters. Jeptha was one of those rare people who have already in childhood much of the personal force that will fall to their lot as grown men, and his mind was agile, and when we were talking I felt smart. We discussed the city and the country, oyster barges, canal boats, and steamboats, the funny way his four-year-old sister Ruth had looked after a harmless mishap, and a remark that his sister Becky had made when a potato had come out of the ground with the face of George Washington, and then, after asking me if I could keep a secret, but otherwise very casually, as if merely to explain more about Becky, he told me why she walked the way she did. When she was three years old, Jacob (drunk, frolicsome) had tossed her so high that her head hit a rafter, and after that she limped but she did not know why; she had forgotten; and I was not to tell her or anyone else. Then not giving me time to respond to this he said that he had become very interested lately in the art of following bees to locate their hives, and that was what he had been doing today (having convinced Jake that they could make a good profit on the honey at the general store). "And that was what I was up to when this tree came by." Then he looked around and said it was pretty here, wasn't it?

I said without thinking, "I pray every night that tomorrow someone will come to take me back where I came from."

And he shot back, "I'm going to pray twice as hard the other way," just as quickly, testifying not merely to the rapidity of his thought processes but to the settled nature of the feeling he had just expressed. And just like that, I was home, as if my grandfather had come for me after all and placed me in this tree, which was home because this boy was in it.

That was the moment Jeptha said, "Let's never keep any secrets from each other," and I nodded vigorously and agreed, though I knew that at some time in the last half-hour, whether it was when he had asked me what an omnibus was, or said that he pitied my uncle's family for their inability to appreciate me, or when he had applied his mind to the problem of finding the current owner of my books, or told me about how his father had hurt his sister, or maybe just before that when he had mentioned the potato with the face of George Washington, I had come to love him, and I would wait for the right time to tell him, and it might not be for years.

I felt that it was all going to come out right. I had been worried and anxious for no reason, because it turned out that I was lucky—some people just are!—and in the end good things were going to happen to me.

A balmy breeze arose, bearing summery scents of grass and pine and unseen unnamed herbs and making the leaves hiss and the branches sway. I closed my eyes, and when I opened them again there he was, looking down at me, his lank black hair fallen over his brow again. I saw that he was taking pleasure in the sight of me. That's right, I thought, I'm pretty. I'm so glad that I'm pretty.

We stayed in that tree, away from our chores long enough to be scolded when we got back, and there was a moment at parting when if we were older there might have been a kiss. But instead our hands brushed for a second, and I went home with my face flushed and my heart telling me that it was there, right there in my chest, and it had been there all along.

At night, on my straw bed, and at milking time and when I was weeding the garden, I went over our conversation again and again, until it was worn out, like an old rag. Weeks became months, and I did not see him again. There was no school, and in three seasons out of four, Jeptha spent all day and much of the evening at his work. The hour in the tree had been a stolen one. On Jake's farm, half the land was good only for rye, which did not fetch a high price even when times were good. Year by year, he fell a little further in debt to the miller and the storekeeper, who were beginning to treat him as if he were their shiftless employee, and whom he hated more than anyone else in the world. To free himself from this bondage, he made barrel staves and butter firkins, cleared other men's land, broke their oxen, and did other piecework. He drove himself like a dumb brute, and Jeptha worked beside him. Whenever Jeptha took a moment for himself, his father would tell him that, thanks to his selfishness, they might lose the farm; and it was very nearly true. Every ounce of effort the family could put forth was necessary.

I grasped some of this at the time—I knew at least that Jeptha had to work a great deal—but I still wondered why he didn't make more of an effort to see me again.

Perhaps it was Mrs. Talbot. My aunt sometimes sent Agnes on errands to the Talbots' farm, and once, when I asked if I could go along, Agatha said, "Better not, Arabella. Mrs. Talbot hates you like poison."

THAT SUMMER, LEWIS ATTENDED SCHOOL in town with the younger boys, one of whom, Andy Miller, said, "Your pa jumped from a roof and is burning in hell for it." They fought, and Lewis won decisively. However, as I have already mentioned, there were several Miller boys, each one larger than the next. When you beat one, you had to face the next older one. A few days later, Tom Miller waited outside the school to fight Lewis. Tom should have won, because Lewis had no more meat on him than a sparrow, but the fight ended with Tom on the ground yelling "uncle."

The following Sunday, when we were singing hymns in semi-darkness, sweat streaming down our faces, a murmur arose among the congregation. From a message passed by whispers, I learned that a crowd of children and a few grown-ups had gathered outside the church, and they included the whole Miller clan, waiting for us to come out so that John Miller, the next older Miller boy, could beat the tar out of Lewis. I touched my brother's elbow. He made a little frown of indifference, as though it would be light work for him to beat this boy three years older, a head taller, and thirty pounds heavier than he. I said, "Well, I guess you'll have to take your licks," feeling bitter that every Miller got to be a bully just because he had five brothers.

A half-hour later, we stepped, squinting, through the doorway. The sun pressed on my head like a hand. A boy sitting on a stump said, "This'll be quick," and another boy said, "If John lets it be quick." Elihu squeezed Lewis's shoulder, and Lewis, not looking up, nodded—they both knew Elihu could not interfere. The boy who had spoken last continued, "John likes to stretch these things out."

Then Matthew stepped beside Lewis and spoke, twice as loud as anyone else had: "Does he? What a coincidence. I'm like that, too."

There was an odd formality to the scene, like a historical painting of a probably apocryphal encounter of kings or generals, as the little mob made room for John to meet Lewis and ask him if he was "man enough." And Lewis said, "Anytime."

Matthew said, "He was man enough to lick two Millers so far. Hey, Tom," he called out to John's brother, "how's that ass you fell on twice, does it still hurt?" Children not of the Miller clan dared to laugh. "Did your ma make you a plaster, Tom?" Lewis was laughing, too.

John said, "Go on, laugh, you little shit. Soon it won't be funny."

Matthew said, "He's little compared to you, John. But you're little compared to me. And you know me, I like to leave a mark."

Agnes and Evangeline went home with my aunt and uncle in the wagon, but I couldn't abandon my brother, so I followed the crowd to the field behind the livery stable.

For a while it was a fight, with Matthew yelling out advice and encouragement to Lewis, but then, since no miracle occurred, it was just a beating, Lewis struggling helplessly in the older boy's grip, and John pounding him in the ribs—"Laugh now. Ha ha ha!"—and grinding his face into the mud. "This will learn you to respect a Miller."

"Stop them," I said to Matthew. I hit him in the arm. "Stop them. He's licked."

He looked at me blankly, then turned and shouted, "That's enough!"

John didn't stop. Titus and Matthew walked toward them, and Matthew yanked John by the hair. The other Miller boys moved in, snarling. "He's licked," said Matthew, putting his face next to John's. "You can meet me here next Sunday, and since you made my brother taste the mud, you're gonna eat it. You're gonna chew it and swallow it."

"My brother," he had called him. That was new. *My brother.*

"Go on and make me," said John, but he did not look confident.

"No, you're tired now," said Matthew, helping Lewis up. "In a year or two you'll whip him," he told Lewis, and he mounted a stump and addressed the gathering. "What's Lewis got to be ashamed of? Not one thing. John's got fifty pounds on him, but did he complain? No, he stepped up like a man. So . . . that's settled. Now let's talk about John. I'm giving John a week to get his strength back. Next Sunday, rain or shine, I'll be here to make him eat mud. Bring your friends. Bring your folks." There was excited murmuring from his audience, and Lewis, oblivious to the dirt in his mouth and the blood running down his face, looked up at Matthew worshipfully.

FROM THAT MOMENT ON (and thus well before Matthew made himself into a legend by beating John Miller and every older Miller boy, including the seventeen-year-old), Matthew and my brother were inseparable. Matthew taught Lewis to shoot, and with Elihu's gun the two of them pursued the bounty the town put on rabbits, squirrels, chipmunks, and other such small enemies of the farmer. On rainy days they played marbles. "Damn you to hell, you little thief!" Matthew would say. "Titus, look what he's doing to me; tell me how he's cheating!" Lewis generally won, and Matthew would howl in outrage and my brother would laugh as he used to when I tickled him.

It had been noticed by this time that Lewis had remarkable eyesight and dexterity. He could hit a bottle with a stone from twenty feet. He could thread needles more easily than any of the women, and he used to do us this service until Matthew wondered out loud if we would succeed in making a girl of him.

When the winter school session started in November, Matthew walked in with his arm around Lewis and said that they probably all knew Lewis had licked Tom Miller, almost two years older than him, but maybe they didn't know that in addition he had the sharpest eyes in the county, and if anyone doubted it, come tomorrow with some marbles.

Lewis began to eat more and to fill out and grow again. He spent less time with me. I despised his new hero—I found Matthew unpleasant personally as a bully and a braggart, and I disliked him on principle; I associated him with everything I hated about the farm. But I could not deny that Lewis was better off. New York City, Bowling Green, Mama, Papa—if he could forget all that, why should I stop him?

❧ XVI ❧

HE COULD FORGET. I COULD NOT—or would not, if there is a difference. Years went by, and still I refused. Anything good in this place was an exception: exiled here, like me. True, Jeptha was here, and he was good. But he was mistreated and made to work like a beast. That proved me right. I preferred Melanchthon's farm to my uncle's farm, any town to any farm, Patavium to Livy, Rochester to Patavium, New York to Rochester, and Paris to New York. I was not always consistent in these views, but when I remembered, these were my convictions. I preferred the rich to the poor. "We're just as good as they are" was the motto of my uncle's family. I hoped it wasn't true.

Like the slender paths etched by rain as it slides randomly down a hill, which numberless later storms carve into gullies, ravines, and canyons, the little choices of the first year gave a lasting shape to our lives. As 1838 gave way to 1839 and 1840, Lewis drew closer to Matthew, who was permitted to run wild; so Lewis ran wild, too, and heeded me less and less. Agnes and I worked side by side, hating each other and mooning over Jeptha, and the grown-ups laughed at our feelings. "What do you *want* from that boy?" my aunt inquired of us both. Once—in a sort of pitying tone, as if she were trying to cure me of a delusion—Agnes explained to me that I couldn't possibly love Jeptha, it made no sense, because I did not love what he loved. I did not love this place. I came here ruining all their innocent fun with my distaste. With my mind twisted by my city upbringing, I noticed only the ugly side, the trivial blemishes of honest, simple things. This idea hurt, because there was truth in it. Agnes and Jeptha had lived here as long as they could remember, and they had deep feelings for every little island in the pond, every gnarled old tree or old gray shack collapsing into the stream. I wished I could feel that way. I wished that Jeptha could make me feel such things.

So things stood, with no showy changes but countless infinitesimal preparations of the kind that make an old tree suddenly topple, roots and all, three days after a heavy rain. Two hired hands, neither of whom had ever talked much, were replaced by another pair, one of whom was very chatty and full of himself, and then he left, and sometime later the other, quieter one left as well. Things broke and were mended. Shoes wore out. Bones lengthened. A little family calling themselves the Boston Traveling Wonder Show parked their caravan on the green behind the livery stable, exhibited a fake mummy, an octopus in a jar, and a hollow elephant, sold pamphlets about Egyptian mummies and elephants, and moved on. A cow with a biblical name wandered off and froze to death and we ate it all winter. One day after school Jeptha handed me volume one of *Peter Simple,* by Captain Maryatt. On the flyleaf, the name "Frank Godwin" had been crossed out, and under it was written "Mrs. Adelia Harding." The peddler had sold all of my old books to Mrs. Harding, the miller's wife. "Come with me," said Jeptha, and we walked to Mrs. Harding's house, and over the years she let me borrow all my old books and many others, one by one.

At last, like the old tree that falls, the thawing river that suddenly cracks, the small hidden preparations announced themselves in the great sudden rearrangement.

In 1841, when Jeptha was fourteen and Agnes and I were thirteen, a religious revival swept the state, running like an electric current to light up all the big canal towns to the north. That summer, my uncle's family and several other families of the community went by wagon train to a big camp meeting on the shore of Canandaigua Lake. Other wagons from towns along the way joined ours, until it began to seem like a great exodus or heavenly migration, and we all felt that something important was happening.

From the moment I had heard of the camp meeting—or, rather, from the moment I had realized that Jacob meant to take his family to it (as many profane people always did, and they were very welcome to come; otherwise, who would there be to convert?)—I had seen it as an opportunity to be with Jeptha again and again, on the two days it would take us to get to the lake and the two days it would take to get back, and the three days in between. The flaw in my plan was of course that it was Agnes's plan as well. Now we both gazed on the object of our desire: he sat at the back of the wagon just ahead, eating an apple while reading, with mildly comical absorption, a book he had borrowed from William Jefferds. Jeptha had become a great reader. Since his labor was needed during the day, he went without sleep and read at night. He collected oily pine knots to burn for their light; he would never have been so wasteful as to use candles.

At the moment he seemed to prefer the book to either of us. We looked away, pretending indifference so as to avoid being teased by the boys, but it was useless. They made their jokes. We ignored them, convinced our rivalry was as serious as anything in life can be. Often, like this, our thoughts marched to the same drum, as we daydreamed side by side of the same blessed consummation with the same innocent absence of detail.

Agnes at this age was lovely, with smooth, pale skin enlivened by a stylish sprinkling of freckles. She had long eyelashes, glossy coppery hair, rosebud lips, and the tender start of bosom and hips. My shape was less advanced. Everyone said I was pretty. Everyone said she was pretty. How pretty? I couldn't find within myself an unmoving plumb line to use in measuring this quality of such awful consequence to me.

At camp, after we had pitched our tents, Agnes brought a small pasteboard bandbox, which she had somehow concealed from us, to the tent of the Talbots (across the street from our own in the orderly little tent village we had created) and presented them with a rhubarb pie she had made in secret at the widow Lyall's. They each had a slice, and I heard Mrs. Talbot say pointedly that it would be a lucky man who came home to baking like that every day. Agnes's meager talents in the kitchen were a theme of humor to everyone who knew her, something odd was happening, it seemed to me, since I considered all this as we sat on rough logs in the open air, while up on the speaker's stand the preacher, who if he had been born in another part of the world could have made his fortune as an opera singer, explained with a piteous, whimpering note in his voice what a long time eternity was, and how much the damned regretted their ignorant mockery of men like him.

The camp stood on a gently sloping covert by the lake. Wavy bars of light, reflected off the water's steady shoreward movement, licked the trees and the canvas tents and the clothes and faces of the congregation in tremulous, glimmering upward strokes, so that they seemed already as immaterial as they would be in heaven. "A wicked and adulterous generation." The ululating voice cleaved the sweet air. "Oh, ye hypocrites," the minister groaned, and I thought about baking and bosoms.

By and by the shimmer faded, clouds gathered, the rain came, and everyone ran for the tents. It rained all afternoon and all night.

The next day was clear. We stood for hours in the mud, or sat on wet logs and slapped our necks and arms to kill mosquitoes, while listening to speakers of varying ability. The most eagerly anticipated was a Millerite. Around fifty years later, I was astounded to realize that the Millerites had been forgotten, their shame lived down at last, though, as always, the world abounds with such people. I don't recall whether I first heard of them before or after I came to Livy. I know this was the first one I ever saw.

He was fat and red-faced, so unlike my idea of a preacher that when he mounted the speaker's stand I expected to hear an announcement about the cooking arrangements. In the high, piercing tones some men use to grip a crowd's attention, often repeating key phrases to give everyone a chance to hear, he told us about William Miller, a farmer, but in his spare time a Bible scholar, who had delved deeply into the book of Daniel, in which the Second Advent of Jesus is prophesied. Miller's research led him to a conclusion he found unwelcome, because it meant he would have to turn himself into an object of public mockery. But the facts were there for anyone to see who knew how to do arithmetic and knew the Bible to be the word of God.

"And what was it, this discovery that made William Miller go from church to church and city to city in the hope that other people would lift off his shoulders the awful burden of warning mankind? Many of you have heard of it, and think that it must be the ravings of a madman. He says that the world will end in 1843. We have, according to this farmer, two years before everything is to perish in a great fire the like of which no man has ever seen, and none to be saved except by the blood of Jesus. So this man William Miller says. Why should we believe him? Why should we take his word?

"Because it isn't just his word," he said, holding up the Bible.

The crowd took his meaning. There was a murmur of approval.

"It's based on the word of God, whose prophecies have come true, one after another, confounding the deists and the mockers time and again throughout history."

If you were willing to entertain the idea, it was thrilling. I looked around. I saw hope on my aunt's face. Elihu had that friendly set of mouth that on him represented small-minded skepticism about another man's claim to superior knowledge of any kind. Becky, who was in everything except her walk an ordinary, shallow girl, living for everyday amusements, wore a look of polite attention appropriate to church. Every time I saw her I thought of what Jeptha had told me about the reason for her limp, and that she didn't know, and I wondered what she would think, what she would do, were she ever to learn the truth. Jeptha looked interested.

There were small-town folk and farm folk, babes in arms, old people whose memories stretched back to the eighteenth century. The poor were among them, and the sick, the twisted, with canes and ear trumpets, people who had been carried to the spot in wicker chairs, people who could certainly use a new body in a new world.

You feel superior? Go ahead, but remember that it was 1841, not 1908. The cosmos under discussion was smaller than the one we inhabit today. We knew nothing of the recent geological discoveries proving that mountains take millions of years to form, and though we had heard that the earth turned, only half of us believed it, and we had no idea of how big or far away the stars were. Most of all, we were Christians, and the Second Coming was as much a part of our creed as the crucifixion and the resurrection. Anyone not prepared to call the Bible a fairy tale had to take this question seriously.

We listened. After an unavoidably complicated explanation of Miller's system of biblical prediction, the speech became a terrific hellfire sermon in which not only the torments of the damned but the pathetic ordeal of the poor earth itself was evoked in merciless detail. The sun would turn black. The moon would fall out of the sky. Everything would burn. Everyone would burn. Unless, by then, they had been saved.

By and by, a murmur passed through the crowd, and sporadic conversions began like popcorn when it first starts to exhibit its magical response to heat: a shout of "Hallelujah!" somewhere, followed, seconds later, by sobbing and wailing, and then six yards away a man falls to his knees, and somewhere else a woman shouts, "Thank you, Jesus!" and after an interval a man says, "O Lord, You've found me," and another woman starts to jerk and tremble, and soon these things are happening with greater and greater frequency, until seemingly the whole assembly is popping off in paroxysms of joy. But always in the end there remain a few hard kernels, roasted but not popped—who knows why?—and I was always one of those.

. . .

MY AUNT FOUND PLENTY OF CHORES for us to do, plenty of cooking and washing, and digging ditches to keep the rain from flooding the tents. Agnes and I raced each other through them, hoping to finish fast enough to give the winner a precious half-hour alone with Jeptha.

Each of us had her moment. I found Jeptha not far from his tent, sitting on a wide old stump, cleaning the family's shoes with a twig—there had been so much mud after the rain. I stood watching until he asked me to join him, and we talked about the end of the world. We talked mostly about what had been asserted, not the likelihood of it, until I dared to ask him if he thought that William Miller was a humbug.

"Probably," he said. "Such people usually are." His glance was contemplative, taking in my face and my hands folded on my skirt, and my feet, as if they had some bearing on the subject, and I really thought that at last we were getting somewhere. Then we heard a rustle of wet leaves. "Oh, look," he said brightly. "It's Agnes."

And so it was, and the next day we broke camp.

❧ XVII ❧

WE WERE A DAY FROM HOME when news traveled through the train that there was sickness in several of the families. "Camp fever," we called it, blaming the decision to pitch the tents so near the lake. My uncle's family was unaffected, but Jake and Becky stayed in their wagon when we stopped to cook by the roadside, and they were both said to be taking broth; a woman from another wagon who had brought some patent tonics along passed them to the Talbots. Agnes and I went to see. Mrs. Talbot, sitting at the reins, told us that Jeptha, too, was sick, and added, "Thank you, children, but don't come nearer."

After the passage of so many years, it is difficult to remember what exactly Agnes and I had in mind when, two days after we got back, we went to look in on the Talbots. Certainly we did not yet realize how bad the sickness was. Had we known, it would not have stopped us, but we did not know. We brought food, sheets and pillows, bottles of patent remedies, and bags of dried herbs.

The Talbots' house was smaller and meaner than our own, and the family was larger. There were eight of them, counting the parents. Jeptha was the eldest child, and the other boys were Ike, Ezra, and Lionel, and the girls were Becky and Ruth. I don't remember all of their ages, except for Lionel, who was not yet a year old and just beginning to walk and Becky who was twelve.

Physicians in those days cast doubt on the very idea of infectious disease; it was an outdated notion. But country people, clinging stubbornly to ideas from earlier centuries, had no doubt that a great many illnesses were catching. We were quite sure that, whatever Jeptha's family had, we could get it by being near them.

We noticed that the oxen had not been unhitched from the covered wagon, and they had dragged it into the hayfield. The house stank like a corpse from as far as ten feet away. The front door was open. As we approached, the Talbots' dog, Zeke, emerged. It made a sort of strangled bark and vomited. Agnes cried out. There was a baby's finger in the vomit.

"You'll want to go back now, Arabella," she said.

I see that this remark is open to the charitable interpretation that she wanted to protect me. Don't be fooled: it was just an insult. We were both happy to risk death for the prize of being the one to nurse Jeptha from the brink of death, and if the other one died in the process, so much the better. She hesitated at the door. My desire to best her in everything gave me the strength to go in first. When I saw what was happening, I shrieked and looked around frantically for a weapon. My eyes lit on the fireplace; next thing I knew, I held a black iron poker in my two hands and I was swinging it onto the backs of the pigs, two of them, who were fighting over the half-shredded corpse of the one-year-old, Lionel. One pig gripped an arm, the other a leg. They had already gnawed at his face. I swung with all my force. With thwarted, outraged squeals, the pigs reluctantly lumbered away from their feast. Gasping, I thwacked them until they were out of the house. Agnes bolted the door, covered Lionel's remains with an empty grain sack, and made sure that there were no other beasts in the house and no other door was open. While she was thus occupied, I climbed up a rickety ladder to the loft, weeping and murmuring, "Please, God, please," and repeating Jeptha's name. It was dark up there, and reeked of excrement and vomit and rotting meat, so that automatically I wanted to breathe through my mouth, and yet I made myself smell, because at the moment I couldn't see, and smell was a valuable source of information. I banged into something, a bed probably. "Jeptha?" I cried, and listened, hearing Agnes busy below. "Agnes, be quiet—I can't hear!" There was silence for a moment as she obeyed me, followed by steps and the sound of her own breathing and the creak of the ladder as she climbed it. I opened the shutters at one end of the loft, letting in a shaft of bright light full of lazily drifting dust motes. I turned to see Agnes moving to one of the beds, and I ran and got there just when she did; it was Jeptha's bed.

He had his coat on and was shivering violently, with hardly the strength to raise his eyelids to see us. His tongue was white and peeling, his skin dripping wet, his breath shallow; his clothes were drenched in urine and sweat, and he had retched and fouled himself. Frightened into a truce, Agnes and I worked cooperatively. We brought clean water and stripped him; asking silent forgiveness for taking this liberty with his nakedness—and looking away at first, but we then had to look to do the job properly—we washed him and dressed him. After a lengthy search through the house for linen, we changed his bedding.

We did all this, the two of us, ignoring the rest of our patients. There was no one to question what we did, as we discovered when we finally turned our attention to other members of the family. Not one had been spared to help the others; they could not rise to use a chamber pot or look out the window; they did not notice us until we were right over them, and then they did not know who we were.

The remedies of the times, which we had brought with us, were tinctures and decoctions of herbs that had been discovered to make you sweat, or puke, or belch, or empty your bowels, or make your heart beat faster, and they were useless now, because all these reactions had been produced already by the disease, and the family's garments and bedding were soaked with the results.

The services we had performed for Jeptha, we performed for the rest of his family. It took us most of the day. To ease the suffering of the cows, we milked them; we put some of the milk in the creek, in jugs, to keep it cold, and used some of it to make clabber. We went to the toolshed, found shovels, and buried Lionel, including the finger Zeke had vomited, in the family plot, which held a stillborn baby and a grandmother who had come with the family to Livy ten years ago and died the first year. We buried him deep and piled stones on the grave, so the dogs and the pigs couldn't dig him up. It was dark by then, and Becky had died, but we were too tired to bury her. We put our ears to her chest to make sure there was no heartbeat, and closed her eyes, and left her in her bed, locking the doors to keep the animals away. Believing that contagion was carried by the poisoned air in the house, and that we were more susceptible to it when sleeping, we spent the night in the barn.

Agnes said her prayers out loud, with her usual exhaustive specificity and precision. She prayed that no others would die. Speculating that the disease had been sent for a good purpose, she expressed the hope that the deceased were already in heaven and the survivors, chastened, would turn their hearts toward Jesus.

I prayed that Jeptha would live and that no one I loved would get sick. I didn't make a list, even in my mind—God was supposed to know, maybe better than I did.

In the morning, we washed Becky, put her in a relatively new-looking dress that we guessed was hers. We wrapped her pale, damp fingers around the hickory cane Jacob had carved for her, buried her without a coffin, and piled her grave with stones. We washed the linen and the clothes in boiling water. We milked the cows. We killed and cleaned a chicken, made broth and spooned it into the mouths of our patients. In the afternoon, my aunt came and was alarmed to see how bad the sickness was, saying that we were both very good children but we were taking a terrible risk. She tried to make us come back with her, but not very hard. We told her that we felt fine; we had already taken the risk, and we were all right. We must be immune.

The crisis had passed for most of the family. After another day, the survivors began to recover—all except Jeptha, who breathed in short gasps, and sweated, and spewed up any food we managed to get into him. I became so angry that at last I directed my prayers to Satan. "Take Agnes instead of Jeptha," I told the devil (I prayed aloud, but in a whisper, and alone). And just in case the universe was as unjust as I was beginning to suspect it was, and Agnes was destined for heaven, I added that he could have my soul when the time came.

The next morning, Jeptha was sitting up in bed. Jacob told him about Lionel and Becky. "They've passed," he said with unaccustomed gentleness.

"Take me to the graves," said Jeptha. Agnes and I, though we had washed every inch of him, turned modestly away as, dressed only in his shirt, he staggered to a chest of drawers and put on his trousers. He walked slowly, barefoot, his father—who was much less weak—leading him, walking not too far ahead, until they reached their destination.

"That's Lionel," said Jake. "That's Becky."

"Becky," said Jeptha, looking down at the heap of stones. He nodded, and was quiet, and looked as if he had thoroughly adjusted to the new situation. He stood like that for about ten seconds while we all waited respectfully, and then, suddenly, his jaw began to shake, and as though she were not buried in the ground at his feet but lost in the woods somewhere, he shouted, "Becky! Becky, where are you?"

His father said, without very much conviction, "She's in heaven."

Jeptha turned on him, his lips curled with some strange, combustible blend of grief, fury, helplessness, and disgust. "Heaven? Where's that?" He laughed. "Heaven?" He marched a few steps closer to his father and began to strike Jacob with his fists. "I'm gonna tear you in two, you worthless son of a bitch. Heaven—I'll show you heaven, you damned killer. I'll send you to heaven, you evil bastard." We shouted variously "No" and "Don't" and "Jeptha" and moved to pull him off his father, but Jacob shook his head to signal us to leave them be as Jeptha struck his father with all the force he could deploy just then, which was about as much as would be available to a two-year-old child. Jacob took it, methodically and patiently deflecting the blows aimed at his face. At last they gripped each other like a couple of exhausted boxers and fell to their knees.

AFTER ABOUT A WEEK, the rest of the Talbot family recovered, and we went home, with their thanks and blessings. Mrs. Talbot, though still shaky, insisted on making us a meal and fixing us two baskets full of Indian pudding and dried fruit and salt pork to take home with us. "You've been a ministering angel," she told Agnes. She did not say that to me. The distinction she made between us, her persistence in it even fresh from the rim of the grave, would have been comical if she hadn't just buried two of her children. "I don't reckon I've ever known any girl so good and brave." And glancing at me and back to Agnes meaningfully, she said, "You're not only good yourself, you make other people good!"

Why did Jeptha's mother hate me? I'm still not sure I know. I never learned it from him, because he loved her too much to understand her. My current theory is that she disliked anything that was a challenge to her mind, which included anything the least bit foreign, and like a child she thought that whatever displeased her was wicked.

Agnes and I walked home in silence. Ten yards from our door, Agnes dropped her basket and collapsed. I dragged her to her feet. We walked with her arm over my shoulder. My aunt, who had been working in the garden, was running toward us when, a few feet from the door, Agnes suddenly bent over and vomited her breakfast in the grass.

I heard my aunt shout, "Oh no, O precious Lord, please, no."

In the days that followed, as Agnes, despite our best efforts, fell away from us, I hardly knew what to feel or to wish for. Certainly I hated her. If ever, in all the time we'd known each other, she had shown me the slightest kindness, it had been only a feint or a temporary expedient in a larger plan to harm me. I had often wished her dead—I had prayed for it only a few days ago—but now I feared the power of my wish, and I nursed her diligently, spooning broth into her, cleaning her, and sitting up with her when my aunt could not.

As for my aunt, she kept up an appearance of calm and good cheer when she was near Agnes, but when we were downstairs she gave in to despair, often calling on God to explain why this was happening, and why of all people to *her daughter*. "Why Agnes?" she kept saying. Once— when we had been talking about Agnes's condition and whether some swallow of broth that had stayed down could be considered a sign of recovery—my aunt remarked, "It's certainly a wonder you didn't come down with it."

"Yes," I said, "I've been lucky."

We were chopping vegetables. Evangeline, Lewis, Matthew, and Titus had all been sent to Melanchthon's farm until the danger passed. My uncle stayed during the day to do farm work, but at my aunt's urging he, too, slept at Melanchthon's house.

"Oh, you both took a terrible chance, I shouldn't have let you. What a mystery sickness is. Remember how sickly you were when you arrived? We thought sure that you and Lewis would both perish before another year went by."

"I didn't know you thought that, Aunt Agatha."

I knew just what she had in her mind. She knew she shouldn't say it; it would be wrong and pointless. But she ached to.

"We did. Remember, it was why you came. Because the two of you had that dry cough. And were both so undersized, and narrow-breasted, and your poor mother had only just died. But here you are, a fine-looking, lovely girl, and safe after being put next to a sickness that felled a whole family and killed two of them in the wink of an eye, and is on its way to . . ." Here she began to sob again. "O precious Lord, why? Why?"

Later that evening, as we sat beside Agnes's bed, the theme was renewed. "Why, Lord? Why Agnes? Why my Agnes?"

"Why not me?" I said finally.

"Yes!" cried my aunt—in a whisper, so as not to disturb Agnes. "Oh, God forgive me, yes! Why not you? Miserable and hateful and envious, when you can't be happy anyway. Living off other people's lives, wishing you were Anne's daughter, and Jeptha's wife, which you'll never be, not even if the Lord takes my sweet Agnes. Why?"

"Oh," I said, my tears surprising me with the news that I wasn't beyond caring what she thought. "Oh. Well, now I know, then. Oh, I hope there's a heaven! I hope there's a heaven, so your sister can see how you treat her daughter!"

"I'm sorry," said Aunt Agatha, "I want you to be all right, of course I do, but I love my daughter, and she's dying—oh, dear Lord—and I'm beside myself."

I couldn't bear these feelings. I reached for her. She held my face against her dried-up bosom and sobbed. "I'm sorry, I'm sorry." Falling to her knees, she meshed her bony fingers in a white-knuckled tangle of prayer. I saw her homely face and puffy eyes from God's perspective, and had a sort of religious vision, of all the faces—black, white, young, old, plain, pretty, simple, smart—looking up at Him, begging for justice, mercy, fair winds, rain, victory, long life, quick death.

"Dear Lord," she implored Him, "whatever I've done, don't judge me this way."

. . .

A DAY OR TWO AFTER THIS CONVERSATION, we heard the dogs barking and the rumble of a wagon, and went out to see Jeptha, his mother, and his father coming up the dusty road, bringing more food and the offer of their labor and such encouragement as they could dredge out of the depths of their grief. Jake was quiet and gentle.

We stood around Agnes's bedside. She seemed to recognize him for a moment, but then she mistook him for Elihu: "Papa, where's Jeptha? Why doesn't he come?"

Jeptha looked down at her, saying, "I'm here, Agnes, I'm Jeptha," and squeezed her hand, and he looked at my aunt with an expression that, though correct in its way, was hard to read, and did not look like grief.

My cousin shivered and clawed the air; she clutched Jeptha's hand while calling him "Papa," "Matthew," and "Titus." At last she fell back with a sigh and slept. My aunt gave a cry and put her hand to her mouth, while Agnes murmured his name in her sleep. "Well, maybe sleep will mend her," he said. "Let's leave her, Arabella."

I followed him out of the house, and there was a moment when he looked at me as though he were about to say something important—some deep truth he had learned from his ordeal—but then decided the time wasn't ripe for it and remained silent. I was curious, but cautious enough to let him bide his time. We strolled about the farm, gathering eggs in the barnyard, milking the cows, and doing other odd chores that were not strenuous, and at last we just ambled around the place with no pretense of being useful. His movements were tentative; he seemed to look about him with unhurried appreciation, like someone returning home after a lapse of years; and I saw him as more precious for having almost died. I remembered having touched his nakedness. At fourteen years old, he was already taller than his father. Years of toil outdoors had given him plenty of lean, hard muscle. Altogether, he had more than his share of animal attraction, and I was just old enough to feel it.

When I alluded delicately to Becky and Lionel, he shook his head. He didn't want to talk about it. Suddenly he said, "She's not dying. Agnes."

"What? But she—?"

"It's a humbug. Watch her, you'll see."

"But she's spitting up her food."

He nodded. "She must be starving."

I thought about this for a moment and realized that he must be right. She had been pretending from the start. For vomiting, she'd had ipecac. She'd had a wide choice of purges, diuretics, diaphoretics, and stimulants among the other medicines we'd brought to the Talbots. When the Talbots came to our house, she had dropped all but the most decorative symptoms; she couldn't bear to be disgusting in front of Jeptha. That was her error. With his intimate knowledge of the sickness, he had seen through her charade.

This, I assumed, was what he had wanted to tell me. I thought of Agatha. "Jeptha, we must go back and tell my aunt right away."

He gave me a measuring look. "I knew you'd say that." He meant that I was good, and despite all the bitterness in my heart, and the little matter of having pledged my soul to the devil, I felt just then that I *was* good. "We'll tell her—just not yet, okay?" he continued, and I nodded, realizing that he had still had something to say or at least a task to accomplish on our walk.

I asked him about *A View of the Hebrews*, the book I had seen him reading on the way to the lake. It propounded the theory that a race of civilized, Christian Indians used to live right here, where we stood, until they were exterminated overnight by the savage, pagan Indians, five hundred years before Columbus. We discussed the idea as today young people discuss the possibility of life on Mars. I asked him again if he thought that Jesus would return to judge the world in 1843, he said that, though it went against common sense, common sense was no use for this kind of problem. "Common sense is all about what usually happens."

Remembering the pie Agnes had given him, I asked him what kind of pie he favored, rhubarb, or apple, or blueberry, or cherry, and he said he liked apple best but he liked variety, too. And so, having disposed of the end of a civilization and the destruction of the world, we talked of pies—whether a pie made from dried apples could ever be made as good as a pie of fresh apples, or whether it should be regarded as a different sort of pie, with its own excellence—and you might be surprised to know what a pleasant conversation it was, despite the idiocy of the topic.

It was unnecessary, but I had to say it: "She didn't bake that pie. Not if it was good. Agnes can't bake. Someone else must have done it for her."

He looked at me curiously and then said, "I want to show you something," taking my hand and pulling me through the broad leaves of the ripening corn, past a place where the rows, fairly regular until then, were interrupted by a stubborn old stump my uncle had not yet gotten around to removing. There we stopped, a little breathless. Suddenly he leaned in, grasped me firmly by the shoulders, and kissed my lips—before letting me go and taking a step back to watch me, as though now it was his turn to wait, and my turn to act. It was hard to think or talk with my pulse loud in my head, my mouth remembering his mouth, wanting to cry, wanting to shout, greedy for another kiss. Then a great joy flooded through me, and I kissed him. We wrapped our arms around each other. We kissed and stopped and kissed more and stopped. We didn't open our mouths. There was only the dead-on pressure of our lips, until, by a lucky accident, we learned that brushing lips side to side could be pleasant, and we sought that pleasure over and over. For the moment, it was actually too much. We stopped, brows touching, faces flushed. We were short of breath, as if the kissing had exhausted us.

WHEN WE RETURNED TO THE HOUSE, I was a person clothed in glory, lit from within, perfected, enjoying the illusion of absolute invulnerability that comes only in the first flush of requited love: Jeptha loved me! Nothing could hurt me or stand in my way. I had no quarrel with the world. Every sorrow I had experienced in my life until now had only prepared the way for this moment, for the express purpose of making it sweeter, like the rough jokes that some fellow's friends might play on him just before he opens the door to where everyone is waiting to sing "For He's a Jolly Good Fellow." I did not hate anyone. I wished only that all these silly fools could be happy, and I thought they all could be—they had only to seek my guidance. I knew all about happiness.

When I told my aunt about Agnes, I expected her to be angry with me for calling her angel a liar, for implying that Agnes had deliberately put her through this hell. But there was no anger. That Agnes might live— nothing else mattered. She seized the hope desperately.

We stood around Agnes's bed, wondering how we could ever have been fooled. Later in life, I saw such illnesses in plays. Agnes gasped musically, arched her back in pretty paroxysms, and freed her hands from the sheets to make interesting gestures. Her arms stretched upward toward unseen angels. In intervals of lucidity, she planned her funeral, gave away her possessions, and delivered deathbed advice.

She asked for Jeptha, who said, "I'm here."

"No, you're Papa."

He insisted, "I'm Jeptha, don't you know me, Agnes?" and he winked at me. I assume that, not really being in a delirium, she noticed and knew the game was up, which must have been horrible for her.

Deception was the mode of our humor in those days, as you know if you have read Barnum's *Life*. We liked stories of elaborate "humbugs," uproarious then, tedious now, and liked to recognize them in real life, so even Jeptha could enjoy Agnes's folly for short periods. Then, remembering Lionel and Becky, he would tire of the charade.

We never said that we knew Agnes was cheating, so she never had to admit it. We simply began paying her less and less attention. Once, she screamed and my aunt came rushing, certain that her daughter was dying after all. The second time, she didn't come. At last Agnes rose from her bed and responded with wan, weak, soulful looks to our inquiries about her health. But she knew she had lost her last chance of having Jeptha. Out of the corner of my eye, as months passed happily for me, I was aware of a time of profound misery for her, followed by a time of keeping company with other boys, so that she seemed to admit she was licked.

XVIII

THE ILLNESS AND THE DEATHS had left both Jacob and Jeptha profoundly troubled. Jacob brooded on his faults, prey to a gnawing and basically superstitious conviction that his irreligion had brought this evil upon his family. Jeptha, who had less to reproach himself with, was overcome with a consciousness that all daily certainties rest on nothing, and life is mystery upon mystery, and it was futile to look for honey in the forest and gold in the mountains while the most elementary questions were in doubt. One day, walking in the woods alone, he heard himself say, "O God, I'm lost; find me." He had a feeling of a hand falling on his shoulder; a profound peace and certainty, such as I only wish I could feel, came over him, and the very next thing he wanted to do was to tell everyone—me first of all—about the wonderful thing that had happened to him, and that it could happen to them, too. He turned his attention to his father, the father whom he had once meant to drive from the house as soon as he was capable of it. He told Jacob that it was all right—God had forgiven him *already*. Within a week, they were both baptized by William Jefferds.

It was understood that Jacob's conversion had to mean total abstinence from drink. Men who make such promises often backslide. So did Jacob, and when drunk he was as bad as ever.

Afterward, he was remorseful. "It wasn't me. It was the demon that got into me. Blame the demon."

The next time his father came home in this condition, Jeptha barred all the doors of his house against him and told him to sleep it off in the barn.

"I'm your father," bellowed Jacob. "Honor thy father!"

"My father?" asked Jeptha. "My father warned me about you. He said you were a demon. You crawl inside him through the neck of a whiskey jug."

And Jacob replied: "I'll show you a demon! Just let me in there!"

The month was January, cold though not freezing; it began to rain. Jacob raved like King Lear, demanding that the wind blow him into oblivion so as to rebuke his unnatural children, calling heavenly judgment down on the whole family, and then switching to tears and swearing that he felt the return of his fever and he guessed he was dying. Eventually, he left. Jeptha stood vigil all night.

In the morning, a sober Jacob appeared, with hay and feathers in his hair. Jeptha let him in, saying, "There was a demon here last night. He tried to get into our house."

Jacob said, "This ain't right. I said I was going on the wagon, and I am, but if I slip that's between me and the Lord. You've got to be punished."

Jeptha followed him to the woodshed and took ten strokes meekly, and no more was said. A week later, Jacob came home drunk again, and the whole scene was replayed without the rain. In the morning, Jeptha quietly accompanied Jacob to the woodshed, but this time it was different. The switch fell to the straw. Jacob sat on a woodpile, palm on his pulsing brow. "Oh Lord, where is this going, where are we all going? I don't know what I'm supposed to do. Tell me what to do, Jeptha."

Jeptha took thought, while his father waited patiently, and at last he said, "You've got to be a strict Christian now. It's what you meant to do when you joined the church. But the devil keeps whispering in your ear, saying it was just the shock of Lionel and Becky and you would get over it, and you kind of hope he's right, since being a Christian means giving up some comforts. But the devil is a liar. And you don't believe a word he says, and he's not your friend anymore, you hate him now. I can tell because otherwise you wouldn't have asked my opinion when you knew just what I was going to say."

A week or so after that, Jeptha and I met near my uncle's place, at the Muskrat Pond; we often went there. I had arrived first, and he walked toward me through the dappled light, and when a bright patch lit his face I cried, "What's wrong? Is everyone all right?" because he looked so distressed.

We sat on a log and he said, "Pa's giving Ike the farm. Leaving it to him."

"Oh no," I said; I knew he had planned all his life to farm; he was the eldest and good and could be relied on not to kick his brother out anyway.

"They want me to be a preacher. They talked to William Jefferds. They want me to study with him and, when he thinks it's right, to go away to school. He thinks he can get a Home Missionary Society to pay for it. At a seminary in New Jersey."

He had told them that it was wrong, that he had never wanted to be anything but a farmer, and he was needed here—they couldn't spare him. But it wasn't true anymore. Times were better, the farm was no longer in danger, and Ike was old enough to help as Jeptha used to. As to Jeptha wanting to be a farmer, he had only wanted that so he could save his family from Jacob; and he had just done that—not with a lifetime of toil, as he had expected to, but instantly, by means of a miracle.

We sat side by side on the fallen oak, and I looked at him. It made perfect sense to me; it was like a puzzle solved. His serious mind, his fervor, his willfulness, his love of justice, his homely eloquence were like parts of a new engine which seem merely curious until they are assembled and the machine begins to do the work for which it was designed. His vocation was so perfect, it was all by itself an argument for purpose in the world. But for me it created a couple of problems.

In the months since his conversion, he had told me many times that he would make a Christian of me. The first or second time I had said lightly, "What do you mean? I *am* a Christian," and he had touched my arm and, with surprising vehemence, insisted, "No, Arabella, you're not. But you will be. Because I won't rest until you are."

I had looked at it from every angle, and I did not see how I could be saved, and though I was happy in those days, still, distantly, it bothered me that there should be this lie between us, that he must want to save me, and I must pretend it was possible.

Now I put my hand on his, and he brought my palm to his mouth and kissed it and put it against his cheek. "They won't let you come along," he said. "I asked. They won't pay for two."

"I know," I told him. "We can wait. I'll stay here. I'll save money for us."

I reminded him that Mrs. Harding, whose husband owned the flour mill and the distillery, had agreed that this year I should become her hired girl and move into her house in town. A salary went with the job, and I was thrifty.

He said that he felt like a fraud, he couldn't measure up to people's ideas of him, and he hated to be under an obligation to a bunch of strangers—what if he wanted to change his mind later?

I saw that he really wanted to go. He wanted to see the world and exercise his talents. And it would get me out of Livy at last.

"I'll wait," I said. "I'll wait. They're right. You're wasted here."

I didn't say, "God wants you to go." He would have known I didn't mean it. Nor did I say, "Become a preacher someplace where people are civilized, and I will be a perfect imitation of a preacher's wife."

❧ XIX ❧

JEPTHA DID NOT KNOW WHEN EXACTLY he would be sent away. There would be at least a year of private study with William Jefferds. We spent as much time as we could in each other's company. I lived for the moment and was happy.

That spring I went to work as a hired girl for Mrs. Harding, sparing me the daily irritations of life with my uncle's family, where I must listen to Agnes brag unconvincingly about her sweetheart of the moment as she hatefully jerked the slop from the spoon to my bowl, and Agatha wonder out loud when "that foolish boy" (meaning Jeptha) would come to his senses (Agnes looking daggers at Agatha, for making her feel worse); where Matthew, now sixteen, quite handsome, utterly repulsive, had begun to look at me in a hungry way that made me feel uncomfortable. Going away from this house also meant seeing less of Lewis, but we had grown so far apart that it made hardly any difference.

Together with their ten-year-old daughter, Eva; their three sons, William, Richard, and Miles; and now with me, Mr. and Mrs. Harding lived on the town's nicest street, in a pretty two-story house full of polished furniture, glass, mirrors, carpets, a grandfather clock, a cookstove, a pianoforte, and many books, including (as I have mentioned already) those my aunt sold to the peddler in 1838. The miller was an important man in Livy. His wife, with money to buy novels and the leisure to read them, was a much more agreeable woman than my aunt, although, I realized fairly quickly, she did not like to be inconvenienced. She professed herself an admirer of my grandfather, for his efforts on behalf of abolition, and I believe that she liked the idea of an association with the granddaughter of a famous man.

It was agreed, between Mrs. Harding and my aunt, that in the winter I would continue to attend school, and I would work on my uncle's farm whenever there was a special need. In the meantime, I wore dresses Mrs. Harding had ordered for me, imitated her finishing-school manners, and read my way through her library. In all my dealings with my employer, there was an extra dollop of the hypocrisy that lubricates the gears of everyday life. She said I was "like a daughter," but worked me as hard as any of her previous girls. I understood her, so my feelings weren't hurt. She did like me a little, and she was nice to me so long as I did my job, and I had far more freedom than I would have had if she had really considered me a member of her family.

I had more freedom to be with Jeptha. As time went by and our young bodies began to strain against the limits we set them, we did everything permitted to Baptists, and such further indiscretions as young Baptists have been known to commit with subsequent apologies to the Lord. We could not go to dances; dancing was immoral. We went to prayer meetings, and Jeptha visited with me in Mrs. Harding's sitting room.

On my day off, or when I was wanted at my uncle's farm, I arranged to meet him in the woods or the fields. Sometimes I would sneak out after dark. I had a room of my own on the ground floor, making it easy. We met in places where we had no other company than livestock, mice, squirrels, and insects. We kissed standing up against the boughs of trees, and lying down in the grass, torturing each other deliciously, stimulating each other to the verge of the act we considered irrevocable. Sometimes we twined our legs together, and as if by accident there would be contact and even a degree of friction between our lower limbs and the parts of our bodies never mentioned by the major Victorian novelists. Once, when he was lying on his back, I straddled him with my legs. He seemed, for a moment, astonished at my shamelessness. I leaned over him so that my bosom was an inch from his chest. Though we had embraced tightly many times before this, there was something different, infinitely naughty and lubricious about this delicate nearness.

According to Saint Paul, he courted damnation even by thinking of me the way he did, and he considered himself a hypocrite for meeting me this way. Sometimes, when his conscience got the better of him, he would say I ought to hate him, because if we died tomorrow we were both going straight to hell, and he would have been the murderer of my soul. "We've got to stop," he'd say, his hair falling over his forehead, his hands gripping my shoulders, his eyes gripping my eyes, brimful of lust and remorse, looking as though he could devour me and yet so worried about my fate that I could not help but surrender my will to his—though my virtue was dear to me, I would have done whatever he asked without question. "I've decided," he said. "We'll stop."

For a week or so, we would stop. Then, without a word, he would take my hand and lead me into the woods.

The next day, perhaps, we would attend a prayer meeting, hear a lecture on Adventism, and learn the exact date on which, according to William Miller's calculations, all good Christians would be taken into the sky to be spared the burning of the earth. Dozens of households in Livy, including my uncle's, found Adventist newspapers waiting for them each week at the general store. From the newspapers we knew this wasn't just a fancy of farm people. It was the talk of the whole country, which made it all seem more real.

As 1842 became 1843, the time of Jeptha's departure was postponed and the time of Miller's prophesy neared, and its implications began to sink in. I looked about me at the world as you would look at a man of whom the doctor had just said that, despite outward appearances, he had a bad heart and could drop dead any minute. Nursing calves, freshly painted signs, new straw hats and the girls who had just plaited them would never live to be old.

People believed or did not according to the way it made them feel. Jeptha, though he could not simultaneously be a Baptist and scorn the Second Coming, pointed out that these predictions had been made many times before, that according to the Bible we knew not the hour, and anyway—as his teacher, William Jefferds, often said—we were all, in any case, always supposed to be ready to die and face God's judgment. But really, like me, he did not believe or want to believe, because he looked forward to our life together here on this planet.

SOMETIMES, LYING IN THE GRASS, we talked about the books we were reading. He would tell me about Hannibal and Cato, about the Crusades, about Cortés and Montezuma. I would narrate the story of *The Last Days of Pompeii*, a novel I was reading for the second time: it was set in that real Roman city in A.D. 79, the year when it was destroyed, buried, and preserved by the volcano which its citizens had been gazing at for as long as they could remember, thinking only that it lent variety to the view. I described the houses of the Pompeiians and the elaborate public baths where some of these people, who apparently never did any work, would while away their time. How civilized were these lives that had been snuffed out so suddenly! It was pleasant to talk about ancient cataclysms while safe in the crook of Jeptha's arm, watching the squirrels and the birds, for whom history did not exist, hop about the branches of the trees above us. A world was lost in a day, and passing centuries had leached away the suffering, leaving only a strange beauty.

"Well," he observed, "that's how it is with all the people of those times. Their world is gone."

We were quiet, until it occurred to me to ask, "Will it happen to us?"

"What?"

"Will we be buried under the years? Will people dig up our houses and say, Look how quaintly people lived back then?"

He thought a bit, and then he sat up and leaned over me, his earnest face framed by the sky as if he were an angel. "We're going to live in heaven forever."

"Will we be together there?"

"Always. I promise. We will always be together."

❧ XX ❧

"I HATE WHAT HAS HAPPENED TO LEWIS," I told Jeptha one day, out of nowhere, and did not have to explain; he knew what I meant. My brother had become my cousin's hound, and as Matthew ran wild, so did he. Under Matthew's leadership, but with Lewis often showing initiative in wickedness to please his idol, the two of them became the town's practical jokers—not the only ones, but the most daring and disrespectful. They tied a live cat by its tail to the ankle of the town drunk. They placed a whiskey jug and a piece of liver under the bench used every Sunday by Mrs. Harris, a pious and quarrelsome old widow, and when the congregation was singing, "How lost was my condition till Jesus made me whole," a dog raced into the church and knocked over the jug in its eagerness to reach the meat.

Everyone knew who perpetrated these crimes. Except for my aunt, whose life Matthew had made a misery for years, nobody cared, so long as the target was the town drunk and an unlikable widow. As time would show, however, the two were only practicing for an assault on Matthew's real foe, William Jefferds. Matthew had never forgotten his old grudge against Jefferds, who had come to stand not only for all the suffering my cousin had endured in the schoolroom, but for all the abstract forces Matthew opposed—for the sly triumph of the old over the young, for the curbing of masculine freedom, for his mother's victory over his father, for effeminacy, civilization, and religion.

Jefferds was a man with defenders, a teacher and the minister of the church Matthew himself had attended until announcing that he was done with church until his mother found a new minister. Matthew approached his degradation by stages.

First came a mild joke. A boy named Solomon Cole performed the feat of memorization that earned him his fiftieth ticket. Jefferds grasped a fat tome, telling Solomon that he had well earned the right to his own private copy of this holy book and he should let no one take it from him, should take it into his heart and be guided by it; he handed it to the boy in view of the class. It developed gradually that a switch had occurred, and in lieu of the Old Testament the nearsighted Jefferds had handed Solomon a copy of *Aristotle's Masterpiece,* an illustrated guide to fornication, which passed from hand to hand among the older boys. Somehow a beautiful mint-new presentation copy had been obtained for the occasion; it had been inscribed, "With love and best wishes, to Solomon Cole, from William Jefferds."

Everyone not a member of the Free Will Baptist church enjoyed this joke. Nothing was done, even by the elders of Jefferds's own congregation, who could not be certain who the culprit was. No one had been hurt.

A month later, Jefferds was attacked by a pair of dogs while he walked on the main road near the millrace. Some spectators figured out that what the dogs were really after was Jefferds's coat—blood was seen dripping from the pockets—and shouted for him to remove it; which he did, and then watched the dogs tear apart the coat in an effort to get at the raw meat stuffed in its lining.

The moment I heard about the incident with the coat, I knew that

Lewis was responsible. We had just done a slaughter, and I had seen him tuck away the lungs.

I didn't like seeing my brother become a hooligan. The next chance I got, I told him that I knew, and that I'd keep his secret, but that if he and Matthew started trying to outdo each other in nastiness they were bound to go too far. He looked stonily back at me. My word had no weight with him anymore. I was now merely a despised member of the other sex. Anyway, I was Jeptha's sweetheart, and Jeptha was a sneak; Jeptha was a fast talker who had taken up religion because it was his ticket out of Livy.

Besides that, though Lewis didn't mention this and I didn't know it, there were already certain rumors about me in the town, and they had reached Lewis by this time.

My aunt was more distressed than anyone when she heard about the dog and the coat, but had no idea who might be responsible until Bill Dodge and Jonathan Wakeman, two church elders, appeared at her door asking to speak to my uncle. Then she guessed everything. She had Elihu get Matthew from the fields, and since his sense of honor did not permit him to run, he sat at the kitchen table under the glare of Dodge and Wakeman while my aunt told him that he had disgraced the family. He said he hadn't done what they thought he'd done. My aunt said, "Then you put someone up to it."

Matthew said he hadn't.

She told the elders, "It isn't like Matthew to lie."

Dodge said, "Matthew, do you know who did it?"

"Yes," he said.

"Will you tell us?"

"No."

"Was it Lewis?"

Matthew didn't answer, and though I wasn't there, I imagine his face showed what he thought of people who would ask him to tell a tale on his own kin.

My aunt wept. My uncle took Matthew to the barn and whipped him, though it was like whipping a statue, and when he found Lewis, he gave Lewis a whipping that meant just as little. The next time we were together, Lewis accused me of telling what I had seen him do.

"I would never tell on you, Lewis. I'm loyal to you. I'll always be loyal." He screwed up his face in disgust and walked away.

Colonel Ashton gave Jefferds another coat, newer and warmer than the one he'd lost to the dogs, and he accepted it with a humility some people found contemptible.

It was from Jeptha, on one of our walks, that I first heard about the next and last of these incidents. Since the beginning of the year, Jefferds had been boarding with Alvin Walters, and each morning he took a constitutional in the forest of honey locusts on the property. One morning, on a path that had been perfectly firm beneath his feet the day before, the leaves turned out to have been a thin covering over a two-foot-deep cavity filled with muddy water. He sprained his ankle. His spectacles fell off, and when he was struggling to get out, he broke one of the lenses with his elbow. From the high branches of the tall, crooked trees came the laughter of the boys who had prepared the trap.

He couldn't see much, but he knew who two of the boys up there had to be.

"It's your uncle's fault," said Jeptha, who had been calm when he began recounting the incident but became angry as he told it. "No: it's your aunt. She took away Elihu's pride, and his revenge was to let Matthew run wild, and now look at him." He walked on a little. "I whipped him once."

"You don't mean that." I had been afraid of this. "You're strong, but you can't beat him. That other time, you were children. You used his vanity. That won't happen again. Besides, now you're a Christian, you can't. It's against your principles."

I looked at him, at his penetrating blue eyes, at his brow that with advancing adolescence had acquired a hawkish, feral ridge, and at the shoulders and arms which mattered to me not for the damage they might inflict on a foe, but for their beauty, and because of the way they felt pressing against me and gripping me, and because they were his. Today Matthew had no match in Livy. He knocked out teeth and broke jaws. And Matthew was envious of Jeptha and hated him, and would have loved to have him at his mercy. It made me sick to think of it.

Jeptha was as annoyed as a young fellow is bound to be when his sweetheart worries that another man is too strong for him. "I'm not stupid, Arabella. It will be a last resort. But if it comes to that, I'll pray and use strategy, and we'll see."

I kept telling him he was supposed to turn the other cheek, and he kept telling me not to worry, but I knew what was in his mind. He ached to punish Matthew, and his pride told him that he could do it, and I wished I could believe it.

True to his word, though, he did not resort to fighting first. First he complained on Jefferds's behalf to my uncle Elihu. Elihu said that he would whip Matthew. Jeptha said that wasn't enough: Matthew must make a public apology and pay for the spectacles.

I was not there, but it was all reported to me in detail, by more than one party to the conversation.

"I'll put it to him," said Elihu with a smile. "But I don't know as I can make him if he don't want to. Matt can be awful stubborn. Maybe you can make him."

Jeptha, who was perhaps a trifle angry, angrier than he knew, at this point—I was angry when my uncle's words were quoted to me—said, "Let's both ask him. And if he refuses, why, then, you should do it for him. You should make restitution. It could be a great lesson for him."

Now Elihu was angry. "What are you talking about?"

"You should humble yourself, and make a public apology to Mr. Jefferds, who is your minister, and has humbled himself before *you:* he's washed your feet, I've seen him do it. You should insist on paying for his broken spectacles, and you should say it's to make up for the shame your son and your nephew have brought upon you."

"Now, see here, I've heard you out. Don't make me lose my temper. Nobody can even prove Matthew did this."

"Yes, but we know he did. Of course nobody blames you. That's what'll make it work. That's how you'll be able to get through to Matthew and Lewis. A thing like that could turn them both around. It could save them, and Jefferds himself would bless that hole he fell in and see the Lord's work in it, since it brought two erring souls to Jesus!"

Now, I am well aware that many of us who are not actually in the grip of religion have a distaste for talk like this. We prefer the citizen who angrily demands his rights to the preacher who, when he wants something, ropes your immortal soul into the argument. We are pleased when we find out that such men are hypocrites. So it is necessary for me to say that I loved this boy and knew him well, and though he had the zealotry of a recent convert and inevitably fell short of the perfection he aimed at, he was being as sincere as he could bring himself to be. It was his duty to interfere with people's souls.

And if you think about it, his proposal made sense. It was what a better man than Elihu would have done. For Elihu to become a better man was a tactfully unmentioned opportunity in this plan. But if there are any forty-two-year-old men capable of taking such advice from a sixteen-year-old boy, my uncle wasn't one of them. Instead, his face turned colors and he shouted, "Leave my house!" When he reported the conversation to my aunt, she said Jeptha was right, but he wouldn't budge, and when the church elders came again, he said he had intended to whip Matthew, but now, because of Jeptha's insolence, he wasn't going to do a thing.

SO, FINALLY, LIKE THE YOUNG HERO in a boy's adventure story, Jeptha challenged my cousin Matthew, the town bully, to a fight. I learned about it first from Matthew, on the day I hate to speak of, the day I have dreaded speaking of as I have watched its steady, unrelenting approach in these confessions.

Agnes and Evangeline were in the house with Aunt Agatha, carding and spinning. Titus was in Patavium, where he now had a job as a clerk in a dry-goods store. Matthew and I were shelling corn in the barn. With Mrs. Harding's permission, I had come home especially to assist with this chore. Lewis was supposed to help us, too, but he didn't show up, and when I asked Matthew why, he said he had told Lewis that he needn't: he could hunt for nests or shoot birds, and Matthew would do his share of the work.

Matthew was fond of Lewis, and might do him a disinterested favor sometimes, but this wasn't one of those times. He wanted to be alone with me. I knew it, and I was nervous about it, but I couldn't very well refuse to stand in the barn shelling corn with my cousin, out of a suspicion so base that I would be considered vile for uttering it. This was work, it was necessary, and there were no excuses for shirking it.

I am reluctant to continue, which seems very odd, considering all I've done and had done to me, and that I'm up to the event that is supposed to excuse my crimes. For days now, as I've approached this incident, I've been going over it in my mind as I haven't in half a century. I feel like an Egyptologist who has said aloud the ancient curse inscribed on the wall of a long-buried tomb, and the curse still works. I wish. I wish I had done things differently.

Anyway, I let myself be alone with him, even though I found his company unpleasant. Lately, whenever I was around him, his eyes raked my form with a candid lust so disconcerting it could make me stumble. While his eyes took these liberties, he practiced gentlemanly manners that gave him excuses to draw his body nearer to mine. He would hand me my coat or lift me into a wagon.

This attention from Matthew had several causes, some known to me at the time. My form was more mature, and my new clothes displayed it to better effect; also, now that I lived away from my uncle's house, maybe I did not seem so much like a sister to him. I think I understood all that. What I did not know was that there was a rumor in town that I had granted my favors not only to Jeptha but to all three of the Harding boys, William, Dick, and Miles. It was said that they had given me or paid for the pretty dresses I went about in.

Furthermore, Matthew himself had recently been initiated into the rites of Eros by Mrs. Caroline, a forty-year-old widow who had employed him in clearing land on her farm, and he had filled out the gaps in his knowledge with the help of Penny Jackson (also called "Five Penny Jackson"), who lived with four bastards in a shack downstream from the sawmill and would take any man to paradise in exchange for a bushel of corn.

Hay blocked one of the two windows in the barn loft. As we moved about, we were sometimes in darkness, and sometimes in the glare from the other window. One moment I'd be peering into the murk, the next shielding my eyes. I heard the hard corn kernels falling through gaps in the floorboards. Matthew was spilling them. He was doing this job, for which he had contempt, in a state of moderate drunkenness.

There were three corn shellers, one for Matthew, one for me, and one for Lewis. Matthew helped himself unthinkingly to the most productive and easy-to-use sheller, a machine with a wheel to turn. I had a board with the points of nails sticking out of it. Turning the wheel, his big hand in the light, his face in darkness, Matthew told me that Jeptha had challenged him to a fight, a formal fight, in front of witnesses on the green, and he wondered if I might have something to say about it. "He was always sly, your preacher boy. He can talk his way round almost anybody. Guess he got round you, didn't he? But talk won't help him now. This is stupid, taking me on like a man, when he could hide behind Jesus. I'm surprised at him. Remember when him and me scrapped that first year you came to Livy? And Agnes begged me to go easy on him."

He began to talk about what he might do to Jeptha. "I could gouge out one of his eyes. I could break an arm so it never set right. I've a mind to do something to him. Talking to Pa that way in front of Ma: 'Go apologize for Matthew, humble yourself, be a great thing for all of you.' That wasn't right. I can't just let it pass."

We both went on working; it took him a long time to say that much. He kept stopping, as if he were done with the subject, and then returning to it, as if he were merely thinking out loud. It was a way of working on my feelings, and it was very effective. I was uncomfortable. I was not yet afraid. At least, I don't think I was, or why would I have remained? Some of it is not easy to remember.

"Or," he said finally, "I could go easy on him. I could make us come out about even. I could make it look like a tie. I could. I could make it a tie and not be hurt myself, and everyone would believe it. Even Jeptha would believe it. I'd have to swallow my pride. That would be hard." In a little while, he went on: "You want me to do that?"

Finally, I answered, "Yes."

"What?"

"Go easy on him."

"Go easy on him, huh?" He said it now as if it had been my suggestion. "You'd like me to go easy on him. Oh. Huh. Oh, I see. All right, but why should I do it?"

There was silence for a long time, and at last I said, "I'll give you ten dollars."

He pretended to consider this. "No. I don't want your money. This is an affair of honor." More silence, more work. "Suppose you give me a kiss. Then I could go easy on him."

More time passed, too much time. "You're a pig."

Perhaps here I began to be afraid.

"Maybe. That's a whole other discussion. But what about the kiss? On the lips?"

"I'm your sister."

"You're my first cousin. Nobody'll know. It won't hurt Jeptha, unless"—he gave a smile which in another context, from another person, would have been suave and charming—"unless you like it too much. Do you really care about him? Come on."

He went on like that; finally, I asked if he was serious. He said yes.

"Just a kiss," I said. As soon I said it, I knew it had been a mistake. He nodded. "Come on," he said, walking toward the hay. Did he expect me to lie down there with him? I shook my head. He stood by the hay. "I'm waiting." I walked halfway there. He smirked and walked the rest of the way. I knew already that I was in trouble. Whenever I thought about it later, I would identify this as the moment when I knew the nature of the danger I faced. In my reconstruction of the event, I would change course, slip past him, and run to the ladder, and in some versions he would grab my elbow and in others I would hit him with the corn sheller. But I did not run. I let him kiss me. He bit my lip and said, "Open your mouth," and, thinking that he would not honor the bargain unless I did, I obeyed him. He thrust in his tongue, tasting of whiskey and chewing tobacco. I tried to draw away. He pulled up my skirt and reached between my legs. While I struggled to free myself, and he expended what was, for him, a very moderate amount of strength in preventing my escape, he talked about my unkindness. "You're killing me," he said. "Oh Jesus, you're killing me, you're a killer, I can't stand it, don't do this to me."

"Stop it, Matt—what are you doing?" I said, but I didn't shout. I felt already that I had a secret to keep. We fell, hard enough to knock the wind out of me. This time I yelled. His hand covered my mouth. I renewed my struggles. For him that just meant a barely noticeable increase in the force needed to restrain me.

"Let me. You'll like it. You'll see you will. I'm better than your preacher boy. Better than those Harding boys." I saw his mistake and tried to tell him that I was a virgin. He kept his hand over my mouth.

My whole body was pounding like a heart; I had all of my strength to use at once; I used it, and the effect was negligible. With my free hand, I pulled his hair and tried to poke a thumb in his eye. His movements were methodical and unhurried—a good workman doing an honest job for the devil. He took his hand away from my mouth and used his own mouth to smother my cries. He pushed my dress and my petticoats up to my waist, driving his knees between my legs, and spread his knees, forced my legs open. I felt his hand between us, moving his own clothes. One hand covered my mouth again as he spat into the other; then his mouth returned, and at the same moment his prick tore through my flesh, over-riding the great *No* within me. Then came the drilling, and the sad, sick-ening rhythmic riding, each thrust a separate renewal of his triumph and my defeat, the relentless repeated delivery of the message that it was to be his way, not mine. I felt as we do when we fall in a dream, a fatal fall, and we have no choice but to wake if we can. I was a worm in a bird's beak. I had wandered down the wrong path, and I was to be nourishment for another creature. This was what it had all come to. This was what I had been headed for from the moment my mother had died.

I lay beneath him like a rag doll. After he had finished, he kissed me, told me that I was wonderful, and that he meant to be very good to me. He was going to treat me like a queen. He talked like that until he noticed the blood on my skirt, and perhaps he remembered the moment when he had encountered an obstacle that had not barred the way to the womb of either Mrs. Caroline or Penny Jackson. He was smart. He got the idea at last. "Oh," he said.

I was distant from myself, as people are at such times, hearing myself speak without advance warning of the words. I did not know whose will moved me now. "I can't be seen like this. People would guess." I told him to go into the house and where to find another skirt, and some rags and a bucket, and not be seen. He must not be seen.

"I didn't know," he said. He looked contrite. I believe, from the way he behaved then, that he had not planned to rape me. He had planned to seduce me, buy me, or blackmail me, whichever method got the desired results. He had gotten carried away.

"No one must know," I told him.

"I swear," he said. "I'll swear any way you like, on anything you like."

I didn't know what he meant, but later, on thinking back, I realized that he had been prepared for a Tom Sawyer ritual, to draw blood from his finger. I did not have the presence of mind to think that Matthew had committed a crime and was afraid of being found out. All I could think was that this must be kept a secret.

On one point I was clear. It wasn't the rupture of the hymen before marriage that ruined a girl; it was other people knowing. No one would ever think the same of me after they had learned of this. They might pity me, if they believed me. In any case, I would be held in contempt. Jeptha would marry me anyway, supposing he survived the attempt to kill Mat-thew that would follow my telling him. But we would always have this between us. I couldn't endure that. He must not know. Whether I was really naïve enough to believe that his *ignorance* of what had happened would not stand between us, or whether I had an inkling that it would, I cannot recall, but in any case I would have believed that his ignorance of it could never be as dangerous to us as his knowledge. I had suffered a small wound, an invisible puncture. Why should I let it change my life? The safest thing would be for no one to know.

Matthew went. When he returned, I changed out of the torn and bloody skirt and into the clean one he had brought, which looked noth-ing like the one I had been wearing; I could only hope that no one would notice. He cleaned the floor. We resumed our work. I imagined having the courage to get close to Matthew, perhaps by promising to let him have me again, and when he was near enough, slamming the nails of the corn-sheller deeply into his neck and killing him. The picture kept com-ing unbidden into my mind while I went on numbly scraping the dry ears on the nails and beadlike kernels of dried corn dropped from my hair.

When we were done, I wrapped the rags and my bloody skirt in a bundle and walked back to town. As I left the farm, I passed Lewis. He was carrying a couple of dead birds. When he saw my face, he asked me what the matter was, and I made myself smile and told him that it was nothing important.

At the Hardings' house, I washed as thoroughly as I could with a basin and ewer. I was afraid of what might be said or guessed if I had a bath in the middle of the week.

❊ XXI ❊

ON ONE EXCUSE OR ANOTHER, I put off spending time with Jeptha. I thought that if I gave myself some time I would begin to feel better, or at least find it easier to conceal my emotions, but after a week had passed, my misery had only grown.

Jeptha came by on my day off, wanting us to go in the fields to kiss and tease each other. I used the excuse of a sudden chill in the air—it was now October—and said I wanted to walk in town, by the millrace. He was going to fight Matthew in a few days, he told me. It was to occur in the field behind the tavern. I became so upset that I felt almost too weak to walk.

I did not think he would be hurt. Matthew kept his bargains. I knew, though, that I must not be present at the fight. If I saw Matthew, my feelings would betray me.

On Monday, the day of the fight, I told Mrs. Harding I would do the wash as usual. I put on an old wrapper, and boiled water in a great kettle in the yard. I lifted and stirred the clothes with a paddle. Often when I performed this chore, one or more of the Harding boys would come out to watch me. When it was William and Miles, who spent much of the year away at school, they disguised their interest as friendliness and propped up this illusion with chatter. Richard, the dolt, would simply stare like a starved dog. As a rule I found this annoying. Now I did not think I could abide it, and I was glad that Richard wasn't there that day.

Richard was watching the fight. When I was hanging the wash, he rushed into the backyard, excited, to tell me of the great upset. Matthew—overconfident, Richard supposed—had missed blow after blow and hadn't ducked when he should have, and finally he had taken one to the chin. He had lain on the grass until someone threw a bucket of water on him, and he had admitted that Jeptha had won, and said he was sorry for what had happened to William Jefferds and was of the opinion that nothing like that would happen again, which was understood to be as close as he could come to admitting he had done it and had been justly punished.

Matthew and Jeptha had shaken hands. I kept picturing that. A crowd consisting mostly of people who had placed bets carried Jeptha through town and toasted him in the tavern and the store. As will happen when the favorite loses, a few malcontents voiced the suspicion that Matthew had bet against himself and thrown the fight, but Richard said he didn't believe that, even though he'd lost a dollar. Abruptly he interrupted his own account of events to ask why I didn't look happier.

"I don't hold with fighting or gambling," I said.

The crowd had wanted to take Jeptha to the Hardings' house to see me. He wouldn't let them, thankfully. But he came alone later. Mrs. Harding, looking through the window, told me to stay where I was, and she opened the door herself. She congratulated him and invited him for dinner. I saw immediately what this would mean. It would be me, Jeptha, Mr. and Mrs. Harding, and Richard at the long table set for company, while Richard and Mr. Harding described the fight from their point of view, and Jeptha from his point of view. It was impossible. I could not bear it. But I could not avoid it.

He was dusty and sweaty, with a red spot above his right eye from some glancing blow that Matthew had given him to make the fight look real. His eyes sought the additional fillip of my approval as Mr. Harding pounded his back, asked to see the hands that had done such impressive work, and told Jeptha he guessed that in the future, whenever warnings of sinners' fates in the afterlife proved unavailing, he could persuade them with the more immediate threat of "the damage those iron fists could do! Yes, sir!" He asked me, "What do you think of your seminarian now, little lady?"

Town notables who had gotten word that Jeptha was here kept coming to pay their respects and to enjoy Mr. Harding's liquor. They toasted our health and urged Jeptha to drink, but he was still a Baptist and had to refuse. I was not offered whiskey. I had been given it as medicine sometimes during childhood illnesses. I resolved to put its reputation as an anodyne to the test just as soon as I was alone.

At least the noise and commotion in the house made it easy to disguise my feelings. The things these people wanted me to say were all simple and obvious. It is very superficial, the manly world of good fellowship and cheers and toasts.

Only Mrs. Harding noticed my discomfort. "Is something wrong, dear?" she asked quietly. I had an answer prepared. I whispered it in her ear. I said "my friend" had come. She whispered back, "Oh my goodness, and we've made you work so hard today." (That was empty talk: my monthly pains never caused her to lighten my work.)

In any case, it was plausible, what I had told her, because she knew when my time usually came—it usually came about now. But it had not come. And it did not come.

XXII

THREE WEEKS LATER, IT STILL HAD NOT COME, and there were other signs which I had learned from Anne and from girls at school. I knew right away. There was comfort only in sleep. My waking hours were filled with disgust and panic. My wish to believe it wasn't true warred with the practical need to find a solution. I had to be rid of this baby. It was like a second rape happening inside me. And whatever else it might mean to tell Jeptha, I knew he would never countenance abortion: he would consider it murder.

Every day, usually in the morning, I threw up. Once, while I was preparing breakfast, the urge came upon me so quickly that I had barely time to find a pail. Mrs. Harding was there, and she felt my pulse and told me to lie down, and she looked at me. "If I knew what you had, I would know what to give you." That gave me hope. Over the years, she had accumulated a great store of patent medicines. I had looked through them already, not finding what I wanted, but perhaps it existed just the same.

Later, when I was scrubbing the floor, she asked me how I was feeling now.

"Tolerable," I answered.

"I'm so glad. This sickness of yours: it seems to come and go."

She looked at me appraisingly. My breasts had already started to get larger. She had four children. Perhaps she knew already.

Still later, we were baking pies, and apropos of nothing, she said, "Belle, is there anything you want to tell me? If there is, you needn't be afraid. I won't judge you."

"Thank you, Mrs. Harding," I said, steeling myself. "Mrs. Harding, you are the doctor in your family, with many remedies at your disposal."

"Yes?" she said.

"I have a woman's complaint. I was wondering if you have anything for menstrual regularity."

"Oh dear," she said after a brief pause; how surprised she really was I could not tell. "But you said—three weeks ago—that your friend had come."

"I was mistaken."

"Oh my goodness." She had understood my request immediately. "No, dear. No, I don't have anything like that."

"I was wondering if you could get something, from a friend or from a store: a store in Patavium, not in Livy. I would be very grateful. I know you want to help me."

She shook her head. "I *can* help you. I can talk to your aunt. Mr. Harding can talk to Jacob Talbot, and Jacob will talk to Jeptha, who is an honorable young man, and it will all come out right, and we'll forget that you said what I think you just said."

"Mrs. Harding, you know what I'm asking you. I hate asking it. But I have to. Do you think you could help me with medicine?" To eliminate any possible doubt of my intentions, I named the remedies I had seen in newspaper advertisements and at the general store.

The temperature lowered abruptly. "Mercy, you aren't short of information."

"Girls talk about these things."

"Do they. Well, I hope you haven't shared your wisdom with Eva."

"No," I said, hurt that her mind would turn this way when I was in trouble.

"And Patavium. That's good. You can't get it yourself without spilling the beans. If I got it here, they might still think of you, so you say Patavium. That shows thinking ahead; yes, it shows very clear thinking. I'm not sure I admire it."

"I don't know what to do, Mrs. Harding! I have no one to turn to. I can't ask my aunt for help. She wouldn't understand."

Mrs. Harding wiped her hands and led me to a chair at the table. "I don't mean to be harsh. I just don't hold with what you're asking. It's a sin worse than the sin it tries to hide, and apart from that, those potions, when they work at all, are dangerous. It's bad enough you got into trouble while you were living here. I'm going to be blamed for that anyway. Dear, it's not so bad as you think. I'll talk to your aunt. You talk to Jeptha. He'll do what's right, and you'll be happy again, much sooner than you think."

I had never taken Mrs. Harding's careless assurances of fondness for me at face value, but now I gave them rather more credit than they deserved. "Mrs. Harding, it's not Jeptha's baby," I confessed. Immediately

I felt her grip on me loosen, and I hastened to add: "It's my cousin Matthew's. He forced himself on me. He took me by force."

"Oh. I see."

I pulled away from her. "Did you hear what I told you?"

"Don't assume that tone with me. I'm not your aunt."

I was amazed. I had taken a risk telling her. I had decided to tell her only if I had no other way of gaining her cooperation. I had not anticipated that she would doubt me.

I understood her perspective a little better when she asked, "Are you sure it was your cousin? Maybe it was Jeptha."

"I was a virgin."

This would have been a sharp rebuke if she could be sure it was true. But girls in my position often lie.

I told her how it had happened. When I was done, she looked at me sympathetically. "Let me show you something," she said, and I waited in the kitchen while she fetched an old book. Its cracked leather covers were falling away from the binding in disintegrating flaps; the insides of the covers were lined with paper in a pattern of marble. I had never seen it before, despite having cleaned every inch of Mrs. Harding's house with an eye out for books of every kind. Yet it was a book I had heard about. It was *Aristotle's Masterpiece*.

We sat down at the table with the heavy volume between us. "This," said Mrs. Harding, "is the book that they tricked poor Mr. Jefferds into giving to young Cole. It was not written for boys to snigger over. It is a serious book for married women."

She turned the pages. I saw woodcuts of women's bodies; of the baby in the womb. She turned the book around and pointed to a sentence: "The greater a woman's desire for copulation the more subject she is to conceive."

Her finger moved lower down the page, to a passage that told me that it is when a woman achieves rapture during intercourse that her egg descends, this egg that, fertilized by a man's essence, makes her conceive.

"What you have told me simply cannot be. A woman can be taken against her will, but if it is entirely against her will, no child comes of it. So the attentions of your cousin cannot have been entirely unwelcome to you. It is simply against nature."

There was silence, and at last I said, "The book is wrong."

"You'll have to forgive me if I take the word of a book written by physicians over the word of a country girl who has gotten herself into a fix."

Probably she just thought I was lying; in any case, I believe, knowing her and knowing more of life now than I did then, that her first thought was of herself. Her mind leapt forward; she pictured me dead from taking an abortifacient, followed by an investigation in which it was discovered that she had helped me obtain it. I know moral considerations had nothing to do with her refusal, because she did not hesitate to advise me of other ways to bring on a miscarriage. She phrased her advice coyly. She allowed that she "had heard" of certain things being done by certain girls in like circumstances. They went into the woods and did violent exercises: jumping vigorously up and down and touching their buttocks with each leap. Or they jumped down from a height, or did heavy physical labor, or fasted. She had heard of such methods. How effective they were she did not know.

Human nature was certainly quite varied, Mrs. Harding noted. She had heard of cases in which an unscrupulous woman, pregnant by a man she could not or would not marry, persuaded another man to sin with her, to fool the second man into thinking the child was his, so he would marry her. So it was rumored. She supposed such things happened.

DECEIVING JEPTHA, I TAUGHT MYSELF SKILLS that would serve me well in my later profession. I had no appetite for him. My body disgusted me. Even washing myself was a grim matter. But, staring Jeptha in the eye with a look that said I was imparting a great secret, I drew his fingers to the buttons of my blouse. I pulled his head to my breasts and dragged his hand under my skirt. By and by I whispered, "I'm tired of waiting."

We were in a clearing by the edge of the Muskrat Pond, on sloping ground strewn with oak leaves, twigs, and pine needles. The winds up high must have been stronger than they were down here: clouds kept covering and uncovering the sun swiftly, and the light kept changing, as if the sky were a great wheel of fortune. A spider had built its web in the branches of a fallen tree just beyond Jeptha's shoulder, and when a breeze blew, parts of the web would move suddenly into the light, showing the tiny bundles of silk-wrapped flies. I felt something round and hard under my back, and I kept trying to shift away from it without breaking the spell I was trying to cast.

At last, red-faced, his voice sounding strange, he said rather grimly, "We could be seen here. Let's go into the cornfield."

We got up. I glanced at the ground and saw the acorn that had troubled me. We walked, his arm around my waist, into the tall corn that had been left standing for the pigs to forage on. I lay down on my back again. It was damp here, too, and the sun emerged from a cloud and stabbed my eyes, and I shut them, while he stepped out of his trousers. Then we heard dogs barking and children's voices coming closer. I opened my eyes, saw his rampant nakedness, which I had washed once when he was near death. Now it was in quite a different mood; the first I'd seen in this condition, and it was large and clumsy, as prototypes so often are. Hastily he hopped on one leg at a time, getting into his trousers. He pulled me to my feet, and we walked out of the cornfield feeling as shamed as Adam and Eve. Except, too bad for me, Jeptha had not yet partaken of the apple. He said, "We were lucky, lucky. We won't attempt that again."

"Then let's get married," I dared to say at last.

As though there were not very much at stake—for *him* there wasn't, he didn't know I was pregnant, he didn't know I was in trouble, for *him* I seemed to be saying that we should marry now to enjoy each other's flesh—he smiled, and pulled a stray hair away from my face, and kissed my cheek. "Sweetheart, you have my promise: we will marry. But to marry now, and do such things we almost just did, night after night, would not be wise: a baby would come of it, and we would have to change all our plans. I'm going away." He was supposed to set off in only two weeks, to a seminary in New Jersey. In partial payment for his education, he would be a church sexton and tutor. "I'll have barely enough for one to live on."

"Leave me here in Livy until you can afford me; I'll stay with Mrs. Harding."

"It wouldn't be just you and me, not for long. Soon there would be three."

Still I pressed my point: marry now. He said neither yes nor no.

He seemed cooler to me the next time we met.

We went to a Millerite prayer meeting in a back room of the Presbyterian church. Agnes was there, with her beau, George Sackett. George was the sawmill owner's son. He was tall and thin, with sharp lines already etched on the sides of his mouth, so that he resembled a life-sized wooden puppet. He was very religious.

Agnes, who did not love George Sackett, rushed up to me and embraced me. "My dear sister, how are you feeling? Have you walked far? I've been so worried about you."

George Sackett and a few others were looking at me for my reaction to this, and I suspected that I had walked into an ambush.

"I'm fine, there's nothing to worry about. And how are *you* feeling, Agnes?"

"Tolerable, thank you. But are you really fine, or just being brave? Mrs. Harding's daughter said you puked three times last week. In the mornings, like Ma when she was first carrying Hosea." Hosea was the child who had died in infancy a few years before I came to Livy.

I did the first thing that came into my head, and denied it. "Does she say that? I don't know where she can have gotten that idea."

It was a stupid mistake, but there was no room for clear thinking in the tiny space left over by the immense realization: *Agnes knew.* She would not have dared to hint that I was pregnant if she thought that Jeptha and I were having relations. She knew Jeptha; she knew that if he thought he had gotten me pregnant he would have married me, which was the last thing she wanted. She had to believe that we were saving ourselves for the wedding day. And how could she know? I could not imagine Mrs. Harding betraying my trust so soon: it was not in her interest. Agnes's information had to have come from Matthew. Perhaps when I had sent him back to the house to fetch my clothes, Agnes had seen him, and asked him to explain what he was doing, and then or later she had interrogated him— she could have threatened to bring my aunt into the matter—and he had confessed, and included the crucial detail that there had been blood, that I was a virgin. She could not, it was true, be perfectly sure that Jeptha and I had not had relations *since* then; with an iron will and no heart, I could have seduced him the very next day, as I had nearly seduced him just a little while ago. Perhaps she had not thought of this, or perhaps she had sufficient insight into my nature to realize how unlikely it would be, or perhaps she simply gambled that we had not. She had always been brave. She pounced on my error. "I guess from seeing you do it. She saw you do it in a pail twice, and one time she only heard."

Feeling the heat in my face, and knowing its color betrayed me, I admitted that I had been feeling unwell, probably from something I had eaten; I had denied it because I had not wanted to worry my aunt; but I was better now.

Agnes said she could see that—in fact, I seemed to be gaining weight. Today I am experienced enough to know that it could not have been true, but by saying it Agnes made her point very clear to all of us. I felt as if I were ten pounds heavier than I had been three weeks ago, and I think that in the eyes of the others at that prayer meeting I looked it. I could think of nothing to say in reply, except that she was mistaken, I was not heavier, but I was well, thank you, I was very well. The pastor arrived, and there was praying, singing, and Bible study. When I had the courage to glance at Jeptha, he was already looking at me. I turned away. My heart was drumming, drumming, drumming.

❧ XXIII ❧

I TOLD MRS. HARDING I HAD TO GO HOME for a few days to help on the farm.

My aunt, who had heard the dogs bark at my approach, stood in the doorway, wiping her hands on a rag, as I walked up to the house. There was no ease between us; nor was there much of a struggle anymore. We were just sick of each other.

"What is it?" she asked.

"I need to talk to you alone."

If you are wondering how I could bear to tell my aunt of my predicament, and what I intended to do about it, remember that I was desperate. She had not been my first choice. But I knew, at least, that I could trust my aunt with my secret, because it was Matthew who had made me pregnant, and I knew that she would believe me when I told her how it had happened, and I knew that she would do anything within her power to prevent that from becoming known.

We went into the kitchen and sat. She offered me Souchong tea and a piece of bad bread. I drank the tea, but though very hungry I refused the bread: I was fasting. Between sips, very quietly, I told my aunt that I needed some medicine to restore my menstrual regularity. She looked at me blankly. Then she understood. "Oh dear," she said, putting down the bread. "Oh my goodness. Well, I won't judge you. You took a chance. You'll have to pay. I can't do what you're asking."

"Yes, you can. You will." I told her what had happened, sparing her nothing.

"No," she said. The word was half denial, half dismay. "Oh my Lord," she said, "oh my Lord, if this comes out. You're lying, aren't you? Oh Lord, I hope you're lying."

I let my eyes answer. "If I've got to have this baby, I'll make sure Jeptha knows how it happened. Everyone will know what kind of a family this is."

"Oh mercy!" She put her head in her hands. Her shoulders heaved. After a while, she looked up, her face red and wet. "You shouldn't have let him be alone with you."

The urge to strike her made my arm twitch. When I was sure that my voice would not shake, I said, "Help me get rid of it."

"I can't."

"What do you mean, you can't? Didn't you hear what I told you?"

"It's in the Lord's hands. You've been hurt, I see that, and you're going to be hurt more, and I guess we all are, but I'm not going to go against God." I stood up. "Where are you going, Arabella?"

I went out and climbed the maple tree we used to hang the hogs from when we butchered them. Standing on the almost horizontal limb, which bore groovelike marks from the ropes that were so often slung over it, from five feet up, I jumped. My skirts puffed open; my bottom hit the ground hard and the back of my head after it. I climbed up and jumped again. I sat on the ground, waiting for my body to react.

My aunt had come out of the house by now. "Arabella, what are you doing?" I looked up at the tree. The stumps of the lower limbs, cut close to the tree, had long ago been painted black with tar, and the bark ringing those cut ovals had bulged so much over the years that they looked like lips. I had once thought of them as a choir, but now they were screaming.

I wrapped my arms around the tree, stepped on those lips and climbed again. "Stop it, Arabella! You'll hurt yourself! It's wrong, it's a sin, stop it!" she cried, but her shout did not sound entirely convincing. I think her feelings were mixed. The sin horrified her. But she would have liked me to succeed.

This time I fell forward and hurt my knee and my wrists. The possibility of spraining my ankle made me stop. Rising to my feet, I thought of Anne. Could she help me? Her views on bedroom matters were broad and easygoing. But I knew that she would not lightly countenance abortion. To win her cooperation, I would have had to break her heart—she adored Matthew.

So I decided first to try Titus, who was boarding with a family in Patavium so that he could clerk in the dry-goods store. It was eight miles away, and I thought I had just enough day left to walk it.

The road had two names. In Livy it was called the Patavium Road. In Patavium it was called the Livy Road. When I'd gone about two miles, a farmer gave me a ride in his wagon, which had no springs or straps. It was a very bumpy ride. Maybe that would do it.

THE STORE WAS OPEN, and Titus was in an apron, all smiles and smart patter for the customers. When he saw me, he yelled a few words to his boss and took me to a tavern a few doors down the street. We talked inconsequentially for a few minutes. At last, with a shrewd look, he asked me why I had come to see him, and I told him everything.

His eyes welled with tears, and I regretted that we were in a public place. "I wish he wasn't my brother."

I swallowed, waited until I could speak without choking, and then told him my plans regarding the little creature inside me. He said very simply that he could help, if I was sure that this was what I wanted to do.

I FORGET WHETHER IT WAS THEN or the next day that Titus warned me—in any case, many weeks too late—that Agnes had been spreading the rumor I was granting the freedom of my person to Mrs. Harding's sons. She spread it by pretending to quash it. Whenever she heard my name come up in conversation, she would leap to my defense. The things that were being whispered about me were *not true*. What things, Agnes?

I remembered that Matthew had said he was better than Miles, Dick, or William. I asked Titus, "Have you told anyone but me about this?" He said he hadn't. I said, "Keep it mum. That way I can threaten Agnes with you telling your mother."

If there was a hell, I wouldn't have hesitated to send her there. But Titus, in a discussion that did not concern Agnes, had assured me there was no such place. Recently, he had become a Universalist, like his employer. Universalists believed that everyone would be saved. God was not a torturer, they said. To hold simultaneously that God is omnipotent and benevolent, and yet punishes people eternally, was just illogical. I don't know why I was never tempted to become a Universalist, since it would have comforted me about my father. Perhaps it seemed too good to be true.

That night, after closing the store, Titus took me to the house where he was boarding. I met the owner, his wife, and their pretty daughter. I saw that she and Titus were sweet on each other, and they were lucky, lucky, lucky. I stayed the night, and in the morning, Titus handed me a bag containing a bottle of Madame Drunette's Lunar Pills. He said that I should be alone when I took them, but not too far from help, because I might get very sick—if I could wait a few days, he could arrange to be with me. I told him I could not bear to wait. He said that he did not want to scare me, but he had heard that it hurt like hell. He had heard that women had died from taking it. That whenever a woman took one of these pills she was rolling the dice.

I set out on the Livy Road, carrying in a carpetbag a wide-necked brown bottle that contained three large pills, each one supposedly sufficient for the purpose, and a jug of water. The day was sunny. I passed farmhouses, smokehouses, horses, pastures. As soon as I came to wild land, I walked into it, pulling my skirts up above the brambles, stumbling, my sick fear growing. The ground began to rise. I sat on an old musty log, the remnant of a forest giant torn from the side of a little hill. Its mighty roots, raised higher than its branches, were twisted, clenched, and hairy, clutching hunks of clay and stones. The violence with which that massive tangle had been torn from the earth spoke to me more plainly than words. I leaned my palm on the peeling bark. A chunk of the log gave way, and I saw tiny white larvae tunneling through the pale, mushy wood. I took the bottle from the carpetbag. I thought of myself lying there beside the log, eaten by insects, to be found months or years later, next to a carpetbag and a bottle of Madame Drunette's Lunar Pills.

Slapping bits of leaf and bark and tiny white eggs from my clothes, I got up and went back to the road and started walking; a little sooner than the last time, a wagon came along and gave me a ride the rest of the way. I went through the house, passing my aunt in the kitchen, and took the pill with a cup of water on the back porch. I came back in and told her that I was tired and was going to rest upstairs for a few hours. She watched mutely while I dragged some worn-out sheets, a bucket of water, a basin, and a ewer up to the loft where I had spent the waning years of my childhood. I lay on my old straw bed and waited.

These medicines could not be advertised for their real purpose then, and are no longer available today. They were made of plants that had been discovered, by trial and error—at God knows what price in suffering to the experimenters—to cause the strong muscle contractions by which women give birth. Physicians and midwives sometimes used them to induce labor in women past their time. Those of you who know that the pains of childbirth are caused mainly by these same muscle spasms will understand that it was impossible to keep entirely quiet. I moaned and begged God for mercy. I bled, not knowing if this was the result I intended or the beginning of a foul, ignominious death.

When it was over, I washed myself and wrapped everything in a bundle, which I handed to my aunt. She took it without a word. "Get me something to eat," I demanded. She slapped together one of her revolting stews, and for once I liked the taste. It tasted like being alive.

"Arabella," she said, to get my attention, while I was eating.

"What?"

"Now that you've done what you wanted to do, you don't need any other folks to know, do you?"

It was the last thing I wanted, but I liked having her beg me, so I didn't answer.

"It would break Elihu," she said. "It would break him. And just think what it would do to Lewis."

"Oh yes, Lewis. Lewis."

I could not decide which would be harder to bear, discovering how Lewis would react to the news of what his hero had done, or letting him go on as Matthew's dog.

. . .

I TOLD MY AUNT I DID NOT FEEL strong enough to go back to town; I'd spend the night here. "I want him kept away from me. I don't want to see his face. Tell him I'm here and keep him away." She did it. She told him to stay away, and his readiness to comply was a sort of confession, as I pointed out to my aunt.

After lying upstairs reading until the light dimmed, I went down to help her serve supper. I didn't have to help, she said.

"Oh, but I want to."

I served each family member individually. Agnes was solicitous about my health, wondering if I should be working so soon after having been so sick earlier in the day.

"I feel much stronger, thank you, Agnes."

"I was so worried; I thought you were dying."

"Oh dear, that must have been so distressing for you. You have such a good heart, Agnes."

"Thank you, Arabella."

"I picture your heart sometimes."

"Where's Matthew?" my brother Lewis asked of us generally.

"In town," said my aunt, and I could see that Lewis was bewildered and hurt because Matthew hadn't asked him to come along.

Elihu and Evangeline continued feeding obliviously.

We went to bed and prayed aloud, one after another. Agnes prayed in her usual highly specific fashion, leaving God very little room for initiative, treating Him as a sort of unimaginative factotum who has to be reminded flowers must grow up and rain fall down, and provided with very exact instructions concerning the management of the farm. I prayed that Agnes be given greater understanding. Not long after she fell asleep, she was woken by pains so unexpected that they startled her almost as much as they hurt her. "Mama!" she cried weakly. "Evangeline!"

Evangeline was still snoring, so it was left to me to go to my cousin's aid.

"What ails you, dear Agnes?"

"These pains! Fetch Mama!"

I sat looking down at her moonlit face. Soon, with her quick mind, she understood. "You've poisoned me. You killed your baby, and now you're killing me."

"You won't die," I said. "Now, be quiet." I put my hand over her mouth and said, "You spread the rumor about me and the Harding boys. Titus told me. If you call Mama now, I'll have to tell her why I've done this to you. Titus has promised to back me up. God knows how long it will take you to pull the wool over her eyes again—it would cause you no end of trouble. And what will you have gotten for it? Nothing. She hates me already. Now, I've just been through this thing, and it's no picnic, but it only takes an hour or two, and then you'll be right as rain."

I took my hand away, not knowing whether she would scream and shout for her mother again. But she didn't, though her pains were obviously acute.

As time went on, it seemed to get even worse. She ground her teeth so hard I thought she might break them. Tears streamed sideways, right and left, from her eyes. When the moon had gone a third of the way across the night sky, I said, "Maybe I gave you too much. It could be that you are going to die after all."

I hated her enough to be at peace with that idea.

She began to pray, commending her soul to Jesus. The whole ordeal took her much longer than it had taken me, for some reason, and she was not really done until dawn and the rooster's crow. She had fouled the bed, but there was no blood.

"I bet you'd like to sleep," I told her. "But you shouldn't. Your mother would want to know why. You'd better get dressed. Oh, and clean yourself up."

"You're going to hell, Arabella."

"I expect so. Maybe when I get there you can show me the ropes. Tell me how to pull the carrots, and which cow likes to put her tail in the milk."

THE DAY WAS CRISP AND CLEAR. I wore a yellow cotton traveling dress, a homespun woolen shawl, and a white bonnet. I carried a carpetbag and walked along the road to town like an innocent, apple-cheeked dairy maid. All was not well with me, and it would not be for a long time. But at least I did not have Matthew's child in me.

I walked up the slate walk of Mrs. Harding's house. "Arabella," she said with a fraudulent smile, and I knew immediately that I had lost my position.

She had me sit on the couch beside her and said I was a wonderful girl. She enjoyed my companionship. I would be a fine wife to the man of my choice one day. However, as I was perhaps aware, there was talk around town about me and her sons. She had thought the matter over while I was at my aunt's house. She'd decided that, to put a stop to the gossip, I should absent myself from her house for the time being.

"But, Mrs. Harding, that wouldn't stop the gossip. That would just make everybody think it was true!"

She knew that. She did not mean to fool me. She expected me to swallow the lie.

"Oh, I don't think so, Arabella. I'm sure you're wrong. It's you being in the house, such a pretty girl as you are, and the boys the age they are, that makes people talk. It's probably best for you to be in a house where the children are younger."

I asked her if she knew of such a house. She said she would ask around. If she heard of something, she'd let me know. "That reminds me. Ephraim Towne was here and brought a letter for you from Jeptha." Handing it to me, she suggested, "I think it is a very personal letter. Maybe you should take it with you."

I realized much later that she must have had a pretty good idea of the letter's contents, and she wanted to be spared the hysterics she anticipated. I didn't think of it then; I could only wonder why he would write me a letter, and why send Ephraim instead of coming himself. I felt sick. I felt a weakness in my wrists and elbows. It seemed to take all my strength to unfold the page. A few bits of red sealing wax fell on my skirt; a heavy clump of it stayed on the edge of the paper as I read:

Dear Arabella,

I know about the baby you tried to make me think was mine; I can't excuse that, I could never forget it. ~~You've~~ It has wrecked things between us. I don't know why you did it. I always thought that you really loved me even when you kept secrets but I guess that is a man's vanity. I can't bear to see you. I'm going a week earlier than I planned so I don't have to see you. I would have given you my arm. I was such a dolt. I would have damned myself for you.

You had me in your grip, you could have made me do anything, but now my eyes are opened. Go and marry Miles or Dick or whoever got you into trouble. Let there be a shotgun wedding and marry him and be a rich woman—be a rich, rich heartless woman and go straight to hell. I can't believe how stupid I was. I wish I could rise above it. I can't. You've torn my heart out. I'm like you now. Empty.

Jeptha

It was too awful for tears. It made me dizzy. I cried out Mrs. Harding's name as if the house were on fire. She came. I asked her if she had spoken to Ephraim when he brought the letter. She said she had. Did Ephraim say where Jeptha was? I asked. Yes, she said, he had taken a coach to Rochester; he was taking a cheap, circuitous route to the seminary. "Isn't that what he told you in the letter?"

"Oh, Mrs. Harding, he's given me up! He thinks I deceived him!"

"Oh dear. Oh, he can't mean it!"

"Do you think so, Mrs. Harding?"

"I'm sure he'll change his mind. How could he give up a lovely girl like you?"

She knew as well as I did what could make a pretty girl unsuitable for marriage. All the same, I threw my arms around her and wept. I'd have wept on the breast of a dressmaker's dummy for an instant of motherly comfort, and to delay the time when I must walk away from this house and face whatever in the world came next.

We then heard the brass knocker on the front door. "Don't, Arabella," said Mrs. Harding, as I ran down the hall to get it. Such was my desire for it to be Jeptha, here to beg my forgiveness, that at first I did not see that standing before me was Emily Johnson, a bucktoothed girl whom I knew from school. She was dragging a trunk.

Behind me, Mrs. Harding said, "This is unfortunate."

"Mrs. Harding said to come at noon," Emily explained.

"I'll get my things," I told Mrs. Harding.

MY LEFT HAND GRIPPED THE HANDLES of two carpetbags. In my right I carried a leather portmanteau that had traveled with me to my uncle's farm when I was nine years old. I walked down to Mill Race Street, past neat two-story clapboard houses, past dogs, past children who knew my name and would soon be telling their mothers they had seen Arabella Godwin leave Mrs. Harding's house with all her things.

I took familiar shortcuts through the fields to Melanchthon's house, and wept in Anne's embrace, giving her a selective account of my troubles that excluded the rape and the pregnancy. I told her that Agnes had spread lies about me, and that I could not bear to go back to the farm, because Agatha always took Agnes's side, and that Jeptha and I had quarreled over that. Anne disliked Agnes, and she believed me, though probably she knew I wasn't telling her everything. She said that I could stay.

Melanchthon brought another bed into Susannah's room. That night, after my dreams woke me, Susannah came and asked me why I was crying. "I had a bad dream," I told her. I fell asleep at dawn, and Anne let me go on sleeping that first day.

I HAD ALWAYS FELT UNDERSTOOD BY JEPTHA. It had been the first thing I loved about him, and it was a riddle and a torment that he could have believed the things he said in that letter; that he could have been so sure of them that he would go without hearing me out. His first accusation ("I know about the baby you tried to make me think was mine") was, of course, no more than the truth. I saw that my furtive behavior in the weeks since the rape, the great fact hidden from Jeptha, would have prepared him to doubt me. I had been deceiving him since then. But what in all the years before that could have persuaded him I was *essentially* a deceiver and there was something false in me at the core? I have given the question a great deal of thought over the years. I believe now that it was religion that came between us. We began to part the moment he was saved, for that was when I began to hide many of my thoughts and feelings from him, and he began to blind himself, incompletely, to uncomfortable truths about me. My falseness was on display for a whole year, in every one of those prayer meetings, every time he preached a sermon to me from the trees, and every time he talked to me about his deepest feelings, which I pretended unconvincingly to share.

WHEREVER I WENT, THERE WERE LOOKS; everyone seemed to know that I had been in a fix, and gotten myself out of it somehow; and that this was why I had been fired, and why Jeptha had left me. How much of the story came from Mrs. Harding, or Agnes, or Mrs. Talbot? It made me feel ill to think about it. In any case, I was disgraced, and because I didn't deserve it, I believed that it could be undone. I had a sense of justice.

This was the source of my second great error, after my decision to permit myself to be alone with Matthew. Instead of taking the stage out of Patavium, going to New Jersey, and meeting Jeptha face to face, I stayed at Melanchthon and Anne's house, and took thought, and formed what I considered a more intelligent plan. I would write to Jeptha, telling him everything. When he received my letter, either he would come here to kill Matthew or he would leave Matthew to God's vengeance and send for me. He would send for me, of course, with a letter. What a wonderful letter that would be! It would make me clean again. I could wave that letter in front of everyone's face: I would show it to Mrs. Harding, I would show it to Agnes, I would show it to Colonel Ashton.

I could not get Jeptha's address from his family; they hated me. So I did what seemed logical. I visited Jeptha's good friend and guide, William Jefferds.

He had moved again by then, to the farmhouse of Nathan Cole—father of Solomon Cole, the boy to whom Jefferds had once mistakenly handed *Aristotle's Masterpiece* in place of the Old Testament.

Solomon's mother answered the door. Time crept as the expression on her homely face went from surprise to pity, and I saw that she belonged to the small class of Livy's women who were inclined to forgive a young girl's weakness. When I said I wanted to talk to William Jefferds, she fetched him and tactfully left us alone in the sitting room. He asked after my health and my family's health, and at last he said, "Why have you come to me, Arabella?"

In the presence of the good man, I broke down and told everything, except for one thing—I did not tell him about Madame Drunette's Lunar Pills; nor had I told Jeptha about them in the letter.

The top of Jefferds's head had gone completely bald by this time. He wore his stringy hair long at the sides, and with the spectacles he looked like a sort of underfed Benjamin Franklin.

He nodded and murmured sympathetically while I told my story, but was silent for some time afterward. At last I asked, "Mr. Jefferds? What is it?"

He cleared his throat. "Do you have the letter?"

"Yes."

"May I see it?"

From his words, I did not know whether he meant to read it or merely to hold it, but I didn't ask; I just gave it to him. It was a relief to put myself in his hands. He stroked the folded pages and wax seal pensively with his dry little fingers. "You're not looking forward to bringing this letter to Colonel Ashton," he said, looking from the letter to me. I felt his gaze in the new way that I had come to feel people's gazes since my disgrace. "Everyone in the store staring at you. And they would ask the colonel who the letter was addressed to, and he might tell them, or he might not, but he would tell his wife, and she'd talk, and maybe they'd find something wrong in it, and anyway they'd be talking about you again, when you'd hoped the talk had died down." This was rather more than I wanted to hear from him, but it was all accurate. There was no postal box in those days, nor was there any post office in our little town. There was only the general store. The contents of a letter might be private, but everything else about it would be noticed and widely discussed. After a while he said, "I'm writing to Jeptha. I'll include your letter with mine."

I went back to see him every few weeks, giving him more letters, and asking if he had heard. I attended school and bore the stares of my classmates because Jefferds might have wonderful news for me. And one day he summoned me to his desk at the end of class and said: "Jeptha has written. See me in Cole's house."

When I got there, he showed me a page of a long letter. Jeptha had numbered it page 3 on one side and 4 on the reverse. It described the habits of other boarders in the minister's house. There was a part about a girl his age, pious, pretty, and "unspoiled." Then this: "As to Arabella, I ask that you do not write to me about her any more, & I ask that you do not encourage her. I've heard what she has to say, & I've heard what you have to say; I've closed that chapter. She ought to do the same."

After that, I went a little mad. In this, by coincidence, I was not alone.

✣ XXIV ✣

FOR THIS WAS THE YEAR OF FERVENT HOPE, when, all around the country, people were gazing up at the sky, waiting for the world to end. My aunt was among the most passionate believers, convinced that Jesus would come back, as Millerites were learning to say, no later than October 22, 1844. If, so far, she had failed to do her duty by me—failed to turn me into someone she could admire, failed to protect me from Matthew—she could make it all right by saving my soul. Unpleasant as she supposed it must be for me to return to the farm, I must not be left with a family of worldly Presbyterians. She and Elihu went together to Anne and Melanchthon's house to demand that I be returned and have a chance of being saved.

Any day now, it was going to be too late for the doubters. Christ would appear in the sky. The righteous dead would arise in a wondrous spectacle of yawning graves and sprung coffin lids. Skeletons would fly off the shelves of medical schools; scattered atoms would abandon their present work in the stems of flowers and the bellies of worms to reflesh the bones. Living men would be yanked out of the fields they were sowing or threaded spinelessly through windows that had suddenly opened themselves and be lifted to the clouds, while 99 percent of the human race remained below to burn. After certain complications and delays whose purpose is obscure, the saved would enjoy an eternity of bliss in heaven, while the damned were tortured forever in a lake of fire.

Would the saved be happy? If so, surely there would have to be something very wrong with them. We were reminded constantly that husband would be torn from wife, brother from sister, mother from child. When a child has a toothache, the mother suffers with him, yet the saints rejoiced while their children burned. It was hard to imagine such people, so very good, yet disloyal to the profoundest human tie. To save them, God had changed the most essential thing about them. Whom, then, had He saved?

If these paradoxes ever troubled my aunt's meditations, she brushed them aside. She had no choice. She was desperate. Her son had raped her niece, who had then murdered their unborn child. Things were so bad that only the Second Advent could save the family. There would be our happy ending, the sweeter for having come on the heels of despair. She never dared in my presence to call Matthew's crime a blessing in disguise, but that it would be was clearly her fervent hope. He was skulking around the farm in misery. He avoided Lewis. He felt sinful. He was ripe for salvation. The rest of us, whether we knew the ugly secret or merely sensed the wrongness in the house, were unhappy, too: and that, too, she was sure, would bring us all joy in the end.

With the rest of us adrift and rudderless, she bent us to her will. That winter, she dragged us to a big revival meeting in a great hall in Lockport. We were all exposed to the oratorical powers of the celebrated preacher Elon Galusha, himself recently converted to Millerism; one after another, Matthew and Elihu wept for their sins and were saved.

As for me, I did not know what I believed anymore. I wanted not to feel and not to think. I went where I was taken and did as I was told.

As a proof of his conviction, Elihu harvested only so much of the crop as we needed for our own use until the return of Jesus on October 22, 1844. All the pests that are a torment to farmers seemed to realize that a special feast had been prepared for them, and they came in greater numbers than I had ever seen before; whenever I walked through the corn, dozens of startled black crows rose skyward, noisily beating the air.

Lewis was the only one among us who was sure that my aunt was wrong. It was a common sight that year to see him pitching stones at a row of sticks on a log behind the house. Each throw demonstrated his view of the matter. Down they'd come, one after another, and the last stone he threw would be his killing stone, a fragment of the rock he'd killed a pig with from the top of my grandfather's warehouse so long ago.

Sometime in July, I watched from the back porch while Lewis knocked the whole row down. He retrieved the sticks and sat down on the log. I sat beside him. "What's wrong, Lewis?" I said, petting the dog. "Lewis, do you think about Papa much anymore?"

"Get off," he said, and put sticks everywhere on the log, excepting the space I occupied. He walked back to the porch and began once again to throw the stones. One flew over my head. "You want to hurt me, Lewis?" Another. "You don't need stones to hurt me. Lewis, you're the only creature left on this earth who *can* hurt me anymore." I stood up. I spread my arms out. "Go on. Show me what you can do."

He pulled his arm back. I saw what was in his hand. The killing stone.
"Do it," I said. "I want you to."

He pocketed the stone and walked away.

❧ XXV ❧

TUESDAY, OCTOBER 22, 1844, the day the world was to end, dawned cloudy.

The sky was white. There were no shadows. Nature had a washed-out look. Some of the colors had been removed, and I wondered if this was how it would be done. Stealthily, no angels or trumpets, no wrath or judgment—a simple undoing. Things would disappear by categories. First certain colors. Then the fish. On the farm, we wouldn't notice it. Suddenly no birds; we might realize it after a while. Next, plant life vanishes, leaving the dry, brown earth and the rocks and the sky. Small animals and insects, suddenly uncovered, creep over the rocks awhile and then they, too, are gone. God takes our clothes. We're all naked, as we were in Eden. He takes away the air and watches our silent agony. We cannot gasp or beg for mercy. In time, we stop moving. He walks away in despair. Why did He do it? Why, why, why, why, why? He takes a last look at the miniature, the picture of His dead wife, and, crouching for a moment, lays it down on the roof. He rises to his feet, looks over the edge, and jumps.

THE COWS WERE LOWING. They needed relief, so we milked them. To show our faith, we did not use a pail, but let the milk spurt onto the ground.

We bade a solemn farewell to the dogs and the horses and oxen, and then we walked to Anne and Melanchthon's family to urge them one last time to ready themselves. We passed Harmon Chase's house; the whole family was standing on the roof. We passed a churchyard where a crowd had gathered to watch the graves open. On the way back from Melanchthon's farm, where no minds had been changed, it rained, and when we got back, we changed into our second-best clothes. It was chilly. We put logs on the fire and huddled near it. We were profligate with the wood. Soon the sap was sizzling, and the young logs sank abruptly into their cradle of glowing twigs.

Elihu sat on the rocker, sucking bits of his last earthly meal from between his crooked teeth. Lewis sat on a high stool, his hair defiantly uncombed. Matthew's black hair gleamed with grease. The women all looked ready for church. I thought how astonishing it was that every living creature had its own private thoughts and desires and importance.

My aunt kept saying that at the last minute Titus would come.

"We must apologize to each other," she said. "If we have anything on our conscience, any secret wrong, we must confess it and ask each other's forgiveness."

Agnes began, admitting that she had paid Evangeline (in chores and in cash) to put the pebbles in a batch of bread I had made and to thwart me in other ways. "I did it because I could see that from the first you had set your cap for Jeptha, and would do anything to get your way, and I did not know how to save him."

This broke through my protective stupor. "So—you did it to help Jeptha."

"Belle," said my aunt, "please, let Agnes apologize without interruption. Whatever you think she's done to you, forgive her. Don't meet this day with bitterness in your heart."

"I want to forgive her, but her confession has to be complete. Agnes, Titus told me that you defended me against the charge that I was selling my favors to the Harding boys."

"That's right, Belle, I defended you."

"Didn't you start defending me before anyone accused me?" I asked. She looked like a saint on stained glass, but I noticed that my aunt and Evangeline were watching her, too, and perhaps I had made them wonder. As if this were a matter that concerned only women, Lewis, Matthew, and Elihu went on studying the fire.

"I see why you've been angry with me, Belle," said Agnes. "It must be very distressing for you to believe such a thing." My aunt nodded to herself, agreeing.

I looked up, wishing Jesus would lift Lewis and me through the roof and leave the rest of them behind, yelling at Him that He had made an awful mistake.

"Forgive her, Arabella," said my aunt. "Forgive her, for your salvation."

"Suppose I forgive her just for what she's confessed. I can't very well forgive what hasn't been confessed."

"Good," exclaimed my aunt, as if a bargain had been struck, binding no matter what the spirit of it had been, and it was my turn. My confessions were more substantial than Agnes's. "It was I who put Madame Drunette's Lunar Pills in your supper, Agnes. I knew you wouldn't like them. Can you forgive me? You do forgive me, don't you?"

Evangeline confessed that she had let her secret parts be touched almost daily by Lucas, a hired hand who had been with us from haying time in 1841 to the spring of 1842, and she had touched Lucas's secret parts. The other hand, Mike, had found out and threatened to tell if she didn't do bad things with him, too, but she wouldn't, because she didn't love Mike. In the middle of this confession, Elihu began to moan with his head in his hands. Evangeline put her arms around him. He turned away, saying she'd broken his heart. My aunt demanded that they reconcile, and grudgingly he said he would try to forgive her.

Aunt Agatha apologized to me. "I tried to love you for my sister's sake when you first came here, Arabella. But your father's death got between us, and your sharp tongue, and I lost my temper with you." She begged me to forgive her. I said I did.

When it was Matthew's turn, I twisted my hands together as he apologized to his mother for grieving her with his fighting and for showing disrespect to the pastor. At last he said, "Lewis, I have to tell you about me and your sister."

I stood up. "Stop him. That's between him and me."

"Arabella, please," said my aunt.

I pulled my shawl around me and walked out to the yard, where the rain had stopped and a purple evening was settling in regardless of our opinions. The mud was so thick that my steps nearly pulled my shoes off; the wind pushed my skirt against my legs and loosed a spray of water droplets from the leaves of the apple trees. The sun, couched royally in the clouds, shed a ruddy glow on distant fields where the corn had been left for the crows to harvest.

When I came back in, I could see that they had been waiting for me.

"Lewis has forgiven Matthew," said Aunt Agatha.

Had he? I could not read his face. Elihu stared at the ground. Agnes looked unsurprised. Evangeline looked placid, as always. Sometimes I envied Evangeline.

"Lewis," said my aunt, "are you sorry for anything you've done?"

"No, ma'am," said my brother, and he would not say another word.

We sang hymns. We took turns reading from the Bible. Every now and then, one or more of us went outside to look up. It grew dark. We lit lamps. Midnight came and went. Evangeline fell asleep at the table. Lewis went up to bed.

At last it was dawn again; the rooster crowed, the cows lowed, we milked them into buckets, and Aunt Agatha began the washing she'd put off. Uncle Elihu hitched the oxen to the wagon, and the girls accompanied him into the cornfields to search for ears of corn the hogs and the crows had left us. Lewis and Matthew were not on the farm, and Elihu swore (using initials, "D-it to H!"), assuming they had gone into town to amuse themselves. We all worked in silence until well after noon, when we broke for dinner.

A little after we had eaten, a wagon came up the drive. It was the owner of a neighboring farm, Barnabas Welch, and his son Elias. Stretched out on his back on the wagon's floor was Matthew, with two bloody wounds on his head, his right leg broken (so a doctor later determined) twice above the knee and once below it, his left leg broken below the knee, and both kneecaps shattered.

Though Matthew was never able to remember the incident that had crippled him, a note found in his trouser pocket explained a good deal, and I learned more later. Lewis, the night before, had put a note in Matthew's hand that said to meet him at the Muskrat Pond, "if bye sum chans the sun duz us the faver of risin 1 mor time." Matthew, no doubt assuming that he was being challenged to a fight over me, went to the appointment, probably planning to talk Lewis out of it. Though Lewis was formidable for a boy his age, he was no match for Matthew and would have lost a fair fight with him.

It was not a fair fight. As soon as Matthew arrived at the Muskrat Pond, a rock whizzed by his head; and when he turned to see who had thrown it, another rock passed his ear. A third struck him full in the brow;

and when he was still reeling, a blow from the end of a rude club knocked him unconscious. He was woken by the pain, as the same weapon broke bones in his legs, and he lost consciousness again.

Then Lewis departed—"leaving him for dead," everybody put it, but that wasn't accurate. Except for the two that had felled him in the first place, there was not a single blow above mid-thigh. Lewis had done exactly what he had planned to do.

Barnabas's five-year-old daughter, Betty, found Matthew, or perhaps it is truer to say the dog found him, and Betty went over to see what was fascinating the dog. She was startled, but got over it and went on playing for another hour at what she considered a safe distance before she wandered home and happened to remember and told her mother about the scary bloody man she had seen asleep in the woods by the pond.

By this time, Lewis had stolen a horse from another farm; it wandered back to its owner the next morning. My uncle, going to Patavium to fetch a doctor, told the justice of the peace what had happened, and it was soon learned that Lewis had taken a stage to Rochester. A horseman was sent to stop the stage, but Lewis, with a three-hour head start, got to Rochester first, and there the trail went cold. The electric telegraph had been invented that very year. Had it come ten or twenty years earlier, perhaps Lewis would have been caught—or perhaps he would have been shrewd enough to modernize his tactics. For 1844, the ones he used were sufficient.

He had taken his own savings, about fifty dollars, and $130 from the old sock where Matthew kept his money, and twenty dollars from a tea box where my aunt kept hers.

The savagery of these events frightened me. I feared that Lewis would be caught, or killed for the money, or would starve when it ran out. I was afraid that the family's grief and wrath would turn on me as the cause of Lewis's crime and perhaps its instigator, or simply as his sister, available to be punished.

Because of all that, at first I wished that he hadn't done it. Nothing in particular changed my mind. Yet a moment came, a day or two after it happened, when, with the whole house in profound gloom, I began to weep in joy and gratitude.

. . .

TWO WEEKS WENT BY, DURING WHICH we should have starved were it not for Melanchthon, whose wagon came up the dirt road daily. On one of those trips he said, "Let me talk to Arabella alone." Agatha and Elihu left us, Elihu taking with him the smoldering, stupid hate that had been his predominant mood ever since Matthew's broken body had been brought back to the farm. ("Why did we ever take them in?" was his constant refrain now.)

We went into the kitchen, where we both sat on straight-backed chairs, and Melanchthon rocked his chair back onto two of its legs. When he was thinking, he had a habit of pinching his nose. "Went to Rochester last week," he began. "Went there about some wheat, but I had you in mind. Had a talk with a man there about you."

He waited, smiling falsely. I looked at his big ears and eyebrows and enigmatic buttonhole eyes. He was one of those men who are always genial, not because they love everybody, or because they are afraid of a fight, but because they are game players and see no advantage in showing their emotions. At last I said, "Oh? What about me?"

As if he were revealing a wonderful surprise, he said, "A job! The man was a mill agent, you see, for the Harmony Manufacturing Company in Cohoes, which is a canal town near Albany. You passed through it on the way to Livy when you first came here. They have a big falls. Do you remember it?"

"I don't think so."

"Guess it's a long time ago for you. Anyway, they make cloth, with machinery, and young farm girls mind the machines, and they want twenty new girls. I asked the man, what's it like at your factory, and he said, well, had I ever heard of Lowell, it was like Lowell. Did you ever hear of Lowell, Arabella?"

"Yes."

I had read about the Lowell mills in Mrs. Harding's copy of Charles Dickens's *American Notes*. The fame of Massachusetts's cotton mills had reached Dickens before he left England. They were regarded as a social experiment. The mill girls—healthy, unspoiled, well paid—lived in clean boarding houses supervised by respectable matrons. In the sitting room, where there was a piano, the girls read books from a circulating library. They went to lectures given by famous transcendentalists and phrenologists. They produced a literary magazine. They were a rebuke to British manufacturing, with its subhuman proletariat doomed to toil a lifetime on a diet of gruel and gin.

I told Melanchthon some of this. He said he had little time for reading, but it sounded like Mr. Dickens had given a favorable report of conditions at Lowell, and, well, the Harmony Manufacturing Company in Cohoes had been started with the example of the Lowell mills before it, and was run along similar lines, paying the same handsome wage. If I didn't like it, I could always come back here.

"I could always come back," I echoed him, trying to imagine that. Not yet sure how I felt about Melanchthon's proposal, I heard myself ask, "When would I go?" As soon as the words were out of my mouth, I knew I wanted it to be that very day.

Book Three

{ 1844–1849 }

Book Three

XXVI

ONE RAINY DAY IN THE 1880s, ON THE VERANDA of a Western hotel where I had nothing to do but develop an appetite for dinner, I happened to pick up a two-year-old copy of *Frank Leslie's Illustrated Newspaper*. My eyes were drawn to a line in the table of contents; soon I was reading with deep emotion. The article told what had become of the three daughters of Thomas McCormick, owner of Harmony Mills in Cohoes, New York, who had died before his children were grown. It seemed that they had all married titled aristocrats, becoming the Marchioness de Bretevil, Lady Gordon Cumming, and the Countess de Miltke. The cost of the jewels, the number of the servants, the acreage of lawn around the three stately mansions—the author breathlessly imparted this information; then, in a queer little spasm of socialism, and with amazing ignorance of modern manufacturing, he noted that the fortune that had purchased the names of three impecunious foreign noblemen had been "spun by the nimble fingers of immigrant factory girls."

He also mentioned the other famous thing about Cohoes, the mastodon skeleton found there in 1866, when the foundations of Harmony Mill No. 3 were dug. Beside photogravures of the heiresses, their homeliness testifying to the majesty of Harmony Manufacturing, was a picture of the mastodon.

Did I want to show the magazine to the ladies fanning themselves and nursing iced drinks beside me; did I think of saying, "I used to work at that mill"? Did I imagine their reactions? I don't recall. Probably I just laid the newspaper in my lap and let the memories return. They come readily enough now. I remember walking on the high ground. I must have walked hundreds of times over the hidden fossils. Tall, slim poplars shimmered whenever breezes turned their double-hued leaves. Men were fishing with poles and nets. I could hear the honks of geese. I could hear the mighty rush of the falls, audible all over town to anyone standing out of doors. That is, I could hear it when I first arrived, but later, after many days at the factory, I heard only the noise from the system of shafts and belts that transmitted water power to the looms. Even when the wheels had been disengaged I heard them. It would take half of Sunday for the hallucination to fade, and when I laid my head on the Harmony Manufacturing Company's pillow, in a room I shared with seven other women, in the bed I shared with one of them, I'd start hearing it again in anticipation of Monday. I'd hear them even amid the whimpers and hastening breaths of my bedmate, little Jocelyn—pleasing herself, under the counterpane, in blithe indifference to anyone's opinion.

In my time, the factory girls were all natives, mostly farm girls from New England and upstate New York. Jocelyn arrived after I had been at the mill for about three months. When I first saw her, she was stepping from the rear of a covered wagon owned by the Harmony Manufacturing Company, which owned almost everything in Cohoes. Her arms held a cloth-covered bandbox that contained all her possessions. Onto the bandbox her mother had sewn a card with the name "Martha Hale," for that was Jocelyn's name then. She wore a gingham dress, yellow with green dots. She was pretty, and beginning to have a shape, but small for her age, fourteen. She struck me as very much on her own in the world, and I could not have been more correct: among the paltry collection of personal oddments in her bandbox was a legal paper which bore the signature of her mother, declaring that she was "emancipated," and didn't have to give her wages to anyone, and no one had to support her. Soon after arriving in Cohoes, Martha had made a discovery made by many another American girl from the country: that she could change her name for the cost of mailing a letter to the state legislature, and after being assured that it would not undo her emancipation, she took the name Jocelyn, which I had suggested. I had read it in a novel.

Not all the girls shared their beds. I had been asked when I first arrived whether I would be willing to, and I had said yes. It was a small imposition, and in any case I did not care very much what happened to me in those days. There were only two people in the world whom I loved—Lewis, a fugitive, who might be dead for all I knew, and Jeptha, whom I tried fruitlessly to forget. It was a relief to be among strangers. In my best mood, I was a mildly curious spectator of my own life, wondering what would happen to me next. They put the new girl with me, and the light had hardly been put out when she began to touch herself. I grunted to show that I was awake, and that I considered her behavior unseemly. She went on. I grunted again. She went on; I did not care enough to make more of a fuss than that, and she simply could not be embarrassed. She had no more shame or conscience than a cat.

I grew to appreciate this quality in Jocelyn. I had been involved, from the moment I went to live at my uncle's farm, in an endless argument as to whether I was a good girl, whether I was hardworking and dutiful or lazy and envious, and whether I was being judged fairly. At the mill, no one knew of my reputation in Livy, but most of the girls, or at least many, would have shunned me if they ever did find out. I knew from the very first that Jocelyn would not have cared about any of that, and when at last I told her—when I was sure she would keep a secret whose gravity she was unable to feel—there was great relief for me in the telling. She responded by telling me of how she had lost her virginity in her home-town, to a much older boy.

She did not strike me as stupid, but she could barely read, and in conversation it developed that she didn't know that rivers empty into the oceans, or that the earth was round, or that there were more foreign-ers in it than Americans; she had never heard of Julius Caesar or Wil-liam Shakespeare or Thomas Jefferson. Since she was careless, when I was around her I felt wise and prudent. I felt responsible for her.

Jocelyn said that her father had been a teamster in Pennsylvania, regu-larly carrying beer to Philadelphia, and he used to take her along. Then he died in a terrible accident. The horses, frightened by the cracking of a walnut board while he was loading baggage, ran wild, and he was crushed by the wheels and caught by his belt and dragged along the highway for half a mile. His fellow teamsters helped her mother open a little store, where she sold candy, bread, kindling wood, and so on. The family lived in a back room. They took in washing and sewing and made straw hats, and still they had nothing. One day, a neighbor showed them an adver-tisement for millworkers. Jocelyn and her mother both applied, but her mother was rejected because she was blind in one eye.

This was the story she told me first. A few weeks later, she admitted that her father was alive. He'd gotten better work in New Jersey, where he remarried without bothering to obtain a divorce. He had never taken

Jocelyn to Philadelphia. But someone had, it seemed to me. She was well informed about the city's amusements.

She had come to me, this foolish pet, this empty-headed friend, about two weeks after I had received a terrible letter about Jeptha. It came from Anne, and it began with an apology for the pain she was about to inflict on me. Jeptha had married Grace, the minister's pretty, unspoiled daughter in New Jersey. I remember holding this letter in my hand in the sitting room, and then finding myself upstairs, facedown on the hair mattress, crying my heart out, as though I had dematerialized in one place and reappeared in another.

As much as I had grieved before, I had never thought I'd seen the last of Jeptha. And as you will learn, I had not. I write it here out of kindness, so you need not despair with me. But you must remember that I didn't know this. I acted in the belief that we were separated forever, and I would never be accountable to him for my actions. Had I known the truth, I would have behaved with more discretion.

A WEEK AFTER THAT, I RECEIVED a letter in Lewis's hand, addressed to me in the care of the Harmony Manufacturing Company. It was posted from Rome, a town on the Erie Canal, about a hundred miles west of Cohoes.

Dear Arabella,

Sorry I had to leave without saying good-by & cood not get you "news" befor. I hope I did not worry you to much. I am also sorry about Matthew not the sad thing that got done to him so I heer but that it did not get done much sooner. If you wood of told me it wood of got done sooner. In case you wonder I got your adres from paying a suprise visit to sumbody we know in Patavium. Rite now all my visits must be suprise. I will come to see you but just when I cant say. In the meen time do not worry about me. I am keeping body & soul to-gether by doing this & that. I toed a canal boat. I did ice mining on a lake. I cleerd a field for a farmer who cheeted me but later he sed he was sorry. Sum other jobs came my way wich I will tell you about by & by. I have made sum frends & am not in trubel. Dont tell anyone you got a leter frum me. I will visit when I can.

Yr devoted brother,
Lewis

Where had he picked up such a fancy closing—"devoted brother"? Maybe he had gotten someone's help. I loved those words: "devoted brother"—*devoted*. There had been two more letters since, both promising visits, both vague about the nature of his occupations. They were sacred to me.

BEFORE DAWN A FACTORY BELL WOKE US. Most of us had grown up on farms and were used to working before breakfast. But this part was new: emerging from our boarding house under dimming stars to join other streams of half-dreaming girls summoned as if by an enchantment to the several doors of the long high brick factory building across the street. By five a.m. we had assumed our various duties in the picking room, the carding room, the spinning room, the weaving room, the cloth room. At seven the bells rang again; we ran back to our various boarding houses for breakfast. Mine was served under the supervision of Mrs. Robinson, a big, fleshy, red-faced woman, almost six feet tall, a widow, and a generous cook, whatever other complaints we had, we did not starve. We had to be back by seven thirty-five. Dinner—with its own bell—was from noon to twelve-thirty, also at the boarding house. Mrs. Robinson made hard-boiled eggs that we could carry with us if we had not had time to fill our stomachs.

As it had been discovered that dry air causes threads to snap, the windows of the weaving room were never opened and steam was pumped in through pipes, and it was always warm and damp. Cotton fibers flew into our throats and lungs. Despite these discomforts, the thing that made the strongest impression on me was the amazing regularity of the place. The one room ran the whole length of the building. We saw the long rows of pillars, the farthest diminishing in apparent size as perfectly as in books that teach drawing. A rotating shaft over each identical loom helped turn a barrel-like cylinder. A black band around each cylinder ran to the loom, somehow causing it to open and close, open and close, while the shuttle flew between the threads, and we mill girls, dressed alike the better to illustrate rules of linear perspective, watched the perfect manufacture of our identical seconds, minutes, and hours. When the falls ran dry, causing the machines to stop, and we left the mill to stroll through the impressive natural scenery of the Mohawk Valley, it was like being woken from dreams too strange for the waking mind to grasp.

At the seven o'clock, evening bell, we went back to the company-owned boarding house, had supper, and did as we pleased until ten, when, by company law, we had to be in bed. We were permitted to go out, but Cohoes was not a lively town, so we spent our few hours of leisure in a large room furnished to resemble the sitting room in a home more prosperous than those from which any of us had come. We played games, drew, made clothes, wrote in diaries. Unbelievably, some girls knitted. I read to Jocelyn from *Godey's Lady's Book* and memorized passages from a cheap one-volume copy of Byron's works, with tiny type in two columns per page.

We were expected to go to church. Jocelyn and I chose the Cohoes Presbyterian Church. It had the most comfortable pews for the price, good heating and ventilation. On Saturday afternoons, young Reverend Adams gave lectures on the terrible vice of self-abuse, an epidemic of which was filling America's insane asylums with madmen, its hospitals with consumptives, and its brothels with girls exactly like us.

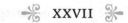

XXVII

ONE DAY, WHEN I WAS IN THE WEAVING ROOM, minding my three looms, I became aware of a stir, an additional alertness among the other operatives. A stern-looking senior clerk was walking in my direction. "Arabella Moody?" he inquired.

"Yes," I said.

"A man is asking for you. He says he's your brother."

An overseer took charge of my machines, and I was allowed to take a half-hour off. I went to the counting house, which was where I went once a week to collect my wages; and there, to my joy, I found Lewis waiting for me. He had a cigar butt in his mouth, which he removed and tossed with careless accuracy into a distant spittoon. We embraced hungrily. Then we stood holding each other at arm's length, to give our eyes the pleasure. In the six months since I had last seen him, he had grown taller and leaner, and he was dressed and groomed in a way that would set him apart from any man in Livy or Cohoes; he had a plug hat, under which his hair was cut very short behind, but long and greasy and puffed out at the sides. These side locks were made to curl forward, in front of the ears, with the help of soap. He wore black broadcloth trousers, which vanished into high-heeled boots; an open tailcoat; a woolen shirt with a bright-orange silk cravat.

I introduced him to the clerks in the counting house, "This is my brother Lewis," I told them proudly. The clerks nodded with wary expressions, and I could tell that they disliked him, resenting the clothes, the hair, even the posture. As I came to understand later, it was the outfit of the New York City "Bowery Boy." That Lewis should be so dressed and groomed was especially odd: since as our conversation progressed I learned that he had not been to New York City during our separation.

We went down the dark, winding stairs and out of the factory. I made him stand on the side of me nearest the street and walk arm in arm with me. "Well, what have you been doing, Lewis? How have you been surviving?"

"One thing and another. I been traveling with somebody."

I have not troubled myself with exact reproduction of people's speech in this memoir; but what Lewis said was really more like this: "One t'ing 'n' anudda," and "I been travelin' wit' sumbuddy." He spoke in the dialect now considered the accent of New York's lower strata, and then as the specific accent of the Bowery.

"Oh? Who?"

"Tom Cross. We met up in Lockport"—he said "Lockpawt"—"and we've been doing this and doing that and getting jobs on the canal and the farms around here. He's a grand fella, Tom is. He's done a thousand things—you'll get a kick out of him. He's from York. We're staying at the Cohoes Inn. He's dying to meet you."

He waited outside while I went into the boarding house. Mrs. Robinson was on her fat white knees, washing the stairs with her great hanging arms and a bucket, her hair pasted to her neck and brow from sweat; from her two talkative grown daughters, who helped in the boarding house and slept in our room, I had learned that she was the widow of a housepainter, who had succumbed to an illness she called "painter's colic" after lingering a year in bed. Her strange manner and physical appearance had frightened me when I first arrived: I did not know what to make of her big, shapeless, sweaty, sour-smelling body, and her bulging eyes, always startled and distracted, as if staring at some horror she alone could see—maybe her husband's illness and the financial ruin it caused. She had nine children in all, some living with relatives, some others, boys and girls, working at the mill.

I asked her if my brother and a friend could visit us for supper. "So long as they act like gentlemen," she replied, and as usual the thoughts behind her bulging eyes were unreadable. I wanted her to think well of me. It was foolish, but there it was.

TOM WAS A LITTLE LARGER THAN LEWIS, and ten years older, blue-eyed, with brown hair and a prominent Adam's apple, which, when he drained a glass of water, the mill girls watched as if it were a circus acrobat. His overall good looks were marred by a crooked little scar that ran from his temple to his right eye. The real Tom resided in that scar. He was dressed in an outfit much like the one Lewis wore. Under his coat, which he kept on at supper, he wore the tight-fitting red woolen shirt of the volunteer fire department. As a member of Engine Company 9, he had put out many fires; until almost a year ago he was led north by the love of adventure and the opportunity of helping a pal (Tom's stories were liberally punctuated with offhand references to unnamed pals). He had been kicking around here, doing manly work on the canal, ever since.

He was voluble, though not always believable, on other subjects: lives and property he had saved, brawls with other fire companies, times he and his pals had defended the honest working women of New York against insulting advances from aristocratic dandies.

He reminded me of Matthew; a more cosmopolitan Matthew from New York. I wondered if Lewis had ever noted the resemblance.

I suppose it was pleasant for a sturdy young fellow to sit down to sup-per at a long table surrounded by man-starved young mill girls. Lewis's and Tom's plates were heaped high. The girls listened raptly to their stories of life on the big freight boats, and of all the "scraps" they had gotten in between Albany and Buffalo. Whenever the boys' big gestures threatened to overturn pitchers or candlesticks, a girl sitting nearby would uncomplainingly rescue these items.

One story struck an unpleasant note: The two of them, adding details and correcting each other, told how, a few months ago, in Rome, they had wanted to get a job together as freight-boat drivers. They befriended two drivers, took them to a tavern, and stood them to many drinks. When these two fellows were corned so badly the last trump wouldn't have woken them, Lewis and Tom showed up for work in their place. Concluding his story, Tom speared a potato with his knife and thrust it whole into his mouth.

And he thought this was something to brag about! It hurt me. I said, "I can't help feeling sorry for those men. Some people would say that was a dirty trick."

Tom, chewing and swallowing hurriedly, said, "Well, sure, yeah, we wouldn't have done it if we hadn't known what those men were like. We did it after I saw the way they was treating the team—ain't that so, Lewis?"

"Oh yeah."

"They was killing them. They just laid on the whip. They wasn't fed right."

"We saved those creatures' lives," Lewis agreed.

Another sour note came when they were praising each other's fight-ing abilities. Tom said, "Lewis looks nice, but he can do harm if he's of a mind to. He's a killer."

Lewis was opposite from me at the table; I saw the smile vanish, then return as a hardened mask of itself. He flashed a look at Tom, who winked.

One girl, who knew that firefighting is an unpaid profession, asked Tom what he did for a living back in New York City. After a brief hesi-tation, he said he was a journeyman butcher. It was a trade that com-manded a good wage, he assured us, and considerable respect in the Bowery, where much of the city's butchering was done.

"What do you do for fun around here?" asked Tom after we had retired to the sitting room, and he and Lewis were looking around for the first time at its grandmotherly wallpaper, rag carpets, framed samplers, big stuffed chairs and sofas.

After a silence, a girl name Rosaline asked, "Would you like to play a game of checkers, or backgammon?"

Tom laughed. "I meant in Cohoes. When you want to get out of this stuffy room. Where do you go for a glass of beer? Where do you go for fun?"

"We ain't much for fun," said Barbara, who had arrived in Cohoes the week after I did: they had cut her braids off because of the risk that they might be caught in the machinery. She had cried bitterly over those braids, but their sacrifice had made her into a company girl. "We've got to save our money."

Barbara had more than the usual suspicion of idle amusement. But none of us were supposed to like it; we were of New England stock.

"Sure, that's smart. But don't the boys here take you out and spend their money on you?"

We had a pretty correct idea of what boys who spent money on girls wanted in return, and those of us who weren't shocked felt obliged to pretend we were.

"When boys come, they visit us in the sitting room, as you are doing. There isn't much of that, though. Mostly we read or sew."

"Sometimes we rent a rowboat and go on the river," volunteered Jocelyn.

Well, one could, but we never did. During the rare daylight hour not spent in the mill or at church, we packed a lunch and walked by the river. We watched the canal boats being loaded, and the men working the locks.

"You gals are wasting your lives," said Tom.

"Would you like a game of checkers?" Rosaline repeated her offer.

"New York has spoiled me for checkers," said Tom.

Behind me, I heard Lewis ask Jocelyn, "Would you go out on a boat with me?"

I heard her say, "Maybe."

"Who else wants to come?" said Lewis.

"You asked *me*!" said Jocelyn.

"But you only said maybe. Say you'll go and no mistake."

"All right."

"All right, what?"

"All right, I'll go with you."

"Good," said Lewis, laughing in a helpless, uncontained way, like a boy. "Who else is coming?"

"You're bad," said Jocelyn. "I knew it. You're no good at all."

"You're right," Lewis admitted. "I spend all my pay soon as I get it. I fight and I cuss. I take all the girls on boat rides and I try to kiss them."

"I knew it," said Jocelyn. "I knew you was bad."

I felt a pang of jealousy and couldn't have told you whom or what I was jealous of—I suppose I wanted them both to love me and not each other. But I could see they made a sort of sense together; they were very alike.

"A rowboat is all right if you're used to checkers, I guess," said Tom, and he started to tell the mill girls of the plentiful and cheap amusements of the Bowery, already known then as the workingman's Broadway. He spoke of firehouse balls; oyster saloons offering "all you can eat" for six cents; ice-cream saloons; pleasure gardens; plays, baseball games, dime museums. In the warm weather, there were steamboat trips in the East River and ferry rides to Long Island; picnics in New Jersey and Staten Island. If you didn't like spending money, just watching the people promenading in their finery up and down Bowery was a thrill. They were *all* spoiled for checkers, all the Bowery Boys and Bowery Gals. Pretty girls, such as we all were, did not need to pay for anything, but if they were the independent type, why, most of them were wage earners and didn't have to take any guff from anybody.

That's where Lewis and Tom were headed. They were on their way to New York City, where Tom would resume his work as a butcher and Lewis would start as an apprentice. "Anyone who wants to come with us is welcome."

Some tittered, as if he were joking. Others took offense, explaining frostily that we were girls of hard-nosed Yankee stock who labored not for a day's amusement but for a dowry, or a home to start our married lives in, or to pay for a clever brother's education. No doubt it was tedious of us, but we were rather inclined to worry that such shortsighted expenditures would lead a girl in time to the almshouse.

"Oh, the almshouse," said Tom. "I don't know about that. Not while we're young." With a smile of conspiracy, he looked past the prudent girls to the fools.

I suppose we all had a little more trouble sleeping that night. Certainly Jocelyn and I did, watching the slow-dying glow through the grate of the heating stove.

"Let's go with them," she whispered.

"You don't know what you're saying. We'd wind up on the streets."

"How do you know that? You sound like Barbara. We'd find work. You heard him. Girls work in New York, and they have money to spend on oyster cellars and ferries."

"We don't know anything about those girls. Can't you see that that Tom is a bad egg? You can't trust him."

"Your brother trusts him."

"I wish he didn't. I'm going to warn him about Tom, as soon as I get him alone."

After a bit more time had passed, I thought she had gone to sleep, and I drifted off to confused dreams of Tammany parades, beach picnics, beer gardens, and dime museums. I woke abruptly to the voice of Jocelyn whispering, "I'm dying here. I hate it. I can't stand it. The cotton fly is giving me consumption. Do you want me to die? I can't stand the wet air, the heat, the same thing day in, day out. Maybe reading Byron and *Godey's Lady's Book* is your idea of a good time, but that won't do for me." I saw she meant to hurt me, but I kept my peace. "If we go to New York, we can work as dressmakers."

"It takes years to become a dressmaker. You start out as an apprentice. Do you know how to make a dress?"

"I can sew."

"Who can't? That's what the good widows do in the newspaper stories, the worthy old widows everyone pities, who freeze in the cellars without the shrift to buy a lump of coal for the stove. They sew shirts; they starve."

"I won't starve," said Jocelyn lightly. "I know how not to starve."

I knew what she meant. She had dropped one hint after another. The moment I first understood had passed without notice. She hadn't lost her virginity in a careless frolic with a boy. She had given herself for gain—not every day, just occasionally, for dollars, and for steak dinners and trips to the city. Though she had been slow to reveal it to me, she wasn't ashamed. It was just the way she managed; she kept it a secret only because of the fuss other people would make.

It is hard to remember how strenuously I resisted the knowledge that Jocelyn had been a prostitute—or, rather, that, as I thought then, she *was* a prostitute, for certainly, once you had prostituted yourself, you were a prostitute forever, and it was the main thing you were from then on. Is the mark invisible? Invisible marks cannot be erased. You can never think the same about someone after you learn she has been a prostitute. If she stops, she is a former prostitute, just as a man who was once in prison is an ex-convict. If she reforms, which is more than stopping, a stale odor of repentance hangs over her until she goes to meet her Maker, with the final disposition of her case still in doubt.

Honest women shun prostitutes. Even if we view prostitutes as unfortunates rather than as sinners, they are unclean, and they ought to keep away from respectable women. My fondness for Jocelyn outweighed these feelings, and I could not wish we hadn't met, but I believed that, without intending to, she had contaminated me.

Certainly I did not want her to return to that trade. "All right, then," I said. "Here's what we'll do. We'll be smart about it. From now on, in the evenings, we'll practice fine sewing and dressmaking. We'll make clothes out of *Godey's Lady's Book*. We'll practice until we're good enough to offer ourselves as dressmaker's apprentices in New York. And in the meantime, we'll visit now and then. We'll try to get positions before we move. If we must, we'll get positions as help. It would be less money, and we wouldn't be together, but maybe it would be worth it to live in New York City."

On Sunday, after church, Tom and Lewis took Jocelyn and me out boating on the Mohawk. The falls roared, seabirds shrieked; Tom boasted. I watched water purl around the oar, and thought: Dressmakers, why not.

We ate—the boys paid—at a tavern near the locks, got back in the boat, and rowed to the shelter of a pretty channel. A breeze combed the water; green leaves, blown off the branches, glided twirling down as their reflections rose twirling upward to meet them; tiny fish darted among the slimy rocks in the drifting shadow of the boat. Jocelyn let Lewis kiss her. As a sort of experiment, to see how I would feel, I let Tom kiss me. His kisses were subtler than his speech, and were not unpleasant. But when his hand reached under my skirt, I pulled away with an unthinking gasp, the boat rocked, and Jocelyn cried out, having banged her head. Tom glanced at Lewis, perhaps remembering that he was my brother, and for the rest of the afternoon had the surliness of a man who has been cheated out of half the price of a boat rental, a plate of chicken and corn fixings, and a sarsaparilla.

Lewis and Tom said that they would be staying at the Cohoes Inn till Wednesday; we would have until then to decide whether we would go with them to New York.

Monday came, the factory bell woke us; we rose in the dark and walked across the gravel street to the long brick factory; I went to the weaving room and Jocelyn went to the picking room. When the seven o'clock bell rang and I crossed the street again to get my breakfast, Jocelyn wasn't at the table. I was worried, but not worried enough. I thought she was with Tom or Lewis. Noon came; still no Jocelyn.

When I came home for supper, one of the girls handed me a message from Lewis.

Deer Arabella,

Don't be mad at us. We are taken Jos to New York. She cant stand it heer. She ses you will cum wuns we get setled & you see we are doing peachy. Dont fret I wil rite agen by & by.

Yr devoted brother,
Lewis

ALONE ON MY HAIR-STUFFED MATTRESS, I lay thinking and fretting, my eyes open in the darkness; in the weaving room, rushing to straighten the threads that had gotten tangled, I worried; and when I came back to the sitting room, I missed Jocelyn and was simply lonely. But what could I do? She had gone of her own free will with my devoted brother and his friend.

A week and a half later, a letter arrived.

Deer Arabella,

Took a steembote to York and got heer in a day. Gang of boys tride
to steel our luggege had to get tuff with them. Jos is a wonderful
gal. Tom and I almost came to blos over her but she sed wel
never mind ther was no fite thanks to Jos. Met Tom's pals in fire
compny 9. Saw plays at the Chathem and the Park. Tom sez it cood
take time to get jobs so we R staying cheep in 5 Poynts. It is not as
bad as they say. Our address is 65 Mott Street. I do not think letters
cum here, so dont rite yet.

Yr devoted brother
Lewis

Another week, another letter:

Dear Arabella,

You wer rite about Tom. Hees a bad egg and a theef wen we meet
agen I wil teech him. He stole my mony and Joses mony and he
tride to make out like it was sumbody else. Jos left 2 days after Tom
then she came bak to take me owt for a feed and giv me mony. She
had lots of mony and a dres. I was skard to ask where she got it but
she came rite out and sed it was in a bawdee hows. She wood not
say wich one. I was working in a grogshop until I cawt up with Tom
we fawt he nifte me. I cant work—to sick. Im at 160 Anthony. Cant
hardlee leev my bed. Dont want to worry you but I think I mite be
dying.

Lewis

"Nifte." What was that? "We fawt he nifte me." I read the sentence
three times before I understood. Tom Cross had cut my brother with
a *knife*, badly enough so that he could not work, and when he said he
might be dying, it could be the plain truth. He was sick, maybe from the
wound's festering, and he lay in some miserable hole in a district whose

reputation I remembered from my girlhood as the gate of hell—a place no one I knew would dare to enter unaccompanied by a policeman. And Jocelyn: in a bawdy house, probably not far from where Lewis lay. I will not dwell on my feelings. I had to go to New York.

I went to the counting house to tell them that I had to be absent for a while—I knew that sometimes girls were given leave to visit parents, even to help with a harvest—but I was told that this was a busy time and it was impossible. I asked to speak to Thomas McCormick, the manager and owner; I said that I was determined to go, and hoping for sympathy I explained the circumstances. I begged him: "I must; I have no choice, Mr. McCormick."

McCormick, who had seemed awkward but kindly in our one or two brief previous conversations, was a different man that day. He wished me to know that, whatever I might think, mill owners were not defenseless against unreliable girls like me. They had a list, which they circulated among themselves; if I left now, I would go on that list and never be hired at a knitting mill or a weaving mill again.

I begged, argued, and wept, to no avail. I stood numbly beside him while he instructed the clerks to give me the forty-three dollars I had managed to save after the money deducted from room and board and the money sent home to Agatha and Elihu, plus the nine dollars owed to me from this month's salary less room and board.

When I returned back to the boarding house to pack, Mrs. Robinson was there with her daughter Amanda. So that we might be alone, she sent her daughter to go clean one of the downstairs rooms. Then she asked me if I had been crying; I told her yes, and why.

"Oh, the bastard," she said. "It was nothing to him and everything to you. Oh, damnit. The rotten bastard."

I had always wondered what she thought of me, and her ready sympathy for my predicament, her certainty that I had done nothing to deserve it, surprised and touched me. After an instant of hesitation, I embraced her shapeless, overworked body. She patted my head, and murmured soothingly for some seconds. When we separated, she asked, "What will you do now?"

"I still have to go on the same errand as I had before, and I guess then I'll look for a job. Maybe at another mill."

She nodded. "You can try, but I should tell you, what he said was true:

when a girl is dismissed for cause, the mill agents put her on a list that circulates to all the cloth mills. You'd better find work in a factory in New York, or as a housemaid there. It's not so bad being a servant when you're young, if you have a good employer. Do you have anyone to go with you down the river?"

"No, Mrs. Robinson. It's been too short notice."

"I wish you didn't have to go alone. A young girl traveling by herself, it gives people the wrong idea. Men: there are men who would try to take advantage of that. But since you must go alone, I have something for you. You won't be coming back, so I've got to sell it to you." She left the room and returned a few minutes later with a leather pouch, from which she removed an object that had been wrapped in several layers of cloth and newspaper and twine. After a full minute of suspenseful unwrapping, it was revealed to be a pocket pistol.

"It was my husband's," she said. "He won it in a card game. He never used it except once or twice, to test it, and I'm sure I'll never use it myself. I can't give it to you: it's like money to me, I've pawned it three times already. But I think you had better buy it, since you're going to York and, at that, to Five Points, where you'll be cheek to jowl with niggers and Irishmen and God only knows what other thieving, murdering scum that sleep in their own filth and kill each other for a dollar."

I didn't want a gun. I could not imagine using it. But I responded to her concern for my welfare, and I didn't want to say no to her. "Thank you, Mrs. Robinson."

"Don't thank me. I'm selling it."

"Thank you anyway. How much?"

"Look at it first," she said irritably. Hiding my reluctance, I took her little killing machine into my hands. It was an English-made pistol of the type known as a "pepper-box revolver" because of the rotating barrel, which was on the front. When you pulled the trigger, the barrel turned and the gun cocked itself. "It's not accurate," Mrs. Robinson warned me. "But it didn't take poor Joe's hand off, and I guess it won't take yours. You ought to keep it loaded, so you can scare them off with a shot."

After making sure the barrels were empty, she encouraged me to pull the trigger, and she showed me how to load it. Again I asked her the price.

"Ten dollars."

I took it on trust that the price was fair, and I supposed I could sell the gun when I was sure that I would never need it. And perhaps, if someone tried to hurt me, I would point it at them and the threat would be enough. I counted out the coins, but when I reached for the gun, she stopped me—"Wait!"—and gave me back half the money. "You were supposed to Jew me down. What a baby you are. Oh, and here's another box of bullets."

Later, as an afterthought, she warned me against men who would try to help me; I should be careful. They might seem merely kind at first, then, later, demand a recompense that no honest girl could give. I must not take money from them. I must not be alone with them. I was very pretty, she observed, and that added to the danger, but some men even took advantage of young girls who were not pretty. She knew.

XXVIII

SO ONCE MORE I WAS ON THE HUDSON, this time heading south, to the city of my birth. I was worried about my brother and my friend and my future, and I had no real plan, yet I felt strangely equal to the situation, for no other reason than that I was young and strong, and I was thriftily determined to enjoy this little trip, which I had paid for with my own money, earned with the work of my own hands.

The steamboat, the *Israel Putnam,* was like a floating hotel, with more people on it than inhabited the town of Livy. Since the word "saloon" in those days still conveyed a sense of luxury and gentility, there was a "gentlemen's saloon," a "ladies' saloon," a "dining saloon," and, for the men, a "shaving saloon" as well as a barroom; there were flying pennants, and two great smokestacks, and people of varying stations in life, most of them friendly and talkative, happy to be of the race of travelers now, whatever they were at other times. All were eager to explain themselves, like actors in some simply written drama. "I'm a merchant on a buying trip," a man would say, as a bearded child in a school play might brandish a trident and announce, "I'm Neptune, King of the Deep."

I made three male acquaintances and had every meal at the same table with them, the first time by accident, the other times by design. We sat by the window, to my left the boats and birds and mountains, and to my right a taciturn, gray-headed Yankee corn-dealer, stiff and straight, who spoke very little but sat with us every time.

The other two men, facing me, evidently knew each other, but it was not clear how far back their acquaintance went. Both were well dressed and, as their conversation soon established, rich. I judged them to be in their thirties. Their names were Eric Gordon and Charles Cora. Eric Gordon was handsome, with straight black hair, smooth white skin, and a big chin. He said he was the manager and part-owner of a celebrated New York City dry-goods store, and was on his way back from a business trip to Rochester and Utica and other canal cities. His home was in Brooklyn, but he kept a separate residence at the Astor House, where his business required that he stay for a few days each week—had I ever heard of the Astor House? I allowed that I had. Had I ever been there? I told him no. Oh, Eric Gordon said, I *must* go there. It was a grand place! I must dine there as his guest one evening soon after we arrived in New York.

I knew that many mill girls—Barbara, for example—would have taken great offense at the suggestion that they should let a strange man buy them a dinner costing more than a mill girl's monthly wage, and they would have made it known in some well-bred way; and I wished I could think of one. I wondered whether the stiff-looking matrons a few tables away had overheard, and, if so, what they thought of me now.

He didn't pursue the subject, but perhaps by not speaking I had given him a tacit permission to continue. When the menu was passed around and oysters were on it, he said he would not have them, for soon he would be dining in the Park Row Oyster Palace, on oysters the size of a dessert plate—had I ever eaten oysters like that? And when I said no, he said it was a crime that I hadn't, I must have them, and he would see to it that I got them. I said I would probably be too busy. That was wrong, he said. While we were young, we must make time for enjoyment. And he listed a series of New York's temptations, some already named by Tom Cross. How well the women of New York dressed. How well those styles would suit me. "Isn't that so, Mr. Cora?"

Every so often, with words like these, he would ask his companion to back him up on some point. Mr. Cora—I will call him Cora now, though he became Charley to me later—was a few years older, and not as handsome; he was slim, with curly black hair, dark eyes, and an Italian accent. He was ordinary-looking, except for a certain watchful self-possession that one noticed in him after a while. He had the table manners of a farmer, conveying food to his mouth with his knife, but all his movements had such economy and precision that they seemed civilized in their own way. When Eric Gordon solicited his opinion, Cora would say that he had to agree, I would look good in the fashions of the day. When Eric Gordon mentioned a restaurant where some wonderful dish was to be had, sometimes Cora would chime in with a comment drawn from his own experiences of the city's delights. But he seemed simply to be making conversation, whereas when Eric Gordon spoke I knew that a practiced fisherman was at work, and I was dining on bait, as pretty girls often do, and I had to keep my wits about me.

At last I said that, though it was entertaining to hear of these places, they did not sound practical for one in my station of life. Eric said, "Station? Station? What a word. Are we in England? We have no fixed stations here. Besides, there is an aristocracy of beauty, and indisputably you belong to it. Don't you agree, Mr. Cora?"

"I ain't blind," said Cora, with a smile more friendly than seductive.

Eric Gordon looked as though he had considered, and decided against, asking the opinion of the Yankee corn-dealer who sat to my right, most of the time as stiff as a wax-museum representation of his type.

To change the subject, I asked Cora what kind of work *he* did.

"Work?" He repeated the word as though it were unfamiliar. "I don't work." He said it not so much as if he were a gentleman but more as if he were a boy.

"How do you live?"

"I play." He said this soberly as a statement of fact.

"Mr. Cora's games are poker, faro, and blackjack," said Eric Gordon. I saw that he wanted me to admire him for knowing someone like Cora, but he also wanted me to know he was Cora's superior.

Cora regarded him without expression. "I like to play these games with sporting gentlemen."

At dinner, I told them that I worked in the weaving room of the Harmony Manufacturing Company's textile mill. I did not tell them I had lost the job. At supper, I told them of my errand on behalf of Lewis and

Jocelyn. When I said that my brother was staying on Anthony Street in Five Points, Eric Gordon became alert.

"Tell her, Mr. Cora," he said, "what she's doing isn't safe." But Cora didn't answer. "Let me help," said Eric Gordon, putting his hand over mine. "A girl as lovely as you shouldn't have to do a thing like this alone."

His concern for my welfare seemed genuine. For my part, I would have loved to have someone's help, but I had seen the white shadow of a wedding ring on his finger, and when he had known I was a mill girl he had proposed to take me to dine at the Astor House, which, considering the social gulf between us, was very little different from asking me to climb into his bed. Eric Gordon's help, I was sure, came at a price; he was one of the men Mrs. Robinson had warned me about. So I thanked him but said that it was a family matter, and I had better handle it alone. At this, his attitude changed rather surprisingly: he looked unhappy, and almost angry. "Is this true, that you've got a sick brother on Anthony Street?"

"Of course it's true. Do you assume as a matter of course that people you meet as strangers are lying?"

"And you're going there alone? A girl like you?"

"I don't see how I can go as any other girl; I guess it will have to be as me."

"I wouldn't go there without a policeman."

"Maybe I will ask one, then."

"They won't help you unless you give them money."

"Thank you. I will."

"Do you mean it?"

"Your manners are getting worse and worse."

When the argument had gone on a minute longer, I blurted out that I had a gun: it would keep me safe. As soon as I said it, I felt I had said something childish. To cover my embarrassment, I told them the story of how I had gotten it.

"Can we see it?" Eric Gordon inquired.

I reached under the table, into my carpetbag, and came up holding the gun as if I did not know which end of it the bullets came out of. Each in turn, the men at the table examined the pistol. Cora held it as if estimating its weight. "It's a good weapon," he concluded. "Probably you don't need it. Try not to need it."

At breakfast the next day, an hour before we were to arrive in New York, Eric Gordon again reminded me that he was staying at the Astor, and he gave me a card with his name on it; if I wanted to see him, I should leave a message with the clerk there. He was often in town, and I should get in touch with him if I was in any kind of trouble.

Then Cora came to sit down with us, and Gordon said, "You look pleased with yourself," though in fact the gambler looked just as he usually did: composed, tranquil, and watchful. Gordon told me that Cora last night had hosted a midnight supper of oysters, canvasback ducks, and champagne, for the sporting men on the boat, and there had been a friendly card game. "I see one of your sports now," he said. At the far end of the dining saloon, a big man in a stained gray waistcoat was glaring at Cora. "Maybe you had better leave, Miss Moody," said Eric Gordon.

"No, stay," said Cora. "Let him come. It's okay."

"I think she ought to leave," Gordon insisted.

Whereupon the Yankee corn-dealer got up, strenuously swallowing his last bite, and bade us a good trip. "You should come, too, Miss Moody," he added. "These fellers are an education, but don't get tangled with them. Either of them."

I was about to take his advice when Charles Cora inquired, "Miss Moody, would you show us your pocket pistol again?"

I found the situation exciting, and something about Cora—his composure, maybe—gave me confidence. I knew he was a sharper, and that tricking people was a part of his profession, but I was sure, I don't know how, that he would never think of tricking *me*, and so from the very first I trusted him. I took out the pocket pistol and put it on the table. The man in the stained waistcoat walked to our table, and said he'd been thinking about what had happened last night. He'd been turning it over in his mind.

"Yes?" asked Cora.

The man's eyes found the pistol, and he looked startled. "What's that?"

"Bacon," replied Cora blandly; there was bacon not far from the gun.

The man's face reddened, and for a moment I thought that Cora was going to have to use my pistol, but evidently Cora did not think so, and the man walked on and out of the dining saloon. Then Cora did something that endeared him to me: he picked up his napkin and patted his brow with it.

"You're a coward," said Eric Gordon. "Hiding behind a woman's skirts."

"He could have called me out," said Cora mildly.

"What would you have done if he had?" asked Eric Gordon.

"Swim."

I could not tell if he was joking.

"I've half a mind to call you out myself. How'd you like that?"

"Please don't do that," said Cora. "It's been such a nice trip."

Despite Eric Gordon's great concern for me, he did not offer to help me with my luggage or to get me a hack uptown. I assumed that this was because someone was waiting to meet him when he left the boat, maybe a wife, or a relative, or a business associate more reputable and less broad-minded than Charles Cora.

IN THE SUMMER LIGHT, EVERY DETAIL of the waterfront sparkled. Each dirty face, scuffed sign, crate, dog, and puddle looked its best, ready to have its picture taken, when I stepped from the mere tumult of the emptying steamboat to the churning chaos of the docks. I walked, disoriented, past bewildered immigrants dragging chests and searching the crowd for their husbands or their brothers; past children running, men holding placards with the names of hotels; past heaps of sacks, pyramids of barrels, streams of spilled rum and oil. Two boys fought on the bricks of the street while boys around them shouted advice. A cabman called out, "Come to the cheapest house in all the world!"

All that in the first paltry seconds, as if New York were saying: "Last Judgment? We have it for breakfast here. This is the Big Town." Waterfront buildings loomed over me, formidably businesslike, warehouses with wide awnings and wooden overhangs projecting from the second story. The names of firms and their trades were blazoned in giant painted letters interrupted by windows. Everything up there was fine and majestic. Everything down here was grimy and chaotic and twice my eyes recoiled from the corpse of some unlucky rat that had been flattened and embossed many times by wagon wheels. Since I had last been here, New York had grown out of human scale. Though it crossed my mind that I might have stood right on this spot with Horace and Lewis in 1837, really I had only a dim idea of where I was, other than smack in the middle of everything. I remembered a few streets from my childhood, and I knew that the infamous Five Points lay in a sort of fat triangle bounded by Broadway, Bowery, and Walker. I reasoned that if I walked east from the North River I would come first to Broadway. Walker would lie either north or south; if necessary, I would take an omnibus. Then I would ask directions to Anthony Street.

It was easy for a newcomer to get lost in the New York of those days. Though the eye found printed words everywhere—on rooftops and awnings, etched into flagstones in front of the stores, on the sides of wagons (and, the oddest sight, on sandwich boards slung over the shoulders of ragged men who trudged up and down the street)—simple street signs were hard to find. They existed, but they were on the lampposts, and small; and since I did not know that, my only clue as to which street I was on was the occasional store sign that included the full address. I walked away from the river and came presently to cleaner, better-smelling purlieus, with fewer stores, and many impressive buildings of brick and limestone, or white marble. I reached a big park surrounded by rails and trees, and at one end of it stood a giant fountain, at the other a white palace with flags and a cupola. During all my years in Livy I had been the girl from New York, and I had taken the characterization very seriously. I had expected that within a few minutes of my return it would all come back to me; and instead I was lost within sight of a prominent landmark.

I approached two well-dressed women, one young, the older one walking with the young one's help. "Excuse me, could you tell me the name of that big white building with the two flags?" I asked. The younger one told me it was City Hall. I thanked her and asked, "How would I find 160 Anthony Street from here?" At this they looked at each other, made a decision about me, and walked on. Several of the men who passed by looked at me and a couple of them attempted to catch my eye. I preferred not to ask directions of them. I kept asking women, who kept pretending they didn't know. At last I put my inquiry to a gentleman. He was walking slowly, smoking a slim cigar, and tapping his cane on the black railing. He was about thirty, with soft, longish, poet's hair, parted in the middle, and dewy, sympathetic brown eyes, and he asked me with an expression of concern if I was certain that I had the right address. I said that I was sure I did. If it was not too bold of him to ask, why was I going there? I hesitated and then told him that my brother was living in a rooming house at that address, which I knew to be a bad one, and that he was sick, and I had come to help him.

"Well, let me think," he said. "You know, it's really not that far. It's—I'm not very good at giving directions. It's no use; I'll have to take you there. No, I don't mind. Don't be silly. Come on." He flicked away the cigar and took my portmanteau in one hand. I was grateful to be relieved of the burden. He hooked his free arm through mine, and we walked on, while he asked me about my trip and talked about New York, how interesting I would find it, and how, even though it was quite a large city, the bad places and the good places were only a short distance from each other. I must be careful.

We turned into a neat, clean, quiet street, where there were only a few carts and people. He said, "I promised my sister I would look in on her. If you don't mind, I need to stop here for a few minutes. You can come up with me."

"All right," I said, beginning to be suspicious, "but if you don't mind, I'll wait for you out here."

"Don't be absurd. It's right inside. You can rest your feet. You must be tired."

I was sure it would be a mistake to go inside with him. I wondered whether I should demand my luggage. Would he keep it? Perhaps he would, making a joke of it, in the hope that I would follow him. I wondered if I should take out the pocket pistol. I wondered if I was being foolish and worrying about nothing.

"All right," I said, and I held onto his arm firmly, while he reached for the key to the door. He had to put down the portmanteau in order to reach into his pocket. I grabbed the bag and ran.

"Wait!" I heard him call after me. "Wait! You don't understand! I'd have made it worth your while!"

Eventually, I slowed to a brisk walk, passed a child who must have been playing hide-and-seek, because he stood with his back flat against a wall and put his index finger to his lips when he saw me; and passed a maid carrying a basket, and a young man helping an old woman out of a carriage. I turned and saw no one pursuing me.

In my panic, I hadn't paid attention to where I was going, but, calmer now, I recognized the street I had fled to: It was Bowling Green. I looked up. Rows of gray chimneys tugged with lethal precision at those mystic chords of memory that have been said to link hearts to hearths, and perhaps I sighed, or perhaps I just stood there with my mouth agape.

I had come to my old house, where a hot meal cooked by Anna or Sally or Christina used to be waiting for me after I had spent a Saturday playing in the snow, where my mother coughed into a bowl and looked at the color and wrote letters her children were meant to read when she was dead, and where she took mercury and paregoric and made mustard plasters and said I was a joy and a boon to her.

I rapped the brass knocker, imagining—I could not help it—that they would all be there, my father, my mother, my brothers as children; my little self, nine years old. And she would say: Who are you? I don't know you. I don't want to know you. Go away.

After a minute the door opened, and there appeared in it a short, fat, blousy, red-faced, brown-haired, blue-eyed woman whose features were crowded into the center of her blotchy countenance, like certain old-fashioned representations of the sun and the moon when they have faces. She was only a little over thirty, as I learned a bit later, but I took her for a woman in her middle years. She wore a dress and an apron. Her left hand held a rag. I asked her who lived here. Glancing at my bag, she said it was a boarding house mostly for young clerks, only men. She had an Irish brogue. I said I had been born in this house and lived here until I was nine years old.

At this her manner changed. "Go on! You lived here?" she said, and she invited me in. "Tell me how it was in the old days. Come, I don't bite."

After a little hesitation, I followed her. She introduced herself as Mrs. Shea; it was her place—that is, she rented it and ran it. With misgivings, because the Irish of New York were known to dislike my family, I told her that my name was Arabella Godwin. She did not respond to the name, except that she called me by my first name often in the first few minutes after I told it to her ("Come this way, Arabella"), as if to help herself learn it. She led me on a tour of my childhood home. I recognized a few pieces of furniture that must not have been thought worth the trouble of carting out and selling, and most of the wallpaper was the same; in two rooms it had been painted over. Everything was drabber and more worn, with nicks in the wainscoting and patched sections in the plaster. There were wooden numbers nailed to the doors. The one Lewis and I had slept in was number 4.

When we made our way back downstairs, she sat me down at a long table, in a room smelling of stale tobacco, and I noticed a Turkey carpet, whose complicated pattern of big orange squares and impossible blue flower petals had mesmerized me as a child. It was badly frayed and stained now, as changed, I thought, as I was. Mrs. Shea served me reheated coffee, bread, and jam. She asked me for my story, and I told it, leaving out the most shameful details but including my parents' deaths (I found out by her remarks then that she knew my father had committed suicide, and that she knew the previous owner of the house had been Solomon Godwin). I told her about Livy and Cohoes, and I told her, in a general way, of my purpose in New York. I said that my friend had disappeared and, I feared, had fallen into bad company, and that my brother was sick in a Five Points lodging house.

When I told her about William Miller and Adventism, she said, "It was an honest mistake. There were many here in New York that made it." She added, "There are those in Ireland now who could wish that Jesus would return and bring the world's end, and a stern judgment, while He's about it." I often thought, in later years, that she must have been thinking of the potato famine, which had not been going on long enough to cause much notice in the United States, except among the Irish.

It had felt strange at first, to be here in my childhood home telling my story to this stranger, but after a while I began to enjoy myself.

When I told her about running away from the man with poet's hair shortly before I stumbled into Bowling Green, I placed great emphasis on his outward respectability, how well-dressed and gentlemanly he was, how improbable it had seemed that such a man could have bad intentions. I said these things because I did not want Mrs. Shea to have a bad opinion of me, but also because I was genuinely shocked. I told her that I was still not sure what the well-spoken stranger had meant to do.

She shook her head. "No honest man would ask you to come alone with him into a strange place when you didn't know him. You showed good sense when you ran."

I showed her the miniature of my mother. "How dear!" exclaimed

Mrs. Shea. "A window on lost times. Oh, I wish I had a likeness of my mother. I know that room. Mr. Holland stays there now."

She told me about her life, a few years of it spent in Ireland and the rest in New York. Her family had been poor, and her story was full of untimely deaths from illnesses and work accidents. Her surviving brothers and sisters were all good honest working people. She told me a little about what life was like in the house now. The young boarders were good sorts who spent most of their evenings around this table, joking or singing songs, and holidays were celebrated here in a splendid, warm, family-like way.

Perhaps an hour had gone by with all of this, and I decided I must return to business. I asked her if she knew the way to 160 Anthony Street.

"Of course, your brother is sick—you'll be wanting to go to him. Let me think," she said. "You can walk it if you're not too tired, and if you get lost, well, if you get lost, ask any man you see wearing a leather apron"—suddenly her fair wide face, with its features strangely positioned near its center, became pink with emotion—"or a man holding a broom or a trowel or a shovel; he may or may not be able to tell you, but he won't try to take a mean advantage of you, like a man whose only tool is a black cane with a brass grip will, if you ask me, who knows something about it. Ask the hot-corn girl or the woman who sells apples; she'll tell you, and she won't want anything for it other than maybe for you to buy an apple, and sure you'll be no worse off for that." Her voice shook. She was angry, but I guessed not at me—or only a little at me, for my divided loyalties and misplaced suspicions. "Better to ask the apple woman than some man who thinks himself the lord of creation because his mother never had to sell apples, and looks on a poor girl's worry and confusion as another gift to him from the gods."

And she gave me the directions. I thanked her and got up to leave.

"Wait," she said. "I know that place where your brother is. It's a bad house on a bad street. I wouldn't let my brother stay there. Get him out. If you must stay in New York for any time, I can tell you where to find cheap board and lodgings."

She left to fetch a pencil and some paper. Then, reciting addresses slowly, she gave me the name of a house where six girls who sewed hats in a factory lived, and another where a widow took in lodgers.

If I had any clothes to sell or to buy, or if I needed to borrow money or to pawn something, I should go to her uncle's secondhand shop on Orange Street, just below Walker—she gave me the address—but I must stay clear of the secondhand stores farther down on Orange: they were all run by Jews. What's more, and this was very important, I must introduce myself to Con Donoho and his wife, Mrs. Donoho, whom I would find at their grocery, also on Orange Street. Donoho was the Sixth Ward street inspector, and might find my brother a job when he recovered; in any case, he was a good man to pay one's respects to, and I could endear myself to him by using her name—I should introduce myself to the wife first, and make it clear that I was a factory girl. "And it's all right that you're a Protestant, if you're civil. But don't say your name is Godwin, for the love of heaven. Not to hurt your feelings, but in the Points, only niggers remember that name fondly."

Since she had brought up the Godwin name, I thought I might as well ask her: "Do you know what happened to them—my grandfather—his wife—my brothers?"

The hard look in her eyes melted. "I heard he was ruined in the Panic and died of a broken heart. That's all I know."

I WALKED, FOLLOWING MRS. SHEA'S DIRECTIONS. Step by step the streets were more crowded with people and incidents, with fewer carriages, more cheap goods being lifted for skeptical examination by short stout women, more children selling things. I came to Chatham Square, a middling neighborhood frequented by rich and poor, with a circus-midway atmosphere created by garish advertising placards and by the presence of men who stood in front of stores praising the goods within.

Another turn, another block, and I did not have to ask, I knew I was in Five Points. Children carrying scraps of wood in their arms, dandified young hooligans, Jews in skullcaps, Negroes pushing carts, staggering drunkards, dispirited men with heavy burdens strapped to their backs, women holding wicker baskets against their hips, men with patches on their trousers, people arguing at the top of their voices in the street—such folk had made up a fraction of the population wherever I had been in New York until now: here the proportions were reversed: here they lived in all their multitudes; this was the source; this was their home. They rushed toward me, they passed me from behind (sometimes tarrying to cast a curious, hostile, or lascivious glance my way), going in and out of places that stenciled wooden signs identified as dime-a-night lodging houses, cheap restaurants, saloons, groceries, old-clothes stores, coal yards and horse sheds. Patches of color, paint from another century, clung to the gray clapboards of which most of the buildings to my left and right were made. In every tenth window broken glass had been replaced with a plank or canvas or newspaper. A long ridge of trash ran along the middle of the street, and the mire on either side was imprinted with crisscrossing wheel ruts.

THOUGH THE CROWD WAS SO DENSE that sometimes I could not see from one side of the street to the other, there were no friendly apple women in sight. Two women stood near a doorway and I decided to ask them where 160 Anthony was. I noticed after I had changed course to walk toward them that they were sharing a bottle, and were only half dressed, and by the time I was close enough to speak to them I had no doubt they were prostitutes. They were both quite young, about my own age, and homely: one thin, missing a front tooth, the other fat with curly blond hair and fair skin but the features of a colored woman. Only my fear of insulting them kept me from turning and walking away. I asked my question. The skinny one said this was 160 Anthony—we were all standing in front of it! I asked if there was a lodging house for men here, and said I was looking for my brother. They asked me his name. When I answered, the thin one, whose missing tooth gave her a juicy lisp, said, "Lewish!" She passed the bottle to the fat one and grabbed my hand. Her grip was tight. She pulled me to a flight of stairs and started down it. "Come on," she said, when I resisted.

"What do you mean? Where are we going? Where are you taking me?"

"To yer brother! Lewis! You'll be wanting to see yer brother, won't ya?" Under the lisp, she had a brogue as heavy as Mrs. Shea's.

She took me down the staircase, which had one turn in it, into a basement with a low ceiling and many beds: some on legs; more in shelf-like tiers, one atop another, set in the walls, canvas hammocks strung between two wooden rails. There were also straw mattresses on the floor. I could imagine how crowded this place would be when night came, and how dear unconsciousness would be then. The air stank, like all the air of the neighborhood, but with mildew, vomit, and drink added to the usual aromas of sewage and rot. On the walls near the floor were wavy stains of varying hues, the geological record of yesteryear's floods.

There were only a handful of men in the wretched room now, most of them pickling in liquor, yet still the girl had to point my brother out before I saw him. He was like everything else here, a chaos of muddy hues. Then his name was torn from my chest—"Lewis! Lewis!" I spoke it not so much to alert him to my presence as to conjure him into continued being, and I ran to him, still crying his name. I saw when I stood over him that I had been right to come. He had been cut badly in at least two places, with bandages around a wound at his waist and others around his right arm, and he was sick, very sick, from the festering of his wounds, and this was no place for him to recover. But I could see that someone was taking care of him. The bandages, though less clean than we like bandages to be today, had been changed recently, and the bedclothes were clean and dry. "Belle," he said wonderingly, when he saw me, and then he told the skinny prostitute that I was his sister. A few seconds passed, and he added, "That's Bridget, Belle."

"Lewis," I said. "Lewis, I was at our old house." Quite unexpectedly I began to weep. "I was in Bowling Green today, Lewis. I was there *just now*. In Bowling Green."

❧ XXIX ❧

I WAS GLAD THAT SOMEONE HAD HELPED my brother, grateful—but I was also dismayed, more than I can express, more than I can really remember now, to find myself under an obligation to a gap-toothed prostitute. She had changed his clothes, bedding, and bandages, and brought him clean water, and broth that she had paid for with her own money, earned through the degradation of her body. Perhaps she had saved his life. I realized all that, and yet I felt invisibly damaged just by being in her presence. People would think differently of me if they learned that I had been here and had touched her hand.

We sat on the edge of an empty bed and talked through the snoring of men who looked as pale as if they had their drink delivered here and the sun's direct rays never touched them. In the most offhand way, she told me things no decent woman should know; and, fearing that no woman could remain entirely decent once she knew them, I listened. She said she had a room to herself in the brothel that occupied the second and third floors of the house, and she took care of my brother when she could. She had wanted to take him into her room—most of her clients wouldn't have cared—but Mrs. Mulrooney would not allow it; she did not want someone dying in the house.

I didn't know where to look, every view was so disgusting. At last, for lack of an alternative, I chose Bridget's homely face. "I must get him out of here. I'm scared to walk around this neighborhood alone."

"I'll go with you," she said cheerfully.

While we were together, she told me more about herself. She told me what she liked and didn't like. She liked whiskey, rum, chocolate, hot buttered corn, the theater, Shakespeare, and the actor Edwin Forrest. She liked dancing. She liked New Jersey—it was beautiful. She liked Yankee Sullivan, the prizefighter. She liked the policeman Tim O'Hara, who had helped her and asked for nothing in return. She did not like Pell Street, where something bad had happened to her that she decided not to talk about. She didn't like what men and women did in bed. Did anyone really like it? She didn't believe even the men really liked it. They just thought they had to do it because they were men.

She told me how she had become a prostitute. She had been born in County Waterford. Her parents died. With the help of her landlord, who wanted to get rid of his indigent tenants, she came to America, and she sought out her aunt Liz, a widow. Aunt Liz was living in a small apartment with three young women who took turns taking men to the one bedroom in the apartment; they paid Aunt Liz for the use of the room. Sometimes the girls served two or three men in the room at once. Soon after Bridget arrived, her aunt kicked out the three girls, to Bridget's relief, but then started bringing men to Bridget, saying that she had to earn her keep and she wouldn't be sorry, it was a good life. "You're sitting on your fortune," her aunt said. Bridget wept and resisted. Her aunt threatened to kick her out to roam the streets, where, Aunt Liz said, she would certainly become a whore anyway; finally, Bridget gave in.

A year later, when she was fifteen, she had left her aunt so that she could keep more of her earnings. By now she was used to the life. It was all she knew, and not so bad. She had all her meals out. A maid did all the cleaning and washing for the girls. Bridget spent far more time standing and waiting than she did in the performance of her duties, and she had money for oyster saloons and ferryboats and theater tickets, and for a drop of whiskey now and then. Even so, sometimes she felt blue, because this was not the life she had planned; of course, it was different for someone like me (I learned gradually from such parenthetical remarks that she thought I was a whore, too, but a fine one, far above the likes of her). She planned to quit any day now. I didn't ask, but she told me that her price was a dollar. She thought that was fair, since she was, she admitted, "no Cleopatra." It could go lower if there was haggling.

When I told her that I worked at a mill, she apologized for her mistake and asked me if it was true that, as she had heard, mill girls had to grant their favors to the bosses. I told her it wasn't true. I could tell she didn't believe me.

I WENT TO SEE THE WIDOW mentioned by Mrs. Shea; she had no room, but knew of another widow, Mary Donovan, on Mulberry Street, who was looking for lodgers and who, for an additional fee, would probably wash our clothes and feed us.

She lived on the fifth floor of a five-story brick tenement that had been built by an enterprising landlord in the courtyard surrounded by his other properties. To reach it, we walked through an alley past sacks of refuse and stray cats. A skylight was the only source of illumination on the stairs, which were in the center of the building, a squarish spiral with an empty square drop in the middle. A small girl sat on the steps between two floors, playing with a whirring, buzzing toy made out of a button and a piece of yarn. She ignored us as we passed. I heard her coughing, and looked back in time to see her put down the toy and cough into her hand and look.

When I knocked at the door at the top, I was met by Mrs. Donovan, who had the permanent squint and roosting buzzard's posture which I later came to recognize in women I saw on the street as the mark of the seamstress. I explained my situation, and she explained hers. She had been widowed for about a year. She had six children, boys and girls. Three of them were out picking rags or sweeping streets. One was being watched by a neighbor down the hall. Two of them, girls, were right here, making shirts, with terrible urgency and concentration.

In the apartment below us, a man screamed, "Get up, you drunken slut!" amid words I could not make out, and "My dinner! My dinner!" The voice was passionate, as if his poor dinner lay brutally slain and he was mourning it and demanding justice. A child cried. A woman spoke. Later, when we were discussing the room, we heard thuds and grunts, and Mrs. Donovan observed calmly, "Now he's beating her."

It was horrible, but I returned that evening knowing it was the best I could do on short notice. It was only temporary, after all. We had to live in New York while I tended to Lewis, and we had to live cheaply until I got a job.

Incredibly, Lewis was reluctant to leave 160 Anthony: he said that that was where Jocelyn would come looking for him. He loved her; he was going to forgive her and, if there was no other way, marry her; they'd put what she had done behind them. I told him that we would leave word where we had gone, and that I had come here to find Jocelyn as well as to take care of him. We would find her, and we would take her away from that place.

I managed to persuade him, and we went to live on Mulberry Street, the two of us in the cramped little room that had belonged to the two homely daughters, who moved into another room already occupied by their mother and their youngest brother. The three remaining brothers slept in the kitchen.

Mrs. Donovan spent a surprising amount of time on her knees beside a pail, weilding a rag, with indifferent results. The portion of the walls beyond her reach were so smutty that if I stood on a chair I could write my initials with my fingernail. The cracked plaster ceiling was brown with the greasy residue of smoke; and whenever I think about that tenement, I always remember the dreadful stench that came through the windows if you were foolish enough to open them under the misapprehension that nothing could be worse than the air inside. I thought the air might actually be poisonous. In a week or two perhaps, Agatha and Elihu would receive word that I had been fired from the mill. What would they think and say? I thought of Agnes, living respectably with her parents until she married some weak-willed man with good prospects—that wooden doll George Sackett, perhaps. I thought of Jeptha, living in his father-in-law's residence, or with his unspoiled wife in a boarding house, as many married couples did in those days. Maybe he had his own house already. If only he could see me now, I thought, feeling that I had reached the depths of degradation and it would be a great rebuke to him.

ON THE FIRST NIGHT WE SPENT IN OUR ROOM on Mulberry Street, Lewis's fever worsened. He shivered and sweated. There weren't enough blankets for him. I felt so helpless that I prayed. I plied him with patent medicines, changed his bandages, and fed him meals of bread and soup from a nearby oyster house. Gradually, he began to gain strength, and one day he said he was all better; it was time for us to find Jocelyn, as I had promised. I looked away while he got into his trousers. Then I heard him stumble; when I looked back, he was sitting on the floor.

"Give it a little more time," I told him, and he got back into bed. In a day or two, he did seem much better, and I told them that I had an idea of how we could begin our search for Jocelyn. I had been thinking about Mrs. Shea's advice regarding Con Donoho, Sixth Ward street inspector, and his grocery on Orange Street, one block below the Five Points intersection. Donoho was a power in the neighborhood, she had said. I thought that if I mentioned Mrs. Shea to him, perhaps he could help us find Jocelyn.

"We're going to ask about Tom Cross, too," I said, mainly in order to see the look on Lewis's face when I did. There was something between Lewis and Tom that I did not understand. Whenever we talked about Tom, Lewis was evasive and looked uncomfortable. "Tom is sneaky," Lewis had said a few times when I was tending him in our room. "He likes to get a handle on people." He said it as if the mistake had not already been made and Tom's bad character was not already well established. I remembered the day at the Harmony boarding house when they had been bragging of their exploits on the canal and Tom said that Lewis could do harm if he was of a mind to; that he was a killer. Whatever it was that worried Lewis so much, it had probably happened before they'd come to New York City.

We went up the stairs of the Donoho grocery Indian-file, because most of the space on each step was taken up by a barrel overflowing with brooms, or charcoal, or herrings. Inside, the idea of a drinking saloon and a grocery contended, with no decisive outcome. Besides cabbages, potatoes, eggs, flour, candles, soap, and coal, there was a handsome bar well stocked with liquor, as well as a crock of tobacco and a rack of clay pipes; a sign said that whoever bought a shot of whiskey was entitled to an ounce of tobacco and the temporary use of a pipe.

Mrs. Donoho, behind the bar, was dispensing beer into a bucket, which she handed to a boy of about eight. Then a man asked for a pound of salt pork. When she went to get it for him, he said, "Not that barrel." She told him, "You're too suspicious," and got the meat from another barrel and wrapped it in newspaper, and finally she turned with a big smile and hard eyes to us. She was squat, pale, and sweaty, with strands of her thin hair pasted to her brow. When I mentioned Mrs. Shea, her manner softened. When I said we were looking for a girl named Jocelyn who we believed was working in a house of ill fame, she said, "A house, do you say, of ill fame? I'm sure I don't know about such places, if indeed there are any hereabouts."

She spoke loudly. There was laughter from men and women within earshot.

"We thought, as many men come in here, and men will be men, you might ask if they have heard about a girl with that name," I said.

"How do you vote?" Mrs. Donoho asked Lewis.

"I'm not old enough to vote yet," said Lewis.

"What a pity. Still, there are other ways to be useful come election time," said Mrs. Donoho, looking right and left, and there was amusement again. "Come March if you're still here, speak to Con about it."

"I will," said Lewis.

"And I will ask about your poor friend Jocelyn," said Mrs. Donoho. "I do hope she sees the error of her ways. Is she handsome?"

"She's beautiful," said Lewis. "But young. She's only fourteen, and looks younger."

"Well, I'll tell you, I've heard about such places, things one shouldn't hear, but folks tell me for the pleasure of seeing me blush, and I've heard that some of them make a point of offering young women, children practically, to men who are shy with grown women. If I were a man and could go safely into such places, I would look there. I wouldn't look around the Sixth Ward."

Lewis asked her about Tom Cross.

"I don't recall a man of that name," said Mrs. Donoho. "Does anybody here know a Tom Cross?" she asked generally, and no one seemed to know.

"He might be known by other names," said Lewis, and he described Tom, naming his profession and his fire brigade, while I watched Mrs. Donoho's face.

Soon after we had left the grocery, and were blinking and squinting in the sudden brightness of the day, a man in a patched coat came up, tipped his shapeless hat to me, and dragged Lewis by the elbow a few yards away.

As a result, I was left standing alone. People of various types passed by. Often men turned to examine me. Two homely young missionary women came by, of the sort who stood outside drinking saloons and brothels telling the men who went through their doors to be ashamed, and to think of the little ones starving at home. One of them put a tract into my hand, and they moved on. Then, a well-dressed man tipped his hat and said I looked lost, and he would love to help me if I would let him. No, I said.

"It's a lovely day. Wouldn't it be fun to take a walk? Walk with me."

"No. Please, leave me alone."

"Oh, don't be that way. I would make it worth your while."

"You have made a mistake," I said. "Here's my brother."

Lewis, whom I had seen give the man with the patched coat a coin, probably in payment for his information, was approaching. The man who had been annoying me tipped his hat again and left us.

"Who was that?" asked Lewis.

"No one. Never mind."

Lewis contemplated the departing figure as he told me of his conversation with the man in the patched coat, who, it seemed, had overheard our talk in the grocery, and was now waiting halfway down the street.

"He says Mrs. Donoho might help us find Jocelyn, but all she'll do about Tom is tell him we're after him. Donoho's in with Alderman O'Daniel, and Tom paid O'Daniel to get him a job. Paid him with my money, and money he got selling Jocelyn to a madam. Because that's what he did, he sold her."

"What was the job?" I asked.

Lewis grinned the special, crooked grin of a person who is about to wise you up. "He's a policeman. That's how they get hired, all of them."

"It can't be true," I said, but by the time I had finished denying it, I believed it.

We were naïve enough so that the foul streets looked more wicked to us, every brick and board of them, as we walked home in the knowledge that Tom Cross was a copper, and that every policeman one saw had obtained his job by means of a bribe.

We went home, and I cooked. When we were eating, I thought of something funny to say. "No wonder he's so hard to find." Even though a half-hour had passed, Lewis understood I was talking about Tom's being a policeman, and he laughed, and the laugh turned into a cough, and the cough got out of control.

"Stop it, Lewis," I said. "Don't get sick."

"Yes, ma'am," he said, but he went on coughing, one of those complicated, percussive coughs that call to mind factory noises—machines in his chest manufacturing some unpleasant fate for us both. He spat into his handkerchief, cleared his throat one more time—his little chest sounded cavernous, a vast chamber full of echoes—and spat again. I insisted on examining the sputum.

"My God, Lewis," I said, for it was green. I did not know why, but I knew that whenever my mother had seen green in her sputum it was a cause for worry. From living in the orbit of her sewing circle—in that other life, in the house where now Mrs. Shea took in boarders—I knew some of the medical theories prevalent in those days before consumption became tuberculosis, before Dr. Koch and his pet bacilli. We believed that you inherited a predisposition to the illness, like a seed, but the seed might remain dormant in you, unless and until you received a shock to the system. A shock was like water on the seed. Should Lewis prove now to have consumption, I would attribute it to his having been knifed in the arm and the gut by Tom Cross.

I gave him a tablespoon of Dr. Wistar's Balsam of Wild Cherry, said in newspaper advertisements to prevent consumption and as many other ailments as could fit on the page without making the print too small.

"Lewis," I said when he had taken his dose, "do you think we're doing the right thing, looking for Tom?"

"What do you mean?" he said. The look was there again, the Tom Cross look. "He's got my money. You know what he did to Jocelyn. He's got to pay for that, don't he?"

"He should," I said, "but people don't always pay for their crimes, and we have to look out for ourselves. Tom is a hornets' nest. Maybe we should leave him be."

We didn't speak for a while, and then he slammed the cup on the table. "Ask me. Go on. Ask what you want to know."

"What happened on the canal, Lewis?"

He hesitated, and said with a firmness that would have been more convincing without the delay, "Not a thing."

"Well, then, what does Tom know about you?"

He gave me a fond look. "Big sister, rest your mind. There ain't a thing Tom Cross knows about me that he can talk about, because I know plenty about him. And that's all I'm saying, because that's all you need to know."

I couldn't get any more out of him. I looked at the tract the missionary girls had given me. The title was *Self-Pollution,* and it identified itself as a publication of the Female Reform Society. It is a generally unremarked feature of life in poor neighborhoods that one is always being handed these insulting tracts.

THE NEXT DAY, LEWIS WENT BACK to Anthony Street and talked to Bridget, who told him where to find a parlor house for men who liked very young girls. He went to this address; there he found Jocelyn; and later that evening, he told me about it.

He had found her, he said, about to go upstairs with "a disgusting old man" whom Lewis chased away. Jocelyn had said he had just cost her more money than he could make in a month. Lewis had told her that she was on the road to death and damnation, and that he loved her, she was wonderful; and she had laughed, saying that the only reason he thought she was wonderful was that she had granted him her favors for free. She agreed that it had been an act of charity, but she was willing to forget it; so should he.

She said she liked what she was doing, and no one could get her to change her mind about it, but she missed me, so I should come and see her and try.

She insisted that I come see her *at the brothel.*

"How was she?" I asked Lewis. "What did she look like?"

"Like a princess," he said, with a sort of gloomy admiration.

"What was the place like?"

"Like a palace."

We had this conversation in the company of Mrs. Donovan and her daughters, as they sewed desperately in insufficient light, eyes narrowed, necks bent, and Mrs. Donovan commented, "It'll be no easy task getting her away once she knows what it's like to work short hours. Thank goodness, my girls are ugly, or I wouldn't know what to tell them." The two girls, Moira and Kathy, gave her rebuking glances—not, I think, for calling them ugly, but for suggesting they'd be tempted to do wrong. They were good girls, and proud of it. It was all they had.

XXX

AS IF TO PROVE THAT THE DEVIL had been given complete charge of this world and procured a license to distribute its choicest properties, Mrs. Bower's brothel, specializing in girl children, was on a good, clean, quiet street somewhat superior to the one on which I had grown up. Its trash was hauled away regularly; you could see every paving brick under your feet, there were black iron fences and polished brass door-knockers, and you would never have guessed that anything amiss was going on inside.

A skinny colored woman with a bright-red rag on her head and a white rag in her hand opened the door, and asked if I was the dressmaker.

I said no. "We expecting a dressmaker," she said, as if it were a negotiation and if she stood her ground I might accommodate her. For a moment, I didn't know my own name. "Looking for a place here?" she asked with a sly smile. "No!" I said hotly. She laughed.

"I'm looking for Jocelyn," I said "Is she here?"

"What she look like?"

I described her.

"You mean Granny," said the colored woman.

Inside, the brothel looked like a rich man's house, which it had been once. Every window had curtains; the wallpaper and furniture were new and no more ostentatious than those to be found in the home of many a well-off New Yorker. The chairs and sofas and ottomans were well uphol-stered, in silk, with plenty of pillows. There were spittoons. The carpets were clean. Paintings on the walls and statues on pedestals depicted clas-sical myths, a Roman slave market, and Truth and Charity as embodied in seminude goddesses. Maybe they weren't very good, but I could not tell, and no doubt the house's patrons felt that their loathsome orgies were transpiring in an atmosphere of taste and refinement. A pair of eleven- or twelve-year-old girls descended a grand staircase, holding hands. They wore silk nightgowns tailored to their boyish forms.

I knew I ought to feel that I was peering over the edge of an abyss at a scene of unspeakable horror. I did not feel that way, for Five Points was already doing its work on me. I had seen girls younger than this sleeping in wagon sheds and alleys. I had seen consumptive children, drunken children, starving children, and children beaten half to death.

I could not help observing that these two girls looked clean, healthy, and lively. They whispered to each other. As they neared the bottom of the stairs, they looked at me rudely. "Who are you?" asked one of them, and I answered, "My name is Arabella."

"Arabella," she repeated. "She's pretty."

"Yes," said the other one. "But, fuck, she's old."

I told them I was looking for Jocelyn, and while one continued to inspect me, the other turned and called, "Granny! Someone's here to see you!"

She appeared at the top of the stairs in a flannel nightshirt. "You came!" Simple pleasure spread across her face, and I guess across mine, too. She embraced me and pulled me into her room, which was furnished like a rich woman's bedroom, with a fireplace, a vanity table, a chest of drawers, two windows, lavender wallpaper with a pattern of vines and flowers, carpets, gilt-framed mirrors, and an oil painting that featured a pudgy pink-and-lavender infant Cupid with a bow. Then I was startled and turned away: a man with a hairy back lay prone in the bed. "Mister," said Jocelyn. Reflecting that the sheets had covered him from the waist down, and thinking, *how can it hurt me?* I looked back. She shook his shoulder; he grunted; she shook him harder, and he turned and pushed himself up. The sheets still covered the salient parts of his nakedness. "Mister," she repeated. He rubbed his scalp in a thorough, practiced way that bespoke many a hangover before this one, and looked at us blankly.

"Go to the kitchen," said Jocelyn. He sat motionless for a time. When he rose abruptly to get his trousers, which lay on a chair just out of his reach, I shut my eyes with a gasp, and Jocelyn laughed. "It's all right, he's got his pants on now," she told me just a few seconds later, and she told the man, "Go on. They'll give you something for your head."

When he was gone, she patted the spot next to her on the bed. I shook my head. She stood, put her arms around me, and held me to her, murmuring that she had missed me terribly, that the only thing she had really not liked about New York so far was the thought that she might not see me again. Then she said, "God, you stink, Arabella. I'm glad you came. I'm happy you're here, but you need to know that you stink."

It was true. How could it be otherwise? Every drop of water I used on my body had to be dragged up four flights. Over my objections, she opened the door and yelled for the help; when the colored woman appeared, Jocelyn demanded that buckets of hot water be brought to the room. A small room adjoining her bedroom turned out to contain a water closet and a large tin-plated tub. I didn't want to accept anything that was offered to me in this terrible place, but the temptation was too great. I bathed, and the hot water was heaven, and then Jocelyn bathed, and we dressed and went downstairs. With my mouth watering, I nobly refused rolls and coffee, and then, when the cook prepared a meal of ham and eggs and sour cream and peach preserves and Jocelyn began blithely eating it, it seemed silly to refuse, and I took my share. I had already given up any hope of getting her out of this place. If something bad enough happened to her here, she might leave, but no argument of mine was going to do it.

"What's it like?" I asked her.

She knew what I meant. "Quick, usually. I know how to make it be over quick, and they don't mind usually, because they're drunk. Oh, sometimes a fellow will surprise me and go on too long or want it twice, but I don't mind it, not compared with picking dirt out of cotton twelve hours a day. I've never minded it. I wash them before. They put up with it because they're getting something special, being here, that they know they shouldn't have. I'm going to have to move next year to another house, where I'll be the youngest. Here they call me Granny."

"How many?"

"A night?"

"Yes."

"Five is the most I've done. A girl here says she has done eight."

It was hard to grasp. You were supposed to have one man in your whole life, perhaps another if the first one died, and Jocelyn had just admitted to having five in one night; she said it as though she were telling me that she had had five sandwiches, or five cups of tea.

She continued innocently, "It's still not that much time, because usually, like I said, it's fast. It's two hours of work, doing what some girls do out of charity. Some will stay till morning, like you saw, and that's the easiest, because they think they'll use you many times, but they never do."

Of course, she hadn't been there very long.

"Do you save any of your money?" I asked her.

"Yes."

"Do you still want to become a dressmaker?"

She laughed as if the notion were absurd.

I asked her what she would do when she got old, I asked her what about the opinion of the world, I asked her about pregnancy and disease— but I asked without passion. It wasn't an argument. I was asking because I wanted to know.

She brought me upstairs again and made me brush my teeth. Then she brushed my hair at the vanity table and put it up with combs and pins. She sprayed me with perfume. A few minutes later, a servant came in bringing a traveling dress, secondhand but nicer and a lot cleaner than the one I was wearing, and Jocelyn offered it to me with a blithe pleasure in her ability to be generous. I sat on the bed, thinking of what occurred there, and what paid for the ham and eggs and the peaches and perfume and pretty clothes. I put my head in my hands. "I can't, Jos. Don't make me say why."

I looked up to see if I had hurt her feelings. She examined the dress in her hands. She knelt and held it under my face, as if I had objected to the color or the pattern. "I could get you another. I could get ten sent up here."

"I can't," I repeated. "I must go," I said, and stood up.

I thought she hadn't understood a thing until, at the door, she touched my arm and with a sad little smile said, "I missed you, Belle. Will I see you again?"

"Of course," I said, not sure if it was true. Deciding to make it true, I added: "But not here. Not again."

As we reached the foot of the stairs that led through the sitting room, I saw a plump gray-haired woman in a sober dress and a white cap, who was looking up at me expectantly, and I knew before Jocelyn said, "This is Mrs. Bower," that it was she, the spider of this place, the madam. *I will run; I must run,* I thought, but I did not feel it. Besides, if I made a fuss, perhaps I would make trouble for Jocelyn. The woman asked me to sit in this parlor where, a few hours later, men would be drinking champagne and eating oysters in the company of little girls.

In appearance, she was a soberly dressed woman of fifty who might be taken for the widow of a rich merchant. The only sign of her profession was a certain briskness, like that of a man of affairs taking time from his busy schedule to speak briefly to a young relative visiting the city. She asked me my name and where I lived, and where I had grown up, and what I did for a living, and how I knew Jocelyn.

I told her. An inner voice castigated me for being civil to this despoiler of lives, who had grown wealthy by catering to depraved appetites. But unless you are habitually rude to everyone, it is hard to be rude to people who give an impression of wealth and power, and who have good manners and are civil to you.

She looked at me appraisingly. "You speak very well. Do you like to read?"

I said yes. She asked me what sort of things I read. I told her.

When I said I liked Byron, she inquired, "Can you recite something from Byron?"

"Yes."

"Well, go on."

"I can, but I don't care to."

"But if you did care to, if there was a reason to, you could."

"Yes."

"And you like that kind of thing. You do it for pleasure. Reading. Novels. Poetry. Scott. Bulwer-Lytton?"

"It passes the time. Yes."

"Do you understand what you read?"

"There would be little point to it if I did not."

"I agree, but people do it. They pretend to like things." She paused briefly. "You have remarkable gifts at your disposal, if you don't mind my saying it." I blushed. I knew what she meant, and it was obvious that she noticed my embarrassment, but she went on anyway. "With the right attention, the right clothes, the right paint, the right corset, you could be a beauty of the first rank. You speak like a lady. You have a good carriage. And with all that reading, you could pass for a girl from a good family, a New England family, maybe Boston, ruined in the Panic, or—or you went bad and now you're dead to them; it all came of reading Byron. You could be richer than me one day, if you're sensible, and don't pick up bad habits like drink or gambling, and make good investments, and don't give it all away to some man."

She paused, waiting for my reply. I thought of Eric Gordon, the handsome, rich man, part-owner of a five-story dry-goods store, whom I had met on the steamboat from Albany. I felt now, as then, that I ought to do something to show I wasn't that kind of a girl.

"I'm needed at home," I said simply, rising from the soft, clean chintz cushions of one of Mrs. Bower's tasteful, pretty chairs.

"When you've got money, you can help the folks that matter to you," said Mrs. Bower pensively. "You lose the respect of the parsons and the churchy women. Everyone else treats you much better."

Neither of us spoke for a while, and then I said, "I'm sure you don't intend me any harm. I have decided not to take this as an insult."

Mrs. Bower nodded. "You've been knocked around some. Otherwise, you'd have been out the door five minutes ago."

I did not trust myself to speak. I left.

LEWIS AND I WERE ON MULBERRY STREET for two and a half months before he was strong enough to work. It would be winter before long, and Mrs. Donovan warned us that employment would be harder to find then. She did not say why that was so; probably she did not know why; but I was a merchant's daughter, and with a little thought I understood that it was because New York's commerce was highly dependent on shipping over water. Each winter, the canals froze and fewer ships crossed the Atlantic. Factories shut down, clothing manufacturers stopped giving out piecework, and young seamstresses and milliners put on their best dresses and accosted gentlemen in the streets.

Lewis, who looked older than he was, found work easily once he started looking, and had series of ill-paid jobs. Some he lost when it was found that, though strong, he tired rather quickly. He emptied trash barges into the ocean; he worked as a porter for the New York and Harlem Railroad; he worked in a Bowery boot-blacking factory.

Meanwhile, I became a maid. I left my first position, for a lawyer and his wife, after I went to my small room on the second floor of their house one evening to find the lawyer sitting on the bed, declaring his love and offering me some cheap trinkets in exchange for my caresses. I returned to the employment agency, determined to find work in a house that did not contain a man. On the third day of this quest, I was interviewed by two elderly sisters, who argued about me without bothering to lower their voices, while I struggled not to show emotion, one of them saying that they might as well try me, the other maintaining that by the time I was trained to their exacting standards I would be either married or a whore. The first sister won the argument, and so I was hired. But don't think of her as the nice one: they were both despicable. If they had no designs on my honor, still they had a very low opinion of it, and even after I had been their maid for three months, they made a great show of locking away their jewelry, counting the silverware, and leaving out small change to test my honesty. The elder sister had an upper lip that was wrinkled like a drawn curtain. The younger sister was in the habit of picking her nose. Though they had several unused guest rooms, they stuffed me into a drafty attic dormer with a small stove and enough coal, each week, to last four days. Once or twice a week, I stood in silence for twenty minutes while either the elder sister or the younger sister told me that in this house they had a very special way of doing things, and it was not the way I had just done it.

On my day off, sometimes I saw Jocelyn. We met in City Hall Park and at an inexpensive Bowery oyster house. She was growing taller, and she had recently graduated from Mrs. Bower's child brothel to Mrs. Bower's house in Washington Square. She had had to spend over a thousand dollars on new dresses and was, as a result, in debt to Mrs. Bower; but when the debt was paid off, she expected to live well. Always I searched her face for signs of corruption, and during every conversation I looked for opportunities to change her mind. I never found either of those things. Instead, I lost my horror of her actions, and she became merely Jocelyn to me again.

Whenever I went out, no matter where, whether it was to do my own business or my mistresses', men looked at me; some of them called out to me, and sometimes they followed me until I escaped into a store; the most determined men would go right into that store and would corner me there. If I met their eyes, they took it as encouragement. Soon I hardly dared to look up when a man was near. "Where are you going, sweetheart?" they would ask. "What do you do, little angel?" and if I told them I was a maid—meaning that I had a job, I worked, I was not to be taken so lightly—they would smile and say, "A pretty girl like you, a maid? A girl like you shouldn't have to work."

Often, following me, they would ask this question: "Why the long face, pretty girl? Why so sad?" Of all their remarks, I hated that one most.

XXXI

WHEN THE SUBJECT OF MY FINAL DESCENT into dishonor came up later, I had one story for patrons, and another for my intimates. I told members of the first group that a handsome man had taken advantage of my youth, and when my disgrace became known, my family cast me out. I told friends that I had entered upon this life in order to save the life of my brother Lewis. I believed this second story, although, with the passage of years, I have come to see that it does not exactly make sense by itself and cannot be the whole story. For what it's worth, here is what I used to say. The facts are accurate, so far as they go.

On a day in January when the road was full of deep ice puddles within which leaves and oyster shells were suspended like exhibits in glass museum cases, I opened the door of my employers' house to see a small, slender man, under five feet tall. His name was Johnny O'Faolin, he said, and he told me that my brother Lewis was in the Tombs, the prison on Centre Street. Johnny had just come back from visiting his own brother there, and Lewis had asked him to come and tell me.

It seemed that Lewis had been walking by the piano factory on Bowery when he saw, coming the other way, his former friend Tom Cross, whose real name was Jack Cutter. Cutter wore a long coat with a silver star pinned to it—it was true, what we had heard: he had become a policeman.

Lewis pushed him in the chest, told him he was a dirty, cowardly, thieving skunk, and announced to spectators, who had begun to gather immediately, that the star Cutter wore had been purchased by a bribe to an alderman, with bribe money obtained by theft from a friend and by the sale of a fourteen-year-old girl to a brothel. "See the man now paid to keep the peace," Lewis shouted. "And there's more I know, and more I could say."

O'Faolin did not tell me, because Lewis hadn't told him, that Cutter at that point said, "Watch your mouth, Lew; don't forget what I know about you."

Lewis told Cutter, "I'm gonna give you a mild pasting, not the mortal pasting you deserve. Then you'll pay me the money you stole."

Cutter swung his truncheon. Lewis evaded it and knocked it out of Cutter's hand. They fought, Cutter getting much the worst of it, until he broke free and ran on Bayard all the way to Mott, with Lewis behind him. New York City's police did not wear uniforms back then, only the star, so this chase did not look as strange as it would today, but it cannot have done much for Cutter's reputation in the Sixth Ward. Cutter was about to escape into an alley on Mott between Bayard and Pell when someone stuck a foot out and tripped him. Lewis leapt on top of Cutter and began punching him in the face.

It began to snow. People who would ordinarily have gone inside stayed in the streets, taking bets and shouting, "Get his eyes," and "Kick his stones," and crying foul as another man with a star on his coat began choking Lewis from behind. My brother was fortunate in the character of the second policeman. He used the truncheon on Lewis's body only, did not use it after Lewis was subdued, and would not let Jack Cutter use it.

So now Lewis, badly bruised but not crippled, was in the strange Egyptian-looking prison a few blocks from the street where he had caught up with Officer Jack Cutter, alias Tom Cross, and with my employers' permission I went to visit him there, bearing a basket full of apple pie, bread, cheese, sausage, candles, and newspapers.

Perhaps you have seen pictures of the famous edifice, whose appearance inspires a feeling less of the law's might than of its mystery—a thing too bizarre to reason with. There was a broad flight of dark stone steps, and massive columns whose capitals, in the shape of palm leaves, were on that day partly obscured by icicles.

After I had gone through the entrance, I was in a large courtyard, facing a second building, which was the men's prison, made of four galleries, one on top of another. Laborers were making repairs on the bottom floor—the prison was sinking into its soggy foundations. The light was dim, the air foul. A jailer on the third tier led me to my brother's cell. On the way, we passed many others, one of which had the door open, so I could see a woman with a bowed head talking to the unseen inmate. Finally, the jailer opened a massive black iron door to a small, bare cell lit by a chink in the wall, with one table and two bedsteads, a sink, a chamber pot, and my brother and another prisoner, whom Lewis introduced to me as Hugh O'Faolin.

"Johnny's brother," I said, and Hugh smiled as if we were old friends because I knew Johnny.

While the two of them shared the food I'd brought, Lewis told me, with a careless air, as if it made a funny story, that he was being charged with robbery, assault, resisting arrest, and half a dozen other things that slipped his mind. Cutter claimed that he had recognized Lewis as fitting the description of a man who robbed a grocery on Pell Street, that *Lewis* had run, and he, Cutter, had given chase.

When I asked how I could help, he said by not worrying. He had sent for me because he knew I would be mad if he didn't and I found out later he'd been in jail. But if I wanted to—if it would amuse me—perhaps I could help him find a lawyer, one who would waive a fee in view of the easy victory he was bound to achieve by representing Lewis. For it was sure to be easy! Dozens of witnesses had seen that it was he, Lewis, who had followed Cutter, shouting "Stop, thief."

My brother Lewis was an open book to me. I knew that under his bluster he was terrified. He had never seen the inside of a jail cell before, and a moment later I learned that his circumstances were in fact graver than he had yet revealed to me.

O'Faolin, who looked several years older than Lewis, said, "You left something out."

Lewis looked at him uncomprehendingly for a moment and then shook his head.

"What?" I cried. "What is it? What? I must know everything."

"I was there," said his cellmate. "I was there at the police station when they brought him in, and the other coppers, when they saw Lewis, and how small he was next to Cutter, they all let go a big laugh. Because they had already heard about the chase. They heard it was Lewis chasing Cutter."

"You see," said my brother, "everyone knows."

"And Cutter being so much the bigger man, that makes it funny. Your brother, he looks just half alive, but he laughs, too. And Cutter takes Lewis by the head and whispers something and gives him a knock."

He stopped, and we both looked at Lewis, who threw another angry look at Hugh.

"What did he say to you, Lewis?"

We just listened to the sound of hammering below, until O'Faolin spoke. "He says, 'A friend of mine is a guard in Sing Sing. You won't last a month there.' He says, 'My friend'll see to that.'"

I looked at Lewis, and then I looked back at his cellmate. "Mr. O'Faolin, do you think this is true? Tell me," I implored him, because I needed expert opinion.

"It happens," he said with a judicious air. After a little pause for recollection, he explained, "They can punish you. They say you broke this rule, and that rule, and they work you to death." He named some men who had suffered this fate, and others who had been stabbed by fellow prisoners who had been paid to do it.

"I can take care of myself," said Lewis, his words belied by a fat lip, and various swellings and discolorations on his face; to make his claim even less convincing, he erupted into a complex, protracted cough.

"But the court, Mr. O'Faolin—what do you say to my brother's chances in court?"

"He needs a miracle."

OUTSIDE THE TOMBS, THE WIND BLEW SNOW horizontally into my face and I did not feel it—I could only think and fret and wish. My brother was the world to me. He was all the family I had, and in all creation he was the only man who had ever stood up for me, really stood up for me so it counted. He had shown me the truest, purest, most absolute loyalty there is: loyalty that had to make up for the absence of a mother, a father, and a lover; loyalty to lift my steps across the mindless drudgery of an ordinary day, or to carry me on beating wings over the sudden abyss of an emergency. He had made a cripple of his hero, just as soon as he learned that the hero had harmed me. For my sake, he had become a fugitive. And now he was killing me with his recklessness. I could not live and see my brother crushed, and he *was* being crushed, he *would* be crushed, without a miracle. Where could I get one?

I have always been a quick study. I had been five months in New York City, and I knew where miracles were sold. I went to the grocery store of Con Donoho, the mighty Sixth Ward street inspector, and asked Mrs. Donoho to speak with me alone. Without a word, she took me down to a musty-smelling basement full of sacks and barrels and broken furniture. She lit another candle to improve the light, and said to me, "This would be about your brother Lewis?" I nodded, not very surprised—glad of it, since her omniscience suggested power, and I needed power—and she went to a barrel and drained a mug of beer from it and handed it to me. "Tell me what you think of this variety," she said. My two elderly employers had a secret fondness for beer and sometimes sent me out to get it for them, so I knew a little about it. I sniffed the mug and guessed that it was stale beer from the lees. A cup of it gave one a killing headache, but it was a cheap way to get drunk, and—so a flirtatious bartender had told me—the Five Points was full of dank cellars in which men determinedly obliterated themselves with this stuff. Supposing that the cup had been put before me to test my good sense, I ignored it. Trying to sound businesslike and not too worried, I began repeating what I had learned while visiting my brother in the Tombs—my brother's words, O'Faolin's words—and after repeatedly nodding, as if she knew all this, Mrs. Donoho said impatiently, "And Cutter has threatened to have your brother killed in prison."

Here I suppose my brave front dropped. "How do you know this?"

"Oh, word gets around."

I was at a loss for a few seconds. At last I asked her, "And is it empty talk?"

She shrugged. "I wouldn't count on it."

"Tell me what I need to do to fix it. I'll do anything."

She blinked at me. "Anything? Is that so? Or is that just a figure of speech?" I didn't answer. She took away the mug of lees without comment, got up, and brought me another mug. "Try this and see if you like it better."

I smelled it and took a sip; it tasted exactly like the drink I had once stolen from the two elderly sisters in an impulsive act of vengeance.

"What makes you think Constantine can fix this?" she asked.

"I guess he'll know who can, and what they'll want in return."

"I'll ask him, and he'll ask around. But if you forced me to guess, I'd say they'd want five hundred dollars. And you a housemaid. Where are you going to get money like that, if you don't mind my asking?"

"I don't mind your asking, but where I get it is my lookout."

"I guess so. Well, you're loyal to that brother of yours. I hope he appreciates it."

I had to get back to the elderly sisters, so I walked fast, and a young fellow in a stovepipe hat noticed me. "Hello! Where are you going in such a hurry?"

I was in that state when one schemes to quell panic and make the next minute bearable. If necessary, you think, I will do this unpleasant thing, and give up that dear thing, and you feel better because at least these ugly choices are your own. I decided that I would really need six hundred dollars, not just five hundred. That way, I could promise Mrs. Donoho an extra hundred when my brother was actually freed. I know now that five hundred alone would have been enough: her cut had been figured into it.

Six hundred dollars was twice my yearly salary. My rich grandfather was dead. I had not heard from my older brothers since I was twelve, or any other relative of mine save my aunt and uncle, who hated Lewis. Distasteful as it might be to ask Jocelyn to loan me the money she had earned by selling her flesh, I would have asked her, but I knew she didn't have it. She owed money to Mrs. Bower.

So my mind turned to my steamboat companion Eric Gordon. He must be very rich, to have one home in Brooklyn and another just a ferry ride away, at the most expensive hotel in New York, so that he could amuse himself with light women while his wife enjoyed a house with trees, a garden, and servants. Such a man could solve carelessly, almost absentmindedly, problems that meant life or death to me and to Lewis.

There was never any doubt in my mind what I would have to give Mr. Gordon in exchange for such a large sum. Shivering in my bed in my cold attic room that night, in the house of the two sisters who had predicted that I would eventually do just what I was about to do, I went through many phases of decision and indecision. What if Cutter had been merely lying or boasting when he said that he would have my brother killed in prison? In that case, the trade was this—either Lewis, thanks to his own folly, would go to prison for a certain time, or I would dishonor myself forever. And after that, what? What would I be? *Who* would I be? Was it a fair exchange?

Perhaps I would not be able to find Eric Gordon. Maybe he was out of town. Whereas before I had calmed myself with the idea of action, now I took refuge in the thought that the final outcome was up to chance and fate, and at last I was able to sleep.

IN A FUR-COLLARED COAT, a pretty blue dress, an India-muslin pelerine, and white kid gloves, all just purchased secondhand with my entire savings, I crossed the street, which was full of dirty snow, big-wheeled, boatlike omnibuses, gigs, hacks, and carriages, and I approached the world-famous Astor House. The great hotel looked majestic from a distance, but at ground level it resembled a bazaar, gripped by a disorderly collection of canvas awnings that put the sidewalk in shadow, by street hawkers, and by hanging placards and bills that advertised restaurants, patent medicines, and theatrical productions in those tall letters that remind one of men on stilts. I passed between a pair of Roman columns, and up a flight of steps into a tall, wide, gaslit lobby. The marble floor was strewn with luggage. Guests handed coats and capes and silk hats to a fellow in a room to the side. In another alcove, a man stood still while a hotel employee brushed his coat.

An imposing, double-chinned desk clerk stood before a great book and near a mysterious glass case full of sickle-shaped pieces of brass. After he had assisted a few of the customers in line before me, I handed him a letter for Mr. Gordon; he gave no sign of whether he knew who Eric Gordon was, or had any opinions about the kind of girl who might leave a letter for him. He turned and put the letter into a pigeonhole in the wall behind him.

The letter told of my brother's trouble and asked for Eric Gordon's help, not saying what I might give in return, or the amount of money that would be needed. I said that I would come back to the hotel desk at the same time next week, on my day off.

As I was leaving the hotel, I saw him. He looked richer to me now than he had before, and nearly as handsome as I remembered. He gave me the glance a man of his type gives a pretty girl, and then his face lit up. "Miss Moody! From the *Israel Putnam*!" He pressed my right hand between his hands. "Look at you. Don't you look lovely. Do you know someone at the hotel?"

"Only you," I said, frightened—it was happening too quickly. "I left a letter for you."

"When?"

"Just now. Only just now."

"I see. Is there someplace you must be right now? Or do you have time to speak to me in person?"

"I have time."

"Then you must dine with me," he said, as though it were a matter of course and he said that he was planning to dine here—would I mind that terribly?—and when I said no, he hooked his arm in mine, took my letter from the clerk, who did not look at me, and led me through the Astor House, which became to me at that point a labyrinth. I suppose if Eric had left me there I would have been able to find my way out, but it did not feel like that as we walked through doorways and down halls; I decided that twice the combined population of Livy and Patavium were contained within these walls and most of them were strangers to each other. The thought was comforting. No one knew or cared what I did.

There were children in the corridors, rich men's children, running and screaming. What an easy life they had!

At last Eric led me into an opulently furnished, gaslit room, with heavy drapes and rich carpets and chandeliers, and a few round tables with lacy white tablecloths. There were women and children as well as men in the chamber. When we came in Eric nodded to a few of the other patrons, evidently casual acquaintances of his—and who, I was sure, must know I was not his wife. Though he had not introduced me, the men, and also a few women in the proximity of children probably their own, returned his speechless greeting in a way that seemed to acknowledge and welcome me into their company, and afterward ignored us, and I felt that I had learned something about the morals and manners appropriate to a fashionable hotel dining room. A well-dressed waiter filled our glasses with clear, sweet Croton water and some chunks of ice, handed us a printed bill of fare, and retreated to a corner. "The *table d'hôte* here is considered one of the best in the city," Eric said. "I don't think you'll be disappointed."

"I'm sure I won't. I have very little basis for comparison."

He looked at me: "I remember that about you. That you talk that way."

It was not clear quite what he meant, but I liked his saying it. It made me feel that he had noticed me for something other than my proportions, and I found a bit of courage in that, enough to mask my nerves.

"Why don't you order for me?" I said. "And then you can read the letter, and we'll have something to talk about."

"You're here in the flesh. Why don't you just tell me what's in it?"

"I labored over its composition. I don't want it to go to waste."

"All right. Do you like veal?"

"I'm happy to try it," I said.

"Wine?"

"Yes, and quickly."

He laughed. I was amusing him already. He ordered with the expected fluency. When I drank the wine I felt its power immediately, as abstemious people do, and was less nervous about the future. What would be would be. The rich man would decide.

He read my letter without a change of expression and put it into his waistcoat. He took a sip from his glass as the waiter came forward to refill mine.

"The Sixth Ward is certainly badly governed. I did not know it was governed out of a grocery, but I can believe it." My letter had mentioned Con Donoho and his wife. "How did you come to meet that woman?"

Sipping more slowly on my second glass of wine, I told him of my experiences in New York, starting with my encounter with the bad man with the poet's hair and the cane, and how, while escaping him, I had come to my old house; and Mrs. Shea, who had given me the name of Mrs. Donoho. "Will you be able to help me?"

"I'm sure I can do something," he said. "What a life of adventure you lead."

The waiter was bringing the dishes now.

"It only seems that way when I tell it quickly. It has been mostly drudgery."

"I hope you'll let me change that."

If that was a question, I was not ready to answer it, so I just smiled at him.

"Do you like the theater?" he asked me.

"Probably."

"We could go to the theater tonight, you and I. Of course I'll help your brother. You can rest easy, knowing that, and in the meantime, we can enjoy ourselves."

"All right," I said, smiling at him.

I thought I had a pretty good idea of what was going to happen tonight, and if I must take this fearful step, I preferred to do it in an atmosphere of music and wine and oysters and such amusements as he had described to me on the *Israel Putnam*. Luxury was supposed to be the thing that tempted weak-willed girls from the path of virtue, and it was a terrible mistake and a bad bargain; I had always heard that, and I believed it. But if I had to be bad, I might as well have the pleasant things that came along with it, and I welcomed distraction as someone undergoing a surgical operation would welcome ether.

The food came to us. Together, Eric Gordon and I discovered that I did like veal, that I had a great talent for liking viands well cooked in the French mode, and that my mouth looked pretty when I was attempting to pronounce their names.

Since it was early for the theater, we first walked arm in arm to the fountain at City Hall, and from there to a great gaudy five-story building with flags on the roof, oval paintings of its attractions between the windows, and the name BARNUM'S AMERICAN MUSEUM running under the fourth-story windows along Anne Street. In the company of visitors from the world over, we went from floor to floor, looking at dioramas, panoramas, models of Dublin, Paris, Niagara Falls (with flowing water); mechanical figures, industrious fleas, educated dogs, jugglers, automatons, ventriloquists, living statues; American Indians doing rain dances in full ceremonial dress, the very club with which Captain Cook was killed in the Sandwich Islands.

We then walked to the Park Theatre, which burned down a few years later. It was evening. Lamps were on. The streets were full of hacks and carriages and elegantly dressed strollers. Men tipped their hats to me. It was a worldly throng, friendly and at ease with each other; the preachers and the deep thinkers were at home, eating their dinners and rebuking their children, and we were safe from their disapproval.

The Park was small by today's standards, but beautiful, with gaslight chandeliers, well-upholstered chairs, and attendants; and Eric had a subscription to a box. We saw a musical number, with a singer, followed by a play featuring Edwin Forrest, Bridget's favorite actor. The play was *Spartacus,* which allowed Forrest—whose figure was much admired, though he struck me as too stout—to stand half naked, waving a sword, while lecturing ancient Romans on modern American notions. The mechanics, who adored Forrest, sat in the pit, eating peanuts and sandwiches, insulting the actors they disliked, and whooping and whistling at each entrance of their hero. In those days, clergymen considered theaters to be cesspools of immorality, and they knew whereof they spoke: one could see the men in the lower tiers leaving their boxes to visit the prostitutes in the third tier, a section reserved for such people back then, as even I who had never been in a theater before knew. After *Spartacus* there was a minstrel show.

Then came the reckoning. Eric said that he knew a place where we could get a nice little supper. Outside the theater, he hailed a hack; once we were in it, he told the driver to circle the park until further orders; he put his arms around me and kissed me; I let him. He said I was a fascinating creature; I had bewitched him, he was under my spell, he was mine to command, I could do what I wanted with him. He said it as a sort of absentminded amorous patter while his expert fingers busied themselves with my clothes, like an Italian barber simultaneously telling a joke and administering a shave. Or like a man who is good with a nervous horse: it would be given a carrot, spoken to softly—it didn't matter what was said—and mounted. He kept moving past barriers, some tangible, some abstract, each a cue for me to protest if I cared to, but I did not, for he was bound to discover eventually that I was not a virgin. Without virginity to bargain with, I must please him enough for him to want to have me more than once. Anyway, that's how I thought. At last his hands found the door to my womb. His fingers stroked me not unpleasantly, delving farther as my responses lubricated the passage. Discovering no barrier, he said, "It is as I hoped." He slipped my undergarments aside and lifted me so that I straddled his lap, with my skirts around us both. As he pulled me closer, the tip of his manhood, which I had not even realized had been exposed, penetrated my depths. I gasped. He drew me closer. I shut my eyes and pulled Eric's head against my bosom.

Without a doubt, the answer of my flesh to his attentions pleased Eric. It was real, and he knew the difference. Otherwise, he would have spared himself the trouble and expense of seduction and been content with prostitutes.

He lifted me up as he was about to have his crisis, and spent his seed in a handkerchief; then, with a consideration rare among men who fancy themselves great lovers, he stroked me with his fingers until I had my own satisfaction. He gave new instructions to the driver.

So at last it had happened; I had given myself to a man, voluntarily, without a wedding. I thought, like countless other girls, that after all it had been easy. The ground had not opened beneath me. Everything was just the same as before, except for a mild physical satiety, as though I had eaten an apple. I felt a bit more warmly toward Eric and wondered what he thought about me now. I was still worried about my brother, and I wondered where all this would lead. Though I felt that I had taken a step down a slippery slope, I realized that I had been on that slope a while.

Supper was at an oyster saloon, near enough to the Park Theatre for us to have walked. We ate in a private room. His manner was altered. There was a frankness, almost as if I were another man rather than a woman, a lack of deference compensated for by an easygoing friendliness.

He said that he wouldn't speak of it if I minded, but it seemed to him that I had a little experience with men, though not enough to spoil my delightful freshness. I told him about Matthew, how he had forced me, how I had had to get rid of the child, and how it had ruined my chance of marrying the man I loved, how Matthew had confessed to his crime the day we all believed the world was about to end, and how my brother had repaid him for his foul deed.

Eric's reactions were different for each stage of my story. He commiserated with me for the untimely loss of my virginity and the ruin of my marital prospects. He made no comment regarding my self-induced miscarriage. The circumstances of Matthew's confession amused him; he told me a few secondhand tales of Millerites in New York City who had stood on rooftops in their white ascension robes. When I told him that, so far as I knew, Matthew was still unable to walk, he said, "It seems a little hard."

"Not to me," I said.

"It's all nonsense," he said, "left over from the Dark Ages, this store that people set on virginity and chastity."

He did not think he was changing the subject. Perhaps, with girls less cooperative than I, Eric himself had used a bit of force to complete his conquest, and thought of it as only natural.

From the oyster saloon we went to bed—to my disappointment, not at the Astor, but at a clean, well-furnished house of assignation, where they were careful not to greet him like the steady customer he probably was. With the lamps still on, he undressed me; he had me turn and show myself to him, every part. He disrobed and showed me his staff, its rigid state "a tribute to your charms," he said. He asked me if I dared to touch it, and when my finger circled it he said, "Brave girl, oh, what a brave girl you are." By morning, it seemed to me that—as they say in books—nothing remained hidden from me.

It was already the afternoon of the next day when I awoke and looked at him. He lay with his head back and his neck exposed, his arm over his brow, one leg hidden by the covers, another out. I thought: *It will be all right, he will love me.*

Perhaps he loved me already. He was attached to the delights of the bedroom, and I had pleased him. He had said over and over that he had never been with a woman who was so perfectly proportioned; that I looked better with each shred of clothing removed; no part of me had disappointed him. I was happy to accept his invitation to forget the old rules, under which I was irreparably destroyed, and accept a new set of rules, under which I was beginning life with great advantages. He had said I was wonderful. I knew it did not always mean love when men said things like that. But maybe it would mean that this time. He would love me. I would love him—I could feel it already, though it was not so easy at the moment to separate the love from need. He would leave his wife (who could not have been very good to him or he would not have looked elsewhere for affection!). We would defy convention, like Byron and Shelley and their lady friends. We would go to Switzerland and Italy.

I reached across the bed and touched his cheek with my finger. His eyes opened, his gaze settled on me, and he smiled. "Look at you," he said.

I kissed him on the eyes. He pulled me to him and had me again, sweetly at first, but then not so sweetly. It turned out that I had not in fact learned everything the night before, and I received the impression that much of what we had done then had been merely a preparation and that he was now doing what he had really wanted to do all along. When he was finished I had a changed opinion of myself, and I believed, with a dismay that I was not quite ready to acknowledge, that this had been an important part of his purpose; that it figured largely in his pleasure.

My face was in the pillow as his body uncovered mine. I lay like that awhile. Then I turned on my back, pulled the sheet up to cover my nakedness, and looked at a bumpy patch of plaster on the ceiling. "Take me away somewhere," I said after a while, and he replied promptly with a list of possible amusements for the day. "No," I pressed him. "I mean far away. After my brother is freed. Let's go to Italy. Take me to Italy. I want to see Florence. I want to see Venice."

There was a pause, and he said, "Italy. Well, it would be a little awkward, this time of year. As I think you know, I have other demands on my time, people who depend upon me."

"Do you love her? Your wife?"

"I must ask you not to speak of my wife," he said quietly. "I alluded to her just now when I saw something had to be explained, something a smart girl like you ought to have understood, but I must insist that you not mention her again." Then, in a be-sensible tone, he said, "When you said your brother was in trouble, I believed you. Is he really in the Tombs for assaulting a policeman?"

I was trembling. "Yes. And robbery. But he didn't do it. Only the assault, and it was less than the bastard deserved."

"I have no way of knowing that, but let's say he didn't. Were you really told that a bribe handled by an Irish grocer would resolve the problem?"

"Yes."

"Well, you see, I find that hard to credit. In my experience, grocers sell salt meat and potatoes and coffee and maybe a glass of whiskey; they don't dispose of criminal-law cases. I can't help wondering if you are being deceived."

"Constantine Donoho is the Sixth Ward street inspector," I said, and then I was silent for a while, gathering my thoughts. "In Five Points, that makes him important, because he has jobs to give out that don't involve any work. He happens also to own a grocery, and does his business out of it. He's a politician, really. He knows the other politicians. They do each other favors. For example, he knows Alderman O'Daniel."

I had more, but he stopped me. He didn't really care, and—though I didn't realize this until much later—he still didn't believe me. Girls like me always had an imaginary friend in dire straits. "How much do you need?"

I told him.

He laughed. "You might as well ask me for a trip to Venice again. It wouldn't cost any more. Oh no, don't do that." I was weeping. "Don't. I can help you out. I can help solve your problem. I just can't be the whole solution. I can give you twenty dollars. All right. Twenty-five. That is my limit, and believe me, it is high praise. I give it to you out of gratitude and admiration, out of my very high regard for you."

"But I've given you everything!"

"Now, don't exaggerate," said Eric dryly. "You had parted with some before we met. And you'll find now, if you do an inventory, that you have stock enough to last you many years. And twenty-five dollars isn't chicken feed. But if you really need more . . ."

"There's no if about it."

"Be that as it may, you can easily get more." Because I was silent then, he added, "There are other men like me." I remained silent, and he misinterpreted me again, this time by overestimating the amount of my knowledge. "I even know some, but I'm afraid I cannot introduce you to them. If I did that, I would quickly find myself in a new line of business, and the dry-goods business keeps me busy enough. Now, don't sulk."

In those days, I thought I was pretty good at giving people my opinion of them. I wanted to do that with Eric Gordon then. It would have made me feel better for a while. Something held me back. Maybe I realized that whatever I said I couldn't hurt him very much, or that it was better not to burn my bridges before I understood the terms of this new life. Perhaps it was just that I didn't want to show this man my feelings. I had surrendered too much to him already.

"I'm sorry," I said. "I was weak for a moment."

"Yes, and bless you for it," he said. To show he wasn't angry, he began speaking again of the day's possible amusements. I told him that I was tired, perhaps another time, and that when I moved I would leave him my address so that he could write me letters or send me messages if he cared to. He said, "Before I forget," and gave me twenty-five dollars in silver.

I DID NOT KNOW WHAT TO DO NEXT. I had to decide. I went back to the house of the elderly sisters, who docked me a full day's wages for having missed half a day of work. For two days I swept out fireplaces, trimmed wicks, and scrubbed floors. On the third day, when they sent me with a shopping list out to the Washington Market, I went instead to the house where Jocelyn now worked. The colored girl who opened the door for me told me that Mrs. Bower was in bed with ague in her home on Lafayette Street. I walked there and announced myself to another servant, who came back saying, "She'll see you."

As I sat by Mrs. Bower's bed, we discussed my future. We agreed that she would advance me the money I needed for my brother, and also some money for new clothes. In return, I would become the new girl at her best house, the finest in this great city, patronized by the city's leading men and important visitors from other states, who were all on their best behavior when they were there—so Mrs. Bower assured me. If I did not like the life, once I had earned the money I owed her I could leave and there would be no hard feelings. Or perhaps I would stay on until I had earned enough to open up a little shop. There were girls who did that. Not many, but such things happened. I thanked her, promising that I would not disappoint her. I was lying, however, for I planned that as soon as Lewis was free I would kill myself.

XXXII

IF THIS WERE A PLAY, AN INTERMISSION would come here. The next act would take place "two years later," and when the curtain rose again I'd be stepping out of a carriage, entering a drawing room looking respectable, or in a bed dying gracefully and repentantly, and all the degrading actions that had intervened would be delicately alluded to in subsequent dialogue. If only life could be like that! In our actual lives, the humiliations authors turn away from must be endured second by second, with only drink or a bad memory to provide a respite.

If, in Mrs. Bower's house, a bit of illusion remained, this was not to make things easier for the girls, but because it was part of our service. Before we went upstairs, there was conversation downstairs, and glasses were filled and sipped and refilled. It wasn't the raucous carousing of a bordello, but an imitation of polite society as the men in society secretly wished it to be. There would be flirting, gallant compliments, and giggling rejoinders. We went to bed under the pretense that a forbidden romance was moving forward at an impossible speed.

How delightful it would be, for the wealthy man about town, if the pretty girl he met in her family's drawing room could, for the right payment to her father, be whisked upstairs and rogered on the spot! How refreshing for the young man who has to worry that a few incautious words might turn him into a husband tied to some dreary job, if he could have the girl right now, then hitch up his trousers and walk away! How pleasant if the fiftyish fellow who plays the avuncular friend of the family, and gives sage advice to his friend's pretty daughter, could do what he really wants to do with her, instead of just imagining it on his widower's bed a few hours later, grimacing, his furious red manhood in his fist! Well, Mrs. Bower's parlor house was the enchanted realm where these things could happen; and I was a crucial element, for, thanks to my unusual life history and natural gifts, I did an uncanny imitation of a girl of good family. I *was* a girl of good family, to whom a series of accidents had occurred which made me available to these men.

Mrs. Bower suggested I take a new name, as most of the girls did, to cover their tracks. I did not care about that practical purpose, but I liked the drop of oblivion a false name provides, and, borrowing a Christian name from a novel and a family name from a newspaper article, I called myself Harriet Knowles.

My first, if we do not count Eric Gordon, was Colonel Jack, a state senator, small, gray, with an asymmetrical mustache and acrid breath. In my life until then I had not seen many naked bodies, and I was startled by the web of blue veins that enveloped the skin of his frail white legs and haunches as he methodically folded his clothes and placed them on a chair. His face pivoted abruptly toward me—I ought not to have been watching him—and I gave him a frightened smile. "Be gentle," I heard myself beg him, he replied coolly, like a gentleman rebuking an untested new servant, a rebuke that is part of her education, "I'll be what I please, as the mood takes me. Lie flat." He was of the school that tries, using their weight, to print the girl into the bed. I could not move—he did not want me to move—and he moved only enough to generate the necessary friction, until, toward the end, he began to shudder. Meanwhile, I breathed through my mouth and returned the stare of his watery eyes, which were trapped within folds so pronounced they reminded me of hardened candle ends.

I do not remember much more from that night. I drank a good deal before we went upstairs, to improve the appeal of Colonel Jack, and again afterward, to flush him from my consciousness, and as a result I did not make a good impression on the next man when Colonel Jack's needs had been met; I was too drunk to behave much like a Boston merchant's daughter. The man took me anyway, because I was beautiful and a novelty, but Mrs. Bower—who supervised right up to the bedroom door at the beginning—told me the next day, "It could be liquor is your weakness. That's your lookout. If your plan is to wind up a used-up drunken whore in the space of a few years, I know better than to try and stop you. But you can't do it while you're here, because these men, so long as they aren't blind drunk themselves, enjoy neither the company nor the caresses of women who can hardly walk for drink. Somewhere lower down the ladder you can get away with that; maybe that's where you belong. You'll decide. Meanwhile, though, my prices are too high for that. You're expensive right now. You have to act expensive."

I didn't argue with her. What did it matter? My plans did not involve a gradual descent to the lower ranks of prostitution, accelerated by strong drink, or the opening of a millinery or a notions shop, or the acquisition of wealth through the astute management of rich men's weaknesses. I planned to do the honorable thing and die, as soon as a few preliminaries had been cleared up.

I went that very morning to the Donoho grocery in the Five Points, gave Mrs. Donoho the five hundred, and promised her another hundred when Lewis had been released, which, according to her, should be within the week. It was part of the bargain that his case would be expedited, for I was haunted by the possibility that Cutter, who said he knew a guard at Sing Sing, might make the acquaintance of a guard in the Tombs and do away with my brother there. I gave her my new address, so that she could send a messenger to tell me the date of Lewis's trial. Very likely she knew what that address meant, but if she had any opinion about it she gave no sign.

I decided that I could not kill myself until Lewis was free—otherwise, Mrs. Donoho might just keep my money. For the next week after that, whenever I was in the parlor, where we pretended, or upstairs, where the clothes came off and truth was supposedly revealed (but really another set of pretenses went into operation), I would always be thinking with longing and dread that this was not going to continue much longer: the end of my life was nearing. I was eager for Lewis to be out of prison, but I was also scared. Though the decision to die had been a comfort and a sop to my vanity (I was better than these other girls, because I was going to kill myself), as the fatal hour approached I began to be afraid.

One morning, the maid knocked loudly on my door, waking me and a man whose name had slipped my mind, though I remembered that one of his testicles was shrunken and that he liked the feeling of being smothered. The maid told me disapprovingly that a rude boy from some grocery had given her a note to pass to me. The note, scrawled in pencil on a scrap of newspaper, named the location and approximate time of Lewis's trial. It would be soon. I had to hurry; I rushed the stranger out of the room, and dressed quickly. I took along the pistol Mrs. Robinson had given me back in Cohoes; I planned to use it on Jack Cutter, in case it went wrong and it turned out that my money had been taken, and my honor lost, for nothing, and Lewis was to go to prison anyway.

I expected to see Cutter, and I hoped to see him ruined. He would be revealed as the monster who had seduced an innocent fourteen-year-old mill girl, brought her to the wicked city, and sold her into shame. Which—as I fully realized even then—would not be a perfectly accurate description of what had occurred between those two. But it was true on the general point, that he was a rotten bastard.

I thought, you see, that for Lewis to be freed, Cutter must be unmasked; at the very least, it would be made public that my brother was innocent of any robbery. But what happened instead was this: Jack Cutter and the other policeman, who would have been the only witnesses against my brother, did not show up. The state's attorney asked that the trial be postponed; Lewis's attorney said that justice delayed was justice denied, and his client had been shut up in the Tombs for too long already. The judge agreed and dismissed the case and ordered that my brother be set free.

I could not say I had been lied to. All Mrs. Donoho had promised was that she would use the money to free Lewis. Now he was free. However, she had known very well that I expected more. I had the feeling the poor often have, that the game is rigged.

With these complicated feelings, then, I met Lewis in the center aisle of the courtroom and embraced him, while at the front of the room the clerk announced the next case and the judge said, "Lemuel Sanders? I know this scoundrel. Bring him up here." My brother smelled like a sour washrag, but I hugged him close a long while, telling myself that it would be the last time we would ever embrace.

"See?" he said. "See? I told you there was nothing to worry about."

Like so many anonymous donors, I was frustrated by the ingratitude of the beneficiary. "You're wrong, Lewis. You've been lucky. You should take a lesson from this."

He shook his head. "I knew he'd be too yellow to come to court. I wish he had, so I could have told people about him."

I knew that most of this talk was empty show, and that he had been far more frightened than he let on. But he was going to forget that fear as fast as he could. As we walked out into the street, I repeated that he was luckier than he knew. "Lewis, I don't care how you do it, but you've got to get yourself a shave and bath and clean clothes."

"Okay, sis," he said, in a funny voice, to show that he was being good-natured about my endless mothering of him when, after all, he was a grown man. I remembered that our mother had told me on her deathbed to look after him, and I felt a pang at the thought that I was about to relinquish that responsibility.

"Let me give you some money for the bath and a shave and clothes," I said. He told me he could pay his own way. We went to an oyster house, had a meal, and talked about Bowling Green. I became emotional. He asked what was wrong. I said I was just happy because he was out of jail; I had been so worried. I pushed money into his hands. "If you take this, I know you'll feel honor-bound to spend it on cleaning yourself up, and I'll feel better. Make my mind easy, Lewis." He rolled his eyes and took it, he said, just to make me stop talking about it. Then I said I had to get back to my job, and I walked away, my throat tight, tears flowing.

My suicide note was in my chest of drawers back at the brothel.

My dear Lewis,

Do not mourn; the life just lost was no longer precious to me. If at first you do not understand what I have done, in time you will see that it was best. Do not feel remorseful; nothing that has happened is your fault. Know that I died loving you and thinking well of you. Now that I'm gone I hope you'll be more careful. You must take charge of your own affairs from now on. Go to Mrs. Donoho and ask her to help you, for she and her husband are a power in the Sixth Ward and have an interest in your future.

Your Devoted Sister,
Arabella

I had torn up four earlier versions into small pieces, not wanting my suicide made into a joke with the discovery of competing notes. Each draft had helped me survive the day on which it was written. The first had been the shortest, just a cry of anguish. The others all began "My dear Lewis." He would know after he got the note that I was in a brothel. Mrs. Donoho would tell him why. He would realize that I had sacrificed myself for him, so, on the same day he learned I had been a whore, he would decide that I was a saint.

It was the dinner hour. Lewis had turned one way on Bowery, I had turned the other, and I had come to the rug district—rug stores for block on block; giant rugs hanging from the upper stories. I had stopped, planning to get on a horsecar, when I spotted, in the busy rush of mechanics, clerks, restaurant patrons, and paupers coming my way, one man who was not moving, and a little taller than most, and looking at me with a mixture of appetite and confidence, as if he were a boy and I an item in a store window that had been promised to him for Christmas. It was Jack Cutter. He had been following me. The copper star was still on his coat.

"Arabella!" he said. "Or—no, not Arabella, Harriet. It's Harriet now, right?"

Just the sight of him had frightened me; it took all my self-possession not to show it, and I had not time to master my emotions before this remark threw me further off balance. My mind was clear, however, and I understood at once. He knew Mrs. Bower. It was he who had introduced Jocelyn to her. If Mrs. Bower herself had not told him about me, someone else at one of Mrs. Bower's parlor houses must have. They need only have said that the new girl at the other house was Jocelyn's friend from the mill.

"Do you like my new coat?" he asked me.

"How are your knees healing? I heard you fell hard on them when you were running away from my brother."

"I'll heal faster than he will," said Cutter, looking very fit and pleased with himself. His handsome face had one expression, sufficiently nasty, and his little crooked scar had another. The horsecar stopped. I got on it, reaching up through the trap to pay the driver. Cutter was right behind me, getting on, too. A portly man offered me his seat. I smiled, a smile full of feminine modesty and good breeding, and shook my head. I wanted to be able to leave the car in a hurry. Cutter said, "I wanted to ask you. Do you think your brother appreciates the sacrifices you make for him?"

I thought how terrible it would be were Lewis to learn the truth from Cutter, and I could think of nothing useful to say back beyond, "You're a pig."

He grabbed my wrist. "Don't call me names."

A few of the passengers gave Cutter unfriendly glances, and a young man, who looked as if he might consider himself capable of defending a lady, said to him, "This is disgraceful."

Cutter put a thumb on his star. "I caught this girl asking a man in a rug store if he wanted to take her to a disorderly house. That's against the law. You look respectable. You don't take strange girls to houses, do you?"

I had the impression that the passengers had become a jury, and the verdict was going against me. I did not think they would believe me if I said he was lying.

I had the pistol, I remembered. It was loaded. If he let go of my hand, I could get it. I would say that there was something in my bag he ought to see, and I would open the bag and shoot him before he knew what was happening. The other passengers would be frightened and duck for cover, and then I would shoot myself.

"I'm sorry I called you names," I said. "Let's be friends."

"That's better," said Cutter, smiling, and released my wrist.

"I have something in my bag I'd like to show you," I told Cutter.

"Let me see it," he said.

I felt myself leaving the decision up to my hands. My hands were unwilling.

Someone tugged the cord and rang the horsecar's bell. The horses rested, the car stopped. I wormed my way quickly into the clutch of people disembarking. Cutter called after me. "Like my new coat?" he repeated, adding this time: "You paid for it!" I was at that moment more ashamed of being unable to kill him than I was of being a whore. It was because I was sober, I told myself. When I was drunk I would find the courage. I lifted my skirts clear of the mire of Bowery, rushed through a brief safe passage between a carriage and a horse cart, and stepped onto the curb. I heard Cutter calling through the horsecar window: "I can afford your prices now. Maybe I'll pay you a visit."

I had thought myself wise beyond my years. I had had an idea of how my brother's release had been arranged, an idea that I considered sufficiently cynical, and it involved many little and big payoffs to corrupt officials. As I walked away—aimlessly at first, but then uptown and back to Mrs. Bower's—I saw how it could have been done much more simply, with greater profit to Mrs. Donoho. Every dollar that she did not keep for herself she had given to Cutter and the other policeman who had arrested my brother.

WELL, WHY THINK ABOUT IT? I was going to leave all that behind. I went to my room. I took out the suicide note. I took the pepper-box pistol from my bag. I had a whiskey bottle, which I had sent for earlier expressly in order to acquire the courage to kill myself. I drank until I was fearless. But then I was shameless as well. When the difference between life and death was unimportant, so was the difference between being virtuous and being a whore. Instead of shooting myself, I went to sleep.

When I awoke, I heard a series of loud, insistent knocks, which hurt as if each blow of that unseen fist were striking my head, and after I had staggered across the room to open the door, there was Mrs. Bower. I asked her the time. She said, "Past time for you to be earning, damn you." I began shambling over to my dresser. She said, "No, you can take tonight off. Sleep it off." I went to the water closet and vomited; then I came back and drank a little more and fell back asleep.

When I awoke a second time, I saw I had left the pistol in plain sight. I put it back in a drawer, put on a robe, and went into the hall. A diamond of light that a window at the end of the hall laid on the carpet hurt me so that I was careful not to look at the window itself. I moved slowly and tentatively, eyes half shut, as if my head were not attached to but merely balanced on my neck, down the back stairs to the kitchen, in search of a solution for my immediate problems. Mrs. Bower sat at a small deal table—things were orderly but never fancy in the hidden rooms of the house—before a delicate china cup of coffee in a matching saucer, and two pens and two identical ink bottles, a small day book, a big ledger, and a green felt ink blotter. When I came in, she closed the day book and the ledger and bade me to sit on a chair at the other side of the table. She wore daytime attire, modest enough for the wife of a Presbyterian minister, with an ivory silk pelerine and a lace-trimmed cap. She had a double chin and puffy eyes.

"How are you feeling, Harriet?" she said, and when I didn't answer right away, she spoke to the kitchen maid in a voice whose gentleness I had to appreciate in my condition. "Juno, Harriet's got a hangover." Mrs. Bower opened the day book and the ledger again. Her writing made it apparent that one bottle held red ink and the other black. "I keep track of every penny. It's the secret of my success. I'm careful. On the other hand"—she put the pen in the bottle and looked up at me—"one can't get rich without taking risks. I took a risk with you." She raised a hand to signal me to silence. "I am sorry for you. This is a cruel world. We are in a cruel profession. It's not good to be sensitive. And to be a weakling is terrible. You don't yet know how terrible. I fear you are about to discover it." Her voice was gentle. "Then you will wish—oh, how you will wish—you had been strong enough to take advantage of your opportunities in this house."

At this point, quietly, Juno set down before me a tall mug of beer. She cracked an egg on the side of the mug and emptied its contents into the beer.

"Drink," said Mrs. Bower. She watched me drink my beer and egg as though she could learn about my character from the way I drank it, and then, as if the manner of my drinking had helped her reach a decision, she said, "I'm going to try you out another week. If you don't improve, I'll let you work off your debt in a bawdy house run by a friend of mine. There you may stay as drunk as you like. But it will take you a year to get what you may get in a month here, and you will have to submit to many more men each night, and they'll be men of a lower class than you meet here, and if you don't get sick or have a baby it will be a miracle. Is that what you want?"

I asked her to give me another chance.

"I said I would give it to you," she said, blotting the ledger with the white cloth. She stood up, tucked the book under her arm, and—picking up her shawl, which she had draped over the chair, but leaving the ink bottles for a maid to put away—she left me to rub my brow with my fingers and to think.

See? Nothing is as easy as it looks. Even whores have a duty to "improve," if they can, and show up to work relatively sober and on time.

For a while, I kept alive the thought of using the pistol on Jack Cutter, and perhaps Mrs. Donoho while I was at it. I tried to think of ways to get them in the same room, so that I could shoot them both before I shot myself.

Gradually, I reordered my mind, as I had to if I was not to sink into despair. I lived among people who had special ideas of right and wrong, and what deserved admiration or contempt. Their views were such as to make a whore's life tolerable, and I accepted them as simply as I would have wrapped a blanket around me if I were cold. I became as changed a person as the possession of such opinions could make me.

THERE IS A STORY ABOUT A YOUNG PURITAN who goes into the woods to meet the devil. He goes furtively. He hides whenever his godly neighbors pass, and more and more of them do pass. There's an amazing amount of traffic in this part of the woods, all in one direction. He realizes that every single person in the village is on the same foul mission. They are *all* on their way to meet the devil! They are all hypocrites.

Whores of the highest type experience a similar illumination. They see society inside out; they meet the reputable pillars of the community on the occasion of their visit to the devil. We do not encounter quite every preacher, to be sure, or every crusader against vice, or every mill owner who claims that a higher wage would deny his workers the opportunity of learning thrift. Some of these folks are just what they seem. But we meet the other ones, and they are a mighty and numerous host. We meet as in the forest, in a great witches' sabbath—fallen women, and eminent men with a name for sobriety and chastity. We drink and we fornicate; we laugh until our sides ache at all you gullible fools.

. . .

I BEGAN TO HAVE THE RECURRENT DREAM I have already mentioned. I was back on my uncle Elihu's farm. I was cleaning the cider barrel, bringing water to the mowers, brewing sassafras tea. I was innocent, I was weeping.

My aunt was there. "Arabella," she said. "Belle, my angel, why are you crying?"

"I had a bad dream."

"Tell me about it."

"I can't."

"Yes, you can. Of course you can."

"I'm too ashamed. I dreamed that I was bad, very bad. Oh, Aunt Agatha, even to dream such things, such wicked things—I'm so ashamed."

"Don't be sad." She held me and patted my back. "Everyone does bad things in dreams. The Lord won't hold us to account for what we do in dreams."

She was so wise! "But what if I really did these things, in real life?"

"Then you would burn forever with your father," she said with a tender smile.

I awoke in my room, my face damp with the tears I had dreamed, and I was not alone, but with Philip Heywood, who was only a year older than I, and not unattractive except for a weak chin. He was fair, with blue eyes, long lashes, and a soft, pudgy white body, never having done a day of manual labor. He was shaking me awake, very gently; he had not been so gentle the night before. "What's wrong? Did you have a bad dream?"

"No," I said, wiping my face and looking in true evergreen surprise at my own tears. The only time I cried was in my sleep, as if another soul, one with more tender feelings, inhabited my body in the night. "Yes. In a way. Not exactly."

He had been with me before, but this was the first time he had spent the night. His father, Mrs. Bower had told me, was Arthur Heywood, the editor and publisher of the *New York Courier,* a penny newspaper with Democratic leanings.

"Tell me about the dream," said Philip.

"I dreamed I was back in Boston." It was time to tell him a version of the story I had made up at Mrs. Bower's suggestion. "I grew up in Boston.

My father was—rather, he is, he still lives—my father is an importer, very pious and respectable. His name—I'm going to respect his wishes and not tell you his name. It wasn't Knowles."

"Yes, of course."

"I had two brothers"—making a snap decision, I added—"and three sisters." I knew the undoubted pain of this memory would account for my silence as I took thought. "My father demands a great deal of himself and his clerks. He was not much seen around the house when I was growing up. My mother is very religious, as the wives of Boston merchants tend to be. She's a good woman, but not a good judge of character." I looked at a picture of Lord Byron that hung on the wall nearest my side. "Or so I tell myself when I want to blame her for what happened. Anyway, a few years ago, she had come under the spell of a handsome young minister, whom she asked to help bring her daughters to the love of Jesus."

"Oh," he said. "Oh dear."

"You guess? So quickly? I guess it's an old story, but it seems my mother hadn't heard it! If my father had been more present, he might have prevented what happened. The minister—I do not feel as obliged to protect him—his name was Jeptha Childe, Childe with an 'e.' He preached to all the girls in the house—we attended him very eagerly."

I stopped a long time. At last he prompted me: "What happened? If it does not hurt too much for you to speak of it."

I laid my head down on his hairless chest and regretted it, because it was sticky. But it was too late: I stayed and endured. He put his arm around me. "He was married," I continued. "His wife was consumptive, and they had stopped having physical relations on her doctor's advice. When Jeptha first began talking to me of hellfire and salvation, my figure was not as well developed as it is now, but I guess I was a temptation for him all the same; he would stroke my neck as I bent down over my Bible. One day we fell into sin. It was quite mutual. I was sixteen. I had a baby, a girl. My mother is raising it. She says it is innocent of my crimes, and my father grudgingly agrees. I am not allowed to see the child." Another pause. "There were three portraits of me in the house, one of them in oils. They have all been burned, along with the compositions I wrote at school, the diaries in which I used to pen my childish thoughts, and the pad in which I used to do my clumsy drawings. Everything of mine that could not be carried in a single portmanteau has been given to the poor.

My name may not be spoken. Even *I* do not speak it, since I use a new name now. They tell my little daughter her mother is in heaven, but they know the opposite is true. They tell each other that I was born bad, and this was always my destiny, even if, unaccountably, they did not notice it when I was small. Maybe they're right. Who can say?"

"I can," he said. "It's rotten, the way they've treated you. It's callous and stupid and rotten. I know you aren't bad. Anyone should be able to see that."

"Your tool says otherwise," I observed, stroking him.

"Oh, that, that happens every morning," he said, as if I were likely to be unaware of this phenomenon. "Oh," he said. "Oh."

"Let's use it," I suggested.

"What are you doing?" he inquired, for he was on his back and I was straddling him, and this was new for him. "Oh." I pulled his hands to my bosom.

"Do you like this? Do you like it this way?" He groaned. "I think that must mean yes! So do I. It helps me to please myself." He was one of a select group of men with whom I could take pleasure. I made lovers of them if they were young, and rich enough to have me often. With the loathsome ones I shut my eyes and pretended I was with one of the handsome ones. I never pretended that I was with Jeptha. "Maybe I wasn't born bad, but I think I must be bad now. I think I must be very, very bad."

"Oh. Oh my Lord. Oh Jesus. Oh. Oh. No, don't!" I dismounted—if I could help it, I never let any of them spend their seed in my womb—and switched to other methods, learned in frank discussion with the other girls. "Oh, you're wonderful," he said at the end. "You're not bad at all. You're fine. There's no other girl like you."

"Do you mean it?"

"Of course."

"And you care for me? A little?"

"Oh, very much."

"And if things had been different? If I were not—oh, if I had never met that minister, if I were still a respectable Boston merchant's daughter?"

"I would have asked you to marry me."

"And Juliette Bowden?"

"What about her?"

"I saw the look you gave her last night."

"I didn't give her any look."

"Would you have married her?"

"Of course not."

"Good," I said, and lay beside him as if very glad to know that he did not care for Juliette. Then I asked him to tell me how he spent his day. I wanted to know how he occupied himself when I wasn't there. Where was he at this hour, where was he at that hour? Flattered, he told me (with a lot of complaints, for he didn't like working and didn't see why he should work, since he was rich), and later that day I sent him a long-stemmed rose, along with a note to say that I was thinking of him.

Mrs. Bower was always pushing me to earn more, but she would not mind it if, as eventually happened, most of my income derived from a relatively small group with whom I enacted a charade of love, accompanying them to restaurants and the theater and exchanging *billets doux* and presents. When I say presents, I include the ones I bought them. Where I had gotten this idea I cannot say—from a novel probably, I drew so many of my ideas from novels—but I had begun, very early, to buy certain of my gentlemen presents (accompanied by a brief note, "Thinking of you . . . wish I could stop thinking of you," or "No man has shown me, never, never, what you showed me last night"). The effect of this had astonished me; it was magical; it was more persuasive than anything I had ever done in bed. Though they might with a little thought realize that the present, a silver pin or a silk cravat, was only a fraction of their own money returning to them, the recipients were at the very least flattered and sometimes virtually enslaved. With every reason to be skeptical they believed, because it was a delightful thing to believe, that while there were other men, they were exceptional; their prowess in the boudoir had taken them through brambles and over high walls into my heart.

I tried to persuade them that they had breached the defenses of a special heart. Portraits of Byron and Shelley and Mary Wollstonecraft hung on the walls of my room, and a shelf near my bed displayed their books, along with the works of similar folk, like Fanny Wright and George Sand. Men who stayed the night tended to ask about them. If the right kind of interest was shown, I would say that these writers were my idols, tell their story and mine, and with numerous small touches present myself as a Boston-bred Marguerite Gautier, awaiting the Armand who would revive her finer feelings. I *claimed* to live just for gaiety—let us revel, revel and forget! I *claimed* to be grateful for the fall that had made me into a fascinating woman, but I was a creature of sudden fancies and contradictions, and in intimate moments I would reveal my tragic self, unable to hide the truth that I would have given anything not to have taken the wrong path. (If only *you* hadn't come along, reminding me of all that I can never possess!)

By special arrangement with me, Sean Donovan, the eleven-year-old son of my former landlady, was on call at the house a few hours each day to carry messages to the various men whose affections I cultivated. I was careful not to endanger their marriages, engagements, or reputations with puritanical employers. Sean delivered the letters to their place of business or to their habitual tavern or saloon. My letters were florid and romantic, and, I realize now, longer than they really needed to be. I enjoyed writing them. To make my state bearable, I had accepted without question the traditional hierarchy of whores, which looms very large for those within the profession, and when I wielded my pen I was always conscious of performing an action that marked me out for a rung near the top, with a skill that Lewis's friend Bridget would never master, though she might do certain other things just as well as I.

Not all men want a Marguerite; I could be other things. I could be shy or naughty or obedient or a good sport; I could be of the opinion that men were beasts and we women loved them for it. Unfortunately, sometimes there would appear in Mrs. Bower's parlor one of those men who cannot have a good time unless the girl suffers. If I was fortunate enough to recognize such a man for what he was, I would avoid him by occupying myself with another gentleman. But my instinct was not infallible. I had my share of unpleasant experiences, and all and all, I received a thorough education in a relatively short time.

Mrs. Bower began to show me special signs of her favor. She would ask me to come with her into the kitchen while she did the books, or invite me to go out riding with her, and tell me how superior I was to the other girls: "I like talking to you. You notice things. My words aren't wasted on you. Gwendolyn can act refined, but it's all tricks, it doesn't go deep, like it does with you." A little later she would say, "Annabel would do murder to have your figure; that's why she speaks ill of you behind your back." She would tell me how lucky I was to be working in her house. She did not do the things that other madams did: She did not bring us to dress shops where we were charged twice the going rate and the madam got a kickback from the dressmaker. She did not take us to be overcharged by druggists and doctors and restaurants with whom she had the same cozy arrangement, so that she might make extra money and keep us in debt. Her competitors did that sort of thing: not she. So she said, and she did not think she was lying, because, although she did in fact take us to a handful of stores where we paid more than everyday people paid, we were not cheated so badly that we would remain her slaves forever. She couldn't do that to us; we had more choices than the miserable girls on lower rungs of our profession and would not have put up with such treatment. Besides, Mrs. Bower did not need to keep us in peonage. Like most madams of fashionable parlor houses, she tried to bring in a fresh girl every few months. She wanted us to stay for about a year and a half and then move on to some other house, in another city. Earlier in her career, she had run a cheaper establishment and had practiced all the mean, dishonest methods she described. I knew better than to trust her.

I had been with her about four months when I broke the lock on her desk and examined her day books, where she entered the payments she had made and received. There was a book for 1845, last year, and 1846, the current year. Every page was dated, and letters beside each of the payments identified grocers, dressmakers, hairdressers, vintners, patrons, policemen. She used abbreviations, but since her memory was not good she made them simple and obvious, and I recognized many names easily. Hurrying because someone might come upon me at any moment, I flipped through the 1845 book to the date of Jocelyn's arrival at the child brothel. I found, as I had expected, a payment explained this way: "J. Cut'r—Jcl'n." That would be Jack Cutter's finder's fee for bringing Jocelyn from Harmony Mills to the arms of Mrs. Bower. With an excitement that had less to do with the risk of being caught reading the day book than with the unpleasant suspicion I was about to confirm, I switched to the beginning of the 1846 book and the date of my arrival at the parlor house. Sure enough, an entry said: "J. Cut'r—HK." HK would be Harriet Knowles, me. It was as I had thought. I had done a lot of thinking by this time, and it was my belief that Cutter's arrest of my brother had been part of a plan to drive me by deceit into Mrs. Bower's clutches. I found no payments either to Mrs. Donoho or Hugh O'Faolin, both of whom I suspected of helping to trick me by insisting that my brother was likely to be killed in prison, but their absence from the book did not exonerate them. *I* had paid Mrs. Donoho; and Cutter could have rewarded O'Faolin either with money or easy treatment at the hands of the law.

It was too late to do anything about it, but I had wanted to know. I did not want to be a fool anymore. I did not want to be a fool ever again. I wanted to know my past folly, to suck all the humiliation out of it until there was nothing left and it could not hurt me again. And then to shrug and say: All right, never mind, the damage is done; it was my fate. I had to believe that somehow I had always been meant for this. Anything else would be torture.

❧ XXXIII ☙

ONE DAY I RECEIVED A LETTER FROM A MAN I had heard of but never met. Its tone was formal but friendly—the message of one potentate to another. It made me feel important. Arthur Heywood, publisher of the *New York Courier,* wished that we might meet to discuss the welfare of a person for whom he was sure we both cared greatly. Though the letter did not say so, I had no doubt that the person in question was Arthur's son, Philip.

We met at a tavern where Heywood could provide us both with a pleasant luncheon but far enough uptown so that no one who knew him was likely to see us.

I took a hack to our meeting. I felt nervous—I must not waste this opportunity—but I complimented myself, too. I was not the suffering creature I had been ten months ago: Eric Gordon, Italy, *Take me away.* I would never be that foolish girl again. When, with a folded parasol, I entered the tavern, I was told that Heywood had arrived first, and I was directed to his table. He was a well-dressed man in his late forties, portly, with a drunkard's twisted radish of a nose, hanks of greasy hair athwart his balding head, jowls, spectacles, dandruff on his coat, bread crumbs on his waistcoat. He struggled stiffly to his feet and bowed, saying that no one could mistake such breathtaking beauty, and a glance was enough to explain the enchantment under which his son had fallen.

It followed from the tone of his letter that he would treat me this way, which flattered us both: he could be gallant and feel like a gentleman. I understood this, and knew that if I showed weakness or frustrated him too much he would change his tone. I removed my gloves, held out my hand; for a moment, I was worried that he would not kiss it, but he did. I sat and then he sat. The two of us spoke as we imagined fine high-tea-taking people in England did; I asked questions about the running of his newspaper and certain stories I had condescended to read therein, and he avowed himself impressed and surprised—though not to an insulting degree—by my knowledge of and citizenly interest in such topics as police corruption and election fraud.

At last, with our meal about finished but brandy still before us, he wondered if I had guessed the matter he wished to discuss with me.

"Does it concern these?" Removing an inch-thick bundle of Philip's letters from a pocket hidden within the folds of my dress, I gave them to his father, whose face showed alarm gradually subsiding to relief, as if a falling pianoforte had just landed a few feet away from him; I thought it had gone very well so far. "I see," I said. "You didn't know about these. Then you're here to ask me to—to give him up."

In fact, I had assumed as much. Philip was a garrulous bedmate; he complained constantly about his father, and I had a pretty good idea of his father's plans for him. I had also retained two of the choicer letters.

"Regretfully," said Arthur Heywood, "and with the utmost respect."

"May I ask why?"

"He's engaged to be married. She's a fine girl, not that you—"

"I'm fine in my own way, but still. Only a stone fence separates her father's newspaper from yours."

"Not a business connection. But they're an old family, and we're new money. He had agreed. Only now . . ."

"He's infatuated with a Cyprian."

He spread his meaty hands. I reached out, and he gave me one to hold. "In my heart," I said, "I knew it couldn't go on forever; it was a beautiful dream, but dreamers awake. I must stand aside. But how? How? How shall I find the strength?"

"I know how difficult it will be for you."

"Does it even mean anything, for *me* to do what's right, just because it's right? Can I afford the luxury of such scruples? Is there not something strangely false in it?"

"I am prepared to be generous."

"I don't want money from you. That is, not for this." I laced our fingers together. He blushed—mostly in his nose.

"What do you want?" His breath came short.

Here it was. Much less confident than I was trying to appear, I took the leap: "Remember, earlier, we were talking of police corruption? There is a very bad policeman in the Sixth Ward who acquired his position through bribery."

"As do they all," he said, with a certain distance still from his own words.

"Let God attend to the others. I'm interested in one who goes by the name Jack Cutter. This tavern is also an inn, did you know that? There are rooms upstairs. I wonder about them. Do you share my curiosity?"

"Yes," he said hoarsely. I reached under the table and put my hand on his knee. "Oh," he said, just like his son. "Oh."

I took him upstairs and applied my skills; before long, he lay gasping on the bed like a fish on a deck. When we were both sure he wasn't going to die, I broached the subject of his newspaper's upcoming investigation of police corruption in the person of Jack Cutter, and the Sixth Ward politicians such as—possibly—Alderman O'Daniel and Constantine Donoho.

I had never before tried to influence a powerful man to do me an elaborate favor, but I had met and talked with many such men when they had their hair down, and I had heard them talking to each other. I had come to know them better than their wives and their employees knew them, and I had an instinctive understanding of what was required. At the center of it was a bargain: I would stop seeing Philip, keeping his father's involvement secret. The father, in return, would conduct investigations and write, or have written, the exposés, timed to hurt O'Daniel and Donoho in the upcoming Democratic primary.

That was not all, however. He would replace his son as one of my regular customers. This was to keep him before my eyes, where I could watch him and urge him on when necessary. It was also another inducement, because, as he was aware, money alone could not purchase my favors: I was popular and I had choices.

He was shrewd enough to guess that I might at the last minute ask him not to mention O'Daniel or Donoho or others who fell into his net, if they undertook to promise—promise *me*—that in the future they would mend their ways. After all, he said, "No human soul is beyond redemption."

It was my turn to gasp. "You put that so well. I see the literary man in you."

"It is no more than I believe."

"So you have shown, by appealing to my better nature today," I agreed.

I WENT TO THE DONOHO GROCERY, and Mrs. Donoho took me to the basement and poured me a glass of beer. I had only to smell it to know what it was. "Is this how you show your displeasure with me?"

"You don't like lees beer. I forgot. Well, you're forgetful, too, it strikes me."

"You mean the one hundred dollars I promised you?"

"You know I mean that."

"You overcharged me."

"It was the agreed price."

"I was ignorant; you would have enlightened me if you thought my opinion of you could ever matter. And you didn't think that Jack Cutter would brag to me that you had bribed him with my money. I would like us to be friends, but you know you didn't earn the hundred, and I didn't come here to give it to you."

Of course I had more against her than this relatively small matter. I believed she had helped Jack Cutter to bring me to Mrs. Bower's house. But I wasn't ever going to let her know of my suspicions. I hoped merely to make her wish she hadn't done it.

"I know no such thing. What are you here for, if not for that?"

"I'm here to warn you, Mrs. Donoho, because, as I said, I think we should be friends. Read the *Courier*. You will find there a series of stories about people known to you, and I fear that some of them will not be mentioned in a favorable light."

"And how would a little slut like you know such a thing?"

"One has only to look at your face to know that you've always been a chaste woman, Mrs. Donoho. So it is left for me to tell you that all kinds of men make fools of themselves for pretty young girls. They tell things to them and promise to do things for them, in order to work their wicked will on them. It's unfair, I agree. Consider this as you read or have read to you the stories about your friends and your husband."

I left her and walked out of Five Points, where some remembered me, and no one was in any doubt as to how I had come by my finery; they acknowledged it with a mixture of cynicism, contempt, and envy. I looked men in the eye now, and often it was they who turned away, shamed, shifting their gaze to painted signs or struggling horses or broken bottles in the street while they tried to imagine being rich enough to fuck a beautiful whore.

ONLY DAYS AFTER MY MEETING with the newspaper editor Arthur Heywood, I learned something that caused a revolution in my ideas about myself and my circumstances. I had been at Mrs. Bower's house less than a year, though it seemed much longer. It was early in the evening. The owner of an omnibus company, a man in the mayor's office, a manufacturer of gutta-percha cement roofing, an India-rubber importer, and a buyer from Cincinnati (being entertained at the expense of the India-rubber importer) were enjoying cigars and champagne in the company of Beatrice, Jocelyn, Juliette, Gwendolyn, and Harriet. They were getting us to drink whiskey, and we kept saying we shouldn't because we had no head for it, it made us misbehave; it made us do what we should not! To show how true that was, ten minutes later Juliette was sitting on the lap of Mr. Martin, the buyer; Mrs. Bower noticed and promptly fined Mr. Martin fifty cents. There was a strict rule in her parlor against such breaches of decorum, with different fines for permitting a girl to sit on one's lap, for kisses on the neck, for kisses on the lips, for curious hands straying to naughty places, and so on.

I sipped and giggled with the others, while the men talked business and politics, and I gave their words more attention than I showed, because

I wanted to educate myself, and also because acting out an obscene travesty of the behavior of a girl of good family required only a fraction of my mind once I had learned how it was done.

So I was already listening, when I heard the syllables that would have snapped me into attention anyway. "Godwin," said the omnibus man. My whole being vibrated like a struck bell, but not even the India-rubber importer, upon whose lap I had just settled, seemed to notice.

"Harriet, what do you think you're doing? Just because Juliette is bad, do you have to be worse? Must you do everything Juliette does? And, Harold, you disappoint me; you know how suggestible Harriet is. Fifty cents," said Mrs. Bower.

They were talking about credit. A man named Godwin had started an ingenious new business, supplying as a service an estimate of the creditworthiness of other businesses and also of the bonds issued by states and municipalities. Mr. Martin said it was a shocking fraud, he supposed, and he wished he'd thought of it, ha ha!

Harold, causing a great deal of movement beneath me as he reached into his pocket for coins, said that it was not a fraud, and the need for such a service was obvious, but it had taken a very special personality to think of it.

"What personality?" said Mr. Martin.

"A Tractarian, an abolitionist, a man accustomed to judging other men."

Then I had no doubt they were talking about my grandfather.

"A prig, but also a phoenix," and they explained to the out-of-town buyer that Solomon Godwin, formerly a silk importer, had gone bankrupt in the Panic. It had taken him a few years to go down; and they must have been gloomy years for the old man, for they had come fresh on the suicide of his only son. The fellow had jumped off his father's seven-story warehouse on Pearl Street, which the father then sold—either because of its unpleasant associations, or because he needed cash. But he had retained enough other property to have recovered financially by now even without the credit business. In the end, no investment was more reliable than New York real estate.

"I knew him," said Harold.

I waited for more to be said. Finally, I had to ask, "Who? Godwin?"

He looked at me as if I were a cat that had suddenly spoken English. "The son," he said, gripping my waist and addressing the others generally. "He used to come to the old place on Anne Street. It was I who brought him first. Do you remember him, Dolly?" Mrs. Bower shook her head. "Sure, you do," said Harold, and he described my father. "He wasn't as religious as the old man, and his wife was so feeble after her last child that he didn't dare use her for fear of killing her. Besides"—he smiled at me—"she was too good to be fun. There was a girl he was fond of. What was her name?"

"Frances," said Mrs. Bower.

"What happened with her?" asked Harold, looking up and squinting.

"Alas, they seldom keep in touch," said Mrs. Bower, as if she ran a school for girls.

"That's not what I meant," said Harold. Turning to me, he said, "Of course, this was long before your time. How old were you in '37? What's wrong?"

I had jumped off his lap. I walked unsteadily to the sideboard, poured myself a shot of whiskey, and gulped it.

"Well, you're a big girl now," said Harold admiringly.

"I'm not feeling well," I said. "I have to lie down."

"I'm sorry, dear," said Mrs. Bower. "Why don't you go upstairs to your bed?"

"I will."

"And, Harold, why don't you go with her and make sure she's comfortable? Help her out of her clothes."

We went up to my room. When I had pleased Harold, I told him that my family in Boston had been connected with the Godwins, who were originally from Boston, as he might know, and I had met the Godwins' grandchildren a few times when I was a girl.

"Is that why you took that drink all of a sudden?"

"Yes, it reminded me of my former life."

"I see." He did not care. He was not romantic. He was forty-five, with a big hairy bottom, a flabby, womanish chest, a narrow face, and a tiny mouth with crowded yellow teeth, almost in double rows on the lower jaw. "I always thought you made that up."

"The children," I said. "The children of the man who liked Frances. Do you know what happened to them?"

"One of them, Edward, is clerking for the old man," Harold answered. "The other, the older one, I forget his name, is a lawyer."

"Godwin's son had four children," I said. "Five—one died."

"Did he? I think you're right. You really *did* know the Godwins, didn't you? I don't know what happened to the others." After hitching up his trousers, he added: "She's dead, you know. You can be sure Mrs. Bower remembers. Frances. She took arsenic. They were always quarreling. It was like a love affair. He was jealous. She said she was finished with him. He jumped off the roof of the warehouse, and she took arsenic."

I HAD A BAD NIGHT. On fresh sheets, studying the lights a street lamp scattered across the ceiling, I was amazed at how much innocence had remained within me long after I thought I had destroyed it all. I had never questioned my father's love for my mother. Hadn't he given it the ultimate demonstration, killing himself because he could not live without her? But, no, he had killed himself because he could not live without a prostitute named Frances. It was an attack on my oldest illusions, a stake in the heart of the girl I had been. I tried to laugh at it—what a joke on that girl—but I could only lie there, pinned, unable to wriggle free from the weight of this knowledge.

My grandfather, not only alive but rich again—that was just as bad. If I had known, when Lewis was in trouble I could have gone to my grandfather. Whether his rectitude would have permitted him to bribe the police I didn't know, but he'd have done something. Why hadn't I tried to find him? Mrs. Shea had told me he was dead, but long before then I had given up the hope of assistance from my grandfather. If you had asked me to calculate his age, I would have been able to say that he was sixty-seven, and that many people lived to be much older. I had never thought to do it. My childhood in New York seemed such a distant epoch to me. And if he was alive, why had he not written? None of the Godwins had been in touch with us, and casual acquaintances had been permitted to receive the impression that we had never existed. They had abandoned me, and Jeptha had abandoned me, and I had been left to wander off the regular paths of life and into the wilderness where the devil dances with his friends.

I gave in and took laudanum, and slept, and had many vivid dreams, of which I remember only the last, the one I had just before waking. I dreamed that I had never come to Mrs. Bower; I had looked my grand-father up as soon as I had arrived in New York. It was not until I had woken from this dream that I realized, with a terrible piercing thrill, that I could go back! I could be Arabella Godwin again, with luck, if I man-aged it carefully. I would have to account for my activities during the gulf of time between my employment as a maid and the time of my reappear-ance. Maybe I could say that I had worked as a maid in some house with some family out of the city, in Brooklyn or New Jersey, some people who had moved west, so we would not expect to meet them again.

Still, I was not sure I wished to be Arabella Godwin again just yet. Perhaps this shocks you. I think I have shown that I did not become a prostitute lightly, and that I suffered, as a girl should, when she becomes a prostitute. The point is, I *had* suffered. I had paid a price in shame, and buried that shame, and I would have to unearth it if I went out among respectable people, once more to see life through their eyes while feign-ing the innocence I had lost. Then I would know shame again, and I would be in virtually constant fear. A former customer had only to recog-nize me and point me out, and I would be humiliated and disowned. If I remained in New York, it was bound to happen.

The life of Harriet Knowles had its compensations. I belonged to the aristocracy of my kind. A handful of rich men were in love with me. Others, less romantic, paid a coarser tribute to my appeal, which I had become coarse enough to appreciate. I had long since paid my debt to Mrs. Bower. I had money. My world was in some ways wider than the world of a good wife or daughter. I had even had a taste of power, through my influence on men like Arthur Heywood. These advantages may strike you as a pathetic recompense for my degradation; I valued them the more for their high price. In my current circumstance, to re-enter my former life was as frightening as leaving it had been. And what were the induce-ments? To see my brothers and my grandfather again—knowing they would despise me if they learned the truth, and I must hide my bitterness at their treatment of me? To be married, to a larger fortune than I could acquire with my own efforts? Yes, but I was still sentimental enough to be dismayed rather than elated by that prospect. I had never wanted to marry anyone but Jeptha. To think of marriage meant thinking of him, and I tried never to do that.

Perhaps you have heard of "caisson disease," discovered when the foundations of Brooklyn Bridge were laid. Divers, breathing through tubes, stayed for hours deep under the water, and those who rose too quickly to the surface were ill for the remainder of their lives. The transition from one world to another is inherently dangerous.

Lewis's situation was different from mine. After his release from jail he had gone back to live with the Donovans on Mulberry Street. He knew what I had become, and eventually he had adjusted to the knowledge. He did not know why I had decided to sell myself. He thought, in his simplicity, that Jocelyn had talked me into following her example, and he often said that he wished he had not asked me to see her.

He lived by unskilled labor, and would not take money from me. I watched him changing week by week. I watched him adapting to life in the Sixth Ward, becoming in reality the Bowery Boy whose external manners he used to ape. He spent his pay immediately. He won money in tenpin alleys which he promptly lost in card games. He drank, he had women. He fought. Men like him had accidents and got sick. They were old at forty. And then, of course, there was his cough.

Since I have last described him, he had acquired a fresh bruise on his temple and a new gold-capped incisor: the tooth had been broken in an encounter a month earlier with Jack Cutter in a gambling hell on Pell Street. Cutter had come for his weekly payoff. Lewis had been there. Cutter had said he was thinking about going to Mrs. Bower's to try me out and see whether, after all the men I'd had by now, he, Jack Cutter, had anything to teach me. He outlined some of his ideas. Lewis, considering himself smart to sit calmly through most of this so he could make his attack unexpected, had finally lashed out. Cutter had struck him across the face with a truncheon. Lewis had told me amiably that he planned to kill Cutter. He would call him out. If Cutter hid behind his star, Lewis would force the issue. There was no hurry.

I believed him. It was one reason I was anxious to get Jack Cutter fired at the least, in prison if possible; and it was another reason to take my brother off the path he was on.

I sent Lewis a note, and we met in a Bowery oyster cellar at four o'clock in the afternoon; at that time of day the place was almost empty. We could see the boots of passersby through high windows on the side that faced the street. Whenever we weren't talking ourselves we heard rattling pots and snatches of conversation from the kitchen, along with the slurps and moans that went to show how much the top-hatted customer a few tables away from us appreciated his soup. "Lewis," I said, when we had asked after each other's health and told each other how fine we were, "do you remember Robert and Edward very well?"

"I wouldn't say well." With a glance at the noisy creature behind him, he removed his own hat. I observed his profile. He wore his hair Bowery Boy fashion, short in the back. At the front and sides were the long, carefully tended soap locks, sideburns oiled and brushed to stand stiffly away from the face. A Bowery Boy could not pass a reflective surface without inspecting his soap locks. "I remember Edward made a lot of jokes, and he would put me on his shoulders and another boy Edward's age would put his little brother on his shoulders and we'd fight, me and the other small boy. I never had much to do with Robert."

During all the years on my uncle's farm, we had had perhaps four or five conversations in which we pooled our memories of Bowling Green.

"And Grandpa and Grandma and the house on Bond Street?"

"Mostly from after we went to live there." As if it had suddenly occurred to him, he said, "Edward could walk on his hands."

A waiter brought stew, bread, and pickles. We talked about old times, Christina, the Great Fire of 1835, my father's stories about the Turk, Lewis's accident-prone years. At last, I said, "They're here, Lewis. Robert and Edward and Grandpa and Grandma. They're all here in this city."

I told him, very selectively, what I had learned, leaving out Frances and our father. "I overheard some men discussing it, and got their addresses at the post office. Lewis, you must announce yourself to them."

I proposed that he do it himself, not mentioning me. In case they found out later from the Moodys, he should tell them what he had done to Matthew, say he had done it in my defense, say that he had lost touch with me and did not know where I was.

Lewis became upset. I had it exactly backward! If only one of us should return to the family, it must be me. He was getting on fine. He was a man doing man's work. He didn't have to go hat in hand to rich relatives. "But you, Belle." He looked around the nearly empty room and spoke in a low voice. "I shouldn't even have to say it. How can you think of going on, when there's a way out?"

I told him that I couldn't stand the shame. "I would always know what I had been. It's easier for me now to stay with my own kind."

"Your own kind!" There were tears in his eyes. "*Your own kind?* But you're not *like* those women, Belle."

"Hush, don't call me that."

He grabbed my hand and kissed it. "You're not like them." Not since he was a boy had I seen him so emotional. I began to pity myself. "I don't care what you do," he said. "You're better than all those people."

His naïve words took me unprepared, and I wanted to weep in earnest. He loved me after all. I was his big sister, I was good—how could I be a prostitute? That wasn't *me*. I saw my fate through his eyes; it was sad that he had to know what I'd become.

I used these feelings. "Lewis, you're all I have now—you know that, don't you?"

"Oh God, Belle. Don't."

"You've got to seize this chance for my sake. You can't let it pass. Or what is my life worth? What's it all been worth if I can't help you? Lewis, remember we were talking a little while ago about the Great Fire? I went to look for you in the fire."

"I know. That's what I *mean*, Belle."

"You can make me happy in spite of everything, in the very midst of everything."

He sang his aria and I sang mine, and I believe it was effective, though it wasn't until the following week, when he had gambled away his pay, that he walked into the offices of Godwin & Co. and asked to speak to Edward or Solomon, whoever was nearest to hand.

I saw him next a few weeks later, when he slipped away to meet me. The soap locks were gone. He wore a new suit of clothes and looked a new man, and he told me of the rejoicing and how many times they called him "the Prodigal Son" and how the help was told, "This is Lewis, my grand-son, who I had thought was dead!"

My grandfather had taken Lewis to his house in Bloomingdale (which was far north of the city in those days); and so, straight from his foul quarters in a Mulberry Street tenement, Lewis moved into a big room with a window, with curtains. Lying on crisp bedsheets, he could see the silvery bow of a beech tree, and if he stood up and got closer to the window, he could see a lawn, a marble birdbath, and flower beds. It was very strange at first. One morning, Lewis came out of his room and asked the servants, "Who stole my shoes? Has anyone seen my shoes?" The shoes had been taken away to be blacked. When they were returned to him, Lewis clutched them to his breast, called them the Prodigal Shoes, and said he loved them better than the shoes that had never strayed. This story reached my humorless grandfather, who considered it a wonderful jest and repeated it ponderously to everyone he met.

Robert and Edward lived in town, and Lewis had met them. I envied no part of his reintroduction to the family so much as the hour the three brothers spent comparing their memories of the old house, of our dead parents, of Frank; of Anna, Sally, and Christina. I could tell from the way Lewis talked that it meant less to him. He found Robert, who was now a lawyer, a little stuffy. He preferred Edward. One Sunday, after church, Lewis watched a baseball game between the men of Edward's volunteer fire brigade and the members of some other volunteer fire brigade; later, in a saloon, Lewis told Edward what he had done to Matthew and what Matthew had done to me. "Solomon must know of this," said Edward, and that evening he had Lewis repeat the tale in my grandfather's study. My grandfather, Lewis said, was moved, and said he understood now why a good boy like Lewis could have become so angry; had he been there, he might have wished for such a reckoning as he had visited upon our cousin. If only they could find me! Then his happiness would be complete.

Though Lewis said he missed his Bowery friends, he missed bowling, gambling, and drinking, it seemed that he was willing to give his new life a try. I suspected, however, that he was sneaking off now and then to his old haunts to show off his new clothes and spend the pocket money my grandfather was giving him. My biggest worry was that a careless word from him might lead the Godwin family to me, and I would have to return to them in the character of a fallen woman. Fortunately, before this could happen, my grandfather sent Lewis off to a place called the Pearson Academy in New Haven.

I did not dare visit my brother at the school, but I went to meet him once in the town, and some hours later, as I walked by the iron gate between the school and the sidewalk, I glimpsed a rambling two-story house and a brick dormitory. Some students in the uniform of the school eyed me curiously. None of the boys happened to be Lewis.

❧ XXXIV ❧

DESPITE THE IMPRESSION that a superficial acquaintance with my biography might create, I am really quite a prudent individual. Although I was not yet ready to change my mode of life, I knew I might one day wish to come up from the diving bell and be Arabella Godwin again, and I became attached to the thought that it might actually be possible. The more I considered the matter, the more anxious I was to neutralize Jack Cutter.

"SHAME OF THE METROPOLITAN POLICE: Police Purchase Stars by Bribery: Bribe Price Lists—Specified Amounts for Differing Ranks and Wards—Corporation Officials as High as Aldermen Involved." So went the headlines of Mr. Heywood's first article, breaking the news that was actually common knowledge. "Proof has been obtained by the *New York Courier* of a scandal which, when its details are fully made public, will rock the city to its foundations and shock the Corporation into a reform of the most corrupt police administration to be found in any city of comparable importance in the world." The article, which promised to be the first of a six-part series, named only one individual, Jack Cutter.

The day it came out, a boy appeared at Mrs. Bower's house, asked to speak to me, and recited word for word a carefully memorized message inviting me to a powwow in the basement of the grocery. I bade him wait and wrote a note back.

Dear Mrs. Donoho,

I was delighted to receive your gracious invitation to share a cheerful glass of lees beer in the lovely basement of your husband's fine grocery. However, I feel disinclined to accept this generous offer, as you have entertained me so often and I have never been in a position to reciprocate. Now that I find I am better placed, I have the great pleasure of inviting you, your husband, Constantine, and the esteemed Alderman Michael O'Daniel to the Sawdust House at 1:00 in the afternoon this Thursday. An important journalist and literary man may also be present, and we shall all discuss the best road to good government and other matters of mutual interest. Please do come and bring your husband and Alderman O'Daniel, or I shall be heartbroken.

Sincerely,
Harriet Knowles

Heywood came. So did Donoho and O'Daniel. It was agreed that future crusading newspaper stories would omit mention of their names and be harsh on their rivals in the Democratic Party, and that Jack Cutter would be sent to Sing Sing for bribery and his replacement would be a man of my choosing. I had no one in particular in mind, but I thought that it would be good to have on the police force someone who was beholden to me. I knew by now that, although bribery and blackmail are useful in emergencies, the usual currency of politics is gratitude.

Philip Heywood gladdened his father's heart by marrying into an old New York family. Cutter went to prison. I took a breath.

❧ XXXV ❧

NOT LONG AFTER THIS, MY ATTENTION was drawn to the one watchful-looking gentleman in a rowdy group that had just entered the house. He was dressed quietly for a man of his profession, but extravagantly for most men, in a soft black hat, a black suit, black boots, a white shirt, and a silk vest, with gold rings on his fingers and a small diamond pin on the shirt. When he spoke to Mrs. Bower, I heard the Italian accent: it was Charles Cora, the gambler whom I had met in the company of Eric Gordon on the *Israel Putnam* between Cohoes and New York. It had been a year and a half. Mrs. Bower introduced him to Juliette, but he turned to me. "You," he said. He snapped his fingers and was about to speak but stopped, noticing my alarm.

"This is Harriet," said Mrs. Bower, who had also noticed; she noticed everything.

"The boat," said Cora.

I nodded tightly, and he took the hint and didn't mention it, and then I made sure that he was the one who took me upstairs.

Later, I asked him if he was surprised to see me here. We were both on our backs. It had been easy and in no way unusual, except for the delicacy of his long fingers, and he said, "Yes, a little." *A little* was a funny way to put it. He added, "I knew I'd see you again. I didn't think here."

"You have presentiments? They come true?"

"The strong ones."

"That must be useful in your profession."

There was more skepticism in that remark than I had intended. He said simply, "All gamblers believe in fortune."

I had been ready to bribe him to keep my secret, but there was no need: he wouldn't think of harming me. He had a comradely regard for women of my type. In this he was an unusual example of his own kind. Most sporting men, though they may admire a fine whore and thank God that some women are bad, are contemptuous as well; to feel otherwise would be to insult their wives and mothers and sisters. In Italy, where Charles Cora was born, an even sharper distinction is made between good and bad women, but he had different ideas, because his mother was a prostitute, and he had been raised in a brothel in Milan.

Though he was—and I liked this about him—as thoroughly a creature of the present as any grown man I have ever known, and not much interested in his own past, now and then during our time together a scrap of it rose to the surface of his talk. With your permission, I will tell it all now, everything I learned in all the years I knew him. He thought that his father might have been a French officer, since he was born in the time of Napoleon, when there were many Frenchmen in Italy. Or maybe his father was the amiable landowner's son who spent as many hours playing with him as dallying with the girls, and gave him his first deck of cards. He did not know who arranged for him to be sent to the school from which he had run away to live on the streets of Bologna when he was fourteen.

He had lived in Brazil and Cuba. He had called himself Fabrizzio

Bologna and Bernardino Blanco. "Charles" was from St. Charles Street in New Orleans, and "Cora" was really his ignorant misspelling of *cuore*, Italian for the suit of the card that was in his hand when he decided it was time for a new last name.

He was a very gifted gambler, with a brain that was wonderful for remembering the play and calculating odds; and hands uncanny for their skill in conjuring the wide, irregular, or slightly nicked card, so swiftly and eyelessly that it was all over before his victims knew it. He could imbibe quarts of liquor without visible effect, and he always knew exactly when to leave town.

He told me that where men were honest he was honest, but America, if he could say so without hurting my feelings, was a very dishonest country; here he had to cheat in self-defense. This was nonsense. Cheating is the whole art of professional card dealing; it had been his study since he was a half-wild boy in Lombardy.

He lost everything he had—it happened all the time—and to watch the methodical, uncomplaining, and perfectly confident way he began again from nothing was an inspiring sight. He was always generous, because money was unreal to him.

CORA CAME BACK ALMOST EVERY DAY for a few weeks. There was something between us, though I couldn't put a name to it; perhaps we were friends. At any rate, I felt comfortable with him; he was comfortable in a brothel and would stay almost for the whole next day, having breakfast with the whores, telling them stale jokes, of which he had an encyclopedic knowledge, playing absentmindedly with a deck of cards (in my room, he would go even further and sit at my desk trimming them and nicking them).

Since his appetite for lovemaking was no greater than average, for a while I wondered if he might be jealous and trying to monopolize me, but if so he was going about it very carelessly: he often went out, and I was with other men; sometimes, when he was busy trimming cards, I was writing love letters, and it didn't seem to bother him. He usually came back in time to be the last man and to spend the night.

I will not say that I fell in love with him, but I looked forward to his visits, and I wondered what he was doing when he was not with me.

When, on occasion, he did not show up as expected, I was disappointed, and when he returned again, I found myself taking him to task for it, as if the absence of obligation were not the whole point of him and me. He had an easygoing, self-possessed manner that was very agreeable—instant intimacy of a low order; I could speak freely, he was never angry or hurt—but which would be frustrating to anyone trying to make the acquaintance of the inner man. Then I'd say something sharp to get under his skin, but he would just smile. I envied Charley his composure, and after a while I learned to take his mood as my own, and to glide lightly and swiftly over the surface of life, as he did.

Once, he was gone for over a month, and I decided that when he returned I would tell him not to come anymore, because I was becoming too attached to him. But when he showed up he was in a good mood, and it seemed foolish to spoil the moment. "Let's go out," he said. "Show, restaurant, dance, hotel."

He had just been to New Orleans, where he had run a faro game in a little storefront, and also played poker in rich men's houses, and he had prospered, and he told me how it all was done.

"I'd like to see New Orleans," I said, and he promised to take me next time.

He suggested later that we go to his hotel room, which, it turned out, was on the second floor of the Astor House. My back stiffened when I learned this, and I told him how I had embarrassed myself with Eric Gordon who often stayed at that hotel. "Let's go somewhere else, then," said Charley. I thought about it and said no, I didn't want to be weak, and he nodded. That was something he understood.

At the Astor House, we registered as Mr. and Mrs. Cora. The next morning, in the bed, with his arms crossed behind his head, watching me dress, he said: "Why not stay?"

"I have to answer to Mrs. Bower," I reminded him.

"That's what I mean," he said. "Where do you stand with her?" He knew how American parlor houses worked. He offered to settle my debts.

I told him that I was paid up, and that I liked him, but I had to be realistic. What was he offering me? Was he offering to keep me permanently?

"No, just while I'm in town."

"And when you go?"

He shrugged. "You won't be any worse off."

He was right, I realized. I had already stayed with Mrs. Bower as long as the average girl did. I was still popular, and she wanted to keep me, but she had nothing to complain of if I left. In a month or a year, I would still be marketable. I sat down at the desk and, with an Astor House pen on Astor House stationery, wrote a letter to Mrs. Bower; I tipped a boy to take it. And so, for a time, I lived in the best hotel in New York City as Mrs. Charles Cora. We lived a life of idle pleasure, going to see races and prizefights out on Long Island, learning to ride horses, taking cruises in schooners and steamboats around the bay and up the Hudson, attending concerts, plays, picnics, and circuses, drinking champagne, and eating saddles of veal and oysters as big as dessert plates. When I was bored with all that, I would sit in the hotel common room, read *The Tribune* and *The Penny Magazine,* and strike up conversations with people from far-off places, people who had uprooted themselves, if only for a few weeks: here they were in New York; and where was I from, they would ask me, what was my story?

Once, when I was on Charley's arm, I ran into Eric Gordon. I had had daydreams about this: that Gordon would snicker; Charley inveigle him into a card game and destroy him. But when the time came, Eric seemed as pleased to see me as if nothing unpleasant had happened between us, and though he must have known I could not be Mrs. Cora, he was perfectly willing to let me pretend I was. He did not wish to hurt me, and as soon as I realized this, I lost any interest in revenge.

Besides, I had other things on my mind by then.

One day, Cora came to our room to find me waiting for him reading the *Courier,* and when I looked up he knew I had something to tell him; I said that I had missed my time, and all the other signs made it very clear that I was pregnant. He said nothing. I told him that the child was his (as it had to be, though I could not prove it).

He didn't comment on that right away, but after more time, he sat down at a small table and asked me, "What do you mean to do?"

"Probably I'll get rid of it; I know how," I said, dismayed. I stood up, telling him I had to take some air and would see him at dinner. I walked through City Hall Park, thinking. I had hoped that he would want the child. He was gentle, intelligent, and companionable. I felt safe with him.

He liked children. He was always ready to spare them a joke, a card trick, a story, and he listened to their prattle. A traveling lecturer on phrenology had shown us a bump on Charley's skull that proved him to be highly "philoprogenitive." In the last few weeks, my eyes had often sought out that bump. But it seemed that the prospect of a little Cora did not make him wish to turn our holiday into a permanent obligation.

Maybe, if the baby came anyway, that would change his mind: he would hold the baby, note its resemblance to him, become attached.

Probably you'll find in such reasoning a simple and contemptible explanation for my subsequent behavior. Perhaps I should just leave it at that. But to me it seemed that there was more to it. Abortion was immoral, wasn't it? I did not regret murdering Matthew's child, but this was different. I had the feeling that I would be wronging Charley by killing his child, even if he didn't know his own mind enough to realize it. And abortion by any method was painful and dangerous. Childbirth, though also painful and dangerous, was several months away.

Time went by. I left it for another day and another. My condition became visible. At last I had decided, without knowing when I had decided. Whatever Cora thought, he did not say. He stopped having relations with me, and the odd long hair that began to appear on his coat made it evident that he had sought the company of other women.

ONE MORNING, HE ASKED ME TO COME down for breakfast with him; it was late, and no one else was in the dining room but one waiter and one guest, an old man smoking a cigar at a table on the other side of the room. Cora watched me eat. You would have had to know him as well as I did to know that he was tense; and though I had come to the table very hungry, I lost my appetite and I waited. At last he said quietly, "I can't have a wife, I can't have a mistress. I can't be reliable. I don't like to be reliable. I think the baby is mine. So. What should I do?" I didn't speak. He was very still for a moment. Then he said, "You've brought me luck. I'm going to give you a thousand dollars." It seemed more than fair—he had been generous already, what did he owe me?—but I said nothing, and my expression showed him nothing. "I'm going to give you two thousand dollars," he amended, as if we had been haggling. "Do what you like with it, but—look—you like to manage things." He raised a hand to get the waiter's attention. "More coffee," he said. "You should open up a house. For the girls, go to Baltimore—there are a lot of houses in Baltimore, you can find girls who are stale there but they'll be fresh here. Get them to come with you. It has to be here." He was thinking hard now; the prospect excited his business instincts. "In New York, you know aldermen and newspapermen and coppers, and they can help you. You know the sporting men. Rent a house in the Fifth Ward, some nice clean neighborhood where gentlemen feel safe. Furnish it out of auctions and estate sales, but make it fancy. Buy champagne, send out cards to the bachelors. They'll tell the husbands." His gaze fell on my belly; perhaps he was remembering the brothel in Milan, and that it was not so awful growing up there. "Men will like the idea that such a young, pretty girl is a madam, the madam the best-looking girl in the place." He looked at me. I knew he wasn't finished, so I didn't answer. "You'll have to be one of the girls, too, at least at the start. But not to just anybody. You're the prize. Make them have the others first. Use some of the money for bribes. I could tell you to try your hand at some other business, but this is the one you know, so you begin with an edge; it's your best chance."

The coffee came. He had it black, and I had it with a lot of sugar.

"Will you help me get started?"

"I'm leaving town. If you can't do it yourself, you can't do it. Write me a letter. You get in trouble, ask me for help."

That's what he said. It was the opposite of sentimental, but for some reason now, maybe just because I am old, I am moved. Eight years later, his trial for murder was to make us both famous. People were impressed by the strenuousness of my efforts to save Charles Cora's life. It has been seen, over the years, as a sort of romantic riddle. I believe I have provided several solutions. He was the father of my child; he treated me with respect and kindness; and we understood each other, which was a comfort. Just look at how many pages I am compelled to write, trying to be understood, now that he is gone.

❧ XXXVI ❧

I VISITED MRS. BOWER AT HER OWN HOME. Her housemaid brought us tea and little cakes in the sitting room. Seeing my belly, Mrs. Bower asked when my baby was due and if I knew whose it was, and if he believed me. She chided me for carelessness, but she was friendly. "Men have been asking about you."

"Have they? Good. Tell them to inquire at 259 Mercer." It was not on Washington Square, but only two blocks away.

Her face fell. She knew every parlor house in the city. The novel address, together with my smug expression, made the situation clear. She liked competition no better than anyone else in trade does. In a house of shame, as in any emporium, there are times when no customers come through the door. The girls sit around eating and drinking, but the landlord and dressmakers and maids insist on being paid. "Your own house?" she cried. "It's a mistake. You're too inexperienced. You'll go bust."

"Then you have nothing to worry about," I said tartly, unsure enough to be hurt by this prediction.

She actually said, with genuine bitterness, "This is how you repay me!" And since I didn't want her for my enemy, I insisted that I was very grateful and would never forget how she had helped me when I was at my life's lowest ebb; that I looked upon her as my model and wouldn't have contemplated this step without her example before me, and that that was why I had come to pay my respects and ask her advice.

This helped to mollify her. As we drank tea from pretty china cups, we talked about doctors and midwives. Thanks to Heywood, Alderman O'Daniel, and Con Donoho, and others I had met through them, my political protection was as good as Mrs. Bower's, and she knew it. In the ensuing months, she limited her campaign against me to intimating that my girls were in poor health and that I had fine wine labels specially printed for me and glued to bottles of cheap wine. (The second charge was true, but I had learned that trick from her.)

Jocelyn, who had gone to New Orleans around the same time I put Lewis in touch with my grandfather, had come back at my request. She helped me not to feel lonely. I had gotten the rest of the girls in Baltimore, as Charley had suggested, and very easily: I had simply made my desires known to the proprietor of a dress shop that did much business with prostitutes. We all stayed at a ladies' boarding house until the current tenant vacated the house on Mercer Street. When we finally moved in, Cleo, the octoroon, got first pick of the girls' bedrooms in recompense for the indignity of posing as my servant at the boarding house. Cleo's feelings were not easily hurt, but she stood up for herself as a matter of policy, being simultaneously the daughter and granddaughter of the same proud Virginian aristocrat. Monique, who had a round, rosy, dimply baby face that would not age well but was very appealing now, was simple, and cried so often that I worried about her until one day, after I had seen her cry over a blind man selling apples, a patron's account of his impoverished childhood, and the news of the death of John Quincy Adams, I realized that she just enjoyed crying. Victoria hated herself and wanted to be dead. Through sheer luck, in that first group there happened to be no girl who made trouble just for fun, or who was envious, or thought the others were plotting against her.

Frank, named in memory of my brother, was born without medical complications on February 24, 1848. It was exactly one month after the day gold was found at Sutter's Mill on the American River, but New York had not heard of it yet. That year, one heard a lot about Europe. They were having the French Revolution again, this time not just in France but in many countries. As, one after another, the uprisings were crushed, my figure resumed its former shape, with improvements, and I learned what it was to hear an infant cry and to feel the tug of milk descending by way of an answer.

I wrote to Charley often. In March, he came north and stayed for two weeks. He picked up the baby with an easy skill that suggested experience; where he might have gotten it I never learned. Sometimes Frank clamped his mouth on the flesh of his father's arm and sucked like a leech until there was a red spot, and then I would put the baby to my breast.

One day around this time, I was playing with Frank when Sean Donovan—whom I had started using as my messenger again as soon as I opened the house—knocked on my door and said a man with a plug hat and soap locks was here to see me.

"Did he give his name?" I asked.

"Jack Cutter."

I straightened my back and was silent for long enough to make my next words unconvincing. "My old friend Cutter!" I told Sean. "Bring him to the sitting room."

"He's already there," said Sean.

"Is that so? Oh. Well, then, let's go down and see him." I put Frank down, and had Sean get the nurse while I looked at myself in the mirror. "Jack used to be a copper," I told Sean a minute later, as we went down the turning stairs together. I glimpsed Cutter's stained sleeve and big grimy hand on an expensive chair, and then his face, a little gaunter than when last seen. The scar noticed me before Jack did. "But he had a misunderstanding with the Corporation, and they sent him away. Hello, Jack. I'm glad you made yourself comfortable. Sean, get Rosie to bring Jack a whiskey, and wake Charley up, too. I'd like to introduce them."

I took a seat on a divan near his chair. "Well, well, Jack, how are you?"

"Get your boss a whiskey, too," Cutter told Sean, who was on his way out of the room. "Bring the bottle, and two glasses."

"Sure," I said. "How are you, Jack?" I asked again. "I heard you had a raw deal."

He let me wait for a while and at last said, "What'd you hear?"

"Why, that you were sent up for something every policeman in New York does."

"That's right."

"But now you're out, and looking up old friends." From the expression on his face, it seemed likely that he knew I was the one who had arranged for his arrest. "What do you know, Jack?"

He leaned forward and said quietly: "Lewis Godwin. Arabella Godwin. Solomon Godwin."

"Oh," I said. "Oh, I see."

"Oh," he said, leaving his mouth fixed for a while in a small "o." "Oh, I see." He held out his big hand, and then he closed it slowly into a fist, as if he were crushing a tiny Arabella Godwin.

Rosie came with the whiskey. Charley was with her.

I introduced them to each other. I had told Charley about Jack. "Jack tells me he knows all my names. Charley knows all about me, too," I told Jack.

Charley and Jack looked at each other, Charley smiling at Jack in a kindly, understanding way. At last Charley said, "Harriet. Could I talk to Mr. Cutter alone a minute?" and I left them.

Charley knocked on my door a half-hour later. I started thanking him for scaring Cutter away, but he said, "You're paying him. Thirty dollars a month. You send it to a P.O. box. He shows up, or asks for more, write me a letter—I'll come."

IN APRIL, CHARLEY LEFT AGAIN. I hired a wet nurse and made myself available once more to a select group chosen from the gentlemen who came to 259 Mercer Street. Once more, Sean began carrying *billets doux* and little presents between me and my spurious beaux around the town. To reprise the role of fallen angel who had found love too late, now that I was known to be a madam, with a baby in a trundle bed right in the house, required a good deal of finesse. Daytime was easy. I could nurse the baby in the front parlor. The girls played with him, and engaged in lively discussions about swaddling and weening and the proper time to introduce solid foods; the atmosphere was quite domestic. At night, the baby lived in a part of the house the outer world never saw, separated by a pair of doors and a long hallway. I kept one room for myself there, and another, for business purposes, on the second floor of the house. To the patrons, Frank was just a rumor. I was very young. I was beautiful in the style of the time. I knew my clientele, I knew what they wanted, and the city's rapid growth created a steady demand for the services available at my emporium. I prospered.

Following the example of Mrs. Bower, I kept a day book and a ledger and did my own accounts, for nothing connected with business was more frightening to me than that I should not realize when I was spending more money than I was taking in. I kept the ledger in a locked drawer in my bedroom writing desk. My father, the chief clerk, the lover of the whore Frances, had kept my grandfather's books, and sometimes he took the work home and I had watched him. I thought of that whenever I wrote in the ledger.

❧ XXXVII ❧

BY THE SPRING OF '49, news of the gold strikes in California had reached the East, and the whole country had gone insane over it. We heard that ships in San Francisco Bay couldn't sail, because their crews were panning for gold in the rivers; the forts were empty, because the soldiers were busy prying gold from the rocks with the tips of their bayonets. In New York, everything that could float was being rigged to take men to California. The newspapers were full of advertisements for gold-washing machines. I got a letter from Charley postmarked Panama City: "When you get this I will be in San Francisco. I'll get my letters at the Parker House. So write me there if you want. If you ever come out this way go by the Horn, not by Panama. People are dying like flies here from the fever."

I had that letter in my hand when I heard a rapid knock on my door, and a shout from the sentimental Monique—"Harriet! Come quickly!"— of such urgency that I thought she must have discovered the corpse of a patron on the floor at the foot of her bed (where, several weeks earlier, just as we were about to open, she had discovered a gentleman who had been sleeping there all day).

She took me downstairs to the parlor. Frank and his nurse sat in a chair by the window. Upon my arrival, at the bottom of the staircase, the nurse put him on his feet and said, "Go to Mama, Frankie!" He looked at me, drooling and gurgling, in his gown, and took one step, and then another. I stood still and let him come—it was a long way, and two paces short, he seemed to decide that he had done his share and stood wobbling with his arms raised and his lips pressed together. I picked him up. "Ma—" he began, and the word, his first, was like a blow to my chest, it wrung my heart with a strange mixture of joy and dismay—I wanted to hear it, but it would shake my resolution if I heard it—and so, before he could finish it, I lifted his gown, put my lips against his navel, and blew noisily, making him laugh instead. To change a fellow's mind, to make him want something it is easier to give him, is a crucial skill in a courtesan.

Still, there was no getting around the fact that soon he was going to be walking around and calling me Mama, and the incident strengthened my resolve in the plan I had made soon after he was born. As a first step, I had re-established contact with my aunt. I told her that, thanks to the generosity of a dressmaker—a childless woman in her sixties—I had completed an apprenticeship in that craft; and soon afterward my benefactress had died, leaving her shop to me. The dressmaker, a devout Presbyterian, had been an active member of the New York branch of the Female Reform Society, to which I now belonged as well. I promised that hereafter I would stay in communication. I wrote in a similar vein to Anne and Melanchthon. I did not tell them that I knew where Lewis was, or that my grandfather was alive and in New York.

Some weeks later—long enough for me to wonder if she was dead—my aunt replied with news of her own. Titus had a general store in Patavium. Matthew helped him there. He had started walking again, for short intervals, with canes, and with the Lord's help would make a full recovery. Evangeline had married a local farmer. Agnes was teaching school in Boston, and affianced to George Sackett, who was now a minister.

Our correspondence had continued from there. Now I wrote as follows:

Dear Aunt Agatha and Uncle Elihu,

As I lift my pen to write to you in this season of snow, when hoar lies on the roofs of the horse cars, my thoughts fly to my dear aunt and uncle and to all the other folks in Livy still living the honest farm life and walking the paths of righteousness for the Lord's sake. I am so happy that thanks to the success of my dress-making shop I have been able to help you out again, thereby repaying your generosity to me in my childhood.

I am writing a little earlier than usual, while enclosing the draft redeemable at the bank in Patavium, for a special reason: I am coming to see you in person, and not alone: I am bringing a surprise with me, as explained in the other letter I am enclosing, which I ask you pass on to Anne and Melanchthon. They will explain it to you.

I continue well. God has blessed my efforts here in the city, and I hope the same is true of you. How often in the noisome streets does my memory harken back to Livy and the old farm!

Yours truly,
Arabella

Here is the letter I asked them to pass on:

Dear Anne and Melanchthon,

As my aunt will probably have told you, I am coming to Livy soon.
I will be bringing a child with me, and if you agree I will be leaving
without him, though the two of us have become rather attached.

Let me explain first, however. As I mentioned in earlier letters to
Agatha and Elihu, I am a member of the New York Female Reform
Society, which does good works among the deserving poor in the
most wretched wards of the city. One sad case, watched by us for
almost two years now, was that of Margaret Wright, a woman not
out of her twenties, a Protestant and a native of good Yankee stock,
employed in a hat-making factory, whose husband, also a native,
had passed away of consumption, along with her two children. She
had consumption herself and was carrying her husband's posthumous child; she had little doubt that she herself would go to glory
soon after she brought it into the world: and so it came to pass. I
was with her when she was taken from us. With her dying breath,
in a voice so frail we all had to move within inches of her lips to
hear, she asked us to take pity on her poor baby, her little son
Frank, and to find a good home for him with a Christian family far
from the poisonous fumes and filth of the city. After much praying
on the subject, I have come to a conclusion which you may by now
have guessed—that I will ask you if you might be willing to raise
the child so that, if Providence wills it, he may grow up strong and
healthy in upstate New York.

If you can find a place in your home for a sweet motherless little
stranger, the Female Reform Society, assisted by an anonymous
donor, has set aside moneys enough to guarantee a $120-a-year
stipend, which should more than cover any additional expenses
that will be incurred as a result of the child's keeping until he is of
age to take care of himself. The donor has said that he may take a
future interest in the orphan, eventually providing assistance in his
education, should he prove of quick mind, and should he live long
enough for it to be an advantage to him.

Little Frank has been examined by physicians who say he is at present free from disease, but, in view of his heredity, will benefit from a rural setting and, when he is old enough, by agricultural labor. He has just now become fully weaned, is a little over a year old, and can toddle halfway across a room before falling—with a startled look upon his face but no tears, for he is a brave little boy—and likes milk sops and crackers broken into egg yolk but does not like vegetables very much, I am afraid!

With fondest regards,
Arabella

Judge me, reader, if it gives you satisfaction. I was not without feelings for little Frank. When I was asked how I could do such a thing—I was asked this question by his nurse, by Monique, and even by a couple of gentlemen who knew I was disposing of Frank without knowing where—I told them that it was because I was growing more attached to him every day, and I feared that if I did not do it now it would be impossible.

Let us think about this, shall we? Think seriously. Even though growing up in a fancy parlor house, where your mother is the madam and can see to it that you are treated well, need not be unremittingly sordid, it doesn't compare very favorably with growing up on a prosperous farm. If I had hated Livy, that was only because of Agnes and Agatha, and because I had missed the city. Frank would not remember it, and so he would not miss it. One day he would enter a world where reputation matters; he wouldn't thank me for letting him start life in the character of a prostitute's bastard. Anne, who had had four miscarriages after Susannah, would be happy to have him. She was the best of mothers. I had often wished I had been raised by her. Melanchthon was a good father, and he would be pleased, both with the child and the $120, which he would use to buy livestock or make other improvements. It was also consoling to realize that my aunt, who would have loved to dandle a baby again, would be rebuked by my conspicuous choice of Anne and Melanchthon.

Finally, like many other women who abandon their children, I told myself that it was temporary. Who knew but that perhaps, in two or four or five years, when I had enough money to feel really safe from the threat of poverty, I would dissolve the parlor house, open a grocery, or a laundry, or even a dress shop, and return for him.

MY AUNT HAD TOLD ME BY LETTER that Jeptha's family had moved to Ohio years earlier. I need not fear meeting them. Still, I could not help wondering, wondering and dreading, what it would do to me to be so near the fields and forests where once we had walked. To make life endurable, I had put the part of me that loved Jeptha to sleep, but I had never been able to bring myself to kill it.

I returned to upstate New York at the beginning of April 1849, in the company of Jocelyn and Monique, and Frank. We took a steamboat up the Hudson, the New York Central Railroad, and a stagecoach. We went in comfort, stopping like tourists to view famous falls and locks. We dressed simply and used plain names. I was Arabella, Monique was Sarah, and Jocelyn was Martha.

It was eleven and a half years since my grandfather's clerk Horace had brought Lewis and me to our uncle's farm, two children who had just lost both their parents. I mentioned this to my companions, and Monique, seizing greedily on the opportunity, began to cry, which helped me to keep my own eyes dry. "There, there, Monique," I said. "It didn't happen to you; surely that's a comfort." But as we went south from Rochester, and the roads became ruder, and I noticed that a certain stream was just the same but the bridge over it was different, and signs announced the approach of Patavium—I had decided to stay there, where there was less chance that I would be recognized, rather than in Livy—I felt a steady loss of strength. "What's wrong?" Jocelyn asked. "You look pale."

"I'm dyspeptic," I said. "That breakfast. This coach. This road."

I closed my eyes and slept, and they woke me when we were in town.

We all wrote our false names in the hotel register. Since there would be talk anyway, when a child appeared in Anne's family and she told the far-fetched story I had given her, it might have been better to have acted less furtively. But I didn't have the courage, not here.

I sent Jocelyn and Monique out to see the town. They were to tell people that they were members of the New York Female Reform Society, charged with the blessed work of bringing orphans of Anglo-Saxon heritage to be raised with good Christian farm families. Yes, the Christianity of people hereabouts was famous. In wicked New York City, everyone talked about it with awe.

I dreamed that I was with Jeptha on my uncle's farm. He took my hand and pulled me into the corn. Willingly I surrendered my precious virtue, and before the end of the dream we had a child and named him Charley. When I woke up, Frank was crying; I lifted him from his trundle bed. He snuggled into me, saying his terrible word: "Mama."

"No, you don't," I told him.

In the morning, I had the egg with crackers sent up to us. "Eggy!" I said, and he grinned pinkly with a little glint of white suddenly show-ing through the gum on top: a new weapon in his arsenal. I broke the crackers finely into the yolk until they had softened enough for him, and I spooned them into his mouth—"eggy, yum yum, eggy"—feeding him, as I thought, for the last time. I felt sorry for him, to lose his mother so young, and I felt sorry for myself, too. I foresaw a very bad time coming in the moment of going back without him. I foresaw many nights of regret. But it was the right thing to do. And he would not be so far away. I could visit him. Next year or the year after, I could change my mind, tell Anne that he was mine, and take him home with me.

When it was time to take him to Melanchthon's farm, I told the other women: "You take him. Say I had business back in New York City, I couldn't come in person."

"Are you sick?" asked Jocelyn.

"I don't know."

"Should we ask about a doctor?"

"No, just take him."

He was asleep with his thumb in his mouth when they picked him up to take him to the carriage downstairs, but I made the mistake of holding him one last time, and he woke; and then, when they took him away, he cried until he turned red, as if he knew he might never see me again; it was a bad few minutes for both of us. "Hush," I begged him, "hush," and to Jocelyn and Monique I said, "Stop looking at me that way."

When they were gone, I wept a little; after a while, I composed myself. Between parting with Frank and being in Livy again, it would have been more than I could bear. Everyone would have read it on my face; they'd know I was his mother.

I read fifty pages of a novel by Eugène Sue, and then they were back, and Frank was with them, sleeping again.

"What's this?"

"Your aunt Agatha was there," said Monique. "Anne says she won't take the baby unless you come."

"But I'm not here, remember? You were supposed to tell her that I wasn't here!"

"They didn't believe us," said Jocelyn.

"Stupid, stupid, stupid," I said, shutting my eyes, and I didn't know whom I meant. "Now I'm going to have to part with him all over again."

Monique, happy to tell me something good, said "Oh—I just remembered—he has a tooth!"

"Dear Lord," I said, putting my palm to my brow. "Precious Lord."

"Don't you want to see it?"

"I've seen the tooth! Do you think I'm made of stone? Help me. Don't make it harder. I won't have him raised in a brothel. I won't have him meet life as a whore's bastard. It's all been decided. I'm doing this. You are supposed to help me."

They apologized and embraced me and cooed, saying that they could tell, from the way I was acting, that I had maternal feelings after all. While I dressed, I had Jocelyn and Monique prepare me for the meeting ahead. What had been said about me and asked about me? Had anyone mentioned Lewis? No. What about Matthew? Was he walking? Short distances, with two canes, same as in Agatha's letters. Matthew greatly reformed, religious now. Fine, I thought: so long as he couldn't walk without canes.

The carriage was driven by Toby, the ten-year-old son of the hostler whose establishment adjoined the hotel. It was a lulling journey. The boy's back swung from side to side like an inverted pendulum, obsidian flies glistened on the velvet rumps of the horses, and twisting gray fences, deeply etched with the lengthwise grain of the wood, seemed to wriggle and leap as we rode by. I held Frank, cushioning the knocks for him.

MELANCHTHON HAD BEEN FETCHED from the fields in expectation of meeting us. His hair was grayer. Anne had become a little plump; so had

Susannah. My aunt looked more intensely herself: haggard, desperate, driven.

Frank kicked to be let down, and I put him on the grass. He walked several stiff steps and fell over on his face in the weeds. He rolled over and sat up. He sat for a while, as if deciding what to do next, and whether it would be a good idea for him to cry. He reached his arms out to me. I picked him up.

"Poor motherless creature," I said. "He's become attached to me, I fear."

I introduced Monique and Jocelyn to Susannah and Melanchthon, who had not met them. I introduced them as "Sarah" and "Martha," respectively. Melanchthon told Toby where he could refresh the horse, and to come and join us when he was done.

Anne asked to hold Frank. When I gave him to her, he began to cry, pushing her away, reaching for me. "Mama! Mama!" I took him back. With the baby between us, we could not embrace, but she pressed her cheek on mine, and I was moved. She had always been kind to me.

"I'm sorry," I said. "As I said, he's been mostly in my care until now."

"Never mind," said my aunt. "I suppose he'll get attached to Anne soon enough when he finds he has no other choice." When Anne and I had given each other that half-hug, Agatha had worn an affronted look. It was not that she longed for my embrace, but she felt, probably, that the embrace was hers by right, that a better girl would have done her that homage in return for caring so wonderfully for her when she was a helpless orphan.

Two tables were put together to make one long enough, and chairs were brought in from other rooms, and we all ate together, including the hostler's son. I asked about William Jefferds. Anne told me that he had died in his sleep while living on the Weemses' farm. At the time, he was no longer our family's pastor—my aunt and some other members of the congregation having quarreled with him over Adventism—but of course it was sad; certainly he had been a good man. I asked about Agnes. Had she and George Sackett planned a date for their wedding?

"Not yet, no," said Agatha vaguely.

My aunt had never been any good at keeping secret the existence of a secret. I knew she was hiding something. I looked at Anne and decided that she was in on it.

"Where exactly are they living now? Maybe I'll go see them after this," I said, hoping that the threat of a visit, where I might find out the truth, whatever it was, would force my aunt to tell it to me now.

Indeed, she looked alarmed and reminded me that Agnes and I had never gotten along very well. I replied that that was all water over the dam, and she said, "Well, I would give you her address, only I don't know it. It keeps changing. You see, she and George are going to California as missionaries, and they, they"—I watched her trying to improvise; she was as incompetent as a child—"the first, the Boston mission society that was going to send them couldn't quite come up with all the money they needed, so they're looking for another, and traveling, seeing people to raise the rest of the money."

This was plausible. Among the newspaper articles we were all devouring about California in those days were some inspired by the mission societies, talking of how wicked it was bound to be with all those unruly men and hardly any good women, and efforts were being made to send ministers. Men in my house joked about it. I had heard, from Lewis, that my grandfather was involved in these efforts. So that much was true; whether it had anything to do with George and Agnes, I didn't know.

"Oh, I see." I sat watching them awhile, thinking about all this. I looked at Jocelyn and Monique, and I looked back to Anne and Agatha.

What secret could be so fraught that both Agatha, who despised me, and Anne, who loved me, would want to keep it from me? I meant to know before I left, but I did not press them right away. I asked about Evangeline and Elihu and Mrs. Harding and other old Livy residents, and at last, careful to keep all emotion out of my voice, I asked if they had had any news of Jeptha. At this, they all—Anne, Agatha, Melanchthon, and Susannah—all stared resolutely at their plates.

I waited a bit and then said, "You're hiding something from me."

"Belle, don't," said Anne.

"What's the point? I'm sure to find out. I'll ask around here. I'll ask in Livy. I'll ask in Patavium. I'll go to Boston and ask there if I think it's important to me."

Leaving them to think about it, I fed Frank boiled milk with soft bread and a little molasses at the table; Anne and my aunt both watched with a yearning that was almost lust. I asked Anne if she would like to take over the chore, and she did; and her handsome face lit up with pleasure when Frank accepted the food from her; he smiled and gurgled and flirted with her, after the manner of babies, and my aunt looked on with a starved expression. When he had gone to sleep, I brought his trunk in and showed everyone his baby clothes and his toys, and I said that I thought it would be best if I left while he was sleeping, to avoid creating a fuss.

My aunt said, "There'll be a fuss. You just won't be here for it."

Anne said, "Belle, before you go, could you tell me what you think about a dress I'm making? Just you and me." I was supposed to be a dressmaker, remember. I went up with Anne to her sewing room, and she pulled out a drawer full of material and then she closed it, abandoning the pretense upon which she had gotten me alone. She turned. She surveyed me from head to toe. "You've become so beautiful, Belle. Those girls you are with, they're very pretty, too. I think the three of you are about the prettiest girls I've ever seen in one place. Do they work for you at the dress shop?"

"Yes. They—they work for me."

"But they don't make dresses, do they?"

I didn't answer for a while, and then I said, "No."

"Oh—oh my," she said, and she gave a sigh with a sob in it, and we held each other. "Is he yours, honey? You can tell me. I won't tell anyone else, not even Melanchthon, and I'll love him just the same either way. But I should know."

"Yes," I said. "I'm sorry, I'm sorry, yes. Be good to him. And please don't tell anyone, for his sake."

"I'll be good to him. I'm glad you brought him to me and not to her." She let me go and looked at me. "You're so young still. Just twenty-one."

"Yes."

"You can start over. Why shouldn't you?"

"I know."

"Don't wait too long."

"I won't. I won't. Don't worry about me."

There was a little hesitation then, and she said, "Well, I guess you'd better get going."

She started for the door, but I didn't follow her. I grabbed a pretty little Windsor chair with a red-and-yellow flower-print cushion tied to the seat, and I sat in it and pointed to another just like it. With a wary expression, she lowered herself into the chair. "Tell me," I said. "What is it? It's about Agnes? And George Sackett? And what else?" Suddenly my heart was beating as if I had just run a race. "And Jeptha?"

She watched me for a little longer, then shook her head, put her hand over her mouth, and moved it over her eyes.

"My father killed himself when I was nine," I reminded her. "Everyone in New York tried to hide it from me. They wanted to spare my feelings, but I was bound to learn. It was left for Agatha to tell me, and it was worse for me that way. I know you love me, Anne. I can hear it from you. You are the best person to tell me. Tell me."

I waited, and at last she said: "I was going to tell you if I thought it would be any use. If you—if your shop was really a dress shop. Now it's just going to hurt you, but here it is. Jeptha was here for William Jefferds's funeral, and we asked after his wife. It turned out she had died the year before. It was the first we'd heard about it. And Agnes was there; and she told him—she told us—that George Sackett had consumption and was unable to go to California, and they had parted company. And we learned by letter a few weeks after, Agnes and Jeptha are engaged, and they're going to California. At least, they want to. The missionary society that was backing George Sackett and Agnes went ahead and sent another couple. Jeptha and Agnes are both eager to go, and now Jeptha and Agnes are looking for another sponsor."

"I see," I said, feeling as if I had been hit by a giant hammer, and I knew I was just beginning to feel it. "Yes, I can see why you might have hesitated to tell me all that. Well, well, Agnes and Jeptha. Agnes and Jeptha at last."

I put my head in my hands, suffering, but in the middle of it doing some thinking, because I knew I had to make the best use of my time alone with Anne, and I asked: "When did she tell you that George Sackett had consumption and they had parted ways? Was it before Jeptha said his wife was dead, or after?"

"I don't know; I wasn't there. I only learned it from Agatha. I see what you're saying, but what does it matter? Anyway, what's the use? Arabella, even if it weren't for Agnes, after what you've told me, don't you see it's too late?"

"Didn't you just say the opposite?"

"Too late for you and Jeptha."

I put my head in my hands again. Anne got up from her chair and put her arms around me. She said, "When we met him a few days after the funeral, he said he had wronged you; he'd been wrong about you. I don't know what he meant by it, he wouldn't say. I don't think he knows how much he wronged you."

AFTER WE LEFT, I HAD TOBY DRIVE US in the direction of Livy, and at a certain landmark I had him halt and let me out. Monique and Jocelyn followed me when I walked off the road and through the woods, to a hill overlooking the Muskrat Pond. I came to a beech tree on whose thick, silvery branches Jeptha had once stood, preaching his first sermons to me, and then to the meadow where we had fondled each other at the risk of damnation. Nothing here had changed. Five autumns had stripped the trees, five winters had frozen the ground and six springs had thawed it, while my aunt awaited the end of time and I sent Jeptha letters that he never answered, and I became a millworker, a maid, a whore, and a woman who lived off the earnings of whores, and had a baby, and gave him away.

A breeze made a noisy rustle in the leaves and combed the pond; reflections of trees and grass were split and pulled apart like a deck of cards being reshuffled; and a squirrel with an acorn looked my way, as if trying to place me. I stood there, remembering and ruing, and then I walked back and told Toby to turn the carriage around.

❧ XXXVIII ❧

ON THE RETURN TRIP, MONIQUE AND JOCELYN were respectfully silent, permitting me to concentrate. I stared out of the window at the buds on the apple trees. There were so many new facts, and they kept coming at me like breathless messengers, bringing dispatches from different parts of a chaotic battle.

He said he had wronged you, Anne had told me. *He'd been wrong about you.* What could he have meant by that? It had to mean that he believed me at last. He knew I had not been unfaithful to him. I had told him in my letters about Matthew. For some reason, five and a half years ago he had not believed me. For some reason, now he did. Agnes's part in my ruin he could not know, surely, or he would not be with her.

I thought until my head hurt. When we reached Albany, I put Jocelyn on a stage to Boston, where she was to act as my spy, helping me to find Agnes, Jeptha, and George Sackett, if they were really in that city, and to discover what she could about their real circumstances.

For what I was about to attempt, no plan would be good enough. Any plan would be overtaken by events. If I won, I would do it by putting myself in the path of opportunities and taking advantage of those that came my way.

Too late, Anne had said, only wishing me well. But she did not really know me anymore. She did not know the resources I had at my disposal, the risks I was willing to take, and how far I was willing to go.

WHEN I RETURNED TO NEW YORK, I arranged for a wonderful coincidence to occur.

Walking along Fourth Street, I captured the attention of a slim, handsome, rather smug-looking young man with a silk hat and white kid gloves. I recognized him immediately. He noticed the look of inquiry and wonder on my face; interested, he stopped and smiled. "Can I be of assistance?"

I stared at him for another second. "Robert?"

"Yes. I—"

"Robert Godwin?"

"Do we know each other?" he asked. He was still a bachelor. He began to flirt. "I think I have a tolerable memory. Could it have deteriorated so much as to allow me to forget so lovely a face?"

"Oh, Robert," I said, genuinely moved, even though I had worked very hard to arrange this chance encounter. I had waited on this street, which I had studiously avoided ever since I learned from Lewis that Robert belonged to the Union Club, whose front door was twenty feet from where we stood. "Robert, look at me."

Curiosity gave way to astonishment. "It can't be."

"It is."

"Arabella?"

"Yes. Yes!"

We embraced, then walked arm in arm to a nearby restaurant, and I told him, very selectively, about Livy and Cohoes, and how, since leaving the mill, I had become a dressmaker with a shop of my own on Grand Street, which he declared that he had passed a hundred times. I had probably been busy with pins and measuring tape, a matter of yards away! But men seldom enter such shops. He told me about the fall and rebirth of our grandfather's affairs, and his own—Robert's—career as an attorney at law, and—oh, wait, hang on to my hat—he told me that in finding him not only had I also found Edward and our grandparents, but I had also found Lewis! Yes, it was true, Lewis had chanced into renewed contact with the family before I had! He was in a boarding school, the same that Edward and Robert had gone to after our mother died.

"It's like a dream," I said. "It's like a wonderful happy ending in a book."

It was not necessary for me to feign strong feelings.

At Robert's insistence, we took a hack north up Broadway, all the way to Bloomingdale—where, according to the maps that the Corporation had already drawn, 100th Street would be one day. We passed farms, and country stores, and ponds whose surfaces were stroked by weeping willows. "There it is," said Robert, about a big house with a white-columned portico: it was the house my grandfather had purchased two years ago and had been living in all this time. "Just wait," he said, and put his hand over mine, obviously thrilled to be reunited with his baby sister.

As the hack turned onto the gravel road to a house I had never set my eyes on before, I blinked back tears. Robert put his arm around my shoulders and watched me, smiling, thinking he knew what was in my heart, but of course he couldn't know. Even if the facts were put before him, he couldn't know. I felt as if I were coming home at last. I felt as if all that was broken could be fixed. If anyone could do it, my grandfather could. All the indelible stains could be washed clean.

At the same time, I knew it was false and dangerous. I would have to be vigilant with myself. I wasn't here to be made right. I couldn't be made right.

To the elderly servant who met us at the door, Robert said, "Tell Mr. Godwin to consult the health of his heart before coming down to greet us; this young lady and I have a great though very pleasant shock for him and for Mrs. Godwin."

We waited in a comfortable drawing room. A vase with daffodils stood on the lid of a piano near a window; Robert idly turned the stool a few times, sat, squinted at the sheets on the music stand, and made straight bars of shadow appear and wink out as his fingers pressed the sleek rods of wood and ivory. The notes were tinny. The rhythm was halting. Never had a piece of music moved me so. I reminded myself that he had not answered a single one of my letters when I was in Livy. I supposed my grandfather had told him not to. He ought to have disobeyed.

There were footsteps, and Robert turned to an archway that opened to the hall; I looked in that direction, too.

My grandfather, who looked much older, of course, after twelve years, was smiling broadly when he came in. I believe he assumed that Robert had brought home a prospective bride, and the presence of a young woman of suitable age and appearance doubtless seemed to confirm the impression.

"Don't tell him," Robert instructed me. "See if he can guess."

This showed my grandfather that something else was afoot. He looked at me a few seconds, walked up to look closer. "Can it be?" he inquired. "Is it?"

"Say it," Robert commanded him.

"Arabella?" he said. I nodded. His old eyes welled with tears, and he enfolded my soft young hands within his hands, which had the cracked translucency that mine have today. He brought my fingers to his lips;

then he released them, and his arms enfolded me. "Oh, what a providence it is." He gazed into my eyes with a tenderness that made me forget the countless times I had cursed him for abandoning me, and I began to tremble and sob. "It's a miracle, a miracle."

He pulled a chair over to the couch, and we sat, leaning toward each other, while he had us narrate the story of our chance meeting on West Fourth Street. He asked Robert if I knew that the family had found Lewis, too, and asked me to tell him what I had been doing since I had left Cohoes. I had just begun the story I had prepared when he said, "But this is unfair to Mother," and dispatched a maid to fetch my grandmother. He told the maid who I was—"Isn't it amazing?"—but instructed her to tell my grandmother only that someone she would be very pleased to see was waiting for her downstairs.

Presently, she came in. The years had been harder on her than they had been on my grandfather; she was wizened and hunched, and her cane was very necessary to her. Also, I think her mind had deteriorated, just enough to make her subterfuges transparent. It was evident that she had overridden my grandfather's instructions to the maid and demanded to know exactly who was downstairs. She recognized me with improbable dispatch and broad acting. "Merciful heavens—can it be?" She opened her mouth and popped her eyes, looked left at Robert and right at my grandfather. "Is it Arabella, my granddaughter? Come to me, my child; a few years earlier I would have hurried to your side, but now I am so frail that I must bid you to come to me."

I kissed her, and felt the chill. I was more convinced than ever that the reason my brother and I had been sent to live with strangers in the darkest hour of our lives twelve years earlier was that my grandmother had not wanted the noise and worry of young children underfoot; consumption's disdain of country air had been a convenient pretext. You'll think it wrong of me to resent it, when I had only just left my son, Frank, in the same place. I see your point, I guess.

EARLIER IN THE WEEK, I HAD MOVED some of my belongings into the apartment of Ann Dunlop, who lived with two other women above a dress shop she owned. For a fee, Miss Dunlop agreed to pretend that I owned the store, giving a semblance of reality to the story I was telling about myself. Soon Robert and my grandfather visited. I showed them the shop. I showed them where I lived: the apartment, neat and clean, but rather cramped for four women, created an effective impression of honest spinsterhood.

As soon as they left, I went back to the house on Mercer Street, where I still in fact resided in order to keep a close eye on my affairs.

At a series of dinners at my grandfather's house, over the course of several weeks, I was reacquainted with the family and brought into my grandfather's social circle. For the first of these, Lewis was brought down from school, and the two of us acted out our conception of the emotions we should have felt on meeting again after a four-year separation. At this dinner and subsequent ones, I met several of my grandfather's business and political allies. Some of them were staying to eat, some were leaving as I arrived, for my grandfather had become busy with politics. He received letters from people who were famous at the time and are in the history books today, and at one of these dinners I met both William Lloyd Garrison, editor of *The Liberator,* and the dusky pastor of New York City's Abyssinian Presbyterian Church.

It was at the second of these meetings that Robert took my arm and said, "He got Arthur Heywood to come, the *Courier* editor. Remember I used to read it to you, about the steamship disasters, though I wasn't supposed to?"

"Yes, I remember." I felt dizzy; my face was burning, and my feet were very far away from me. I wondered if I ought to plead a sudden illness. "Isn't he a Democrat?"

"Yes, but Grandfather hopes to make him a Free-Soiler, at least when it comes to California." In a lower voice, Robert added, "Be prepared, Heywood's not far above the majority of his readers; the wife is a little more refined."

I could feel my pulse in my face, so frightened was I, but I determined to brazen it out. His wife was here. Even if she hadn't been here, he would have wanted to keep his relationship with a whore a secret. Each of us had something to lose. On the other hand, the story that Solomon Godwin's daughter was a parlor-house madam—what a wonderful story for a Democratic newspaper.

"Jonathan Wheeler is here," Robert added, as we walked up the stairs and into the dining room. "You remember we mentioned Mr. Wheeler?"

"The young Presbyterian minister."

"That's right."

"With his fiancée?"

Robert didn't answer.

I had waited impatiently through three evenings with my grandfather before he had finally gotten around to mentioning his work as the chairman of the California Missionary Committee and their search for a suitable young couple to send west to minister to the miners. The committee was determined to send a man and his wife. By all reports, good Christian women were so rare in the gold regions that they were accorded a respect scarcely short of worship. A wife would not only be a comfort to the missionary but multiply his effectiveness tenfold. But of the candidates they had interviewed so far, one married couple was too old for the journey and not terribly keen. Another, though young and zealous, were a pair of Methodists, and the committee was lukewarm on this sect. Finally, there was Jonathan Wheeler, a recent seminary graduate, young, ardent, a Presbyterian, but, unfortunately, a bachelor.

"What a coincidence," I had said, and I added that when I was back in Livy, placing an orphan there for the Female Reform Society, I had learned that my cousin Agnes and her fiancé, Jeptha, a seminary-trained clergyman, were determined to go to California as missionaries, and were trying to raise money for the trip. I didn't know their address, but perhaps my aunt Agatha would. My grandfather said he would write to Agatha.

He then asked what religion they were; when I said "Baptists," his enthusiasm waned a little, but he said he would contact them; perhaps they would do if Mr. Wheeler failed to find a wife. But he rather thought he would. Mr. Wheeler was a handsome man, and my grandfather had a woman in mind for him.

AS ROBERT BROUGHT ME IN, the men who were standing bowed and the men who were seated rose. Most of them were members of the California Missionary Committee, important, established men, variously equipped with bushy eyebrows, nostril hairs, bald spots, double chins, wattles, warts, and crow's feet. Except for Edward and Robert, only one man was young, so he had to be Jonathan Wheeler: tall, with a Roman nose, a prominent Adam's apple, and a clean suit that fit as if he had borrowed it for the evening from a smaller, less impecunious friend. He was very stiff, and became even more nervous when he saw me, and suddenly I understood that the woman my grandfather had in mind for Wheeler was me. It was very good news, really.

Arthur Heywood, who had been eating an hors d'oeuvre when he saw me, stopped chewing with the soft mass still in his mouth. I was introduced here and there, taking their hands. By the time I got to him, he had swallowed without mishap, and was composed, though with an almost imperceptible look of disbelief in his eye.

By then I felt comfortable enough to say, "You look familiar to me, Mr. Heywood. I wonder if we have crossed paths sometime, on a steamboat or a horsecar, some place where newspaper editors may encounter their readers in the flesh."

His tuberous nose crimsoned, and his smile reproached me for teasing him, and he bowed.

We had met in the forest, dancing with Satan, and had to keep each other's secret.

Later in the evening, when we were near to each other and no one else was by, Heywood said, "Have pity. Say you are who I think you are."

"I am."

"And an impostor? Or . . . ?"

An impostor. That had not occurred to me—that he might wonder if I were pretending to be a girl who had disappeared, last seen here when she was a child. The idea was no stranger than the truth. "Well, I'm not exactly what they think I am, but I'm Arabella Godwin. I began as Arabella Godwin. How is Philip getting on?"

"Tolerably."

"I'll send you a message. We'll meet. I'll satisfy your curiosity."

WHEELER WAS SO FRIGHTENED OF ME—of any woman, I think. When we stood apart from the others later that evening, he spoke about his mother, who had encouraged his religious calling over the objection of his brute of a father. He thought that his mother and I would like each other. He had heard that my mother had died when I was young.

"Yes, and my father at the same time."

He reddened and said haltingly, "So—so I heard. But I don't—I don't—it's all right. That doesn't matter."

He meant the suicide, and the disgrace of it, and perhaps the bad blood, all of which he was willing to overlook.

I cast my eyes downward. He cleared his throat twice, wiped his chin with his hand, and cleared his throat again.

He was clumsy, but people were helping him, and on a Sunday afternoon only a few days later, I found myself alone with the young minister in my grandmother's garden, the landscape of which was her main occupation when she was not arranging social gatherings in aid of my grandfather's good works.

Jonathan Wheeler and I were left alone to stroll through these grounds. It was May, the sky almost clear, with songbirds, and a gravel walk lined with cherry trees with silvery bark and pink blossoms. He walked with his hands behind his back; the gravel crunched beneath his boots; there was a sprinkling of dandruff on the dark jacket of his suit, which was his own this time, and was rubbed to a shine at the sleeves and cuffs. He wasn't well-off; he wasn't claiming to be. He claimed only to be righteous.

He coughed into his hand, gave me a smile, asked me to sit on a bench, and paced. "Do you believe in Providence?" he asked me.

"I suppose so," I said.

"I do as well. Nothing, I find, happens entirely by chance. I have often discussed it with my mother. She sees instances of it everywhere. Did we but know it, we are surrounded by miracles!" And he told me a story, which went on far too long for the occasion, about meeting my grandfather by accident, and how it had led to his candidacy for this missionary work. "And now, a matter of weeks before the date set for the ship's departure, when I may leave my mother perhaps forever"—here he paused, and there was a catch in his throat—"at this very time, you meet your long-lost brother, also by accident. Do you see what I am trying to tell you?"

"I have to say that I do not."

"I do not believe this has occurred by chance."

"Jonathan, if you would wait a moment . . ."

"I believe it was meant, that we are to be—"

"Jonathan, I must go into the house. I'm unwell."

"Oh," he said, and I left him.

I found my grandfather in his study, sitting in a chair that he must have kept from his old house on Bond Street, though nothing else in the room was the same. "He's an honest fellow," I said, "and with his good looks, and help from friends and relatives, I have no doubt that in time he will find a young woman who does not frighten him too much, and he will marry. But I do not think it will happen this summer, and I am bound and determined that it will not be me."

My grandfather was still for a moment, and nodded, accepting my judgment. "Forgive us. We thought—we thought we would try. We never had any daughters."

Despite my grievances, I felt a stab of affection for him—each time I saw him he seemed a miracle, alive after all, like the youths in Daniel stepping unhurt from the fiery furnace, and I stood here in his study as though nothing much had ever happened to me. "It's something you would have done if I had grown up in this house."

Had my mother and father lived, or even if they had died but I had not been sent away, such scenes might have occurred—eligible prospects sighted, dinners arranged, the old folks retiring discreetly at the right moment. They'd have done it like this, except that the young man left alone with me would have been rich.

What exactly was it that made them put me in a garden with a penniless seminary graduate? Was it my father's suicide? If so, it showed them to be extremely ignorant in these matters. Such tragedies occur in the best families. People overlook them. As the granddaughter of Solomon Godwin, with my beauty, a little luck, and ingenuity, I could have snared an Astor or a Vanderbilt. Then, if I stayed in the East, I'd have been ruined. Too many prominent men knew me as Harriet Knowles. But my grandparents didn't know about Harriet Knowles, so it could not be that. I thought perhaps it was the rape. Lewis had told them about it.

"Would you speak to the young man?" I said. "I'd rather not see him again. If you don't mind, I will stay in here until he is gone."

He nodded, rose with a grimace, and walked to the door. As he passed me he said, "I wrote to your aunt yesterday," which alarmed me—I thought he'd written to her a week ago. Now it would be better if he had *not* written to her; I could have claimed that I had written to her myself, and told him where Jeptha and Agnes were—I had just learned it from Jocelyn, my spy in Boston. They were right here in New York.

❧ XXXIX ❧

THEY WERE IN NEW YORK CITY, Jeptha and Agnes, living in two down-town boarding houses, his for men, hers for women. I had to wait while my grandfather's letter wended its way to Aunt Agatha and she wrote back. For all I knew, they would be married by then, but I had no choice. I had to wait and to suffer.

Since my meeting with Robert outside the Union Club, I had sent Sean once a day to the dressmaker's shop, where Ann Dunlop would give him any letters that had been sent to me at that address and let me know, through Sean, if anybody had been there to see me. One evening, when the champagne had begun to flow, the maid called me away to meet Sean, who handed me a letter from my grandfather.

Dear Arabella,

Wonderful news. Your aunt has written back that Jeptha Talbot and your cousin Agnes are both living in this very city! I have been to Talbot's boarding house and met him and am favorably impressed. He seemed like a serious fellow, experienced beyond his years, and decisive, with energy for the task, and sturdy, though thankfully more refined than his Biblical namesake! He has had hard times with his wife, who was ill for years before she died. I would like us to meet the day after tomorrow at my house, so that you can become reacquainted with your cousin and your old friend, now her fiancé, if you can spare the time from your shop. Then probably a dinner at which the CMC can get a look at him; everyone understands that we have to hurry now. If I can expect you, send a messenger to my place of business and I will pay him for his trouble.

Grandfather

I took Sean up to my room and had him wait while I penned a reply, which I gave to him with a reminder of how careful he must be and what a circuitous route he must now take when traveling between the parlor house and every other destination. Finally, I tipped him, and held out a box full of zanzibars, gibraltars, lemon drops, and peanut brittle that I kept around especially as treats for Sean. It used to be fun to watch him agonize over which kind to pick. If he always picked his favorite, he'd never have the others. Lately, in a show of arrogance, he would take a handful of them, eat one, and put the rest in his pocket. Sean was beginning to worry me. Any day now, he was going to comprehend the full value of the secrets stored in his mind.

ROBERT WAS GOING TO PICK ME UP in a hired coach on the day of the meeting, for Agnes was his cousin, too, and he was curious to meet her. So, frightened to the bottom of my soul by the prospect of the encounter I had done so much to arrange, almost wishing it would be delayed, so that the possible wreck of all my hopes would be delayed, I went early to the dress shop. There I tried on and discarded several dresses and caps, and was ready too early, and spent an hour with nothing to do, unable to read or eat or think or stay seated or pace back and forth, until Robert called me with a shout. I came outside, where the light was very bright, and he lifted me into the coach, which was very dark inside. I had expected to meet Jeptha and Agnes at my grandfather's house, but I soon became aware that there were other people in the vehicle, who could see me better than I could see them, because their eyes had grown accustomed to its darkness. "Who's with you?" I asked Robert, and before I even knew what I was seeing, I began to tremble, as my eyes' adjustment to the darkness and my mind's accommodation of the unexpected assembled, piece by piece the face whose memory I had struggled sometimes to preserve, sometimes to erase, which I had addressed in a thousand imaginary dialogues full of rebukes and defenses. Jeptha's face—mature now, its lines clearer—was clean-shaven, framed by long black hair. His mouth was thin, shaped like an archer's bow, a little solemn in repose. The eyes were the most striking feature, not just the blue but their setting, which was deep, hooded, and feral. They made me feel naked, revealed, in a way that was insupportable unless I could know there was love in them.

Robert laughed at the surprise he had arranged, but Jeptha nodded to me seriously, and said my name—"Arabella." His voice—sonorous, lower than I remembered it—made my body vibrate like a plucked string. To cover my feelings, to show myself playful, I punched Robert in the arm, which made him laugh again. Then, with my whole self taking a running leap up to the name, I turned back and said, "Jeptha," and I was happy that my tongue did not falter. It took a little more time for Agnes to come into focus; she gave me a polite smile which did not involve her eyes, which took stock of me very skeptically and warily.

"Dear cousin," I said. I kissed her, and I took her hands in mine, and with a consciousness of not looking at Jeptha, but of his sober gaze resting on me, I told Robert, "We're more like sisters than cousins. It was Agnes who first instructed me in the duties of a farm girl. Do you remember those early days, Agnes?" I asked, cocking my head as we sometimes do when we wish to express sympathy for sick people, and giving her the gentle smile that used to be her specialty.

"Of course, Arabella."

"We were both sweet on Jeptha," I said, and turning to Robert, I added, "It's true! We were rivals, oh, it went on for years. And then for a time, Jeptha and I were keeping company, but that was long ago, and many joys and sorrows have intervened. I was so sorry to hear about your wife, Jeptha."

"Thank you, Arabella," he said. Again the voice cut right through me.

"And now Agnes has him, and I must learn resignation a second time. How lovely she's become. I can't wonder at his choice."

"You're not such an eyesore yourself," Robert consoled me.

"It's true," said Agnes. "I wonder that you haven't married by now, Arabella."

"There's still time, I'm sure," said Robert.

"After all, you're such a good mother," Agnes observed, and paused, and added, "I mean to that little orphan child, what is his name?"

"Frank."

"Frank, whom you brought to Anne and Melanchthon." To the others in the close interior of the coach, she continued, "My mother wrote a long letter to me about it. She said that the infant had become greatly attached to Arabella—he called her Mama, and cried bitterly to be parted from her."

"I had the care of the little fellow for almost a year," I explained. "I must say I miss him, too."

"What was the name of that society?" Agnes inquired.

"The one that arranged for the adoption?"

"Yes."

"The Female Reform Society."

"What good work they must do. I should like to meet with their officers and learn more about it all."

"Do you think you'll be able to make time for it? You have so many preparations to make, for the wedding."

She put her hand on Jeptha's. "It will be a plain ceremony." Addressing Robert and Jeptha, she said, "The ladies at my boarding house have heard of the Female Reform Society, whose members are famous for preaching outside of saloons and houses of ill repute, but none of them had heard that they also found homes for orphans. It should be more widely known. Not everyone thinks it is right for women to thrust themselves into such work, which puts them into low company, but I expect it is all right for women of strong character, with male supervision. Is there, by the way?"

"We consult with learned reverends."

"While I'm still in New York, you will introduce me to the officers of this fine institution?"

"I'd be happy to."

Through all this, Jeptha did not say a word, but as we stepped out of the coach, he took Agnes aside and spoke to her. She cast her eyes down, and it seemed to me that she had been rebuked; and in her display of contrition I observed more variety and subtlety than I remembered: a daunting advance in skill.

HAD HE CHANGED? HOW COULD HE NOT? I watched him furtively. I looked at whoever was speaking, and since he was the center of attention, often enough it was him. When he was behind me, I watched him with the back of my neck, and if he happened to be elsewhere in the house, my spirit haunted those other rooms. He had told Anne that he had wronged me. What did that mean?

Sometimes, stealing glimpses of him this way, I thought that I had changed too much, and it was impossible that we should ever be together again. Then there were moments when the intervening years fell away like a fever dream, and it was 1843 again.

Only my grandmother and grandfather and my brother Edward were added to the company when we got to the house, and we talked in the drawing room, and ate ham in the dining room. I told my grandfather that Jeptha was a fine judge of character, and to prove it, look at his choice of a bride, she was so *good*. I said to Agnes, "Remember the time when, to save me a licking, as you thought, you replaced my mending with yours, so soon after Lewis and I arrived in Livy? And Aunt Agatha praised my sewing, but I noticed it wasn't mine and told her, like a fool."

I had told this story to Jeptha long ago, so it was meant as a reminder of the kind of woman his betrothed was.

My grandmother expressed surprise that Agnes's intervention had been necessary. She remembered my sewing as being very creditable for a girl my age.

"It's a lovely story, Arabella, but I'm sure I would remember such an incident had it actually occurred," commented Agnes. "Are you quite sure you aren't embellishing the past? You always had such a rich imagination; you always told such amazing tales." To the table: "She was such an exotic creature to us. We never knew what she would say next. We didn't have the imagination to guess."

You would think that after all I'd been through I would feel stronger than my cousin Agnes, who had had a much less eventful life, but I did not. Perhaps fewer things had happened to her because she was too smart to let them happen. She loosed fewer arrows, but more of them hit the mark.

I observed, "It is strange how differently people can remember things, for I remember myself as clumsy. I remember you as the subtle one."

"You seemed to think so then, too. I wonder if it was because we were too simple for you—you could not believe we meant no more than what we said."

"Am I wrong to consider that a subtle remark, Agnes?"

This received polite, relieved chuckles from the company, which must have been puzzled by our evident antagonism. A little after that, Jeptha, who had retreated into a wary silence while Agnes and I fenced, whispered to her. For the rest of the day, no matter what I said, she did not rise to the bait and did all she could to show me that we could put aside our childhood rivalry and now she intended to be my good friend.

Over dinner, Jeptha was gently interrogated on the subjects of California, gold, politics, and street preaching. Edward, who, like Lewis, was itching to go to the gold fields, was rude enough to ask Jeptha if he wouldn't be tempted to imitate all those sailors who, it was said, had abandoned their ships and the soldiers who had abandoned their posts. Didn't he think he would be tempted, once he was there and heard of all the fortunes being made?

"I think you are really asking if I can keep a promise," said Jeptha.

"I meant no offense by it," Edward rejoined.

"On the contrary, I consider it a fair question. Money has been raised to send a man to California to preach God's word in the lap of temptation, and the man you send should be able to keep a promise." He paused, but everyone knew that we were about to hear a sample of his preaching, and no one interrupted. "When a man cannot keep a promise, it is a weakness. We shouldn't blame him for it, any more than we blame a man for having a frail body; but we must not burden him with our trust, any more than we would burden a frail man with a heavy hogshead. It would not only be foolish, it would be cruel to the man, who would blame himself for failing." He looked around the table, at the assorted sound, middle-aged men of the California Missionary Committee. "If it is thought that I may not be able to keep a promise, you ought to wait, for the next ship and the next, if need be, until you have found someone suitable to the task. You owe it to this great cause. However, I believe I *can* keep my promise. I judge this not because I feel called to preach the Gospel, though I do, or because of my conviction that the gold fields will pauperize many more men than they'll enrich, but simply because I have always kept promises in the past. Others, whose letters I have as references, will attest to my disposition in this vital matter of keeping promises. Of course, a man's character can change. Almost anything in this world may change. Against that, we must go to the only perfectly reliable source of strength and pray for His help."

"Hear, hear," said Robert, who occupied the seat next to mine, and there were general murmurs of approval.

"If I get to California, I promise not to be pauperized, but to be enriched," said Edward.

My grandfather looked at Edward a little nervously, not wanting the parson to disapprove of his grandson. Jeptha responded with an easy grin, "In that case, I'll come to you for a donation," and Edward smiled, and there was a sprinkling of laughter around the table.

THAT EVENING, USING SEAN AS A MESSENGER, I sent Jeptha a note, asking him to meet me the next day; and a message came back saying he would. I arranged to meet him at Jefferson Market, a place frequented by wives and servants rather than by gentlemen of fashion, and I could tell Jeptha that I had chosen it for its eight-story watchtower, which was visible from a great distance. I would walk to it in the company of Monique and Ann Dunlop: thus I would not offend propriety by walking alone, and when they left me with Jeptha, neither of them would be walking alone, either.

They came to my room at 259 Mercer, where Antonia, my lady's maid, dressed my hair before a mirror, her face as grim as if she were a squire dressing a knight, but with more anxious choices than there are to trouble knights and squires: first with a bun in the back, in the fashion of the day, and then, thinking it over, with a bun on top, in the manner of the 1830s, as Agnes wore it, and then, after I had more time to think, with no bun at all but braided, the braids wrapped into a crown, and with spiral ringlets dangling from the sides. Then we agonized over whether to festoon my hair with pearls, which Monique and Ann—their studious faces at angles in the mirror over my face—both insisted were so perfectly in the mode that they could not but compel any man's admiration. But I wanted a particular man and could not afford to look rich, and so I decided against them, and punctuated it instead with a plain black comb. To the bewilderment of my companions, I spent an inordinate amount of time over the choice of gloves. I remembered how Jeptha had been about my hands when we were in Livy—how often his eyes had been drawn to them, and how sometimes he had taken my wrist captive and stroked his own cheek with my right hand, and then he had kissed my palms, one and then the other. My dress was of figured gauze over satin, with a low corsage and sleeves very short and perfectly plain and tight, ornamented with double rows of ribbon bows, and with a third row of very small bows around the skirt, a short distance below the waist. We went through several cardinal pelerines and settled on one of watered silk trimmed with lace. As an afterthought, I had Antonia undress me and remove two petticoats, to the horror of my advisers. But I insisted: "I'm not going to a ball, just to Jefferson Market, and I'm trying to win the heart of a Baptist preacher. I have to seem practical."

It was a fine day at the beginning of May, pleasant to walk in except for one moment of foul odor when a wagon passed carrying away the offal of the streets, which were being cleaned and strewn with lime to keep off the cholera. On West Fourth Street, two men, each in the humiliating costume of the sandwich sign, had gotten into an argument, waving their fists at each other, and a crowd was collecting at the prospect of combat between gladiators dressed in wooden armor.

The western sidewalk on Sixth Avenue, outside Jefferson Market, lay permanently in the shadow of wooden awnings, and there were produce wagons labeled with the names of towns to the north and west. Sawdust covered the floor of the indoor market. Jeptha, not noticing us yet, stood between a barrel of ice, several cages of dispirited chickens, and a coffee-and-pie stand, telling a couple of pushcart men what Jesus had done for them. Something about his stance, and the way a shaft of light from a high window hit a portion of his face, the way a lick of his black hair fell over his forehead, and his expression as he spoke to the men combined to produce in me a sharp, sudden stab of carnal need. When we got close, we were both shy and awkward. I introduced Jeptha to Monique and Ann; we all went together to a nearby oyster saloon, and Monique and Ann left with the understanding that they would return in a half-hour.

In the oyster saloon there were many men but few women, none like me, and I attracted the glances of the clientele. I gave Jeptha my cheek to kiss, and his sweet musky odor, special to him, brought a pang of memory as surely as a whiff of mown grass may conjure some lost moment of a childhood summer. I asked him what he thought of New York, and he looked around at the pandemonium of the oyster saloon and said that in a day here there was raw material for a lifetime of philosophy. We talked about the places he had visited since his arrival. We were polite and distant. There was a wall between us. It was his object to keep it there, and my object to break it down.

A waiter came and went. We each had soup with crackers. I began to remove my gloves. I saw him glance at my hands. Because of this, I took the gloves off extra slowly, and made a big show of putting them safely aside. I lifted the spoon very slowly to my mouth, and I opened my mouth slightly, but I didn't sip; I put the spoon back in the bowl. I said, "You can't marry her. It's impossible."

He looked levelly back at me. "You know we can't talk about that."

And though I was sure we *had* to talk about it, there was something in the speed of his response that encouraged me. It was as if a second before there had been twenty yards between us, and now he was right there, and five years had fallen away.

I shook my head. "I see how you are with her. How she plays the naughty child and then you scold her and she's contrite. So you think that you see through her saintly pose. That's her cunning. She lets you see her most trivial crimes. You feel agreeably superior to her. But in this sort of thing, Jeptha, almost anybody is your superior."

He dipped his head in a way that said he grasped my point—honest men are not the best judges of deception—without conceding its truth, and changed the subject: "I was glad to see you reconciled with your grandfather after all these years," he said, and asked me a series of light questions about my grandfather and the California Missionary Committee. I was supposed to show my good breeding by letting him lead me into small talk.

I let this go on for a little while. Finally, I said, "Jeptha, is it your plan to tear my heart out with politeness? Do you know what it does to me for you to talk to me as if we are a couple of old friends who have grown apart?"

He became serious. "You're right to rebuke me. I apologize."

"As to a stranger you jostled in the street."

He sat silent for a while and responded: "I'd just better say what I came here to say. It's about what happened in Livy."

The wrong he thought he had done me. I had wanted to know this ever since my visit to Livy, and now that I was about to learn it I was afraid, I didn't know why; maybe I was afraid that it would amount to less than I had hoped it would. After a pause full of the clinking of silverware and china and the voices of other patrons, I said, "All right."

"You know that William Jefferds died recently—that is where Agnes and I met again, at his funeral. I was given his books and papers. He left me a note, amounting to a confession, and your letters to me, which he had never sent on as you had asked. That was the subject of the confession. Until then, I never knew what had happened to you. He did not want me to know. He did not think it was in my interest to know."

My hand covered my mouth. It was only because I didn't want people to stare at us that I did not put my head in my hands. Then I had a thought: "Did you read my letters and Jefferds's confession before or after Agnes got you to promise to marry her?"

"Please don't put it that way, and what does it matter?" he asked. "I told you. That's all decided."

"Oh dear—that means *after*."

Gently: "It means it would be wrong for me to answer."

I looked down for a few seconds, gathering my thoughts, and then, feeling sure of myself, feeling right, I lifted my head and watched his face to assess the impact of my words. "My darling, all those years when you thought I had betrayed you, did you ever wish you had acted differently? Did you ever, even with your wife beside you, wish it had been me, even with the crimes you thought I had committed? You did. I know it. Because you love me, Jeptha, through and through, down to your feet. I'm an arrow in your heart, and you will never get me out; and I'm the same way about you."

"This has to stop," he said hoarsely.

"Just imagine how it has been for *me*. I was innocent. I suffered unfairly. I suffered more than you can know. I've thought of you every day. Alone, without you to guide me, I've wandered down strange paths into terrible places. I've been in danger. I *am* in danger. But you can keep me safe now if you will. You can fix everything."

He stood up from his chair. "I can't listen to this. If this goes on, I've got to leave."

"She *tricked* you. If you've read my letters, you know what she did. She's as responsible in what happened as Matthew."

He stood indecisively, sat down again, and shook his head. "I did read your letters. You said you'd heard, from Titus, that Agnes spread a

rumor about you and the Harding brothers—a rumor that came to my
ears (though I never believed it in its worst form, but never mind, what I
believed was bad enough). So I talked to Titus. He said you came to him
to tell him what Matthew had done, he remembered that day clearly, but
he was sure he never accused Agnes of spreading that rumor; he said you
must have misunderstood him. That kind of gossip can start so easily,
anywhere. I would revile Agnes if I believed she had done what you say.
She didn't do it. She couldn't have done it."

"Do you remember when Lionel and Becky died, Jeptha? And we
nursed you? And afterward, Agnes pretended to be sick herself, and how
it tortured her mother?"

He shook his head, not to deny the truth of what I said, but to deny
that it would convince him.

I felt like a regiment that repeatedly attempts the storming of a citadel. Within the citadel was a prisoner, wishing himself free, wishing I
would succeed.

Just to keep him here while I recouped my forces, I asked him about
the ship to California. What was its name? The *Juniper*, said Jeptha. And
what was the route? After rummaging in his coat for pencil and paper,
he drew a map. It would go south from New York, he said, and cross the
equator. It would stop for provisions—and, probably, repairs—in Brazil,
and stay there a week, maybe more. It would go south even farther, and
around Cape Horn, where it would be very cold and stormy, and then
north, with a stop in Valparaíso, Chile, and north again, till it arrived in
San Francisco, a dirty little village which was growing very fast now. And
what were the accommodations like? I asked. Very primitive, cramped,
and crowded. And how long would the journey take? I asked him. "It
depends. Four months with good luck and a skillful captain. Seven
months if there are a lot of problems."

Staring at my palms, I pictured it. I pictured them together on deck,
against the rail, one of his arms wrapped around her shoulders, and the
other stretched out to indicate some interesting sight. I grieved, and
then, thinking more, I rejoiced.

"Four to seven months," I said, raising my head and looking at him.
"And you think you can spend all that time, in crowding and discomfort, with a woman you don't love? You will live that lie, you who live for

truth, you who hate lies so much that when I say you don't love her you cannot bring yourself to tell me you do, and I'll bet you haven't told her either?"

We were silent. I took a sip of my soup, and he took a sip of his, but the soup was quite cold, and we weren't hungry, so we stopped. I wiped my mouth with the napkin and asked, "What would you have done if you had gotten my letters?"

His head inclined and righted itself. "It's idle for me to say. I would have come to Livy. Beyond that . . . it was Jefferds's belief that whatever happened then would have been the ruin of all his work on my behalf. He sat on your letters. I married Grace. The life you and I would have had together, whatever it would have been, it didn't happen. It can't happen. I can't make it up to you. We're different people now."

"I am not different," I said—a giant lie, yet there was truth in it. "And you are not different. Not in any way that counts to me."

"I have given her my promise."

"Your promise. Well, if it's a matter of law, you promised me first. In '43. Let her sue if she thinks she has a case. We'll be in California."

He gave me a sad smile. "California? Arabella. California? You want to be a missionary? Bring souls to Jesus? You?"

I felt closer to him at that moment than at any time during this conversation, and I waited, and then, in a small voice, I said, "I have a soul, don't I, Jeptha?"

He shut his eyes.

"For you, Jeptha, I can do it. I can be a missionary's wife and help-meet. I will not disgrace you. I will make you happy by day and by night." I reached across the table and stroked his cheek, and his head jerked slightly from the surprise of it, but he did not pull away, and I could almost hear the blood rushing around his body, upriver and downriver, on many errands.

We talked a little while longer after that, but I was no longer advancing my cause, so I sighed and stopped. All in all I thought it had gone very well, and I had a general idea of what was needed now.

I WENT BACK TO MY HOUSE ON MERCER STREET. When I got there, Sean was waiting for me with a message from the dress shop. We climbed the stairs to my room, and I stood watching him eat peanut brittle, and then I read the note.

Dear Arabella Godwin, Arabella Moody, Harriet Knowles,

It's funny that you think you can change your plans without talking to me first. I watch you. I know your gambler friend is far away. I know you're back with your grandfather now, and you want to be respectable again. Go ahead, but pay me first. Meet me at my house. Bring $2,000 and bring an extra dress, because I mean to rip off the one you're wearing.

—Jack

I sat down at my desk and thought, feeling trapped and raging at my fate: was it all impossible, everything I had planned, was it all to fall apart because of this mindless beast who had already done so much to wrench my existence out of its proper shape? It was an insult to me, to have so unworthy a foe. Sean was still in the room, and, showing more emotion before him than perhaps I should have, I got up and paced, sometimes putting my palm on my forehead, or covering my mouth with my hand, and somewhere in the middle of all this, even then I did not know when, I decided what I must do. I sat down and wrote a few versions of my reply. I asked Sean, "Why do you think he brought the note there? Why didn't he bring it here?"

"He thinks you're living there now to fool your folks."

"You're sure?"

"He said so. He saw me; he knows what I do: he said, So she's running the house by messenger."

"Very good, Sean."

I gave him a letter to take to Jack Cutter.

Dear friend,

I see the force of your argument, but I cannot meet you in your rooms. I am being watched very closely by another person who wishes to unmask me. For this reason I am avoiding my house, and I can't be seen with you near the shop. Let us meet then on neutral ground. I am supposed to go to a late dinner tomorrow at my grandfather's house. There is a tavern close enough to the house so that we can transact our business and I will be able to reach my appointment in good time. Ask for me by the name Olivia. I am writing letters to be opened in the event of my death or disappearance, in case you mean me harm. If your intentions are peaceable and reasonable, though, I am sure we can arrange matters to our mutual satisfaction.

I told him to meet me at the Bloomingdale Tontine tomorrow, and I did not sign my name. After Cutter wrote back agreeing to the terms, I used Sean to send a couple of other messages, because I had no intention of meeting Cutter unaccompanied. That evening, I took a hack up to the tavern; my companion was a short but brawny little Englishman who was called Tom London to distinguish him from three or four other, equally unpleasant Toms who frequented the Almanack Dance Hall in Five Points. I wore a hat and silk kerchief that covered up most of my face; to the tavern proprietor I am sure I looked like a woman misbehaving in the usual way. I brought a change of clothes and had London do the same, to confuse witnesses. If escape proved necessary, we would do so by a second-story window, using a rope I had brought in my bag.

I made these preparations not cold-bloodedly but in a constantly changing state of mind, one moment strengthened by hatred for Cutter, and the next wishing I could hate him more, so that I would seem more human to myself; it horrified me most of all that I was about to do something I could never tell Jeptha. There were many things I could never tell him, but this was of another order, this would be in a special locked chamber of its own. I was not sure I would have the courage to go through with it, and I almost hoped that I would not. I made it clear to Tom London that he would get the same pay in any case. It might not even be necessary. That depended on Cutter.

❧ XL ❧

THE BLOOMINGDALE TONTINE WAS BY NO MEANS the fashionable establishment its name attempted to suggest. On the ground floor there were tables, and also curtained booths where one could meet in private. Rooms upstairs could be rented by the hour or the night. My plan was to rent a room, and have London waiting in it—he must get into it without being seen. Then I would wait for Cutter in one of the booths on the ground floor, telling the proprietor to direct him toward it when he arrived and asked for Olivia. If Cutter wondered about my efforts at concealment, I would explain that I could not risk being recognized so near to my grandfather's house. Though I had told him I was afraid to be alone with him, I did not think I would have much trouble persuading him to come upstairs with the promise of my flesh, and then London would deal with him. If I decided that Cutter was not too dangerous, I would not take him up to the room. I would simply pay him the money.

Signing the register with a name I had never used before and have never used since, I took the room for myself, the night before Cutter and I were to meet. I made London wait until after dark and come around the back of the tavern, where I let down the rope for him. He made a great deal of noise coming up, but no one came to see what was going on. Then he wanted to have his way with me in the bed, and seemed to consider it an outrage to his manhood to be asked to spend the night with me chastely. If he had thought I had the money with me, he would probably have killed me instead of Cutter, and congratulated himself for doing the smart thing. But I had paid him a little on account, and the rest of the money was not on my person but was promised for performance. Thus I had influence on him; at least this was my hope. Eventually, with much grumbling, he bedded down on the floor.

The next day, there was a lot of waiting. London, like most such men, was not good at waiting. I let him drink a little. We played cards. He was impressed with my skill in shuffling and dealing. I showed him card tricks Charley had taught me, and while I watched him attempt them, I noticed his hands. The nails were very dirty and cracked, the thumbs exceptionally long and strong, and not as clumsy as they looked. Stains were dyed into his skin. One could not help imagining that blood had made a contribution to them. He chewed tobacco and had brown teeth and spat a lot. He also picked his nose. The dried mucus was black.

In the afternoon, I went downstairs and waited for Cutter in a curtained booth. I had a bottle of whiskey and two glasses brought to me. My terror grew as the time of our meeting approached. Fear this great could not be hidden. I could only hope that Cutter would think it natural for me to look frightened.

There weren't many customers in the tavern at that time of day. I heard Cutter come in, and I heard him talking, and then nothing, and then he was pulling aside the curtain. He looked confident, but his confidence looked misplaced. His clothes hung loose. His cheeks were sunken; he had been ill, maybe seriously.

I gave him a timid, ingratiating smile. I poured the whiskey for both of us. He waited for me to drink first, as a blackmailer should, and then he said with satisfaction, "Well, well, not so high and mighty," and in general spoke like a villain in a melodrama, except in a Bowery accent and with a profanity unsuitable for the stage, and with more self-pity. He asserted several times that his luck was changing. Things were going to be different now. Certain people were going to be sorry for the way they had treated him. He took his shot and poured another and started telling me what he was going to do to me.

"Business first," I said. I told him that before we could agree on a price I had to know exactly what he knew. He replied that I was in no position to bargain. "Very well," I agreed meekly, "tell me what you want to tell me."

"I know you're after your grandpa's money and he thinks you're an honest woman with a dress shop. I'm going to California to make a new start. Pay me two thousand dollars and be shut of me."

We argued, and finally I told him that I might find the money but that he was still asking too much. At that price, it would be worth more to me to keep my old life.

"What about your little brother?"

"What about him?"

"Oh, that's right, I didn't tell you about that," he said, and looked at me; a sick feeling in my stomach said that at last he was about to tell me.

And so he did. Back in 1845, before the two of them had visited me in Cohoes, they had been involved in an argument with two canal drivers in Lockport. Lewis had pitched a stone, and one of the drivers had not gotten up. Lewis and Tom had run away. They saw later in Albany newspapers that the one Lewis had hit had died, that the other driver had recognized Lewis as Lewis Buckley—the name Lewis had gone by at the time—and someone had written anonymously to tell the paper that Lewis Buckley was really Lewis Moody.

There had been many hints of something like this, one or two from Cutter when I knew him first in Cohoes, and later from Lewis, who had a way of reminiscing right up to the point of his crime and then skirting clumsily around it.

"Why didn't you use it earlier?"

"You know why. You said I was in it, too. But now I'm going to California with your money. They won't chase me to California for what I did."

Now, this did not quite make sense. If Cutter had to be in California in order to use his blackmail against my brother, wasn't that a reason not to give him the money to go to California? It was foolish of him to say this. I might have argued with him if money were my sole concern, if I had been as willing as I had claimed I was for him to unmask me as Harriet Knowles.

"All right," I said. "I'll meet your terms." I told him that I would have to give it to him in installments. I would have to sell property; I would have to earn some of it. All I had brought was a hundred. We discussed our future arrangement. Then, predictably, he told me to give him the hundred. I told him I had it in a room upstairs.

"You took a room here?"

"I thought that was part of our bargain."

He smiled, took another drink, stood up, and grabbed the bottle by the neck, while I put on the hat and the scarf. I walked with my head down, my knees weak; with each beat of my heart, my whole body seemed to vibrate like a sheet of iron struck by a sledgehammer. There was a moment of extra panic at the top of the stairs when I forgot which room it was. There was a moment when I decided to pay him: anything was better than this; this was damnation if anything was, to kill a man just because he is an inconvenience to you. But if I paid him, he'd go to California, and he'd still have what he had on Lewis, and he was the kind of man to use it just for spite.

I opened the door. He followed me in, and, as drunk as he was, he suspected a trick immediately. He sniffed. "You've got a man in here." He looked under the bed, and then he went to the closet door and jerked it open. London, who had been waiting in the small, dark, hot closet for two hours, lunged at him with the knife, but his eyes had no time to adjust to the light, and Cutter was able to evade the knife and grab the wrist that held it. They fought over the knife and Cutter took it from him. They rolled over on the floor, London trying to pin Cutter's arm, Cutter jabbing wherever he could and finally thrusting upward repeatedly just beneath London's ribs. Then, with London gasping and shuddering, Cutter pulled out the blade, and swiftly but somehow deliberately, like the journeyman butcher I suddenly remembered he was, he grabbed London by the hair and slashed him across the throat.

My emotions were etherized, they existed but they belonged to someone else, as I looked down at Jack Cutter, that very inconvenient man, who sat gasping beside the killer he had slain. My carpetbag lay under the bed, a few feet behind me. Turning my back on Cutter, I took a step and bent down and found the bag. As I rose, I caught a glimpse of my face, flecked with Tom London's blood, in an oval mirror in an elaborate brass frame on the wall just inside the door. Smiling at Cutter—as if I could fool him now!—I jerked the bag open, reached into it, and for a despairing second could not find Mrs. Robinson's pepper-box pistol. Cutter was rising to his feet. To explain the noise the people downstairs were about to hear, I shouted, "Put the gun away, Harry, you fool! You're gonna hurt somebody!" For a second, Cutter wore a puzzled look, and then I shot him. I had seen guns used but had never used one myself, and the recoil surprised me. As for what happened to his face, my mind could not make sense of it. "You fool!" I shouted. "You're crazy! You can't do that in here!" He fell forward. I stepped away.

I grabbed the bedsheet, spat on a corner of it, and walked to the mirror to wipe my face.

I had planned carefully to make sure that I would be far away before the body was discovered—I had planned so that there would be time, and there was no time. Trying to keep from getting bloody, and succeeding, except for my hands, which shook along with the rest of me as if I were freezing, I emptied Cutter's pockets and London's pockets, stuffed everything into a pillowcase, and put it in my carpetbag. By that time, men were knocking on the door and shouting at me to open it up. I could barely stand on my feet. I was quite sure that it was hopeless, but I was going to do what I could, until the very last minute, to get away safe.

"It's all right!" I called back. "I'm sorry. We're very sorry! There was a pigeon! He shot at some pigeons out the window!"

"You can't shoot in here!"

"We're sorry! Nothing is broken! I told you, Harry! As if you could hit anything in your condition!"

"Are you all right?"

"It's all right. I told you. It was just a pigeon. Leave us be. He won't do it again!" I shouted as I hurried to the window. I stood there, looking out and down and around. They weren't talking. They weren't ramming the door down. With luck, they had gone away. I climbed out the window and let myself down by the rope. I ran through an empty field and into a wood, carrying the carpetbag, which contained a skirt, a blouse, a shawl, a bonnet, all clean and different from those the men in the Bloomingdale Tontine had seen me wearing. I did not look back to see if I was pursued until I was in the trees. The loudest sound was the pulse in my head. I spat on my hands and cleaned them with my handkerchief. I changed my clothes, stuffing the ones I'd discarded into the carpetbag. I put on a pair of white gloves and walked, holding the carpetbag, through the woods, to the road, and down the road to Broadway, where I opened my parasol and strolled down the street until I took an omnibus downtown.

The pepper-box pistol was in the bag along with the bloody clothes and the contents of London's and Cutter's pockets. For a moment, I had considered wrapping London's hand around it. Then I had reflected that men shot in the head cannot cut throats, and men with their throats cut cannot shoot pistols. Even New York City's metropolitan police would probably realize that.

At home, in my room, I poured the contents of Cutter's and London's pockets onto my bed. It was a curious collection—dirty pawn tickets, and folded handbills, and sundry scraps of paper bearing names and addresses. My letter to Cutter was not there. There was a clipping from the Albany newspaper, with the name of the dead man and the name of my brother Lewis.

I HAD LIED WHEN I TOLD CUTTER that I was invited to my grandfather's house that evening. There was to be a gathering, with me and Jeptha and Agnes and Edward and Robert and the members of the California Missionary Committee, but not for another three days. I spent most of the intervening time in my bedroom, every so often sending out for a newspaper. The murders were recognized as a mystery, and the fact that at least one of the killers had been a woman—or maybe a small man dressed as a woman—gave the story added interest. It shared the front page of the *Sun,* the *Herald,* and the *Courier* with headlines about the cholera and California gold. Ragged newsboys shouted: "'He was shooting at pigeons,' cried the murderess!" The *Courier* called it "a conundrum worthy of the skills of Monsieur Vidocq," Vidocq of France's Sûreté Nationale having at that time a reputation for crime solving similar to that Scotland Yard enjoys today.

Sometimes the fear of being caught was separate from the horror of being a murderess, but most of the time the two ideas were mingled in a poisonous brew. I told myself the world was well rid of Jack Cutter. That helped for brief periods.

To bring on sleep, I took laudanum, which gave me long, elaborate dreams involving Lewis, Cutter, and Tom London. In one it was 1837. We were on the deck of the steamboat to Albany. A voice said, "Look." Shadows raced across the deck, and with a murmur of astonishment we looked up to see that the sky had become an undulating ocean made of pigeons endlessly crossing the river. Sounds of gunfire came from the riverbanks. Birds dropped into the water, splashing, spinning, and drifting, as dogs swam into the Hudson to fetch the corpses. Horace handed me the pepper-box pistol. I knew something terrible would happen if I pulled the trigger. I decided I would only pretend to shoot. I pointed. I shot, whereupon every bird in the sky came down and buried the boat. Then we were in a vast deserted ballroom littered with dead birds, and I knew the way out, but my poor lost friends Jack Cutter and Tom London didn't. I was leading them. "This way," I said. "Follow me. I'll help you."

On the second day, I saw Jocelyn, who was just back from Boston, where she had done an important favor for me. She came with news.

"But this is wonderful," I told her. "Wonderful."

I wrote to Arthur Heywood, and we met, and I told him how he might help me. He was delighted. "It'll be like an amateur theatrical," he said, assuring me that he was very gifted in that line. This worried me. He had nothing at stake in the outcome; for him it was a lark.

✳ XLI ✳

THERE WERE ALREADY CARRIAGES OUTSIDE my grandfather's house when I arrived. It was evening. The moist air smelled of lilac and hay, the leaves shivered and hissed on a rising wind, and the long shadows grew blurry and vanished as clouds gathered overhead. Agnes and Jeptha were in the drawing room, along with the other guests, talking in little groups of two or three near the punch bowl, the fireplace mantel, the piano, the window. More than one of these groups was discussing the deaths of the two men found at the Bloomingdale Tontine, not a quarter of a mile from the room where we stood. Even civic-minded abolitionist merchants and attorneys can be titillated by news of murder committed so recently and so nearby as to give them a feeling of proprietorship over it.

Robert had invited a pretty dark-eyed female, Amanda, the daughter of his law partner. She was about eighteen, small, her oval face framed by sausage curls, with a tiny waist accentuated by a big flouncy skirt. As we nodded to each other, I found myself thinking what I would name her and which of my gentlemen would like her best. This thought fled my mind when she began speaking of the murder, scandalizing the company with her naughty relish for the gruesome details. She was an adherent of the theory that the men had fought first and the woman had slain the winner—rather than supposing that she had killed both of them, one by knife, one by pistol, as an opposing camp idiotically maintained. She saw no reason to insist, as some did, that the killer must really have been a small, delicately featured man dressed as a woman. She did not agree that the crime was too bloody to have been committed by a woman. Women differed in their propensities.

Robert remarked that Amanda's enthusiasm for the discussion was itself a revelation about the capacities of Woman. John H. Harrington, of the New York Carpet Lining Company, asserted that women have broader scope than men: they are capable of greater self-sacrifice but also greater depravity. With a certain formality, this silly question was then debated.

Jeptha, when his opinion was solicited, remarked, "Saint Peter, who asked to be crucified upside down, was a man, and so were the fellows who obliged him. So it would seem men have a great deal of range, too."

My grandfather was pleased with this comment. "What say you to that, John?"

"I think it an excellent point for a clergyman to make."

Robert enumerated history's best-known female assassins and murderesses: Judith, Livia, Messalina, Agrippina, Lucrezia Borgia, Charlotte Corday.

Agnes apologized for her inability to take any amusement in the tragedy. "I'm sorry, but I can't help thinking it a grave matter, and that these men have souls that are being judged now; and each of them had a mother who never dreamed they would meet such a sordid end. And as Christians we should try to wish that the woman who committed this terrible, unwomanly deed should find her way to repentance and Christ's forgiveness."

She sought Jeptha's eyes, and he gave a slight nod of acknowledgment. Robert said, "That's a rebuke to you, Amanda. That's how a woman should respond to terrible events."

"Oh no," Agnes protested. "I would never say so."

"Of course not," said Robert. "You're too good to say it. But we are able to make comparisons. Amanda is bad. She should follow your model and improve."

"He wants us to fight," said Agnes. "Let's confound him and be friends."

Agnes was pretty, too, it had to be admitted, and would command high prices from discerning gentlemen.

"What about you, Arabella?"

"I'm just like Agnes. Mostly, I pity the mothers."

"And the woman?" asked Robert.

"I suppose she had a mother, too."

"Though there are some, like that poor babe you brought to Livy, who never know their mothers," observed Agnes.

"It is certainly sad when that happens," I agreed. "Though there is hope that Frank will find some happiness in the place where I once spent so many happy hours."

"I'm sure he will. It is a miracle, what you have found the time to do, Arabella. That you, a woman on your own, have been able to manage your own shop, and yet to have time to care for another woman's child, is almost more than I can believe."

For the part of the company that had not heard of this, I explained about Frank and my work for the Female Reform Society. "But Agnes has an exaggerated idea of my contribution to Frank's first year of life. I was only responsible for a portion of his care."

"That's not the impression one would get from my mother's letters. She said it called you 'Mama' and cried its heart out to be parted from you."

"I'm surprised to hear that. As I recall, he was sleeping when I left."

"Perhaps my mother's memory is faulty." She was interrupted by the arrival of Arthur Heywood, who greeted me with too much formality, almost winking at me, and I became more nervous. I was afraid he would not play his part very well, though I was sure he would play it with enthusiasm.

"This is Arthur Heywood, editor and publisher of the *Courier*," said Robert.

"I have heard of you, of course," said Agnes.

"Arthur Heywood, this is my cousin Agnes Moody," said Robert, "and our young minister Jeptha Talbot."

"Agnes," repeated Heywood. "So this is Agnes. And Jeptha."

"Mr. Heywood," said my cousin, "we were just discussing the good work that my cousin Arabella, whom you know, has done for the Female Reform Society."

We heard a crack of thunder, followed by a hiss of falling rain. Lawrence Jameson of Jameson Ironworks—a pious, awkward, middle-aged widower, very thin, with a white streak running through his hair, not quite down the center—went to the window and shut it before a servant on the same mission could reach it. Jameson never spoke at these gatherings, but was rich and dedicated to the cause.

"Indeed, I have heard of that society," said Heywood. "I regret that in the past scoundrels in my employ have made light of their efforts."

"I am glad you disassociate yourself from them," I said.

"What I find so curious, though . . ."

"Yes, Agnes?"

"Since I've been in New York, I've spoken to many people who know of the Female Reform Society, and none have ever heard of them having anything to do with placing orphan children in homes anywhere. All anyone has heard of them doing is standing outside of brothels and barrooms, exhorting those within to amend their lives, for which well-intentioned work, very unfairly, they are sometimes mocked."

I took the risk of glancing at Heywood. After a hesitation, he coughed and interposed, "Is that so?"

"Yes," said Agnes.

"Well, I guess their information is out of date. The society has for the past few years dealt in orphans—as an outgrowth of their other work. Realize, in Five Points there are children whom it were better to treat as orphans in any case, so vile are the parents."

The conversation turned to conditions in Five Points, Irish immigration, cholera, topics of mutual interest to newspaper editors and pious reformers, and Heywood had a lot to say, none of it useful to me. He passed up half a dozen opportunities to do what I had asked of him. Occasionally, he smiled at me as though he were noticing my beauty for the first time and wished he were young and single; I wanted to strangle him.

Someone mentioned orphans again. "That's right," said Heywood, as if just remembering. "A minister I know in Boston told me the society approached him, seeking suitable families among his acquaintance for placing orphans. So, you see, that *is* one of their good works. George Sackett, that's right."

At last. I watched Agnes and Jeptha separately respond to Heywood's words, which meant something quite different to each of them.

"Who?" inquired Jeptha.

"The minister I know in Boston," said Heywood. "His name is Sackett."

"George Sackett," said Jeptha.

"Yes, do you know him?"

"We grew up together, near the same town—George, Agnes, Lewis, Arabella, and I. Really, the rest of us were farm children, but George was a townsman's son."

He described Livy, how small it was, the old days.

"Amazing. What a coincidence," Heywood prodded him. "And both of you ministers now! Do you correspond?"

"No," said Jeptha, and he cast his eyes on Agnes, who looked back at him, thinking God knows what—racking her brains, I suppose. Whether Jeptha expected her to mention her prior relationship with George I could not tell. Perhaps she and Jeptha had discussed what should be said if the subject arose. At any rate she did not comment. So I had to speak. I spoke gently, since I was supposedly touching a tender spot. "George and Agnes remained friends," I told Heywood, and I looked around at the guests, about a third of whom were paying attention. "In fact, they were going to be wed. Isn't that right, Agnes? Until George took sick."

Agnes nodded, and Jeptha said, "Well . . . ," and tilted his head to acknowledge the sad fact of George's illness.

"Sick," exclaimed Heywood, a little too loudly. "Is he? When did this occur?"

"Several months ago."

"Consumption," said Jeptha.

"He is not expected to live," I explained. "And so, very bravely, he released Agnes from her promise."

"Yes," said Jeptha innocently, looking from Heywood to Agnes.

An unhappy little smile came to Agnes's lips. That was all she showed of what she must have known was the collapse of her fondest hopes. Her eyes sought mine. I cocked my head and returned her look. I did not smile; Jeptha was watching. The moment was sweet. I might still hang, but this could not be taken from me.

"Truly?" asked Heywood, in whom I had come to have much more confidence by now. "I had not heard of this development. Perhaps we've been speaking of two different George Sacketts after all. Is this one a Presbyterian reverend?"

"Yes."

"And his association is with Christ Church in Boston?"

"Yes, it must be the same man."

"Well, when did you see him last?"

"Some years ago."

"Then you know of his illness only by report?"

"Yes."

"Then I have good news for you—good for Sackett, anyway."

"What?" asked Jeptha.

"What?" asked Agnes.

"Simply that I saw George Sackett when I was in Boston not three weeks ago, and he had no complaints whatsoever about his health," said Heywood. He tried to keep the delight from his face, but he couldn't; this was his great moment. "All he could speak of was his broken heart. His fiancée had disappeared without a word of explanation."

"You," said Agnes, turning her whole body toward me, and she spoke loud enough to stop the two or three other conversations that had been going on in the drawing room. Amanda, Robert, and John Harrington, who were standing to the right of the piano, looked our way. My grandfather and Ronald, the male servant who was now called a butler, were talking near the window, and they, too, looked silently at us.

"Agnes?"

I have no doubt she had given her cause up for lost and was about to vent her rage at me, but she recovered quickly. With everyone in the room looking at her now, she moaned, "I see it clearly at last, Arabella!" and put the back of her hand to her head. "I'm faint," she said. A high-backed chair was found and moved near her, and she was held by the elbows and lowered to it, a satin pillow placed beneath her head. She spoke in such a weak voice that we all had to lean in to beg her to repeat herself. "I have been deceived. Dear Arabella!" She reached her hand out to me and I took it, and she spoke with glistening eyes and cocked head. "You told me once that George was not what he seemed, and now I know."

"I don't remember saying that, Agnes."

"Oh, you did, long ago. You knew. You saw clearly, when I was blinded by love."

Give her her due. She never quit. Every man in the room was bent over her, including the one who counted most. Jeptha's eyes flicked just once toward mine. Lawrence Jameson of Jameson Ironworks brought her a glass of punch.

"He was a coward," Agnes continued, looking at the floor, and then at the faces of the company. "A moral coward. You saw that, Arabella, when you warned me against him. I would have freed him from his promise if he had simply said that he had changed his mind, and asked me. By this time, I had doubts about the engagement myself. But he was not as forthright as are better men"—and here, lifting her head, she gave Jeptha a tender, brave smile—"and he had to pretend that he was sick—and to have picked consumption for his imaginary affliction, knowing that both my aunt and my grandmother died of it, was an added cruelty I attribute to his selfishness and thoughtlessness rather than a determination to wound me."

Yes: with me standing not two feet away, the chief tormentor of my childhood demanded sympathy on the grounds that *her aunt* had died of consumption. There were times when I wondered if there was any soul lurking within Agnes, or if she was just a complicated piece of clockwork designed to manipulate other people's misconceptions about woman-hood and honor and decency.

I looked at Jeptha, who was looking at her, and tried to determine if he believed what he was hearing. He gave me a quick glance, which I felt like a stab, before saying, "What a blackguard."

"Yes, my dear."

There was something hidden and steely in his expression as he said, "Let me know your wishes, dear. I'll go to Boston and have a word with George."

"What good would it do, my darling? Do I want to be betrothed to a man who doesn't want me and is so cowardly that he was afraid to tell me?"

"No, of course not. Yes, I see what you mean."

"I'd have released him if he'd been forthright enough to ask."

"Yes. You're sure you don't want me to go to Boston, Agnes?"

"Yes, dearest."

A servant opened the door to the dining room and invited us in. We did not speak to each other much throughout the meal, but often Jeptha gave me warm glances and his demeanor for the remainder of the evening confirmed every theory I had formed about his relationship to Agnes and his feelings for me. He talked very freely and enthusiastically with everyone else at the table, especially with Arthur Heywood, whom he seemed to regard as his new best friend; also, he ate heartily, and I could see that for a man who had just been shown how easily he could be made a fool of by a woman, he was in an extraordinarily fine mood.

THE NEXT EVENING, SEAN HANDED ME a letter that Jeptha had left at the dress shop.

"Agnes and I have broken off our engagement. I would like to see you tomorrow morning somewhere, anywhere, you pick the place. I want to ask you a question."

❧ XLII ❧

I DID NOT SLEEP THAT NIGHT. The cause was not just the anticipation of our meeting; I was worried about the police, who were being propelled into a state of unusual diligence by the attention the newspapers had given to the murders in the Bloomingdale Tontine. If Tom London was identified, the police might know enough to go to the Almanack Dance Hall. From there the trail might lead to Sean, who had found Tom London, and eventually, inevitably to me. If Cutter was identified, and his name printed in the newspapers, I would have to worry about Mrs. Bower, and half a dozen other people who knew of my feud with Cutter.

Sometimes a pedestrian out in the street, or a gentleman coming into the parlor house, would look like Cutter for a moment, as happens with the face of loved ones recently deceased: a part of me wished him alive, so that I would not be a murderess. Sometimes I simply could not believe that I had killed a man. Other times I was glad or indifferent or frightened by my cold-bloodedness. Each of these feelings seemed in its moment like a candidate for my permanent state of mind.

I had so much to think about, and so little of it bore any resemblance to the thinking of a young woman hoping for a proposal of marriage from the man she has loved for over half her life.

JEPTHA STOOD WAITING NEAR THE FOUNTAIN at City Hall Park, and I saw him before he noticed me. We sat on the fountain's cool marble edge. "What an imbecile I am," he began. "I wonder if it is wise of them to send such a fool to California." With no more introduction than this, folding his hands in his lap, and looking out at the passing parade of New Yorkers—young women with parasols, dandies with canes and old ladies also with canes, and mechanics and their sweethearts—he proceeded to tell me about his first wife, Grace, the clergyman's daughter, who had revealed on their wedding night that one doctor had predicted she had two years to live, another gave her six months, and another said five, and that she had wanted to tell him, but her mother had warned her not to. Was it wrong of her to lie to him? she asked, so pitifully, and childishly, that it hurt him to have to say, "Yes, my dear, it was." But would he have married her if he had known? she asked. That was why it was wrong, because it was so unnecessary, right? He said, "Yes, I would have," and thus began their married life with a lie of his own.

"She's gone, and I should not speak badly of her."

But bad things were essential to the tale. She spent money like water. He felt like a brute when he got angry with her. He gave up the ministry in order to take a job as a drummer that promised more pay. When she took ill, only the nature of the expenses changed. When she died (it took two years), there was sadness, but also relief, and he was able to free himself from debt.

Abruptly he turned, bringing his face closer, and in the summer light I noticed a scar on his lip not there when I knew him in Livy. He looked at me intently, and I had a feeling of being inspected and probed, that his words were meant to stir me while his eyes noted my reactions. "So you see why it's been such a shock to me, to realize that I was fooled a second time, with Agnes. I'm very glad you spared me that. It was you, wasn't it, who found those things out about Agnes, and told them to Mr.

Heywood?" I nodded, and he finished, "Who likes you and was happy to help. Well, that was lucky for me. I'm grateful." He touched my cheek. "But you didn't do it out of kindness, I hope? You want something, and you've told me what it is."

Well, yes, I had said so at the oyster saloon, but it wasn't gentlemanly of him to remind me. "This isn't very romantic," I observed.

"I'm a lout," he agreed. "Still—" He looked out at the park, where two well-dressed children had begun to fight and a matronly woman scolded them, and he said, as if thinking out loud, "I love you, Arabella, and you know it; and for the rest, you have to make allowances." He put his hands between his knees. I watched them struggle with each other. "We had a courtship once. It was ruined. We'll never get it back. You've been hurt. I've been fooled." Once again his eyes interrogated me.

It would come now. He would ask me now. *Hurry*, I wanted to tell him.

But instead he stood up, walked a little away, thrusting his hands in his pockets, and looked back at me this time as if I were some work that could be done in different ways, and he was deciding on the method and where to start. "I feel as if I know you."

"You do. You always have."

He nodded. "But I have to be skeptical about that feeling. Your manner changes to suit whoever you're with. I see that. I ask myself, is my Arabella the real one?"

"She is. You see my heart. You see to the core of me. The outer details—perhaps the details do not matter so much as you think."

"Don't you think that's too convenient a philosophy? Not just for you. For me, too. I can just look away. I don't have to think." I smiled, until I saw from the look on his face that something quite serious was coming. "Back in Livy," he said, "our last walk in the woods. We hid in the corn, do you remember? We stopped when we heard the children coming. Do you know what I am talking about? I alluded to it in . . . that very cruel letter I wrote to you that year."

"Yes." I saw what was coming.

"You thought that you were carrying Matthew's child."

The wrong answer and I would lose him after all. An assortment of denials and evasions passed through my mind—all obviously no good. It wasn't gentlemanly of him to bring such a thing up; but it was honest, and I respected him for it. It was perfectly obvious that I had tried to trick him into thinking Matthew's baby was his. I didn't know what to say. I put my palms together and rocked, truly beside myself.

"So," he said, with a sigh. "So that part of my letter was true."

"Jeptha," I whispered, "I was terrified. I was fifteen years old."

"And what happened?" he asked, as I knew he would. "With the child."

Agnes would have told him about Madame Drunette's Lunar Pills. To a Baptist it counted as murder. Fortunately, Agnes's testimony had no authority now. But had he asked Titus?

"I lost it," I said. "The day before I got your letter."

I waited for him to challenge me. Instead, his arms reached out—tentatively, as if to give me a chance to escape if I wished. I fell against him, pressing my face on his coat, while he kissed my hair and held me close, and he said, "Then I'm not cursed after all, and we can be happy at last, praise God. This is how we should be, this is how we'll be from now on. It's better to tell me things, don't you see? I love you, and you can tell me." But what I felt was his relief that I had not murdered a baby, and I drew a different moral. "We may be poor for a long time."

"I want to be poor with you," I said, and it was true. We had struggled separately; now we would struggle together. Let troubles come, trial on trial, victory on victory, until they made a great heap dwarfing the events of 1845 to 1849, and the various errors I had made during our separation.

"We've got to trust each other," he said, putting my palm to his cheek. "You mustn't keep secrets."

"I won't."

I told myself that I would keep no *new* secrets from him. I daydreamed about telling him everything someday, when we were two or three hundred years old.

He stood up again and took my arm in his. "Let's take a stroll around the park."

We walked, discussing the church, the guests, the ship, the voyage. At last I asked him, "Are you under the impression that you have proposed to me?"

He laughed, and kissed the palms of my hands, first one and then the other, and he got that detail out of the way.

· · ·

THE SHIP WAS TO SAIL WITHIN A WEEK. We had to rush. I was glad of it. I lived in terror that at any moment a passing gentleman might greet me as Harriet; or that Agnes would appear, bearing irrefutable proof of my true profession. Every conversation about our experiences during the years of our separation held pitfalls for me. I thought there would be less to worry about once we were at sea, dealing with the difficulties of the voyage.

When we were apart, I said goodbye to my girls; some were sentimental, and some were cold. I sold the parlor house as a going business to Mrs. Bower. I met with bankers and lawyers. I bought jewels and racked my brains to think of a place to hide them. I kept looking over my shoulder for the police.

I wrote to the Parker House in San Francisco.

Dear Charley,

I'm going to try being respectable again. If all goes well I'll be in San Francisco before long, and if we meet there you'll have to pretend you don't know me. I'll be Arabella Talbot and you're going to laugh when you see what I'm passing myself off as. All the same, you're going to be glad for me, too, because I'll be happy. I'll get you my address once I'm there. I'll be living very simply, but I'll have money put away for a rainy day, and if you ever need a stake I want you to come to me.

Jeptha wanted us to be married by his friend and guide, Reverend Charles Danforth of the Wall Street Baptist Church, and we visited the reverend and his desiccated wife, both of whom looked at all times as stiff and astonished as if they were posing for their daguerreotypes. Mrs. Danforth took me aside for a dismal talk about my bedroom duties, which she presented in the light of a martyrdom. She left me with several pamphlets expressive of her views: the one I remember best was called *Marital Chastity*.

From there we walked to the offices of Godwin & Co. to receive congratulations and discuss arrangements. "Well," said my grandfather, "well, well," and shook hands with Jeptha. There was a forced jollity to my grandfather's manner that I remembered later.

I intended to insist that my grandfather increase Jeptha's stipend—which I had learned was shockingly parsimonious, less per year than the money that had been spent on the banquets of the California Missionary Committee—but I knew that Jeptha would not approve of the conversation, and I thought I would postpone it till the next day, when we were all to meet at my grandfather's house and I could buttonhole Solomon Godwin while Jeptha was otherwise engaged. But now my grandfather, with an unconvincing smile to cover the impropriety of his request, said that since Jeptha and I were not married yet, he hoped it would be all right for him to discuss a small family matter with me alone, and took me to a small office.

"Do you have something you wish to tell me?" he asked.

"Yes." I told him that after proposing to me Jeptha had mentioned the size of the salary he was to get from the California Missionary Committee. "It's worse than parsimonious—it's impractical." For two minutes I spoke, adducing this reason and that one, but with a mounting uneasiness. There was an unfriendliness in my grandfather's gaze, and I knew something unpleasant was in store. I ended with a hint that if better arrangements were not forthcoming, Jeptha and I might have to stay in New York after all.

All at once, his rheumy old eyes emptied of all sympathy and lingered coldly on mine. "I don't think it's very likely that you will do that, Arabella."

I became very still. I waited.

He continued, "I think you'll do all you can to get that unfortunate young man to the other side of the continent before your past here catches up with you."

"Oh," I said, stung. "Grandfather, think what you will of me, but don't go on."

"I try to be a good man. I know I'm just a worm before God, but I have my vanity, and I don't like being thought a fool, even by a clever young harlot."

"You've been listening to Agnes, a proven liar."

"My information does not come from Agnes," he said quietly—the whole rather brutal conversation that followed was conducted in low voices. "You know I am a member of the Magdalene Society, which keeps close track of all such people as Mrs. Bower and Miss Harriet Knowles. I know which dress shops serve them. It made me unhappy to think that yours was one of them. And after that, the only serious impediment to my discovering everything was my own reluctance to know it. But now I do know, and you are in no position to dictate terms to me."

I put my head in my hands. He said, "Your life has turned you into an actress."

Well, that was a very unfair remark; I felt that, and it helped me get through the rest of the ordeal. For years I had been rebuking him in my imagination; I had wished he was alive so I could tell him what he had done to me by sending me away to live with poor relations—Elihu, Agatha, Agnes, Matthew—and then when he had turned out to be alive the circumstances made it impossible to tell him. Now that had changed, and at last I could say it all. There was no question of thinking of hurtful things to say; it was only a question of choosing and organizing. "You *are* a sinner, Grandfather. You should not speak that way. It is weak and cruel." I could see from his face that he didn't like this. "How strange," I said. "You want to cover me with scorn yet keep my good opinion and until today you did. Even after you'd forgotten me utterly, your own blood, banished to live among poor relations, crude, ignorant people—"

"You know very well why we sent you there. It was for your own good."

I thought that probably he had not expected the conversation to take this particular turn and I had him at a disadvantage. I leaned in close to him, so close that it was itself a gesture of disrespect. "Do you still say that to yourself? That you sent me to upstate New York, where it is colder and wetter than it is here, to keep me from getting consumption? Are you quite sure you weren't trying to *give me* consumption?"

He shook his head vehemently. "We had physicians' advice; we weighed those elements; it was thought that country air and farm work counterbalanced them."

"What of your wife's preferences?" I cooed. "Her love of peace and quiet and leisure? Her disinclination for having little children about at her age, especially difficult children like Lewis? How much did that weigh? Enough to tip the balance in favor of Livy?" Perhaps he winced—if he did it was very small. "I begged you, *begged you* to take us back, away from the vicious girl who plotted night and day to destroy me, and the brute who forced himself on me just as soon as he was old enough to be capable of it. Look what happened to me. Look at it whole. Look at me. This is your doing. This is your work."

Though I had not been shouting, my throat hurt, and I swallowed the last few words. In the end he seemed to be a good deal less upset than I was, and whether he felt more remorse than he showed, or whether he dismissed everything I had said as vain posturing, I still don't know. He shook his head again. "I only did what was right in my eyes; I regret what happened to you; it does not excuse your actions since then. You see my emotion but you misunderstand it. I mourn. I mourn for what my granddaughter has become."

"Tell the world, why don't you."

We sat with that for a while.

"I should," he said at last.

"Conceive what it would do. To you, to everyone connected to this family. And, oh, the worthy causes you espouse, they would hardly benefit. Think of it. Newsboys shouting it in the streets. I've stain enough on me to dye you all scarlet for generations. Worldly people would be snickering in the next century. I think, when Jeptha and I are rounding Cape Horn, you should do what you can to close up your investigations of unscrupulous dress shops and who owns them."

"Who do you think you're talking to? Do you imagine you can make me do your bidding as you make others—as you make Arthur Heywood; as you make those benighted girls you lure onto the paths of shame?"

"I'm just advising you, Grandfather, because I love you. I'll be in California. It won't affect me as much." I stood up. "I hope you will reconsider Jeptha's stipend. He deserves better, and so do I. You want to help fallen women? Begin with me. I should like a chance at a decent life doing God's work."

WE WERE MARRIED BY REVEREND DANFORTH on July 7, 1849, at the Wall Street Baptist Church, on the morning of the very day our ship was to sail. Jocelyn and Monique were in the pews, happy for me. Lewis looked appreciatively at Jocelyn but gave no hint of their prior acquaintance. My grandfather did not have to disguise the change in his attitude toward me. His habitually formal manners took care of that. From my grandmother's behavior, I judged that he had not taken her into his confidence.

A few hours later, we were on South Street, staring up at the *Juniper*, a 110-foot, 325-ton square-rigged three-masted whaling barque refitted to carry passengers.

The day was sunny. Passengers on the decks, high above us, were squinting and shielding their eyes with their hands, but down by the piers we walked in crisscrossing shadows of bowsprits, masts and yardarms, pulleys and ropes, pyramids of barrels, high placards announcing the names of the crafts and their destinations, several bound for California. My eyes followed the lines upward to a sailor hooking one thing to another high in the rigging; the sun at his back turned him into an inky silhouette.

Members of the California Missionary Committee acted as our porters. My grandfather put a hand on my shoulder and whispered: "He's a good man, and loves you, and I believe you love him, so—I wish you good luck. We will never meet again, very likely."

He flinched when I embraced him, but I held on for a moment, feeling as I did how narrow, old, and frail he really was.

When the passengers were on deck, together with wives and relatives, members of the California Missionary Committee handed out Bibles. Reverend Danforth, with Captain Stormfield's permission, gave a sermon comparing us to the Pilgrims and commending us to the guidance of my husband—they were lucky to have a man of God on board this ship. Then the captain, a fiftyish fellow with brown teeth and a glass eye, gave a speech that, although not directly contradicting Danforth, made it clear that on the *Juniper* Stormfield was God. Then it was time for friends and relations to go ashore.

I embraced Lewis. At the wedding, he had tried to raise money from me, from my grandfather, from anyone who looked prosperous, for a trip to California. He couldn't bear the thought of spending another year at the Pearson Academy while other men were taking gold out of California's rivers. "Stick it out," I told him now, a moment before he left the *Juniper*. "Go later if you must; and if you go, go by the Horn, not Panama. If you go by land, go by Oregon."

The wind stirred up white peaks in the East River and pushed our clothes against us. People squinted and gripped their hats. Someone said that if it was this rough here it must be worse on the open sea. Already, thanks to the sail that had been let out, the ship was rocking; everything was rising and falling. The deck's pressing upward and dropping away, endlessly repeated, was a third involuntary rhythm added to those of breath and heartbeat. It was strong and insistent. There was no arguing with it.

The first mate was shouting at the men to lay this and lay that. And then: "Let go the bow line, let go the stern line, pull away." We moved up and down in one place while everything else moved away: the men below us, the hulls and masts and rigging of the other ships, the heaps of barrels, the cobblestones, warehouses, signs, red chimneys, and pointed roofs. The lifting and dropping of the deck became more forceful, as if it were a sort of pump pushing away the island of Manhattan. The nearest buildings shrank. The ones behind them rose. The piers seemed to turn like the spokes of a great wheel as the shoreline began to simplify, a wiggly thread gradually pulled straight; the wind blew my hair into my face. Jeptha wrapped his arms around me, and if our story had ended there, it would have had a happy ending.

Book Four

{ 1849–1850 }

FIVE WEEKS LATER THE SHIP WAS BREATHING like a live creature beneath us. I sat on a barrel, Jeptha at my feet. A three-legged dog was pursuing a wispy hare across the sky when we heard a voice shout "Land Ho! Land Ho!" Murmuring "At last," Jeptha lifted me off the barrel. All around us men were shaking themselves out of their torpor, dropping the journals they had been writing in and the cards they had been gambling with, rising and stretching their limbs: all sorts of men—carriage-makers, coopers, farmers, clerks; a schoolteacher, a homeopath, a small-town mayor, a daguerreotypist, a traveling lecturer on animal magnetism; the man who had not left his stateroom until the third week, the man who only talked about how thrifty his little wife back home was, the man who had dreamed last night of drinking fresh water from a cold stream. Several climbed into the rigging for a better view. The rest swarmed to the side, and those with the best eyesight discerned a strip of blue one shade paler than the ocean and one shade darker than the sky. For five weeks they had had nothing to feed their eyes but this ship and the water around it, and they studied that faint line with a good deal more interest than it deserved.

For two days, the blue line grew and acquired details, eventually yielding to our starved eyes a clump of strange bald mountains set like monstrous eggs in a colossal nest of greenery; a cliff-top fortress; church spires; paradisiacal islands; terra-cotta roofs of white villas among orange and banana trees—wonder on wonder, until our patriotism was offended. "To think that all this was given to the heathens," murmured George Ewell, the reformed drunkard, about to be tested by a wicked port city full of brothels and grog shops. With Jeptha's help he had been good, for the first time, at sea. Could he be good on land, too? He didn't think so. We must let him stay near to us. We must help him. We promised him we would, although the truth was, we wanted desperately to be alone.

It had been crowded aboard that heaving ship, and belowdecks, where

Jeptha and I spent our nights. It had been dark, cramped, filthy, and heavenly. For weeks we had walked in a protected sphere of our own, invulnerable to every care or danger, indifferent to every other human being. Other passengers stared, amused, envious, as we fed each other the dreadful food (usually a pasty hash of soaked biscuits and bits of pre-served codfish) and poured the stale water down each other's throats as if under the misapprehension that it was wine. We noticed other people only when it came time to quench our desire for each other: then, each night, we confronted the sobering fact that the California Missionary Committee had not purchased the stateroom we had been promised; for sleep we had just two narrow shelflike berths, one over the other, amid a hundred such berths, all occupied by men. For privacy we had darkness. A greasy cleat had torn a wide rent in my traveling dress when we were two days out and everyone was seasick, and the replacement buttoned in the back, so each night, when the time came, I would whisper from my shelf to his above me, "Dress me"—it would not do to be overheard by all these men saying, "Undress me." He would come down, undo the but-tons, and shuck me of my clothes, either slowly and teasingly, or quickly, with imperious impatience, as the mood took him. Later, as we caught our breath, we would begin to hear the snores and coughing all around us. Then we would rummage under my bunk for a secret jar of plum pre-serves and sit face to face. I would slip a plum into his mouth. He would slip a plum into my mouth.

After about twelve days out, Jeptha recalled that we were missionar-ies. Sometimes alone, sometimes with his arm around me, he made the acquaintance of the other passengers and talked religion to them. He held services each Sunday on the quarterdeck, on rainy days beneath a canopy. The pious men were drawn to him immediately, and they seemed to feel that he ought to have been satisfied with their company, but Jep-tha insisted on preaching to the unbelievers, too, and in the three weeks between this decision and the sighting of the Brazilian coast, he had made eight converts and given each of them a dunking in the ocean. The most impressive of these acts of reclamation, a soul snatched directly out of the devil's claws, was Ewell, who had been sent to California by his father in a last, desperate effort to make a man of him, or maybe just to be shut of him. Care had been taken to keep his baggage free of stimu-lants, but he had managed to find plenty of liquor aboard the ship. In those days, the scent of him used to linger in a room long after he had left it: but not anymore.

Now Jeptha stood behind the nervous Ewell and clapped his right hand on his shoulder, while with his left hand he blew me a kiss. "We're not worried about you, are we, Arabella?" he said, and I murmured that it was not my husband who had taken Mr. Ewell in hand; it was God Almighty, who never leaves us. But we would help him, too.

Within sight of Rio, there were frustrating delays, boardings by inspectors and agents. At last, in the morning, Captain Stormfield assembled us and sternly repeated the date and time of day by which we must return to the *Juniper* or be left behind.

Jeptha, his arm around my waist, whispered, "Tonight in a bed."

We went ashore in a *falua,* a boat with a lateen sail and oars. A Negro at its helm commanded four rowers of his race: half naked, sweat-spangled, faces scarred into beadlike designs. Near shore, the water was full of refuse. A rower invited me to hop on his back, but Jeptha took off his boots, rolled up his trousers, and carried me himself.

The city was reached by great stairs that put us abruptly in the middle of everything: hackney coaches, carriages, omnibuses, men in foreign uniforms, women walking with platters of fruit on their heads, a man in a metal mask—scenes that would have been strange to us even if our receptiveness to every novelty had not been heightened by our long confinement aboard the *Juniper.* Fifteen barefoot Negro coffee carriers, big men clad only in short white pantaloons, rounded a corner at a trot, each with a sack balanced on his head. The leader carried a flag and a rattle. We passed a boy about four years old. Our necks all swung to keep him in view a little longer, as though we'd seen an elf or a fairy—so they really existed, this fabled other order of humanity, the race of children!—and I thought of Frank.

Ragged, underfed-looking porters took our bags without permission, for all we knew stealing them, and—waving their bony arms and pointing—led us to the Custom House, a stately domed building swarming with soldiers and clerks. It was going to take hours. With a secret anxiety, I told Jeptha that I could not bear to wait here doing nothing, and I volunteered to go to the General Post Office, where we expected to find letters waiting for us: mail came by steamboat, much faster than by sail, and friends and relations back home had been told to send their first letters here. I offered to retrieve mail addressed to several other passengers as well. There would be newspapers, too, and that worried me. Mary Dunn (the wife of a Fulton Street fishmonger now turning miner, and the only other woman among us) insisted on going.

In the Correio Geral, the letters were piled randomly in heaps behind a counter. I positioned myself near a stack of *New York Couriers*. My worry must have shown. "Is something wrong?" Mary asked.

I shook my head perhaps a little too emphatically, and, feeling that there was a risk in reading the newspapers with such fascination under Mary's scrutiny, I did it anyway, murmuring, "I ought to be ashamed of myself, Jeptha would scold me, but before I left I was following the story of that mysterious murder in Bloomingdale. Perhaps it is solved by now."

After all, it would be absurd for her to imagine the preacher's wife was the murderess. I had nearly persuaded myself it wasn't true.

Days were missing from each paper, but between the *Couriers* and the *Heralds* I had almost the first two weeks since our departure. If the mystery had been solved, or even if there were any promising clues—if the victims were identified, and one of them had bragged to a friend that he knew something an unusually young parlor-house madam would pay to keep quiet—both newspapers would be sure to mention it. But there was nothing. As I thumbed through issue after issue, I was relieved to watch the story sink from the front page to the inside pages, from a column to a paragraph, until it drowned in the ooze of local history.

"Did they find out?" asked Mary.

"It seems they've given up," I said in a disappointed tone, and we began looking for letters addressed to the several passengers whose mail we had agreed to retrieve. We made piles; there were many, more than we had money to redeem. Jeptha and I had four: one addressed to me, one for us both, and two for Jeptha only. His father had written him from Ohio. One letter had no return address: I recognized Agnes's special round loops and capital "T"s. The letter for both of us was from Solomon Godwin.

I gripped these letters in my hand, and considered. Sometimes Mary talked to Jeptha. "The gall of this woman," I said, waving Agnes's letter.

"What? Who?"

"The woman Jeptha kept company with before me. She's written to him, and has not put her name to it. If I didn't know her handwriting, I would not have known, I might never have known. That is to say—I only hope he would have told me. Mary, might I ask you for a favor?"

She put a fist in front of her pursed lips and made a little gesture of turning a key. Begging her pardon, I crossed the room to read in the light of a deeply recessed window.

The letter that was addressed to me alone was from Anne. I expected it to contain news of Frank. If any mishap had befallen him, this letter would tell of it. For a moment, I stood judging myself. Exactly how bad a mother was I? Was I heartless enough to open my enemy's letter to my husband before the letter that might inform me that my son had been bitten by a snake and died? I opened Anne's letter first.

She knew it would be awkward for me to receive mail that Jeptha could not read, and had the elementary cunning to assure me first that everyone was well, and to congratulate me on my marriage and tell me other news, before adding, "Maybe you would like to know how Frank, the orphan you brought to us, is adjusting to his new home." Then she described his growth and health and latest accomplishments and adventures in a detail that might be attributed to her own doting enthusiasm.

Perhaps it was disgusting of me in view of what I had done about Frank, the thousands of miles I was willingly putting between us, but in fact I hung on every word I ever received about him. I pictured him as he was when I saw him last: the dimpled elbows and the sweaty sweetness of his neck; his cries and babbling and chubby thighs. When Anne alluded delicately to his unnatural quietness in the first week after his arrival, I felt as sorry for both of us as if we had been separated by some tyrant's decree and not my own free actions. I got a lump in my throat over the news that he was climbing stairs and going into closets. He had bent a silver fork double, such was his immense strength, and was not afraid of anything except all dogs other than the two family dogs. My baby, my boy, my little man!

I experienced all those thoughts and emotions without for a second forgetting the letter from Agnes. And at last I opened it.

Dear Jeptha,

I hope this letter finds you well. I would love for you to write and tell me, and it makes me sad to doubt you will. It seems improbable enough that you will even read this, but I will ask anyway the questions one asks: How are you? How is your journey? What is it like on the ship I was supposed to be on, that we were going to take to California together? Do you think of me? Can you imagine what it is like for me to sit at my writing desk picturing you and your new bride aboard the *Juniper*?

Do you sleep well, Jeptha, on the rolling waves, on the deep waters? I do not sleep very much. I weep, and I pray, and often during the daytime, on an omnibus, I nod for a moment or two, but I do not sleep. When I lay my head on the pillow your voice comes to me, usually uttering the last words you said to me, perhaps the last I will ever hear from you, all so deservedly harsh, and most of them quite true: yes, I deceived you; yes, for selfish reasons (though, you will certainly find out one day, and probably soon, my reasons were not entirely selfish, unless it is selfish to hope to prevent someone you love from doing himself a great injury). I deceived you, and you said that because of it you could never trust me again; I hope that isn't true. You said I meant little to you now. I do not believe that is true. But I will mean more, the more you learn about her.

In the grip of your anger, you said that you can never again believe anything I say, but that is not logical: if I say the sky is up and Monday follows Sunday, you must believe me. Other propositions you can put to tests. Write to the Female Reform Society and ask them if Arabella Godwin is a member of their organization. They'll tell you they never heard of her until I asked about her! Ask them if it has ever been their practice to place orphans in homes. They'll tell you it has never occurred to them. Write to my mother, and ask her whom Frank resembles, whose child he obviously is: the little boy is Arabella's child! Even Anne obviously knows, though she hides it to spare him the indignity of growing up as a bastard, as people would quite naturally and I suspect justifiably assume he is.

Ask your wife if she is the mother of a child whom she has abandoned. She will deny it, but I would love to hear you ask.

There's obviously much more to unearth, and I will do my best in your service, Jeptha, whether or not you thank me for it. Perhaps she is still married to her first husband, who will not give her a divorce. In that case, your marriage to her is not valid, and you are under no legal obligation to her. I can imagine how difficult this is for you to read, but it seems unlikely that she has really amassed the money she has at her disposal as a dressmaker. Either one rich man has given it to her, or many men have given it to her. It is an ugly possibility, but consistent with her character. It must be faced.

Certainly, even if your marriage to her is technically valid, you have excellent grounds for a divorce.

Arabella, if it is you, and not Jeptha, reading this, you must realize how hopeless your position is in the long run. You can intercept one letter, but there will be more. Sooner or later, one will get through; and even if it doesn't, he will see through you finally. You are one kind of woman pretending to be another. You are brass passing as gold. Every gesture, every word rings false. It has to. He will know I was protecting him. You can't win.

Jeptha, you are my heart.

Your sister in Christ,
Agnes

I stood there, fearing the pain she would inflict on us should one of her letters reach Jeptha, yet certain that her lies (even to myself I called them lies; they were lies *in spirit*) could never destroy our love. Poor Agnes, my poor old enemy, was telling Jeptha about a woman who no longer existed. She could not know how changed I was, she could not imagine the delight we took in each other every day and night aboard that foul, musty, uncomfortable ship. Husband and wife, we had grown into each other, we were inextricably entwined and woven, turning Agnes's collection of nasty facts into so much biographical trivia—into, at worst, a history of my misfortunes.

MY GRANDFATHER'S LETTER READ AS FOLLOWS:

Dear Jeptha and Arabella,

Greetings from New York. I expect that about now you are glad to have land under your feet and relief from the monotony of shipboard life. You may know from reading New York newspapers that the cholera is taking a terrible toll of life here. Sadly, there have been deaths in the families of my business acquaintances. We pray each night that Almighty God will show us greater mercy than we deserve.

While I hate to worry you when you are helpless to act, I must apprise you of disturbing news from the Pearson Academy, where Lewis boards as a scholar. Lewis is not there. He left, along with two other students and a man—we have reason to believe it is Edward—three days following your departure aboard the *Juniper*. From the testimony of other young men at the academy, it is clear that they mean to go overland to California. Perhaps it is only to be expected. They are young, and wish to "see the elephant." I now regret opposing their desire, since they are undercapitalized for such a journey, and I would have seen to better preparations. If all goes well, they may arrive in California before you do. When you are in San Francisco, try to establish contact with them—I am hoping they will leave some word in the post office there.

On another subject, I have been making inquiries here among New York and Boston merchants and importers who are setting up branches in San Francisco. They will receive letters in advance of your arrival and will expect your call. I append a list to which I will probably be adding more names later.

Write to us; we look forward to hearing of your adventures so far.

Sincerely,
Solomon Godwin

I decided to open the letter from his mother and father, in case Agnes had reached them with her suspicions or asked them to enclose a letter of hers in the same envelope with theirs. But, fortunately, she had not yet thought of that. The letter wished Jeptha luck in California. It did not congratulate him on our marriage but acknowledged it, saying that he was a smart man, so he must know what he was doing.

. . .

WE RETURNED TO THE CUSTOM HOUSE to find Jeptha arguing with his flock. He proposed to send George Ewell to find us a hotel; the others thought it was a bad idea, since this mission would take the young man past many purveyors of sin. Like one of the Bible's timorous prophets, Ewell pleaded his inadequacy to the task. Jeptha gripped the drunkard by the shoulders and swore he was ready. I told Ewell that I, too, had faith in him, and added to his instructions various specific demands as to the cleanliness of the rooms and, in particular, the beds. He was to see for himself and not take the proprietor's word.

A few hours later, still sober and godly, Ewell led us to a hotel. It was sealed off from the street with a high wall, with gardens around the central building, whose walls were climbed by vines, and another garden in a courtyard, and many broadleaf plants in pots, and cross-ventilation. A square, narrow, turning staircase rose up to our room.

Jeptha let me walk before him, as a gentleman should. Our previous couplings aboard the *Juniper,* with only the darkness for privacy, the repertoire limited by the slender berth, had been an experience *sui generis,* reminding me of no others. But now, as I walked before him, with Agnes's letter fresh in my mind, I thought of all the times that I had mounted stairs with a man behind me, his eyes level with my hindquarters; and I felt as nervous as a virgin, though for the opposite reason. In the room there would be the freedom of a wide bed. I must not seem to know too much. As he prepared to open the door, I smelled his closeness, which I loved, but I remembered the smells of other men. This had always been an anxious moment, the seconds before I was alone with the stranger who was paying for the privilege of taking me to my depths, ransacking the most secret, forbidden chambers of the temple's holy of holies and, if such was his whim, fouling it, because he could, because he had the price.

Then we were in the room, and I expected to examine it, to see if the bed was clean and firm, but as impatiently as any of my gentlemen in former times, my husband turned me and pulled me toward him. As if someone were flipping a deck made of a hundred face cards, all jowly kings and tumescent knaves, the visages of a hundred men passed before my mind's eye while he stripped and unwrapped me, layer by layer, kissing each new patch of flesh as it was revealed, to claim it, to make it his. He lifted me. He took me to the bed, my Jeptha, whom I had known since I was a girl of nine, and his knees drove mine apart, and he bit my lips gently with his teeth, and he smiled down at me teasingly in a way that was at once cruel and compassionate, and what happened then was an exorcism, as, thrust by increasingly urgent thrust, he filled me up until there was simply no room left for anyone else. I felt as thoroughly claimed and possessed by this one man as I could wish. I was convinced that he had performed a magic rite which turned the world right side up again. We lay side by side. He stroked his face with my fingers. Then he rummaged through our bags and took out a jar of preserved plums, and I fed one to him and he fed one to me, and we licked each other's fingers.

Later, he rebuked me, gently, for opening a letter addressed to him. I told him that I had had a premonition that it might contain bad news and I could not bear to wait. I admitted that my impatience was a great flaw in me. To change the subject, I asked him if his family thought he had married Agnes (his father's letter had not mentioned my name). He assured me that they knew the facts and apologized for the tone of their letter. "They'll come around, I hope." He did not seem to be too sure of this, and added: "Anyway, who knows when we'll see them again?"

DOWN BY THE SHORE, HALF-NAKED MEN sold fish out of canoes, and for two cents women who stood under large linen umbrellas would serve you a bowl of hot coffee or a stew of meat and black beans. We walked by heaps of outlandish fruit; green parrots; a small white monkey with a devil's face; a giant rat in plate armor; stores with striped awnings; work gangs and soldiers; and a priest wearing about twenty pounds of black cloth and a black tricornered hat. This was Rio. We spent two weeks there, enjoying the honeymoon our swift departure from New York City had denied us. We saw cathedrals, forts, mountains, plantations, churches, and gardens, and learned the stories of natives and other travelers.

Every paradise has its serpent, however. Jeptha, chosen by the California Missionary Committee partly because of his strong Free Soil views, was troubled to realize that nearly all of the Negro laborers we saw in Rio were slaves. Each morning, their owners sent them out of doors to get money; when they returned, they must, in effect, pay their masters not to whip them. The rowers, the coffee carriers, the porters, street vendors, charwomen, maids, and cooks were all slaves; and the prosperity of Brazil rested on the sugar plantations of the interior, where men fresh from Africa were regularly worked to death because it was more economical to import new ones than to keep the old ones alive. Since cheap labor makes low prices, many of our incidental pleasures were implicated in these crimes. But we told each other we could not immediately perfect the world. Happy with the drugged irresponsibility of lovers, we did not feel this injustice keenly, just as we had not minded the bad water aboard the ship.

❧ XLIV ❧

BACK ON THE *JUNIPER*, WE RECEIVED the thrilling news that two stateroom passengers were languishing in a Rio jail. This meant that, with a little reshuffling and for a fee we were glad to pay, a whole stateroom might be free for Jeptha and me. But before we could rush to take possession of it, we were told that the stateroom had already been given to a woman and her son. She was French, a widow. Her name was Marie Toissante. The boy's name was Philippe.

Philippe was eight years old, an active, healthy, intelligent child, curious about everything that went on aboard the ship; soon he became the pet of the passengers, who tousled his hair, gave him candies, played card games with him, and let him hold the fishing line. The boy followed anyone who interested him. His favorites were Jeptha and a tall, sandy-haired, round-shouldered fellow named Herbert Owen, who spoke French and was very happy to make himself useful to a handsome woman and her son. After a while, one saw that really Jeptha was the boy's favorite, and Owen was being used as a translator.

I have not mentioned Herbert Owen until now since we saw little of him in Rio, but from our first weeks aboard the *Juniper*, he was the person whose company we best enjoyed. He was twenty-eight years old—one of the oldest passengers—from a good old Boston family. About a year earlier, his reading of German philosophers had turned him into an agnostic, which did not stop Jeptha from liking him. In fact, I could not help but notice that Jeptha's efforts to change Owen's mind were rather feeble, as if he did not want to spoil him. For Jeptha, Owen was a relief from some of the pious men who treated the pastor as their very own private property. He was gentlemanly and cultivated; he had traveled, had studied the law and practiced it briefly. For Owen, who knew himself to be a dilettante and a tourist, untested by life, indifferent to ideas—his freethinking was just a toy—Jeptha was someone with convictions, an enviable and admirable trait.

Owen agreed to attend Jeptha's Sunday services on the quarterdeck if in return Jeptha read Thomas Paine's *The Age of Reason,* famous in our day as a Deist tract. Jeptha read it openly, high in the rigging or on his back on the deck. When people asked him about it, he told them of his bargain with the agnostic, and said that it was never good to suppress a mistaken book: one must read it to refute it. Book burning was for priests, not ministers. The Gospels need not fear a fair fight.

He believed this in the face of powerful countervailing evidence, as I learned one day when he was twenty feet above me on the mast; the book slipped and fluttered down open, like a gunshot bird, and I caught it. I remarked that Owen and his friend the devil would be grateful to me for saving their book, and Jeptha said, "This isn't Owen's copy."

"Oh?"

"Look on the flyleaf," said Jeptha.

I looked. In the tropic heat I felt a chill: "*Ex Libris:* William Jefferds."

Climbing down to retrieve the volume, Jeptha informed me: "His name is also on the flyleaf of Voltaire's complete works, and he had a book by another Frenchman, Volney, who says that all religion is one, and a *Life of Jesus* which tells the Gospel story without miracles, and some reviews of German books which try to prove by Hebrew grammar that God did not write the Scriptures. I saw some of them when I was still in Livy. He said he read them to refute them, but I should wait to read them until I was older."

I returned *The Age of Reason*.

"How did he refute them?"

"He didn't," said Jeptha. "They convinced him."

That night, we slept on the deck in our clothes, holding each other, lit by the stars of the Southern Hemisphere, cooled by a steady breeze, enjoying an experience common to drunks and children: our bed was in motion, conveying us to dreamland. And Jeptha told me that Jefferds had lost his faith many years before he died. It was in his diary.

"Many years?" I asked. I could hear his heart. "How many?"

"I have the diary. You can read it if you care to. There was a time of doubt and wavering, and there had been earlier episodes when he lost it and found it again. The first time you saw him, he spoke what he believed—maybe adapting his terms a little for country people."

"And when we went to Canandaigua Lake and heard the Millerite?"

"Then he was telling his diary that perhaps Jesus was merely an excellent man."

"And when he baptized you and Jacob?"

"He had gone deeper into infidelity. Religion was a lie, but people weren't strong enough to live without it. If you took Christianity away, they would make up something else. 'The human imagination will always populate the heavens with gods,' he wrote. 'At least monotheism keeps it to a minimum.'"

I asked carefully, "And what has knowing this done to your faith?"

"The world without the Gospel makes no sense. Are we here on this ship? Am I me? Are you you? It's like that. It's a fact before my eyes. It's not faith."

The ocean lifted us up and plummeted us down to remind us that we were tiny beings borne on a little chip of wood over inconceivable fathoms of water. After a while, he went on: "This is my first congregation, the people on this ship. I preached before as a guest in other pastors' churches, and at revivals, and in the street to whoever would listen. Then, for two years, I didn't. I felt like a dead man. I need to preach; when I didn't, like most people, I believed in my religion but I didn't feel it." He stopped. I knew there would be more. I waited. He went on: "I don't prepare sermons anymore. I get up. I wait for the spirit. It comes. It lights me up. I watch it working—I see their faces and bodies, I see them put down their armor, hear them cry out, their hearts melting—each time a miracle."

"It must be fine to be able to touch people that way," I said, thinking, though I did not want to think it, of the many times when I had persuaded men to put down their armor. I had made them gasp and cry out, and even thank Jesus, or at the very least say His name. *Me, too*, I could have told him. *I've done that, too.*

"There's nothing like it," he said. "Only I wish I could reach you."

"You do reach me."

"No, I don't. You wear so much armor. You resist so much. I think that is why God has put us together. You're a hard case. You need special attention."

THE *JUNIPER* WAS BY NOW PUSHING INTO climes so far south that it began to be cold. The sailors took down the upper yards and sails, checked the rigging, and changed new sails for old ones that had so many patches and extra seams they resembled the clothing of tramps. Little Philippe followed these preparations with his wide brown eyes, asking Jeptha questions about it all with the bits of English his quick mind had by now absorbed.

"He's smart," Jeptha said to me the night we had begun again to sleep under blankets. "He doesn't need Owen for translation anymore." After adducing other evidences of Philippe's intelligence, he added: "He hates heights. Did you notice? He doesn't even like to look over the gunwales. When he sees the sailors climbing, he feels ashamed. Being brave is important to boys."

Jeptha began taking pains to help Philippe overcome his fear, encouraging him, in calm weather, to climb a little higher each day, while his mother watched nervously. You had only to see the absentminded way she stroked his hair and the happy way he leaned into the stroke, or the pleasure on both their faces when they talked to each other in French, to know that she was a loving mother. She was lucky to have her child with her.

WE WERE SHIVERING IN OUR BERTHS, wearing our coats and under all our blankets, long before someone said we were at latitude 50 degrees, and our misery counted as rounding Cape Horn. Strong winds were dead ahead, the breath of a giant determined to keep us in the Atlantic, where we belonged, and the ship zigzagged ten or twenty miles for every actual mile of progress. During a lull in the violence, Jeptha and I bundled ourselves as warmly as we could and went up top to look around, shielding our eyes with our free hands. The ropes and much of the canvas were encased in clear and milky ice, which made a tinkling sound amid the wind's roar. Snowflakes fell at a slant. They were so densely packed that they hid the ocean from view, and thus everything, ship and ropes and canvas, seemed to be rising at a slight angle into the sky.

At last, we were on the other side; the good sails were put back; the ship headed north again. We had a long stop in Valparaíso, a city of labyrinthine cobblestone streets, brightly colored houses and churches, and pretty brown-eyed girls. As in Rio, a few men were left behind in jails. New passengers joined us, Chileans male and female. The women, all prostitutes, began to earn their passage, and probably the passage of their men, immediately, using the stateroom of a man left behind in Valparaíso. I feigned ignorance, then shock, then the lofty sympathy suitable to a missionary's wife.

As we neared the equator a second time, and Philippe sought Jeptha's attention more anxiously than before. I was reminded of the way Lewis had behaved with my father's clerk long ago on the canal boats to Livy, how he had laughed too much at Horace's jokes, bothered him with questions, and performed childish feats in hope of a compliment. "Look at me, Jeptha," Philippe would shout, pronouncing the "J" in the soft French way. When Jeptha looked, the boy jumped onto his small eight-year-old hands and walked a few paces across the deck. He loved Jeptha but couldn't pronounce his name; I thought it said something sad about love.

We pushed north. It grew colder again. All around us, the passengers were becoming more alert, and they forgot the hobbies that had helped them pass the time during the voyage and began talking of what San Francisco would be like, and the methods of recognizing and extracting gold. Jeptha began to think more of his mission in California and spent more time in prayer and study. One afternoon, he sat on the deck, intent on his Bible, while Philippe, I noticed, hovered about for some minutes, looking at him expectantly. Finally, I touched Jeptha on the shoulder. He looked up, startled, then nodded at the child, explaining patiently that it was time for Philippe to play and for Jeptha to work, and they would play together later on, or perhaps tomorrow.

About ten minutes after that, just as the wind was starting to rise, we heard Philippe's mother, Marie Toissante, calling Jeptha's name. We turned. She pointed up. There was Philippe, clinging to the mizzen-mast, above the yardarm of the topgallant, the third above the deck of the ship's five rows of sails—perhaps he was forty or fifty feet up, several times higher than he had ever gone before with Jeptha's encouragement. He had climbed there, certainly, to surprise and impress Jeptha; but we could see he had become paralyzed with fear as the ship began to roll.

For a moment, Jeptha's face was tight with worry—the wind was blowing stronger, and the sea became rougher as we stood there. Then he smiled and shouted, "Look, Belle! Look how brave Philippe is! Look how well he holds on! How about that!"

"I want to come down!" Philippe yelled.

"Of course you do, but stay another moment, my brave lad," cried Jeptha, as the ship began to roll more violently. "Stay where you are, Philippe! I'll get you!"

"Maybe we should get a sailor to fetch him down," I said.

Jeptha shook his head. "No time," he murmured, and called out: "Hold on! I'm coming to get you. There's nothing to worry about!"

Jeptha began climbing. "I'm coming! I'm almost there!" Other passengers, including the schoolteacher, the small-town mayor, and two Chilean prostitutes, began gathering below. They were pointing and talking to each other, while Captain Stormfield emerged onto the deck and began shouting advice. Jeptha climbed quickly: before long, he stood close below the boy. Herbert Owen was beside me now, and next to him Marie Toissante, one hand on some rigging and another over her mouth, as still as if carved of wood, as if she were afraid her slightest movement would shake her child off the mast. We heard Jeptha shout, over the creaking ropes and timbers and the moaning of the wind: "Take a step, Philippe! You can keep your arms around the mast as you do it. It is better if you do it yourself!" But Philippe would not move. Jeptha called down to Herbert Owen to translate for him, but still the boy did not move.

"All right, then," called Jeptha. "That's all right. I'll carry you." Rain was beginning to fall, a slick, slanting drizzle, as he maneuvered to the other side of the mast and took the boy's right arm, intending to wrap it around his own shoulder. Then Jeptha's foot slipped, and for a moment he teetered on the mast. When we fall, we clutch thoughtlessly at whatever we are holding, and though he had lost his grip on the boy's shoulder, Jeptha instinctively clutched Philippe's wrist. Together they fell—for an instant holding hands in the air, as if leaping, not falling. Passengers gasped. I screamed. Marie Toissante shrieked and rushed to the other side of the mast, where her son was falling. Then everyone heard the sickening thud, the sound of Philippe landing headfirst on the deck. Jeptha fell into a sail, then clambered quickly down and sprinted to where the boy lay.

We crowded around Philippe, rolling him over, listening for breath and heartbeat. The pupils of his black eyes were large. His expression was as empty as a doll's. The mother fell to her knees, stroking him, kissing him, and repeating his name. The whores from Valparaíso were sobbing and holding each other, and I ran over to Jeptha, who stood shaking, his hand against the mast. Meanwhile, the rain-whipped sky was darkening, the wind wailing, and the ship slanting sharply leeward. We were in a squall. Yes, I thought: Distract us. Wash this away. The first mate shouted. Sailors scrambled up the tilting masts.

"Bring them into my cabin," commanded Captain Stormfield, and Jeptha stepped in to lift the boy, whereupon the mother looked up, her face a mask of torment, and shouted, "No! Not you," and shouted something else in French; she rose to her feet and spat in Jeptha's face.

I grabbed Jeptha's arm. "She's beside herself, she's hysterical," I said. "It was just bad luck. It could have happened to anyone, only she would blame you, no one else," and so on. Jeptha steadied himself with one hand on the mast, and with his other hand he gently touched the spit, wiping it from his face after a delay. She walked to the gunwales, evidently meaning to jump over the side. Owen, Ewell, and some other men struggled with her.

I led Jeptha belowdecks, where he sat on the edge of his berth, holloweyed and wordless. The boy was in a better place now, I said hesitantly. Such a sweet boy had gone straight to heaven, surely. Jeptha didn't respond. Did I foresee that I would not be a good wife to have in this particular crisis? I don't remember, but I'll tell you now I wasn't. Where faith, steadiness, and conviction were needed, I had only lies and secrets.

Supper came, night, and at last sleep. I dreamed that Frank was up high in a maple tree—the very tree that Jeptha had been in long ago, when he had called me from it, saying, "Do you dare?" The tree had grown much taller. Its top was hidden in the clouds. Frank had climbed it, much too high for him, and called for help. Jeptha, standing on the ground beside me, said, "I will save him," but I said, "No, Jeptha, you're tired, you rest, let me do it," and I began to climb. I woke up drenched in sweat.

Jeptha preached one last time on the *Juniper*. It was his best-attended service. He preached on the death of children, on our ignorance of God's plan, and the weaknesses of God's servants, using the example of Jonah, and it was like watching a man flog himself.

In deference to the mother, who abhorred the prospect of a burial at sea, the boy's body was packed in ice and placed with some of his toys in a pine box made by the ship's carpenter. Two days later, we sighted California.

❧ XLV ❧

THE EARTH, TO PROTECT ITS VALUABLES, mixes them with sand and mud, heaps mountains on them, hides them in Indian burial grounds. San Francisco it wraps in mist. Now a ship's prow, now a lone sail, now a sheer rock face emerged from the void. Around nine o'clock on the morning of December 15, 1849, like the colored smoke of a stage magician, the fog dissipated. We beheld the strange, makeshift treasure city, gorged on tribute from every continent, yet still incomplete, not fully incarnate, ready to change its mind and return to elemental chaos.

Where did the land end and the shore begin? Who could say? The harbor was clogged with brigs, barques, schooners, men-of-war, and Chinese junks. Some vessels had been wrecked to make new land. Others bore painted signs announcing their conversion into warehouses, restaurants, offices, rooming houses, visibly in the process of becoming part of the city's advancing edge. Beyond that, the flat land and hillsides teemed with houses, tents, shacks, and tens of thousands of diminutive toiling men.

It was past noon by the time we disembarked. Boatmen charged a staggering sum to row passengers to shore. Most of them turned out to be immigrants from the British penal colony of Australia, either Cockney or Irish in their speech—emancipated convicts, Herbert Owen observed, who had graduated from robbery to extortion. Then we found a cheerful fellow with a New England accent, a plug hat, and a coat with a shoulder seam so torn we could see the white cloth of his soiled shirt through it, who claimed to have been a college professor in Boston. We went with him, though his price was just as high as the others'. He told me it was rare to see a woman here and warned me that my clothes were impractical—it was the rainy season. Until a month ago, it had been all dust here; it got into eyes and mouths whenever people faced the wind. Now they missed the dust. Now it was all mud.

Ewell, who had bought flour in Chile, asked what it was selling for. The boatman replied, "It is being used for landfill." Ewell turned away, insulted. We found out later that it was literally true. A passenger said he had ten fresh oranges. "Are they juicy?" asked the boatman, and, hearing that they were, he gave him five dollars he had just collected from the rest of us.

Jeptha, who was haunted and speechless when he was alone with me, and in public cheerful and voluble, a cheap imitation of his former self, said, "Tell us about conditions here." No doubt a common request. The boatman answered readily: "You do a month of living in a day. You meet every kind of man. You hear every language. Mining is killing labor." That was his general wisdom. Next came news items. "A fourteen-year-old boy found an eleven-pound gold nugget and sold it for twenty-eight hundred dollars last Thursday. A Philadelphian was shot by a New Yorker yesterday at the Bella Union. The gamblers didn't take their eyes off the roulette wheel." At last, he settled to his chief enthusiasm, prices, and we learned that we had all made the wrong decisions about what to bring along and what to buy once we got here.

As soon as we reached shore, the boatman began to shout: "Oranges! Sweet, juicy oranges!" He had sold them for a dollar each before the last of us set foot on land.

By then I understood. Everyday rules were suspended. Things that had hardened into their final shape at home were fluid here. If *Alice in Wonderland* had been written yet, it would have come to mind now. With a bite of magical cake or mushroom, a ship could become a lodging house, a Yankee teacher a boatman or a fruit vendor, and flour worthless. I could become a good woman.

The black cast-iron bodies and pipe joints of about a dozen heat stoves waited on the slimy boards at Clarkes Point. Grimacing, with yellow teeth and red faces, suffering men were loading them onto a sinking wagon; the driver was yelling at them to stop. There were buildings of all kinds, many half finished, some mere canvas sheds open in front, covered with signs in several languages, hand-painted with words that in another city would be carved in stone: GOLD EXCHANGE. DRY GOODS. HARTLEY, DAGUERREOTYPES. JONATHAN STODDARD, ATTORNEY. There were gray barrels and crates and lumpy coarse-woven tan sacks, heaps of merchandise. There were men, hurrying, waiting, determined, exhausted, as diverse in character as the houses. They say gold has no magnetic properties, yet look what it had dragged to this spot, all these foreign-looking people, thousands of miles from their customary haunts, their many shades of skin, shapes of noses, angles of eyes, in pea jackets and oilcloth hats, in ponchos and sombreros, in knee-length blue tunics and pigtails. They all seemed strangely unsurprised to find themselves here, walking in the sticky mud, their images in caramel puddles mingling with bits of cloud and sky and circling birds.

Red, brown, bluish, green-gray muck, dense as potter's clay, noisily sucked our steps and gurgled over the tops of our boots. Some fellows were laying planks. Others tried to dig out a frantic mule sunk up to its belly (two hours later, I thought it was sleeping until I noticed the dark stream of congealed blood and the bullet hole). Jeptha, solicitous but distant, pulled me out when I was gripped above the knees. Our predicament was more absurd than dangerous, and he laughed. "Don't leave me stuck like that mule," I said, to fan this little flame of laughter. Instead, he grew pensive. His mind had moved from my remark to the general idea of rescue, and thence to the boy's death.

Men who had been looking away while we approached were suddenly surprised by the sight of a female, and they removed their dripping hats with wonder writ on their faces. Other men, many yards away, recognizing this sign of a woman's presence, began trudging toward us. Jeptha introduced himself as a preacher and me as his wife; the men nodded absentmindedly while staring at me as if I were Niagara Falls or a two-headed calf.

All who had been here over a week spoke like old-timers, eager to disabuse newcomers of foolish Eastern notions about mining, California, and Life. Some, fresh from the hinterlands, looked unhealthy—undernourished, missing teeth, or walking on a leg that had been broken and set improperly by amateurs. We asked if they had seen Lewis or Edward, and I searched each new face, expecting it to belong to one of my brothers. Sometimes I was fairly sure I recognized a face from New York City.

Around Portsmouth Square were substantial edifices of wood and adobe, and hotels and gambling houses in two-story buildings with wood frames and canvas walls. We were dumbfounded to see men crouching with pans and buckets before the United States Hotel, washing the mud: a Connecticut Yankee told us that, indeed, gold had just been discovered in this mud—whether it was here naturally or some drunken miner had dropped a bag of gold dust, who knew. He offered to sell us the equipment. "You have made up this story to sell pans and buckets," said Jeptha, and the fellow shrugged. We heard later that he had been playing this trick on greenhorns for months.

We bought coffee and pie being sold from the back of a wagon. By then it was evening. The gambling houses were open. Having paper-and canvas walls, they glowed all over like giant lanterns, and we used their light to find our way as the music from the different houses clashed in the festive discord heard today in carnival midways.

A drunk staggered out of the El Dorado, throwing the door wide, and with this gesture, like a dimpled Cupid uncurtaining a bathing Venus, he laid bare a lavish world of gilt, mirrors, and crystal, voluptuous furniture, obscene oil paintings, young sirens in lace and muslin, every type of hat, cravat, and mustache, and lifetimes of toil rising in sinuous golden towers on the tables. It occurred to me that a Harriet Knowles could become rich very quickly in this unnatural city, where there was so much sudden wealth and the mere sight of a woman made men gasp in wonder.

Though I looked on my former life as a disaster that had befallen me long ago, I could not control these thoughts about what could be done with the materials at hand. I thought this way automatically, as a man who had once been a cooper might look at a barrel and think, *I could have made it better.*

We walked on. Jeptha put his hand over my eyes to spare me the sight of a man urinating in the street.

WE SPENT OUR FIRST NIGHT BELOWDECKS on the *Juniper,* our second in a wood-frame lodging house in which a canvas curtain separated us from several men in the next room. On the third day, we moved into a permanently moored schooner formerly called the *Flavius.* Nailed to a short pole where the mainmast had once been was a large hand-painted sign, FLAVIUS FOOD AND LODGING. Its owner was Captain Austin, a Mexican War veteran who had bought the vessel, along with several water lots and nearby town lots, with twenty thousand dollars in gold dust, after which his wife had come out by steamship, almost dying of yellow fever in Panama. I helped Mrs. Austin cook and bake, and I cleaned and served meals, for which Jeptha and I were given free board and lodging and I received another twenty dollars a week; Jeptha brought in about forty dollars by helping to put up houses four days a week. On the other three days, he preached in the streets for nothing. At night, he collapsed on the bed and never attempted to be intimate with me.

Captain Austin was short and had a head too large for his small body, like a funny man in a children's book; he was clean-shaven, with sleepy, protuberant eyes. His sloping nose had a bulb at its end, and one of his small hands was missing half a pinky finger. Mrs. Austin described this gravely as a war wound. She was short and stout, with a face like her husband's, and the same storybook proportions. He wasn't around much except at meals, at which times his bulging eyes followed me in his unmoving head as though he were a lion studying a grass-eating creature from a hilltop.

Mrs. Austin did not seem to notice. She dressed like a farm wife, in a baggy calico wrapper—she owned three—and a long, stained blue apron I never saw her without. She did not bathe as often as I would have liked, and this mattered to me, since we were constantly together. For several

days, she did not speak except to tell me what to do. Then, one time when
we were in the *Flavius*'s tiny galley, she paid me a compliment. She was
mixing a tablespoon of saleratus into a bowl of corn flour. I was using
an empty tin can to stamp out disks of dough for soup dumplings. Taking note of my speed, she said she had been afraid that, being pretty
and refined, I would not be a hard worker, and she had been pleasantly
surprised. But I mustn't slack off now that she'd said this. I promised
I wouldn't (reminding myself that life is a wheel, as I believe Herodo-
tus mentions somewhere). She said, "Everything happens fast here. Back
east, Captain Austin would have taken twenty years to make his fortune.
Other men might take ten years to admit they've failed; here that takes
just months. Men who would do murder one day in Philadelphia do
it here the first time they walk into a gambling hall; and the ones who
would turn into broken-down drunks after twenty years, here you see
sleeping in their puke a week after they arrive."

I was impressed by this observation, and I thought I might enjoy her
company once I got used to her physical liabilities, but it turned out to
be the sum total of her special wisdom; she was a one-idea person, like
a minor character in a novel by Charles Dickens, and once the topic was
introduced, no day passed without a discussion of Time in the West.
For example, when I spoke to her about Jeptha's prospects, and whether
he would become known and have a church, she said, "Whatever happens, it will happen fast, you'll see," and she repeated the speech that had
impressed me so much the first time I had heard it.

Once, I carelessly described Captain Austin as "lucky." Mrs. Austin,
shoving equal proportions of red meat and white fat into a grinder, denied
it so hotly I was afraid she would lose a finger. The *country* had been lucky
to acquire this territory—with Captain Austin's help, remember—just
when gold was found on it. Captain Austin had seized the opportunity.
His character was such as to make it inevitable for him to become rich:
the gold discovery had merely hastened the process.

There was something rather anxious about this insistence that her
husband's success was grounded on his talents: perhaps she was afraid
it would turn out to be a mirage. And so it might. When she was not
expounding her single insight, Mrs. Austin fretted out loud about her
husband's business, and I learned that Captain Austin had taken a great

risk by sinking his money into the water lots around the *Flavius*. He had
bought too late, when the market was high. Besides, he had purchased
them during the time of transition between Mexican and American rule,
when it was not clear who had a right to sell land. There was sure to be a
legal battle, and if things went badly in the courts—perhaps even if they
seemed likely to go badly in the courts—he might lose them.

Even if Captain Austin held on to his wealth, that might not help
Mrs. Austin. They often quarreled. One night I heard him say he wished
he hadn't sent for her.

Really, there was nothing sillier than to deny the role of luck in everything that occurred in San Francisco in those unnatural years. The whole
city was a vast casino; a fortune hung on every decision. Walk into this
lodging tent; you and a fellow you happen to meet there start a mighty
business enterprise still in operation in 1910. Walk into that other tent;
die of cholera next week. Earn good pay loading riverboats; but lose the
fortune you would have found in the gold fields.

Philosophers know that all choices are fateful. Each decision destroys
worlds of possibility and permits others to survive at least a little longer.
In a gold rush, the process is visible to ordinary men, and since they're
not philosophers, it unsettles them, and they begin to do strange things.

SOON AFTER WE ARRIVED, I woke to the noise of crackling and the
smell of smoke. I shook Jeptha awake. "Wake up, wake up, the ship is on
fire!" He jumped into his trousers, I wrapped myself in the blanket, and
we hastened out to the deck along with others who had been roused by
the commotion. It was determined pretty soon that the fire was not on
the schooner. It was in the city. To wake us here, it must be big, but we
could not see it until the fog lifted. By then, Jeptha and some of the other
men were fighting it: his tasks for much of the day were to shovel mud
onto burning walls to tie ropes to the tops of buildings in the fire's path
and to help to pull the buildings down.

That day, Jeptha met David Broderick, the Tammany politician who
had come from New York round the Horn in steerage, with the express
purpose of becoming a U.S. senator from California when California
became a state. Volunteer fire companies were the heart of Democratic
Party politics, and Broderick showed considerable experience and con-

spicuous bravery in battling the flames, as did several other men who would come to have dubious reputations in San Francisco. Jeptha mentioned the name to me repeatedly, and later, when Broderick's name was on everyone's lips, its syllables would conjure a memory of Jeptha as he was during the fire—in a good mood, full of interesting news, pleased with his small but creditable role that day—and how grateful I was to the fire, hoping its salutary effects on my husband would last.

The most popular explanation for the fire was that Australians set it in order to loot the stores. Another theory, told to me in several versions, was that the fire had been set by a Negro, who had been thrown out of the saloon where the conflagration began. Other people—Australians, Negroes, workingmen—insisted that the merchants had set it, to raise prices by destroying excess stock. The city was awash in tales of conspiracy, as might be expected when such a varying group of men are brought together and there is a treasure for them to fight over.

JEPTHA MADE TEN DOLLARS A DAY helping to put up new edifices that were only a little more substantial than those that had burned down so easily. Many of them were portable houses of wood or iron that had been shipped in pieces around the Horn. He continued to preach in the streets outside the gambling saloons, and along the wharves, and among the tents on the hillsides. I noticed that when he talked to me about putting the houses together he spoke with pride, but when he spoke about his preaching, whether it went well or badly, there was a new distance in his voice, as though it had been spoiled for him. Once, in our cabin on the *Flavius,* he rehearsed to me the outline of a sermon he planned to give. "But I thought . . . ," I began, and stopped myself.

"What?" He turned to me abruptly, as if I had caught him in the midst of some furtive crime. "What did you think?"

"Nothing—just that you used not to prepare your sermons in advance."

He said nothing for a moment, and I saw he was sorry he had snapped at me. "I said, I think, when we were on the *Juniper,* I said that I *used* to plan them, and then I stopped planning them and just waited for the spirit to move me. But that was on the *Juniper.* Now I'm here in California, and a great deal hangs on the success of what I do here, and it would be remiss of me not to plan."

He had begun gently, but by the time he was done, the tone of his voice was nasty and defensive, a tone I had never before heard him assume with anyone. "I see," I said.

That night, a gasp woke me. I felt him leave the bed. I heard him moving in the dark. A match sputtered to life and lit the candle in its lamp on a small table we had bought for the cabin. I sat up and saw him reading the list of names of well-connected men my grandfather had sent in his last letter. This was the part of his job he hated most, going to these practical men, these proud adventurers in the world of trade, and asking them to subscribe to a church, or to help him to rent space for worship in some schoolhouse or the back room of some store, and working on their vanity and their ambition to be big men—founders of a great city's oldest Baptist church—since it was no use working on their religious feelings. Even their vanity was a weak force, compared with their greed. He wrote in pencil next to some of the names. He knew I was watching him. "I'm a beggar," he said. "Parsons are beggars."

Most professions have their little indignities. In the past he had always borne his cheerfully, sure of his abilities and his destiny, and believing that nothing was more important. "You work," I reminded him. "You work as hard as any miner, for me and for God. They live for money; you have a higher purpose. Come to bed, Jeptha."

Eventually, he did. We lay together. He stroked my hair in a way that he sometimes did before he took me. I yielded to him, needing this comfort, too. He threw his flesh into mine as though he wished he could drown in me; and I felt that, after all, I was learning something new about the uses of carnality. But after our crisis, before we drifted off to sleep, I recollected that when his gasp woke me I had been dreaming of Philippe. And I thought that probably Jeptha had been dreaming of Philippe as well.

Everything had been about Philippe since the moment the boy fell to the deck of the *Juniper*. Jeptha was like an animal running through the woods with a hunter's arrow in him. The arrow had not taken him down yet, but it was bound to finally. Nothing I said was any help. The truest things I could think of saying—that no one is perfect and everybody makes mistakes—seemed banal and inadequate, and I made them weaker by hiding them among a lot of lies about Providence and tests from God, and everything being for the good in the long run, things he must have guessed I did not believe. In completely separate conversations, sometimes he would say he didn't deserve me, and I would say, "Just the same, you have me, you always will." Then we would go to bed.

The next day, he came home carrying an empty light-brown sack imprinted in Spanish with the name of a Chilean flour company. He opened one of our trunks and stuffed into the sack every one of the forbidden books he had inherited from William Jefferds's library—Paine, Volney, Strauss, Lessing, etc.—threw in rocks for extra weight, tied the sack, walked out of the cabin with the bag over his shoulder; I followed him, feeling that something very grave was happening, whose nature I did not quite comprehend. The hard edges of the books bulged, receded, and bulged again in temporary lines and rectangles on the coarse-woven cloth as they swung behind his back. He walked to the schooner's stern, which was in the deepest water. I saw what he meant to do. "Must you?" I asked; he nodded, and he threw the sack into the bay.

I didn't need to tell him that the books might fetch a great deal of money here. Nor could I believe his character had deteriorated to the point where he feared it to be known that he had possessed them. No, it had deteriorated to this point: he saw them as dangerous—to him and to others. Destroying books was no longer just for priests.

I asked him how his day had gone. He told me that he had preached to excellent effect outside the old adobe Custom House on Portsmouth Square.

"You're doing well," I said. "You're becoming known."

"I think so."

"This is what you are made for. You're good at it because you are made for it."

"Yes, no doubt." He was quiet for a while, and then, as if he had just been reminded of a completely different topic: "I've lost my faith." He said it lightly, as if he meant his gloves, and they were bound to turn up.

"No," I said. "You don't mean that. Do you?"

"No, of course not. I was just joking," and he talked a little about the sermon he would deliver next Sunday at the First Presbyterian Church.

I had sometimes hoped he would lose his faith, so we could be of like mind; but I had wanted it to happen gradually, over the years, taking it all a little less seriously as time went on, with maybe just enough complacent, nebulous credulity left over to ease the passage to decrepitude and death. Not like this; I had no idea where this might lead.

XLVI

ABOUT EVERY TWO WEEKS, the placement of two long black boards on a high tower on Telegraph Hill announced the arrival of the Pacific Mail Steamship Company's side-wheeler. Then for a few days, the post office—a small wooden building with a porch and square columns, at Clay and Pike Streets—would be surrounded by a homesick mob while the clerks inside frantically alphabetized. Two lines formed, one before the window for mail in foreign languages, the other before the window for English mail and newspapers. Some men made a regular occupation of standing in the mud half the day, while slanting rain beat their hats and puddles deepened, so when their place was close to the front they could sell it.

To be sure of intercepting letters from Agnes, I always went straight to the front of the line and paid one of those men for his place. I would pay cash on delivery for Agnes's letter, read it to follow the progress of her investigation, and burn it, the first moment I was alone, in the cookstove in the galley of the *Flavius*. I left all the other letters for Jeptha, so that he would think he was getting the mail.

Our room on the *Flavius* was a sailing vessel's stateroom, with a few chairs and a table and a washstand, and a spring bed with a feather mattress in place of the shelflike berths. It was damp and chilly and smelled of the wharf. I expected that in a few months at the most we would find better accommodations; in any case, the discomforts of my existence did not make me long for my former life with a cook, a lady's maid, carpets, fireplaces, a water closet, theaters, and restaurants. I wanted everything to be different, so that I could be different. I cooked, cleaned, carried water, and made fires. With every sweep of the corn broom, I was becoming a better woman.

Memories of the *Flavius* come back to me easily: calm days when each vessel sat on its quivering, upended watery twin; clear nights when lights on the ships were reflected as shimmering yellow streamers in the bay. Up in the hills, the tents and canvas houses, lit from within, resembled paper lanterns suspended in the blackness.

I don't remember the exact date when I went to the post office and saw Jeptha stepping out from the shadow of the porch and into the light, a clutch of envelopes in his hand. I do know that it was in late February, and that I was a month past my time, with all the signs of pregnancy, but I had not told him yet. As soon as I saw him, I formed a plan to distract him with the news of my condition and get the letters before he read them.

It was chilly but clear. The wind rose, sending handbills into flight, making ripples in the shallow tawny puddles and the deep silver-black puddles on the undulating streets, while men pulled their coats tight and grabbed their hats. Jeptha looked dazed and lost, sadder than his fellows, and when he saw me there was something else—shock, fear—and he turned his face away as though consulting with the horizon or a wheelbarrow or a sparrow; when he turned back, he looked on me with a sort of shyness. I knew he had just read one of Agnes's letters. I felt I was in terrible trouble, but not beyond hope. We walked toward each other and embraced. I realized *again,* as if in the previous second I had forgotten it, that he had read the letter. "Arabella," he murmured, and the knowledge was present in the way he uttered my name, with a hint, suppressed, but detectable, of helpless grief.

We walked down the muddy hill, his arm around my shoulder. "You're trembling," he said.

"I'm cold," I said.

"Arabella, I have just read a letter from Agnes," he said, and though I had been as sure, as sure as that I was standing on a wet hill among a crowd of men sporadically putting their hands to their hats, that he had read the letter, to hear him say it made my knees buckle, and though it was in my interest to seem indifferent to the news, I could not. I would have fallen in the mud if he hadn't caught me. "Are you all right?" he said, and we walked again, facing in the same direction, toward a little rise of mud and sand and rocks that hid the bay from view just then. "This isn't her first letter," he said. "You've read her earlier letters. You read them and you destroy them. Isn't that so?"

"Yes, Jeptha."

There was silence as, perhaps, he waited for me to speak. It was a hopeful silence. It was an invitation for me to explain it all away. I had thought a thousand times of what I would say, worked out half a dozen speeches, and I saw now that none of them were any good.

"When, Arabella?"

"In Rio. That was the first letter. That's what you mean, isn't it?"

"Yes," he said, squeezing my shoulders. "What else would I mean?"

"I don't know."

The bumpy street of mud and pebbles and scrub began to rise. At the top of it the bay came into view, the geometrical lines of the wharves, the tidal stretch of mud flats which grew and shrank daily, the crescent-shaped little city of wooden ships, the watery expanse gleaming and shadowy, here blue, there silver, in constant watchful motion.

"Arabella," he said.

I turned and looked up at him. He was troubled, but he wasn't cold. I had hope.

I said, "You've read it; it's the fifth one. I know most of what's in it—she adds something new to each one and repeats the old accusations. She seems to know I'm intercepting them, and she keeps on, knowing one is bound to get through finally, and now one has. I know what you'll say, that you know she is a liar, that I should have trusted you not to believe her, but—" He began to speak; I put my hand over his mouth. I was inspired, I felt as if I were telling the truth; I was telling the inner truth. "I couldn't bear it. Do you understand? I couldn't bear to let her put those pictures in your mind. To be thinking those things when you looked at me. She scours the mire of the streets, she is willing to abase herself and pick up the dung of the streets to fling at me. She wants to poison our marriage. And now she has."

"No, she hasn't," he said.

I shook my head. "You will never be able to forget."

We walked, bending our heads down against the wind, to the foot of Clay Street, where several rowboats labeled "Flavius" waited in the mud. Jeptha rowed us to the *Flavius,* which rocked, straining against its tether, amid the musical knocking and drumming of moored boats on restless water. "Give it to me," I said, when the hull of the ship rose before us. He handed me the letter. I opened it. I read just enough to see that she said I was Frank's mother and had lived as a prostitute and a madam under the name Harriet Knowles; and then, partly because it was difficult to read it under Jeptha's gaze, and partly because I thought the upright woman I pretended to be would have found these disgusting lies unbearable, I crumpled it up hastily into a ball and threw it into the bay.

The ball of paper rose on the wavelets and fell and rose again, while slowly opening like an ugly white flower. Jeptha took an oar and reached with it until he nearly fell out of the boat, so he could catch the pages, which separated from each other in contact with the flaring end of the oar. Carefully, as though performing a delicate operation that would save our lives, as if ultimately everything, including guilt and innocence and suspicion and trust, were a technical matter calling in the main for dexterity and finesse, he coaxed the paper nearer to the boat, pulled the oar in slowly so as not to send the sheets swimming away from the rowboat, and reached out slowly for them. Like a killer drowning a man by holding his head beneath the water, he submerged them. When they were wet enough, he picked them out dripping and shredded them in his glistening, dripping hands. "We don't want to send it out like a message in a bottle," he explained. "We want it to end here."

I reached out to stroke his cheek. He leaned his face into my caress. "You won't think," I began.

"Of course not," he said.

"You won't look at me, thinking of what she said."

"I promise," he said, stroking my hair, kissing my cheek.

"I wish I could tear it out of your mind."

"I understand. I don't blame you for keeping it to yourself—I can see why you would try to—but it would have been better, don't you see, for us to have discussed it earlier."

"Yes, Jeptha."

"Then you wouldn't have had to bear it alone."

"Yes."

What could he do? Agnes was telling the truth. On the other hand, this truth was highly improbable, and she had been proved a liar, and he didn't want to believe her. His faith in God was shaken, and his faith in himself. How could he bear to lose his faith in me at the very same time?

"She must be crazy," he said.

We took our other letters to our cabin. We embraced, inhaling each other's smell, which was like a drug to us; both feeling that we had had a near escape, we were hungry for each other, but Mrs. Austin was calling my name. I did not tell him about my pregnancy until we were together again that night. He kissed me, said it was wonderful, and, like any good man in such circumstances, he began to worry about money.

I felt immensely relieved, but later, recalling that celebratory moment, it made my heart sink to realize how pallid it had really been. There had been nothing like the joy we would both have experienced if this good news had not had to creep into the world under the memory of the boy who had fallen from the mast, and in the shadow of Agnes's words, which rang true because they were true. I could not make myself believe that I had escaped detection forever. With my head on my sleeping husband's chest that night, I told myself that at least I had postponed it, perhaps for years, and I could enjoy those years.

For a week or two, he was often testy and irritable. He complained about the rain, the mud, and the soulless dollar-worship of the men around us. He seized eagerly upon any little mistake he made—a shirt or a belt that eluded him until it turned up in some place he had already looked—to accuse himself of being a fool. In all this I recognized anger directed away from its proper target.

JEPTHA HAD MADE ELEVEN CONVERTS during the journey from New York to San Francisco. Four of them left for the gold regions as a group, pledging to keep each other Christian, after bidding us a solemn farewell, and a few others went by themselves, also shaking my husband's hand and thanking him for bringing them to Jesus, and promising to keep the Ten Commandments in the mining camps. A few decided to stay in town until the end of the rainy season, but whether seeing him made them sad or they realized that seeing them made him sad, in any event they stopped visiting. He preferred the company of Herbert Owen, who now had a law office in one room of an old adobe-brick cottage on the wharf. When I was alone with Owen, he told me that Marie Toissante had been spotted dealing cards in the Bella Union. The *Juniper* was anchored within sight of the *Flavius*. Stormfield wanted the government to turn it into a hospital.

A letter came from Edward. It was four months old and written on a letter sheet that had been printed a ten-minute walk from where we stood. On one side, a series of humorous verses about the miner's life were arranged in a ring around a picture of San Francisco Bay. On the other, blank side, my brother Edward had written in tiny print:

Dear Arabella and Jeptha,

If you're reading this, you are in California. Guess what, so are we! Both well, after ups & downs. Albert Mitchell, one of Lewis's Pearson Academy friends, got the cholera on the way to Independence; died. Lots of hard luck with wagons, oxen, ponies. The funniest part of the trip is a desert you get to near the end where you pass all the family heirlooms, sideboards & chests of drawers stuck in the sand.

Our camp is in Tuolumne County. We eat well thanks to hunting & the friendship of a clever Frenchman who keeps a garden. Had a misunderstanding with some Sonorans thanks to Stephen McPhereson, another one of Lewis's Pearson Academy friends. We wrote his family, saying how we'd miss him, but just between us their dear Stephen spent everything he made on vice & dissipation & then he nearly got us all killed, but never mind RIP.

We met an interesting man named Billy Mulligan, who Lewis likes better than I do. Mr. Mulligan runs boxing matches in the mining towns. Lewis fought for him, acquiring more specie in this way than all us together have gotten with pick and shovel, but he hurt his hand, which is why it is I who mar this helpless fair page with my scribbling & not he. Write to us c/o the Imperial Hotel in Mariposa. Lewis sends his love & will write himself when able.

Affectionately,
Edward Godwin

Two inches were left blank at the foot of the sheet, ample room to tell us what made Billy Mulligan interesting, what fate befell Stephen McPhereson, and other questions that naturally came to mind.

In the same post, we received a letter from Agnes. With matches we had brought along for the purpose, we burned it, unopened, within twenty yards of the post office. A man with a dusty black frock coat, muddy pants, and a chin-muffler beard stopped to watch us. Soon afterward, there came a man in a boater and a butternut shirt and striped pants. A third spectator arrived, wearing a flat cap and smoking a clay pipe, and finally a gentleman with a round hat and a cigar. They accumulated like birds on a ledge and stared as if they had each paid us a dollar for the privilege. It seemed that the one with the pipe wanted to ask us the meaning of our little auto-da-fé, but a look from Jeptha changed his mind.

I was not ready to relax. I knew he had not forgotten anything.

Breakfast each morning on the *Flavius* was at a long table under a canopy where the mainmast had been. Like most meals in San Francisco, it was conducted as a race, which I began by hitting a small brass gong with a hammer. As many men as there were seats would fall with frightful efficiency—with a simultaneous working of jaws and elbows and darting arms—upon the highly miscellaneous and occasionally surprising comestibles I kept rushing to the table. Anyone who lingered over ten minutes would be asked to hurry by others waiting for seats, and usually, by tacit consensus, the eaters rose all at once to make way for the next shift. A day or two after we burned Agnes's letter, a short but sturdy-looking fellow in his early twenties took a seat among the others, and Mrs. Austin told the company, "This is Justin Nugent, our new boarder."

The blue flannel shirt was new. The red kerchief and the stained brown hat he doffed politely had been through a lot. He was bronzed and bearded, and would have been handsome had he not been cross-eyed, a doll with a fixed expression of bemusement. Where had I seen those eyes?

There was a flurry of handshakes. I decided not to wait for Jeptha to introduce me; the whole company had noticed that Nugent was staring at me. But I was too slow. "Harriet! Harriet Knowles from New York," he said, as if pouncing on the correct answer in an oral examination. Instantly I remembered him—clean-shaven, with white gloves, silk hat, cape.

Jeptha was a few places away at the table, behind me. I dared not turn and look at him. For what it was worth, I was going to tell Justin that he was mistaken, but I heard Jeptha say in a stranger's voice, "So you know Harriet. You know her from her establishment on Mercer Street, I suppose?"

"That's right," said Justin. His eyes, in perpetual conference with each other, made his expression hard to read. I do not think he wanted to harm me. I think his main emotion was nostalgia: after many strange experiences, a hard voyage here, hard living in the mountains, it was delicious to remember New York City. Possibly it had slipped his mind that some people come west to leave behind a bad name, that a woman who condescended to be a waitress in California might not wish it to be known that she had run a parlor house back in the States. Having drowned his pancakes in molasses, he sliced them all into small squares with a series of efficient strokes. "Do you remember a girl named Monique? And what was her name, Alexandra, who never talked, but Miss Knowles here said she was the daughter of a ruined Polish aristocrat?"

Jeptha stood up, and everyone was looking at us, and if they were too stupid to guess what sort of establishment was being discussed, they could read the dismay on my face as Jeptha rose and took me by the wrist and out to the deck and into our cabin.

I sat on our bed, rocking, my face in my hands, while he paced the tiny cabin, his hands squeezing and wringing each other. "Tell me now," he said. "Tell me all."

He waited.

"You know what happened to me in Livy."

I reminded him that he had abandoned me, believing Agnes's lies. He mustn't think that the bad things I had done since then made those lies true.

As I spoke, he moved restlessly about the cabin, sometimes stopping by the window as I spoke. All the light in the room came from that one window. Whenever he was facing me, I tried to catch his gaze, to guess his emotions and adjust my tale accordingly, and also to seek the balm of his sympathy, but there wasn't any. I knew that he would not be satisfied with a confession of sins already proved or be distracted by a reminder of someone else's misdeeds; and that probably nothing I said could help.

I told him most of it. I left out the parts about Eric Gordon and Jack

Cutter, except in the most general way, saying that, as a young girl without guidance in a sordid world, I had done many things I wished I could undo. Abandoned, misused, I had lost my self-respect. I had suffered blows worse than any that Agnes had ever endured. I had been tried in a way she had never been tried. For that matter, I had been tried as Jeptha had not been tried—not even, in my expert opinion, after the death of Philippe. "You think you know what remorse is, but you don't—oh, my darling, not yet, I hope not ever. I don't hear you sobbing in your sleep as I did, night after night. You don't know what it is to be kept alive only by the fear of death. You don't know what it is to feel your heart grow cold, and your spirit die, and wish that it would happen faster."

I told him about Jocelyn and Mrs. Bower, and how I had learned too late that my grandfather was alive and arranged for Lewis to return to him. I told him about Cora. I said that Frank was the child of a gambler who had treated me with great kindness, and I had thought it better that my son grow up with Anne than with me.

He was quiet, and whenever I stopped we heard water splashing on the beams of the *Flavius*, footfalls making its boards creak, distant shouts and nearer conversations. The whole cabin went dim for a while—out there some clouds must have gone before the sun—and presently it brightened again. "Through all of it, I was true to you in my heart; I loved you only, though I thought you had treated me cruelly. I thought that you had read my letters, which Jefferds kept from you. I thought that you knew about Matthew; I thought you were heartless; and still I loved you. And the instant I knew that your wife was dead, I turned myself inside out and my world upside down and gave up . . . many things to get you back."

As I spoke, I began to think I might keep him after all. Surely he was still enough of a Christian to believe in forgiveness. I was carrying his baby. There was some justice on my side. I grabbed the sleeve of his frock coat as his steps took him near the bed. I took his wrist and made him face me. I looked up at him. "All these months, I've been in terror that you would find out; that you would throw me aside in disgust, as any ordinary man would—as anyone out there would think you had a right to do. Now my time of reckoning has come. All I can cling to is the hope that you will show yourself different from other men, better than other men, as I have always believed you are."

He looked down at me as if attempting to recall whether we had ever met.

"Help me—there are some things I don't fully understand," he said.

"What, my darling?"

"You said that you—put yourself into the employ of this woman, Mrs. Bower, in order to pay a bribe and thereby, if I have this right, keep your brother out of prison."

"Yes, Jeptha."

"And then you had to go on because you owed her money for the fine dresses that she had bought for you to make you more attractive."

"Yes," I said.

"But this went on for years. It went on after you had found that your grandfather was alive. He would certainly have paid whatever was needed to free you from this woman. You went away with a gambler and had his child. He did not want to marry you, so he gave you a large sum of money. With his help, you started an establishment of your own, in which you employed other young women. You left the child with Anne."

"I had lost you. I was without guidance. I was weak."

"You don't seem to have been weak. You seem to have been very capable."

"I meant the weakness to want money. I was confused. I was in a wilderness. You can't know. You can't understand. I was lost. I was among other lost people. None of us knew right from wrong."

"Put aside the question of what was right. If you found that life unpleasant, and had a way to leave it, why didn't you? If it was money you wanted, you could have gotten more than you had as Harriet Knowles, by hiding your past and marrying."

"No, I couldn't."

"Don't you think so, a lovely, well-spoken woman like you?"

"It was too late!" I expostulated, really thinking out loud—understanding it myself for the first time. "The damage was done. I could never go back to being like another girl when I had crossed all the lines they say you can never cross without being destroyed, but I had crossed them, and here I was, alive and strong. And then comes this chance, the world saying: Here is the life we stole from you to see if you would crawl, and look at you, you *did* crawl. Isn't that funny? Well, here it is back again." I stopped for a moment. "Well, in that case, keep it, I thought. I don't want it anymore, keep it. What, I'm supposed to spend the rest of my life in a parlor, sewing, while my husband goes around town free? Do that now, when I know how these good men live away from their dutiful wives? Restrict my society to the company of these smug, stupid women who would shun me if they knew what I'd done? Why should I, to what purpose, when I'm free, with money of my own, and I'm an aristocrat among my kind, and a newspaper editor does my bidding, and I don't care that much"—I snapped my fingers—"for anyone's opinion and could tell anybody to go to hell? And if I did, there would always be the chance that someone like that cross-eyed miner would come along and recognize me from my old life. There had to be a reason, Jeptha. And there could only be one reason. I was ready to do all of that the moment there was the slightest possibility of having you. You see that, don't you, Jeptha?" I asked, walking to him, reaching my hand out toward his face, but not quite daring to touch him.

He nodded. "Before you said you had given up things to marry me, you were going to say something particular; then you amended it to 'many things.' You didn't mean the chance of marrying wealth. You meant the satisfactions of the life you were living."

"I suppose I did." I touched his face.

His head was perfectly immobile on his shoulders, while my fingers stroked his face and felt some bristles the razor had missed an hour ago. Remembering his feeling for my hands, I flattened it against his cheek, and I thought: That was smart. Perhaps, after all, everything was a question of technique, and the right combination of deft moves could save the direst situation. Then he said, as if just reaching the conclusion in his own mind, "Do as you like from now on. I'm finished with you."

"Oh, Jeptha, please. Show mercy!"

"I'm not better than other men."

I gripped his coat by the lapels. "You are! You are!"

He pulled my fingers free and writhed out of my grasp, his elbow knocking my jaw so that I bit myself and tasted blood. I clutched him again and collapsed to my knees. "You're wrong. I'm not better than other men." His voice did not express his emotions but merely informed

me of them. "I'm not different from other men. I don't want to be married to a whore. I despise you. You don't have a shred of decency or morality or honesty. You don't recognize any law beyond your own desires. You
don't set any value on truth. I don't want to see your face again or hear
your name again. I want to forget I ever knew you."

I threw my arms around his legs. "Go on and talk that way; hurt me
if you want."

"Get up."

"Hurt me, you have a right to, I've hurt you, but you can't mean all of
it. You can't. I'm carrying your child."

He looked down at me. "How do I know you're carrying a child?
Because you've told me? That means nothing; your word means nothing. And if it turns out that you are carrying a child, how do I know it's
mine?"

"You know I am and you know it's yours!"

For a second he seemed to be at a loss. Then he yelled, "How do I
know it's mine?" loud enough for everyone aboard the *Flavius* to hear,
as he pulled me to my feet, and across the room, and kicked the door
open, and dragged me out onto the deck. "I don't want you. I don't want
you, and I don't want your bastard!" he howled, letting go of me. Before
I could scurry away, he swooped me up and threw me over his shoulder and walked toward the stern. I remembered him throwing over the
books, and I guessed his intention.

"Stop it, Jeptha!" I cried, struggling. It was noon by now. There were
other men on the deck, boarders, miners, some amused—a young woman
over her husband's shoulder is comical to certain minds. "Stop him!" I
called out. A few floppy-hatted men approached, but they were unsure
whether it was right to interfere, or wise: in the San Francisco of those
days, quarrels had a habit of becoming deadly affrays, and when not
under the influence of spirits, men were cautious.

He lifted me over the rail and threw me clear of the ship. The shock of
contact with the chill bay water went unfelt, lost in the shock that he had
really done it. I went down a few feet, swam up, and treaded water, tasting salt and beginning to feel the cold. Dress and petticoats ballooned
around me. I could swim, as Jeptha knew, and shallow water lay nearby;
but the situation was not without danger. There were splashes nearby as

men dived in to fetch me. Two men pulled me to the ladder. One climbed ahead of me, and the other stayed below to catch me if I fell.

I stood on the deck in my dripping clothes, shivering, looking around me. "Where is he? Where is he?"

"Over there. There, that way," said Mrs. Austin, pointing over the side, and I saw Jeptha on the wharf, getting out of one of the *Flavius* rowboats.

"Jeptha!" I screamed. He didn't turn. I was shivering so violently I could not speak.

"You'd better get out of those clothes," said Mrs. Austin.

It was at this point that I became aware of an urgent cramping in my womb, a sensation until then lost in my emotions and the shock of my immersion into the bay. "Oh no," I said. "Oh no."

Later, after I had lost the baby, Mrs. Austin brought me clean sheets, took away the old ones, and came back with some broth in a cup. Standing over me, she said, "A Baptist minister—if that don't beat all. Well, he's baptized you, all right. You know what? I'll bet, if you had gotten him to some other city, you could have gone on fooling him for a good ten years. But here everything goes fast. Now, you can stay overnight, while you recover, but I want you out by tomorrow afternoon. I draw the line at whores."

XLVII

I SAT IN THE BED WITH MY HANDS FOLDED across my lap, thinking at first mostly of the bloody mess, my child somewhere in it, that I had glimpsed for a moment before Mrs. Austin wrapped up the gory sheet that had received the contents of my womb. I felt as if I had been struck all over, equally. Though my thoughts were disordered, I understood that this was the good part. When rational thought came, it would bring suffering of an as yet incalculable size. After what could have been a minute or an hour, Mrs. Austin re-entered the cabin with a bucket, a scrub brush, and some rags. Without giving me so much as a glance, she got on her knees—that good woman, that good, stupid, honest Christian woman—and, with her fat bottom a little higher than her head most of the time, she scoured a place on the floor where a puddle of my blood had left a residue. When she was done and had left, the spot was noticeably cleaner and lighter than the surrounding wood; and when feeling came back to me, it came back first through that tawny light patch, which delivered a stab of grief whenever I looked at it. Gradually, it became a symbol of everything I wished not to think about: of the unborn child and all it would never be; of its absent father, who had spurned us both; of the future that had been proved a silly daydream, the impossible things I had wished for with my poisoned heart's last ounce of innocence.

It was afternoon, probably, not late. The walls of the cabin were thin, and the schooner was small. Often I heard footsteps, clanking, grunts, and muffled conversations; once, I thought I heard the name "Harriet Knowles," and a burst of laughter. In time, my eyelids became heavy and I thought that I might sleep. If someone had told me I would never wake again, I would have hoped it was true. I wished I were made of sand and a wind could blow me away. I had as lively a distaste for Arabella Godwin as any of my breast-beating Puritan forebears ever cultivated for themselves. Creation groaned with the burden of me; the earth was an unwilling stage for my wickedness. These facts had been established by an expert in morality whom I had long ago denominated the expert on me. I had told myself that if he knew the truth he would love me still; but I had known all along that he would not. Who was I, really? I was a whore. Anyone who knew my history would agree. He had agreed, because it was true. I was a whore, whatever I did. If I should devote the rest of my life to charitable work in a home for crippled orphan children, I would still be a whore: not only was I a whore as a matter of personal history, I was a whore in my character, in my instinct to deceive and manipulate, in my readiness to turn anything to use, to be dishonored in ways good women would die rather than permit. I was also a murderess, but that was of less account to me, as it is to mankind generally. Though the punishment for murder is very severe, the world holds murderers in far less contempt than whores.

I woke in the middle of the night, and lay burning like a wound for hours. I slept again. When my eyes opened next, there was a crack of daylight through the door, which shook repeatedly, and a sound of loud knocking. I wanted it to be Jeptha. It could all be made right again, we would mourn together and forgive each other. I pulled the sheet up to my shoulders. "Come in."

The door swung open, and a sudden brightness hurt my eyes. I could see from her silhouette that it was Mrs. Austin, but I could not make out her expression. She half closed the door, and after a moment she said, "You can stay if you get back to work right away."

I blinked. "Why?"

"Do you want to or not?"

I thought a little longer, and her patience while I did so was instructive. "Have the men been asking for me?" She didn't answer. I supposed this meant that they had been. "I'm not well," I told her finally. "I need more time."

In an unconvincing tone of authority, she said that I could not take up space here without working. I repeated that I needed time to recover.

I spent the rest of the day in the cabin, sleeping when I could and mourning when I was awake. A little after nightfall, it occurred to me that I should eat. I went out to the galley to get a piece of corn bread, but when I had it in my hand I wasn't hungry. I went back to my bed.

The next day was the same. In the evening, there was a knock, and upon lighting the lamp and opening the door, I saw Jeptha, with Herbert Owen behind him. I guessed from his grim expression that he had just heard of my miscarriage, but all he said was "I came for my trunk."

I watched in the quaking lamplight, which shook our tall shadows, while he dragged it from under the bed and to the door. He stood still for a moment. "She told you?" I asked. He nodded. I rose from my bed slowly and stood before him for a second. I tried to slap him across the face. He caught my hand. "I hope you never have another," I said.

"Just as well," he said, and released my hand. Herbert Owen, who looked very sorry for both of us, helped him drag the trunk down the deck and into a rowboat.

On the following day, I left the cabin. I had thrown on a bedraggled dress, and had not washed or combed my hair, but still the men I passed doffed their hats and bowed. A few were bold enough to say that they had heard I was indisposed and hoped I was feeling better. When I said I had decided to take a walk through town, three men volunteered to row me to shore. I picked a homely-looking young man who was missing so many teeth he must have had to eat only soft food. When we got to the other side, he refused the payment I offered him. I walked to Portsmouth Square and on the streets around it, past lodging houses, cafés, assayers' tents, and canvas gambling halls. Everywhere, the men showed me elaborate courtesy. When I was about to cross Washington Street, a tall man with a big droopy mustache offered to carry me in his arms. It was a custom that year: women, who were so precious, were carried over the filth of San Francisco's unpaved streets. Until then I had declined, but this time I accepted. He carried me to the other side, not speaking except to say, in answer to a question, that my weight was not enough for him to notice, and he tipped his hat and did not presume any further upon our acquaintance.

I went to the steamship office and asked the price of a ticket to Rio de Janeiro and to other destinations, but I did not buy one. A carter with a load of lumber gave me a ride to the top of Telegraph Hill. I stood on a cliff, the wind buffeting my face and making false thunder in my ears. As I had many times in the last few days, I pictured Jeptha being shown my broken body and the note in my coat pocket, which I had written not with a fixed intention of destroying myself, but just to be prepared in case I did. It would blight the rest of his life, I was fairly sure, for I had some little experience in this matter. He would suffer then as I was suffering. It would crush him. I wanted that. The trouble was, I wouldn't be here to enjoy it.

I bought a tamale from a Mexican woman down by the wharf. It made my mouth burn, but I had not eaten in three days, so I finished it quickly while walking, and then turned around, deciding to buy another. Now there was a line, but the man at the front insisted that I go ahead of him, and he insisted on paying for the tamale.

I walked on, and with my emotions dulled by exhaustion, I began to consider my position in practical terms. There were many ways a woman willing to work and, even better, a woman with capital might make money in the boomtown of San Francisco. Women were getting rich just doing laundry that year. They were getting rich running restaurants and boarding houses. I could do that. Or I could invest my money in water lots, which were going cheap just now. Or I could peddle my beauty at the altar to the richest bachelor in the territory. But there was only one way that was, for me, perfectly reliable—one business I knew inside and out, one way I knew in my bones I could rise to a kind of glory, commanding a host of pretty underlings, in a little kingdom I would rule, while humiliating and shaming the man who had been supposed to save me and instead had damned me. I returned to the *Flavius* and spent another day in bed. In the morning, Mrs. Austin appeared again. "I need you in the galley. Come now, or out on your ass."

"I'm not ready."

"Then pack."

"But I'm busted, Mrs. Austin," I lied. "How will I live?"

"I guess you know how you'll do it," she said, and shut the door.

Presently, there came another knock, and there was big-headed, pop-eyed Captain Austin, in a new shirt, with a tie, and fresh from a bath, smelling of rosewater, his hair slick with grease, the hat in his hands.

"May I sit?" he asked. I nodded. He took a stool. "I heard what happened, and want to say that I think it was raw, it was too rough, I don't agree with it."

"And you know—you know what your wife said to me."

"That was raw, too. I don't hold with that, either. Cast a woman into the street just after she's been through an ordeal like that, if you ask me, I can't see the right of it; it's heartless, and we have no call to act so high and mighty. Well, I guess you know, just from being on the *Flavius* the time you have, me and Mrs. Austin don't see eye to eye on much, and I've decided . . ." He looked down at the hat in his right hand and stroked the underside of its brim. "I've decided we're going to divorce." He looked up, and once again the bulging eyes regarded me. "It's easy to divorce in California. It's a territory. The courts here are easygoing. I think it's safe to say that you and your husband are going to do it. So there you'll be, without a husband, and me without a wife."

"Good God in heaven."

Astonishing myself, I began to laugh.

"Now, hear me out. I'm not offering myself up as a Romeo. I'm rich, and if certain things work out, I'm going to be a whole lot richer. Let's be hardheaded. Neither of us are fools."

"And what would happen to your poor wife after that? Would she be thrown out in the street?"

"Well, I don't know. That would be a little hard."

"I would insist on it," I told him.

"Well, then, we could talk about that. Maybe—well, all right."

I nodded. "That's good. That shows you're serious. And it would certainly give me a great deal of satisfaction. But I can't accept your offer."

"Don't answer so quick. Think about it."

"No, I know now. I won't. Do you want to know why?"

"Why?"

I gave a shrug. "Because you're not rich."

Now, for the first time, his feelings were hurt. "Of course I'm rich. Do you know what I own?"

I nodded. "You own a bunch of land with contested deeds. These water lots are already losing value, because no one can say if the courts will uphold them. They could be worth a fortune one day if the gold holds out, but who knows if it will. Meanwhile, you might lose them. You don't have enough cash to make land, or build a wharf here, or pay a judge to come down on your side. To get it, you went to a bank, Captain Austin, and if that bank would put on a new shirt and some pomade and propose marriage to me, why, I guess I could learn to love it in time."

He shot off the stool like a jack-in-the-box, furious now. "She told you all that? Damn her, she did it to poison your mind against me! And I was going to leave her provided for!"

"What? Behind my back?"

"You didn't say don't provide for her. You just said throw her out."

He put his hand on the door; still, he was only a few paces away from any part of the little cabin. "Wait," I said, because a thought had been germinating quietly in my mind for days—I had glimpsed parts of it in the corners of my eyes, between the tears. I had seen fragments that could not survive by themselves. Now they were assembled, terrible and glorious. I touched his arm. He turned his homely face toward mine, and I think it was the first time he really saw me. "Sit down," I said. "I have a proposition."

I would crush him, that pious upright psalm-singer. I would grind his face in the mud. Whore? I would show him a whore.

I gestured toward the stool. After a moment he sat. "Are you a religious man, Captain Austin?"

"Well, not so you'd notice. I've got nothing against it."

"Nor do I. Religion has its place. But I'm glad you're not too religious, because I don't want to offend you. You've heard of my house on Mercer Street in New York City, and you're willing to overlook it, which is kind of you, but why overlook it? Why not make the most of it? I know how much the *Flavius* brings you now. It could make ten times more as a place of entertainment for men who have been lucky in California. I am not talking of some low bawdy house, but a fine house like the one I had in New York. I would do everything, find the girls, manage them, buy the wine, and arrange for some improvements to make the *Flavius* a place of refinement and luxury for the very best people—including, probably, the judges, merchants, and legislators whose favorable decisions could help your affairs prosper. We'll need fewer, bigger rooms, with better furnishings. I have capital of my own to help pay for that. We'll need female help of other kinds, and since you are sentimental about her, we might keep the former Mrs. Austin on as a general maid and housekeeper. She would have to know she was subordinate to me, be respectful, and stay up to the mark, but if she did all of that, she'd be welcome to stay on at a good salary. Oh, and she must bathe twice a week."

And so we made a bargain. I didn't marry him, nor was I his concubine. It was a business arrangement. Mrs. Austin became a maid of all work. How did she take this treatment? She learned. We must all learn sometime.

A FEW DAYS AFTER CAPTAIN AUSTIN AND I reached our agreement, one of Mrs. Austin's boarders handed me a note from Herbert Owen, suggesting a time and place where we might meet to discuss the divorce. The day after that, I took my best dresses out of my trunks and spent a day freshening them and ironing them, with the help of the recently subjugated Mrs. Austin. Tight-laced, in boots, holding my skirts over the mud, I walked carefully to a French café on the south side of Kearny Street, which had an appearance that might generously be called picturesque: narrow, steep, and irregular; its buildings—some of canvas, some of wood—set low or high according to the level of the ground on which they had been erected; signboards and painted cloth banners in Spanish, French, and German; and sidewalks made out of barrel staves and packing cases and upended tin cans.

Inside the café, beneath a tin ceiling stamped in the shapes of flowers and vines, were rectangular tables. The diners, wearing dirty linen shirts and vests and rumpled frock coats, ate with the usual velocity. I spotted Jeptha and Herbert and walked to their table. As I moved, the patrons swung their heads to keep me in their field of vision while shoveling food into their mouths without pause. As an afterthought, just before I sat down, I looked back at one of them for a few seconds. He rose, took off his hat, and bowed; a few more followed his example, and then the rest of them did, all except Jeptha and Herbert Owen.

"Do you know that man?" asked Jeptha.

"Oh, I know all of them," I said.

Owen put his hand on his friend's shoulder and said sadly, "Jeptha prefers to keep the occasion of your quarrel a secret from these men, and he supposes you want that as well. So we'll discuss what needs to be done in general terms, if you're agreed."

A greasy blackboard gave the bill of fare in French and English, and a waiter in a dirty shirt and torn trousers added to this the astonishing statement that, with sufficient advance warning and for a small fortune, one could have a grizzly-bear steak brought to the table. I ordered extravagantly: fresh eggs, biscuits, and coffee with cream (five times as costly as black coffee). Herbert Owen had soup and mutton. Jeptha had black coffee.

Even here, said Owen, one party in a divorce must sue the other, with grounds, creating a public record and a blot on the sued party's reputation. Our choices were: natural impotence, adultery, extreme cruelty, habitual intemperance, desertion, willful neglect.

"You ought to let me be the petitioner, don't you think?" I said.

Jeptha and Owen looked at each other and back at me. They were inclined to let me have my way: they did not want a court case making Jeptha famous as the Baptist preacher so dumb that he had unknowingly married a parlor-house madam. "All right," said Owen.

"Recite the grounds again," I asked, just to be mean. He did. "Desertion," I said finally.

Owen would prepare the petition. We would appear before a judge in district court, and it should not take long.

Jeptha asked me if I was planning to stay in San Francisco.

"Why? Do you think I should go away? Where should I go?"

"Anywhere, I guess. You're free." '

"I think I will stay here. There are many opportunities for a woman here. A woman could get rich here just doing men's laundry."

"Is that what you plan to do here, laundry?"

"I haven't decided."

I planned to run my business under the name of "Mrs. Jeptha Talbot." Mrs. Talbot's, they'd say, the best damned house in the whole damned town.

I asked him what his plans were. After a hesitation, as though he hated to say a word to me not spoken in contempt, he said that he and Herbert Owen were going to try their hand at prospecting.

Then he was going to give up preaching. I was so shocked that for a moment I forgot I hated him, forgot I didn't believe in God, and I wanted to talk him out of it. The moment passed.

"If you like," he added, and he cleared his throat—I could see this took effort—"if you like, I could ask about Lewis and Edward."

I thought about this, what he might mean by it. When I tried to find a clue in his tired face, I decided it was his essential decency, and I wanted no part of it. "What a gentleman you are. What a good man. What a knight," and I watched him react to each of these compliments as though he were a disgraced officer being ceremoniously stripped of various ribbons and chevrons and epaulettes. "Yes, thank you," I said after a little more time had gone by.

For a moment, nothing was said, and then I took thought. "Not a preacher anymore, really? So quickly?"

He didn't answer. I took another look at him. He was brushed and neat and shaven—he would never neglect such things. In fact, his neck had been scraped pink by the razor; and his hair, which I had cut two weeks ago with scissors that had been mine when I was Harriet Knowles, was pasted and combed across his brow like the hair of a farmer dressed for church. But otherwise he did not look well: his sunken eyes told me he had not slept; his face looked thin, as though he hadn't been eating; and he bore as well, I thought, the subtle marks of an inner struggle over God and Tom Paine and Philippe and me. His deterioration bothered me for a moment almost as if he were still my responsibility, but I pushed the feeling aside. I had to be hard now; I had to show myself stronger than he was.

Of course, if he was not a preacher, perhaps it would hurt him less when I became a madam again—that was too bad, since I wanted so much to hurt him (so I told myself, though at that moment I did not feel it). When we were on Kearny Street again, outside the café, I had another attack of worry for him and said, "But you will go back to it. To preaching."

He gave me a look that reminded me that it was none of my business, and, as if speaking to someone past my shoulder, he said, "I haven't decided."

It was pathetic, really, this show of indifference, and only to be expected after the bile I had spent the last hour feeding him, but it angered me. "Well," I said. "Well, well, well. You sure pulled a fast one." He realized that I was about to shower him with abuse and started walking away. Herbert tipped his hat and followed. I spoke in a normal conversational tone to their backs. "You sure fooled the California Missionary Committee. Here you are, sitting pretty, where everyone wants to be. And those fools paid for it."

They had turned the corner before I was done, and I didn't say the last two sentences out loud. I only thought them. Just the same, he heard me.

IN THE END, I REMEMBERED HOW EFFECTIVE the threat of staining the family name had been with my grandfather, and I decided not to go by "Mrs. Jeptha Talbot." Better to keep a weapon like that in reserve. For that reason, I gave myself a new name and a new past when I became a madam a second time. I became Arabella Ryan, a clergyman's daughter from Baltimore. My precautions did not need to be elaborate. On occasion, someone would tell me the beloved story of the man who threw his wife into the bay when he found out that she had been a parlor-house madam back in the States, and if the storyteller dared to ask me if I had been the wife, I would reply, "Would you like me to say I was?" Often the husband in the story was a minister. But Jeptha was never named. So it did not link us, or link me to my old name. The few people who knew had various reasons to keep quiet. It has remained for me to reveal the truth.

❈ XLVIII ❈

THERE WAS A RESHUFFLING OF CABINS on the *Flavius* as boarders were ejected. Captain Austin and his wife, who remained together, moved into a smaller cabin. I moved into theirs. I let them take their bed, but kept Captain Austin's writing desk and his whale-oil lamp. I also kept the chair. Sitting there, amid the noise of water beating the hull and footsteps on the deck and the hammering of carpenters I had hired to change the boat into a floating palace, I thought and thought. Every item in my world put up its hand, asking for re-examination, and as I made each decision I felt a little better, a little stronger, the voice of my old self saying: Fool, fool, so you thought you could be a minister's wife? Aren't you ashamed? Isn't this better after all? And though I was starting up a new place from scratch, inevitably much about the experience was familiar. It was like returning to a room you had left six months before, and while the servants take the sheets off the furniture and draw the drapes, it all comes back to you, and there is a spurious feeling of immortality in the proof that you can so easily reassume your old life. I bit my lip and chewed on the pen. I wrote to Jocelyn, assuring her that she would be treated like a queen here and I would pay her fare. And I asked her to bring a friend or two—the most beautiful she could find, and they must have wardrobes, and I would pay their fares as well.

Since I did not want my old friend to get yellow fever while waiting for a boat in Panama City or Chagres, I told her to come round the Horn. If she followed my advice, it might be six months or even eight before I saw her. I would have to find my first girls nearer to hand.

Charley, I suddenly realized: I had to see Charley. I went to the Parker House, where I was recognized immediately—not as Harriet Knowles, but as someone like her, as a prosperous denizen of the sporting world—and was treated with friendliness and professional courtesy. When I said the name Charles Cora, there were smiles of fond recognition. He was a legend among gamblers as the man who, in one six-month period, had broken the biggest faro banks in New Orleans, Vicksburg, and Natchez. But Charley wasn't in San Francisco anymore, and his forwarding address had been lost with the burning of a previous incarnation of the Parker

House in the December fire. "Ask Big Pete Hughes, at the El Dorado," I was told. "Big Pete will know."

I went up the street and walked into the El Dorado. Its atmosphere was an agreeable assault on the senses, like a friend grabbing your hand and pulling you onto the dance floor without a by-your-leave. I was enveloped by the music of fiddles and concertinas, by the aromas of slow matches, cigars, and whiskey. Past the hats and heads and shoulders of the crowd, I glimpsed, to my left, a massive bar. Its far end was lost in smoke, and it was accompanied along its vanishing length by the customary appointments of crystal chandeliers, mirrors, and oil paintings of reclining odalisques. A row of slender columns ran down the center of the room; another, crosswise, row supported a balcony. Hung on ropes from the ceiling, rings of globular lamps lit up the gambling tables. The faces of the dealers were childlike and innocent. The faces of the suckers, clutching the dollars they insisted on gambling away, were determined. Pretty French girls sat at some of the tables, not doing anything, merely present, like the wallpaper and the crystal, as reminders of what money can buy.

It was a nice place. I liked it, and I felt at home there right away.

I came in, chin up, back straight, the hook of my parasol lifting my skirts over the sawdust. I sat at a vingt-et-un table, ordered wine and a cigarita, drank and smoked, and lost two hundred dollars with a shrug.

By and by, a fashionably dressed woman—pretty, quite small, red-haired, with freckles and green eyes—sat beside me. She introduced herself as Irene Grogan and said she was the close friend of Mr. Peter Hughes, who was the owner of this establishment, as I might already know. She pointed to a mustachioed ruffian at a table on the mezzanine not far above us; he tipped his hat and nodded. Would I like to meet him? she asked. Yes, I said, and we went up the stairs to his table. He rose to greet me, and I saw that he stood well over six feet. He wore a Prince Albert frock coat with a fur collar, and a crisp white shirt and silk cravat and striped waistcoat and striped trousers, all clean, which was the biggest luxury of all in San Francisco in 1850. On his head was a misshapen, worn-out leather slouch hat, the brim permanently turned up here and down there, so ugly and in such contrast to the rest of his outfit that it couldn't just be his favorite hat; it had to be his lucky hat.

The two of them began feeling me out by asking if I had ever been to New Orleans or New York, and if I knew this or that street or person, and by what route I had come. I answered truthfully but evasively, and finally said I was looking for Charles Cora, who was a friend of mine. Big Pete said he was well acquainted with Charley, a fine feller, "straight as a string," and last he heard he was at the Belle Vista Hotel in Sacramento City. I thanked him.

Then Irene invited me to live and work at her parlor house, a few blocks away from the El Dorado. It was the best in town. I said, "Let's see it," and we walked there. It smelled of sawdust and paint. The girls were pretty, but otherwise it wasn't much. She explained that the previous house had perished in the big fire; curtains and carpets were on order. I told her I would think about it, and she said, "Damnit, I knew it. I told Pete. You're a madam."

"I'm not going to lie," I said.

"You want my honest opinion? Don't do it. We don't need another house here. Go to Sacramento City. They're growing fast. You can get in on the ground floor."

"Sacramento. Oh. Sounds like good advice. I'm glad we met."

"Go fuck yourself." Her face got red. "You're not taking any of my girls. My girls are loyal. I treat them like daughters. They're like daughters to me."

"Your daughters are lovely, but I'm not going to get anywhere here with girls from another house. Gentlemen want fresh girls, and getting them is my lookout. Irene, don't be sore. We shouldn't have to start out this way, but I'm new here, and I had to look things over from the inside before I started throwing my money around."

She said that if I had been honest with her she would have told me anything I needed to know. That was nonsense. Even so, eventually, we became friends. We were competitors, but we also had a community of interest and outlook.

I got to know Big Pete and Irene pretty well. He ran a square gambling house, as such places went. He considered it bad luck to possess a coin smaller than a silver dollar; so every morning, at four o'clock, he collected all the small change the El Dorado had taken in the night before and threw it out among the Indian boys who had come to feed their goats on the refuse of the vegetable market. Irene was volatile but sweet. She and Big Pete were famous for their fights, and once, after a big one, she drugged his wine and shaved his head. That was her idea of vengeance. Big Pete eventually moved to Denver without Irene, and finally I lost track of both of them. Many times, years apart, I have thought that I saw her face, hurt by time, in a restaurant, or among the bathers at an oceanside resort, or in the run-down lobby of a hotel full of aged, indigent women.

SOON AFTER MEETING PETE AND IRENE, I dressed in clothes selected with the intention of dazzling Charley and took the Pacific Mail steamer to Sacramento City, a monstrously overgrown trading post which announced itself with a stench of rotten groceries a few minutes before it came into view. It struck me as a lonelier variation on the theme of San Francisco. Recently, the river had overrun its banks, drowned the city, and receded, leaving dead fish and burlap sacks in the branches of the sycamores. The hillside was littered with heaps of lumber—shacks carried and then abandoned by the swell—and on every standing edifice, a flood line of mud and small leaves like a bathtub ring told me where the waters had reached their highest level. Yet in the streets, by now dry, men were hammering, carrying sacks, leading mules, unloading covered wagons. The gold rush was a flood, too. There had never been anything like it, and there was no stopping it.

The Belle Vista Hotel was a two-story building with a façade that made it look a yard taller than it was. I stood before it, readying myself. At last, I walked in. There was the usual gaudy interior, as though a genie had transported a piece of Monte Carlo onto the unpaved main street of a scrubby town in the middle of nowhere. When I mentioned Charley's name to the bartender, he directed me to a back room, and there he was, in darkness and lamplight in the early afternoon, in the middle of a card game.

"Belle," he said quietly, and put his cards down and gave me a little smile that acknowledged the time that had passed since we had last seen each other. "Gentlemen, this is my old friend Belle." He stood up, and the other men followed his example. He bowed, and looked at them as though a little surprised to see they weren't bowing, too, and so they did.

I sat at the big table in a seat that was brought for me, and he spoke about me in flattering terms in a tone that put me under his protection. I needed to know what was going on with Charley, and I needed to know how I felt about him. Something told me not to pause for one long look but to gather information in a series of glances, from various angles in various lights. His shirt and his vest were of the finest silk, but they were stained; when he put an arm around me, I could smell a history of meals, drinks, cigars, and all-night card games, along with the distinctive smell of Charley's sweat, which I had once grown to like, but not in so highly concentrated a solution. He was a dandy, and in New York he had kept himself immaculate; I wondered if he was down and out, as I knew he was every so often, or if this was the effect of the gold rush, a world of men, a shortage of laundresses. I burrowed into him, not only for comfort but to answer the important question—could he comfort me?—and to help him find a way into my heart. "Papa," I surprised myself by murmuring. It seemed to surprise him, too. I felt him startle and relax, and gradually he pulled away and looked at me quizzically. Perhaps it was then he remembered that he was indeed a papa. We were mother and father together. But what else did I mean by "papa"? I don't think I really knew.

Behind me, the door of this little room opened and shut, changing the light for a moment, and I heard one of the gamblers call for whiskey, and another for sandwiches and a fresh deck. I had another look at Charley. He was past forty now. His face was etched by his habits, by several cigars daily, and whiskey drunk like water from the moment he awoke (generally in the afternoon) to a nightcap just before his eyes closed in sleep (a little before sunrise, sometimes a little after). Fine lines webbed the corners of his eyes. He never did a lick of manual labor. His body was soft. The impression of strength it gave, the strength it actually had in an emergency, was entirely a product of his character.

He won the pot—enough to buy a thousand silk shirts. "You always bring me luck," he said, and I realized he had been down and out after all, for weeks perhaps, but now he wasn't. Now he'd be on a winning streak.

When we were upstairs in his room, I bade him sit in a chair and wait and watch while I stripped to my undergarments. As I sat with my legs across his lap and my arm around his neck, I brought him up to date about Frank, and about Jeptha. I got up and took Anne's letters about Frank out of my carpetbag. "Read them to me," he said.

"Later, Papa." I put the letters back in the bag, and I got on his lap again, this time facing him and straddling him, undoing his shirt buttons, kissing him, making him moan. I gave myself to him and brought him to his crisis right there in the chair, and my flesh had responded just enough to hide that inside I grieved, inside I was waste and desolation. The sadness I thought I had managed to push away rose within me like a whirlwind. I had never known such grief. I felt a kind of panic, fearing that I would break down and cry right in the middle of it, fearing what would happen if Charley saw it, and fearing more than anything that Charley would be no use to me after all, that nothing in the world could really help me and I would die of this grief.

When we were done, I pushed the feeling away, and was cheerful with him—cheerful, as I well knew how to be with a man when I was unhappy—and hoped that he did not notice the falseness of it; most men didn't.

We had supper sent up to the room with champagne. I read the letters, and we talked some more. We undressed down to our skin; he took me again, and we fell asleep. But when I woke up, not long afterward, the awful sorrow had returned, and the tears streamed down. Charley mustn't see those tears. I got up and pulled the chair to the window. I sat looking at the street through a crack in the shade and wept as quietly as I could, until, just behind me, I heard him say softly, "What is it, Belle? What's the matter?" This opened the floodgates—sobs so loud they must have been audible all through the house and outside it, so powerful they hurt my back and made me gasp. It was all there was of me. I could hardly breathe, but I had to speak: "He's broken me, I'm nothing anymore, I'm not even here, I'm in pieces. Oh damnit. I'm so sorry, Charley. It isn't fair. It isn't fair to you. Damnit, damnit, Charley, forgive me."

"You can cry," he said. "Cry it out, go on," he said, kissing me and pulling me to him. "So you're not made of wood. Look, you've got feelings, you're miserable, that don't mean you're broken. You've been down before. You always come back."

"I'm scared. I'm so scared."

"It'll pass. I'll get you through it."

"I'm scared you won't be able to help me."

"You want it, it's yours."

"I'm—you don't understand. I want to love you. I want you to make me love you. I'm scared you won't be able to make me love you."

This stopped him. Neither of us said anything for what seemed like too long a time, so that I thought, *That's it, I've wrecked it.* "Oh," he said at last. "Well, that'll be harder. That's a tall order, all right." A few more seconds passed during which I believe he considered the question quite seriously and objectively; during which—for the first time in his life, probably—he weighed his chances of getting a woman to love him. "What've we got to lose? I'll give it a shot, and we'll see, okay?"

"You're not reliable. You don't want to be reliable."

He laughed, which made me laugh, too, in the middle of the tears and the terror.

"I'll work on that," he said. "Now that I'm a papa, I gotta work on that."

"All right," I said.

"Feel better?"

I nodded. "A little."

"Good."

We were both quiet for a while. Then he said, "California is a good place for people like us." He thought a little bit more and said, quietly but with a good deal more force than was usual for him, "I mean . . . just look at you. Look at what you've got—inside and out. Show me anybody else like you."

"Oh, Charley."

"You'll show them."

"Say, 'We'll show them,' Charley."

"Sure. Okay. We'll show them."

He looked at me a little longer and said, "Why don't you come to bed? You gotta cry, cry where it's comfortable."

I went back to the bed, and I didn't feel the need to cry anymore. I laid my head on his chest, and sleep came.

HE HAD AFFAIRS TO WRAP UP in Sacramento City, and, with one thing and another, it took a month for us to be together again. After that—he was right, it was a symptom of California's freakishness in those times that it was an excellent place for people like us. In San Francisco especially, where many rules were suspended as unworkable until certain necessary equipment had belatedly arrived from the States, we were as close to respectable as anyone in our professions could ever be. This acceptance was never perfect, nor was it the same for both of us. In houses that contained lawful wives, Charley was welcome and I was not. We were both shunned by a few prudes who, it turned out, had principles, the simple, honest prudes discovering right here, for the first time, that they alone actually believed the things that most everyone back east pretended to believe. But generally, in this city ordered by the appetites of young men a continent from home, we stood high in the social pyramid, friendly with fellows whose names today adorn equestrian statues, multi-volume biographies, and street maps. One day, chins up, standing partly to the side and a little out in front of their wives, they would demand that I leave the city that it might purify itself of evil, but now these men, who knew us from Big Pete's El Dorado and from my parlor house, were openly friendly to us in restaurants and theaters and at races and base-ball games. They doffed their hats to me, and they were so respectful to my girls I almost forgot there was shame in what we did.

Though Charley had a fine practical understanding of men and women, I never heard him say a word against a single one of them. He never aired his views on general matters or spoke of his philosophy. Yet his whole life was like a studied insult to the Protestant convictions of the people among whom my childhood was spent. The black-clad men who handed out Bibles on the New York waterfront and the pioneer farmers who washed each other's feet in their puncheon-floored church had divided humanity into the saved and the damned. They had believed in hard work and self-denial. They were builders. Even at their most superstitious they were modern, whereas there were men like Charley in Carthage and Babylon. For him the great division was between sporting people and all the others. He believed in skill, luck, fate, pleasure, and loy-alty. He did not believe in equality or progress. He was a hunter. He exer-cised his profession, which was also his passion, in short, intense stints. The rest of his life was a vacation spent in the company of his friends in barbershops and saloons, cock pits and shooting galleries, theaters and hotels and gambling halls. He was useful only in his seignorial generosity, supplying funds to any friend who needed to be helped through a hard time, good to waiters, washerwomen, cripples, and shoeshine boys. There are white-haired men today, cutting hair, tending bar, cadging drinks, in the bits of old San Francisco that survived the earthquake, who still speak of him fondly.

He was flush or broke—that was the nature of his profession—but flush much more often than broke. I was always flush. We lived well.

. . .

SOMETHING WAS MISSING. Something always is. Is anyone ever really perfectly content? Unless we are crushed by care, or in a desperate struggle that leaves no time for reflection, we are all restless and dissatisfied, if only because none of us can have his cake and eat it, too. As in some houses certain rooms are locked and left just as they were on the day a child disappeared, so certain rooms in my heart were left unvisited, but dimly remembered amid the gayest revels.

Sometimes I felt blue. I would watch myself from the outside and say, "She only thinks she's having fun." Sometimes I was sure I had made a terrible mistake: better to live out a life of starchy repentance somewhere my secrets would never be discovered, send for Frank, tell everyone his father was dead, start again—nothing for me, everything for the blameless product of my sin, my boy! That looked good in a daydream. Then, moody and irritable, I would pick a fight with Charley, but Charley wouldn't fight. In a fight with Charley, I was the raging sea, he the immovable cliff; my victory was certain if I persisted a million years. He formed the notion that I had moods. He put on his hat and found other company until I was feeling better.

"Send for him if you miss him so much," Charley would say, when I fretted out loud about Frank.

"You don't understand. I can't have him growing up in a brothel," I'd say.

"Rent a house for him. Hire a nanny. He can live two blocks away with the nanny. You could see him all the time. You don't have to say you're his mother."

"But by the time he grew up he'd figure it out. He'd hate me."

Once he said, "You keep thinking of reasons why it can't be done. Maybe you don't really want him." I didn't talk to him for a week, and after that he never said it again, and I didn't bring it up again for a long time.

Another time, we had one of these conversations, and he said just what he always said, with the same words and the same shrug, but somehow his reasoning found me in a receptive mood. I sat at the desk that had once belonged to Captain Austin and wrote a letter to Anne in Livy, thanking her for all she had done to help Frank, the little orphan, while my life was unsettled. Now, though, as I had told her earlier, Jeptha and

I had divorced, I had remarried; and my new husband, a prosperous banker, was eager to adopt the infant with whom I had formed such a strong attachment in the first year of his life. I would make arrangements for a woman who was making the trip west to take him to San Francisco by sea.

A little over three months later, a letter came back from Anne, politely refusing my request—saying that I could not mean it, I must not have been thinking straight when I wrote that letter. That, hard as it must have been for me, I had done the right thing by bringing Frank to Livy. He was happy in their house. It would be wrong to uproot him. Besides, Frank was a frail child, and such a journey might kill him. I wouldn't want that to happen, would I? (The suggestion that I needed to be told how to feel about the prospect of my son's death made me so angry that I wasted paper on three replies I had to tear up.) I realized that my request must have hurt her, and I wrote to her apologizing, and making my case again, more subtly. She was not moved, though she held out a little thread of hope that when he was older perhaps things would be different.

I had always assumed that Anne would consider the bond of a child and mother sacred, so her resistance was a blow to me. But it made things easier, too. It was out of my hands.

In San Francisco, I was never one of the attractions in my own house, though I traded a good deal in false hope, as I believe even respectable women do if they are pretty. According to my fictitious life story, I had been seduced long ago by a rich man whose family would have disowned him had we married, I had buried that fellow's child, and except for him I had never known any man but Charles Cora.

He was, so far as I ever found out, faithful to me, and scrupulous in his insistence that I be treated respectfully. He took it for granted that this was our town. Towns like this, if they served any purpose, existed for the convenience of gamblers and whores.

Today, when people like us are spoken of, we occupy a position some-where below the Indians in a Wild West show. We are symptoms of law-lessness, villains, necessary only so that in defeating us the heroes may exercise their fortitude. What did we produce? Nothing. We dug no gold. We built no wharves, warehouses, or factories. We fed on the dreams of reckless young men. That's one view. I understand it perfectly, but I can't help feeling that it overlooks important truths about gold rushes, cities, and the world. Though it is true we added nothing practical to San Francisco, we were in perfect harmony with the spirit of the place. I think we resembled the gods of ancient times, who could be selfish and cruel, yet were never really useless. Why do men arise in the morning, work, risk, endure, if not for desire, which is as necessary to human progress as the sun? For a few years, Charley and I were the incarnations of greed and concupiscence, Mammon and Venus; and whatever lying prayers your lips may utter, in your hearts you pray to us.

Book Five

{ 1851–1861 }

THE ATTENTIVE READER WILL OBSERVE THAT sometimes in the course of this narrative I claim the playwright's prerogative of leaping forward in time. I skip over months or years, to the moment of a crisis in my affairs; and we discover that certain cast members have disappeared, while others, who spent the whole previous act in exile, have apparently returned long ago. It all happened in the interval, while the audience perambulated in the lobby, smoking cigars and drinking refreshments.

Still, even in a play, when the curtain rises, there is a moment for learning all we can from the new props we find on the stage, and a helpful line in the playbill tells us where we are and what the year is. Very well: We find ourselves in a fancy house with entrances on Dupont Street and Washington Street, in February of 1851, in a city that is still in flux. San Francisco has burned down three times more since the fire I saw from the deck of the *Flavius* a little over a year ago. It has been in each instance quickly rebuilt, larger and more substantial than before, in a miracle wrought by the gold of California. Ships more full of treasure than the galleons of New Spain leave our port monthly, and each day from the States—as we still call the main body of the country, though California now *is* a state— come other ships, laden with every simple necessity and idle luxury that human labor can provide, all cheaper to sail around the Horn or drag across Panama than to make here. Even brick and limestone, trousers, apples, and ice are cheaper to import. Men send their shirts to be laundered in Hawaii.

I am twenty-two years old. It is a year since Jeptha threw me in the bay. But as Mrs. Austin has remarked, things happen quickly in this city. It seems much longer, and I feel much older. I've been busy. Eighteen forty-nine, the *Juniper*, Rio—that was another life. I don't think about it. Edward and Lewis are back in town, after a falling out in the mining camps. Edward, after trying his hand at many things, now works as a reporter for the *San Francisco Herald*. Lewis lives very irregularly; he has done things that don't bear close examination. He and Edward see each other sometimes, but they aren't on very good terms.

I meet them both occasionally, but not at my house, because I don't want their family connection to me known.

Edward has said: "I know how it is between you and Lewis. But I have to be honest with you: if you want anything in this life except worry and heartbreak, you have to know that Lewis is a dead man. It will be a miracle if he sees twenty-five. He lives by the sword. He likes hurting people. I've seen it. And he's reckless. Men like that die young. We've got to resign ourselves."

And I have said this in reply: "Our mother told me what my responsibility was toward Lewis. I have lived up to it, and *he*, what *he* has done for *me*, what *he* and *I* are to each other—don't pretend you understand that. Only Lewis and I understand that. We're a family of two, he and I. You're an agreeable fellow, Edward, but I have no notion what you use in place of a heart."

We made up and agreed to be friends. Edward was shocked to learn how I make my living, but that did not last long, and he is by now quite comfortable with the idea. I think he actually likes me better this way. It confirms his view of women. From Edward, I found out that Robert knows. My grandfather must have told him. Robert loves me, so he is heartbroken, but wishes to have no further communication with me.

From the street, my house looks plain, two stories tall, with an unpainted exterior. It is not meant to excite the curiosity of pedestrians. Still, anyone who has been in San Francisco for over a week has heard all about it. They know that when you knock on that unassuming door on Dupont Street you are met by a Negro maid or footman, better dressed and cleaner than ninety-nine out of a hundred of the inhabitants in this raw and grimy city. Your eyes, long accustomed to disorder and squalor, behold what appears to be a hallway in some European palace—Brussels carpets, damask curtains, crystal chandeliers, mirrors, paintings, mahogany surfaces rubbed by servants until their laboring hands are reflected in the wood. Perhaps briefly you glimpse one of the inhabitants, the sweets in this improbable candy box, the costliest luxury of all.

To the best house in San Francisco come the best men of San Francisco: bankers, merchants, ship owners, real-estate developers, judges, the mayor, the aldermen, the collector of the port. Their friendship helps me in several ways. They spend money in my house. Thanks to them, no laws hostile to my business are passed, and ruffians do not break into my house and mistreat my girls. Thanks to them, my house is popular even when the city is in one of its periodic business slumps. There is still money to be made during hard times if you know the people who pull the strings—and they are all here, the leading bankers, merchants, and ship owners, the judges, the mayor, the aldermen, the collector of the port. All I have to do is keep them happy.

A GENTLEMAN SITS ON A SOFA in my parlor. His left hand strokes the leaves of a potted palm. His right hand stroke's Pauline's cheek. He has made his fortune, never mind how, and will leave by steamer tomorrow, and have no further part in my story. I mention him solely because of the information he is about to impart.

Give him wide-apart eyes and a wide mouth: a frog face. Not old, maybe twenty-five. He's smart. He likes people to know it. He talks about the war that is coming to San Francisco. "You girls are going to be in the middle of it," he declares, and he offers Pauline his wineglass and watches her sip.

I recline on a sofa that faces theirs, and though he talks to Pauline, he often glances at me. I'm the one he wants to impress, or help—I'm not sure which. "On one side, it's State Senator David Broderick and his friends—immigrant laborers who cast their votes for the Democratic Party. On the other side, it's Sam Brannan and his people—Know-Nothings."

Pauline licks her lips. "Know Nothings," she says in a careful way that draws attention to her mouth. "Am I one of those?"

He taps the end of her nose. "Soon, my pet, we'll go upstairs and discover what you know." He looks at me. "The Know-Nothings are simply men who hate immigrants and the children of immigrants. They especially despise Irish Catholics.

"Now, you know that in San Francisco many of our laboring men are Irish Catholics and members of the Democratic Party, and they all worship David Broderick, because he used to be one of them. They think he walks on water. They made him a senator. They'll vote for an old shoe if he tells them to. Against Broderick, and hating him like poison, are the bankers and merchants and auctioneers and newspapermen, who are mostly Protestants and Know-Nothings. Their leader is Sam Brannan, the richest man in San Francisco—he comes to this house sometimes, doesn't he?" (So he did; special requests; money no object.) "Have you ever had Sam Brannan?"

"I?" says Pauline deliciously. "I told you, I'm a virgin." She does this very well, and as a result, we both realize, the frog-eyed gentleman is ready to take her upstairs.

But I want to hear the rest, and to her annoyance, I say, "So it is Brannan, and the rich natives, against Senator Broderick and laboring immigrants."

He blinks, nods, and says distractedly, "With, in between, a lot of native, Protestant laborers who, at election time, might go either way."

"And who is the bad one?" Pauline asks, squinting at me: Is this really what you want? Are we in a lecture hall? Time is money, no?

His fingertip toys with a corkscrew curl beside her brow. "The honorable Senator Broderick does lots of dishonest things. He's from New York—so, you know, New York politics. Uses his boys, tough fellows, to keep his opponents away from the polls at election time. When he wins, he rewards his cronies with city jobs and he plunders the treasury."

"So David Broderick is a thief," I say, "and Sam Brannan is a hero."

He smiles slyly; he knows I've made a joke. "Sam Brannan is a slippery fellow. You know how he made his fortune—what he did to poor Mr. Sutter." I do; it is the founding legend of our city and everyone here knows it, the way everyone in ancient Rome knew the story of Romulus and Remus. But he repeats the tale anyway. "Brannan used to be a Mormon elder . . ." he reminds us. In 1846, he came to San Francisco (then a small village with another name), leading fifty bigamous families who shared his dream of turning the West Coast of North America into a Mormon republic. In 1848, several of the families found work in what is now Sacramento City, building a sawmill for a man named John Sutter—building Sutter's Mill, later to be inscribed in numberless schoolchildren's composition books as the place where gold was first discovered in California. Brannan, who was always starting small business ventures, opened up a general store near the mill. One day, his people showed him some gold nuggets they had found while at their work. They told him of Sutter's predicament: gold was a fine thing, but his claim to the land was uncertain; he must keep the discovery quiet until he was firmly in possession. Brannan urged his people to keep the secret, telling them that that way they could look for other gold deposits around here without having the whole world pour in to elbow them aside. Very quietly, Brannan purchased every pick and shovel in the West, and choice waterfront property in San Francisco. Then he ran down the street with a horn full of gold dust, screaming, "Gold! Gold from the American River!" The gold seekers came like locusts. Sutter was ruined. The Mormon laborers stayed broke. There was no Mormon empire, since the hordes that came to California from all over the world were not Mormons. But Sam Brannan became the prototype of the rascal who gets rich by mining the gold in the pockets of the miners.

"Now Sam Brannan and his friends have all the money in the city, but David Broderick controls the government. Brannan means to change that. And I know how. I—who was privileged to be present when Mr. Brannan was even drunker than usual—I know his plan. With the excuse of all the crime that you have in any city this size, and the fires that keep destroying the town because it is made of kindling, Mr. Brannan and his friends will form a Vigilance Committee like the ones in the mining camps. They'll say they're going to clean up the city. They'll lynch a few robbers to show they can do it, and then they will run Mr. Broderick and his men out of town. Only Mr. Broderick is not the sort to go without a fight; the bloodier it gets, the more he likes it."

He stands up and takes Pauline by the hand. He looks back at me. "I don't have a dog in the fight, not anymore. But you do, Belle. Because you have to be friends with whoever comes out on top, and you don't know who that's going to be, do you."

He bows to Pauline—*After you*—and they retire to her room on the second floor.

❧ L ❧

A FEW DAYS LATER, I HEARD a tremendous clamor in Portsmouth Square, one block west of my house. I went up to the roof and observed a great mass of people packing the streets and the field near City Hall and looking upward, as if someone was giving an address from the balcony. I went out to the plaza to see what was going on, but by the time I arrived the crowd was dispersing. As the men walked off in various directions, I noticed the handbills scattered all around me. Some of these pages, caught in a breeze, quivered like live creatures on the wooden streets and sidewalks. Others momentarily took flight, or floated in puddles, or were firmly trodden into the mud. "What's happened?" I asked a young man in a miner's outfit, who, coming closer, emitted a yeasty reek of whiskey, bobbed forward and back on his feet, and stared at me as if I might be a product of his delirium. Another man, in a long black coat, having overheard my question, said, "They called off the hanging; maybe they'll have it later," in the same tone as one might mention the postponement of a boxing match. He removed his tall black hat and knelt; with his free hand he picked up a page that bore a boot print, and held it open before me. The handbill invited "all those who wish to rid our city of thieves and murderers" to come to Portsmouth Square today.

I heard my name shouted. I saw a familiar misshapen slouch hat (now with patches) and a black silk hat, and a moment later, as a clutch of men between us happened to move away, I saw Charley and Pete. I walked toward them. Charley kissed me and took my arm, and the two of them told me what had happened.

Three days earlier, a store owner had been knocked on the head and robbed of two thousand dollars. The police had caught the man suspected of the crime: the notorious English Jim, from London by way of the vast British prison that was Australia. Somehow or other, Sam Brannan and his friends had gotten English Jim away from the police and had sent out these handbills calling for a rally in Portsmouth Square, where, just now, from the balcony of City Hall, Brannan had given a speech in favor of hanging the thief immediately ("No courts! No lawyer's tricks!"). The mayor had then spoken out on behalf of constituted authority—don't be hasty, let the law take its course—and at last a man with the heroic appellation of William Tell Coleman had suggested the compromise of a small trial, a people's trial, free of legal technicalities and guaranteed to be over by sundown. The crowd had not been told where the trial would take place, but Big Pete had a tip that Brannan had commandeered the recorder's office on the second floor of City Hall, and curiosity led us to the office.

The recorder's office, ordinarily a place where deeds were registered, smelled so strongly of stale sweat, unwashed feet, whiskey, and rotting teeth that one greeted the lighting of cigars with relief. Men tipped their hats and offered me their seats, and I sat near the front, close to the windows; Charley and Pete stood along the back of the room, near the door. There were many silk hats and black frock coats, but also many flannel shirts and bandannas, not because any laboring men were here but because San Francisco's rich thought of themselves as frontiersmen and took their tone from the miners. In the front row, turning to speak to some men behind him, sat Sam Brannan, looking moderately drunk, as he always was by this time of day. He was tall and angular, with a nar-row, goatlike face, shaggy sideburns like two big brown brushes down to his chin, a long skinny nose, and sleepy eyes that never participated in the rest of his expression; they had the same fatigued look whether he was saying that tonight he would take three of my gals to bed with him at once and use them in ways I had never imagined—how much would that cost?—he had the money!—or screaming that gold had been discovered at Sutter's Mill; or that a man should be hung right away, without any lawyer's tricks. Fantastic overnight success, success such as no man could achieve by his merits, had gone to his head; only his complete destruction could teach him anything now. Brannan was talking in a friendly way to a long-haired, clean-shaven fellow, uncommonly handsome, who I later found out was William Tell Coleman, the man who had suggested giving English Jim the courtesy of a mock trial before they hanged him. (The prisoner kept on insisting that he was not English Jim and had never even heard of English Jim, and furthermore that he had not robbed any store, but no one believed him.)

I searched the room for habitués of my house. With an impact as palpable as a stone striking my chest, I saw Jeptha seated beside Herbert Owen on the side of the room farthest from the windows: I watched them until Jeptha looked up. He returned my glance calmly. I thought perhaps he had seen me first and had time to collect himself. Certainly I hoped that's what it was. To demonstrate my indifference, I gave him a tepid smile. He turned away from me. With a dry mouth, I asked the man beside me, "Who's the preacher?" for Jeptha was wearing a white clerical collar, and another man said, "Reverend Talbot, he's the new minister at the Unitarian church on Clay Street."

My heart beat against my ribs as if to say I could stay here if I wanted, but *it* was getting out of this terrible place. I had seen him last almost exactly a year ago, when he was about to go to the mines with Herbert Owen. I knew from advertisements in the newspapers that Herbert Owen had returned to San Francisco and opened up an auction house. I had wondered what had happened to Jeptha of course.

At two o'clock, the trial began. Despite its location in a government office, it was an illegal trial, circumventing regular judicial processes so that a man might be hanged that very evening by the men now playing the roles of prosecutor, defense, judge, and jury.

I kept trying to see it through Jeptha's eyes, but that was hard, because I did not know what his opinions were now. Was he a Brannan man or a Broderick man? Unless he was changed beyond recognition, he would think that the prisoner was innocent until proved guilty. But Jeptha had not spoken. Perhaps he was planning to speak up if it actually came to the rope. Jesus had been lynched—he would make that point. And I would stand up and shout out: Gentlemen, don't let this man confuse you. I know him. He's a killer. He killed a child on the *Juniper,* and another, our child, on the *Flavius*. Do you admire me, gentlemen? Give me justice; enjoy my gratitude. And the cry would go up: Hang him! You heard the lady! No lawyers! Hang him!

WITH ALL THE DULL PARTS LEFT OUT, the trial went quickly. There was an intermission while the jury went to question the injured store owner in his home a few blocks away. Spectators shared flasks of whiskey. I got up to talk to Charley and Big Pete.

"You'll never guess who's in the room," I murmured as coolly as I could. "My former husband. The preacher," I said, and I pointed toward

Jeptha, and just as I was pointing, a young woman who had come in by way of the door behind us walked to his chair; I had not yet seen her face, but I knew who she was without quite believing it. When she reached the row where Jeptha and Herbert Owen were sitting, she took out a jug and some sandwiches. I wanted to sit down or lean on something, but there was nowhere to sit, and nothing to lean on except Charley, while he watched me with his tranquil brown eyes that missed nothing and revealed nothing. "That's my cousin Agnes."

Agnes sat with Jeptha for a while, talking with him and watching him eat and drink. She offered him her cheek and he kissed it; he rose to escort her out, but she shook her head and left. Her clothes were simple and becoming. She looked cleaner than soap. The men's eyes were on her, and if for me men had removed their hats, for her they laid their hats solemnly across their chests, as if she were the American flag. They *did* make a distinction between her kind of woman and mine, after all.

There was a wedding ring on her hand. I felt the bile rising in my throat.

THE JURY RETURNED, HAVING SPOKEN to the wounded shopkeeper in his home and given him an opportunity to identify the prisoner. Witnesses came forward to say that English Jim had also committed a murder in a mining camp, so the jury need not feel uneasy about hanging the man merely for theft. The jury retired. When they filed back into the room an hour later, the foreman said they had not been able to reach a unanimous decision.

"Hang 'im! Majority rules!" yelled Brannan, and some like-minded men cried, "Who bribed the jury?" and "Hang the jury!" The jurors drew their guns. I rejoined Charley and Big Pete, and we left.

THE NEXT MORNING, I WENT TO Herbert Owen's auction house. Though I had furnished my house from auctions, until now I had avoided Herbert Owen's establishment, because I did not think it would be good for my peace of mind to hear of his adventures with Jeptha in the gold fields. But now my peace of mind was gone, and I was trying to restore it.

Herbert's place was located half a block from the edge of the fourth great fire. The neighborhood still smelled of ashes, and I passed the misshapen remnants of the prefabricated iron buildings that had been put up after the third fire, the insides of which had been intolerable in warm weather. Their owners had been willing to work in buildings that were as hot as stoves in exchange for the confidence that they would never burn. Instead of burning, these iron buildings had melted.

Owen stood at a high desk, running an auction, when I came in. I sat in the back row. He wore a black frock coat, a black satin waistcoat, and a silk hat. When he noticed me, he gave me a big smile. A year in California was like ten years back east, and to him I counted as an old friend from his pioneer days.

When I had been there about twenty minutes, he announced "Lot Seventeen" and lovingly put a handsome wood-and-leather case on the desk. With a stage magician's sign language—with the salesmanlike dexterity that makes objects look justifiably proud—he snapped open the brass catches, turned the case, and raised its lid to afford us a forbidden peek at two solid-gold-handled derringers on a green baize lining: virgins both, fired just once, at the factory, to make sure that they could do their duty when the fatal hour arrived. A few bids later, they were mine. Some of the men in the room knew who I was, and I heard this well-informed group telling the others that the pistols had been bought by a parlor-house madam, no doubt as a gift for her lover, an Italian gambler.

When the day's business had been done, Herbert Owen invited me to a quiet room full of curious objects and uncorked a bottle of champagne that came from the cellar of a man who had briefly flourished as a waterfront developer. Owen had found success here; he seemed much more confident than the man I had known aboard the *Juniper*.

I drained my glass. "Tell me about Jeptha and Agnes," I said, unable to wait any longer. "How in the world could such a thing occur? Did he ever tell you what she did?"

"I think . . ." he began carefully. "I believe, yes, that I know what you refer to."

"Are we still friends, Herbert? Did he poison your mind against me?"

"No, I like you both. I always have."

"Then be candid with me. Don't spare my feelings. Tell me everything."

"I guess you deserve to know," he said, rubbing his chin, and he began:

"Last year, when we were getting ready to go to the mines, he started drinking a great deal."

"We're talking about Jeptha."

"Yes. We walked into a saloon one day, and . . . he said something peculiar. He said he hadn't had strong drink since he was a boy."

I shut my eyes for a while, remembering 1837.

"After that, every evening he'd drink. He'd toss four or five drinks down his throat, and then he'd pick a fight with a stranger, which would come to fists. Once, while he was drunk, he posted a letter. I asked who it was to; he said, 'The girl I left behind.'

"This all happened over about a week. By then we were outfitted and we left town. There'd been so much rain, the roads were like porridge. We started prospecting one place and another. At a few places we made enough to meet expenses, and about six months after we left San Francisco, we found a placer that we were experienced enough to know was going to be very good. We started working it. In the camp, he was sober all day; he saved his drinking for the evening. By then people had gotten wind of our strike, and we had lots of neighbors, and we couldn't stop them—the rule is, we're only entitled to twenty feet apiece. In the camp, in the evenings, after he drank, he would quarrel until punches were thrown, and it was dangerous now, because there were serious things to fight over, like water rights and boundaries, and every other man had a Colt in his belt. I tried to be his friend, but it was difficult: he was dirty, he stank, he let his beard grow. His ribs showed, and he had a festering ulcer on his shin. One day we heard a loud noise up and down the river. Men were shouting and whooping. But it wasn't gold they were shouting about. It was a woman. It was Agnes. She found Jeptha, and he was dumbfounded. She took his hand, and looked him over, and started sobbing, and . . ." Owen stopped, his head down, looking across his brows for permission to go on.

"I told you, don't spare me."

"She said, 'Look what she's done to you. I will do better.' I left them to talk in private. The next time he and I were alone he said, 'She came all this way—by Panama. She risked her life.' He told her about Philippe, but she said she already knew, because it had been in his letter. 'She says I wrote to her,' he said. I told him he had. He said, 'I don't remember! I must have been drunk. What am I going to do?' I said, 'I don't think it's up to you anymore.' I judged that just from what I'd already seen of her. She'd traveled two thousand miles for him. She must have set off as soon as she got his letter."

I looked at the ceiling for a while, picturing that scene, letting it work on me.

"How much gold did you find?" I asked after a while. "Did you get rich?"

"I was already rich; my family is rich. But it was enough for me to start this business without their help, and enough for Jeptha to buy a house in Happy Valley and put up a third of the money needed to build the church. Really just enough so it counts as success, which is everything here. At all events, Agnes took him in hand, cleaned him up, and nursed him, and she talked to him about God, and I don't know what was said, but I'm pretty sure it was she who decided that he had become a Unitarian, or maybe just that he could still use his gifts and do some good, and not think that he'd cheated the people who sent him here. It couldn't have been more than two weeks before he married her."

"Well," I said at last, "if I were a vengeful woman . . ." I stopped, and when I was sure my voice would be steady, I began again: "If I were vengeful, I could embarrass him. He's a minister, and his ex-wife is a parlor-house madam. I could turn them into a pair of clowns with that news. But I won't. Tell them that when you see them. I'll keep the secret so long as they do. And you won't tell anyone, either, will you, Herbert?"

"Whatever you want, Belle."

I felt restless and agitated. I wanted to take a walk, to be alone with my thoughts, but I didn't want to show Herbert Owen the full degree of my distress, so I made myself stay awhile longer. We talked over old times on the *Juniper,* and what had happened to various passengers we knew from those days.

At this time, I was asking everybody about David Broderick and Sam Brannan. It turned out that, like most of the businessmen in town, Owen was a Brannan man.

I ARRANGED THROUGH A RESPECTABLE INTERMEDIARY to rent a seat on a pew at the Clay Street Unitarian Church. It was a new wood-frame building smelling of paint and sawdust, between a bank and a saddle-

and-harness store. From the outside, it looked more like a Masonic temple than a church. Inside, one crossed a lobby into a cavernous room where services were held. Heavenly rays complete with swirling dust motes shone down at steep angles through tall, narrow windows along high walls left and right, on men prosperous enough to have brought their wives to California. Nearly a quarter of the congregation was female.

And here I was, hardly understanding why, trying to look brassy and be a hussy, but terrified to be in this big hollow room because of the man here, this tyrant over my emotions. I felt at that moment that everything I had done this last year I had done only for the purpose of pushing him out of my thoughts; and now he had ruined it; he had started a war against me, by returning to my city and marrying my enemy. I could not let him alone, because he wasn't letting me alone.

As I walked with a folded parasol down the center aisle, most of the men and women who turned to look at me did so because I was lovely and dressed like a delicious confection. A few of the men gave me knowing or surprised looks; one wagged his finger at me—waist-high, to keep it a secret between us. My pew was the third from the front, as close as I had been able to get. Jeptha was only a few yards away, standing at the pulpit, looking strong and healthy. She had accomplished that. She had taken him in hand. He gave me a nod of welcome appropriate to a pastor seeing a new face in his large, well-attended church; but I was confident I was making him uncomfortable. He was trapped. This was what I had come for—to remind him that he was a hypocrite with a sin on his conscience, like that preacher in *The Scarlet Letter*. Agnes played the harmonium, sitting at a bench behind the instrument, a little to the rear of the choir but visible to the congregation, which she faced at a slight angle. So she, too, was trapped. She certainly would not want it known that I had been married to Jeptha once, and my presence was perhaps a torment to her, but she was more resourceful in these things than he was—she returned my look and filled her eyes with pity for my degraded condition.

When I left, it seemed to me that I had gotten the worst of it. The following week I didn't come, but I couldn't think straight, wondering what was going on and whether Jeptha and Agnes were discussing my absence, my defeat. So, on the third Sunday, I was back, and then I went Sunday after Sunday, though it tortured me to watch him, knowing he belonged to someone else. I wondered what their fun was, and what they talked about, and what they did together in bed.

Eventually, I learned from one of my Unitarian customers that I had created a controversy. Several female members of the congregation had signed a petition demanding that I be banned from the church, because respectable women should not have to be in my presence. Several others had replied with a petition that I be allowed to attend, because Mary Magdalene had been such a good friend to Jesus, and because the hope of my redemption was more important than the disagreeable feelings I aroused; and though there were fewer names on the second petition, it was the one that prevailed. It bore the most important signature, the signature of the pastor's pretty wife.

The congregation's developing attitude toward me was reflected in the changing composition of my pew. One awful Sunday, I was alone on my bench, while the godly were jam-packed hip to hip in all the others. The next Sunday, some bachelors joined me on my lonely bench; and the next Sunday, well-meaning wives, one of whom handed me a tract from the Magdalene Society. The week after that, thanking her, I made her a gift of *Marital Chastity,* the very copy presented to me a lifetime ago by Mrs. Danforth just before my marriage.

From behind the harmonium, Agnes smiled at me. I smiled back. We hurt each other. Were his dreams troubled by the memory of my flesh? She had to wonder.

Charley generally woke up long after services were over on Sundays. I was ready with explanations for my behavior, some of which I believed, should he ever ask.

LI

THAT SPRING, THE CITY WAS FULL of worried men. My business was good, but business in general was bad. Out there in the mining camps and the towns, people weren't buying much. Fewer were coming to California in the first place. Warehouses were glutted. My gentlemen talked about conditions while spending liberally to distract themselves. Tom had gone bankrupt. Harry had gone back to the States. Dick had gotten bad news from home and shot himself.

Even successful men had to worry, for California riches were so often temporary. They seemed *by nature* temporary. One heard constantly of newspaper peddlers and street sweepers in San Francisco who, a year ago, had been "worth a hundred thousand," and lost it by trying to corner the market in rice, or by being sued for the actions of a dishonest partner whose present whereabouts were unknown.

With their nerves in this excited state, men began to look around, not so much for a group to blame as for a magical solution to the problem, a human sacrifice with which to bribe the gods. There was an ominous spirit in the air. This new creature we had not yet learned to call the Gold Rush was undergoing a metamorphosis possibly natural to its kind. We felt a little of what the French must have felt during the various unfolding phases of their revolution. What came next? No human being knew, but the thing knew, *it* knew.

I recall the spring of 1851 with the split vision familiar to people who have participated in famous events. Every few years there is an article or a book, and even if I quarrel with its contents, some little part of it is a revelation: so *that's* what was going on! I have, today, a mountaintop view of matters that were then too near to be understood.

I remember the flavor of the jam on my biscuit and the name of the newspaper in my hand when I learned that English Jim (still claiming, first of all, that he was innocent of the robbery, and, secondly, that he was not English Jim) had been convicted in a regular court and sentenced to hang. And I remember hearing bells and smelling smoke, and going out to see what was happening, and almost losing control of my frightened horse, and paying laborers, all Australians, to empty the house in case the fire's rapid march brought it as far as Dupont and Washington (it did not). It was Angelique who told me solemnly over breakfast that the fire had been started by friends of English Jim, to punish the city for convicting him. So she had heard: it was a popular theory at the time.

Angelique was a big, splendid girl with stubbornly medieval notions of the world. She knew that red-haired men could not be trusted, and that her sister in North Carolina was a coward from birth because her mother had been frightened by a horse during the pregnancy. Half of what she earned each night at my house she lost at the El Dorado's roulette wheel, because she knew that lucky numbers were predicted in her dreams, as interpreted by *Old Aunt Dinah's Policy Dream Book*. She knew, having been told it was so by the newspapers that Pauline read aloud to her, that all the crimes in San Francisco were the doing of one well-organized gang directed by English Jim, who was still calling the shots from his prison cell. And either Senator Broderick was in the pay of English Jim, or English Jim was paid by Broderick, she wasn't sure.

One day I overheard Pauline read to Angelique an article from the *Alta California,* San Francisco's leading newspaper, which had been founded by Sam Brannan and expressed his views. The best men of the town, the paper reported, had banded together to form a Committee of Vigilance. Out of fear of reprisals from the vigilantes' targets, the membership of the committee could not be revealed. It was organized as a secret society, with secret passwords, and weapons. But any honest citizen could join, and the committee was not to be feared, because only dangerous and lawless people would be hurt by it—only criminals, and incendiaries, and the corrupt politicians who helped them. No name was mentioned, but everyone knew whom they meant.

So it was true. There was to be a little war between Brannan and Broderick, and I must see to it that both sides would feel themselves beholden to me. Sam Brannan, during his last debauch at my house, had warned me that even whores and madams were going to get off the fence, and if he saw Judge Edward McGowan or any of Broderick's other cronies in my house, he'd see me shut down. Later, McGowan himself had asked me where I stood and what it would take to get me to be a partisan of David Broderick.

This McGowan, a great patron of parlor houses, was particularly fond of a small, big-eyed, redheaded girl I had that year. I wrote to him now, and he agreed to meet me. Late that night, we sat at a table in the back room of a Commercial Street restaurant—me, Charley, Big Pete, and Judge McGowan—and I told him that I wanted to meet Broderick. I could be useful to him, but it had to be secret; secrecy was the key to my usefulness.

Judge Edward McGowan, "Ned" to his friends, was to be sought for "questioning" by the Vigilance Committee five years later, and his image is preserved in letter sheets created at that time by printers sympathetic to the committee. He was corpulent, with the sloping shoulders of royalty on playing cards. His typical dress included a high collar, a linen shirtfront, a bow tie, a fancy waistcoat, and a fine gray herringbone-tweed frock coat and trousers, usually rumpled and worn at the cuffs and elbows. He kept his fair hair greased into a lank mass covering his ears and topped it with a pale-brown silk hat. Presiding over his appearance, making sense of it all, was a mustache like the cowcatcher on a locomotive, its tips extending past the outline of his face, its lower edge shrouding his lips. It made his expression hard to read.

He had the habit, which Irish politicians share with their priests, of asserting his faction's official opinion as a dogma, with an air of having secret reasons he was not at liberty to discuss: Tim is a hero; Jasper is a scoundrel; the proposal of the other party is a scheme to enslave white men. It was his duty wherever he went to promote a given version of events, as it is a sandwich-board man's duty to patrol a given sidewalk, bearing witness to the Excelsior Paint Company. At times a fugitive smile or a quick remark would admit to otherwise unacknowledged subtleties. It was when you were his ally, and he was advising you about tactics or explaining the enemy's strategy, that he came closest to acknowledging the elusive intricacy of the universe.

We were discussing places where Broderick and I could meet when a young man came into the restaurant and talked for a moment privately with McGowan. When the judge returned he said, "I will not be able to convey your message to David Broderick tonight. Tonight Mr. Broderick must save a life." He sat and ordered dessert from within the invisible cloud of expectation he had created, and only then did he explain: "Mr. Brannan, Mr. William Tell Coleman, and their newly anointed Committee of Vigilance have begun their attempt to subvert the elected authority of this city. This evening a man named Jenkins was caught stealing a safe. Some boatmen caught him, and instead of giving him to the police, they gave him to the committee, which wants to show its strength by hanging him. Mr. Broderick will talk reason to the mob."

Not long after that, we heard fire bells. They stopped and started again. McGowan said, "It's a signal; they're taking Jenkins to the plaza."

"Let's go see," said Charley quite casually: it would be interesting, that was the idea. We all walked to Portsmouth Square, and stood on the plank sidewalk outside the Union Hotel. "There they are," said McGowan after a while. Just atop the façade of the Jenny Lind Theatre was a full moon, which had survived a bout of smallpox as a child, and its light, assisted by torches in men's hands and by lamps in the windows of gambling houses, gleamed episodically on the faces, hats, hands, and tools of the crowd pushing up the square. I could not grasp what was happening all at once; I saw this detail and that, and my mind created the picture gradually in a series of small puzzles solved. The captive—Jenkins—staggered and stumbled a little in advance of the vigilantes, a cigar in his mouth, his feet in shackles, hands tied behind his back, urged forward with an occasional shove from a couple of men behind him. Just to the rear of the two men doing the pushing walked Sam Brannan, recognizable by his rangy body and his ear-to-chin sideburns. As the crowd surged up the street, people in the hieratic costumes of the West spilled out of the hotels and the saloons and gambling houses: bartenders with white aprons, men in flannel shirts and neckerchiefs, men in white shirts and vests, men in trousers and suspenders, prostitutes in balloon-sleeve dresses and long white gloves.

Big Pete pointed to the other side of the square: "That's David Broderick, ain't it, Ned?"

"Standing on the wagon. Yes," agreed McGowan.

Pete nodded to me. "That's the boy you want to meet."

I looked: a lean, bowlegged man of middle height in an ill-fitting suit stood on a wagon, his face lit by a torch in the hands of a man beside him. At this, my first sight of David Broderick, I remembered how often I had heard his foes speak of him as "that ape," and "that monkey." He had a battered-looking face, a sunken nose wide at the bridge with flaring nostrils, and with the long distance between nose and upper lip so important to satirical illustrators who want to make Irishmen resemble chimpanzees. But the eyes of this ruthless political boss who had risen from the streets, his eyes were the anomaly of his countenance: they were suffering eyes, sensitive, compassionate. They looked as if they were about to cry.

His wagon faced the 110-foot flagpole made of a single tree—given to the people of San Francisco, California, by the people of Portland,

Oregon—which an advance party of vigilantes had already prepared as a gallows. "This is murder, don't fool yourselves!" shouted Broderick from his perch on the wagon. "Don't you know these vigilante fellows are bigger thieves than this man they're in such a hurry to hang? If you help them, *you're* a criminal. If you stand by and let them do it, you're handing them the power to roll over anyone who won't lick their shoes! It ain't about this Jenkins fellow, don't you see; it's about who's next."

Someone shouted, "You're next!"

"And after me, some friend of yours!" Broderick shouted back. He started calling out the names of people he recognized in the crowd, telling them he thought they had better sense than to be here, keeping such bad company.

Charley touched my arm and pointed.

"Oh no," I said. "Oh my God. Oh, damnit."

Broderick was surrounded by a group of tough-looking fellows, and to his immediate left was my brother Lewis.

"Lewis!" I cried. "Lewis, get down from there. Get away from him!"

I shouted it as I might have when he was a boy and I had caught him playing on the roof or taunting some ferocious dog. But of course he couldn't come down from there: being there was his job. He was working for Broderick. He was one of his shoulder strikers from New York. I had seen him and talked with him only last week, and he had not told me, and I had no idea how long he had been hiding it from me. We had both learned a great deal about hiding things, it seemed.

When Brannan's men were forty feet from the flagpole, they put the noose around Jenkins's neck. Broderick and his associates, including my brother, got off the wagon and rushed the vigilantes. They were joined by a handful of men from other directions, including several policemen. I felt sorry for the stupid thief being hurried to his death and began to hope that Broderick would prevail.

Big Pete said, "Five to one he hangs."

Charley had his arm around my waist, and a barely perceptible tightening of his grip told me that, for the first time tonight, he was interested. "How much?"

"A hundred."

"Make it a thousand."

Big Pete handed me his lucky hat, but Charley and McGowan kept theirs on as they rushed in to join the fight—Big Pete to help the vigilantes, Charley and McGowan to stop them. The two sides fought, hundreds of men, a churning mass of arms, shoulders, and heads moving in and out of the flickering light. My attempts to follow the individual efforts of Lewis and Charley and McGowan did not help me to understand what was happening. Eventually, I became aware that Broderick's men had captured Jenkins. They had their arms around him. Some were trying to get the rope off his neck; some were trying to pull him free of the vigilantes. But Brannan's men held the rope, and that turned out to be the most important thing. I inflicted further damage on Big Pete's old hat, twisting it in my hands, as I watched the contest devolve into a tug of war. The noose was still around Jenkins's neck, and he was slowly strangled in the mêlée; still the struggle continued. The corpse, jerked this way and that with a puppet's borrowed life, had lost its own meanings. It was no longer a man hoping to be saved or, if necessary, to die bravely, but a ball two teams were fighting over. The vigilantes made steady progress. At the last minute, whether out of respect for Oregon or because the flagpole presented unforeseen difficulties, they put the rope over a beam on the old adobe building. Brannan yelled, "Pull together—let every honest citizen be a hangman." The body rose. It wasn't on a pole, but it was a flag now, just the same.

I looked around for Lewis, but I couldn't find him. Charley and Big Pete returned, both sweaty and gasping for breath, in good humor, having enjoyed the sport. David Broderick, slapping his clothes and twisting his shoulders as if to loosen his muscles, walked to his wagon, ten yards away from us. Strangely calm, he stood in the street before a wagon wheel, listening to Ned McGowan. As I watched, Ned stretched his arm out in my direction, and David Broderick turned his head and looked at me.

❧ LII ❧

AT AN INQUEST THE NEXT DAY, after Jenkins was taken down, a police officer refused to testify, saying that if he did he would be killed by the secret organization that now ruled the city. The day after that, there was another battle in Portsmouth Square, with fists, boots, and sticks, when Broderick's people broke up a meeting of Brannan's people.

I was very worried about Lewis, so I sent a note asking him to visit the house, by the back entrance, during the afternoon. He came at the appointed time and place, but he disobliged me by bringing three friends: men of a sort that my servants would have never let through the front door. "This is Billy Mulligan," he said proudly. "This is Jim Casey. Billy, Jim, this is my old friend Belle, who I used to know in New York," and he winked, making me angrier.

I brought them into the parlor. On their best behavior, they waited for my invitation before settling comfortably into the furniture and looking all about them in hope of seeing beautiful women. Each was dressed in his own garish combination of plug hat, swallowtail coat, plaid trousers, and brightly patterned waistcoat. Their manner was sweet and easygoing. I knew them by reputation. Billy Mulligan, a short-legged fellow with an acne-scarred baby face—like a badly deteriorated fresco of an adorable cherub—was the onetime boxing promoter who had befriended Lewis last year; probably it was he who had introduced Lewis to David Broderick. He was going to die in 1862, during a shoot-out and in a condition of *delirium tremens,* soon after he began firing his gun randomly out of the window of his room in the St. Francis Hotel. James Casey, a slim young fellow with a sad, puzzled face and prematurely receding hair, had done a term in Sing Sing Prison. He was going to be lynched in 1856 for the shooting of a newspaper editor who had mentioned Casey's prison record in print.

As for Lewis Godwin, soon after arriving in California, he had gotten a reputation by winning prizefights, and then won a small fortune by losing them, until no one, including his brother Edward, would bet a penny on him ever again. Then he and Billy Mulligan were hired by a couple of men to win a dispute over a contested mine. Then they had been involved in a shoot-out in which a woman selling tamales across the street had been hit by a stray bullet, whose bullet was never determined, and then they had come here. And the date and circumstances of my brother's death will be related in their proper sequence among the other events of this narrative.

I sent word that the girls were not to come down, but I had Niobe bring out some wine, along with bread and oranges and dates and cheese, which counted here as delicacies, and talked with Lewis and his friends for almost an hour, just so they would not feel slighted. Then I begged them to go, on the grounds that members of the Vigilance Committee often came here during business hours, and if they stayed there was bound to be a brawl—for I knew what caliber of men they were!—and that the breakage would ruin me. They laughed and they departed, except for Lewis, whom I asked to stay a little longer.

As soon as they were gone, I said, "These men you call your friends—they're no good, and they're not going to do you any good."

He stood up. "I came because you're my sister and I need to see you sometimes. I didn't come for this." He thrust his arm into a coat sleeve. I clutched his gaudy silk vest. "Let go."

"If you could hear the things I've heard about that man," I said. He knew I meant Broderick. "You're such a fool. If you heard what is said . . . ." I was vague as to details, because I was too upset to remember. "No one respectable likes him—a politician who surrounds himself with hooligans. Hooligans like you, who he'll toss aside the minute they're not useful to him."

"What do you know about it? He's not like a politician. I've seen him go into fire—a real fire, that could have killed him—to get a friend out safe."

I released him, as if his argument about Broderick's heroism had moved me, and he was in less of a hurry to leave. "Well," I said, "that takes courage, to be a fireman."

"It does," said Lewis.

"Jack Cutter was a fireman. I suppose he wasn't all bad."

He went for the door again, and I didn't grab him this time, but I did say, "I thought you'd want to stay and visit Jocelyn."

He hesitated a moment. "You know she won't see me here," and he went stomping down the hall in those big boots that make all the men of the West feel a couple of inches taller than they really are.

A FEW HOURS LATER, when I told Jocelyn what Lewis had said, she shrugged and told me he was right. I changed my clothes and left her in charge, and went with Charley to the house of Tom Gallagher, where Judge McGowan had arranged for me to meet David Broderick.

Gallagher, who had built the city's first theater, the Jenny Lind, lived with his wife, their maid, their cook, and an occasional lodger, just for company, in a three-story house on the plaza. Ned McGowan was already there when we arrived. Gallagher's wife, who had come from nothing, just as Gallagher had, was friendly and natural with me, and we all had a fine dinner served on real silver and good china. Broderick recognized Charley as one of the men who had tried to save Jenkins's life, and commended him for it. Charley said he was glad of Mr. Broderick's good opinion, but he had to be honest: he had been trying to win a bet, and his friend Big Pete of the El Dorado had been helping the other side only because of the bet, and Mr. Broderick shouldn't hold it against him. Broderick did not reply. McGowan said that anyway Charley had tried to do the right thing, though the results had been unfortunate.

At last the table was cleared. Gallagher and his wife invited the rest of the company to enjoy cigars and brandy in another room, Broderick and I stayed behind.

We examined each other, and I found him quite frightening on close inspection. His associates lived to satisfy their immediate appetites. If there were such elements in his own character, he had mastered them. At dinner he had drunk only water and had eaten the capon as if it were a bowl of mush; when he glanced at me, the sorrowful expression on his ugly face seemed to say various things: that we were both mourning someone, or that he still loved me even though I had disappointed him in some profound way. When I had first seen those saintly, grieving eyes of his up close, I had wanted to tell him: don't do it, you can't win against Sam Brannan, he's heartless, and nature has given you a mother's heart. But by this time I had sensed the steely purpose behind the sad eyes, and I had concluded that David Broderick was a fanatic. To feel himself another inch nearer his destiny was the only pleasure that meant anything to him.

Now, having no small talk for the likes of me—or for any woman, I supposed—he said, "You said you had something for me. What is it?"

"Four members of the executive committee of the Committee of Vigilance are regulars at my house; they come, they drink, they have a good time. They brag, to impress the girls. They get drunk enough, they brag about the committee and what they know, the secret signs and signals and plans. I thought that might interest you."

"Do you know the watchword?"

"*Fiat justicia ruat coelum,* which is Latin. 'Let justice be done though the heavens fall.'"

This was a secret at the time, supposedly known only to committee members. "I knew that," said Broderick, and I believed him. "Now tell me something I don't know."

"I must find it out first. I will, don't worry."

"And what do you want in return?"

"Three things. If and when you come out on top, I'll want your protection."

"All right," he said. That was easy to promise.

"Good. But there's something else, and this is important to me. I have a family connection to Lewis Godwin. I'd like you to keep an eye on him."

"I always look out for my boys," he said calmly.

"I am attached to him. I don't want to see him sacrificed to your noble causes. If he's hurt, I'll be your enemy, for what that's worth." Broderick's lips tightened. He had a bad temper—that was what got him killed, in 1859, in a duel with a former chief justice of the California Supreme Court. But he wanted to use me, so he kept listening. "If he's killed, I'll use everything I've got, call in every favor. I'm sorry if it offends you, but I need you to know it."

There was silence while the sober mind behind the saintly eyes performed various measurements and calculations. "You said three things."

"Tell me things I can tell the committee. Things you can afford to let them know, but which they'll see as useful. It doesn't have to be big, but it has to be true. I'll tell it to them, and they'll be beholden to me; if they win, I'll have their protection."

After considering this for a while, he called out, "Ned, come here," and McGowan joined the discussion.

When we were done, Charley came back and we said our thank-yous and goodbyes to Mr. and Mrs. Gallagher. Near the door, the maid handed Broderick his hat. With an expression I had not yet seen on his face—a warm smile—he thanked her and patted her on the shoulder. Turning to me, he said, "Sam Brannan has money and influence. But he hasn't got any persistence. He gets an idea in his head, and he runs with it as long as it's fun. Who dares to say no to him? Nobody, except Coleman, but Coleman's a fool." He put his hat on. "These vigilantes may have their way awhile. But they're impatient. They'll get bored, they'll get tired. I don't get tired. It's their hobbyhorse. It's my life."

I HAD NOT BEEN ENTIRELY CANDID with Broderick. I did have an excellent source of information about the committee, but it wasn't pillow talk. Though these men didn't have the mighty minds they thought they had, neither were they stupid, and I didn't dare ask my girls to wheedle secrets out of them.

Instead, Herbert Owen was my spy; it was he who gave me my privileged view of the committee's inner workings. Sam Brannan and William Tell Coleman, wanting to have a lawyer on the executive committee (the committee's head, the select group that made the big decisions), had invited Owen to join. Owen was flattered to have his judgment and expertise solicited by such important men, and tempted by the promise of their future support. But he had been against the quick hanging of Jenkins, and hurt when his advice was ignored. He had thought of the committee as a kind of trade association full of men it was useful to know. He had not really expected them to do anything, certainly not so quickly. He felt that he had been swept into criminal actions that his family back east would never understand. Two days after the hanging, he contacted me, and he began supplying me with the committee's secrets, aware that I would pass them on to its enemies.

Herbert Owen wasn't the only man with doubts, but whenever public opinion seemed about to turn against the Vigilance Committee, something would happen to direct people's fury elsewhere. On the very day when David Broderick was to hold a big anti-vigilante rally in Portsmouth Square, there was another big fire, and nearly everyone was convinced it had been set on purpose, and that all the fires had been set on purpose. Frightened people, wanting to be saved from this chaos, were grateful to the Committee of Vigilance when its private army conducted street patrols and searched houses and ships in the harbor.

A week or two after the fire, I opened the *Alta California* and read that a suspicious character caught hiding out in the high brush of California Street Hill had been turned over to the Committee of Vigilance, and this man had confessed that he was the real English Jim, the notorious thief and killer (and according to the newspaper he bore an uncanny resemblance to the unfortunate fellow who had already been hanged). The committee kept the new English Jim in a secret location, where he was confessing to many other crimes, and naming his associates and the dirty politicians who had helped him, and from these confessions the committee was already compiling a secret list of men to be hunted down and hanged or driven out of the state.

It seemed clear that the committee was going to add everybody they disliked to this list. Herbert Owen memorized it and gave me a copy to slip to Ned McGowan, who passed the names on to David Broderick. In July, English Jim was hanged. In August, on the authority of his secret confessions, two more men were hanged. Several more were put on ships to Honolulu and Shanghai. With forewarning, Broderick arranged to have some of his men leave town in advance of their capture, though he didn't bother to warn a couple of fellows who had become a liability to him.

"I thought your man would fight harder," I told Ned McGowan.

McGowan had a way of stroking his triangular mustache as if it were an abacus or an oracle to be consulted on important decisions. "We decided it was better to duck this time. We will melt into the hills, Indian-style. Brannan will get his candidates elected, and they'll have the government for a year. Then we'll be back. Don't worry. You didn't back the wrong horse. Well, I guess you backed both horses, right?"

OFTEN DURING THIS TIME I WENT to the Clay Street Unitarian Church, where, week after week, Jeptha preached against the vigilantes. In this respect, he was unique among the city's clergymen. The rest of them stood in their pulpits asking God to further the Vigilance Committee's noble work, or else they preached against the "criminal element" in a way that complemented the committee's efforts. An Episcopalian priest lent dignity to the hangings by wrangling privately with the condemned in their last hours, afterward passing on the news that this one had died repentant and that one blaspheming to the last. Meanwhile, before a congregation that included three members of the executive committee and probably hundreds of regular committee members, Jeptha hunted in his well-thumbed Bible for verses that spoke of God's monopoly on vengeance, the bad judgment of mobs ("Give us Barabbas"), etc., and moved quickly from the text, which really gave him little support, to tell his audience that they were surrendering rights for which English-speaking people had been giving their blood since the days of bad King John and the Magna Carta, that a city of thirty thousand young male transients was bound to have crime, and if they wanted less of it they ought to employ more policemen and pay them better. Next he dwelt on the horror of the hangings and the bestial emotions they aroused. (Fool, high-minded fool—my eyes told him that. But I could not help taking a secret pride in him. He had preached his first sermons to me from the boughs of trees.)

There was much angry murmuring the first time Jeptha spoke against the vigilantes. The second time, one man stood up. It was a signal: fifty others promptly rose in a body and walked out, and most of them joined other churches. The men who remained were the least passionate ones, but even among these there was talk of dismissing Jeptha—impossible, since Jeptha himself had contributed a third of the money to build the church, and unpalatable, because he was a talented preacher, not easily replaced.

I had many complicated feelings about all that, but I did not examine them very closely; I was thinking of other things. By the time English Jim was hanged, Agnes was visibly pregnant, completing her victory over me—her victory over him, too, as I thought. I lost sleep trying not to think of the child Jeptha and I hadn't had; of their happy life, their serious, churchy life elaborating itself. It was like watching a ship with my heart on it sail away from me. Only a few weeks later, in September, I learned from a couple of male members of the congregation who snubbed me in church but were talkative in my house, that Agnes had lost her baby. I went to church the following Sunday. Her pew was in the front row, and mine five rows back. Twice she looked at me and looked away, unable to keep up her charade of pity for me. She was still stout from her pregnancy. Jeptha saw me from the pulpit, and as always his eyes rested on me just long enough to acknowledge our prior acquaintance, but not long enough to announce it to the congregation. The ship had returned, and I was relieved, but I did not triumph. What had I won? I had won nothing, and it was all too sad.

Did Jeptha find himself thinking, lately, that, but for his actions, *we* might have a child? Did he remember my saying that I hoped he would never be a father? Did he believe in God now, or did he see religion as a big white lie? Or had he become even more cynical than that? I told myself that I was curious about these things. I thought I lived without illusions, but really no one does.

CITY ELECTIONS WERE HELD IN SEPTEMBER. David Broderick and the men he supported were voted out, and were replaced mainly by Know-Nothings chosen by Sam Brannan and his friends. The Committee of Vigilance promptly announced that the city was safe and officially ceased its operations, with a warning that they would keep an eye on evil-doers and return if the people needed them. They were to return five years later.

⚜ LIII ⚜

A MAN WHO CALLED HIMSELF JAMES KING OF WILLIAM, and who was to become famous as a newspaper editor and as my enemy, came to my house for the last time a month after the 1851 Committee of Vigilance disbanded. He had been an occasional visitor for almost a year.

He was a banker then. With help from his connections back east, he had become very rich in San Francisco; he was vain of that accomplishment. He was vain generally, and sensitive, and vindictive. He came to my house with his customers and colleagues. He did not touch the girls; he said that he was married. When I told him that half my patrons were married, he raised his chin absurdly (no one dared to smile) and said, "I don't look to what other men do." Everyone could tell he was here for Pauline, poor fellow. When any other man went with her, King's nose would lift and his head turn in a transparent parody of indifference. Evidently a great drama was unfolding in his breast. He was torturing himself. Perhaps somehow he enjoyed it. I hoped so. I felt sorry for him.

He had a stage hero's face, placed, like a cruel joke, atop a small, narrow-shouldered body. To the girls, the combination was funny. How he might have reacted had he heard their talk, I shuddered to imagine, for his self-esteem was exquisitely tender. Yet he tempted the world's laughter with his oddities, beginning with the ridiculous self-chosen name. Why "of William"? people would ask innocently. Is that your home town? With icy vehemence he would reply that William was the Christian name of his father back in Georgetown, Maryland, where there were several James Kings. Calling himself after the town would have been "quite useless." But hadn't John Smiths and Tom Browns the world over solved this exact problem by means of middle initials? "I *told* you: I don't look to what other men do."

I hope I need not point out that a man who says such things is a slave to his obsession with the doings of other men.

He told me about his mostly ordinary life: he had been a printer, and a bank clerk, and apparently he had come west in emulation of his big brother, Henry, who froze to death in the Rockies and was eaten by his starving comrades while James was on a ship rounding the Horn. There was also a younger brother, a black sheep, named Thomas.

He liked me. He showed it by expressing disapproval of the company I kept.

"I don't care for your friend Mr. Cora," he said one day. "He's one of Broderick's scoundrels."

This was in August; the committee, of which King was a member, had already hanged four men.

"You're mistaken, Mr. King."

"I believe I am not. I saw him down at the Metropolitan, drinking with Mr. McGowan, the crooked judge, who is Broderick's brain."

"Charley is friendly, like me. He is nobody's man."

"I hope for his sake you're right," said King, and delivered a quiet little tirade against David Broderick, after which I told him that it was good to know a man of strong convictions, but I hoped he did not feel the same way about all things foreign: we had a new shipment of a fizzy French wine, from grapes trampled under the feet of girls who went to mass and confessed their sins to the priest. King accepted a glass. Over its rim he studied the happy accidents that were Pauline's lips and chin and shoulders.

If I could show her to you as she was then, perhaps you would understand King's obsession. Or maybe not; there are fashions in figures, faces, and personalities as there are in dresses and hats, and many of the women one generation adores would be wallflowers if they were born in another time. For the men of the 1850s, her petite form was lithe and inviting, her face was lovely and piquant, her movements were seductive, and her eyes hinted that you and she were in a conspiracy together.

Beauty misleads without lying, like an ambiguous prophecy in a Greek play. We read into it our hopes, to which it is indifferent. We ask it to be true and good, but it has its own way of measuring worth, its own standard and authority.

At last, one cool evening in October, James King of William grabbed her little hand—she was just over five feet tall—as she passed his chair. "Finally," she said. He had come alone and early. He was the only guest in the house. Perhaps that gave him the courage to act. I watched them mount the stairs. I had a premonition that it would not go well—Pauline was so careless, he was so sensitive. I could not help wondering why he had delayed so long.

He had been up in her room for less than ten minutes when I heard shouting, in three different voices: King's, Pauline's, and Angelique's. I knocked on the door. "What's happening in there?" There was a sound of furniture falling.

"Unhand me," I heard James King of William say. I opened the door. Pauline, in silken undergarments, crouched in a corner, face in hands. Angelique had her arm around King's head. King was naked; he struggled in vain, his face much redder than his soft, white body.

"Angelique, that's enough. Let him go."

"He'll strike me," she said.

"No, he won't," I said. "You won't, will you, Mr. King? She'll let you go, and, whatever went wrong here, we'll all pretend it never happened."

"No," Angelique persisted. "He needs a beating."

"Angelique, please," I said.

"Show her your face, honey."

Pauline took her hands away. Half her face was pink, and her left eye was beginning to swell. That was going to cost us both money. But she was not sobbing, as I had assumed. She looked as if she had a funny little secret to impart to me, and what it was I understood when she cast a quick glance at James King of William's groin, a place my eyes had until now tactfully avoided.

"Oh," I said. I couldn't help it. I looked away, and I knew I shouldn't look again, but I did. It was the smallest I'd ever seen. I thought, later that evening, of words I might have said just then to soothe him, but nothing came to mind.

Knowing Pauline and King, I did not think the mere sight of his diminutive organ would make her laugh. She was too much of a veteran for that; she knew the variety of God's creation; in her time she'd had to hunt for a penis within fleshy folds so copious that success required all her avarice and dedication to her craft. No, there must have been a time when her eyes flicked toward it in a neutral way and she was observed by King—here was the moment he had dreaded, the reason he had hesitated so long—and he gave her one of his imperious looks. That would have been the funny part. He was so sensitive that that merest trace of amusement would have been enough to infuriate him. He struck her, she cried out, and Angelique, whose room connected with Pauline's—for they were very particular friends—came to her rescue.

"Let him go," I repeated, and finally she did. "Both of you, leave," I said, and I looked the other way while King got dressed.

It was my intention to smooth his feathers, but before I had spoken three words he said, "Shut up," and after a few attempts, each merely increasing his shame and fury, I left, and waited for him to manage his own exit.

❧ LIV ❧

IN '52, THE MINES BEGAN TO YIELD gold again. Good times were back. Clipper ships and covered wagons brought immigrants; steamboats returned others to the States. Old faces kept giving way to new ones, for whom San Francisco had the anonymity, the loneliness, and the freedom of a great metropolis. Over their heads, by secret signs, the residents of a more lasting and intimate city saluted each other. We the madams, the gamblers, the politicians, the merchants, the bankers—remained year after year, like the faculty of a university or the proprietors of a great hotel. Conflicts among the members of this permanent city, supposedly about crime or the condition of the wharves, were really about the money in the pockets of those transients who spent a little time here and went home in defeat or victory. Yet we were not simply, not *only* cynical. We loved our great hotel. The hills kept bringing the whole city before our eyes. At every turn we saw wide vistas, many levels, streets paved with long wooden planks, lined with street lamps, choked with people, carts, and horses; a thousand rooftops, giant signs painted on bricks, black smoke rising slantwise from chimneys; factories; wharves; fleets of ships. We could not escape a feeling of civic pride. It had all happened so quickly, yet it looked as if it had always been here.

With still relatively few women in the town, and most of them prostitutes, there wasn't much home life. Our home was the city. It was normal to sleep in lodging houses and eat in restaurants. Pedestrians threaded their way through the merchants' wares that spilled out of doors each morning, and as in a town of the Middle Ages, there were unlimited excuses for pageantry: a political rally, a new fire engine, a march by the Sons of Temperance, the launch of a hot-air balloon. There were children now, precious and spoiled, flying kites, fishing through holes in the wharf, running with torches before the fire engines. Wives and maidens could be seen shopping on Commercial Street and picnicking on Meiggs Wharf. It was said constantly that when there were enough of them, these respectable, white Christian women were going to civilize us.

During this second boom, when everything seemed substantial and lasting, and steamships and the Panama Railroad made the journey quicker, big theatrical names began to show up in San Francisco. I was mad about them. I dined with the actors, generally at the residence of Tom Gallagher—not at my house—but they knew who I was. I was a part of their Western adventure. I met the Booths, but not John Wilkes; he never made it this far west. I have sometimes wondered if I had, and he had held my hand and drunk up my eyes with his, whether I would have sensed the dark deed abiding within him, awaiting a war and a president. I met Murdoch. James Murdoch—please don't say you've never even heard of Murdoch. How awful, when we all loved him so. He was wonderful in *The School for Scandal,* but he didn't shoot Lincoln and is forgotten.

As for the actresses and lady singers, I had candid chats with them in their dressing rooms. They did not have supper with me. In the fifties, these ladies were not yet confident that the public appreciated the difference between prostitutes and actresses. Trying to be respectable, they were less inclined than their counterparts today to keep pet tigers, bathe in milk, or cultivate an association with the demimonde (which many of them knew well enough from earlier phases in their careers). Lola Montez, then fluttering pulses and outraging clergymen with her notorious spider dance, was an agreeable exception. I have only good things to say about Lola Montez. But when Ingrid Strom was in town—the Swedish nightingale, at the end of her triumphant American tour, with theaters, towns, and children named after her at every stop—I was prevented even from going backstage to meet her. I was told that when she heard that the wicked madam Belle Cora was in the audience and would no doubt want to meet her, for Belle Cora always went backstage to meet the performers, she shut her eyes, shook her head rapidly like a spoiled child in a tantrum, and begged to be protected from me! I don't even know if this report was true. Maybe it was her manager who thwarted me. In any case, I was deliberately delayed, three nights in a row, and each time when I got to her dressing room—a room I knew as well as my own, I had been to it so often—she was gone. She had run away from me—imagine!—when all I wanted to do was to give her the urgent message that she was wonderful and that I, Belle Cora, was refined and sensitive enough to appreciate her. As ridiculous as it seems now, I was deeply hurt, and for years I could not hear the name Ingrid Strom, or see it in print, without feeling the pang of an insult unavenged; I searched newspapers from distant cities in the hope of reading a bad review of her performances. Alas, nobody ever said anything bad about Ingrid Strom; there was a conspiracy that she was perfect, though if you look at the photographs it is evident that she was already becoming portly and had a peasant's nose, rather like a potato growing in the middle of her face.

I BECAME MODERATELY RICH, and I acquired, quite cheaply, many deeds to property on the hills—then despised, later choice—so that today I'm very rich. I owned three boarding houses, a laundry, shares in a shipyard, and shares in a wharf that one year brought me more money than the parlor house, but the next year the developer disappeared with all my profits. In '53, I began to notice a sad trend in my principal industry. One by one, the little French courtesans working out of their own apartments came under the control of pimps, and men became silent partners in most of the brothels. I eluded this fate. I closed my old house and opened up a new one, the grandest yet seen in the city, on Pike Street, which is now called Waverly Place. It stood one block away from the ground the post office had occupied three years earlier. Charley and Lewis made it their permanent residence, and their presence in the house discouraged men who might otherwise have tried to take my business from me.

I saw Edward once a month, and through him I learned of my grandmother's death, after a long illness, in '53, and my grandfather's death, which occurred during an afternoon nap around six months later, at the beginning of '54. Robert was the executor of the estate. Along with substantial bequests to charity, every grandchild but one received tens of thousands of dollars and an income of around $1,250 per annum from rental property managed by Robert. Even Lewis, the other black sheep of the family, received his share. I was not mentioned. You will say, how could I be surprised? I had not expected anything; I did not need anything. Yet, when I learned of my absence from the will, it was as if my grandfather had reached up from the grave and across a continent to strike me a final blow.

Back in Livy, Anne had hurt me, too, though more gently. It had become my habit to write letters to young Frank, who was now beginning to read. I called myself his godmother, and along with the letters and on holidays I would send him presents—a small telescope, a set of toy soldiers, a stereoscope viewer, a collection of rare crystals found in the vicinity of the gold fields, etc., etc., and, best of all, packed very carefully in cloth and old newspapers, two framed photographs of myself (one just the head, and the other down to the waist) beautifully dressed and coiffed, in rich, respectable surroundings. I signed my letters Mrs. Arabella Dickinson—the explanation for my wealth being that I had become first the wife, and promptly afterward the widow, of a San Francisco banker of that name.

When Anne wrote nowadays, she was more candid than she had been in her earlier letters, because she knew that Jeptha wasn't going to read them. But she was elliptical by habit, and always gentle, because that was her nature, and thus when she did write plainly the effect was more abrasive than another woman's curses. One day I got a letter from her saying, about as nicely as such a thing could be put, that I must stop sending presents. "It causes talk in the school and town. I'd go on hiding it from you if I could, dear. The problem is that people here have a pretty good idea that Frank is your child. I don't know how they know, but they know, and if they're my friends they don't talk about it, but not everybody is a friend. Every time you send an expensive present it stirs up talk again. We let him have the stereoscope. We put the crystals in the eaves. We couldn't make ourselves throw out something so beautiful. Anyway, when packages arrive at the general store, folks see the postmarks and the return address, and that stirs up talk. Of course we want to hear from you, and we want to tell you how Frank is doing. I have thought of a way to avoid this, if you are willing. From now on, let the envelopes have your brother Edward's return address on them, and let them be sent to Agatha. Agatha will pass them on to me unopened. That way there's no talk and it will be easier on Frank in the long run. And please don't send any more presents."

I had opened this letter expecting a description of Frank's delight with my latest gifts, and by the time I was done with it, my head was swimming and I had to lie down. A couple hours later, Charley found me insensible on my bed, and picked up the letter from the carpet and read it. While I wept on his shoulder, he stroked my hair and patted my back, saying, "That was hard, all right. Maybe she's right, but that was a hard one."

Anne had suggested that I make use of Edward in this subterfuge because I had mentioned that I was seeing him more often. And Edward saw Jeptha fairly often, because the *Herald* sent him as a matter of routine to cover the founding of civic institutions, and, as people who paid attention to such things knew, Jeptha Talbot was the principal force behind the creation of the Protestant Orphan Asylum, the Temperance Society, and the Protestant Drunkard's Mission, which did a great deal of practical good on its own account and because its existence prompted the archdiocese to set up a competing Catholic Drunkard's Mission. Sometimes Edward would meet Jeptha for lunch at a restaurant in town, and sometimes he dined with Agnes and Jeptha at their home in Happy Valley.

Jeptha had been very eager for Edward to visit. "It will do her good," he had told my brother (who told me, when we had lunch). "It will take her out of herself." Edward had expected to find Agnes sad, or at least quiet, but over dinner she was lively—only, he said, strangely rapid in her speech, and he noted in Jeptha a nervousness, a springy readiness to intervene, whenever Agnes directed the conversation toward the possibility, as she put it, "of communicating with other worlds," or with "those who have left the physical plane." Edward told me that ever since the loss of their only child shortly after it was born, this had been her obsession, and Jeptha hated it.

"Her brother Titus is a spiritualist, too," I noted.

"She caught it from him," said Edward, nodding. "He writes to her."

Anne, in her letters, sometimes passed on news of my cousins in Livy and Patavium; and from her I had learned that Titus and his wife, after the death of their four-year-old girl, had begun inviting friends to sit holding hands around a table in a darkened room, and to listen for raps, hoping for news of their daughter. Eventually, they had sought the assistance of a spirit medium from Rochester, who for no charge except the price of her trip had passed on the message that little Laurie was growing and thriving in the Summer-Land; that she had playmates, was looked after by older spirits, was learning to read and figure; that she visited them and stood by their chairs at the dinner table, or sat at the foot of her father's chair while he was doing the store's accounts. Laurie had tried to speak with them to tell them not to mourn, and in fact, though they were unconscious of it, it was her gentle prompting that had led them to contact the medium so that they might learn the truth and rejoice.

An individual who converses with the dead, or thinks the world will soon end, is not counted insane if, nearby, many thousands of others share this same belief. However, whenever such a sect does spring up, crazy people are drawn to it, hiding themselves in a throng of believers like brown deer in the autumnal forest. Apparently, it was Jeptha's conviction that Agnes was one of those. He considered her attraction to the new teaching a symptom of mental disorder, brought on by her repeated failures in childbearing.

There had been three miscarriages, two soon after the quickening, one brought halfway to term, and an infant born blue, whose headstone in the churchyard bore the unusual inscription "Jonathan Talbot. BORN February 9, 1853. TRANSLATED February 11, 1853." Several months later, at a séance in the house of the wife of the owner of the San Francisco Water Works, Agnes established communication with Jonathan and some older spirits, the souls of a wagon maker and his wife, who had become his adoptive parents in the afterlife; and together all these spirits were working to solve the mystery of the curse on Agnes's womb.

EDWARD LEARNED THIS OVER A SERIES of meetings, a few more pathetic facts each time. Jeptha hated Agnes to talk about any of it, yet it was certainly preferable to the melancholy which had earlier afflicted her, when for weeks at a stretch sometimes she would refuse to rise from her bed and would eat only when Jeptha spoon-fed her. On other subjects, she made perfect sense, Edward reminded me, and she could be very good with the poor and the sick. Jeptha did what he could to involve her in this sort of work, and he hoped that whatever this was would pass as she overcame her grief; most of all, he hoped she would get the child she so desperately wanted, though he dreaded the suspense of another pregnancy.

Edward told me about this when we met one afternoon at the Clipper, a restaurant on Washington Street popular with workingmen because they could get three dishes for a quarter; because a little railway—a scientific marvel—ran the length of the room, conveying plates of food from the kitchen to the tables; and, finally, because of the dexterity of the waiters, who with two long-handled tin pots would pour coffee and hot milk simultaneously into one's cup from a thrilling height.

"I feel sorry for them," Edward said, stretching the words a little, so that he seemed to mean: I can understand why you, on the other hand, might feel differently.

"He doesn't have much luck with wives, does he?"

"I guess not," Edward agreed cautiously.

"Do they ever mention me?"

"No."

"Does he know you and I are in touch?"

"I feel sure he does."

"But he doesn't ask after me."

"No. But after all . . ."

"What?"

"He knows. You are known."

By this time, Edward had become a part of our circle; he was on good terms with Charley, with Big Pete Hughes, Ned McGowan, and many people we both knew. So I said, "Edward, do me a favor, will you, don't tell anyone we have spoken about Jeptha."

"Well, of course," he said.

"I mean, don't even tell Charley," I said.

I PICTURED THEIR HOME LIFE, its dreary apprehensions, its moments of humor and tenderness. I pictured it one way; I turned it around and pictured it differently. I could see his anxious face when she began to talk strangely, or when he wondered whether it was wrong to let her harbor a belief he considered foolish; or him in the bed beside her, hesitant to start, and her hoping and fearing. If ever copulation had been chastised, theirs had, and there had to be a shadow over it for both of them. Did he ever think about our happy days aboard the *Juniper*? Surely now and then he must.

A few days after my conversation with Edward at the Clipper, I woke much earlier than I was used to. I sat up and looked at Charley in the bed, sleeping with his mouth open, one arm bent across his chest, and the other flung out straight, with the hand dangling over the bed. I had a tender feeling for him. I loved him, but not in the same way I loved Jeptha. He could never torment me as Jeptha could. I was ashamed of what I was planning to do.

I walked to the window, which was misty, and raised it; a chilly breeze came into the room, making me feel lonely and fearful of the rush of time. I watched the fog rolling in from the bay; how fast it came, ghostly battalions enveloping the masts and yardarms of the ships and the chimneys of the houses and pushing through the streets, looking for me, looking for my truth, looking for my heart.

Later that day, I wrote to Jeptha.

Dear Friend,

I have learned in conversation with my brother that your poor wife is behaving and speaking very strangely, so much so that he is worried about her, and I am sure that you are worried, too. As you know, your wife and I grew up together on the same farm. I am very familiar with her character, and I believe that I have knowledge which will be of great value in helping to mend her disordered mind. We should meet, don't you agree? In view of the differences in our stations now, I suppose it would be better if we met clandestinely, perhaps out of town. I know of a tavern in Sacramento City where we could discuss delicate matters in private.

Sincerely,
Arabella

Jeptha replied two days later. A few more terse messages went back and forth between us, and a week later, I took a steamboat to Sacramento City. I arrived at the tavern first and waited outside, wearing kid gloves and holding a silk parasol, and nodding to acknowledge the approving glances of the men who passed by. At last, Jeptha approached, in a frock coat too heavy for the weather, walking with his hands in his pockets. He looked at me warily and gave me a small unfriendly nod, as if we knew each other but not well. I made him take my arm, and he walked with me very stiffly into the tavern. We sat down, and I ordered a sarsaparilla, he a whiskey, which he didn't touch for a long time.

There he was, fifteen inches away from me, for the first time in five years, and, like a thief taking a look around a bank he plans to rob tomorrow, I took a surreptitious inventory of his face: the high brow, the thick eyebrows, the ice-blue eyes in their hawklike setting. There he was. Still there.

"My grandfather died," I said, to break the silence.

"Yes, I heard," he said, giving me a glimpse of the little gap in his mouth made by the ancient chip in his tooth. He hesitated: he had mixed feelings about my grandfather, and he knew that I did, too. "He was an interesting man. He did many good things."

"He disinherited me."

To that Jeptha said nothing, and the conversation continued in this lifeless manner until he finally said, "What did you have to say about Agnes?"

I smiled. "I think you know that I didn't bring you here to talk about Agnes. Do you believe everything you read?" He scowled and stood up. "Stop. Wait." A little more slowly than necessary, with my left hand I pulled the kid glove off my right hand, and placed my hand over his, stroking his thumb with my own. "I have rented a room upstairs," I said quietly. "Come with me, up to the room. Come with me, and if you don't know why you are here, why, I'll do my very best to explain it."

I rose and looked at him, waiting. At last he stood, and put his hand to his brow, and dropped it to his side, and I led the way and he followed me. When we were in the room, with its small bed, and I had locked the door, I said, "Don't take off your clothes yet. Stand there a moment." I put my hand on his lips, and kissed them lightly. "Don't kiss me back yet. Don't move a muscle. Not yet. Don't move." I slipped a hand into his shirt and up his chest. I dipped my fingers into his trousers. "What do you think of me, Jeptha? What do you think of my character?"

"You're loathsome," he said.

"I see how you loathe me," I said, gripping him. I let go and turned, inviting him to undo the small hooks at the back of my dress.

I could estimate, just from the temperature of his breath on my hair, how far he stood from me when he performed this task. He stood at arm's length. In my narrow shelf aboard the *Juniper*, he had raced through the unfastening. But now he seemed to have taken my cue that everything should be done slowly and cruelly. A hook came undone, and there was a wait so long that I began to wonder if he had changed his mind and was going to leave the room. Then, quickly, the next hook. My knees vibrated. I began to turn. He gripped my shoulders and turned me away again, and I waited for him to undo the next hook.

The bed thumped and migrated across the floor, etching marks into the soft pine floorboards. Our coupling was angry. It wasn't a reconciliation; it was a fight. Our bodies traded insults and recriminations; his body spat out its contempt for me. Then we rested. Then we did it again, twice more, and we didn't talk at all except when I asked him if he thought he was done for the day. When he said he was, I said, "You go first. I'll let you know when I think it's time for another discussion." I looked at him while he got into his clothes and went out, and then I stood at the window and watched until he had left the tavern and was walking up the wooden street and turned a corner. It was late in the day, under a clear sky, and the people and the horses down there had long shadows that they pushed or dragged, depending on whether they walked up the street or down. I stood at the window a little longer, watching the people come and go, and then I sat on the bed for a long time, doing nothing.

I TOLD CHARLEY THAT I WAS THINKING of opening up another house in Sacramento City. Using this excuse, I went there every other week, and Jeptha and I would go up to a little room to satisfy our animal need for each other. We did not speak very much. All the words we said to each other over the course of the first few months were like one conversation, like a series of messages sent back and forth by carrier pigeon. I would ask him, one week, how he felt when he went home after our little meetings. He would reply two weeks later, as if that much time had been needed to investigate the matter, that he felt rotten. He was betraying his wife. He was betraying all the people who believed in him.

Another time he said, as if talking to himself, "They should see me now. Rutting like a dog with the worst woman in California."

I thought about that for a while, and then said: "I see. You do this so you, at least, will know what you are really like."

He nodded, and I was going to say more, but he put his hand over my mouth.

At our next meeting I said, "You do it to degrade yourself."

"Yes."

"Well, in that case, you must do things with me that no good man would ever do with any woman, especially not with his wife."

He agreed. Naturally, I had to lead in this, since I had so much more experience with degradation, and over the course of a few months, I proceeded to unlock cupboard after cupboard, door after door, opening to him the whole treasury of human sexual depravity, everything a man and a woman can do, everything known to me as a harlot and a bawd. While we were doing it, at a moment when my mouth happened to be free, I asked him, "Do you ever think how I learned all these tricks?"

"Yes," he groaned, thrusting harder.

"And do you think of the men who taught them to me?"

"Yes, and shut up," he said, and pushed my face into the pillow, and I laughed, and then I groaned like a dying woman and grunted like a pig.

During all that time, not a single kind word ever passed between us. Both of us had to rid ourselves of burdens we had carried for years. I had to be rid of my desire to win, to triumph over Agnes and revenge myself on him. He had to be rid of the illusion that he was being with me in order to be dirty, to live a truth that fit his low opinion of himself. That's what we did, time after time, over the course of several months. When all those impulses were burned away, we were left with the fact, at once comforting and uncomfortable, that we were in love. It crept up on us so slowly that there arose a secret bashfulness between us in the midst of our debauch—whether to express tenderness, whether the feeling would be returned—until one day, afterward, he held me gently and kissed me as one would a sleeping child. I lifted my hand to his cheek, looking at him. The tender touch given and returned brought the happy, lucky thrill that two love-smitten children might feel the first time they squeezed each other's hands. Grateful, I wept, and I said, "I'm sorry, I'm sorry, I'm sorry, I'm sorry," and he said, "No, don't be, no, no, no, no, *I'm* sorry, *I'm* sorry," stroking my head and kissing the tears away.

AFTER THAT, OUR PREDICAMENT WAS CONVENTIONAL. His wife had a disordered mind, and was incapable of supporting herself, and he held a position that depended on the purity of his reputation. He told me that he was willing to relinquish them both. I did not believe him. I did not think he himself realized how much he liked the authority and influence that he wielded as a pastor. To leave that would be bad enough; to leave a helpless wife would destroy him. He could not touch the earnings of a madam, and I was not prepared to give them up; I had grown accustomed to luxury and was unwilling to be poor.

Besides, I couldn't bear the thought of telling Charley. He would be a man about it, but he would be hurt, and I was ashamed that I was not playing fair with him, after all his kindness to me. Outrageous as it may seem, I did not want to lose him. I loved Charley. I liked having him around me. It made me proud to have this formidable man at my side when I walked down the wooden streets of San Francisco, and it calmed my night fears to have him in my bed. I wanted to have my cake and eat it, too.

So we went on this way.

Jeptha and I talked more freely, more truthfully, than we could while we were married. I told him many things about my time in New York, though never quite all (never about Jack Cutter); and we reminisced about Livy, and our voyage to California, and the hotel in Rio. Once, I told him, "I've lived pretty high, but I never tasted a food I liked as much as the plums we had aboard the *Juniper*."

The next time we met, he brought a jar of plums, and we fed them to each other, face to face, just as we had so long ago. "They're still good," I said, tears running down my face.

"They're still good," he agreed, and our foreheads touched.

I reminded him of the time the Danforths gave us each a copy of the pamphlet *Marital Chastity*. I told him, for the first time, that I had been worried he would try to live by its principles, and he said that even the Danforths had eyes and must have known how doomed such a plan would be; he also told me that he knew I had given my copy of the pamphlet to the woman who had given me a Magdalene Society tract a few years ago. "And did you laugh?" I asked.

"No," he said. "I wasn't ready to laugh about any of it. You know, Agnes and I had been to see the Danforths before I went with you, and she had received her copy."

We talked about Philippe, and how he had died—a grief for Jeptha bigger than the death of his sister Becky, because it had been Jeptha's fault. "It broke me," he said.

"Well," I said, stroking his face, "I'm not saying it was good, I would never, never say that, but I think it's the reason we can be together now, talking like this. It's the reason you can understand me."

"I think I have always understood you," he said.

"Oh, you did." I nodded quickly, putting my fist over my heart. "You did when we were children, and when we were happy in Livy you did, you were the only one who did. But then so much happened to me—I did so many desperate things—and I told myself it hadn't changed me inside, but it had to, didn't it? I had to die or be remade." I sat up in the bed, and he watched me and waited while I gathered my thoughts. "You used to say, when you were a Baptist, that we all had to be born again. I used to think of that when we were on the *Juniper,* that I had been born again, *really* born again, and you had not." I was choking and shivering; I could hardly get the words out. He started to speak; I put my hand on his lips. "I thought that was good then. I would hold you, and think that your innocence was my innocence, your goodness was my goodness. But it couldn't happen that way."

He sat up and wrapped his arms around me from behind; I pushed my head back against him, feeling content.

"We fit before," he said. "And now we fit again."

I told him what Herbert Owen had told me about the letter he had written to Agnes. When I first touched the subject I was careful, since she had been his wife a long time now, and she, too, had suffered, and in her way I guessed she had been remade, but I could not bear to leave the question unanswered. "How could you do it, knowing what she'd done? She *did it,* you knew she had, she helped ruin me in Livy, and all we've suffered since is due to it. Did you hate me that much?"

He paused, casting his mind back, I supposed. "I burned. All day long. Over you. Philippe. My religion was supposed to help." He rubbed his neck with his hand and didn't speak for a while. "I was too proud to accept the consolation I urged on everyone else. It seemed more honest to soothe myself with whiskey. I don't remember writing to her, but it couldn't have been just a mistake I made while drunk. I was flailing about; I needed to stop flailing; I needed someone to stop it."

We lay there a moment, staring at the ceiling and contemplating all that, and then he continued: "Turns out it isn't so easy to toss aside your religion. After we struck gold, I started hearing a voice, inside my head but very persistent, calling me like Jonah, telling me to take that gold and build a church with it, and preach the Word. I drank to drown out the voice. I drowned it out with drink by night and with a hangover by day. Agnes came. I stopped drinking. I listened. The voice, which I knew was just another way of thinking, the voice wasn't telling me the Bible was all true. It wasn't telling me about the truth of any creed. It was telling me that there was a spirit in me and a spirit in the world, and I should honor it by making myself useful to people in the best way I know how, and to be as true as I could to the people who had educated me and sent me here, even if they might not think I was doing that by starting a Unitarian church in San Francisco."

"But marry her, Jeptha?"

"I was drowning. She was my lifeboat. And I thought, At least one of us will be happy."

"And she had traveled two thousand miles."

"There was that, too."

We managed to see each other once or twice a month, no more, sometimes out of town, sometimes, with various subterfuges, on the outskirts of town. I had a lot of freedom to move about, and I did not think that Charley suspected anything. And so we rolled along until the trivial incident between Charley and General William H. Richardson, which led to the formation of the Second San Francisco Committee of Vigilance. Soon we were fighting to save the life of the man I had betrayed.

LV

IT WAS A DAY IN NOVEMBER 1855, either six or seven years into the Gold Rush, depending on when you date its beginning. I had turned twenty-seven, and in exactly one month it would be six years since I had stood on the deck of the *Juniper* and watched the mist clear to reveal a bedraggled city of mud and tents and shacks spread out in a crescent on the bay. I woke up at around eleven, Charley woke up around noon, and we had our separate days. We had a plan to meet at seven that evening to go to a show.

At six-thirty, with the help of my lady's maid, I dressed, choosing my garments with a consciousness of my duty toward a following of respectable ladies who took their ideas of fashion from the town's best-dressed prostitutes and madams. They hated me. They wished their men would not visit my house. But we had a tacit understanding in this one matter, and I arrayed myself as much for them as for anyone else, in a walking dress of patterned blue organdy, a small scarf mantelet of embroidered lace, and a bonnet of fancy straw, blond lace, and crepe flowers. Describing it now, I realize how ridiculous a woman would look wearing it today.

Charley and I walked arm in arm a distance of several blocks to the American Theatre—*our* theatre, as we thought of it—then located on the intersection of Sansome and Halleck. We had attended hundreds of performances by scores of famous actors there. We were friends with the manager, and had been loyal to the place in its two previous incarnations—for, like so many San Francisco institutions, it had been destroyed more than once. Each time, we had mourned, and then rejoiced at the news that it would be rebuilt. It was now more beautiful than ever, as fine as anything in New York, with two thousand seats, thick carpets, red velvet curtains, gilt borders, bas-reliefs of scrolls and medallions and painted wooden infants tugging painted wooden drapes. House and stage lights were coal gas; earlier that year, with much fanfare, management had installed a complicated mechanism consisting of a block of lime, an oxy-hydrogen flame torch, and numerous mirrors, able to envelop a lone actor in a brilliant cone of light that *followed him across the stage*—I cannot exaggerate the astonished animal delight with which audiences in our upstart city greeted this effect that is so commonplace today, and which made pleasurable the performance of many a mediocre play and cast.

The play, called *Nicodemus; or The Unfortunate Fisherman,* was a performance by the Amazing Ravels, a French troupe beloved for their feats in gymnastics, ballet, and pantomime. There was a man on a tightrope, and a clown walking a chalk line across the floor in imitation of him, and it was well done, but at the midpoint of the performance a misunderstanding occurred which diverted my attention from the rest of the show. Two fools way down below us, in the pit, were trying to catch my eye. One wagged his hat over his head. Smiling, I waved my hand, and Charley waved, too, to remind them that he was there and to keep their enthusiasm within bounds, but even after that, from time to time they looked back at us again.

Two rows forward of us in the gallery sat William H. Richardson, who had supported the presidential ambitions of Franklin Pierce at the Democratic National Convention and as reward had been made United States Marshal for the Northern District of California. To his left, in a dress not unlike one I had worn in '52, was his new wife, Sarah, a recent arrival to our state; seated to her left was her friend Jane Matthews. Mrs. Richardson was small, bony, with a narrow bosom, a hatchet face, and protuberant eyes. If she'd been here in '49 or '50, the men of San Francisco would have slogged through acres of mud to gawk at her; but not anymore. Women were still outnumbered by men, but they weren't scarce enough to be mistaken for angels. Her friend Jane noticed the men in the pit and touched Sarah's elbow: Jane was so homely that both assumed the men were leering at Sarah. With apparently enough force to hurt, Mrs. Richardson rammed her elbow into her husband's arm. He turned. She pointed to the pit. "See that?" Charley asked me. I nodded. Richardson, a little bulldog of a man, rose to his feet; mumbling something, he stepped over many pairs of legs and went up the aisle. A minute later, we were looking down at the top of his head; he was in the pit, talking to the fools, presumably telling them to stop annoying his wife. "Now they'll all look up," I told Charley, and they turned their faces up to us and toward Mrs. Richardson. They understood—oh—and, it was evident, they apologized for the misunderstanding and explained that I was Belle Cora, well-known madam of a fancy house on Pike Street, and they had been gawking at me, not at his lovely wife. Jane and Sarah were watching this pantomime and seemed to understand the kind of mistake that had been made. At any rate, Jane turned toward me, and so did Sarah Richardson, and then she turned away, flushing. She did not yet know who I was; she only knew that the gods, for their amusement, had given me the beauty that ought to have been hers. Her husband went back up the aisle, and a few minutes later he was in the gallery again, talking to Mrs. Richardson.

Then that silly tin-hearted woman, with her delicate self-regard, turned toward me, furious, and spoke my name—not addressing me, merely pinning the syllables on me—"Belle Cora."

She spoke heatedly to her husband. After a moment he turned and said to Charley, loud enough for the Ravels to hear, "The woman with you is Belle Cora. She runs a disorderly house." I suppose that was meant as a preface to his remarks. He meant that he knew what we were, and our proper place was the soiled dovecote of the third tier.

Charley said, "Are you trying to save me from her?" People around us laughed, and Charley put his arm around me and said, "Don't worry about me. I like this kind of danger."

Richardson smiled back, while saying: "Get out. Both of you. Get out of the theater. I am General William H. Richardson. I'm the U.S. marshal."

In our section of the gallery, most people were watching us and ignoring the show.

Charley stood up. "General William H. Richardson, you tried to help me, so let me help you. You're letting your wife tell you what to do, and that would be fine if she was giving you good advice, but she ain't. She's making you look like a jackass. So I say, don't listen to her. Sit down. Watch the Frenchmen."

"William?" said Mrs. Richardson to her husband in a tone that reminded him of his duty.

"Don't you talk about my wife," said the marshal.

"Don't talk about mine," said Charley. We were not married, but Charley called me "Mrs. Cora," and referred to me as his wife, and that was why I was known as Belle Cora. Richardson sat down. His wife hissed in his ear; he hissed back. After a while, he left his seat again, was gone for ten minutes, came back, and spoke to his wife. He may have had a drink in the meantime, because he didn't bother to keep his voice down, and he turned his head to glower at us as often as he looked at her. "He won't. They come here all the time. He'd rather lose us than them."

He had spoken to the manager. We had known the manager of the American Theatre since it was built. We remembered the first American Theatre, built on landfill then so infirm that the whole house had sunk several feet from the weight of the opening-night audience—we were there—and after that, at high tide, the patrons had to walk over a plank bridge *inside the theater* to get to the show. We had seen the city burn six times. *We were forty-niners.* Mrs. Richardson was the Johnny-come-lately.

"I knew it. *I* should have talked to him," she said. Down on the stage, the Ravels were doing a selection from a famous ballet, but I gave all my attention to Mrs. Richardson. Suddenly she said, "My *mother*," and then she stopped herself and wept silently, now and then sniffing and wiping her eyes on the backs of her white gloves. He touched her elbow. She jerked it away from him. A minute later, she said in an out-of-doors voice, "I could have married Francis Randolph Hayes. I could be Mrs. Francis Randolph Hayes." She stood up, and here is where, I have to say, she made a spectacle of herself, looking out at the audience as if accusing them all. "American Theatre, indeed. Nothing but a great big cathouse, that's what it is, really. Cathouse!"

From above and below, from left and right, people peered at her through opera glasses, elbowed their neighbors, pointed, and grinned. She was causing herself serious, lasting damage. She tugged at her friend Jane's arm, saying, "I won't stay a minute longer in this *cathouse*," and Jane got up, and Richardson got up and followed them out. As they left, I heard her mutter, "U.S. marshal. U.S. marshal indeed."

WHEN THE SHOW WAS OVER, we walked to the El Dorado, which had been rebuilt for the third time, grander than ever. We went up to the balcony, from which we could eat and drink while watching the small-time gamblers milling around the bar, the roulette wheels and the faro tables and the monte tables. Up here, there were well-appointed rooms with carpets and potted plants and spittoons and windows, but usually the shades were down and a few oil lamps sufficed for illumination. To be in these rooms, wagering fantastic sums, winning without vainglory, losing without complaint, was a matter of pride to the big men of San Francisco.

We ordered steak, oysters, caviar, and champagne. Big Pete spotted us and came and sat at our table. We told him what had happened at the American Theatre. He said that he had met Richardson: about time somebody put him in his place. Big Pete looked over the rail and said, "Speaking of shit, look what's coming through the door." Charley and I looked down in time to glimpse the face of the man who had just entered the El Dorado. "I know him," said Big Pete. "Owns a bear."

"Abner Mosely," said Charley. We had both seen him before, at a match in which Mosely's fighting bear, Kicks, had competed against a bull. He had been here since '47. He was a veteran of the Mexican War. He had had many little doomed business ventures, but his luck seemed to be changing. The bear had won.

As he walked nearer the faro table, which was just below us, his hat gradually eclipsed his face. He walked out of view entirely. Then he reappeared on the second floor and approached our table. He was a man whose looks gave a perfectly accurate account of him. His short nose proudly displayed its hairy nostrils. In his wet mouth, whenever it was open, one saw acres of gum and Niagaras of saliva. He had freckly skin and a bushy red beard.

"Just the folks I came to see," he said, apportioning a hideous leer evenly among Big Pete, Charley, and me. "Gonna clean you out. Ready for that?"

"All right," said Big Pete, running an oversized finger across the irregular brim of his absurd hat. "Only, suppose we win. What do we get? I've got no use for a bear. What about you, Charley?"

Mosely said he'd have us know he had the money, thanks to Kicks, who had surprised a lot of folks who didn't know as much about bears as they thought they did. He was here to play, and this was going to be his night.

"All right," said Charley, and Pete said, "We'll take your money."

And Abner Mosely, because he was insulted, because he thought it might rattle Charley, and finally because he just liked to be disgusting, said that with the money he won from this game he planned to spend a night of rapture with me.

Immediately, yet it was not unexpected, I felt Charley's hand release me. The legs of his heavy chair made a sort of musical groan as Charley shoved it a few inches back across the hardwood floor. He rose to his feet, and walked briskly to Mosely, who flinched when Charley put an arm around his shoulder. Mosely was probably armed. So was Big Pete, who put his hands in his trouser pockets and watched alertly, and so was Charley, who said gently, as if talking to an errant nephew: "Mr. Mosely, you need to realize that you are in the El Dorado now, not some low gambling hell. We don't talk that way here. Besides, you didn't realize you are speaking of Mrs. Cora. Now that you do realize, I guess maybe you want to say you're sorry."

"I won't dance to your tune so easy," said Mosely, pulling away and showing us his slimy mouth.

"Of course you won't, Mr. Mosely," said Charley. "You're a proud man, who knows about bears. But if you don't say you're sorry, Mr. Hughes here will ask you to leave the El Dorado and not come back. And you won't win my money in a poker game. That's what you really want, ain't it? Unless, maybe, maybe, you've decided that this place is too rich for your blood, and you are looking for an excuse to leave."

Mosely appeared to think about that. Perhaps there was some truth in it. Certainly he had been over his head from the moment he had come through the door. He bowed to me with mocking ceremony. "Madam, my humble apologies." Looking from Big Pete to Charley, he said, for the second time, "Gonna clean you out." But I could see he was scared, as he had every right to be, and he went into the game hoping that things were not as they appeared to be and would turn out better than they usually did.

I remained at the El Dorado, for the pleasure of seeing Mosely when they were done with him. A waiter brought me coffee and some sweet biscuits. Someone had left an old edition of a fat British paper that serialized novels: in this issue, part of *The Count of Monte Cristo,* and I occupied myself with it. I had not read the earlier episodes, and there was no synopsis, so I had to guess at the parts of the plot I had missed. What made this count so determined? Why was this other man scared of him?

Another, much slimmer journal peeked out from behind a napkin: it was the *San Francisco Daily Evening Bulletin,* edited by my old acquaintance James King of William. King's bank had failed, ruining hundreds of people, including him, and badly tarnishing his reputation. He had turned all the opprobrium onto his former associates, by writing letters to San Francisco newspapers, which helped to save his name and had the incidental effect of bringing his talent for vituperation to the attention of the public. Only last month, with the backing of some Know-Nothing merchants, he had started the *Bulletin,* full of gossip, scandal, and highly personal attacks on local politicians. It sold briskly. Charley and I both read it. It often mentioned friends of ours.

The band played downstairs; waiters came and went. Laughter and curses emerged from behind the door to the little room where Big Pete and Charley and a few others were playing with Mosely. When I say they were playing with him, I mean like a toy. At last the door opened. Mosely staggered out, followed by the men who had his money, and who also had, I learned later, a makeshift but legal bill of sale for his fighting bear. He looked at me blindly. I said, "I'm ready, Mr. Mosely. Do you have the money?" Laughter.

Big Pete spoke to a waiter, who went downstairs first, and I watched from the balcony as Mosely made his way under the chandeliers and past the roulette wheel and the faro table. The waiter, having spoken to the bartender, handed Mosely a big bottle of whiskey, telling him it was on the house; Mosely took it without a word and stumbled into Portsmouth Square. Later, he claimed that he had been cheated. I don't doubt it. As events were soon to show, he was on a winning streak.

THE NEXT DAY, I LEFT CHARLEY at noon to stop at the post office, where I picked up a letter from Anne, and I read it on the carriage ride home. Frank, whom she referred to, in every letter, as "the precious gift you brought us from New York," would be eight years old in three months. He had shown himself so bright that he was already attending the winter school and using the fourth-grade reader, and the teacher, a young widow, doted on him, as proved by the fact that she had intervened to stop a fight between Frank and another boy, who was only half a year older than Frank but much bigger and stronger because of Frank's illness, which had worried us so much last year. The doctor—Livy had one now—had said that Frank was not consumptive, and would catch up in growth. Though delicate, Frank was brave, as one could tell by the things he dared to say to larger children.

I put the letter in my lap, and, as usual with Anne's letters, I tried to guess what she had left unsaid. It had to do with his character, I supposed. Five traits emerged consistently. He was "quick," frail, stubborn, acquisitive, and tactless (he had often hurt the feelings of Anne's daughter, Susannah, who doted on him). I did not know whether to count it a sixth trait, or simply the logical outcome of the others, that he was evidently friendless: if he had friends, Anne would certainly have mentioned them. Anne always put everything in the best possible light. I wondered if he was a sissy, or a loner, or just unlikable.

AROUND NINE-THIRTY THAT EVENING, my establishment was open. The wine flowed. The girls exhibited various degrees of lacy dishabille. The fleet, sensitive fingers of Mr. Rice, a talented freedman from New Orleans, were coaxing an iridescent Chopin waltz from the piano. Charley was out. By midnight he was still out, but that was hardly unusual or any cause for worry.

Lewis came by. He was a man of consequence now. David Broderick (who over a year ago had returned to power, as he had predicted he would) had made Lewis a clerk in the Board of Supervisors. He went to an office in City Hall almost daily; what he did there, I cannot say. He and Jocelyn had become a couple, secretly, and broken up, and reunited; recently, she had said, with a shrug, that she would let him make an honest woman of her—in a few years, if at that time he still had the notion. I urged her not to show him more public affection than she did to half a dozen others, and she tried to comply, but it must have been suspected, because Lewis had, with his fists, knocked out a tooth and, with his boots, broken two ribs belonging to a man who had suggested that Lewis lived off Jocelyn's earnings.

Edward and Lewis had patched up their differences, and we all got along better now, because we had gotten more used to the kind of life we lived in this city, and because, you might say, we had all reduced our expectations of one another and did not worry as much about each other's character flaws or whether our wicked ways would lead to a bad end.

I was sitting on a sofa with my back to the piano, and facing the double doors that led to the hallway. "Guess who me and Charley met today?" said Lewis, walking toward me. "General William H. Richardson."

That was odd. We'd never met Richardson until the night before. A moment later, Edward came in; he watched us in a way that made me uneasy. I could tell he knew whatever story it was that Lewis was about to relate, and that he expected it to worry me.

"Where?" I asked them. "When?"

Mr. Rice finished his waltz and began playing "Long, Long Ago." "Not here," said Michelle, slapping a gentleman's hand lightly. "We don't do that sort of thing here. You know that." By "here," she meant "in this room."

"A couple of hours ago," said Lewis, and with much enthusiasm he told me the following story.

Richardson, who had apparently been asking for Charley in cafés, barbershops, and saloons all over town, finally caught up with him in the Cosmopolitan, saying, "That's the man who insulted me." He was very drunk, and he had three friends with him. Some of Charley's friends were already present, and, as usually happens in such cases, the two groups both worked to cool tempers (mostly Richardson's temper) and brought about a truce. Richardson and Charley shook hands and stood each other rounds of drinks.

Everything seemed to have been settled amicably, until Charley and Richardson went out to the sidewalk to answer the call of nature. (I'm afraid it was usual even for men with pretensions to good manners to do this in San Francisco back then.) Charley finished first, and went back into the Cosmopolitan while Richardson was still doing his business. For some reason, unexplained to this day, this enraged Richardson—that's what Lewis told me, and it came out later in the trial, and no one said how strange it was. Richardson went back into the saloon, declaring that he would slap Charley's face. He had his left hand out, and his right hand in his pocket. In 1855, many men kept their guns in their coat pockets, and everyone present assumed that Richardson had his right hand on his gun and meant to follow up the slap with an immediate shootout. One of Richardson's friends said, "You're in liquor, Bill, you're not thinking right," to which Richardson replied, "I'll slap your face, too." A second member of Richardson's coterie stepped in front of him, whereupon Richardson did draw his gun, causing just about every other man in the room except Charley to draw his. The friend, who was either a very good friend or very drunk himself, put his hand on the barrel of Richardson's pistol, his palm flat against the hole from which the bullet emerges. There followed, I assume, a tense pause, after which the marshal cocked his pistol. "Don't! You'll blow my hand off!" cried the friend. A third friend grabbed Richardson's gun and pushed it down, even as the crazy drunk growled, "I'll kill all you scoundrels. I'll say you resisted arrest."

In a few minutes, he was weeping and apologizing, saying he was a swine and he didn't deserve such friends as these, and among his friends, guess which one was the very best? It was Charley, his *new* friend. Before his mood turned again, the men he had come in with took him home to his wife.

"Where's Charley now?" I asked.

"He's at Frankie Garcia's," said Edward, "with Ned McGowan and Jimmy O'Meara. We just left them."

I sent a servant for my coat, and we walked to Frankie Garcia's café while Lewis told me the tale a second time. I had to hear it twice before I could picture it all.

Taking note of the briskness of Lewis's step as we neared the café, and the animation with which he told the story, acting out the parts and imitating the voices, I was nearly as worried for him as I was for Charley. Lewis loved violence. If things were peaceful for too long, he became confused and sulky, and Jocelyn would say, "Go out and get in a fight, Lewis, you'll feel better." Few events were so cheering to him as the advent in his circle of a mean bastard just begging to be taught a lesson.

When we got to Frankie Garcia's, Charley was at a table in the back with Ned McGowan. Next to the walruslike McGowan, and in sharp physical contrast to him, sat James O'Meara, a diminutive, redheaded newspaperman. They were the advisers, respectively, of the political bosses David Broderick and William Gwin. Broderick and Gwin loathed each other, but their servants McGowan and O'Meara were easygoing. One often saw them together, conspiring against their common enemy, the Know-Nothings.

Charley, as tranquil as ever, ordered Imperial Punches for Edward, Lewis, and me, while O'Meara told me what he knew about Richardson. It was usual for the marshal to pursue these quarrels, and to hound a man until something happened. "I was telling Charley here to stay clear of him. If there's a shoot-out and Richardson dies, it would look bad. It would be, if you'll excuse me, a case of a gambler, who, ah, lives . . ."

"In the finest house in the state," I finished his sentence.

"That such a man has shot the U.S. marshal, who represents the law."

"It would be very bad now," agreed McGowan, as his fingers conferred with his mustache. "It could be like '51. They could seize on it to embarrass the government, saying we were letting criminals run loose, shooting marshals. It would be bad for both of us." He and O'Meara nodded at each other.

"But if he kills me," Charley observed, "then *I'm* not happy."

"Somebody ought to fix him now in privacy," said Lewis mildly, with an expert's pleasure in his craft. "Put him down quietly. Tell him there's a fast woman waiting for him in some shack in the middle of nowhere."

"Well, now," said McGowan, smiling, "in a perfect world."

"Lewis," I said, "if people heard you, they might misunderstand."

Charley said, "Let's hope somebody else hurts his feelings and he forgets about me," and he asked McGowan and O'Meara if they knew anyone who might be interested in a half-share of Kicks, the fighting bear he had won from Abner Mosely.

I sipped my punch, contemplating the lessons of the evening. There were at least three. One, guns and whiskey don't mix. Two, even Richardson's friends feared him when he was drunk. Three, tomorrow he would forget that his quarrel with Charley had been settled.

AT ELEVEN THE NEXT MORNING, Niobe woke me, as she did every day, and helped me dress. In order to bring the girls all regularly under my eye at once, I had a rule that we ate a late breakfast together every day. One or two were always in rebellion. "Where is Lydia? Marianne, fetch Lydia." Lydia appeared, sullen: my silly rule had forced her to evict from her bed a gentleman who had paid well to stay the night. "Lydia," I said, "when you have had my experience of life, you'll realize that you can't break a rule every time it's inconvenient."

Except for Jocelyn, all the girls had been in the house for less than two years. That was the nature of our business. The girls, who had worked in the States, made the expensive journey here to obtain their share of California's gold. Each upon her arrival in my house was the "new girl," and I made her famous, sending out cards urging the chief men of the town to come and see this exquisite creature. After a year or two, she went to Stockton or Sacramento City, where she was a novelty again. Then, unless something unexpected happened, she returned to the States. So the population of my house was like the population of San Francisco, ever changing.

The kitchen maid brought in covered trays with eggs, toast, corn bread, kippers, bacon, sausage, fried oysters, cream, coffee, tea, oranges. Some of the girls ate heartily. Others had coffee and hangover remedies. Margaret and Genevieve, who had been feuding over some petty matter yesterday, were still feuding, I noticed. Antoinette was angry with me for insisting that she accommodate Mr. Dixon despite his unusual proclivities—which I had known about beforehand, as she realized when she complained to me and instead of banishing him I insisted that she grant his request. I had assured her the next day that it wasn't because I liked her less than the others. She must look on it as an opportunity. "You'll get used to it," I told her. "I can't. I can't," she said, weeping, and I almost weakened. But Dixon had to be pleased, and the girl who had put up with it once was the girl most likely to put up with it on a regular basis.

All day long, I was nervous and jumpy, but I kept telling myself everything would be all right: Charley could take care of himself. After breakfast, I did my accounts. Lewis was already up and in City Hall. Charley went out to have breakfast and a shave on Montgomery Street. I wanted to tell him to stay home, in case Richardson came looking for him again, but I didn't; it would be pointless. I didn't even tell him to be careful. He would be exactly as careful as he always was, no matter what I said.

I got into my carriage and picked up my friend and fellow madam Irene Grogan, Big Pete's girl, whom I had arranged to meet at this time the day before.

My house, on the corner of Sacramento Street and Pike Street, was a massive two-and-a-half-story building with a mansard roof. Irene's place, next door on Sacramento, was narrower and higher, New Orleans style, with a second-story veranda and fancy iron grillwork. The famous Chinese madam Ah Toy presided over a house nearby. A neighborhood of parlor houses had arisen at this spot quite naturally, as other streets accumulate doctors' offices or dry-goods stores.

We went to the auction house of T. Kilmer & Sons, where according to the *Herald* the property of several ruined bankers would go to the highest bidder. I bought a cedarwood chest that had belonged to the wife of James King of William. There was a painting of pine trees and robins on its lid.

Irene and I had a late lunch at Frankie Garcia's as twilight fell and Frankie turned the key in all the café's lamps, one by one. Through the

window, we watched the lamplighter, his neck craned back, deftly insinu-
ate the end of a slender pole into the four-paned chamber of a street
lamp. It was time to return to Pike Street, but my driver was late. When
at last he showed up, it was about six-thirty. It was quiet. Within the carriage we heard the hollow impact of horseshoes, the creak of the wheels,
and a gunshot. "Stop," I ordered. Irene and I got out of the carriage and
listened.

There were no more shots.

For thirty minutes we walked up and down various streets, poking
our heads into saloons, looking for Charley. We saw a crowd gathering in
front of the Oriental Hotel, and I ran toward it, picturing Charley lying
dead or wounded at the crowd's center.

I noticed a stovepipe hat hovering and dancing above the hats of the
men in the crowd. The hat was crying out for justice. It jerked with the
shouted words. Pushing nearer, I glimpsed the arm waving that hat, and
below it a pair of sleepy eyes and a narrow face gripped in a vise of sideburns. It was Sam Brannan, the highly talented promoter, urging all the
men here to be men and make the town safe by breaking into the jail and
dragging a prisoner out of it. "A United States marshal! His poor, sweet
wife don't even know she's a widow yet! She sets at home, writing a letter
to her mama back east, while a man walks up the hill bringing the awful
news! Her husband, murdered by a professional gambler! And where is
this gambler? Resting safe in the basement of City Hall . . ."

Irene grabbed my arm and nodded toward a street lamp under which
stood the sheriff, David Scannell, his great belly lit halfway around like
the moon. Deputies surrounded him, doing nothing. I pushed my way
through the crowd with Irene in my wake, and waited until I was close
to say, "Sheriff Scannell!" When he didn't respond, I shouted it: "Sheriff
Scannell!" Men turned toward us. "How can you let him go on that way?"
We knew each other, but he looked at me as if he did not care to be told
how to do his job. I took a more womanly tone. "Sheriff, I'm scared."

"I was going to stop him," he said, and spoke to the deputies, who
told Brannan to consider himself arrested for incitement to riot.

"Arrest me?" shouted Brannan to the crowd he had gathered. "You
mean, *take me to the station house*? Gentlemen, see how quick on the mark
Cora's friends are. They're taking me to the basement of City Hall to sit
in a cell next to the murderer of General Richardson. Of course I'll go

peaceably. Why don't you come along! Follow me to the station house and see what happens."

About ten men took his meaning and followed him, and I was beside myself with fright. Scannell put his hand on my shoulder and leaned down, smelling of anise and wormwood—he was a habitual drinker of absinthe, which, they say, gives one interesting dreams. "The minute Brannan showed his face, I had Charley taken to county lockup."

I thanked him and went with Irene to find my carriage. As I passed by, someone in the crowd said, "That's her."

THE COUNTY JAIL WAS STONE AND BRICK with windows in arches, set in a niche carved from Telegraph Hill. The lowering of Broadway since it was built had put its front entrance eight feet above the street, and a narrow wooden stairway led to it now. Fifty men were guarding it. They let us in. We sought out Billy Mulligan, Lewis's old friend, now the chief jailer, thanks to the same election that had made Scannell sheriff.

Mulligan insisted on going with me and taking another guard to watch the cell, because I was a woman and it would be indecent to search me for a pistol.

"Search me, Billy. Search me all over," I said, but he wouldn't. From the very beginning of this thing, he was scared to do anything irregular.

The hall was dark. The cell doors were massive assemblies of oak reinforced by strips of black iron. Each door had a small window at eye level. Inside, it was a stinking, dark, damp box with a washbasin, a straw mattress, a piss pot, and an invisible residue of lonely despair left behind by previous occupants. "Papa," I said when I saw Charley. We embraced. Along with the familiar scents of peppermint, tobacco, sweat, and whiskey, I smelled the burnt powder that had come off Charley's derringer. Mulligan insisted on searching Charley for a pistol again, in case I had slipped him one. Then we sat down on the bed. Charley told me his story, sometimes looking at me, sometimes at his hands, in front of Mulligan and the guard.

"I was in the Blue Wing with O'Meara and some others. Richardson came in, looking for me, ornery again. So people talk to him, he's friendly again. He says, let's go somewhere, we're buds now. I figure I'll walk with him awhile, shake hands, ditch him. So we walk, we talk. It's all right. Then he says, 'What do you think I am? Who do you think you're talk-

ing to? Let me show you something.' He draws his pistol. He cocks it."
Charley demonstrated. "With my left hand I grab it by the barrel. I keep
my right hand free for my own pistol, because this ain't no joke. I push
on the barrel, like his friends did yesterday, only up, instead of down. I'm
twisting the hand with the gun. He's small, but he's stronger than he
looks. He won't let go. I push him into the door. If he didn't mean to fire
that pistol before, he does now. You know how folks say, it all happened
so fast? This happened slow. Like wrestling." Charley put his long, skillful index finger to his neck. "The end of the barrel of his pistol is up here,
on my neck—it could blow a hole through my throat. I'm thinking, what
about the other gun? O'Meara said he carries two, right? What do I do?
I can't run. I can't let him go. I need my right hand for my own pistol. I
feel him move the other hand." Charley stopped. "I can't take the chance.
I shoot. He goes loose, like he's dead. But I'm thinking, maybe he's pretending; I keep him against the door. I check his pocket for the other gun;
nothing." Charley gave his head a little tilt, his quiet version of a shrug.
"I go up the street and a copper arrests me."

"You shouldn't have gone with Richardson, Papa. That was stupid."

He shook his head. "I know every kind of drunk there is. If I told this
man I wouldn't walk with him, he'd have drawn on me in the Blue Wing.
I thought—I still think—it was safer to go outside with him. But in the
end, nothing was safe."

I promised him that I would get him out, and the next thing I did was
to get Billy Mulligan alone and tell him to name his price. I was not surprised when he refused. Escapes had been common in '49 and '50, when
there had been no proper jails and no one had cared for anything except
instant wealth. The newspapers, to drum up support for a second Vigilance Committee, would soon be pretending that this was still true, but
it wasn't. If there was any escape now, Mulligan would be finished in San
Francisco, and he was under the impression that he had a big future here.
The best I could do right now was to make Charley more comfortable. In
the weeks that followed, I arranged for him to be moved to a larger cell,
and to have some furniture from our house taken into it, and his favorite
whiskey and cigars. Three times a day, one of my servants brought him
hot meals prepared by my cook.

❧ LVI ❧

I KEPT THE NEWSPAPERS THAT CARRIED STORIES of the trial under my bed, in the cedarwood hope chest that once belonged to the wife of James King of William. Years later, I pasted the articles into a scrapbook. Even today I can't read them without picturing the men at whose behest they were written, and I still want to hurt them, wherever they are.

The *Alta California* reported the incident in this way: "Gen. William H. Richardson was assassinated in the streets of this city last evening, under circumstances particularly atrocious," from "no inciting cause but an unnatural thirst for blood." After a grossly prejudiced account of the incident, a summary of the medical examiner's report ("The ball entered the body about two and a half inches above the left nipple: it perforated the fourth rib . . ."), and a short biography of the deceased, the article concluded: "Gen. Richardson was brave and chivalric to a proverb, and withal so gentle and quiet in his demeanor towards all, that none could know him and not love him. He leaves a young wife overwhelmed in grief, and whose situation is such as to call forth the strongest sympathy of every individual."

James King of William added his voice to the chorus with an editorial in his newspaper, the *San Francisco Daily Evening Bulletin*. "Murder & Gambling, etc." was the headline. "The cowardly-like assassination on Saturday of a U.S. Marshal, General Richardson, on one of our public thoroughfares and within a few yards of Montgomery Street, calls for some expression of opinion from us. We are told by those who knew the deceased, that he was a good citizen and an efficient officer, ever diligent in the discharge of his duties. Cora was an Italian assassin and a gambler . . ."

Like the *Alta California*, King mentioned the vigilantes right away, using his favorite technique of strenuous insinuation—it would be a shame if government corruption left the People no choice but to form another Vigilance Committee. It was his custom to put his most reckless libels into fictitious letters to the editor from imaginary irate citizens. Then, as himself, he would comment on the understandable frustration that inspired those intemperate words. Give the courts a chance, give them a chance, and if justice was not served (meaning, if Charley didn't hang), why, then, it would be no surprise if a Vigilance Committee again arose to punish malefactors as it had in the heroic early days of San Francisco.

It was a conspiracy from the start. But though I had been warned that it was, and sometimes I said it was, I didn't really believe it. More often I told people—my girls, my servants, storekeepers, gamblers, gentlemen at my house—that James King of William had the penis of a four-year-old boy, that Sam Brannan's was just a little bigger, and they both hated me because I knew it. People liked hearing this; it was the kind of thing they expected a parlor-house madam to say. For that very reason, it did not make much of an impression, and after a while I stopped saying it.

❧ LVII ❧

ON THE NIGHT OF THE SHOOTING, I had a messenger deliver letters to Ned McGowan, Herbert Owen, and two or three other men who knew about courts and lawyers. McGowan came to see me. We talked for several hours about the shooting, and he bedded down in an empty room upstairs.

I had the kind of long night that Charley used to help me through, in our early days in Sacramento City and San Francisco, when Jeptha had left me and I felt as if I were someone else, some innocent soul deposited into the body of this wicked woman who dared not even use her real name. Charley had been my anchor. He had saved my life.

Then, last year, I had begun to betray him, on a regular basis, with Jeptha.

I thought a lot about that now, in our big half-empty bed. I tried to sleep. I reminded myself that I must be wide awake tomorrow, when I would have many decisions to make. Of course, that did no good at all. I got up. I lit a lantern and went to the room where I had put Ned McGowan and looked in on him. He was sleeping soundly. I thought about shaking him awake. I almost did—he would be company at least. But, after all, he wasn't Charley, and he would be of better use to me tomorrow with a clear head. I grabbed a book—*The Count of Monte Cristo,* which I had sent a servant to purchase for me the morning after our encounter with Mr. and Mrs. Richardson at the American Theatre—and I went downstairs to the kitchen and fixed myself a hot toddy with plenty of whiskey and began to read it. Edmond Dantès (I remembered this from the excerpt) was imprisoned for fourteen years in the Château d'If. He languished in the Stygian shadows, deprived of sunlight, for so long that even after he escaped, for the rest of his life, he had the unnatural pallor of a prisoner: it was too late for the sun to darken his skin. I wondered if such a thing could be, if skin could lose its ability to absorb sunlight. I made myself another hot toddy.

Early in the morning, I became drowsy and drank coffee to stay awake. A couple of hours later, I went with McGowan and Lewis to the place in City Hall where the inquest was to be held.

There were three factions present among the spectators: curious neutrals; sporting men (Charley's friends); friends of Richardson.

Mrs. Richardson was there in black bombazine, more becoming than the dress she had worn at the theater, and such a perfect fit that I could not help thinking of it hanging impatiently in her closet, awaiting this day. When she saw me, her right arm rose in a slow, unbending gesture learned from melodramas. "That's her. Dear Lord, she dares to come here, she's here to gloat! How dare you!" Everyone looked. "Get her out of here! Get her out of here!" A burly fellow, one of Richardson's friends, patted her hand and spoke to her softly. She jerked the hand away. "I don't need your help, I need a *man's* help. They say there are more men in San Francisco than women, but I haven't met one here except my Billy, and this woman has had him killed!" The last part was spoken in a crybaby whine, eyes on the ceiling, head wagging.

"You ridiculous woman," I said. "You know damned well it was you who killed your husband, by calling him a coward and egging him on into a fight."

McGowan tugged my arm. "You can't win against her now."

"Get her out of here!" wailed Mrs. Richardson like an infant.

"It was you," I said, unable to stop. "You told your Bill to prove he was a man. So he filled himself with Dutch courage and wagged his stupid pistol at my Charley."

"Oh!" she cried as if stabbed. "Oh, help me, someone!"

After murmuring to each other in low tones, several men approached the sheriff's deputies. "Are you going to let a common prostitute talk that way to the general's wife?"

As the deputies turned toward me, my eyes sought Ned. "Judge McGowan," I said, using his title to remind everyone that he was a man of importance, "would you speak for me?"

Ned called the sheriff's deputies each by name, and said, "I know you're not going to let these fellows bully you. Charles Cora is her man. She has as much right to be here as Mrs. Richardson."

"Well, okay," one of them replied. "But keep her away from the widow."

Except that the dead brute had rejoiced in the plum of a lucrative federal appointment, the incident was not unlike many a whiskey-soaked affray of the type San Francisco newspapers dispensed with in two paragraphs: a drunk had drawn a weapon, forcing another man to kill him. That would come out. Charley would be released. The *Bulletin* and the *Alta California* would cry foul, but it would happen, because facts were facts.

But when the eight-man inquest jury was impaneled, McGowan became serious. "What is it?" I asked. "They're all Know-Nothings," he said. "Every last one."

There was much smoking and chewing and spitting. The judge called repeatedly for order. Three guns and a knife were laid out on a table. When the witnesses were called, a court stenographer and three newspaper stenographers scratched furiously away in their notebooks.

I knew from reading the papers that one of the chief witnesses to the shooting was to be Abner Mosely, who had lost everything to Charley in a card game only a few days ago. When he was sworn in, I rose from my seat, ready to tell the jury that they couldn't trust a word this man had to say—he hated Charley. But McGowan warned me that I could be kicked out if I said anything.

When I heard Mosely's testimony, I thought it would be clear to everyone that this man, standing where his own account placed him—twenty yards away, on a dimly lit street at dusk—could not possibly have seen what he claimed to have seen or heard what he claimed to have heard. He said that he saw Charley push Richardson into the door. He said he had heard Richardson plead, "You're not going to shoot me, are you? I'm unarmed." He said that Charley had Richardson pinned by both his arms while he pulled the trigger, which would seem to require that Charley have three arms of his own, as I remarked to McGowan, who said, "Good point." But the jury, though it asked other questions, said nothing about this.

The remaining witnesses told conflicting stories. Three men said they had found a derringer—no doubt, Richardson's gun—near the body when they moved it. One witness had found a knife lying on the ground. *See?* I thought. He *was* armed. But then another man said that when Richardson's body was moved he saw no gun at all; the gun appeared later. And a couple of subsequent witnesses told stories implying that someone had rushed to the scene and planted the gun and the knife. (The someone, I learned later, was generally supposed to have been sent to the spot by me.)

The foreman of the jury, reading from a page, said it was their conclusion that "William H. Richardson came to his death by a pistol shot fired from the hands of one Charles Cora on the night of Saturday, Nov. 17, between the hours of six and seven o'clock . . . and the act was premeditated and that there was nothing to mitigate the same."

THE ONLY REALLY GOOD ATTORNEY I KNEW was Hall McAllister, who used to patronize my house on Dupont Street in the company of his brother Ward, later famous as Mrs. Astor's social secretary. The morning after the inquest, I went to McAllister's office, telling him that I wanted Charley to have the best defense money could buy. He said that he would love to take the case, but public opinion was so inflamed against Charley that it would be the ruin of him: the lawyer who defended Cora could lose all his other business. McAllister had a family. Besides, his father, Judge McAllister, would never forgive him.

"Fortunately, I know just the men who can help you," said McAllister. First, I must hire James A. McDougall, the former state attorney general. McDougall loved a fight, did not mind representing unpopular defendants, and was friendly with Colonel Edward D. Baker, whose services I must obtain at any cost. Baker was one of the finest orators in the country, a man of unimpeachable integrity, admired by the sort of people likely to end up on our jury. His mere presence in the courtroom, at Charley's table, would help us. Baker, however, would have to be persuaded, and he would be very expensive.

McAllister sent an errand boy to fetch McDougall, telling him to look for him in his office, and if he was not there to try this saloon, and that saloon, and that other saloon; this bothered me, because it was early in the day for drinking. Then we waited. I raised the second-story window's shade, revealing the elaborate ironwork of the exterior windowsill, the arched windows of a bank across the street, and the naked masts and yardarms of ships in the bay. Below me were the bricks of Montgomery Street, signs, canvas awnings, hopping sparrows, men in stovepipe hats, a silent shouting match between two cart drivers. It occurred to me that the birds and horses, and some of the people on the ships, did not know that Charles Cora had shot William Richardson, but everyone else out there did, and it was the first thing that many had heard about either of these men. That amazed me. I could not quite grasp it. I thought of Charley in his cell. I thought of Jeptha and Agnes. With everyone they knew talking about the case, would they mention it to each other, or avoid discussing it so that they could avoid discussing me? Jeptha was not easily fooled, but I hated to think of him reading the newspapers and not getting Charley's side of the story. I wished I could tell him about it now.

At last McDougall came in. He was small and spare, with a goatee, a Mephistophelian expression, and agate eyes surrounded by crow's-feet. Newspapers sprouted from the pockets of his frock coat. When he saw me, his mouth stretched in delight, but he looked at McAllister inquisitively.

"I'm just helping her find counsel," said McAllister. "I was thinking you and Baker. Baker likes you. You help bring Baker in."

McDougall's glittering eyes inspected me. He nodded absentmindedly when McAllister rather belatedly said, "Mrs. Cora, allow me to introduce Mr. McDougall."

The little man exuded eagerness and confidence—maybe justified, but how, really, could I judge? I had seldom used a lawyer in my business.

McDougall took me across the street to the headquarters of Baker & Wistar, Attorneys at Law. Baker was out. His partner let us wait in Baker's untidy office, where a window was propped open by books, and stacks of papers bound in twine stood against the wall. I told McDougall about the events at the American Theatre and about Richardson's actions the following evening at the Cosmopolitan, when he had threatened to shoot Charley and anyone who got between him and Charley. McDougall, after hunting for ink and paper on Baker's desk, had me repeat all of the names that had come up in my account. "The prosecution will try to restrict the testimony to the shooting itself," he predicted. "When we bring witnesses against Richardson, they'll say we're soiling his name, putting him on the level of a gambler who lives on an immoral woman's earnings."

"He does not! He's just not flush enough now to pay for his defense."

McDougall looked up, a little surprised.

"Is Baker really a fine lawyer?" I asked him.

"Yes."

"Which of you is better?"

He smiled. "I am, I think. But that's a minority opinion. When Baker gives an address, the newspapers print all of it, word for word. They don't do that for the rest of us. Nor is his value merely ornamental. He changes minds. We need him."

Baker came in at last, a tall man, untidy in his person and evidently proud of it. His head sat in his upturned collar like a cauliflower in a garden; the sparse hair was wild yet stiff, reminding me of those mountain cedars that look permanently struggling and windblown. It was a studied dishevelment speaking of eccentric genius indifferent to appearances. He had shiny skin, a piercing gaze, a long straight nose, and a double chin. From some angles he resembled a middle-aged baby.

He made a visible decision to treat me like a lady (unlike McDougall, who was equally indifferent to my profession and my feelings). He sat in royal silence as McDougall told him that if he did not take the case Charley was doomed. If I had not guessed that Baker was vain, I would have known it from the way McDougall spoke to him. Encouraged by McDougall, I made my own plea on Charley's behalf.

Afterward, Baker sat for some time with his hands folded. A mighty mind was at work: we were not to interrupt. At last he rose to his feet and addressed me as if I were a foreign potentate or a vast crowd. "The most basic principles of equal justice under the law are at stake in this case. I am at your service, Belle Cora. I will do everything in my power, use every tool at my command, all my skill, my knowledge, and all my heart, to vindicate this man attacked by a drunken bully in the guise of a marshal, traduced by a bought press and all but abandoned by the legal profession. Though he had led a dissolute life and kept evil companions, he deserves justice, and I shall not abandon him."

I thrilled to this free sample of the mysterious natural force that was Colonel Baker's power over the English language. Of course it was expensive: it was the best.

❧ LVIII ☙

WHEN THE NAMES OF THE LAWYERS I HAD HIRED were made public, it was understood immediately that Belle Cora would spend vast sums of money to save Charles Cora. My house promptly became the site of its own little gold rush. In the weeks before the trial, half a dozen people came to me claiming to have witnessed the shooting, or to know those who had seen it; with varying degrees of subtlety they would offer to change their testimony, or threaten to change it. I would tell them that they should not have come: my house was being watched, and any suspicion of bribery would hurt Charley's case. But I added that, just the same, whoever helped Charley was my friend, and whoever hurt him was my enemy, and that I was both generous and vengeful.

One of these people was a woman named Maria Knight, who had testified at the inquest. She arrived early in the afternoon, wearing Sunday clothes, looking her best given that her head was too small for her body, her nose was the right size but too complicated, and standing near the nose, like an ill-conceived distraction, was a pink mole from which a long hair sprouted. With her was a sober-looking man with bad skin and round shoulders whom she introduced as Thomas Russell. I bade them sit, sent for tea and a seed cake, and said as usual that though she was welcome I was afraid that her visit might be misunderstood. It might be thought that she intended something dishonest, especially if later her testimony changed in a way that proved favorable to Mr. Cora.

"It would? Really?" she asked, holding out her cup while I poured. "What kind of thing would folks think you'd like me to say?"

That was a plain enough invitation to make an offer, and I would have struck a bargain with her if it hadn't been for the presence of her companion, Russell. Perhaps she had brought him so that she would feel safe in a brothel. But he was also a witness to this conversation; I was afraid of a trap. "I'm not sure I want to give an example. Unless—would you mind if we continued this conversation in private?"

"Oh, don't worry about Mr. Russell; he's the soul of discretion, ain't you, Tom?" Her companion nodded. "You see?" said Maria Knight. "Let me guess what you'd like. You'd like me to say that I saw a pistol in General Richardson's hand. I could say that."

"If that's what you saw," I said, "that's what you ought to say."

"Oh, I didn't see anything of the sort. But for five thousand dollars, I could say I had." With the nail of her pinky finger, in a gesture that she almost succeeded in making refined and ladylike, she scraped a caraway seed from between her teeth.

I spoke carefully. "I know that Richardson drew his pistol, and Charley pushed the pistol up, and it was evening. People could make mistakes. You could realize that you made a mistake. As for the other thing you mentioned, all I can say is, I'm the friend of anyone who helps Charley, the foe of anyone who hurts him, and I have a long memory."

"Well," she said, after a while. "Well, I never. Come, Thomas." Keeping her back very straight, she rose from her chair.

"I don't mean to be unfriendly," I said. "I want you for a friend."

She turned. She said, "My friendship has a price."

I smiled. She blushed. I repeated my vague promises. They weren't enough for her. "You shouldn't have treated me this way," she said. "I've got a long memory, too."

It is my belief that she had other resources. I was not the only one with money.

AT MY SUGGESTION, LEWIS SPOKE to Abner Mosely in the Cosmopolitan and nebulously alluded to the rumors of my generosity. People said that I was willing to pay men to change their testimony. Had Mosely heard that? Did he ever daydream about it? "I daydream of Charles Cora going out dancing in a hemp necktie," said Mosely with a well-lubricated smile.

Well, Lewis said then, what did he think of the rumors that Belle Cora was willing to pay ten thousand dollars to the man who killed Abner Mosely?

"There ain't no such rumor and ain't going to be. She knows that if I'm killed they'll bring back the Vigilance Committee, and Charley will be hanged for sure."

We were afraid he was right. Still, we discussed it. Lewis wanted to take a personal hand, and long after I had definitely decided that it would be too dangerous to murder Mosely, I thought, simply for my amusement, about how it might be done.

CHRISTMAS NEARED. MEN WALKED THROUGH the streets carrying bread, plucked turkeys and geese, apples, and small evergreens. Lewis, Jocelyn, Edward, Ned McGowan, and I spent Christmas Day with Charley in his cell; and we were there together again on New Year's Eve and New Year's Day.

On Thursday, January 3, the selection of the jury began, with four lawyers for the People and four lawyers for Charles Cora. Our lawyers insisted that I stay clear of the courtroom. I could do no good there. The prosecutors need only glance in my direction to remind the jury that Charley was a gambler who lived in a brothel. I followed events through the newspapers and conferences with McDougall or Baker. Every day, as Charley was moved under heavy guard from the county jail to a carriage that would take him to the court, I stood on Broadway to greet him, and we both tried to look cheerful.

The jurors were isolated from the rest of the world, and were never supposed to separate during the trial. They were all moved into the Railroad House, a three-story hotel with entrances on Clay Street and Commercial Street. Three or four would be lodged together in a room, and sheriff's deputies would sleep with them. They would not be permitted to leave, even to visit their families. When I first heard this, I borrowed a carriage (so that it would not be identified as mine) and examined the Railroad House. It was exposed on every side and would be impossible to leave or enter without detection. On the other hand, it had a staff: cooks, waiters, maids. They did not live at the Railroad House. They had to come and go. Perhaps some of my people could become acquainted with them. And the sheriff's deputies. Most of them were very poorly paid.

THE TRIAL PROPER BEGAN. One after another, dozens of witnesses swore on the Bible, stated their names and occupations, when they had come to California, and what part of the States they were from. Several had known either Richardson or Charley back east. To read this testimony now is to be reminded of the unusual conditions of San Francisco back then: strangers from faraway places were mingled here, retaining their old accents, beliefs, and grudges. There had been another life back home, which some of us would rather forget, and right here, just a few years earlier, we had lived under special rules that were not easy to explain to more recent arrivals.

Several men who knew Richardson, including some of his friends, admitted that he was extremely disagreeable when drunk, and went about armed with a knife and usually two pistols. Others testified that he was a knight errant. Our case was hurt when both of our witnesses to the shooting admitted, on cross-examination, that they had gone to my house to talk to me about their testimony. It did not matter that they had come of their own accord, and it would do no good to call me in as a witness and say I hadn't bribed them. What else would anyone expect me to say?

Abner Mosely repeated the testimony he had given at the inquest. Later, Baker called several witnesses as to what manner of man Mosely was, and made him look pretty bad.

Maria Knight's evidence about the shooting was not important. It was on cross-examination, when Baker tried to get her to admit that she had visited my house, that she ruined us. She said that she had been "tricked" into coming. I had begged her to come, and two prominent men had assured her it was safe, and in her version she spoke with me alone, with Russell waiting in another room; she said that I had threatened her life.

She loved being up there, testifying. Today, whenever I see the work of a "still life" painter, who struggles to interest us in a chipped cup, a hunk of bread, and a bunch of dusty translucent grapes, I think how much simpler his task would be if he could say these items were exhibits in a murder trial. The trial is a beam from the clouds, selecting a few trivial objects and telling us that, despite appearances, they're important—a stupid quarrel in a saloon, how many drinks each man had and who bought them, the position of a street lamp, a young woman with a dime-novel imagination. Maria Knight, in her best shoes and best shawl, turned her face up happily in the sunny beam and danced.

Colonel Baker had not expected this. He must have felt as if he'd stepped into a bear trap, and he was obviously rattled. He didn't press her on the weakness in her story—what earthly purpose could she have in coming to my house if not to ask me for money?

When the prosecution questioned her again, she described my parlor and also one of my serving trays, but on the tray, instead of tea and cake, she put a single ominous glass of wine I kept urging her to drink. She told me she was an abstainer; I brought her tea—again, just one suspicious serving, which she refused (but really she had devoured an entire seed cake and tossed three cups of tea down her gullet, just because they didn't cost her anything). "Foiled in her two attempts to poison me," said Miss Knight, "she told me a pathetic story of her childhood." Then, her thrilling tale continued, the folding doors of the parlor were thrown open and she saw two men, one of whom had a pistol in his hand and asked if now she would change her testimony. "I was afraid for my life; one of them cried out to know of Belle Cora if the doors and windows of the house were all barred; I then asked for Mr. Russell, who had accompanied me to the house, but they would not allow him to come in; the men however permitted me to leave when they saw how frightened I was."

After Maria Knight spoke, I felt betrayed and desperate. I had kept within the law, and where had it got me?

❧ LIX ❧

I TALKED IT OVER WITH JEPTHA. We discussed it in our squalid Sacramento hotel room, in the bed where we betrayed his half-mad wife and my gambler lover currently on trial for murder.

Whoever was there before us had spat so much tobacco juice on the carpet that at my request Jeptha rolled it up and put it out in the hall, and washed his hands in the basin afterward. In the meantime, it began to rain outside, wetting the floor beneath the window. Jeptha shut the window, and we lit a lamp and listened to the hiss outside and the drumbeat on the roof. For a few minutes before we had slaked our thirst for each other and for a long time after, I questioned Jeptha about the opinions of his congregation, and the prominent men he knew who were connected with the city's schools and charity hospitals and the several boards where he was a trustee—for Jeptha knew a lot of important people. So did I, some of the same ones, and between the two of us we had a rounded picture.

From the way he had been musing about his congregation and their opinions, I knew he was building up to something. He sat beside me in the bed with his head flung back against the dirty plaster and said, "Maria Knight hurt you with them."

Was he asking me for a confession? I touched his shoulder, inviting his glance. "She came to me. They all came to me, all the witnesses, with their hands out, but I knew I was being watched. I won't lie. I'd have bribed them if I thought I could get away with it. But I was good, and look what's happened."

By then the rain had stopped. On the other side of the thin wall behind our bed, someone coughed and opened a window. Jeptha said quietly, "I know one of the jurors."

I became very still. He had known this an hour ago. Why was he telling me now?

"Albert Patterson. It's been on my mind, because he's in my congregation; I know him, I know his wife. He's an ardent Know-Nothing, and before the trial he said—he told his wife—that it would be a pleasure to see this Italian gambler hang."

"Oh," I said, laying my head on his chest. Giving it some more thought, I said, "Tell me about him. What's he like?"

I couldn't see his face, but from his voice and the pauses I knew there was something more, and that to confide it he had to overcome his own reluctance. "He works for Pacific Mail, came in '51. His family is here. I know his wife, too."

He had mentioned this already. "What about his wife?"

"I respect her. She's a good mother. From a prominent Philadelphia family. Her brother is a clergyman there. Her father is wealthy, and Patterson's connections are mainly through her. They had a maid. Albert Patterson and his wife."

"Had, no longer have?" I asked, wondering why a maid was worth mentioning.

"They still do, but the maid they had quit, and she went to work for us—for Agnes and me. So, in addition to knowing a little bit about him from Martha—the wife—I know something from the maid."

What was he saying? Did I dare believe it? "And what is it that you know?" I waited for an answer. Several seconds passed. I sat up and regarded him. "Jeptha, you've got to tell me if there's anything that can help."

"And I tell you, and you use what I've told you to blackmail a juror."

"Yes. A juror who lied with his hand on the Bible when he said his mind wasn't made up, so he shouldn't be on the jury in the first place. To help an innocent man. Yes, if I can get to him at the Railroad House—and I think I can."

He put his hand on his brow.

"Oh, please," I said. "Oh, I hate your innocence. This is about keeping a man's neck out of a noose—the neck of a man we've been betraying for over a year. And would he hesitate for one second if he could save your life at no cost to himself? I promise you he wouldn't—not even if he knew what we were doing here! That's the kind of man *he* is! Should we let him die to prove we're better than those who want to kill him? Let him die so we can congratulate ourselves on our honesty? Don't be childish. You knew that once you'd told me this much I'd insist on knowing it all."

"You're right," he said, massaging his brow and rubbing his eyes wearily. "You're right. Once I brought it up with you, the decision was made.

It's ridiculous for me to be coy. I won't be coy. It's too bad, if I'm to be a villain, that I can't do it with more enthusiasm. You know just what you're willing to do. I'm always going to be a Hamlet in these things, afraid of being worse than I need to be, and always trying to cover myself with a little fig leaf of principle. So you'll have to forgive me if I hem and haw a bit before I tell you."

"What is it? The maid? He misbehaved with the maid."

There was one small last pause as he took what was for him a leap across a treacherous gulf. "Yes, and Martha knows. But he doesn't know that she knows; he would be very surprised to learn that she does, because he is completely in her power. He depends on her family, who don't like him and help him only for her sake. Besides, he embezzles money from his firm and speculates with it, and she knows that, too, and could send him to prison, though she doesn't, for the sake of the children. She wouldn't harm him, but he doesn't realize that."

"She knows all? Martha? Martha is the wife."

"Yes, but, as I said, he doesn't know she knows."

I was too nervous to stay in the bed. One firm vote for acquittal was enough to hang the jury, and this information (that Patterson was not only an adulterer, but an embezzler) could bind him absolutely—if we could reach him. I put on my gown and my coat, put some wood in the stove, and paced the room, while Jeptha watched. I was thinking of the Railroad House, and how to get to it. I talked about it, as if soliciting Jeptha's advice, but really so as to feel a little less lonely in my scheming. I had already bribed one of the sheriff's deputies. Perhaps I would get him to pass Patterson a note. But the deputy would be sure to read the note and use it as blackmail on his own behalf, which would defeat my purposes.

At last Jeptha said, "Hire someone to rent a room in the Railroad House and get me the key to it. I will go in and wait there—no one will connect me with you. Let the sheriff's deputy bring Patterson to that room. I'll talk to him, and I'll convince him. The man who rents the room won't see me. The sheriff's deputy won't see me. If it is done right, and that is for you to arrange, only Patterson will know that I have met with him. Only you and Patterson and I will know what has been said."

I had been staring at him in astonishment throughout most of this speech. I sat on the bed and touched his arm. "You know I wasn't think-ing of this, don't you, Jeptha? When I discussed the difficulties, it was only to have your opinion. I didn't mean to involve you so personally."

"I know," he said.

"I'd spare you if I could. But what you've said makes very good sense."

"I know. It's all right."

"Oh, thank you, Jeptha, thank you." I kissed him, and soon my coat and gown were shed and we were enjoying each other again.

Because we understood each other thoroughly, I did not have to say that I knew that just in telling me about this juror he had damaged him-self, breaking profoundly with his deepest beliefs. To take it further and do the dirty work was to sacrifice his honor at the altar of our love. I was moved beyond words, and I would have loved Jeptha more if I did not already love him beyond measure.

THE TRIAL CONCLUDED WITH TWO SUMMATIONS by the prosecution and two by the defense. Only Colonel Baker's speech, the longest he ever gave, is remembered: the rhetorical part of it, omitting his discussion of the evidence, may be found in *Masterpieces of E. D. Baker,* edited (*With Glances at the Orator and His Times*) by Oscar T. Shuck and published in San Francisco by the Murdock Press in 1899. I thought Baker did a good job of alerting the jury to the contradictions in the statements of the witnesses who had testified against Charley. He painted an unflattering picture of Richardson's character—true enough, God knows.

As for his remarks concerning me, I have always had mixed feelings about them. I did not think he ought to have brought me into the speech. His client was Charley. We needed a speech that would bring an acquit-tal, not one that would exonerate me or add to Baker's fame. I wondered if, vain of his gifts, Baker thought he had something new to say about golden-hearted prostitutes, and simply could not resist the topic.

However, today, having spent five decades hiding my past and deny-ing my reviled name, I cannot read his words without having to dab my eyes with a handkerchief. When you read them, remember that Baker's speeches were all extemporaneous and he never even made a single note beforehand.

"I will now proceed to grapple with the great bugbear of the case. The

complaint, on their side, is that Belle Cora has tampered with the witnesses. The prosecuting attorney has chosen to declare that the line of
defense was concocted in a place which he has been pleased to designate
as a haunt of sensuality. In plain English, Belle Cora is helping her friend
as much as she can. It may appear strange to him, but I am inclined to
admit the plain, naked fact; and in the Lord's name, who else should
help him? Who else is there whose duty it is to help him? If it were not
for her, he would not have a friend on earth. This howling, raging public opinion would banish every friend, even every man who once lived
near him. The associates of his life have fled in the day of trouble. It is a
woman of base profession, of more than easy virtue, of malign fame, of
a degraded caste—it is one poor, weak, feeble, and, if you like it, wicked
woman—to her alone he owes his ability to employ counsel to present his
defense.

"What we want to know is, what have they against that? What we
want to know is, why don't they admire it? What we want to know is,
why don't they admit the supremacy of the divine spark in the merest
human bosom? The history of this case is, I suppose, that this man and
this woman have formed a mutual attachment, not sanctioned, if you
like, by the usages of society—thrown out of the pale of society—if
you like, not sanctioned by the rites of the church. It is but a trust in
each other, a devotion to the last, amid all the dangers of the dungeon
and all the terrors of the scaffold. They were bound together by a tie
which angels might not blush to approve. A man who can attach to him a
woman, however base in heart and corrupt in life, is not all bad. A woman
who can maintain her trust, who can waste her money like water to stand
by her friend, amid the darkest clouds that can gather, that woman cannot be all evil; and if, in vice, and degradation, and pollution, and infamy,
she rises so far above it all as to vindicate her original nature, I must confess that I honor this trait of fidelity.

"This woman is bad; she has forgotten her chastity—fallen by early
temptation from her high estate; and among the matronage of the land
her name shall never be heard. She has but one tie, she acknowledges but
one obligation, and that she performs in the gloom of the cell and the
dread of death; nor public opinion, nor the passions of the multitude,
nor the taunts of angry counsel, nor the vengeance of the judge, can sway

her for a moment from her course. If any of you have it in your heart to condemn, and say, 'Stand back! I am holier than thou,' remember Magdalene, name written in the Book of Life."

Well, in fact, all over the world, wretched women cling to the ankles of the brutes who kick them and sell their flesh; I realize it better than you do. God knows it is no recommendation of a man to say that his whore is loyal. Still, in a faithless world, the spectacle of loyalty moves us. So it was a touching speech, and I wish I had been present when it was delivered. I have imagined it often, and, having heard Baker speak since, I feel as if I remember it: his sonorous vowels; his high collar, wild hair, stagey gestures, one hand gripping his coat, the other flung out toward the accused or his persecutors, or pointing at heaven, or clawing the air as if gripping the jury's collective heart.

"They were bound together by a tie which angels might not blush to approve." Newspaper editors took special note of that sentence; soon even people who could not read knew it. Many were shocked, and more were derisive, including, I should think, most whores: whores look with disfavor on free love. But we have our sentimental moods, too, so some probably adored it.

For two days the jury deliberated. Each of those days, all day long, I sat in Frankie Garcia's café, usually with Lewis and Jocelyn, waiting for a messenger to bring me the news. A few men, strangers to me, stayed for the entertainment of seeing my face when I heard the verdict. At last a man from McDougall's office came. I stood up, my fist before my mouth. Lewis put his arm around me. "Hung jury," said the messenger, and I relaxed in Lewis's grip and sat down again.

The results of the final ballot were four for murder, six for manslaughter, and two for acquittal. One of those for acquittal was Albert Patterson.

❧ LX ❧

CHARLEY WAS NOT FREED. He was denied bail, and returned to the county jail to await a second trial. Baker warned me that it might take months. He said the delay would work to our advantage. In time, public hysteria would abate; we would have a less partial jury. There was simply not enough evidence to convict Charley. He would be released.

"Not if this man has any say over it," said McDougall mildly from across the room—we were in his office—and he held a copy of the *San Francisco Daily Evening Bulletin,* in which the editor, James King of William, had written, on the subject of the deadlock, "Rejoice ye gamblers and harlots!" and "Hung be the heavens with black!" and that only bribery and corruption had saved Charley's neck, and he could well understand why so many good people were calling for a revival of the Vigilance Committee.

I began telling them the story of James King of William's love for the courtesan Pauline, and the anatomical misfortune that made his love so tragic, though I knew they had heard it before. I told them—I had told them often—how envious this feeble excuse for a man was of Charley, who was his superior in every way.

And little McDougall, in his plain laconic way, and big double-chinned Baker, in his florid, high-flown way, explained, as they had often done before, that it was nothing personal. It was all politics. King's masters were Know-Nothings. They wanted to do in 1856 what they had done in 1851, and we must keep cool heads and not give them an excuse.

That year, San Francisco was James King of William's city. He set the tone of the place. He created its mood. The *Bulletin* had the widest circulation of any newspaper in the city. King packed each thrilling issue with libelous editorials and partly true articles harmful to the reputations of sundry rogues, fine men, and men no worse than average.

I had seen him on the street once, during the trial. "King! Wait!" I called out, and crossed Montgomery Street. He started, not wanting to dishonor himself by running. I stood there haranguing him about the case, in the helpless, obsessive way of people embroiled in legal battles. As I spoke, the sun came out, bringing shadows and color: King's eyes

became pink, and within his pale skin I saw blue and red blood vessels and a feverish flush; on the hand gripping the lion-faced brass handle of his cane, the nails were cracked and flattened. "Diathesis." I suddenly remembered the word. "You're consumptive. Well along. And this wet climate is killing you. You ought to take your family and go—somewhere dry—you'll last longer." Whereupon he turned with a swirl of his short black cape and walked off. In that evening's *Bulletin*, King wrote that Belle Cora, the murderer's paramour, had told him he must leave town or lose his life.

It was certainly true many people wanted to kill James King of William. Lewis, for one, had often announced his eagerness to dispatch him. But it was just talk. He knew it was impossible. It would be wonderful if, tomorrow, King coughed his life out, or was found hanging in his office near a suicide note. But if any of his enemies killed him, the vengeance would fall on us all.

MONTHS DRAGGED BY. I VISITED CHARLEY in his cell every day. Once a week, twice as often as before, I saw Jeptha. We met as furtively as ever, far out of town. When we were done slaking our bodies' thirst for each other, I complained to my lover Jeptha about the hard luck of my other lover, Charley; and Jeptha agreed that it was unfair and promised me that it would come out all right in the end.

Sometimes we talked about Agnes. Did she read the *Alta California* and the *San Francisco Daily Evening Bulletin*? Now that the trial had put Belle Cora in the newspapers, and so many strangers were speaking of Charles Cora and Belle Cora, did she speak of me, did *they* speak of me? Or was her mind too disordered for that?

"We talk of it," he said the first time I asked him. "She takes your part."

"I can imagine," I said, remembering her looks of pity from on high in the Clay Street Unitarian Church.

"No," he said. "You don't understand. She means it. She's different that way. She hates herself for what she's done to you. She'd do anything to make it up to you."

You don't know her, I wanted to say. But by now, surely, he knew her. The truth was, I didn't want to believe it. I did not want her to change, and demand forgiveness, and force me to say, in front of Jeptha, that I would never forgive her.

ONE MORNING IN THE MIDDLE OF MAY, a boy from Baker's office came to my house. Gasping like a messenger in a play, he told us, "Casey has shot James King of William. He's in the jail. There's a mob outside it."

The boy didn't have to say "James Casey." We all knew. Casey had started a newspaper of his own, hostile to the Know-Nothings. A day earlier, an anonymous letter in Casey's paper had attacked King through his brother Thomas. The charge made in that letter didn't amount to much; it wouldn't have meant anything to an ordinary man. But this was James King of William, whose whole being was as sensitive as a blister. On the front page of last night's *Daily Evening Bulletin*, James King had fired back with every piece of dirt he had on Casey. We had all been apprehensive. Casey was as touchy as King, and much more violent.

"Adelia," I said, "Fetch Lewis. We're going to the jail."

Within two blocks of the jail, the crowd was too dense for the carriage to get through. Lewis and I got out and pushed forward on foot. Draymen and their carts stood immobilized, islands in the human sea. Everyone was talking so loudly that we could not hear the words of a man two yards away. People craned their necks out of windows, stood on roofs, and clung to lampposts. At one point, a wave of movement traveled through the bodies massed in the street, pushing us to the sidewalk, as men with rifles held before their faces trotted in two columns toward the jail. "What's going on?" we kept asking, and were told, among other things, that toughs were assembling all over the city, determined to spring the murderers, Casey and Cora, and behind it all was the notorious madam Belle Cora. We were told that the riflemen we had just seen were here to prevent the two assassins from being freed.

With Lewis's help, I reached the steps of the jail, and by begging and pleading and insisting and reminding them that I was only a woman—have pity, had they no hearts?—at last I was let in to see Charley.

The jailers I had come to know so well were outnumbered three to one by people who had been hastily deputized, including members of the militia, who would join the vigilantes just a few days later. Two of the most hostile of them brought me to Charley's cell, along with a sheriff's deputy who had the key. One of them suggested I take off my clothes to prove that I had no weapons. The other told him to shut up, but, to prove that he was not on my side, either, immediately added that if I moved any closer than two feet away from Charley, he would shoot us both. The key turned in the big padlock, the heavy door swung open, a man walked in before me, another after me, Charley rose to his feet, and we embraced.

"I told you not to touch him!" growled the man who had made that foolish threat.

"Oh, Papa, Papa," I said, nuzzling his face with mine. "You know what happened."

"They keep coming up to the door to tell me."

The sheriff's deputy searched Charley to make sure I had not passed him a gun, and then we sat on the bed and talked over what we knew so far about the shooting of King. While they were bringing in Casey, the guards, for their amusement, had let him stop in front of Charley's cell for a few minutes. Casey had said that it had been a fair fight and he had given King plenty of time to draw his weapon. Charley had replied, "You've put the noose around both our necks."

"Oh God, Charley, let's hope not."

"Sure, let's hope," he said.

On the way out, I left the militiamen behind me for a moment, impulsively thanked Billy Mulligan for his goodness to Charley all these months, and clasped his hand—putting into it a note that read "$10,000."

EVERYONE KNEW THAT THE VIGILANCE COMMITTEE was busy recruiting members; already, twice as many had joined as last time, and it was going to be a lot bigger. That night I got messages to Baker and McDougall, asking them to get me in touch with men who were likely to be accepted as vigilantes. With their help, within a few days I had three vigilantes on my payroll, but none of them were very high up in the organization, and they could not tell me much or do anything to influence events.

Morning and evening editions of each of the town's newspapers contained the latest news about James King. Half a dozen doctors were working on him. Edward's paper, the *Herald*, published an editorial roundly condemning the idea of reviving the Committee of Vigilance. By the next day, every businessman in town had removed his advertising from the paper, and the vigilantes were burning stacks of it in the streets.

The *Alta California* and the *Bulletin*—now, supposedly, edited by Thomas King—published the preamble to the committee's otherwise secret constitution, which said that the citizens of San Francisco had no security of life or property and their rights had been violated because of election fraud. A paramilitary junta led by a few of the town's richest men was the only way the people's will could be manifested.

SOON THE NUMBERS OF THE VIGILANTES SWELLED to the thousands. The city bristled with rifles, bayonets, and marching men. I was woken by the sound of their boots rhythmically stamping the wooden planks of the streets. I raised my window. I observed their newfound pride. A great many of them had become unemployed or had been forced, by the recent business slump, to take jobs they considered beneath their dignity. Now they were part of a force that had, without a struggle, usurped the regular government and was able to shut down gambling hells, open jails, and hang men.

The leaders were millionaires. They thought of themselves as righteous men, and they needed to make a lot of excuses whenever they did anything violent. But in the ranks were men of assorted character, as may be found in any army.

The committee claimed the right to search any house it wished without a warrant. On Friday morning two days after Casey shot King, a detachment of ten vigilantes pounded on the door of my house on Pike Street. I looked out the window of my bedroom and saw them. When Niobe opened the door, they pushed her aside and walked in, carrying rifles and pistols. I was downstairs just as they entered. The parlor filled with the stink of chewing tobacco, body sweat, and whiskey. Big and little, fat and thin, bearded and clean-shaven, they looked around as though to say, So this is Belle Cora's place.

A fellow with long blond hair, wearing stained breeches and a faded blue shirt too small for his fat belly, sat on a divan and began stroking the red satin fabric and squeezing a cushion with his dirty hands. "Stop him, that's expensive," I said to another man, who seemed to be the leader—he had given orders to the others. He had a short mustache and a neat little chin-puff beard, and a resigned-looking expression, as though he had learned not to expect much of people. "Off the sofa," he said, and the fellow in the too-tight shirt rose, taking his rifle. "Stand by the door," said the leader, and announced generally, "We're searching the house. Let no one leave." He gave orders, calling his men "you"—"You by the clock . . . You with your hand on the rail"—telling them to block the doors front and back and to let no one out, and telling each man which floor to search. He did not use a single name. Could it be because they had been organized so recently that he did not know the names of his own men?

"What are you looking for?" I asked, worried that it must be Lewis and glad that he wasn't here. He was keeping watch on the jail, along with my lawyers and assorted other members of San Francisco's Law and Order Party, who opposed the vigilantes.

"Shut up," said the world-weary man.

"What is the name of your company?" I asked—the Vigilance Committee was organized on military lines into companies and battalions. He didn't answer. "Who sent you?" I asked. "What's your name?"

With a blank expression on his face, he rammed the butt of the rifle into the middle of a big mirror. He examined his work, cocking his head skeptically, and struck again. Cracks spidered from center to frame; long, knifelike shards hit the carpet. They weren't looking for anybody.

Jacqueline began walking briskly toward the hall. A man held a rifle to block her path.

I knew then that they weren't looking for anybody. I knew what they were here for.

"I'm sorry," I said. "We got off on the wrong foot. Why don't we talk it over upstairs, you and I?"

"That's better," said the sad-eyed man. He followed me up the stairs. I turned just once to say, "Girls, show these boys a good time," and then he kicked me and I fell on my face. I rose without complaint. He kicked me down again, and after that I understood what was wanted: I crawled.

The house resounded with thuds and crashes as furniture was toppled, china vases were smashed, and doors were kicked in. By the time I reached the landing, there were also cries and unheeded shouts for help.

They left after about two hours. My driver, Neil, and the pianist, Mr. Rice, the only men on the premises, had been badly beaten while trying to help us. Neil, it was found later, had two broken ribs. Mr. Rice had lost two teeth. The women had been beaten and kicked, and been taken more than once, by different men, in different ways—the servants Niobe and

Adelia along with the rest of us. Two of the girls, another maid, and the cook could not be found.

In a crooked piece of mirror I examined my face. The worst of the bruises were in places Charley would not see. I gathered up the women. Some stumbled aimlessly from room to room in the rags that had so recently been their finery. A few I found weeping, and a few methodically taking drink after drink of whiskey and rum and whatever route to forgetfulness was near to hand. Everywhere were pieces of glass, spilled liquor, broken chairs. I sent Antoinette to fetch a doctor. I spoke to each of the girls in turn. I told them that I would arrange for them to go to a hotel in Sacramento City until things in this city had settled down. We went to the kitchen. I made coffee, and we had hard-boiled eggs and bread and ham, but not all of the girls could eat, or keep the food down once they had eaten.

One of the girls had mentioned overhearing the men carelessly calling each other by name—first names only. I found a pen and nib and a bottle of ink and made a note. I decided to ask the rest if any of them had overheard names, but the ones I asked first became so upset that I decided to postpone these questions until we were all feeling a little better.

You may wonder if such an ordeal was less upsetting for us than it would have been for women who do not sell their caresses. I don't know how one would confirm such a theory. Certainly even fancy prostitutes must expect to undergo harsh experiences eventually—some at the very beginning. My girl Marianne had been introduced to this life by a man who had kept her in a locked room, raping her, beating her, and letting his friends use her every day until she was tame enough to be let out. Though it had happened thousands of miles away, and years ago, I had more than once known her to give a start and look for a place to hide, thinking she had seen him in the street or in our sitting room.

As for me, and my feelings, I must have had a lot of them, but all I remember is that I didn't want Charley, helpless in a jail cell, to hear one word about any of this and I wasn't ever going to tell Jeptha.

Our regular doctor came. A few days earlier, he had joined the Vigilance Committee. He could not deny the evidence, but insisted that the men who had done this must have been impostors. I saw no purpose in arguing.

We swept and cleaned. The two girls and the cook who had escaped came back and apologized. They had hidden in an outhouse behind a saloon, too frightened of the vigilantes to go for help. At first, wanting everything to be just as it was, I forgave them, happy that they had been spared. But after thinking about it some more, I changed my mind and told them they must take their things and leave.

Lewis returned, bringing news, which he forgot to tell me when he saw the wreckage and I explained its cause. Frightened of his reaction, I followed him as he rushed through the house. He demanded that each of its vacant-eyed inhabitants tell him where Jocelyn was; one after another they shrugged or said they didn't know, or stared at him without answering. He went to her room and stood in the doorway. The mattress had been dragged halfway off her bed. On the floor was a broken terra-cotta pot, its dirt, a potted palm, puddles of piss, an oil painting, and a nightgown. Both the painting and the nightgown bore the muddy prints of three different pairs of boots. I whispered soothing words to him, words I do not remember, while he walked rather more slowly down the stairs. He found Jocelyn at last, sitting at the kitchen table in a fresh dress, drinking whiskey. He held her and kissed her. She was unresponsive. Finally, she returned his gaze, reached out her hand, and patted his cheek. "Tell me their names," he begged her. When she said she didn't know any of the names, he looked, for a minute, as if he was ready to throw his life away in a reckless attack on the vigilante headquarters.

"Lewis, I'm going to find out," I said, gripping his shoulders. "They won't be able to keep their names a secret. There were too many. Some of them will brag. You have to be patient and take my advice. If you go after the men who hurt Jocelyn, the others will gang up on you. And if you kill anyone, even in a fair fight, while the committee is in charge, they'll hang you."

"I'm not just going after the ones who hurt Jocelyn," he corrected me, taking a seat on a torn sofa and playing absentmindedly with a tuft of exposed horsehair. "I'm going to kill all of them."

In his right hand, he held the rock he had possessed since he was a boy of six. It was the size of a baseball, partly smooth, partly jagged, identifiable by its shape and by a cross of some darker mineral set in a white patch.

"Well, Lewis," I said, as you might say to a young boy who has voiced a laudable but unrealistic ambition, "that's a big job. If we want to be able to finish it, we'll need to plan well. We'll need to use our heads."

Naturally, I assumed I would be able to reduce his plans to more manageable dimensions after a little time had passed.

Then he told me the news. The governor of California had met with William Tell Coleman, the head of the Vigilance Committee. He had promised that Casey and Cora would be tried by an honest judge and an honest jury, and agreed to let a company of vigilantes into the county jail, supposedly to prevent Casey and Charley from escaping. In return, Coleman promised that his men would not do anything hasty—that, in particular, they would not kidnap the prisoners. Since there was nothing else I could do, I hoped that Coleman would keep his word.

I sent letters to the newspapers by messenger, complaining that vigilantes had forced their way into my house, insulted my girls, and stolen the equivalent of two thousand dollars in money and valuables. A story in Saturday's *Alta California* said that an "angry mob" had forced its way into Belle Cora's house, damaged property, and frightened its residents. The editors, though understanding the community's fury, deplored their lawless behavior; it would be absurd if the Vigilance Committee had to divert its resources to the protection of houses of ill repute.

No man from the newspapers or the police came to my house to ask the girls what had happened to them, and I thought it was just as well. I did not want Charley to know; besides, girls as expensive as mine do not admit to being raped.

I had the house cleaned and arranged for the girls to go to a hotel in Sacramento City. That night, when I went to see Charley, I was turned away.

ON SUNDAY, THE VIGILANCE COMMITTEE broke its promise to the governor. Thousands of men surrounded the jail. The muzzles of two mobile cannons were directed at its entrance. Vigilantes in top hats and frock coats, holding rifles, stood on a nearby roof. Others, with rifles and bayonets, controlled the street. They cleared Broadway and brought a coach pulled by two horses. Crowds watched from windows and from rooftops. Lewis, Edward, and I stood on the top of a building on the corner of Sacramento and Front Streets. We saw William Coleman and another man go into the jail and come out a half-hour later. Ten minutes after that, a murmur arose from the crowd as Casey walked out, under close guard and shackled.

There was a strong wind coming in from the bay that morning. One of the vigilante guards lost his hat and couldn't break ranks to fetch it. As Casey climbed into the waiting coach, he turned to look at the hat skidding and spinning and flipping end over end down the street. A man closed the coach door. One horse raised its tail, the other dipped its head, the whip flicked, the coach moved slowly, and armed men walked behind it.

"They didn't take Charley," I told my brothers, and we all tried to comfort each other with that thought; but a few minutes later, they came back for him. His head was tilted down as he came out of the jail with a vigilante at each elbow. Once he looked up, but his back was to me. All around me, people were saying things that I could never forgive. I threw my arms around Lewis's neck and whispered, "Not now. Patience. Patience."

The headquarters of the Committee of Vigilance was only two blocks from my house. I thought about that, how near Charley was, as I lay awake at night in my room, which was sparsely furnished now, with pale rectangles on the walls where ruined pictures and dressers had been removed. In the meantime, a sort of trial was under way. Over the course of two days, the executive committee read the records of the earlier trial, debated the evidence, and took a vote. Some said murder, some said manslaughter. Two voted to acquit. According to the committee's rules, a majority was sufficient for hanging.

ON MONDAY, JAMES KING OF WILLIAM died of a botched operation. A sponge had been left inside him.

Every daily newspaper in San Francisco had been busy for a week, calling King the city's noblest citizen, and anyone who disagreed had been prudently silent. Stores, saloons, and all public resorts were closed. Every flag was at half-mast except for the flag of Ten Engine, Casey's fire company. The ships in the bay were draped in black; men wore black armbands. People were waiting in line the length of Montgomery Street to view King's remains. I knew all this only by report; the one time I went outside, a man pointed at me, a hostile crowd began to gather, and after that I kept to the house.

Thursday was the day of King's burial. The crowds, thinking it was to be the main focus of the day's pageantry, packed the First Presbyterian Church and massed on the pavements, in the windows, and on the balconies and hilltops along the route that the funeral procession must take to the sand dunes of Lone Mountain Cemetery. Around eleven, there was a knock on my door. It was Jason Rickey, one of the three men I had paid to join the vigilantes. He hesitated a moment, then said, "They're hanging them both today. They'll let you see him."

I walked quickly, putting everything I had into the effort to make one foot follow the other. In the two minutes it took me to get to the jail, I realized that the committee must know Rickey was in my pay: they had used him to deliver their message. It didn't matter now.

Men took me to a rear entrance to the second-story rooms. At the turning of the stairs, I saw a poster made by a firm of printers and engravers who had joined the vigilantes. It was the seal of the committee, and it consisted of some Latin mottos and an enormous open eye. Then I was brought to a chamber whose entrance was draped with flags, and I found myself being scrutinized by the members of the executive committee, including Samuel Brannan and William T. Coleman.

"Why did you bring me to this room?" I asked, hoping to hear that, in view of the disagreement over the evidence, they were going to show clemency. "Have you got something to say to me?" They looked at each other. "You're going to admit that you've made a mistake."

A few of the men, including Brannan, chuckled. Others, who thought this was no time for levity, threw them disapproving looks.

"We wondered if you had anything to request," said Coleman.

I saw how it was. They wanted to suck the marrow of it, the little courtesies, the last meal, the last visit, the last confession. The prisoner's cooperation in these matters suggests a docile acceptance of the people's judgment.

Would it have done any good to tell these men what I thought of them? I had no heart for it. Time was short. "Is there a priest?" I asked.

"Father Accolti is with Casey now."

"Bring him to Charley," I said.

CHARLEY'S ROOM CONTAINED A BED, a table, some chairs. There were two windows. Both had been boarded up. Two guards with rifles sat on chairs outside the door, and two guards with pistols sat inside, playing cards with Charley, who was picking his teeth. On another chair were the remnants of his last meal, which had consisted of oysters, scrambled eggs, and bacon. This dish is known in California as "Hangtown Fry," and I would have suspected a cruel joke if I didn't know how much Charley liked it.

He had gained weight during the months he had gotten no exercise beyond a daily walk around the jail yard, and food became more important to him in jail than it had been outside. At the trial, he had been slim and elegant. Now he was almost as portly as his picture in the letter sheets the vigilantes later made to celebrate their crimes.

Charley laid his cards facedown, and the guards set down their cards and put their hands on their weapons as he got up to kiss me. I held him as if I meant to crush him. He murmured to me soothingly, as if I were the one in trouble. "Go on, go on," he said. "It's good to feel you next to me. This is real good."

In case you are wondering, no one feels as alive in your arms as a man about to be executed. We heard hammering—the scaffold. I stiffened in terror. He said, "That's some sound, all right, when it's for you."

"Oh, Papa, Papa, I can't bear it, I can't bear it. You know the first thing I did back in November was to try to bribe Billy Mulligan. He's going to wish he took it."

"I know. I mean, I know you did."

"I didn't do it the stupid way the papers say I did. I used my head. Even now, I don't know what I could have done to make it turn out better."

He shook his head and looked at me awhile, then blinked and said, "Once, in Rio," and interrupted himself to kiss me, and began again, softly but clearly: "One time, it was in '39, I had a dinner with some friends, and an hour later I got sick, so, woof, I'm in bed, chills, I'm off my head, talking in Italian. I saw angels. I saw a railroad train in the sky. I saw a snake swallow a church. When I'm making sense again, they tell me it's been *nine days*. I ask, Where's Ramón? '*Ramón está morto.*' Okay, what about the other two—Hector? Alejondro? 'Oh, those two; in the ground a week already. We got you a priest. But it wasn't your time.'" He tilted his head and righted it. "In Natchez—in Natchez, that time I broke the bank, afterward there was a fracas in a saloon, a bullet meant for me killed a waiter, ripped a hole in his neck. He had a wife. I gave her some money. Her kids were there. She took it, but she said I ought to be hung. She thought *I'd* shot him—my English wasn't so good then. I said to myself, Look, your time will come. So . . . okay. I don't mean I'm not scared—but okay."

Father Accolti came in. I explained, "I want him to marry us, if it's all right with you. Then I'll really be Belle Cora."

He was still for a moment, and then he nodded. "All right. Let's do it."

Somehow the priest—a slender young man in a black robe, with a round black hat, a white collar, a crooked nose—managed to obtain two rings for the ceremony. Our guards acted as witnesses, and the priest led us through our prayers. He asked us the usual questions, and we answered them as if many years of married life lay before us. Charley and Father Accolti talked in Italian, and Charley said the priest was from Lombardy.

Later on, I said, "I've brought something to show you, but I don't know if I should—it might cheer you, but it might make you sentimental."

"What is it?"

"It's one of Anne's letters."

"Oh. Sure."

I reached into my purse and gave him the letter. He had read all the other letters from Anne about Frank. But this was the first time he had read one in the certain knowledge that Frank was his only posterity. He sat at the table with the letter in his hands. His lips moved. He took a slow breath. "He seems like a smart boy."

"He's a wizard with numbers."

"Tell them to keep him away from cards."

It was the first time I'd ever heard him voice regret about the kind of life he had led. "You mean that, Papa?"

He thought about it. "Yeah."

We talked over old times, the day we met on the *Israel Putnam,* and our times together since, and his times in Milan, Rio, Natchez, New Orleans, and New York. Around twelve-fifteen, Accolti came back, took his confession, and gave him his last communion. At one o'clock, a distant bell tolled, and a triangle rang closer by. James King of William had been put in the ground, and now the committee was going to perform the two executions King had demanded. The burial was to be followed so promptly by the double hanging that it might justly be called a rite of the great man's funeral. Guards came into the room to take Charley away. We held each other, and I said, "Now, Papa, I know what you're like, so I know you're going to show them what a man is."

He nodded. "You'll see. Goodbye, Belle. Go down and watch me."

Two guards took me out the back and around and onto the other side of Sacramento Street, where people were gathering to watch—not many, thanks to the committee's subterfuge. Why had they not waited another day, as everyone expected? Perhaps, despite the cooperation of every newspaper in the city save one, they weren't as sure of their popularity as they pretended to be. Some of the spectators had dragged chairs to the spot so they could view the hanging in comfort. A few of these men stood up and gestured to their chairs. I realized much later that they had been inviting me to sit. Just then I couldn't understand. I turned numbly toward the vigilante headquarters.

Men with bayonets were as dense on the rooftops as fields of corn. Cavalry and infantry lined the streets around the building. The carpenters had built a platform on the roof, from which the ropes were suspended, and another platform outside two adjacent second-story windows, which were tall enough for men to walk through without crouching. I stood looking up at the ropes and the windows, aware that the space around me was filling up with people all craning their heads up, pointing, talking to each other. The sky was overcast, and a cold wind from the bay made the men around me turn up their collars. High above us, an arm in shirtsleeves reached out of the window of a second-floor room and dropped a piece of white paper, which was evidently a signal. Commands were shouted. Men on the streets and on the rooftops brought their weapons to their chests. A moment later, Charley shuffled out on the east platform, arms pinioned to his sides, feet bound with cords. Another man came out beside him to put the noose around his neck. It was Abner Mosely.

Casey came next, onto the west platform. His right hand gripped a cambric handkerchief. The noose was put around his neck, then removed. He had asked to speak. He talked for seven minutes. I don't think anyone there, including the newspaper stenographers who had been alerted at the last minute, could make out much of what he said. The first words, as later printed, were: "Gentlemen, I have been persecuted most relent-lessly by the *Alta,* the *Chronicle,* and the *Globe.* I hope these editors will desist and allow my name to pass into oblivion and not publish it as a murderer. Gentlemen, I am not a murderer. I did not intend to commit murder. I do not feel afraid to meet my God on a charge of murder . . ." I do not know if his speech became rambling and incoherent, a sign of cowardice, as was alleged by the *Alta,* the *Chronicle,* the *Globe,* and also the *Bulletin,* the only paper he had failed to mention.

During all this, Charley stood still, staring ahead without focus, as people do when they are lost in thought. He had trained himself, long ago, not to let his face show his opinions regarding the immediate future. Mosely slipped the noose back around Casey's neck, then turned to Charley and said something the newspapers did not record: not a kind word, I think. I could not tell whether Charley answered, nor, from where I stood, could I discern any change in his expression. Mosely went back inside. It was 1:21 p.m. A bell rang sharply. My knees turned to water, and I gasped, thinking this was it, but it hadn't happened yet. Some men in front of me took their hats off. At a second bell, the platform fell away. "Papa"—I felt the word in my throat, but it was only an inaudible croak. Charley and Casey dropped till the rope jerked them, and they turned a few times this way and that, as Casey's handkerchief floated down to rest delicately on the point of a bayonet. I heard the ropes creak. Then there was another noise. After a second, I realized that people were cheering.

LXI

AFTER THE CORONER'S INQUEST, I had Charley embalmed and laid out in Mr. Rice's house on Broadway. Only our friends knew where he was. The coffin, mahogany trimmed with silver, lay on two tables, between a pair of silver candelabras. A Byron collar and a dark-blue silk cravat hid the rope scar. The next day, a few black carriages followed the hearse to

Mission Dolores. Irene sat beside me. Lewis and Big Pete talked quietly while I looked out the window. Once, when I turned back toward them, I realized something was different about Big Pete. At last I said, "Where's your hat, Pete?" because he had brought along a black silk stovepipe hat instead of the strange misshapen object he usually put on top of his head.

"Thought I'd try something else today," he said.

"I think Charley loved that stupid hat as much as you do," I told him.

Near the end of Powell Street, Lewis suddenly told the driver to stop: "I've got an errand. I'll try and catch up later, but don't wait."

"Lewis, we're only burying him once," I admonished him.

"He won't mind," said Lewis, looking at me gently. He considered himself the stronger one now, and for the moment it was true. "I'm going to do something for him."

"What? What? Be careful, Lewis," I said, and Big Pete and Irene seconded me.

"Don't worry."

"Lewis, I'm begging you. I need you to take special care, do you understand me? Any plan you've got, you need to let me in on it. Today is Charley's funeral."

I wanted him with me every minute now. I would have wanted him under my eye even if he were not a reckless man sworn to a blood feud. Repeating that I was not to worry, he got out and walked off; the carriage started up again.

I looked helplessly at Big Pete and Irene. After a while, Pete said, "Right before he stopped the carriage, I told him there was a man at the Cosmopolitan selling pieces of the rope for twenty-five dollars each."

"Oh, the dirty dogs," I said, wringing my hands and rocking. "Oh God, what's he going to do?"

"He didn't say," said Big Pete.

Irene put her arms around me. "Lewis is closer kin to you than you let on, ain't he?" I didn't answer. "He's no fool. He's very able."

"So was Charley," I said.

The mission lay out of the city back then. We took the Old Mission Road, paved with planks worn down almost to the sand. Breathing dust, we rolled past dunes and chaparral and shacks and gardens, and past a raffish neighborhood of boarding houses, hotels, saloons, racetracks, and cockfighting pits, where Charley and I used to go sometimes, and finally we saw the gaunt old mission building, which, so it was said, had once been the seat of religion and government all rolled into one here. Now the adobe walls were pocked and leprous; according to a painted sign, the long, low building beside it, where the priests used to live, had become the Mission House hotel, and it all looked so shamed and derelict that I wished I had not picked it to be Charley's final resting place.

Brown-and-green stone slabs, bearing Spanish inscriptions weathered almost to illegibility, tilted at many angles in the mission yard; a long heap of sandy soil waited beside the pit where Charley was to be buried. We noticed another open grave not five yards away, and just as the one priest still attached to the mission was finishing Charley's burial service, we heard the approach of James Casey's much larger funeral cortege, with more carriages, and men and boys on foot, including the firemen of Ten Engine. As we left, they acknowledged us respectfully, and I was touched. In the midst of oppression, one is touched by any small act of kindness.

When we got back, I told Pete and Irene that I wanted to be alone. I had some whiskey and a few stale crackers and sat trying to realize that Charley wasn't ever coming back. So often when I was lonely and helpless he had comforted me. I would never have that again, and I was afraid of the changes these feelings would work in me. I ached for Jeptha more than ever, but he was with Agnes.

The door swung open. And you know how it is when someone dies; for an instant I thought: Charley. It was Jocelyn. We drank together and talked and reminisced. I told her how Lewis had missed the funeral, that he had jumped out of the carriage right after he had heard that a man was selling pieces of the rope Charley was hanged with. "Where do you think he went?" I asked her.

She sat thinking for a little while, and then said, "Why, to buy the pieces, of course. All of them if he could."

I wasn't thinking very clearly. "I don't understand. Did you meet him? Did he tell you that?"

"No. I just know Lewis."

THE *ALTA CALIFORNIA* SAID THAT FATHER ACCOLTI had refused Charley absolution unless we were married. A letter in the *Bulletin* praised the committee for its work, then added:

But, gentlemen, one thing more must be done: Belle Cora must be most firmly requested to leave the city. The women of San Francisco have no bitterness toward her, nor do they ask it on her account, but for the good of those who remain, and as an example to others. Every virtuous woman asks that her influence and example be removed from us.

The truly virtuous of our sex will not feel that the Vigilance Committee have done their *whole* duty till they comply with the request of

MANY WOMEN OF SAN FRANCISCO

A few days after that, the *Bulletin* printed this compassionate response:

A woman is always a woman's persecutor. In my humble opinion, I think that Belle Cora has suffered enough to expiate many faults, in having had torn from her a bosom friend, executed by a powerful association. She has shown herself a true-hearted woman to him, and such a heart covers a multitude of sins. This very circumstance of expulsion might be the means of utter desolation of heart. As for the house of ill-fame she runs, I have heard that it is one of many serving the base appetites of the men of this city. I do not see how the removal of just one, while leaving a hundred others standing, can make our city virtuous.

AGNES

"Agnes" was a common name in that generation. There may have been three or four in San Francisco at the time. But I did not doubt the identity of this one.

The next day's issue contained the report that Abner Mosely had been found dead in the room of his boarding house. An empty whiskey bottle and several empty packages of medicinal arsenic were discovered near the body, and the coroner said he had died of arsenic poisoning. Mosely was busted and three months late on his rent. Only the *Herald,* now reduced to a single page, mentioned the rumor that a piece of rope had been found in Mosely's mouth. The same issue of the *Bulletin* reported that the corrupt judge Ned McGowan, the hooligan Lewis Godwin, and the notorious madam Belle Cora were wanted for immediate questioning by the Committee of Vigilance.

By then, my house was empty. My girls were all in Sacramento. Lewis and I were hiding in the house of my first husband and his wife.

❧ LXII ☙

WE LIVED IN THE ATTIC. If we went into other rooms, we had to creep on the floor whenever we passed windows, which were left with the shades up: otherwise, the neighbors might notice that something was different. Since there were two windows on the stairs and we took all our meals in the kitchen, I must have crept under a window over a thousand times, my palms on the runner, my eyes inches from a place where a knot reminded me of a hawk's eye, and another place where the planks were loosely joined and I could see the corner of a desk on the floor below.

A porch and a line of trees hid the inside of the kitchen from the neighbors' sight, and it was in this room, during our second week in hiding, that Agnes began telling us about the afterlife. She spoke not as a lunatic exhibiting her symptom, but as a hostess making conversation. I had given her the excuse—I had asked her about it. But I knew she had been dying to tell me; and once she began and warmed to the topic, I could sense, woven through and around the authentic heartaches of dead and unborn children, her old love of having expert knowledge and monopolizing our attention.

The maid, Phoebe, short and plump (in this she resembled her mistress), ladled split-pea soup into the bowls set before me, Jeptha, Agnes, and Lewis, while Agnes told us how the transition from life to afterlife was depicted in the book *Geography of the Spirit World,* by the noted clairvoyant James Victor Andersen. What we call "death" is really the moment when the spirit body (visible to certain gifted individuals) leaves the earthly body, according to Mr. Andersen. "Just over the head of the dying person there is a slowly throbbing ethereal emanation attached by a slender life-thread. The emanation is smaller than the physical body, but a perfect reproduction without the disfigurements of disease. As life slowly leaves the body, the thread grows slenderer, until at last it snaps free. Mr. Andersen has seen it."

I thought of Charley when the noose jerked the life from him. What would a clairvoyant have seen then? Watching Agnes, I wondered if she guessed my thought. I examined the others. Jeptha looked resigned; he was used to his wife's strange opinions. Lewis was happy to hear Agnes talk like a fool. Since his arrival, he had treated her just as he used to years ago, as his absurd stuck-up cousin, and she seemed to like it. It must have been refreshing for her to find someone who did not treat her as if she were made of glass.

Phoebe took her seat in the remaining empty chair, and I passed her the bread. The bread was good. Otherwise, the food was terrible—it was Agnes's view that meat and spices rendered people insensitive to otherworldly messages.

According to Mr. Andersen, we were surrounded by ghosts, who were mostly helpless witnesses to our lives, but at the end of life they acted as midwives to this second birth into the spirit world. They performed many small actions to help guide the freed spirit out of the body. For example, since they could not open doors and the new spirit could not walk through walls in a rare act of interference, they would implant the impulse to open a door into the mind of a grieving family member. The spirit of the deceased would exit by means of that door.

"If only people could see, they wouldn't mourn," said Agnes, looking at Jeptha to rebuke him, for of course she wasn't content to be humored, she wanted his active support and belief, which he could never give. "If you wept, it would be because you were the sentimental type."

I found these ideas interesting. I found *her* interesting, and I believed in her suffering and her conversion without feeling sorry for her or friendly toward her.

When the meal was finished, we went back up to the attic, and Lewis threw himself on his mattress, saying, as if it didn't matter very much, "So she's good now."

"I guess," I said.

"Still, you can't help wondering."

He obviously had more to say, but he waited for me to ask. This was something he often did, but I had never noticed it until we were stuck in the attic together with few distractions. It was beginning to get on my nerves.

"Wonder what?" I asked finally.

"If it's smart for us to put our lives in her hands, seeing as she doesn't consider death a misfortune."

"She's not crazy, not that way. These things make her feel better."

"How do you know?"

"Because they make me feel better," I said, striking a match.

He let the subject drop. Basically, he trusted my judgment. My story to him just before we came here was that Jeptha had contacted me through Edward—offering to help us for old times' sake, because no one would think to look for us here. It was possible that he noticed there was something more between us. He did not ask me about it. I think he felt the topic was delicate, and wasn't going to bring it up if I didn't. Anyway, it was not the kind of thing we talked about.

ONCE A DAY, JEPTHA WOULD VISIT US in the attic, either alone or accompanied by Agnes or Phoebe. He would bring the newspapers and whiskey and glasses; by some unspoken arrangement, it was always one shot for himself, one for me, and two shots for Lewis. We sat on stools and crates and read to each other about the developments in the city: there had been two more hangings; the famous prizefighter Yankee Sullivan, who had been told he was going to hang, had committed suicide in his jail cell; the Law and Order Party, which had opposed the Committee of Vigilance, had been overwhelmed and forced to surrender; hosts of men had been put in irons on ships to Hawaii and China. David Broderick, it seemed, had melted into the hills again.

It was awkward between Lewis and Jeptha. They had not been friends when they were boys, and friendship did not come easily to them now. Neither one of them could see the point of the manner in which the other man had chosen to live. Lewis stood for the side of my life that Jeptha could never accept—for the parlor house—for a life he objected to on half a dozen different grounds. For Lewis, Jeptha was a prig, living by right and wrong instead of by friend and foe (really a perfect mate for Agnes). They tried to like each other for my sake. They traded memories of old times in Livy, choosing the most trivial topics, and people I have not bothered to mention because they have played no part in my story.

One day not long after we had gone into hiding, Jeptha read to us a fiery oration delivered in the United States Senate by Charles Sumner, the abolitionist senator from Massachusetts. Sumner was already a hero to Jeptha, and for days he quoted felicitous lines from the speech—including the famous passage in which, speaking metaphorically, Sumner says that his honorable colleague South Carolina Senator Andrew Butler keeps a mistress whose ugliness he is too besotted with love to see; and her name is Slavery.

I could see that Lewis, though very bored and hungry for any distraction, found Jeptha's excitement over this faraway quarrel rather bewildering.

Since the news from the States reached California after unpredictable delays, it was not until two weeks later that we all read what had happened to Sumner only two days after he made his eloquent remarks about the senator from South Carolina. Butler's nephew had struck Sumner in the head with a cane when he was sitting alone at his desk on the Senate floor. While he was reeling from the first blow, the Southerner had beaten him half to death, making Sumner—it was believed then—a permanent invalid. Jeptha, highly agitated after reading this, stood and walked away and walked back; I think this gave him a better understanding of how cramped our quarters were for us, because at the moment they were too cramped for him. One could see that the story spoke to the man in him and the schoolboy in him, and, like a million other Northern men, he pictured himself on the Senate floor with a cane in his hand, avenging Sumner. Lewis did not share these emotions, but at least for once they were of a kind he understood, and he watched Jeptha with an approving smile.

HAPPY VALLEY, NOW A PART OF DOWNTOWN west of Market Street, was then a suburb of San Francisco, with houses that were surrounded by big yards, vegetable gardens, trees that had been here before '49, and with broad meadows on the hills. Jeptha's house was two stories tall. On the walls along the stairs were framed daguerreotypes of Jeptha's mother and father and of Agatha and Elihu, looking much older than when I had last seen them, dressed in the finest clothes they had ever worn, and staring with the grim Calvinistic fixity of expression and shocked eyes which people in these pictures have, partly because of the long exposure times and partly because of the old-timers' sheer astonishment that likenesses can be preserved by mechanical means. The walls throughout the house were papered in wildflower patterns, a different flower and color for each room. Casting my eyes over the fringed chairs, the lace curtains, the fading rugs, or the broken chairs and stools awaiting repair in the attic, I had a great sense of having surprised Jeptha in his home, of seeing the life he lived with his lawful wife—a life not necessarily happy but complicated and with, until now, no visible sign of me.

It was hard for me, living there and never being alone with him: hard just to hide in an attic and not even be able to look out a window or take a walk outside. It was hard for me, and for Lewis it was impossible. Often I would wake to the steady creaking of the boards under his pacing feet. He would sit for an hour, staring through a chink in the shutters of the window, waiting for the slim section of a live-oak branch to shake with the departure or arrival of a finch; then, for variety, he would go to watch the view from a crack in the other window's shutters; or he would stay on the stairs, just to vary his surroundings. He spent many hours honing his already impressive skills with coins and cards and his pocket knife: he whittled pine blocks into the shapes of boats and birds and fish, and one day, while I begged him not to do it, he whittled them all down into wood chips. When I woke the next morning he was gone. I crept swiftly downstairs—like some supple lizard, I had become so good at it—and sounded the alarm, and Jeptha and Agnes and Phoebe went through the house and the yard.

I searched my bag for the list of names I had compiled based on information given to me by the three men whom I had paid to join the Committee of Vigilance:

Jason Babcock
William Bagley

Richard Boggs
Herbert Corothers
Edgar Dent
Andrew Gray
Robert Gray
Eugene Howard
John Hubbard
John Lyon
Henry Teal

These were the men who had broken into my house and raped all the females they could find, including my maids and me. At the bottom of the page were the addresses of seven of these men. I emptied my bag onto the floor, but the list was nowhere to be found. I paced the attic in sick fear, muttering, "Lewis, Lewis, you fool, you fool."

Jeptha and Agnes were at pains to comfort and reassure me. They did not know of my list or the true story of what had happened at my house, but they both knew what Lewis was like. They reminded me that Lewis knew he was being hunted and would continue to hide. He would know enough to stay away from San Francisco.

Jeptha went about his usual duties, preaching sermons on Sunday and visiting members of his congregation, and seeing to the affairs of the Orphan Asylum, the Drunkard's Mission, and the Mariner's Hospital. A few days after Lewis left, Jeptha officiated at the funeral of a small child, and he and Agnes had an argument. She wanted to talk to the parents about the spirit world, and to tell them that they could hear the voice of their child again if their need was great and they took certain amazingly simple steps. "You don't even believe in heaven anymore; and people can tell you don't," she said. "You're torturing these people. You're torturing them, and they don't have to be tortured, there's no reason for it!"

In the attic I listened like a child spying on her parents' quarrel. There was more, some in low voices, so that I couldn't hear, and she said, "You can't stop me!"

I heard her making preparations to leave, and watched through chinks in the shutters as she walked out the door. My heart leapt when

I saw that Phoebe was going with her. I watched them take a shortcut across an empty field.

I went down to the second-floor landing. Jeptha was standing by a window, watching them go. I stood with my back to the wall, waiting until he turned toward me. I beckoned to him; I took his hand and led him to the bedroom and the spring bed and the feather mattress where each night he slept lawfully beside his wife.

"I can't feel like this anymore. I need to feel something different," I told him. He looked down at me and over at the bed, as if to say that it was the marriage bed and we would be doing it under her nose and nonsense like that, and I grabbed him by the collar, my two fists under his neck, and whispered, "Right here right now. I don't care about her at all." I ran my fingers down his cheek with one hand, and, with as much confidence of possession as if I were in my own house reaching for a comb in a dresser drawer, I unbuttoned his fly. He raised my skirt and my petticoats, and put his palms under my bare thighs, and lifted me onto the edge of the bed. "Hurry," I said, reaching between my legs to guide him. With that my work was over. It was all up to him now. I felt sleepy and helpless. My movements were feeble. Taking me beneath my shoulders, he dragged me roughly farther up the bed. He seemed to realize that tenderness didn't fit the occasion. I wanted to feel his weight on me. He stretched me out flat and pinned my arms to my sides.

When we were done, we lay content for a long time; at last I asked, "When is she coming back?"

"An hour, maybe."

"Precious hour," I said, resting on his chest. After a while I said, "Is this the first time she's gone out? How often does she go out?"

"Now and then." He thought for a moment, then said, "She has just one fixed appointment, on Wednesdays, for a séance across town," and, guessing my thoughts, he added, "Phoebe goes with her. One o'clock. Back by four."

"It isn't easy for me in that attic, Jeptha."

"It isn't easy for me down here," he said.

So after that our time was Wednesdays between one and four. We had our fun, and we lay and talked—we talked about Charley and Agnes and

Lewis. We talked pretty freely, but still there were things I kept from him, and I was sure he knew that.

ONE DAY, WHEN JEPTHA WAS OUT and I was reading by candlelight, I heard footsteps on the stairs, and a moment later Agnes and Phoebe stood in the doorway. "We were wondering if you would like to join us in a spiritualist experiment," said Phoebe.

The three of us crept backward down the stairs. We came to the kitchen, where a small round table had been put in place of the larger rectangular table where we had our meals. When I had last seen this table, it had been covered with oilcloth. Now it was bare. Around its perimeter, inlaid into the oak, were pieces of a darker wood shaped into the numbers "0" through "9," the letters "A" through "Z," and the words "Yes" and "No." In the center of the table was a heart-shaped board equipped with little casters so that it could move around the table when our hands were on it.

"This is a talking board," said Agnes. "Before we begin, there is something I want to say to you, Arabella." She turned her melting eyes toward me, and my stomach clenched with my old hatred at my first, deadliest enemy, who had never offered me a token of kindness that was not the envelope of a secret poison. "Phoebe knows what it is. I have confessed to Phoebe. I have told Phoebe about our childhood in Livy."

"Have you," I said, smiling, with inappropriate lightness.

"I *have*," she said. Her emphasis admitted that I had a reason to be skeptical.

"I am not sure I want to discuss this," I said. "I would love to hear from Charley, or to have word of my brother Frank, my father, my mother, but I'm afraid that if we talk over old times we will quarrel. I doubt they will put me in a receptive frame of mind."

"That is why we must clear the air. While we are still in the body. I think we ought to try. Arabella: do you remember the day some of us thought the world was going to end, and we sat around the fire, and my mother wanted us to confess and apologize to each other, and I used my turn to accuse you rather than to confess, and you said, 'Agnes, can this be, that you really think that Jesus is about to come and take away the saved and leave the rest to burn, really believe it, and yet you are using the occasion to add to the calumnies you heap upon me'? Do you remember that?"

"I remember thinking that; I don't remember saying it."

"You did say it." She wiped her eyes with the palms of her hands. "You said it and you were right; I did believe it! I really did believe that the world was coming to an end and almost everybody in it would be tortured forever, and I could not stop myself from damning myself, as I thought, by slandering you, when I had already slandered you so criminally, when I had already done everything I could to ruin you!"

Her voice shaking, she kept looking at me and then looking away, looking around as if to seek help. Phoebe, touching her arm, said, "Agnes, perhaps not all at once. More when you are feeling stronger."

"Phoebe, this will *help* me; let me go on. Arabella, let me do it now, what we were supposed to do on that day in 1844, let me really do it. I don't know if we can ever be friends. It is too much to hope. The debt lies heavy on me. I can never do you a good turn that would equal it. I could give you Jeptha, but what is that when I no longer want him myself! It seems almost a fresh insult for me to ask your forgiveness—I have no right to your forgiveness when I have done so much to turn your life away from the path it should have taken, and I have only myself to blame. I was such a proud girl, Arabella. I told myself that I hated you because you were wicked, but it was really because you were the first girl I had ever encountered who possessed a force that was stronger than mine; I feared that if I let you be my friend you would rule me, and I could never brook being ruled by anyone."

"You were religious. Weren't you ruled by God?"

"I chose a ruler who lived far away, as I thought, so that I would not have to submit to anyone here. And I kept God far away: I never felt anything like grace."

There was more; she admitted what she had always denied, never asking my forgiveness outright, but making her need of it plain.

At last I said, "Agnes, you must give me time. I perceive that you have changed and that you are sincere, but I think it will take a long time for my feelings about you to change. You've known the new Agnes for years; I've only known her a few weeks."

She bowed her head. "It is more than I hoped for." When she looked up, she put her hands on the talking board. "We can begin. If you feel up to it."

"Yes. All right."

With the help of her little machine, we had our séance. There was gibberish, which Agnes said might be an ancient language or a language from some other planet. Then the spirit of Philippe Toissante announced itself, saying that he was happy in the Summer-Land, and Jeptha should not trouble himself about his death. (He often visited, said Agnes, but Jeptha would not believe. Jeptha would not be comforted.)

Charley did not speak to us.

We put the oilcloth back on the round table and replaced it with the long table and ate a meal—whether in the company of incorporeal spirits, I cannot say. A few hours later, Jeptha came home. He had been to the post office, and the catch included an envelope with no return address, but it was in Lewis's handwriting. Inside was a letter sheet, one of a series produced in those days whose illustrated side glorified the actions of the Committee of Vigilance. The picture was of a supposed "Mass Meeting Endorsing the Acts of the Vigilance Committee."

On the reverse, in Lewis's handwriting, was this:

Jason Babcock
William Bagley
Richard Boggs
Herbert Corothers
Edgar Dent
~~Andrew Gray~~
Robert Gray
Eugene Howard
John Hubbard
John Lyon
Henry Teal

Michelle, while pinned by a man who kept his hand on her mouth, had heard a voice saying, "Let her yell, Andy." That must have been Andrew Gray.

I was happy he was dead, but I couldn't be happy that it was Lewis who had killed him. I hoped fervently that he had the sense to lie low now. If he had been careful and gotten Gray when he was alone, and not left a piece of rope in his mouth, there was a chance that the other men did not yet know there was an assassin on their trail. If another died, they would suspect they were in danger. A third would erase all doubt, and they would begin to take precautions.

After dark, whenever there were noises in the house, my heart beat faster, for I hoped that it was Lewis sneaking in; he would be wet and bedraggled, I would scold him for the risks he had taken, and he would answer all my questions. But he did not come, that night or any other night. With each newspaper Jeptha brought home, my pulse would race until I had scanned its columns and made certain that it did not contain news of Lewis's capture or death. At last Jeptha began to arrive home having performed this chore himself; I would hear him on the stairs and anxiously interpret his face during the second before he said, "Nothing about Lewis."

The *Bulletin* reported that Andrew Gray, a wheelwright, had apparently hanged himself from a rafter in an empty warehouse. He was married with two young children.

Another letter sheet came to the post office. This one showed the vigilante 756 infantry and field pieces pointed at the entrance of the Plaza Market, headquarters of opposition to the committee, and was entitled: "Complete Triumph of the People! Exciting Events of Saturday, June 21st, 1856." On the writing side of the letter sheet, in Lewis's handwriting:

Jason Babcock
William Bagley
Richard Boggs
Herbert Corothers
Edgar Dent
~~Andrew Gray~~
Robert Gray
Eugene Howard
John Hubbard
John Lyon
~~Henry Teal~~

Agnes lent me a book from her library, *Geography of the Spirit World* by James Victor Andersen, and I read it, the better to understand Agnes and because I had time on my hands. I found much to admire in Mr. Andersen's vision of the universe, and especially in his account of an afterlife in which the deceased, like wounded soldiers brought to a hospital behind the lines of a terrible ongoing war, were gradually healed—a process that might take more time than they spent in the flesh. No one was damned. They all came with various burdens, and slowly, tenderly, they were helped. When they were ready, they moved on to other, unknown, higher spheres. Oh, it ought to be like that! If only it were true!

I assisted Agnes and Phoebe with household chores. Sometimes I cooked meals in the kitchen, and Agnes and Phoebe kept me company there, busy sewing or knitting. On a day like that, when Jeptha was out of the house, Agnes remarked casually that she thought Jeptha, at least until recently, had been unfaithful to her. "He used to go out of town every two weeks. He was secretive about it. I think he was seeing a woman."

Phoebe, knitting, nodded. "There's no doubt of it."

I would say they spoke as if of a stranger's infidelity, but there was actually even less disapproval than that. I watched the tips of Agnes's needles repeatedly sliding and separating like the heads of two whispering gossips while I considered and discarded several replies and at last, after too long a delay, settled on, "Oh dear, Agnes."

"I've upset Arabella," said Agnes to Phoebe. "Cousin, we mustn't blame Jeptha too much. Nature has given him strong masculine urges, which I am no longer able to satisfy. I become pregnant easily, whatever precautions I take, and then, every time, I lose the baby, and it is like a great hammer, it crushes me to bits, and I am months putting myself together again; and always after this reassembly we see a piece or two lying about and we don't know where it goes. I can't let it happen again. I can't, and . . . I am human, but my urges have never been particularly strong."

She raised the knitting up to examine it. "I no longer believe in the institution of marriage." She began again: slide and separate, shifting the little loops of yarn. "I don't believe that men and women should be in bondage to one another. Swearing eternal fidelity is romantic, but impractical, for everything is change, as the philosophers tell us, and you can't dip your hand into the same river twice. We must permit those we love to change, even if it means they grow away from us. And I think, for love to last, there should be no pecuniary dependency of one upon the other. Dependency poisons love. It is true, as long as women are so poorly educated that they cannot make money, men will have to take care of them. But I can't regard these arrangements as satisfactory. I believe we should reconsider them."

❧ LXIII ❧

GLUED INTO MY SCRAPBOOK ARE FOUR PARAGRAPHS from four different newspapers; they report the official dissolution of the Second San Francisco Committee of Vigilance on August 18, 1856. To be extra careful, I stayed at Jeptha's house two days longer before creeping quietly out, after dark, with Jeptha as my escort. He took me as far as Portsmouth Square, and I walked the rest of the way alone. It was a delight just to feel the wind on my face. I walked to my house, turned the key, and opened the door, hearing small creatures scurrying away. When I investigated the next day, I found that rats had broken into sacks of flour and sugar in the kitchen. Two ground-floor windows had been forced open. The wine, whiskey, and perfume were all gone. The sheets had been stripped from several beds. Someone had defecated on a carpet and urinated on a pile of dresses that had been dragged out of the closets apparently for this purpose. It was unsystematic, and looked like the work of petty thieves and young boys.

Lewis joined me about a week later. All the people who had been sought by the vigilantes could come out of hiding, because none of us were wanted for any crime; we had been hunted merely as undesirables by men who held themselves superior to the law. I immediately began to rebuild my business. Though the vigilantes and the men whose election they supported had made a great noise about closing the gambling houses and the brothels, this never happened. We continued our operations, paying different men for protection.

On a sunny day one year later, I went down Montgomery Street in an open barouche with several girls who had come to me from New York and New Orleans. On my left was Georgette, who was slender with a childlike face. Men who enjoyed soiling purity appreciated her, yet under her doll-like exterior she was a careful girl, conscious of the dangers of her profession, determined to be an old woman one day. On my right was Suzette—the very one I mentioned at the beginning of this narrative, who was to take poison in a Five Points dive some years later. In those days, she had such a tiny waist that she would not have worn a corset if it had not given men such pleasure to see her in it. She gave good value in bed and was a gold mine for me, and was excessively generous to any invalid, bum, or other girl feeling blue. She grew angry only at injustice, and even then forgave readily. When I suggested that she ought to withhold more of herself, she agreed vehemently, like a drunk swearing to give up the bottle come next Monday, and I foresaw everything, but there was nothing I could do except be glad I wasn't like that. In the backseat were Jocelyn, Michelle, and Francesca (or, as we also called her, Mrs. King), each splendid in her own particular way.

Men on the wooden sidewalks tipped their hats, leering, sighing, gawking. I wore black, with a lace veil. My girls wore white and held parasols. Rosy-cheeked, as sweet as cream, as fresh as flowers: ordinary men could dream of one day being able to afford them, as you might hope one day to live in a Venetian palazzo. The barouche slowed. "Girls, all of you, stand, smile, keep your balance." We rolled down the street like a float in a parade. "Behold, you citizens of Sodom! Look, you misshapen gnomes and hunchbacks. This is beauty. This is why you must become rich."

Children followed us. From a basket at my feet I showered them with little bags of zanzibars, candied almonds, and polished pennies.

Snarling wives snapped at their men and curled up the corners of their lips, showing purple gums and sharp dog-teeth. "Hello, you crones and charwomen!" I wagged my finger. "How good you are, how hard you labor, and for nothing, nothing! How life mistreats you. But you like it, don't you? Do you scrub floors? Would you like to come to our house and scrub the floors? And wash our clothes? They need a lot of washing, these white clothes."

As we neared the *Bulletin* offices, I said, "Girls, sit down, all except Mrs. King," and when they had obeyed I asked loudly, "Has anyone here seen Thomas King? I owe him money. Where is Thomas King?"

People laughed. Everyone knew what I had done to Thomas King, James King of William's younger brother. I had found out that his ex-wife, back in Baltimore, was a prostitute. It was true! Ned McGowan had published it in the *Phoenix,* the newspaper he had started in Sacramento City, and all the San Francisco newspapers except the *Bulletin* had picked up the story, whereupon, to almost universal delight, posters suddenly appeared all over town declaring that Belle Cora had offered a thousand dollars plus the price of the first-class steamship ticket to Mrs. King if she would be the new attraction at my house on Pike Street. Which was also true, and fortunately she turned out to be pretty.

I was still here: thriving, mocking my enemies, and making a display of myself in ways appropriate to a parlor-house madam. People spoke of it as Belle Cora's revenge; but it was a paltry revenge. Men who had killed my Charley were in barbershops having their faces lathered, in opera houses applauding the show, at picnics tossing their babies into the air. If I had been able to murder them all I would not have hesitated, and I often imagined it; but I was not going to do it, any more than Jeptha was going to walk into the U.S. Congress and pick a fight with the man who had beaten Charles Sumner. Revenge on such a scale requires a specialist.

I BOUGHT A SMALL COTTAGE between Happy Valley and Mission Dolores. Jeptha and I would each of us separately make our way there on horseback. A miner had owned it before I did. There was a vegetable garden in the back, which a local man tended in exchange for most of the product, with manzanita in the yard and huckleberries growing close to the house. Traveling to and from the cottage, I dressed in trousers and a frock coat. I would arrive first and change into a house dress. When Jeptha came on his horse, I would be standing in the doorway like a wife. We met more often than we used to.

We enacted a simple life and daydreamed about it, but the moment we took these daydreams seriously we were confronted by enormous obstacles, mostly of my making. He would have had us leave California and start a life fresh somewhere else—in Oregon, perhaps, or Australia. He would give Agnes the house, and she could stay in it or sell it, as she pleased. She had told him many times that he was free to go, she could get on without him; he would take her at her word. Naturally, wherever we went, we would start out poor; we couldn't live on the money I had amassed by helping young girls destroy themselves. My fortune must be given to charity.

I did not like to argue with him, but it was all impossible. He was wrong about himself if he thought that, with his overactive conscience, he could leave Agnes, now so fragile, to make her own way. As for me, surely he knew better, and it was thoughtless of him to make me say it: I could never do what he proposed. It suited me to be a madam. I did not envision stopping. If I did stop, I would keep my fortune. I would never willingly become helpless again, unable to assist my friends and hurt my enemies. I wanted, one day, to be an influence in Frank's life. I would need money for that.

Besides, I *had* Jeptha, the man I had loved since I was a child—loved not in friendship and kindness, as with Charley, but through and through, down to the soles of my feet, with my heart and my womb and everything. He was here with me. It was not perfect, to be sure, but the life he had in mind would not have been perfect, either. I wanted to have my cake and eat it, too, and it seemed to me that I could.

I would tell him, "We shouldn't waste our time arguing."

And he would say, "What do you want? Do you really want me just to take pleasure with you, and pretend with you, and not care what you really think and do?"

"Yes, that sounds lovely; let's do that," I said, but I didn't mean it. I wanted him to try to save me; and a part of me, though perhaps not enough of me, had always hoped that he *would* break down every barrier in my heart and make a good woman of me, make me, if not a Christian, at least a better person, less vengeful, more scrupulous, more like him. But, as he had told me aboard the *Juniper,* I was a hard case. I needed special attention.

We quarreled about other things. Ned McGowan had come out of hiding soon after Lewis and I had. The little newspaper he published out of Sacramento was devoted entirely to printing tittle-tattle about the private lives of former vigilantes: this one didn't pay his gambling debts; that one was so hated by white women that in his native Maine he had taken up with a Passamaquoddy Indian (and Passamaquoddies were lower even than Digger Indians); another had Negro blood; another was half Jewish. Jeptha despised the *Phoenix*. I can see now it wasn't anything to be proud of, but then all that mattered was that Ned was making these men suffer. Besides, though I didn't mention this, I had given McGowan money to help him start his paper. Jeptha and I had an argument about it in which I accused him of feeling sorry for murderers, and he said that there had to be limits in any fight, and I reminded him that to help Charley he had blackmailed a juror. Immediately I knew I had gone too far. "I know you did that for me. You wouldn't have done it otherwise."

He didn't answer for a long time. He kissed me to show he wasn't mad. He put on his clothes, and I made the bed. He lit the fire in the stove. I made coffee. When we sat down to drink it, he said, "That boy on the *Juniper* would be sixteen now if he'd lived. I think about that a lot. But I haven't spent my life atoning. I take my share of pleasure just like other people. I threw my wife in the bay; killed my own child, too, maybe. With your help, I break my marriage vows every chance I get. I've blackmailed a juror. Evidently, I'm no paragon of virtue. That doesn't mean I yield the government of the world up to villainy. We are of thrifty Yankee stock, you and I; we don't throw a thing away just because one piece is rotten. We salvage what can be saved."

When he was done, I said: "I could listen to you talk all day. If you would learn to move your arms a little more, E. D. Baker would have nothing on you."

LIKE SNOWFALL IN A PLACE SO COLD that snow never thaws, numberless incidents of every size bury the dead deeper from the moment they expire. They are not here to see this, and that, and that. We said we would never forget them. We do forget them, for minutes at a time, from the first day. Each day we think of them a little less, until at last we join them.

One day in July 1858, in our cottage between Happy Valley and Mission Dolores, Jeptha read a speech from the newspaper, which everyone would be talking about soon: it was Abraham Lincoln's famous "House

Divided" speech, given upon his acceptance of the Republican nomination for senator from Illinois. Jeptha was very excited by it, and in church that week he called it "the sermon given last June by Mr. Lincoln," and he recommended Lincoln to his congregation as "a close personal friend of Edward D. Baker," because Baker, at that time, was widely admired by the people of San Francisco, and most of us had never heard of Lincoln. That Lincoln and E. D. Baker were warm friends, I had learned from Baker, and Jeptha had learned it from me.

Lincoln gave many other speeches that summer as part of a series of debates he held with his opponent for the Senate, Stephen Douglas. The San Francisco papers reprinted them, and Jeptha followed them closely.

That fall, to celebrate the opening of the transatlantic electric telegraph cable, our city held a parade so grand that it took an hour and twenty minutes for it to pass one spot. The militia marched, along with the fire companies, the Odd Fellows, the Hebrew Societies, the Masons, and the brewery wagons. A man wrapped in the American flag and a man wrapped in a Union Jack, each standing on a different omnibus, rolled down the street linked by a long rope representing the cable. Colonel E. D. Baker gave a speech. It had been two years since I had seen him in the flesh.

When I got home, I picked up a hand mirror. I was thirty. Was I beginning to look hard? Less so than you would expect from the way I had lived.

The following year, when I was thirty-one, Baker delivered the most famous oration of his career. It was at the funeral of U.S. Senator David Broderick, who had loomed so large over our lives throughout the Gold Rush years. We had watched him rise and fall and rise again. Toward the end, a reversal of his political fortunes had made him temperamental and erratic, and one day he challenged another politician to a duel, and he was shot dead. The funeral was held on Portsmouth Square. You may find Baker's speech in the San Francisco newspapers for September 19, 1859, and in *Masterpieces of E. D. Baker*. I was there, seated on a horse for most of the time, and Jeptha was there, too, with Agnes; we saw each other but made no sign.

Lewis was not present. He had other business. He went by hack and then on foot toward a ramshackle one-story house with four rooms and a front porch. It stood beside an abandoned horse shed and a shack that stood over a cockfighting pit, but was otherwise in a waste of mud and weeds and stale water in the neighborhood of Mission Dolores.

A few days earlier, he had learned that Eugene Howard, one of the vigilantes who had forced their way into my house in '56, was infatuated with a girl who used to work for Irene Grogan. Lewis offered this girl five hundred dollars if she would help him lure Howard, who was married, to that shack. She agreed to make it their regular place of assignation and notify Lewis in advance when they were to meet, and on the second occasion—today—Lewis would be there with her. The placement of an asymmetrical board at the edge of the porch, its narrow end pointing east, was the signal that the girl was in the house alone and it was safe for Lewis to enter it. They would then wait there together for Howard.

When Lewis arrived, the narrow end of the board was pointing east. It lied. All six of the surviving members of his special list were in the building, waiting tensely, with pistols and rifles. They had laid this trap months in advance.

Despite their advantages of numbers and surprise, they were very frightened of Lewis. When they asked around town about him, they found that he enjoyed a reputation for excellence in his profession, and they were sure that it was he who had killed nearly half of their number already. No doubt they had their weapons trained out every window. Something or other—perhaps the condition of the mud around the house, for it had rained the night before—must have made Lewis suspicious. He did not enter by the front door but approached from a side entrance, with his hand inside his coat, in the belt of his trousers, where he kept a Colt six-shot revolver. The men inside could see that something had alerted him, and though their plan had undoubtedly been to let him enter and dispatch him silently, one of the men decided it was better not to wait. "No!" shouted one of the others, and Lewis dropped to the mud. The shot went where his head had just been. Almost anybody else in his situation would have run, becoming an easy target, but Lewis was clever about these things; he rolled quickly toward the house, near the window the shot had come from, as numerous bullets raked up the patch of mud where he had just been.

Lewis knew by the rapidity of the fire that there were several men in the house and that they would be splitting up so that they could come at him from different directions. But they could not know which exit he was covering. He ran, in a crouch, close to the building, to the front porch, and shot twice at John Lyon, the man leaving the door. The first shot missed; the second shot went through Lyon's throat, and he dropped his gun and fell, mortally wounded, clutching his neck with both hands. Lewis noticed where the pistol had landed on the porch. He would have liked to have gotten this extra gun, but of course he did not dare stop to pick it up. Supposing that men would be coming from the other exit, and hoping that at least for a few seconds his enemies would be too scared to come out the front door, Lewis turned back the way he had come and ran into William Bagley, who put a rifle bullet clean through Lewis's side, just under the ribs. Before Bagley could pull the trigger again, Lewis shot him, fatally, in the chest. He then shot twice at Jason Babcock, who was right behind Bagley. The first bullet caught Babcock's left shoulder; the second went through his right eye into his brain, and he fell dead.

Lewis had one bullet left and needed more, because he expected with good reason that more than one foe remained. Weakened but not stopped by his wound—excitement carries us forward in such situations—he circled the building and came at the porch from the other end. He looked under it and on top of it. There was no noise but a horse whinnying and snorting somewhere and the hiss of the wind in the trees. Lyon's body lay on the front porch, and beside it a Colt revolver. Lewis picked up the long board that had deceived him about who was in the house, and used it to sweep the revolver off the porch. He ran for the pistol: as he picked it up, a bullet from the house caught him in the right shoulder, and he dropped his own gun. He ran away from the house and rolled into a gully, and waited as the three remaining men, Corothers, Robert Gray, and Howard, advanced on him, firing rifles. On his back, with Lyon's pistol in his left hand, Lewis put a shot into Corothers's stomach and another into Gray's face. Their weapons fell to the mud. Howard turned and ran. Corothers bent over, clutching his stomach. Gray staggered blindly back in the direction of the house.

This had all taken about three minutes. Growing weaker and weaker, until he could not lift his arm, Lewis waited for Howard to return. Ten minutes passed, during which Howard, in terror of his life, chased a horse that been hidden in the shack over the cockfighting pit. The horse had been unnerved by the shooting and would not allow itself to be mounted.

Eventually, Lewis heard shouting in English and Spanish, horses whinnying and clomping in the grass and mud, and men talking: "Stop. It's
over."

The shouts had come from several bystanders, most of them customers and workers at a cantina about fifty yards away who had heard the
shooting, armed themselves, and waited at a discreet distance. In the
meantime, Howard had finally managed to get on his horse, and they let
him get away.

"You there, are you alive?" they called to Lewis cautiously. By then
he was unconscious. They brought him into the house, along with
Corothers and Gray, who were also still alive.

Later, in his delirium, Lewis mentioned my name. I was sent for, and
when I came I brought along a doctor, Matheny, and a surgeon, Blair,
both of whom I knew to be good at their work, though with vigilante
sympathies. I arranged for a fast carriage to take us to the scene together.
On the way, I offered them bonuses if Lewis lived. Blair protested that the
Hippocratic Oath required him to do his best in any event, which made
Matheny, who needed money, very angry. I said that nevertheless there
would be a bonus in it; whereupon Matheny, a clever man, suggested
that I arrange as soon as possible for a shipment of ice to be brought to
the scene.

Lewis woke long enough to recognize me, and he asked for his lucky
stone to grip while the surgeon took the bullet out of his shoulder. When
I looked in his pantaloons, the pockets were empty. "Don't operate yet,"
I said, in what I can only describe as an overpowering fit of superstition.
Matheny and Blair said that any delay would endanger Lewis's life, but I
got them to stop while I went outside. Then I saw that it was laughable
to look for his stone amid so many in the grass, in the mud, in the gully,
and I turned and spoke to the men who had come upon the scene. "A
rock was found in Lewis Godwin's pocket, or else"—I had just thought of
this—"maybe it was in his hand; maybe when he knew the shooting was
over he reached into his pocket for it and clutched it in his hand as though
it was important. There's no gold in it, or anything else that most people
think is precious. It is a good-luck charm just for him—it is without value
to anyone else." A small grizzle-faced man in a serape, with gaps among
his teeth, reached into his pocket and produced the stone. "Thank you,"

I said, giving him a gold coin; I rushed back into the house, wrapped my brother's hand around the stone, and covered his hand with mine.

The surgeon's instruments were not especially dirty, but no one back then had ever conceived of such a thing as sterilization. A fever developed. Matheny had a theory that high temperatures themselves were dangerous, and he put Lewis in a bath of ice to bring the fever down. For days, my brother's life hung in the balance.

At the beginning of this long ordeal, Corothers and Gray were in the shack with us. Their physician, Pratt, a small, stocky young fellow with close-together eyes who did not have a professional degree, I think, was clearly less skillful than the doctors I had hired for Lewis. Drs. Matheny and Blair had time on their hands while waiting for my brother's fever to respond to their ministrations, and a professional distaste for their colleague's clumsiness. They would have liked to help with Corothers's and Gray's cases, for when you are good at a thing you hate to see it done badly. But when they stopped to intervene, I shouted out in alarm that Lewis had taken a turn for the worse, and they had no choice but to return to their patient.

Corothers expired early the next morning. He talked some of the time; I worried about that. I asked Pratt what the fellow's last words had been: Pratt said that Corothers had spoken about his poor mother and his poor sister back in Missouri, and his spotted hunting dog, Danger, who had run off one day many years ago and had never been seen again. I did not think Pratt was cunning enough to lie. Corothers had, however, identified himself. When no one was looking, I searched his pockets and found a copy of my list of vigilantes, which Lewis, with his usual reckless bravado, had anonymously mailed to the targets.

Gray, whose name was indicated by a letter and a bill of sale in his pocket, lasted two excruciating days. He spent both those days on his face, because he had trouble swallowing and whenever he was on his back he would start choking on his blood and spit. Dr. Blair wanted to give Pratt an ingenious little hand pump, equally useful for draining wounds or fluid collecting in the mouth, and I could not stop him from mentioning it. Fortunately, Pratt was reluctant to accept help. I said, "Dr. Pratt is a member of the rising generation. Let him do as he thinks best."

Lewis was in a bedroom at the time, where he had been made as comfortable as possible with linens and pillows and a spring mattress. Now and then we wrapped him in canvas and ice. Gray was on the table in the kitchen. He lay on his stomach, gurgling and moaning. I spoke to him. "Mr. Gray. You can't see me. I'm Belle Cora. I think perhaps we have met before. This would be a good time to consider your sins, Mr. Gray. Were you ever burned, for example, by touching a hot frying pan? Imagine that happening all over your body for all eternity." Then, remembering what one of my girls had reported about his behavior back in '56, I thought a bit and added, "But perhaps, for you, the punishment will be gagging. Gagging forever—that would not be very agreeable, either."

The sheriff at the time was a Mexican War veteran named Charles Doane. He had been grand marshal of the Second Committee of Vigilance. As soon as Doane heard about the incident, he ordered that Lewis be arrested on a charge of murder and moved to the county jail, which since '56 had become a rat-infested hell by reason of Doane's embezzlements and the thrift of Know-Nothing government. Not that the destination mattered: moving Lewis at this point would have killed him. Matheny and Blair, who had some standing in the community, said they would call it murder. Doane posted a guard at the shack while an investigation was conducted.

Doane himself handpicked the grand jury, but all the witnesses had the men in the house firing at Lewis first; it was obviously an ambush, and the jury was forced to rule that there was insufficient evidence to bring charges.

IT WAS A YEAR BEFORE LEWIS FELT quite himself. He never recovered a full range of movement in his right shoulder, but with practice his right hand reacquired its former speed and accuracy with a pistol. By posting anonymous advertisements in the *Bulletin* and the *Globe,* offering a reward to anyone who could find Eugene Howard, he learned that Howard's wife was receiving letters from a mining camp in Coulterville. "It's a trap," I told him. "Don't go." But he wouldn't listen. He returned two weeks later, his eyes glittering, and the first words he said to me were "That's finished." He had killed every man on my list.

I have wondered, from time to time, how accurate that list was.

Book Six

{ 1861–1919 }

Frank Moody
c/o Melanchthon Moody
Sawmill Road
Livy, New York

March 3, 1861
Mrs. Arabella Dickinson
Post Office Box 28
San Francisco, California

Dear Godmother,

Forgive me if I get right to the point as I am poorly educated with
no graces. I have just found out that you said you would pay for me
to go to the Pearson Academy. I should be writing you from there
now. Instead, I was not even told of your offer. Anne knew that if
she asked me I would want to go, so she didn't tell me. Now the
cat's out of the bag everybody here agrees that it is a good idea for
me to go. They're dying for me to go, except Anne. She says I'm too
young and won't be liked which is nonsense. She's the only hold-
out, but she's the boss now. She as good as owns the farm. Melanchthon can't even sign his name anymore. Daniel and Susannah
are for me going, but they don't dare cross her.

It's like death here. I wish you had never brought me here. I
know I'm an orphan, Godmother, I guess I would have been worse
off in an orphanage. Or if those good people, my parents, the sickly
mechanics, had lived to raise me to be like them, then I'd really
be in a fix! So maybe I should be grateful. But Godmother please
don't leave your good deed unfinished. You put me here. Now I
need you to get me out of here. Whatever power you have over
them, use it.

Sorry it's not a nicer letter. I'll write you another one full of thank yous and cheer when I'm in a better mood.

Yours truly,
Frank

No, it wasn't a very nice letter, but I loved it. It was bracing, it was thrilling to have my son, whose last word to me had been his very first word, suddenly appealing to me, surly and forthright, as a third party in the middle of a family argument, bold enough and clever enough to track me down. I remembered the passionate letter I had once written to my grandfather, begging him to take me away from the very same place, and the patronizing reply that I had received. Frank was not going to get that kind of answer. He was luckier than he knew.

At the little table in the cottage where I would make Jeptha eggs and toast and bacon and coffee, I had put the letter into his hands and watched him read it. When he put the letter down and dipped the end of his toast into the yolk of the eggs, I asked if he did not think it was remarkably intelligent, and if Frank did not seem like an unusual boy. After a telltale hesitation he replied, "Yes." After a while he added, "He doesn't write like an orphan."

"No, he doesn't," I said proudly. Then I saw that he had not meant it as a compliment. "What's wrong with that? You don't expect him to sound like one of the orphans in your asylum?"

He looked at me awhile. "No. Of course not. Still, I would expect him to sound like a country boy—who with other children might talk disrespectfully about his elders out of their hearing, but would never write in that vein in a letter to a grown man or woman. A country boy with such manners would be horsewhipped every single day. If Frank isn't, maybe it's because Anne has been his sturdy shield, but it hasn't done his character any good."

"It's absurd for you to conclude all that from one letter. He's angry. They lied to him. And he's writing to *me*. He knows instinctively that he can share these thoughts with me and I won't judge him. Even if he thinks I'm his godmother, his blood tells him there's more between us. Where he says, 'It's death here,' I know you never felt that way about

Livy, but you and I are different that way. Frank is my son, and he's more like me."

"Of course," said Jeptha soothingly. "It's just one letter. And he was angry."

For days, and then for weeks, I thought of nothing but Frank's letter—I thought of it while I bid on linens and china at the auction houses; when I went to the theater with Jocelyn and Lewis; when I presided over the ball I held each spring. I thought of it while all around me men talked of the election of Lincoln and the breakup of the United States—which must be saved at all costs some (including Jeptha) said, or which had gotten too big anyway others said (I was with that group)—and the inevitability of war and the improbability of war. That was the year when news from the East came halfway by telegraph and the rest of the way by Pony Express in a mere ten days, and it seemed as if the States had drawn closer to us at the very moment they were falling apart.

I decided that to help Frank I must go myself. I wrote ahead to tell Anne I was coming and began my preparations immediately. To my surprise, Edward and Jeptha announced their intention to come along. Edward would visit Robert and his family. Jeptha would accompany me as far as Baltimore and then go on to Ohio to visit his mother and father, who was ailing. On the way, the farther we got from California, the more freedom we would have to be together and stroll on the deck together and stay in hotels together without damage to his reputation or his livelihood.

And so, one sunny day in the first week of April, not quite a month after Lincoln's inauguration and two weeks after his speech about graves and hearts and hearthstones reached San Francisco, we all went up the gangplank of the North American Steamship Company's S.S. *Nebraska*.

❧ LXV ❧

THE *NEBRASKA* WOULD TAKE US TO PANAMA. We would go by rail across the isthmus, and another ship would take us to New York after a stop at New Orleans, now a foreign port, and another in Baltimore. It would take three weeks.

Amid the usual commotion—the fluttering flags, busy porters, hand-shakes, embraces, and last-minute panics—I felt emotions appropriate to a forty-niner who has prospered in California. I looked back to the shore. Where there had been water there were now theaters, hotels, and banks. Montgomery Street, formerly on the beach, was four blocks inland. Where shacks and tents and crawling bedraggled humanity had swarmed the hills there was now a mighty city, its roofs and chimneys daubed with the fool's gold of morning sunlight, each edifice raked by the shadows of its neighbors; and from the deck of the *Nebraska* my eyes sought the roof of my current parlor house on Pike Street, and the roof of my old par-lor house on Dupont Street, now a legitimate boarding house, and with effort, elsewhere in the town, bits of my boarding houses and my laundry, and several sandy acres on California Street Hill that also belonged to me and might be valuable one day. I could see the American Theatre, where Mrs. Richardson had initiated the chain of events that turned us both into widows.

I had left the management of the parlor houses in the hands of Georgette and Mrs. King. Niobe and two women who have had no other part in this narrative looked after the boarding houses and the laundry. They were all diligent, and liked me as much as was consistent with fear-ing me.

Lewis was not with us: he had gone to Nevada Territory, where silver had been discovered; Jocelyn had gone with him. Agnes was not with us, of course; a year before, she had divorced Jeptha and gone to live with a friend, also a spiritualist and freethinker, in Monterey. There she worked as a schoolteacher, two or three men there wanted to marry her, and one she liked very well, but still she hesitated. Was Jeptha, then, at last free to marry me? No. A sickly wife had never been the only obstacle to our union. Jeptha was also the pastor of his flock, the head of the Orphan

Asylum, and the moving spirit behind the Drunkard's Asylum, the Mariner's Hospital, and other civic projects and worthy charities that would be deprived of his guidance as soon as it became known that he had associated himself with Belle Cora, the notorious madam. We would have to leave California and start over. And he still had his old objection to living off my earnings.

Aboard the *Nebraska*, officially I had a stateroom to myself, and Jeptha shared a berth with Edward, but when we were under way, Jeptha would come to my room in the late hours. Outside our berths, the three of us spent much of our time together, feeling almost like a well-off family on a vacation abroad.

For Jeptha and me it was like a honeymoon in reverse, undoing—by a different route and much more quickly—our voyage from New York to California in '49. Once we were a hundred miles from California, Jeptha seemed to throw off all caution and held my hands and draped his arm around my shoulders in full view of the other passengers. One day, when there was music and others were dancing on the deck, the former Baptist asked me to teach him to dance. For Jeptha to show himself so openly infatuated with a woman some of the passengers surely knew as a madam struck me as extremely rash, but I could not bring myself to tell him to stop. "We're going to have to go back," I whispered when the band played a waltz, but he only gripped my hand tighter and pulled me up. "We shouldn't; it's too risky," I said, and he gave me a peck on the cheek right there on the deck, in front of everyone; because it was in front of everyone, the little kiss was like strong drink to me, making me woozy and confused and happy.

Neither Jeptha nor Edward agreed with me about Frank, so we avoided speaking of him. We talked about the Civil War, by comparison a neutral topic. Lately, Edward was hinting that he might enlist in an Eastern militia. I did not think he was serious, but in case he was, I made many arguments against the plan.

I told him that, first of all, there would be no war. This was the general belief in the spirit world, which had access to the secret counsels of both sides. So I had learned in a letter from Agnes, who had it from her dead son Jonathan. (I believed in the spirit world when it suited me.) If the spirits should prove to be in error, Edward would be of more use in California's militia, ready to repel a Confederate attack on the treasure ships.

WE WERE ON THE TRAIN crossing the Isthmus of Panama when we heard of the firing on Fort Sumter. Newspapers passed from hand to hand. All the Americans on the train felt suddenly very serious and important. We were of varying sympathies and origins; arguments erupted, and one saw right away from the speech of various Prussians, Frenchmen, and Englishmen what their countries' attitudes would be.

The captain of our next ship decided to skip New Orleans, which was a relief to me, because I had always associated New Orleans with Charley and I knew that being there would make me feel sad and angry. Then we skipped Baltimore, too, since the situation in Maryland was uncertain at that time—if it did not secede it was expected to be a scene of fighting. I was pleased with this, too, since it meant that Jeptha would have to take a different route to Ohio, and he would be with me longer.

As the *Nebraska* pushed its way into the lower bay, the day was as clear as it had been when Jeptha and I had left on the *Juniper* twelve years earlier, and we could all see that New York City had not stood still. There was twice as much of everything—piers, clipper ships, steamboats, people. When we disembarked, all was pandemonium. The walls of the warehouses on the East River wharf were covered with posters calling in giant capital letters for VOLUNTEERS and announcing a MASS MEETING IN UNION SQUARE. Several men who had commanded at Fort Sumter would speak, along with about twenty others, among them "Colonel E. D. Baker, Senator, of California." The hack driver, while bringing us to a moderately priced hotel, told us that a Baltimore mob had attacked federal troops who were on their way to protect Washington. In the hotel lobby, a boy sold us a *New York Times,* in which we learned that Robert Godwin—my brother!—was the secretary of the Union Defense Committee, which had organized the meeting to be held in Union Square the next day.

We spent the night in a New York hotel and attended the meeting— along, it is said, with two hundred thousand others, pressed at every side by sweaty, agitated strangers' shoulders, necks, and faces, so that letting go of each other's hands would mean being pulled farther apart, to be inexorably moved to the place where our section of the crowd meant for some unknown reason to head; to imagine how long it would take to get out of here, should it be necessary, was to feel the stirring of panic. We caught only the occasional glimpse, heard only the odd shout, from the men at the speakers' stands. It didn't matter. The point was proved: we were many. At least, that is how I remember it over half a century later, now that the generals have died and been replaced by bronze statues, the battlefields are cemeteries, and the tombstones are green with lichen. It was proved in Union Square that day that the North had an overwhelming numerical advantage in human flesh, as well as in telegraphs, railways, ships, and factories. I was a speck among specks carried forward by a great wave, and I knew that there was indeed to be a war. The forces that decide these things had decided.

I held on tight to Jeptha, and just before the movement of the crowd dragged Edward from us, we agreed to meet near the bronze statue of Washington, which now held the flag that had recently flown over Sumter. When we met Edward again, he brought news that the Union Defense Committee had its headquarters at the Metropolitan Hotel, where Colonel Baker was recruiting for a regiment consisting of men from California, and Robert Godwin was there. Edward and Jeptha decided that they would visit and announce themselves to him.

On the last leg of our journey, when we were not discussing my son, Frank, or the brewing war, Robert had been a frequent topic of conversation. Edward and Jeptha meant to meet him—there was never any question about it—but what of me? Ten years ago, on learning what his sister had become, he had wept. Sorrowfully but adamantly, he had decided for the sake of the family name to cut off all ties with me and never to speak of me, and generally, as the song has it, to turn my picture to the wall. He had not even bothered to make a vow of it—it was to him so obviously a necessity, he could not conceive of the circumstances that might persuade him to change his mind. Should I try? How would I feel if I made the attempt and failed? We discussed this, Jeptha, Edward, and I. We discussed it several times without reaching a conclusion. Jeptha said he would make arrangements to have me brought to our hotel while they went to the Metropolitan, and at last, impulsively, I decided. "No. Let me come."

We walked there in the mire of Broadway. When we were a block away from the Metropolitan, it started to rain, and I remembered the rain long ago, when I was small, when we were on our way back from our visit to the roof of my grandfather's warehouse on Pearl Street, the day Lewis dropped the stone that killed a pig. I told Edward: "I don't care if I see Baker, but bring me to Robert. Make Robert acknowledge me."

At the Metropolitan, a suite of rooms was being used by the Union Defense Committee. Many people were coming and going, and there, as big as life, sat Colonel Baker, at a long table in a crowded, busy room full of flags and brevets, papers and ink bottles, and patriotic civilian volunteers. He rose and bowed. He was about to introduce me to the men around him when I pre-empted him quickly with the name Arabella Dickinson, and he took the hint, that I was not Belle Cora here. I could tell that he was puzzled to see Jeptha, whom he knew as the pastor of a Unitarian church, a man unlikely to be seen with me.

At our request, Baker sent a man to a nearby room to fetch Robert, with instructions not to mention me, but to say that Edward Godwin and Jeptha Talbot were waiting to see him. A moment later, Robert came out, smiling broadly and stepping quickly. When he saw me his pace slowed; the smile vanished. But what could he do? His brother Edward was there, and Jeptha, whom he knew to be a Unitarian minister, apparently not afraid to be in my company; and his problem was made more acute by the fact that his pretty wife was there, too, showing men where to sign and encouraging them with her admiration. He had never told her what had become of his sister, and he didn't want her ever to find out. He introduced me to her—as his sister Arabella—with sickeningly false cheer, all his movements a little delayed, his eyes looking in slightly the wrong direction, as if he were being operated on strings, his own clumsy marionette. He must have felt as if he were exposing her to some terrible contamination. The idea of his wife even occupying the same room as a whore was hideous to him.

Her name was Amanda. "But we've met," she said, looking from me to Jeptha. "We met at your grandfather's house. Shortly before the two of you were married and left for California." I remembered her, the lucky girl with the easy life who could make light of murder. Her face was a little broader and her skin was not as smooth, but she was still pretty, dressed quietly, with red, white, and blue ribbons in her hair and a flag pin on her white pelerine. "We were talking about the murder at the Blooming-dale Tontine, which was never solved. Jeptha was there, and also your cousin Agnes"—here there was a split-second pause, and a subtle change of pitch, as she reflected that the subsequent course of events might have been painful for me. "And then we had our own excitement. I'll never for-get that night." Her look was gentle. "And later—I'm sorry—we heard that you and Jeptha were . . . no longer together. And"—her glance shifting between me and Jeptha—"and—how do things stand now?"

"We're all friends now," said Jeptha.

"I'm so glad I've married into an interesting family. Come to dinner. You and Jeptha and Edward."

"Oh," said Robert, looking at me with panic.

"How kind of you," I said. "We'd be delighted."

"But we're very busy now, and Arabella can stay in town only a short while," said Robert.

"She said she'd be delighted. That means she has time. I know I have time. If you don't, we can spare you. It needn't be fancy—you don't mind if it's just what our cook can do on short notice?"

"Of course not," I replied.

Robert's house was in Brooklyn. We all took the ferry there the next evening, and spent the night, and stuck to the stories we had agreed on.

TWO DAYS LATER, EARLY IN THE MORNING, Jeptha and I walked to Chambers Street, where there was now a railroad depot. We stood in line together, and he bought my ticket, and then, because we were early, we wiped the soot off a bench on the platform and watched the southbound train disgorge a crowd of passengers. I was excited by the prospect of the journey, and I enjoyed the freedom of being out in public with Jeptha. My mind raced, and I commented on the little dramas of arrival: this one disembarked alone and was met by a passionate family; those gentlemen came as a group of revelers and left together; that lonesome fellow had been stood up. All the while, Jeptha held me around the waist; when I looked back at him, he had been looking not at the scene I was describ-ing but at my face. When my train came, he got on with me and stayed until the last minute, kissing me with such tenderness and for such a long time that when he released me I laughed and said, "I'm only going to Livy, Jeptha."

I took the train to Albany and then to Rochester, and from Rochester I took a stagecoach south. In Patavium, I rented a gig and drove it myself to Melanchthon's farm. I passed hilly pastures and wrinkled fields, and I was there. There was now a second farmhouse, forty yards from the old one.

When I had last come here, it had been to leave Frank, and I had been pushed and pulled by the memories of Jeptha and my shame in the town. I didn't feel that this time. That old Livy of regret and nostalgia was not a real place on earth anymore, but a place in my memory. All I could think of was that I was about to see my son.

With mounting excitement, I brought the gig into the barn myself and wiped down the horse. When I walked out, I encountered the hired girl, a stranger to me, who took my portmanteau and went in to announce me. Anne, stout and gray-haired, pulled me into the house and embraced me: "I would never have asked you to come, but I'm glad you did." Frank, she told me, was in town, at the livery stable, where he had been working since the end of Livy's four-month school term, and she observed in a way that was neither doting nor judgmental, "Frank works hard when it puts money in his pocket."

She took me to Melanchthon, who sat in a wicker chair on the back porch, watching two yellow wasps drink from a puddle of cider. Half of his face drooped like a sack. "Melanchthon," his wife said, "it's Arabella! Arabella has come all the way from California to visit us!" He turned his face to me, pursing his wet lips asymmetrically, and Anne said that he was happy to see me. I kissed his damp brow, patted his shoulder. Shooing the wasps and wiping away the cider puddle, Anne told him in a cheerful voice that they would be having bread pudding with dinner. She gave him some good news about the weather and a field and a fence; when the porch door had closed behind us, she said that she had always known this might be the price of marrying a man already middle-aged, and that she had not really been taken by surprise.

"Daniel and Susannah will eat with us," she said, and sent the girl to tell them. "Do you still cook? Will you help me?" I said I would, and we worked in the kitchen, which had been improved since I had been here last. There were two cooking stoves, running water from a cistern, a big steel meat-grinder, and numerous wax-sealed glass jars in which seemingly every product of the farm had been jammed, jellied, potted, or pickled.

In my letters, I had always maintained the pretense that my money was from my marriage to a banker (now deceased), but I assumed that Anne knew everything. I spoke generally of life in California, and she spoke about matters here.

She chose her words carefully, and I knew that I was supposed to read between the lines. Susannah, whom I remembered as my little friend from my first years here, had married Daniel, a good fellow, who now ran the farm. Unfortunately—and I had best avoid the subject—Susannah had so far been unable to conceive, and probably this was why she doted on Frank. She loved Frank to idolatry, without understanding him at all, and it was painful to watch how hard she tried to bind him to her, since it was all in vain and done so badly. At every turn she opposed his wishes. "Frank is sharp as a tack," Anne said, chopping walnuts with machine-like speed. "I don't worry much about Frank. But Susannah will never make him into a farmer."

"If he's sharp as a tack and he wants to go to the Pearson Academy, and I'm willing to pay for it, why won't you let him go?"

"Weren't you listening? It's not me. It's Susannah. She won't part with him. I take the blame for her."

I surmised that Anne had a weakness for her only daughter, and was afraid to make her angry.

We worked a little more quietly, and I asked, "Does Susannah know about me?"

After a few seconds she said, "Yes."

Another pause. "Well, I could use that, couldn't I? I could threaten to tell him. You couldn't, but I could."

"I see what you mean," she said after a while, with a contemplative expression that, in her, stood for disapproval. "No, you can't use that."

"It would be a bluff," I assured her. "I would never tell."

Anne shook her head.

We talked over other arguments that might be used to persuade Susannah, but it seemed clear enough that they had all been made already and had not moved her.

At last, when the hired girl was lighting lamps, which made it seem suddenly darker outside, Frank came up the walk and I went out to greet him. He had his father's dark eyes, long lashes, and wavy black hair. He reminded me of Charley, most of all, in his mature, self-possessed expression, which was all the more striking because he was quite small for his age. I could find nothing of myself in his face or form.

The son of a parlor-house madam and a man hanged for murder, he strolled toward the house with his hands in his trouser pockets. He saw me, and for a moment I did not know whether I was going to run to embrace him or run away and hide, I so longed for his touch and feared his judgment. His brow knit. "Godmother?" he asked—he knew me from my pictures! I nodded. He smiled, which made me very happy, and I embraced him with less emotion than I felt and forced myself to release him long before I was ready. He returned my embrace politely, as one would expect from a boy his age who did not know that he was holding his mother for the first time since he was an infant.

I said lamely, "It's so good to see you after all these years," thinking, as I had often on the way here, that very few of the methods of ingratiating myself to grown men would be effective on a boy.

"It's good to see you, too," he answered mechanically. "You're just like your pictures. I work at the hostler's in Livy." I opened my mouth to say that that was fascinating and I wanted to hear so much more about it, but he added, "I wash up after work there, but Anne makes me wash up again here. So—I'd better do it."

"By all means," I said, hurting. "I'll see you in a little while. We'll have lots of time to talk. I've brought you presents."

We had supper, usually a simple meal, on the best tablecloth and the best plates, and along with Daniel and Susannah. The hired girl spoon-fed Melanchthon. A couple of times he contributed to the conversation, words that the others seemed to understand, though I could not.

I was overdressed for any possible occasion on this farm—I had forgotten, I had miscalculated—and a few minutes of awed conversation were devoted to my clothes. I noticed that Susannah could not utter a word without bringing a look of disgust to Frank's face, and that she feared and despised me—Susannah, whose flaxen hair I had combed on a hundred different days when her father's house was my refuge from Aunt Agatha and Cousin Agnes. Now she was very stout, stouter than Anne, who was twenty years older. Her flaccid white arms shook like jelly, her face was as round as a pancake, and some minor ailment made her skin look red and bruised. She didn't try to hide her feelings. She must have been dreading my return for years.

After Frank went upstairs, and Daniel wheeled Melanchthon back to the porch, we drank cider and looked at the stars until I jerked my head toward a lit window behind us on the second floor. "Is that Frank's room?"

"That's right," said Anne. "You haven't seen Daniel and Susannah's house, have you, Arabella? Let's walk there." Susannah, grasping that we were about to talk about Frank, looked angry and scared, but she complied. Daniel took a lamp, and we walked on a hard dirt path through air that was sweet with honeysuckle and apple blossoms. Anne said, "Arabella, we never thanked you for your generous offer regarding the Pearson Academy," giving me a cue to begin, but I didn't wish to: I couldn't see the others' faces without a conspicuous effort, nor could Susannah see mine, and I planned to use many subtle effects. So I talked inconsequentially until we were in Susannah's parlor and she had served us homemade sassafras tea and we had praised its flavor and discussed its tonic properties.

I began by saying that whoever had raised Frank had done a wonderful job. "Was it you, Susannah? It looks to me like it was you." She sullenly regarded her tea, but Anne and Daniel said I was right. "I knew it. Anyone could see what you mean to him." She looked up with desperate hope. I had her heart in my hands. "It's you he loves. He loves you the way a boy loves his mother." I was glad that I had waited until I was where I could see her face, because I had been about to say that his habitual rudeness to her was clearly the rudeness that boys show to their mothers when it is time to cut the apron strings, and I saw from her expression that this would be much too subtle. She needed a very pure reassurance, and only I could give it to her, because I was his actual mother, dying for his love, and surely I wouldn't say it unless it was true. I dwelled on the topic until she had the certainty of his love within her grasp. Then I handed her Frank's letter and watched as she read it. "What he doesn't know is that you're the only one standing in his way."

There was more to my argument, there were all the reasons why going away to school was best for him and that it was what he wanted, and the unspoken fact that he must never know that his mother was a prostitute and his father a gambler. But the heart of it was the threat that if she didn't let Frank go I'd tell him that she was the one keeping him here. He'd know that in a matter so important to him she had pretended one thing while doing the opposite, and he would never trust her again. After about an hour of this, Susannah, hating me more than ever, agreed to let Frank go; Daniel was holding her and comforting her, but it was plain that he was grateful to me.

It was agreed that I would deliver Frank to the Pearson Academy myself. A few days later, we took the stage out of town.

WE WERE SHY WITH EACH OTHER. On the stagecoach, our fellow passengers—a corn jobber with a storybook witch's face, a handsome drummer, and a jowly sawmill owner smelling of peppermint—talked about the war, and asked me about California. Out the windows, the scenery jogged by, tame and orderly, the houses painted, the roads gravel or plank, the bridges covered. I told Frank how different it had looked when I came here the first time, as a girl. He nodded firmly, obviously not the least bit interested. The only thing about this road that mattered was that it was taking him where he wanted to go.

Savoring each moment with my son, I made the journey last longer with two stops overnight in towns, and meals at the most expensive restaurants I could find. Once, at our hotel (where, to respect his privacy, I got him a separate but adjoining room, and he was amazed by my extravagance), he noticed a deck of cards I had used for a game of patience; and he invited me to play gin rummy, which Anne had taught him. Charley had told me to keep Frank away from cards, I remembered. With some misgivings, I shuffled the deck and we began.

"Play well," he said after a few minutes. "You'll need to."

I lost. We played other card games, and backgammon and checkers. I remember how it felt, losing to Frank. There was motherly pride, there were memories of Charley, there was helplessness. Struggle was useless. It wasn't personal. You were his food. In after years, I would think of these games whenever I heard that some little businessman had discovered that a new zoning ordinance was forcing him to sell his factory, and that

Frank had come to him saying, "If you had sold out to me the first time I asked, you'd have gotten a better price."

At the Pearson Academy, I spent a few days making things smooth for him, buying him clothes and things for his room, imagining the day when I would tell him everything and he would love me.

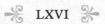

LXVI

I RETURNED TO NEW YORK A DAY BEFORE I was to meet with Jeptha, and asked at my hotel if any messages had been left for me. The clerk gave me a letter, which I tore open where I stood.

> Dear Belle,
>
> Belle, my love, I'm about to make you angry, and I have to ask your forgiveness, because I have tricked you and lied to you. My father is not sick. It was never my plan to visit my family on this trip back east. It was my plan from the first to join in this fight which is the most important we are likely to see in our lifetimes, and certainly the only one that could have induced me to point a weapon at my fellow man. Ever since South Carolina seceded I've known there'd be a war. For months now my sermons have been thinly veiled recruiting speeches, and I couldn't go on telling other men to enlist while I stayed safe and comfortable in San Francisco.
>
> You'll say I should have told you. But how could I? I know you, Belle. You would have made it hell for both of us. If you had suc-ceeded in changing my mind, it would have cost me my self-respect. In any case it would have been a desperate struggle. It would have spoiled the wonderful time we've had together these last few weeks, which have been the sweetest of my life.
>
> Edward has joined, too. We are both in the 71st Pennsylvania

Regiment under the command of your old friend Colonel Baker. We are staying now at a place called Fort Schuyler, in New York, and you may write to us there for now.

Arabella Godwin, Mrs. Cora, I love you more than life. I wish there was a way I could do my duty without causing you worry, but there isn't, so I am asking you to be brave, not in the uncommon way that you have always been brave, but with that resigned, enduring bravery that men are forever recommending to women. I am learning that a soldier's lot is mostly obedience, too. So we must both be patient and hopeful.

Jeptha

After I read the first line of this letter, I skipped right to the meat of it, in the third paragraph. Then, with many anguished gasps, and my hand on the edge of the high desk for support, I read it through from the beginning. "Are you all right, ma'am?" asked the clerk, turning the register around to let a middle-aged couple inscribe their names.

"Yes, thank you." I was already crossing the lobby with the porter when, as an afterthought, I turned back to the clerk. "Could you . . ." He raised his chin and eyebrows, ready to serve. "Where is Fort Schuyler?"

"I will find that out for you," he promised.

The man who had just finished writing in the register put down the pen and said, "It's north of here. On a place called Throgs Neck."

And his wife spelled out, "T-H-R-O-G-S."

"Thank you."

"You're very welcome," said the man. "That's where they're putting the troops before they head south," he told his wife, and they both glanced at me sympathetically.

I went to my room, where I paced the floor with clenched fists, sat down, got up, and slapped the furniture. How could he do this to me, when he knew what I had suffered with Charley, when he claimed to love me more than life? I paced and I cursed, and then I formed a series of increasingly risky plans, each to be undertaken only if the one that preceded it had failed.

I knew it would be at least a few weeks before the regiment headed south, so I wrote first to Jeptha, asking when I might see him.

I went the next morning to the headquarters of the Union Defense Committee, hoping to find Colonel E. D. Baker, or at least Robert. Neither of them was there. The men who were in charge made it evident that at thirty-three I was still adorable and trivial, and they promised to convey my message to Baker. I wrote to him, explaining that an awful mistake had been made. My men could not be soldiers. They were badly needed by me, by me much more than by their country.

When I received Baker's reply, I saw that it had been an error to include Edward in my request. It made me sound absurd. I sounded like every other woman—every actual woman not invented for a patriotic speech or a recruiting poster—demanding that *her* man be spared to plow her fields and warm her bed.

I decided to try Robert. I must use Robert to get to Baker. It would be unpleasant for both of us, since he had hoped not to see me again for years, perhaps ever.

The sun shone brightly the next day, bringing out the color in the striped window awnings along the streets. The East River was as placid as a pond, so that the ships all had long, pale wakes, and the air was so still that smoke from chimneys went straight up but smoke from steamboats slanted back toward their sterns. A ferry took me to Brooklyn, and a hack took me up over a few steep hills to the home Robert shared with Amanda and their children and three servants. The housekeeper recognized me from my previous visit. She let me in, and I played hide-and-seek with the children until Amanda came home. We had a pleasant meal on the veranda with a view of the harbor, ships, factories, wharves, fisheries, and warehouses. The water turned from quicksilver to slate as clouds moved in from the east, and at last over New York City these same clouds were stretched out wide and pressed down hard until they bled.

I discussed my problem with Amanda. At first, with those red, white, and blue ribbons in her hair, she counseled me to be brave. I asked her if Robert was planning to go. With eyes cast downward, she admitted that she was preventing him. After a few quiet minutes, she warned me that Robert did not like pulling strings to make exceptions for his friends, and would not like doing what I proposed; she began advising me of the best way to get around him.

"Put me alone with him," I told her. "I know what to say."

Wheels crunched the gravel, the door-knocker rapped, and we watched from the landing of the stairs while my brother gave his black stovepipe hat and his black frock coat to the maid. He looked in the mirror, running a hand over his thinning hair, while the servant spoke to him. I saw his back straighten—he had been told I was here. He had thought he would not have to go through this again for years. And what could I have been saying to Amanda all this time, what might I have revealed? When he looked into the house, the first thing he saw was that we were both watching him. He made himself smile—"Arabella! Again!"—and went halfway up the stairs, while I went halfway down. We reached our arms out and gripped each other's elbows.

He took me into a study which was full of dark carved furniture gleaming from the maid's attentions, and high shelves of multi-volume *Complete Works* with gilt lettering on the binding, the kind of books in which the author's picture is protected by a flap of gauzy transparent paper (my mother's diaries were up there, too, but I didn't learn that until many years later, after Edward had inherited them). Its windows faced east, so the room was already dark, and as we entered he turned up the gaslights; I noticed two battered high-backed chairs and a rolltop desk, all in much worse condition than the room's other furniture, and which I recognized instantly while Robert watched. I walked toward them and ran my hands over a row of brass knobs that covered the back of a red leather chair—it had been reupholstered, but the exposed wooden parts bore remembered nicks and scars, including one that I used to think resembled the profile of a man in a sailor's cap.

With my hand on the chair back, I looked up at Robert. "You remember Sally, Robert? Sally came after Anna, and before Christina. Christina was the last one. I sat in this chair while Grandfather commended me for my part in getting Sally dismissed."

He stood stiffly. To say the names of our last three servants was to evoke the time of my mother's worsening sickness and our father's sudden death, the jagged crack that ran across our lives; it was to remind him of what we had once been to each other. After a while, he nodded.

"She had talked to me while she was packing. She said that she was going to buy a nasty dress and go on the town. And she said that there was something wrong in our house, there had to be to explain why we could afford only one servant, and it must have to do with Father. Years later, I found out that she was right."

I gathered my skirts and sat. He took the other chair, first moving it a little closer to mine.

"What do you want from us, Arabella?"

"I want you to save a man's life," I said. "But let me tell you what I discovered about Father."

"You're going to say something unpleasant."

"So I am, and it's because I'm a coarse, corrupt woman that I can say such things. But you can take it, can't you? You have to. You're a man. You must be without illusions, so that you can protect Amanda and the children. They can stay pure if you face the ugly truth."

I told him what I had learned while sitting on the lap of a rubber importer named Harold. Our father had jumped off the roof of our grandfather's warehouse, not out of grief over our mother's death—or at least not solely—but out of grief over a whore calling herself Frances. "Her real name we do not know; such women use false names. I've known so many girls like her that I almost feel as if I've known her, too."

He was quiet, and I did not know what he was thinking, until he said, "I never despised you, Arabella. My concern has always been for the family name. I'll never understand the kind of life you've lived. I don't think you realize how changed you are. But I still feel our kinship, and I trust the Arabella I used to know is still somewhere within you, and I wish you well in anything that does not bring harm to other people."

"Good. Then you can help me for my own sake, and not for the sake of Amanda or your children."

When we came out of the study some twenty or thirty minutes later, Robert told Amanda that I would be staying the night. She was delighted: we would become such good friends! She was even happier a few hours later, when she received word, by telegraph and special army messenger, that Colonel Baker was coming to dinner the next day.

The dinner that followed was interesting for her and dramatic for the rest of us. Baker realized for the first time that Belle Cora, who also called herself Arabella Godwin, was the sister of his new friend Robert Godwin; and he learned that Robert knew this but Amanda did not, and that we must keep the truth from her. In her innocence, Amanda brought up the subject of the Cora defense, in which Baker had made one of his most famous speeches, printed in all the newspapers here. She urged him to repeat it; he was too modest; she recited some of it for him. "'Devotion to the last,'" crooned my brother's wife, possibly remembering better than Baker, who did not reprise his roles—"'amid all the dangers of the dungeon and all the terrors of the scaffold . . . a tie which *angels* might not blush to approve.' Oh, Colonel—forgive me, you see it still affects me, it was so beautiful, it was your best." She wiped her eyes with the heel of her hand.

The children had eaten separately and been put to bed, and only the servants, wearing their best for the colonel, and removing dishes and refilling wine and water glasses, were a witness to our party. Amanda drank nothing alcoholic, so if her face had grown blotchy it must have been what happened when she was in the grip of high emotion; it must have been for the sake of Belle Cora. Noticing that I, too, was moved, she said, "I suppose we women feel it more—you were there at the time, Arabella."

I nodded, and croaked, "Yes," not trusting myself to say more, because her sympathy, and the new life she had given to Baker's magical incantation, had broken through my defenses. The words were hogwash, yes, but they had been spoken on *my* behalf; I, whose voice would never be heard among the matronage of the land. How astonishing that those words had reached the heart of a good Christian woman a continent away, persuading her to give her approval to the madam of the best house in San Francisco.

"What a remarkable woman she must have been," said Amanda. "Forgive me. What happened to her, Colonel, after . . . after her gambler met his unfortunate end?"

Baker hesitated, glancing quickly at me, and I spoke: "Oh, everyone in San Francisco knows that." I heard Robert's chair scrape the floor, and he cleared his throat noisily, but I pretended not to notice and continued: "She shut up her house. She dismissed all the girls, giving each of them enough money so they could start a new life, and one or two may have done so, but I'm afraid most of them simply went to live in other houses of ill fame. She lives with a few servants in her house on Pike Street, which is now a respectable house, though the street it is on is still disreputable. She lives, they say, very simply and dresses only in black; she goes to church regularly, and gives openhandedly to many charities, and she goes quite often to the Mission Dolores"—I made my voice softer—"to put flowers on the grave of Charles Cora. So I have heard."

"How beautiful," said Amanda. "Is that what you have heard, too, Colonel?"

Baker had no choice but to agree, and Robert asked him what he thought of the situation in Maryland.

TWO DAYS AFTER THAT, I WAS ADMITTED into Fort Schuyler, a note from Baker speeding my way, and with his informal assurance that if Jeptha was willing he would find him, on some technicality, ineligible for service.

The fort was a colossal medieval star-shaped monster. Lawns around it, receiving heavier wear than usual, were torn by hooves and wagons. Some fellows were driving bayonets into a straw mattress. A couple of stone-faced officers led me into a five-sided courtyard full of men and horses and guns and wagons. I saw Jeptha walking to me, and I was about to embrace him, but then I saw that the officer meant to leave us here, and I began to argue with him, showing him Baker's letter. "We're supposed to be alone! I'm his sweetheart; we can't talk here. It may be the last time I ever see him. Have some pity—have some decency. Put us in a room for a few minutes or Colonel Baker will hear of it. I am a personal friend of Colonel Baker," and so on, while Jeptha watched with restrained amusement. We were taken to a room dimly lit by windows and skylights, and full of barrels and shelves and blue shirts and blue trousers.

To make him look like a hundred thousand other men and give the enemy's bullets a bright target, they had made him wear a forage cap with a sloping visor and a dark-blue sack coat over light-blue trousers. I hated every stitch of it. As soon as we were alone, I lifted the cap by its visor and tossed it into the straw with such an expression of disgust that he laughed. He sat on a barrel and took me on his knee, and I ruffled his hair and kissed him, while crying, saying, "What a fool you are, you're a fool, a fool." He kissed me on the eyes, and then I pulled away so that I could study him. He understood what I was about, and thinking, no doubt, that I had a right to memorize his face before it was carried away from me, possibly forever, he let me turn his head this way and that so it caught the spotty light from the windows set into the thick walls.

He was much changed since I have last described him to you, reader. He was still lean and strong, but his face, in leaving behind young manhood, had lost the beauty that used to make women catch their breath at the sight of him. Though it did not make me love him less, it hurt me a little to see the work of time in him. His hair was receding. His nose and ears were larger. It was a less handsome, less troubled, wiser face, halfway to genial grandfatherly old age. It was my duty to see that it got there—to see that, whether or not we had children, we could be grandmotherly and grandfatherly together one day. It was my right to have him by me at every stage of life.

"You can't go, Jeptha," I said at last. "I won't let you."

"Sweetheart, it's done. It would be desertion for me to leave now."

"No." I waved my hand at the door and the windows. "For those men out there it would be desertion. They're all prisoners now. You can walk out anytime." I told him of my agreement with Baker.

He put his hand on his tall, receding brow. "You must have gone to a lot of trouble. You meant well. But you've wasted your time."

"I hope not," I said. "Listen to me, Jeptha."

Perhaps the things I said then do not matter very much, since they did not change his mind, and if you have read this far you have pictured me in all my modes of persuasion: logic, poetry, pleading, lies, bribery, blackmail. I used every mode except the last two. I made every argument: that he was a thousand times more necessary to the people of San Francisco, the dear, helpless orphans of San Francisco, the fragrant drunkards of San Francisco, the reasonable Unitarians of San Francisco, than he was to the Union Army; that he was too old; that he should wait a year and see if soldiers were still needed then; that he was abandoning me a third time; that after what I had been through with Charley it was heartless that he should let it happen again.

We were sitting on two different barrels a few feet apart by that point. He rubbed one palm against the other, looking down at his hands. "How was it with Frank? Did you get them to change their minds?" I told him, and he said he was happy for me. "And how was it with Baker?" I told him how I had obtained Baker's cooperation, and of my supper with Amanda and Robert and Baker.

Then I got off my barrel and stood. "What are you going to do, Jeptha?"

"You haven't changed my mind," he said—and watched in bewilderment as I hiked up my dress and took, from a pocket in my undergarments, a recently purchased product of Colt's Patent Fire Arms Manufacturing Company. I pointed it at him, which made him smile. "Doesn't that defeat the purpose?"

"I can't let you do this to me. Don't move. If you move, I'll shoot."

My hands trembled, which made it serious for him. He stood up. "Belle, no!" he shouted. Well, I had warned him. Aiming for his foot, I pulled the trigger. The recoil hurt my hand. I aimed again, this time with two hands, but it was too late. We were struggling. I decided I must not have hit him; if I had hit him as I'd meant to, he'd be in far too much pain to fight for control of the pistol. I didn't dare pull the trigger again until I was free of him.

He was strong, and soon he had the pistol. I was sobbing, and he was holding the pistol and kissing me, murmuring, "She loves me, oh, how she loves me. Well, it's a fine thing to be loved this way. I only hope you don't go to jail for it. Hush. Listen." We listened. "Maybe no one will come. It's not so unusual to hear a gunshot around here."

"Does it hurt, Jeptha?"

"Yes, it hurts," he said. "But I can walk." He let go of me, taking the pistol with him, and walked a few steps.

"You win," I said.

"Maybe. My socks are wet."

Wet socks: blood. That gave me hope. The door opened. Soldiers rushed in.

I HAD TORN A HOLE THROUGH his boot and blown a small chip off the medial malleolus of his left tibia; it was the little knob just below the ankle. Better aim and I would have put him out of the war for the duration. As it was, he was laid up for a week. It was agreed, officially, that it had been an accident. A determination that I had shot him deliberately, after having been left alone with him on orders from Colonel Baker, would have been too embarrassing to all concerned. But everyone in the regiment knew better. I would never again be allowed on an army base or in an army camp.

Unable to do more, forbidden even to see my man until he was discharged, I took a steamship down to Panama and the rail across Panama and another steamship back to San Francisco, a journey as grim and bleak as the one before it had been hopeful and fine. I was helpless to control events and helpless to control my thoughts. Having nothing else to distract me, I resumed the management of my properties, including the parlor house on Pike Street. Like all the other anxious wives and mothers and sweethearts, I fell on each new issue of the *Alta California* and the *Bulletin* for news of the fighting in the East, and felt easier as soon as I was sure the headlines did not name the 71st Pennsylvania Regiment. The casualty lists came at the article's end, in the smallest type.

Like the other women, I hoped for letters, and fortunately Jeptha was a good correspondent. During the war he wrote to me 137 times.

❧ LXVII ❧

WITH MY HEART ON THE OTHER SIDE of the continent, I held a grand ball—as I had been doing annually for some years—sending out invitations to all the wealthiest and best-regarded men (including all the clergymen, just for the talk it caused) and to every surviving member of the vigilantes' executive committee. I would also hold a soirée, smaller and even more select, whenever a new girl arrived.

Now and then I wrote a letter to Frank at the Pearson Academy. On occasion he answered. His letters were brief and uninformative.

I had always to be on the lookout for an interesting new girl. Those leaving me sometimes recommended a replacement. Occasionally, I made use of an employment agency. I know it sounds strange, but it is true. There existed in those times several organizations in New York that would arrange for young girls to go to California, promising them highly paid work as maids, housekeepers, or cooks; the girls need pay no fee, thanks to the great demand for female help in the West. Three of these agencies were really professional procurers whose fees were paid by madams and pimps, as some unsuspecting young females learned only upon reaching their destination; and if the girls offered resistance, they were treated, I am sorry to say, very roughly, until their will to resist had been broken. I had sometimes used these agencies—insisting that they send me only girls who knew exactly what they were getting into. However, as you may imagine, the men and women who ran these businesses were not very scrupulous. One day late in August of '61, there appeared at my door a fresh, slender, willowy seventeen-year-old girl, apparently under the impression that she was going to be a maid in a hotel. Her face was not beautiful, but it was pretty; she had good skin and teeth and a splendid figure; and she was pleasing enough in her apparent innocence to have made a small fortune for both of us, providing she was game and cooperative.

When a servant had taken her coat, I said, "You have a good figure." She smiled nervously. I had her bags brought up to the room I had prepared for her. We sat in the parlor. Girls in various states of undress, who had already heard from Niobe that this child had identified herself as the new maid at the "Cora Hotel," came in to get a look at her. I watched as she responded shyly to their sly inquiries, and then I shooed them away. At last I said, "Colleen Flynn. You're Irish."

"Yes," she said, sitting—I had insisted that she sit—with her knees together and her hands folded, leaning forward. "They told you what my name was. They told me that they told you."

"Did they? Well, they have lied to both of us. But I don't mind an Irish girl so long as she doesn't steal and her manners are good. Many San Francisco employers are less broad-minded, and if for some reason you must seek employment elsewhere it may be an obstacle to you. Do you go to mass?"

"I used to."

"You speak well for an Irish girl." In this at least the agency had followed my instructions. "Were you born here or there?"

"Here. In Brooklyn. I was a maid in New York."

"So was I, once. Do you have family?"

She nodded. Her father was an iron molder in Troy. One sister made hats, another was married, two brothers were in the Army of the Potomac. Her mother was dead.

"Why have you come here, Colleen?"

"I wanted to see California. I heard wages were good."

"Forgive me for asking, but where you were a maid, did the man of the house do anything improper? Try to get you in his bed? We're alone here. You can tell me."

She blushed easily—to some men an exciting feature. She hated the question. She didn't think I had a right to ask it, but she had come a long way and had no idea what awaited her in San Francisco if she did not get this job. At last she made a small, almost imperceptible nod.

"He did," I said. "Well, it's natural. It's human nature. Did he succeed?"

"No!" she said hotly. "Why do you ask these questions? What is this place?"

"Don't you know?"

"Oh," she said. "Oh no. Oh no. Oh no. Oh, please let me go. I won't tell anyone that you brought me here. You can have my things that your servants took."

I rang a bell, frightening her even more for a moment. I told Niobe to have Colleen's bags brought down. "I would never make a girl stay here against her will. You can ask anyone here, or anyone out there where they hate Irish girls."

The only way to make her believe that she was really free was to let her go. I called my driver to bring her to the Railroad House, where I had her put up for the night at my expense.

The next day, I visited her and persuaded her to come back to be my lady's maid. I told her quite openly that I hoped exposure to the other girls would lead her to change her mind. She would see that they were comfortable and about as happy as most people are. They were not really any different from other women, and the men who visited them were a very high class of men. To know such men was a privilege which a girl like her was unlikely to enjoy in any other profession. She would be proud of her ability to please them; whenever she felt dirty, she could take a bath; whenever she felt guilty, she could go to confession. She would begin to think of the tidy nest egg she could save in just a year of this work, after which she might move somewhere else, as so many women who were now respectable wives and mothers had done, with no one the wiser.

She didn't say that she would rather die; she just said that her mind was made up. I liked her for that. She was bright and, whatever her private opinions, not openly judgmental. She became friendly with the girls, who were amused by her innocence, some teasing it, some protecting it. I enjoyed her company. It seemed to me that in time she would come around.

I received the following letter from Jeptha:

Dear Arabella,

I enjoyed your parcel and its contents, some of which I shared. The tinned plums I devoured in guilty joy alone. It amazes everyone to think these goods rounded Cape Horn twice.

We saw a boy from Pennsylvania punished today. He had joined up with his brother, who died of camp fever. The mother wrote a letter begging him to come home for the harvest. When denied a furlough, he acted like the child he is, & was flogged on a wagon wheel before us all.

The long wait has taken a toll on the men, who were so cheerful at the beginning. The constant refrain is that they are sick of marching & drilling; just let them fight & finish it. Everyone feels disgraced by Bull Run & wants revenge, yet is cynical about the war. There is much ill feeling against Lincoln, who is called a tool of the bankers. The bitterest suspicion is that he secretly plans to free the "niggers" (no other word is ever used). There will be riots if that happens. Yet I hope it does, or what am I here for? Not to keep down the price of cotton, I hope.

I am still often pointed out to new recruits as the man whose sweetheart tried to shoot him in the foot—sometimes it is said in the heart—so that I would not leave her; & it is often said that they wish their sweethearts cared *almost* that much. I have seen Baker again. He has forgiven you. He asked meaningfully if I had heard from my lovely friend on Pike Street, & told the men standing around me that I was a dark horse with many a secret in my breast.

You are never out of my thoughts. I have only to shut my eyes to be cheered by your image. How I regret the years when you and I were apart. How I wish I could bring them back. Not only that, I regret all the hiding, I regret that we were not together every day, even if it meant living in a parlor house and being your fancy man. Do you want a fancy man, Belle Cora? Say the word. I will be that man. My plan when this other matter has been settled is to walk arm in arm with you down Montgomery Street at high noon on a sunny day, waving my hat with my free arm, with the whole town watching. I will be shouting the words "Gold! Gold! Gold!" and I will be the proudest man alive.

Yours truly,
Jeptha

This letter, because of its last paragraph, had an overwhelming effect on me, with three distinct phases. For a day, I was very happy. On the second day, I was overcome with terror. It was too good to be true. I was bad. I didn't deserve such happiness. Something terrible would occur to prevent it. Four more days passed. It was unbearable. I decided that I must make a bargain with fate. I made a resolution, and relief came instantly. I knew that I couldn't cheat, I couldn't hesitate, or it would all come back.

Over the following two months, I sold my boarding houses and several other properties in San Francisco, retaining deeds to many lots of wasteland in places likely to become more valuable with the growth of the city. I bought shares in Eastern railroad stocks and Western silver-mining stocks. I sold the house in Sacramento to the woman who had been managing it for me, and the girls currently there stayed. I closed up the house on Pike Street and lived there alone with Colleen. When I went out, I walked into the stores, carrying a handkerchief before my face and coughing in the way my mother had coughed for years before she died. As a final measure, I bribed the city coroner, who gambled and was always in need of money, to write out a death certificate and a report asserting that Belle Cora had died of consumption, hastened by opium poisoning, self-administered.

My death was announced in the next issue of each of the city's newspapers, and I had the satisfaction of reading my obituaries. The majority treated me as a relic of San Francisco's legendary past, recounting the events surrounding Charley's trial and his hanging as if they had occurred a century ago. Others defamed us both one last time.

A black wagon came to my house, picked up a coffin weighted with bags of sand, and brought it to the Pleasant Valley Cemetery, to which I had long ago moved Charley's remains; his tombstone was replaced with another, which bore both our names as well as a bas-relief carving that depicted our wedding in the vigilante headquarters. I took up residence under the name Frances Dickinson in a two-story, brick-and-clapboard house on Stockton Street. From my top window I could see Alcatraz, Angel Island, and the mountains on the other end of the bay.

I had already written to Lewis, Edward, Agnes, Anne, and Jeptha, telling them what I was doing and that they should address letters to me to a post-office box until further notice; I communicated my new name, circumstances, and address to Frank as well. I asked Jeptha what he thought our next move ought to be. I had written him exactly 152 letters.

I had by then received from him exactly 137 letters.

HALF A YEAR HAD GONE BY—longer than I had thought the war would last—with no fighting for the 71st Pennsylvania. In 1861, no one knew the magnitude of the slaughter awaiting us. Soon, we thought, a decisive battle would settle everything.

Meanwhile, holes were dug and telegraph poles put in them and raised, mile on mile, until the end of the wire was a few days' ride away from San Francisco. The Union defeat at Ball's Bluff occurred on October 21, 1861. On the morning of October 24, Colleen was walking along Front Street, with her arms around a wicker basket containing pork loin and some dried peas, when she was approached by a large, portly, bearded man in a dusty Mexican army uniform with gold-fringed epaulettes and a saber. In his left hand he held a bunch of carrots, and with his outstretched right hand he demanded what he called a "tax." She had met him before, and she had read about him. He was the celebrated Norton I, Emperor of the United States and Protector of Mexico; that is, he was a harmlessly insane beggar, recently made famous by a couple of newspaper reporters who devoted a column to his antics now and then. As she was rummaging in her bag, she heard him say, "My poor colonel has given his life to protect me." Up close, his odor was rank. When she had given him a dime and walked about ten feet from him he called out, "Tell the provincial governors. A day of mourning in every corner of my dominion. Colonel Baker is dead."

I had by this time made Colleen familiar with that name, and she hurried off to a bookstore to purchase the *Globe,* the *Herald,* and the *Alta California,* the front pages of which all described the battle, and the inside pages of which contained the lists of the wounded, the missing, and the dead.

When she reached the house, she knocked on my bedroom door. I saw her face and gave a shriek, and then I was silent.

"Bad news," she said.

I couldn't look at her. "Go away, I'm not feeling well." She didn't move. We regarded each other. I saw the newspapers in her hand. "A battle?" She nodded. "His regiment." Another delay, another nod. "But you haven't read the list yet," I said. "You don't know for sure yet." She stood immobile, and I guess it was about the third second with no nod and no shake of the head that the unspoken truth went into me like a sharp sword, from the tip down to the hilt, slowly, unrelenting. "Oh," I said, "oh," with my mouth open, and she came to me, and the newspapers fell to the carpet as we wrapped our arms around each other and I wept and moaned, "Oh . . . oh . . . oh . . ." I fell to my knees. I remember nothing more of that day.

WEEKS LATER, I RECEIVED A LETTER from Edward, telling me that Jeptha had been shot in the battle's opening minutes and had died immediately; Edward had seen the body, and Jeptha looked very peaceful.

I had not yet found the will to leave my bed, where I lay numbed by whiskey and laudanum day and night. Colleen forced me to eat, though I could not manage very much, and insisted that I walk about the house sometimes for exercise. After about a month of this, Colleen began to ration my whiskey and ignored my commands for more. I felt literally that I couldn't fend for myself and I was at her mercy. She obeyed me about everything else.

When Edward's letter arrived, I told Colleen that I wanted to write a letter to Lewis, telling him that I was all right but I needed to be alone. Colleen told me that I had already dictated, signed, and sent this very letter a few days after I had heard the news of Jeptha's death. Two days after that, she brought me a parcel that had come for Mrs. Frances Dickinson at the post office. It had come from Carson City, a cigar box filled with straw as if to preserve a fine porcelain bowl, but the contents were not delicate. It was Lewis's killing stone, his lucky rock. It was wrapped in a note that said, simply, "Your devoted brother."

Colleen began reading to me. I begged her not to read the newspapers, but I could find peace twenty minutes at a time when she read articles unrelated to the war in the *Atlantic* and in *Harper's*. She read me *The Old Curiosity Shop* and *Little Dorrit; Don Juan;* Agnes's copy of *Geography of the Spirit World,* by James Victor Andersen; and Buffon's *Natural History,* which I had acquired secondhand in 1857.

Months went by like this. When, at a certain point each day, I could no longer bear to be read books, she distracted me by talking. She talked about anything that came into her mind. She talked to me about her life in New York and Brooklyn, about a nice boy who had been sweet on her but had gone to Indiana and was married now, and about her adventures here when she went out each day. Sometimes, though she was an intelligent girl, she said silly things, and I knew it was because she was racking her brains to say anything at all; she was doing it to keep me sane.

She talked to me about Ireland; she had been raised on stories of Ireland, by her father and mother, who each emigrated in the first year of the famine and met here one day at a Tammany picnic. Her mother's younger sisters had died, "after standing in a draft and catching cold, so my poor ignorant mother always told me, and when I was an infant I believed it, and when I got older I didn't—poor Ma—but just today it came to me that she was right: they were starving, so a chill was enough to finish them off."

She had been told, of every New York river and lake and meadow, that it was a poor imitation of the real thing in County Clare or County Kildare; from early childhood, she learned to speak the strange names that felt curiously right in her mouth. Her mother on her deathbed had said, "I'll never go back there now."

"To think," said Colleen, "that they could talk that way after all their families had been through. Ireland must be the most beautiful country in the world. Do you agree, ma'am?"

She asked me just to make me talk, I was fairly sure. My silence frightened her. But I didn't like talking. I didn't much like anything except my bed.

"What do you think, ma'am?" she asked again.

"Yes, I suppose it's pretty," I said listlessly. "I'm sure it's pretty."

"I'm going to go there," said Colleen. "And you know what I think? Maybe we'll go there together."

"I doubt that very much," I said. "I think I'll sleep now."

She raised the subject again a few days later: Ireland and its beauty, and the relations she would want to look up there, and that I must go with her—I must go, and take her as my lady's companion. And when we were done with Ireland, we could go to England, the land of *my* ancestors, and then to France, which was somewhere nearby, wasn't it? And Italy, to visit the churches and ruins and the famous paintings that we had seen reproduced as tiny monochrome engravings in *Harper's* and the *Atlantic*. The countries over there were all jammed together. You could walk, once you were on the Continent. But we would go by coach, and by boat down rivers and canals, and stay at fine hotels, because I could afford it, couldn't I? How pleasant that would be.

She often spoke of this.

"Don't talk about Ireland anymore, Miss Flynn," I told her one day.

"Why not, ma'am?"

"Because I don't wish it, Miss Flynn."

The next day, she returned to the topic.

"You're doing it again," I told her.

"Doing what, ma'am?"

"Talking about your stupid imaginary country. I told you, no more."

"Oh, but you meant not anymore yesterday."

"You know very well what I meant."

"I don't believe it, ma'am. You couldn't have, when you know what it means to me. It would be too cruel."

"I wish I had a dollar for every Irishman that left the minute he was old enough and told me what a fine place it was, and how he was going to return as soon as he had made his pile. But they never do, never. Even when they strike it rich. They never see Ireland again. And you'll never see it, either. And you're certainly not going to talk me into taking you there. And, talking of cruel, what could be crueler than to take advantage of my state, the tenderness of my emotions, the weakness of my will, to satisfy your whim to see your relatives in the old country and travel in luxury on my dime through the capitals of Europe. I thought you were good. I thought you had a good heart. I was obviously mistaken. I wish I'd turned you into a whore while I had the chance. It would have been easy enough. You were considering it. It was only a question of time."

That silenced her. A few days afterward, she said, "In the market yesterday I got to talking with a woman with a big straw hat, and she was Irish-born. I asked where, and do you know what she said? County Clare! And do you know what she told me?" And so on. I didn't stop her. There was no more fight in me, and, after all, she was only trying to save my life.

IRELAND IS ALMOST AS PRETTY as the Irish believe it to be. There are ancient roads of ancient stone; mountains; cottages with thatch roofs, and vine-smothered castles that seem to have grown out of the high cliffs naturally, without human help. There is a River Shannon, a part of which we traveled, and there used to be many, many people named Flynn, relatives of Colleen, but most of them left during the famine. Ireland was less real to me than my own thoughts and memories. I walked through it like a consumptive strolling the well-tended grounds of an expensive sanitarium. Colleen pointed to a destination on the map, took my hand, and said, "Let's go *there* next," and I said, "If you wish," as though I were granting a boon, but really I had no will and needed to be told what to do.

We also went to England, France, and Italy. Sometimes in crowds I saw his face, an imbecilic part of me reasoning that this infinity of persons could reproduce every possible human being. Anything remarkable was primarily a thing that Jeptha would never see.

By late June of 1862, we were staying on the second floor of a Roman palace whose attic was inhabited by the owner, an Italian prince; the rooms needed days of cleaning before an American woman could inhabit them. In the company of a tiny, birdlike Italian in patched trousers who swore to us that he was a count, we visited the Roman Forum, the Palatine Hill, the Capitoline Hill, the Pantheon, and other famous sights. At the Baths of Diocletian, suddenly I covered my face with my hands. The baths had called to mind *The Last Days of Pompeii*, which I had read a couple of lifetimes ago when Jeptha and I were sweethearts in Livy. I had been fascinated by the idea of an ancient city at once destroyed and preserved by a volcano nearly two thousand years ago. I had asked him if we would be buried under the years, and if people would dig up our broken dishes and dry bones, and he had said, *We're going to live in heaven forever.* I had asked him if we would be together there. *Always,* he had said.

Colleen started to put her arm around me, but I waved her off. Our scrawny guide was at a loss. Behind me, a strong voice with a New England accent said, "You are thinking about your husband who died. Second husband—no, the first, yet you had a second." I turned and saw a tall man in a frock coat. "A spiritual man, and yet a soldier."

I began to sob, telling Colleen, "I'll die, I swear to you, I'm going to die of this."

"No," said the tall Yankee. "Forgive me. You will live many years, and be happy again, and when it is time, you will meet him again in the Summer-Land." He held out his hand and waited while I wiped my eyes.

Then he introduced himself.

"I am James Victor Andersen."

"Oh," said Colleen, astonished, remembering the name from the book.

"I am Mrs. Frances Dickinson," I told him.

We spoke for fifteen minutes. Then, realizing by natural or supernatural means that I could not bear male company, he made up an excuse and left. I was to meet him again a few years later.

When I did, he said he had foreseen it.

IN '84, WHEN I HAD GROWN OLD enough to be confident that no one would ever imagine I had once been Belle Cora, Mr. Andersen and I—by then married—built a house on some land I had retained for that purpose at the summit of what was by then called Nob Hill. Thus we became the neighbors of many wealthy scoundrels, assorted mining, shipping, banking, real-estate, railroad, and manufacturing kings. Several of them had been in San Francisco in the old days, and ought to have remembered me. It lent a frisson to my relatively quiet declining years to nod to these men, and to meet their wives socially, and to wonder if the truth ever crossed their minds. They are all dead now.

To keep the first thirty-three years of my life a secret was strange. I felt at times deeply homesick, like the last survivor of Atlantis yearning to hear her language spoken once again. At least twice a year, unable to sleep, I would rise from my husband's bed and go to my own room. Sitting at my writing desk, I would unlock a small brass chest containing Jeptha's letters from the camp of the 71st Pennsylvania Regiment. Like the strange flower that a man in an H. G. Wells story finds in his pocket, proving that his trip to the distant future was real, these letters proved to me that my past was real. They helped me remember not only Jeptha, never older than he was the last time I saw him, but the woman he had loved and forgiven. I have watched the lines of the writing bleach and grow slender, vanishing slowly before my eyes. The paper has become damp with the oils of my fingers, while the skin of my hands, the hands that exerted a special fascination on my Jeptha, has turned semi-transparent, flecked with irregular dark spots, and traced with prominent blue veins. I have come over the years to require reading glasses, but I don't need them for these letters. I know them by heart.

❧ LXVIII ❧

AND SO I HAVE SURVIVED TO WRITE THESE PAGES, and the years have passed, and the red slayer thinks he has slain nearly everyone who has ever mattered to me.

Lewis married Jocelyn. They bought a farm in Ohio, and he lived to see the funerals of three grandchildren. Four others were still young enough to enjoy his stories of the Gold Rush and the Comstock Lode. One night, he and Jocelyn were woken by a clamor from the kitchen. He pulled on his trousers and went downstairs, with Jocelyn behind him yelling, "What's the matter? What's the matter?" and a Swedish farmhand shouting, "De barn! De barn!" A lantern had tipped into the hay. Soon every adult on the farm was hunting for pails; they were filling them with water and bringing them to the blaze. Lewis alone went into the barn, first flinging a blanket onto an old mare's head and leading her to the door. He returned with the same blanket and rescued the workhorses, taking all six, one by one, to safety. When he came out the last time, his clothes were on fire, and the farmhands threw pails of water on him. Then he got up and went to save the cows. The hands, shamed or maddened by his bravery, began to follow his example and risked their lives to help him save the cows. The Swede shouted, "De colts! We forgot de colts!" Though it was clearly too late to save them, Lewis went in, and the roof fell in on him, and that was that. He was sixty-eight.

Robert and Amanda had five children. Two, Rosemarie and May, died in infancy—within a week of each other—of diphtheria; two more, Solomon and Stephen, died in youth of scarlet fever; one, Robert Jr., who survived the scarlet fever, had a rheumatic heart and was never strong, and died, a bachelor, at the age of thirty, in 1881. Robert, heartbroken, died the year after that, and in 1883 it was Amanda's turn. Edward, who had lost his leg to a minié ball in the West Woods at the Battle of Antietam, died alone in a small apartment on Great Jones Street in New York City in 1884.

Agnes died in 1902 in Monterey, survived by her second husband. She was childless. I had seen her fairly frequently over the years, the intervals between my visits growing shorter until, during her last year, when she was ill, I saw her every week. I miss her every day.

In Livy and Patavium, the tombstones read:

ELIHU MOODY
Born May 3, 1800
Died December 14, 1871
In Hope of His Deliverance

AGATHA MOODY
Devoted Wife and Mother
Born July 22, 1802
Died August 3, 1874

MATTHEW MOODY
February 2, 1826–June 16, 1872

DELIA MOODY
May 11, 1831–June 16, 1872
Perished in the Sinking of the Steamboat *Jackson* on the Ohio River
"In Their Death They Were Not Divided"

TITUS MOODY
Born Into His Earthly Body
February 1, 1827
Moved to Summer-Land
April 9, 1890
"Weep Not"

Evangeline, who had married and moved to Wisconsin, died there in 1898 and is buried in her husband's family plot, beside him and three of their children who died in infancy. Several other children survived.

My enemies have all fled to the spirit realm. William T. Coleman discovered a mountain of borax in Death Valley, adding to his already considerable fortune, and then lost everything in the Panic of 1887. His physician ascribed his death six years later to "a general breaking up of the vital forces." Sam Brannan, also broke, died in 1889, in Escondido, California. He was seventy.

MISS PEABODY,* WE HAVE ASSEMBLED an impressive tower of paper together, telling my story. As I exhume these potsherds and dry bones, arguing my case before the invisible panel of as yet unborn judges whom I imagine turning these pages, what amazes me most is how often I have managed to surprise myself.

I see things now. I do not see the wonderful plan that we are supposed to comprehend when we are dead. But I do see meaning and connection now in events that had remained for many years stubbornly distinct and random. It goes without saying that if my father had lived and kept me with him, my life would have been very different. But I believe it would have been very different even if he had died

---

* The reference is to Margaret Peabody, who was for twelve years Mrs. Andersen's stenographer and typist. —Ed.

of natural causes. I would have accepted the religion of my forebears in the modified form my new family practiced it, and Agnes and Matthew would both have found me less vulnerable. They protect us, these vast lies the whole community embraces. People are almost always more intelligent than freethinkers realize. If they believe in an absurdity, it is because they know deep down that it is more useful to them than the truth.

As it is, I was thrust off the wide, well-traveled path and into a wilderness, and I saw the underside of the comfortable world that I had known as a child. As, in wars, the great questions of the time are written onto men's bodies in the form of terrible wounds, so, admittedly in milder ways, arguments about shame and pride, morality, power, and religion were written on my young flesh.

Readers, to some of you I am a monster. Under my roof, many lovely young women were hurried down a road that ended, for an unknown proportion of them, in misery and early death. I claim that I was fair to my girls, but clearly, had I a daughter, I would have moved heaven and earth to keep her feet off that path. This crime is the foundation of my fortune and the ease I enjoy in old age. I do feel sad about that sometimes. But I am very forgiving of human error, and I include myself in the general amnesty.

Do I fear to meet my maker? Of course I do. But no more so than if I had not done all these things. Who can say what is accounted a crime in the heavenly courts? Maybe they reward everything. Maybe they punish you for living to an old age. Maybe no such place exists. When our time comes, each of us will see, perhaps.

I make these defenses to Frank sometimes, when I meet him—usually either in the dining room of this hotel or at some anonymous Sacramento eatery where he is confident no one will recognize him. I tell him: what I did, I had to do. He wasn't there, so he cannot judge. If I had not acted in ways he disapproves of, he would never have been born, and, whatever the world would think, it is no shame to be the son of Charles Cora and Belle Cora. It is because such blood flows in his veins that he has been successful in his own endeavors. After all, he is far more ruthless than I ever was, and has broken the law in the pursuit of his business interests, so how can he be my judge? I tell him that it is inhuman for a man to prevent his own mother from seeing her grandchildren, to let them grow up without ever permitting them to see her.

And he says, "I can't have this. Mother, if you go on this way, I can't discuss them with you." I promise to be good, and drop the subject, and I beg him to tell me about the grandchildren. "No," he says airily. "No, I don't think so. No, I'm not in the mood. Next time. Talk about something else. Tell me about this book you're writing."

"What book?" I say. Then: "Oh, I know what you mean. I'm not doing that anymore. I couldn't finish. I'm too frail now to go outside and make the observations."

"What was it about again?"

"Wildflowers of northern California," I say.

He smiles and says, "You're lying."

I don't think he knows, not really. Not yet.

In my haste to finish this story before death overtakes me, inevitably I have left out many things, and often I have expressed myself inelegantly, and no doubt here and there I have said more than I meant to. When you return, my dear type-writer, we will review what we have done, and add this and subtract that. This work has become my hobby and my consolation, and I enjoy it. I enjoy your company, and I feel that we have become friends, perhaps because I have confided so many of my secrets to you.

Just now I'm tired. Oh, where have they gone, where have they gone to? Their voices are in the wind over the Gobi Desert and the China Seas; other men and beasts breathe the air that once inflated their lungs; in the place where mobs of terrified women ran carrying babes in arms down to the harbor, while the sky rained black ash, two thousand years later there are only the ruins and the dry dust and tourists with guidebooks, their minds already looking forward to their dinners. Go now; go and type it; come back on Tuesday. I'll be ready then, but in the meantime I plan to spend the next few days in quiet conversation with the shades of my beloved dead.

Belle Cora is, in the words we sometimes see at the start of a movie, "inspired by a true story." Since this is a highly elastic formula, which applies to *Alice in Wonderland* and *Treasure Island,* readers may welcome a more precise accounting of the proportions of fantasy and truth in this book. Though Belle Cora was a real person, she did not write a memoir; so it was not published by the Dial Press in the 1920s or the Obelisk Press in the 1930s or a Sandpiper Press in the 1960s, and nobody named Arthur Adams Baylis wrote the foreword. I have treated a historical figure as if she were a product of my imagination, providing her with a childhood, youth, family, husbands, lovers, and death that are in conflict with the handful of known facts about Belle Cora.

On the other hand, the major public events of the novel, the fires and earthquakes, William Miller's prediction of the Second Coming, Charles Cora's trial, the San Francisco Committee of Vigilance, even E. D. Baker's speeches, are true, and I have tried hard to honor the historical novelist's implied promise of accuracy concerning props and manners. I attribute all mistakes and anachronisms either to the imperfect memory of Mrs. Frances Andersen, writing many years after the events she describes, or to stenographic errors by Miss Margaret Peabody.

For convincing corroborative details, I have relied on the scholarship of many serious historians. I wish to give special notice to Sheila Rothman's *Living in the Shadow of Death,* important for the behavior of Belle's mother in Book One; Edwin G. Burrows and Mike Wallace's *Gotham* and Tyler Anbinder's *Five Points* for the New York passages. For the underground sexual culture of antebellum America and in particular of New York City, I drew on Patricia Cline Cohen's *The Murder of Helen Jewett,* Helen Lefkowitz Horowitz's *Rereading Sex,* Timothy J. Gilfoyle's *City of Eros,* and Christine Stansell's *City of Women.* For the trip around Cape Horn I used Oscar Lewis, *Sea Routes to the Gold Fields.* My depiction of Gold Rush–era San Francisco owes much to Roger W. Lotchin, *San Francisco, 1846–1856: From Hamlet to City,* and I recommend this book to anyone who wants a realistic picture of the urban politics Mrs. Andersen drastically oversimplifies. For readers wishing to know more about the actual Belle Cora, the most complete account is found in Curt Gentry's *The Madams of San Francisco*. The version most sympathetic to Belle is provided by Pauline Jacobson, in a series of articles which were written, ironically enough, for the *San Francisco Daily Evening Bulletin*, the newspaper founded by Belle's enemy, James King of William. These articles were reprinted in *City of the Golden 'Fifties*, a collection of Jacobson's writings about early San Francisco.

I would like to acknowledge, before anyone else does, that the death of Lewis Godwin closely resembles the death of Henry Fleming in the story "The Veteran," found on pages 324–328 of the 1977 edition of *The Portable Stephen Crane*. The quotation on the gravestone of Matthew Moody and his wife is from 2 Samuel 1:23, and also appears on the last page of *The Mill on the Floss*.

The literal translation of François Villon's "Ballad of Dead Ladies" was found, unattributed, on the website *Bureau of Public Secrets*, created by the writer and translator Ken Knabb. I left out the famous tagline because I wanted to make the poem sound less familiar, and give greater prominence to the list of dead ladies.

ACKNOWLEDGMENTS

Before I had written fifty pages of *Belle Cora,* I started forcing the manuscript on anyone too polite to say no. Among the early readers I would like to acknowledge are Nancy Culp, James Radiches, David Rosaler, Helene Rosaler, Barbara Samuels, and Sarah Sands. I would like especially to thank Elizabeth Meister, who met with me for hours each week to discuss the first drafts of every chapter in Books One to Three.

I became acquainted with Dorian Karchmar, the world's best literary agent, in the following manner: One Saturday, when my neighborhood Starbucks was very crowded, she asked me if it was okay to sit at my table. She sat down and took a big fat manuscript out of her bag and started to work. After a short conversation (I asked: "Are you an editor?" She replied: "A literary agent." I said: "What a coincidence . . ."), she handed me her card. For several months thereafter when she came in to grab her morning coffee, she would ask me how it was going, urging me to take my time and make it good—"You've got one shot." Later she nursed the book along with sensitive editorial guidance, and finally, in the spring of 2008, she had, it seemed to me, every editor in New York City drop what they were doing to read my novel.

In that awful season of bankruptcies, desperate mergers, and dying bookstore chains, only Doubleday's Alison Callahan had the vision to ask me to complete Belle's saga in one volume, gambling on an unfinished work by an unknown author, and later, she had the patience and fortitude to guide me through many drafts.

I owe more than I can ever express to my wife, Maxine Rosaler, who has always been my first reader, giving me moral support, exacting criticism, and love while I crossed and recrossed the floor shaking my head, breaking pencils, and telling her that she didn't know what she was talking about, though we both knew full well that I would come around to her view the next day. Whenever during the composition of *Belle Cora* I needed a model of an unconquerable spirit, I had only to look across the breakfast table.

ABOUT THE AUTHOR

PHILLIP MARGULIES is the author and editor of many books on science, politics, and history for young adults and is the recipient of two New York Foundation for the Arts fellowships. He lives in New York City with his wife and two children.